THE YEAR'S BEST

Fantasy & Horror

THE YEAR'S BEST

Fantasy & Horror

FOURTEENTH ANNUAL COLLECTION

Edited by

Ellen Datlow & Terri Windling

St. Martin's Griffin  New York

www.stmartins.com

ISBN 0-312-27541-2 (hardcover)
ISBN 0-312-27544-7 (paperback)

A Blue Cows–Randall Vilas Production

First Edition: August 2001

10   9   8   7   6   5   4   3   2   1

To Gordon Van Gelder
Our knight in shining armor.
Thank you.

— E.D. and T.W.

Contents

Acknowledgments

The Year's Best Fantasy and Horror series requires the cooperation of a number of people. I'd like to thank the publishers, editors, writers, and readers who send material and make suggestions every year. And this year I'd particularly like to thank Alice Turner, Kelly Link, Harlan Ellison, and Bill Congreve for their recommendations and help.

Thanks to Jim Frenkel, our packager, and his assistants, Tracy Berg and Jesse Vogel. To our former in-house editor, Gordon Van Gelder, who shepherded the series through St. Martin's for over ten years, and to our current editor, Bryan Cholfin; also thanks to Tom Canty for continuing to produce such a beautiful-looking package. Finally, thanks to my co-editor and friend Terri Windling for her graceful and complementary participation in our annual marathon.

I'd like to acknowledge the following magazines and catalogs for invaluable information and descriptions of material I was unable to get a hold of: *Locus, Science Fiction Chronicle, Publishers Weekly, Washington Post Book World, The New York Times Book Review*, the DreamHaven catalog, *Hellnotes*, the *DarkEcho Newsletter, Jobs in Hell*, and *Gila Queen's Guide to Markets*.   —E.D.

It takes a large team to put together a book as extensive as this one. Many folks contributed books and music for review; many magazines and Web sites were consulted; many librarians provided assistance in Tucson and Devon; and I'm grateful to all of them. In particular, Charles N. Brown's *Locus Magazine* is an invaluable reference source. (Thank you, Charlie.) The fantasy half of this book would not exist without the hard work of the following people: assistant editors Richard and Mardelle Kunz, and library scout Bill Murphy. I owe deep thanks to them, as well as to my series partners, Ellen Datlow and Thomas Canty, our series creator/packager, Jim Frenkel, and his assistants, Tracy Berg and Jesse Vogel, and our St. Martin's Press editor, Bryan Cholfin.

The following people also contributed to this volume in various ways: Gordon Van Gelder, Charles de Lint, Charles Parsons, Joe Monti, Jane Yolen, Midori Snyder, Terry Dowling, Steve Pasechnick, Greg Ketter, Victoria Ingham, Lindsay Herron, Tom Harlan, and the ladies of Endicott West. More information (including submission guidelines for future volumes) can be found on the Endicott Studio of Mythic Arts Web site: http://www.endicott-studio.com   —T.W.

Special thanks to Bryan Cholfin, our new St. Martin's Press editor, heir to two huge anthologies this year. And thanks, of course, to both Ellen and Terri for an especially fine job of finding marvelous, complementary rosters of stories and poems for this year's compilation; and thanks to Mardelle and Richard Kunz for their own year-long efforts. And thanks to Ed Bryant and Seth Johnson for their terrific columns. Great thanks as well to my staff, Jesse Vogel and Tracy Berg, both new to this enterprise, who helped mightily with many aspects of the project, and also to our interns, Erin Flynn, Holly Sonnleitner, and Nick Thalhuber, all of whom contributed to the quality of the finished work. Thanks also to Tom Canty for his typically gorgeous art and design, and to Jessi Frenkel for the original cover concept. Someone asked me early this year if this was a difficult project. The answer is, "Yes, and worth every minute, hour, day, week, and month of the effort!"   —J.F.

Summation 2000: Fantasy

Terri Windling

Welcome to the fourteenth volume of *The Year's Best Fantasy and Horror*, an anthology series created to celebrate the best in nonrealist literature published in the English language each year. For this purpose, our definition of fantasy is a broad and inclusive one, ranging from Tolkienesque works of "imaginary world" fiction to Márquezean magical realism, whether published as genre fiction, mainstream fiction, children's fiction, or foreign works in translation. The selections in this book come from sources as diverse as *The Magazine of Fantasy and Science Fiction*, *The New Yorker*, *Francis Ford Coppola's Zoetrope All-Story*, *The Iowa Review*, small press editions, the Internet, and collections of Native American, Bolivian, Irish, and children's fiction. Although I'm a great believer in the fantasy genre, a field I've devoted myself to for twenty years, and which has produced a number of the finest writers working in America, Canada, and Great Britain today, I feel that confining the definition of fantastic literature within rigid genre boundaries simply serves to constrict the imaginations of writers working on both sides of the divide. Thus, in this volume, all nonrealist works rooted in myth, magic and surrealism are considered eligible for inclusion, as well as dark fantasy ranging from stories of supernatural magic to psychological horror.

Ellen and I believe that the sister fields of fantasy and horror literature are enriched when their stories are viewed side by side—but for readers who maintain a unremitting preference for fantasy over horror, or vice versa, please note that the fantasy stories carry my initials after their introductions while the horror stories carry Ellen's. Selections that fall in the shadowland between the two carry both our initials, with the acquiring editor listed first—with the exception of Carol Duffy's poetry, which Ellen and I acquired together. For readers new to the series I should explain that the following introductory Summations will provide you with an overview of fantasy and horror publishing in the year just past, along with lists of recommended novels, children's books, art books, nonfiction, etc. Separate essays cover fantasy and horror in comics and the dramatic arts, and the Obituary section notes the passing of people who've been important to our field.

1999, you may recall, was a disappointing year in genre publishing, but I'm pleased to report that the malaise was temporary and 2000 was exceptionally strong. The area of "imaginary world" fantasy (a.k.a. "high fantasy" or "traditional fantasy") has made a solid comeback after too many years when all we saw were those endless Tolkien clones clogging the bestseller lists. The Tolkien clones are still out there, of course, and still outselling everything but Harry Potter, but now there are some fine alternatives for the serious fantasy reader— books that are literary, complex, and restore one's faith in the fantasy form. For a while there, it seemed that our field's best writers were giving up on high fantasy—but books by George R. R. Martin, C. J. Cherryh, Guy Gavriel Kay, Patricia McKillip, Philip Pullman and others are succeeding in taking imaginary world fiction to a whole new level. Magical realism continues to influence our genre in fascinating ways, as seen in the fiction of stalwarts like John Crowley, James P. Blaylock, Jonathan Carroll and in the works of innovative younger writers like Kelly Link. In the 1980s, a group of writers came into the field with strong backgrounds in mythology, folklore and folk music, creating a blend of fantasy and magical realism that has come to be called mythic fiction. In 2000, Charles de Lint, Kij Johnson, Tanith Lee, Greer Gilman and a number of others published interesting new novels and stories in this area, and in the related area of "adult fairy tales" (a sub-genre deeply influenced by the late, great Angela Carter). The field of "alternate history" was also well represented in the year just past, with good novels from the likes of Thomas Harlan, Louise Marley, and J. Gregory Keyes. As for new trends, the strongest one I see is for works of interstitial fiction—that is, books that fall between categories, or that meld the conventions of two or more genres with exuberant disregard for categorization and genre boundaries. There were a number of strange and wonderful interstitial books published in 2000 by Sean Stewart, China Miéville, Pat Murphy, M. John Harrison, Terry Dowling, Michael Moorcock, Storm Constantine, and Nalo Hopkinson, among others.

In mainstream fiction, the best magical realist literature is still coming from outside the country (Latin American writers like Julio Cortázar, Caribbean writers like Gisèle Pineau, European writers like António Lobo Antunes), but a terrific strain of magical realism North American-style can be found on the mainstream shelves in the works of writers like Alice Hoffman, Steven Millhauser, Barbara Gowdy, Joy Williams and others. In particular, we find it in contemporary Native American fiction, which over the last few years has been one of the liveliest areas of American literature—and almost as critically ignored as fiction from the fantasy field. Thomas King, Louise Erdrich, Gerald Vizenor, Carolyn Dunn, and newcomer Eden Robinson were among the First Nations writers who produced fine magical fiction last year.

The field of children's books, after years of editorial resistance to fantasy (with the exception of a few pioneering editors, such as the late Jean Karl of Atheneum), is experiencing a fantasy boom—due, of course, to the huge success of J. K. Rowling's "Harry Potter" series, and the smaller but still substantial success of Philip Pullman's "His Dark Materials" trilogy. I expected to see a flood of Potter clones, and yes, there have been a few of them—but surprisingly, mercifully few (at least so far). What I'm also seeing are works by talented writers finally getting some of the attention they deserve—ranging from established fantasists such as Diana Wynne Jones, Lloyd Alexander, and Jane Yolen to extraordinary newcomers like Donna Jo Napoli, David Almond, and Garth Nix. Children's book editors report that commercially-oriented fantasy series hastily thrown together to cash in on J. K. Rowling's success aren't doing terribly well for them, but sales of authors like Diana Wynne Jones have picked up among young Potter fans. (This comes as no surprise, since children's librarians are neither cynical nor stupid.) It still remains to be seen whether the current post-Potter popularity of children's fantasy will last. My best guess is that it will, and that it's the over-emphasis on "problem novels" and strict realism that's been the aberration. The immense popularity of television shows like *Charmed* and *Buffy the Vampire Slayer* has caused a demand for supernatural novels (despite the ire of religious fundamentalists), particularly romantic tales about teenage girls with Wiccan powers. Fairies are another popular trend among adolescent readers, taking over from the previous fad for angels, with books by "fairy artists" Suza Scalora and Brian Froud particularly popular in this age group. At the older end of Young Adult publishing, the taste for magic becomes a little more gothic, as exemplified by the noir fantasy fiction of Francesca Lia Block, and the cult status of Neil Gaiman's "Sandman" series among older teens. With both the children and adult book industries more and more influenced by film and television (alas), publishers are now waiting to see what the effect on fantasy sales might be of the success or failure of the three forthcoming films based on *The Lord of the Rings*. So keep your fingers crossed.

In the following pages of this edition of *The Year's Best Fantasy and Horror*, you'll find short stories and poetry representing each of these areas of fantastic literature: magical works from the genre shelves, the mainstream shelves, and from children's fiction. Writers in 2000 used the symbols of fantasy in a wide variety of ways, and the stories presented here reflect that broad diversity. The one area of magical fiction that continues to be underrepresented in these volumes, however, is imaginary world fantasy of the J. R. R. Tolkien sort. This type of world-building fiction is very difficult to write at short story length, and tends to be most successful in novel (or multiple novel) form. We have a few good tales set in invented worlds (see the stories by Justin Tussing and by Gavin J. Grant & Kelly Link, for example), but for a better representation of this currently vibrant form of literature, I encourage you to try some of the excellent novels recommended in the Top Twenty below.

Once again, my hard-working assistant editors Richard and Mardelle Kunz gathered over five hundred magical books published in 2000 for review. We think we've found some real treasures among them, and we hope that you'll agree.

Top Twenty

The following top twenty books of 2000 are ones that no fan of magical literature should miss. As a group, they demonstrate the wide diversity of fantasy fiction being published today, ranging from genre titles to those found on the Young Adult and mainstream shelves. In alphabetical order [by author]:

Daemonomania by John Crowley (Bantam) is the third installment in a splendid quartet by one of our field's best writers. (This volume follows *Aegypt* and *Love and Sleep*—and if you haven't read the previous books, don't try to dive in here.) Crowley's novel is a fantasy of ideas—specifically, the ideas of Renaissance alchemist John Dee and astronomer Giordano Bruno—and how those ideas play out in the lives of the inhabitants of a contemporary small town in the American northeast. Linked to the late autumn/winter season, this volume of the quartet is an elegy for things that are crumbling and passing away . . . and thus it's a darker read than the others. Yet spring's renewal is not far behind, and I'm looking forward to the final volume.

Forests of the Heart by Charles de Lint (Tor), the latest novel from this leading Canadian author of modern mythic fiction, is part of de Lint's on-going "Newford" saga set in an invented North American city where myths of indigenous and immigrant groups are recast in an urban context, among a group of interlinked characters. (A familiarity with Newford enriches the book, but it can easily be read alone.) In this volume, de Lint ranges from Newford's wintry climes to the heat of the Arizona desert, mixing Greenman and other Celtic folklore with spirits out of Mexican and Indian tales. Suspenseful, romantic, and chock full of mythology, folklore and folk music, *Forests of the Heart* contains some of this pioneering author's best writing to date.

The Books of Ash by Mary Gentle (Avon Eos) have had a complex publishing history, but finally all four volumes are available in American editions. Book one, *A Secret History*, came out in 1999, and the subsequent three books—*Carthage Ascendant*, *The Wild Machines*, and *Lost Burgundy*—were published in 2000. Gentle's quartet is an interstitial work of fantasy with science fiction and historical elements. The concept here is that the story purports to be a twenty-first-century translation by a certain Dr. Pierce Ratcliff, Ph.D., of a suppressed medieval Latin text which chronicles the life of a fifteenth-century female mercenary commander. You could call this swords-and-sorcery, but it's also so much more than that beleaguered term connotes these days. Gentle, who is a scholar of Medieval history and War Studies, is a terrific writer; and these unusual, entertaining volumes are first-rate.

Wild Life by Molly Gloss (Simon & Schuster) is a fascinating book that I wish more readers of fantasy fiction knew about. Set in the Cascade Mountains of the Pacific Northwest in the early 1900s, it's the story Charlotte Bridger Drummond: freethinker, single mother of five sons, and writer of women's adventure stories. Emulating the heroines of her own fiction, Drummond journeys deep into the wilderness in search of her housekeeper's missing granddaughter and finds rather more than she bargained for, including herself. The story, told through Drummond's journal entries, draws upon the Big Foot legend and wild-man mythology, using these themes to paint a vivid, thought-provoking portrait of frontier life. It's a remarkable novel, masterfully written, and *highly* recommended.

The Fox Woman by Kij Johnson (Tor) is an enchanting first novel expanding upon Johnson's short story of the same name, winner of the Theodore Sturgeon Memorial Award. Set in medieval Japan and based on traditional kitsune (fox wife) legends, it's a sensual, poetic tale recounted in the form of "pillow books" (diaries) narrated by the three main characters: a nobleman, the kitsune obsessed with him, and the nobleman's wife. Johnson's tale is bewitching, seductive, and dangerous, much like the fox woman herself. I look forward to seeing more from this talented new writer.

Year of the Griffin by Diana Wynne Jones (Greenwillow) is the latest novel from an author who's been writing rollicking tales about wizards and magic since long before the Harry Potter craze, so do the Potter fans of your acquaintance a favor and introduce them to this wonderful book—which is the sequel to *The Dark Lord of Derkholm*, yet can also be read alone. Elda, a griffin, is the youngest daughter of the Wizard of Derk, enrolled by her mother into Wizard's University behind her father's back. With a group of friends who are also hiding their magical studies from assorted relatives, they battle together against various foes from trained assassins to exasperating professors in this hilarious send-up of a college novel. It's Young Adult fantasy (with science fiction elements); it's good fun; and it's Jones at her best.

Lord of Emperors by Guy Gavriel Kay (HarperCollins) is the second, concluding volume of "The Sarantine Mosaic" (following *Sailing to Sarantium*), and I'm pleased to say that it's even better than the first. Taken as a whole, Kay has created an important work of fantasy literature here, and I hope these books receive the award attention they deserve. They read like panoramic historical novels, but the history is the wholly invented history of the city of Sarantium—a city of art and alchemy, political intrigue and philosophy, private feuds and impending war. There's plenty of magic, action, and suspense if what you're looking for is a page-turner; but there are also complex characters, and layer upon layer of nuanced text. Kay is a fiercely intelligent writer, using the symbolism of fantasy to explore the nature of human relationships, large and small, and the power of art.

A Storm of Swords by George R. R. Martin (Bantam) is the excellent third book in the "Songs of Ice and Fire" sequence. For readers who love big, sprawling, multi-volume series of epic fantasy, forget the formulaic books that tend to clog up the bestseller lists and dive into Martin's beautifully written fantasy sagas instead. *A Storm of Swords* explores the aftermath of the harrowing events of the previous volume (*A Clash of Kings*), deepening the personal, political, and religious conflicts that form the core this magical tale. If you're new to the series, you'll have to go back to the beginning—don't try to start it here. Once again, Martin proves that epic fantasy can be both highly literate and thoroughly entertaining.

The Tower at Stony Wood by Patricia A. McKillip (Ace) is yet another utterly magical, beautifully crafted "imaginary world" novel from a writer who's been called "the secret master of American fantasy." There were larger, flashier books published in 2000, but even in a year that gives us new work from the likes of Pullman, Crowley and Kay, this quiet yet exquisite tale has my vote as the best of them. McKillip's language evokes the imagery of ancient myths, folktales, and ballads without ever devolving into preciousness, fashioning new tales that feel as though they've been passed down through generations. Her latest novel, very loosely based on the Tennyson poem "The Lady of Shalott," involves a dragon, a troubled knight on a quest, a mysterious woman locked in a tower, and magical creatures of sea and sky—all standard fantasy ingredients, yet transformed into a lyrical story that is unique, mesmerizing, and wise.

Spindle's End by Robin McKinley (Putnam) is a novel based on a fairy tale from an author with a well-deserved reputation for precisely this type of fiction. McKinley's latest (a Young Adult novel recommended to adult readers as well) is a gentle, romantic, feminist version of the classic tale "Sleeping Beauty," set in an imaginary kingdom full of good-natured royals and meddlesome fairies. McKinley's version of the story involves a tomboy princess (who talks to animals), a snubbed fairy's curse, a magical quest, and the bonds of female friendship—all told in classic McKinley style.

Silverheart by Michael Moorcock and Storm Constantine (Earthlight, U.K.) is an interstitial work falling somewhere between science fiction and fantasy, but borrowing most heavily from the "magical quest" format of the latter. Set in the crumbling city of Karador (where the decadent, privileged "Lords of the Metal" are deeply resented by the underclasses), a charismatic thief, a rebellious aristocrat, and the dangerous tenets of forbidden magics become part of an intricate plot threatening to undermine the ruling class. Borrowing on the strengths of both writers, while also reminiscent of Mervyn Peake's *Gormenghast*, this novel contains a weird, wonderful mix of ancient and modern magical tropes. Moorcock and Constantine together in one volume—it's an inspired combination.

Wild Angel by Mary Maxwell, by Max Merriwell, by Pat Murphy (Tor) is yet another good interstitial novel, this time falling between the fantasy, mystery, and western genres. Like the Gloss book above (but lighter in tone), it involves a writer of adventure stories in the American West, recounting the tale of an orphan raised by wolves in 19th-century California. Mark Twain is quoted throughout the book, and his dry wit has clearly influenced Merriwell's . . . er, I mean Murphy's prose. Murphy's Afterward explains the dual pseudonyms. All in all, this one is a treat.

The Saddlebag by Bahiyyih Nakhjavani (Beacon Press) is a magical, Chaucerean novel by a writer of Persian origin about a caravan traveling between Mecca and Medina in the 19th century. The saddlebag of the title links the tales of ten colorful characters from divergent ethnic and religious backgrounds, creating an overall narrative that is fascinating, entertaining, and exotic. A religious allegory underpins the novel but never gets in the way of Nakhjavani's story, which is likewise rooted in Middle Eastern mythology and South Asian folklore. Critics have compared the book to early Salman Rushdie, and I wholeheartedly agree.

Beast by Donna Jo Napoli (Atheneum) is the latest from a writer who, like Robin McKinley, has earned a considerable reputation for spinning fairy tales into delicious Young Adult novels. This time, she turns her attention to "Beauty and the Beast," and comes up with a winner. Napoli's unusual reworking of the story begins in the distant courts of Persia, where a prince unleashes an ancient curse and is transformed into a lion. As a beast, he makes his way across the face of Europe until he reaches France—where he'll meet a young woman named Belle and find his life transformed once more. Beautifully penned, and filled with the lush imagery of Persian fairy tales, Napoli has created a fresh new version of one of the world's oldest stories.

Declare by Tim Powers (William Morrow) is another novel with an Arabian flavor, but completely unlike the Napoli and Nakhjavani books above—in fact, completely unlike anything else, period. Only Tim Powers could throw the *Arabian Nights*, *Le Morte D'Arthur*, T.E. Lawrence, the British spy network of World War II, the fall of the Soviet Union, and biblical Mount Ararat together into one taut supernatural thriller and actually pull it off. It's a dazzling book, and the best one yet from a writer who always surprises.

The Sterkarm Handshake by Susan Price (HarperCollins), a finalist for the Carnegie Medal, is a terrific Young Adult time-travel story that is equal parts fantasy and science fiction. Andrea Mitchell, a young anthropologist from the twenty-first century, is sent back to the sixteenth century to work among the Sterkarm—a group of warriors in the disputed border region between England and Scotland. The Sterkarm believe all time-travelers to be elves—including Per, the wounded son of their leader, who winds up in the "Elfland" of Andrea's century. It's a complex, philosophical story of two vastly different cultures in conflict, beautifully told, enriched by historical detail and Celtic folklore.

The Amber Spyglass by Philip Pullman (Knopf) is the third, concluding novel in Pullman's "His Dark Materials" trilogy. When this book finally came out last year, there were many of us who found it a far greater cause for anticipation and celebration than the release of the new Harry Potter volume—for when it comes to children's fantasy, this is destined for classic status. (If you haven't read the previous volumes yet—*The Golden Compass* and *The Subtle Knife*—you're in for a real treat.) *The Amber Spyglass*, I must report, has become a controversial book. It's as richly inventive as the previous volumes, and ties up most, if not all, of the plot threads. But this time, the allegorical nature of the story lies much closer to the surface. If overt allegory bothers you, then be forewarned. Otherwise, it's simply brilliant.

Monkey Beach by Eden Robinson (Houghton Mifflin) is a first novel, and a fabulous one. Set in Kitamaat, the homeland of the Haisla people, five hundred miles north of Vancouver, it's the story of twenty-year-old Lisa Hill, caught—as all her family is caught—between modern Canadian culture and traditional Native American life. The novel follows Lisa up the Douglas Channel as she searches for a brother who is lost at sea, alternating with flashbacks of her childhood in a colorful extended family. Funny, moving, gripping, tragic, woven through with mythic imagery (animal spirits, ghosts, Sasquatches, and other elements of Haisla and Heiltsuk lore), I recommend this one to fans of mythic fiction of the Charles de Lint or Louise Erdrich sort. Not since Susan Power's *The Grass Dancer* have I read a debut novel this assured.

When the King Comes Home by Caroline Stevermer (Tor) is from one of the leading writers in the sub-genre critics call "Fantasy of Manners"—that is, fantasy that owes as much to Austen and the Brontes as it does to Tolkien. This elegant, understated book is a work of "imaginary world" fantasy, and the best one yet from Stevermer (author of *A College of Magics*, etc.). Set in a Renaissance-flavored kingdom, the story involves a wool merchant's daughter who strives to become an apprentice painter in the atelier of a famous court artist—and a man who appears to be Good King Julian (who's been dead for two hundred years). It's a droll, enchanting coming-of-age tale about art and identity.

Galveston by Sean Stewart (Ace) uses tropes from the fantasy and science fiction genres to create an ingenious work of twenty-first-century Texan magical realism. It's the third volume in a sequence that includes the novels *Resurrection Man* and *Nightwatch*, and yet (like the previous books) it can also be read and enjoyed alone. The setting is the city of Galveston, Texas in the near future, where the floodwaters of a hurricane echo the devastating impact of floods of magic which have turned society back to a pre-technological level of existence.

Moving through this darkly dramatic setting are a host of vivid characters, each struggling to survive with ingenuity, wit, and a modicum of grace. Anyone interested in checking out the cutting edge of the fantasy field would be well advised to read the collected works of Stewart, one of the most consistently original writers to emerge in the last decade.

First Novels

2000 was a very good year for first novels from both genre and mainstream publishers. The best of those published in genre, in my opinion, was *The Fox Woman* by Kij Johnson (Tor), listed in the Top Twenty above. Runner up: *The Chosen* by Richard Pinto (Tor) is another accomplished first novel, distinguished by its exotic locale—a vividly rendered imaginary world with an "Asian empire" flavor. The first book in a projected trilogy, Pinto's novel is darkly sensual, sophisticated, and highly inventive; I found it hard to put down, and look forward to seeing what this author does next. Also of note: *Daughter of the Forest* by Juliet Marillier (Tor) is an interesting reworking of Celtic swan legends and the "Seven Swans" fairy tale recast as a novel that falls somewhere between fantasy, historical and romance fiction. *The King's Peace* by Jo Walton (Tor) is a more muscular story, set in an imaginary world inspired by, though not strictly connected to, the Arthurian mythos. Rich characterization and graceful prose lifts Walton's work above similar fare from lesser writers. *Transformation* by Carol Berg (Roc) is a fast-paced work of swords-and-sorcery. Though not flawless, the story is entertaining and Berg is a writer to keep an eye on. *Fire Bringer* by David Clement-Davies (Dutton) is an epic animal fantasy likely to appeal most to younger fantasy readers. Set in thirteenth-century Scotland, it's a tragic story enriched by naturalist lore and folklore about deer.

On the mainstream shelves, the best first novel was Eden Robinson's *Monkey Beach*, listed above in the Top Twenty. Runner up: *Ghostwritten* by David Mitchell (Random House) is a dazzling novel connecting the lives of nine protagonists around the world, reminiscent of Michael Moorcock's more mainstream works, or the fiction of Don DeLillo. Also of note: *The Better Man* by Anita Nair (Picador) is a charming book which beautifully conjures small village life in India, involving a protagonist who is literally haunted by his past. *I Am of Irelaunde* by Juilene Osborne-McKnight (Forge) is a novel based on Ireland's famous St. Patrick and the warrior-poet Ossian, a spiritual work informed by historical and mythic scholarship. *The Wishing Box* by Dashka Slater (Chronicle) and *The Realm of Secondhand Souls* by Sandra Shea (Houghton Mifflin) are two first novels in the "American magical realism" tradition of writers like Alice Hoffman. Slater's book is the better of the two—a gentle tale of two sisters in northern California, the father who once abandoned them, and a troublesome magical box that grants wishes. The latter is a novel about vintage clothes, family ties, and coming-of-age the hard way—too self-consciously stylistic to be entirely satisfying, but an interesting debut.

Contemporary and Urban Fantasy

This category consists of contemporary tales in real-world settings infused with magic, including tales of "magical realism" published within the fantasy genre. This wasn't a particularly strong category in 2000, yet three books of this sort were very good indeed: *Daemonomania* by John Crowley (Bantam), *Forests of the Heart* by Charles de Lint (Tor), and *Galveston* by Sean Stewart (Ace), all listed above in the Top Twenty. In addition to these, I recommend *Legends Walking* by Jane Lindskold (Avon Eos), which fell between the cracks of the 1999 and 2000 publishing years. This volume is the sequel to Lindskold's novel *Changer*, and it does not disappoint. The tale involves ancient myths in modern New Mexico and Nigeria. Also of note: *The Last Hot Time* by John M. Ford (Tor) is an urban fantasy of the *War for the Oaks* or *Borderland* sort. It's a very short gangster novel, set in a magical version of Chicago. *The Ozark Trilogy* by Suzette Haden Elgin (The University of Arkansas Press) is an omnibus edition reprinting Elgin's three homespun fantasy books set in the Ozarks: *Twelve Fair Kingdoms, The Grand Jubilee,* and *And Then There'll be Fireworks.*

Imaginary World Novels

This category consists of novels set in wholly invented worlds (Tolkien's Middle Earth being the best example), and in magical realms that lie "beyond the hills we know," to borrow Dunsany's phrase. 2000 proved to be a strong year for imaginary world novels, both dark and bright. Foremost among them were *Lord of Emperors* by Guy Gavriel Kay (Viking Canada), *A Storm of Swords* by George R. R. Martin (Bantam), *The Tower at Stony Wood* by Patricia A. McKillip (Ace), *Silverheart* by Michael Moorcock and Storm Constantine (Earthlight, UK), *The Amber Spyglass* by Philip Pullman (Knopf), and *When the King Comes Home* by Caroline Stevermer (Tor), all previously listed in the Top Twenty. In addition, I recommend the following works of imaginary world fantasy: *Fortress of Dragons* by C. J. Cherryh (HarperCollins/Eos) is the fourth volume of Cherryh's "Fortress" series—dark, forceful, intricately plotted, and rooted in fine mythic scholarship. Cherryh continues to be one of the best writers around, with a sharp and distinctive voice. *The Grand Eclipse* by Paula Volsky (Bantam) is a sweeping novel of grand adventures with a quasi-historical, nineteenth-century feel. Flamboyantly inventive, Volsky's book is that rare thing: a literary page-turner. *The A'rak* by Michael Shea (Baen) chronicles the further adventures of Shea's master thief Nifft the Lean, from the World Fantasy Award-winning book of that title. Though not quite as good as the previous volume, this is smart adventure fantasy nonetheless, reminiscent of classic works by Fritz Leiber or Jack Vance. *Knight of the Demon Queen* by Barbara Hambly (Del Rey) is the follow-up book to *Dragonshadow,* which subverts the usual fantasy formula with complex middle-aged protagonists, sending the "knight" of the title to an alternate world that resembles our own. (Fair warning: This is the middle book in a trilogy or series, and it doesn't really have an end.) *Ship of Destiny* by Robin Hobb (Bantam) is the concluding book in the "Liveship Traders" trilogy by Megan Lindholm, writing under the Hobb pseudonym. This energetic story, set on the high seas, provides the trilogy with a rousing end. *Prophecy* by Elizabeth Haydon (Tor) is a strong sequel to Haydon's memorable first novel, *Rhapsody*—epic fantasy made fresh by the author's deft use of world folklore and myth. *The False House* by James Stoddard (Warner Aspect) is the follow-up volume to Stoddard's first novel, *The High House*, a gem of a book set in a marvelous house that contained all creation. Not nearly as strong as the debut novel, more action-oriented and episodic, *The False House* is still better than much of what's out there and thus worth a look. *Wheel of the Infinite* by Martha Wells (HarperCollins/Eos) is a lush, unusual fantasy novel set in a realm with a Far East flavor. Wells avoids all the quasi-medieval, quasi-Celtic clichés that abound in the fantasy genre, creating a distinctive setting for a nuanced, mature, and well-structured story. Eve Forward's *Animist* (Tor), about a young student mage, will probably appeal most to younger readers. There's nothing startingly original here, but engaging characters (both human and animal) give the novel a certain charm. *Sir Stalwart* and *The Crooked House* (Avon) are the first two books in the new "King's Daggers" sequence by Dave Duncan—recommended if you like series books that don't leave intelligence behind. It's popcorn, yes, but tasty popcorn, and darker than his previous novels. Or try Jocelin Foxe's *Child of Fire* (Avon Eos), the second book in her "Wild Hunt" series—adventure fantasy with a mystical bent, steeped in Celtic mythology. *Silver Wolf, Black Falcon* by Dennis L. McKiernan (Roc) is notable as the twelfth and last book in the author's long-running "Mithgar" series, which has been variously praised and castigated for being extremely Tolkienesque. The series has matured over the years and closes rather gracefully, thus it will be interesting to see what McKiernan chooses to do next.

Historical and Alternate-history Fantasy

The best historical fantasy novel of 2000 was *The Gate of Fire* by Thomas Harlan (Tor), sequel to Harlan's impressive first novel *The Shadow of Ararat*. These fat books are alternate-history novels, richly panoramic in scope, set in a seventh century in which the Roman empire still stands. Harlan's command of history is first rate, as is his tightly woven plot. Runner up: *The Glass Harmonica* by Louise Marley (Ace) is a much smaller book, but it charms nonetheless. Falling comfortably between genres (fantasy, science fiction, and historical romance), it's the story of a girl in eighteenth-century London, assistant to the brilliant inventor Ben Franklin, played against the story of a musical prodigy in Seattle in 2018. *Empire of Unreason* by J. Gregory Keyes (Del Rey) is another historical fantasy that paints a magical portrait of Ben Franklin, set in an alternate, alchemical version of the 18th century. This is book three in "The Age of Unreason," a sequence of literate, thought-provoking novels of speculative history. Set largely in the New World this time, Keyes's saga becomes ever more complex, then ends with its plot threads dangling. For resolution, we apparently have to wait for the fourth and final volume. *Lady of Horses* by Judith Tarr (Forge) is one of this author's most engaging tales, billed as "a prehistoric fantasy" with terrific mythological embellishments. Set among the tribes of the Asian steppes who eventually will become the Celts, it's a shamanistic story of a young woman's coming-of-age among hunters and horses. *The Black Chalice* by Marie Jakober (Edge) comes from a small publisher and may get overlooked, which would be a pity. Setting her story in medieval Germany just after the first Crusade, Jakober spins a suspenseful tale shadowed by the conflicts between the pagan and Christian belief systems. It's a dark, violent, visceral tale carefully rooted in Dark Age scholarship.

On the mainstream shelves, several historical novels with mythic or magical elements deserve your attention. I particularly recommend three gripping novels set at the turn-of-the-century: *Affinity* by Sarah Waters (Riverhead Books), a fascinating story of Victorian spiritualists, set in a London women's prison; *The Fig Eater* by Jody Shields (Little, Brown), an atmospheric whodunit set in turn-of-the-century Vienna, flavored with Gypsy mysticism; and *The Knowledge of Water* by Sarah Smith (Ballantine), a delicious murder mystery set in France at the time of Colette. (There's no overt fantasy in the latter book, which is part of the author's *Vanished Child* sequence, but fantasy readers are likely to enjoy the novel's sly gothic theme.) You might also try *Grange House* by Sarah Blake (Picador), a ghost story of the Wilkie Collins sort. Blake is so faithful to the Victorian tradition that she occasionally stumbles into pure melodrama, yet she tells an intriguing nineteenth-century tale set on the New England coast. Also of note: *The Merciful Women* by Argentine writer Federico Andahazi, translated from the Spanish by Alberto Manguel (Grove Press), is a short, stylish novel set in a nineteenth-century Switzerland, involving Mary Shelley, Percy Bysshe Shelley, Lord Byron, and the birth of *Frankenstein. Marley's Ghost* by Mark Hazard Osmun (Twelfth Night Press) is billed as a "prequel" to Dickens's A *Christmas Carol*, portraying the life story of Jacob Marley—the ghostly partner of Ebenezer Scrooge. The prose suffers by comparison to Dickens, of course, but it's an interesting conceit. *The Problem of the Evil Editor* by Roberta Rogow (Minotaur Books) is the quirky third novel in a series that pairs Sir Arthur Conan Doyle and Lewis Carroll up as sleuths. As a mystery, it's not terribly suspenseful or well-plotted, but the cast of characters includes a number of other famous Victorians, making for an entertaining read. *Mrs. Shakespeare* by Robert Nye (Arcade) is a randy little novel about William Shakespeare as seen by his unsentimental widow. Nye's ideas, though rooted in Shakespearean scholarship, contain enough whimsy to put his mischievous new book in the fantasy camp. *Dream of Venus (Or Living Pictures)* by Miles Beller (CM Publishing) is a quirky jazz riff of a novel that both re-creates and reinvents the Town of Tomorrow from the 1939 New York World's Fair. *The Ascetic of Desire* by Sudhir Kakar (Overlook) is a lyrical speculation on the life of Vatsayana, the mysterious author of the *Kama Sutra*, as seen through the eyes of one of his students in the 4th century A.D.

Mythic Fiction

This category includes novels directly inspired by myth, folklore, and fairy tales. The three best novels of this sort published in the year 2000 are: *Beast* by Donna Jo Napoli (Atheneum); *Spindle's End* by Robin McKinley (Ace), and *The Fox Woman* by Kij Johnson (Tor), all listed above in the Top Twenty. I would be remiss if I failed to mention another fine book, *White as Snow* by Tanith Lee (Tor), published in the Adult Fairy Tales series edited by yours truly. Lee's novel-length version of the "Snow White" fairy tale is dark, disturbing, and fascinating, twined with the Persephone-Demeter myth and old pagan lore of the forest. Also of note: *Sometimes the Soul: Two Novellas of Sicily* by Gioia Timpanelli (Vintage) is a lovely book by one of Italy's most acclaimed traditional storytellers. The first novella weaves Sicilian fairy tales into the story of a woman locked away in an old Palermo villa; the second is an unusual retelling of "Beauty and the Beast." *The Palace of Tears* by Alev Lytle Croutier (Delacorte) is a dreamlike, spiced and perfumed little novel rooted in the language of Persian fairy tales. Beginning in 19th-century Paris and traveling on to the Orient, Croutier's magical realist story follows the adventures of a young French winemaker as he pursues the object of his heart—a woman known only through her portrait. *The Snow Queen* by Eileen Kernaghan (Thistledown Press) is a gentle, enchanting retelling of the Hans Christian Andersen fairy tale, set among the cold northern woods and Sami people of Finland. It's a small press edition out of Canada, handsomely packaged with a Dulac cover.

Mad Merlin by J. Robert King (Tor) takes a rather unusual view of the Arthurian mythos, using Roman, Norse, and Irish Celtic mythology to reinvent the figure of Merlin. There's more action than characterization here (try T. A. Barron's work if you prefer the latter), but it's certainly original. *The Knight of the Sacred Lake* by Rosalind Miles (Crown) is the second book in the "Guenevere" series by a feminist scholar and best-selling writer of excellent historical sagas. *Gilgamesh* by Stephan and Melodi Lammond Grundy (Morrow) is a fat heroic fantasy novel based on the ancient Sumerian epic of that title. The scholarship behind the book is sound; the story is dark and well told. *Honk if You Love Aphrodite* by Daniel Evan Weiss (Serpent's Tail) is a thoroughly contemporary mythical saga—a sassy retelling of Homer's *Odyssey*, set on the streets of Brooklyn. *The Minotaur Takes a Cigarette Break* by Steven Sherrill (John F. Blair Publisher) is an eccentric modern mythic novel about a minotaur working as a steakhouse cook. It has some delightfully wonky moments, but overall the symbolism wears thin. *The Snowfly* by Joseph Heywood (The Lyons Press) is another eccentric book, larger in scope. Heywood's novel, concerning the folklore of fly fishing, travels halfway around the globe in pursuit of the possibly mythical snowfly, perfect for catching trout. *The Keeper of Dreams* by Peter Shann Ford (Simon & Schuster) is a mystical thriller by a writer billed as the "Tony Hillerman of Australia." Ford's novel has some flaws of craft, but its vivid depiction of Aboriginal mysticism kept me turning the pages till the second half, where it picks up steam. *Truth & Bright Water* (The Atlantic Monthly Press) is yet another brilliant story from Native American author Thomas King. Although not quite as myth-infused as his previous novel (*Green Grass, Running Water*) there's still enough quiet magic in this contemporary story of reservation life to delight fans of American magical realism of the Charles de Lint or Louise Erdrich stripe. *Chancers* by Native American author Gerald Vizenor (University of Oklahoma Press) is a short, powerful fantasia set on a college campus in California, about wiindigoo, tricksters, and a collection of Native remains in an anthropology museum. *Soul of the Sacred Earth* by Vella Munn (Forge) is historical fiction with mythic underpinnings, depicting the clash between Hopi, Navajo, and Spanish missionary cultures in the sixteenth century.

Humorous Fantasy

Depending on your taste in comedy, the funniest fantasy of the year is either *The Fifth Elephant* by Terry Pratchett (HarperCollins), the sprightly, clever twenty-fourth installment in Pratchett's "Discworld" series—or it's George Saunders's fractured fairy tale, *The Very Persistent Gappers of Frip* (Villard), a short but completely hilarious book, splendidly illustrated by Lane Smith. (The Saunders tale has got my vote. It's utterly, wonderfully wacky.) Also of note: *Valhalla* by Tom Holt (Orbit, U.K.) is a mordantly funny fantasy novel exploring the concept of life after death—darker in tone than the Pratchett book, but just as smart and subversive. Kurt Vonnegut also writes about death in his odd little book *God Bless You, Dr. Kevorkian* (Seven Stones Press), consisting of interviews with famous dead people—Shakespeare, Hitler, "Kilgore Trout," etc. The book began as a series of radio spots for WNYC in New York. *Ray in Reverse* by David Wallace (Algonquin) is a quirky but endearing novel about a man who has recently died, examining his comically shiftless life during his time on earth. Wallace's brand of humor is quiet, folksy, and insightful. *Damned If You Do* by Gordon Houghton (Picador) is yet another book about life after death, and the very best of the four—a dazzling novel of biting black humor chronicled by a man (recently deceased) who becomes Death's apprentice.

Buddha's Little Finger by Victor Pelevin, translated from the Russian by Andrew Bromfield (Viking), is the latest novel from a young Russian literary star, weaving history and Buddhist philosophy into a trenchant comedic fable. *Fierce Invalids Home from Hot Climates* by Tom Robbins (Bantam) is the latest work from a homegrown comic fabulist. Robbins is something of an acquired taste, but for fans of his relentlessly zany style, the new novel (his first in seven years) has some wonderful moments. It's the story of a CIA agent who finds enlightenment with a Peruvian shaman and thereafter cannot touch the ground. I could have done without the pedophile subplot, but otherwise it's pretty funny. *The Miserable Mill* and *The Austere Academy* by Lemony Snicket, illustrated by Brett Helquist (Harper-Collins), are two small, wicked books relating the unfolding adventures of the Baudelaire orphans—volumes four and five in Snicket's Edward Gorey-esque "A Series of Unfortunate Events." *Alix in Academe* by Jeanne Purdy (Creative Arts), a reworking of *Alice's Adventures in Wonderland* set on a college campus, will be of interest primarily to "Alice" completists and diehard academics. A far better satire of university life is *The Lecturer's Tale* by James Hynes (Picador), a vicious reworking of the Midas legend with a deliciously gothic edge. *Mr. Spaceman* by Robert Olen Butler (Grove Press) is a book I shouldn't be listing here at all, since it's technically science fiction and not fantasy—but this wise and funny book by a Pulitzer Prize-winning author is just too good to miss. It's the tale of a Louisiana tour bus abducted while en route to a gambling casino, and of the sixteen-fingered alien who is studying humankind.

Fantasy in the Mainstream

Magical novels on the mainstream shelves can be more difficult to find than those grouped under a fantasy label, so each year we make a special effort to point the way to books you might otherwise overlook. For instance, be sure not to miss *The River King* by Alice Hoffman (Putnam), a contemporary murder mystery with magical realist elements, about the lives of teachers and students in a New England private school. Hoffman is one of America's best writers, and the tale is both moving and chilling. For magical realism Caribbean-style, I recommend *The Drifting of Spirits* by Gisèle Pineau, a prize-winning novel translated from the French by Michael Dash (Quartet Books, U.K.). This engrossing book—about a Guadeloupean family and the ancient spirits who play havoc with their lives—comes out of the Créolité literary movement and is a real gem. For Latin American magical realism, try *Final Exam* by Julio Cortázar, translated from the Spanish by Alfred Mac Adam (New Directions), a darkly comic novel set in the streets of a surreal version of Buenos Aires. I also recommend *A Place Called Milagro de la Paz* by Manlio Argueta, translated from the Spanish by Michael B. Miller (Curbstone Press), a splendid but harrowing new novel from this fine El Salvadoran writer. The author uses magical realism along with a fractured narrative style to portray the lives of women in a family fractured by poverty and violence. *Caracol Beach* by Eliseo Alberto, translated from the Spanish by Edith Grossman (Knopf), is a brutal, phantasmagorical story about a ghost-ridden Cuban soldier in modern Miami. Alberto was a student of literary master Gabriel García Márquez, to whom the book is dedicated. *Playing with Light* by Beatriz Rivera (Arte Público Press) is a gentler Cuban-American novel, also set in Miami, about the interconnected lives of a community of Cuban women. It's an offbeat, slightly surreal, and funny story about love and family ties. *The Natural Order of Things* by António Lobo Antunes, translated from the Portuguese by Richard Zenith (Grove Press), is another novel about family ties— this one darker and harder hitting, using the story of one family to tell a larger tale about the history of Portugal. *Tula Station* by David Toscana, translated from the Spanish by Patricia J. Duncan (St. Martin's Press), focuses on the history of one remote town in the mountains of Mexico. Toscana's engaging novel weaves past and present together into a portrait of a small community.

There were several interesting ghost stories last year, including the Sarah Waters and Sarah Blake books discussed above under Historical Fantasy. I also recommend *More Than You Know* by Beth Gutcheon (Morrow), set in a coastal town in Maine, which involves a ghost, a murder, and small town secrets that reverberate through the generations. *Polly's Ghost* by Abby Frucht (Scribner's) is a less successful ghost story, so lyrically over-written that it devolves into preciousness. The ghost here is the narrator, who died giving birth to her youngest son and now hovers over her family, watching as their lives unfold. *Saving Elijah* by Fran Dorf (Putnam) takes a somewhat sentimental theme—a mother's desperate desire to save her ill son—and turns it into a contemporary version of the Faust legend. The ghost in this thriller seeks the use of the mother's body in exchange for the salvation of her son. Three novels use magical symbolism to underscore coming-of-age stories. The best of them is *The Quick & the Dead*, the latest work from Joy Williams (Knopf), a sharply comic novel about three teenage girlfriends in the Texas desert. It's a quirky book, but Williams is a terrific writer and her language soars. *Pobby and Dingan* by Ben Rice (Knopf) is a much-lauded novella about the imaginary friends of the daughter of an Australian opal miner. It's a sentimental little story, but the unusual setting is beautifully evoked. *When Kambia Elaine Flew in From Neptune* by Lori Aurelia Williams (Simon & Schuster) is primarily a realist story, but it uses folktale themes and imagery to tell a hard-hitting tale about child abuse in a Houston neighborhood. The subject is grim but the book is not, and William's prose is lovely.

Also of note: *The Verificationist* by Donald Antrim (Knopf) is a short novel about a self-centered psychotherapist who, while dining with colleagues in a pancake house, leaves his body and floats to the ceiling. The book comes with glowing reviews by the likes of Thomas Pynchon and Annie Proulx, but I confess it didn't work for me. Nor did *After the Campfires* by Per Jorner, translated from the Swedish by Laurie Thompson (Toby Press, U.K.). Though published by a small literary press, this is pure quest-style genre fantasy involving four friends in a magical realm endangered by wizardly machinations. The publisher claims it's a huge success in Sweden, but I found it unreadable. Another odd one is *Outfoxed* by Rita Mae Brown (Ballantine), a murder mystery involving the rituals of fox hunting and life in the American South. The fantasy element here is that the foxes and hounds all talk. And yes, that's as silly as it sounds.

In Other Genres

Each year there are books published in the science fiction and horror genres that fantasy readers might also enjoy. Here are several novels published last year that I recommend seeking out: *Perdido Street Station* by China Miéville (Macmillan, U.K.) is a sprawling interstitial novel that falls in the cracks between several genres, set in a magical city much like a surrealist's vision of London. It's an extraordinary book, both brutal and redemptive, inviting comparison to the works of such great writers as M. John Harrison, Michael Moorcock, and Mervyn Peake. This is Miéville's second novel (after the excellent *King Rat*) and I, for one, am impressed. *Midnight Robber* by Nalo Hopkinson (Warner Aspect) is set on another planet and thus must be categorized as science fiction, yet the story is magical in flavor, rich in Caribbean folklore and myth. This, too, is a second novel, and Hopkinson is a writer to watch. *In Green's Jungles* by Gene Wolfe (Tor) is the second volume of his "Book of the Short Sun" trilogy. This is fiercely intelligent, beautifully written science fiction with a mystical bent. *Indigo* by Graham Joyce (Pocket) is a dark fantasy thriller that roams from Chicago to Italy, about the secret of invisibility, and the secrets that hide within families. *Dreamside* by Graham Joyce (Tor), is a suspenseful story of college friends involved with lucid dreaming. It's Joyce's first novel, finally available in an American edition. *Shadows Bend* by David Barbour and Richard Raleigh (Ace) is a dark fantasy "road novel," following two men on a mystical journey. The twist here is that the protagonists are pulp fiction writers H.P. Lovecraft and Robert E. Howard, en route to meet up with a third writer of classic pulp fiction, Clark Ashton Smith. It's a clever, unusual book.

Oddities

The Best Peculiar Book Award for 2000 goes to *The Temple of Iconoclasts* by J. Rodolfo Wilcock, translated from the Italian by Lawrence Venuti (Mercury

House), a wonderfully bizarre work of surrealist fiction disguised as a series of biographical essays about (mostly) imaginary people. Wilcock was an Argentinean-Italian writer who was part of the Borges circle, and this seems to be the first of his works to be translated into English. Runner up: *House of Leaves* by Mark Z. Danielewski (Pantheon), a wild, sprawling postmodern novel about an imaginary academic monograph about an imaginary documentary film about an imaginary photojournalist who discovers a supernatural house. The prismatic story comes with footnotes, lists, and invented interviews with real academics. It's a creepy and unsettling first novel, alternately infuriating and rewarding.

Briefly Noted

The following fantasy novels hit the various bestseller lists in 2000. Beloved by large numbers of readers across the country, they deserve a mention: *Angel Fire East* by Terry Brooks (Del Rey), *The Voyage of the Jerle Shannara: Ilse Witch* by Terry Brooks (Del Rey), *Soldiers Live* by Glen Cook (Tor), *Krondor: The Assassins* by Raymond E. Feist (Avon Eos), *Fortune's Stroke* by Eric Flint and David Drake (Baen), *Hero in the Shadows* by David Gemmell (Del Rey), *Faith of the Fallen* by Terry Goodkind (Tor), *The Kingless Land* by Ed Greenwood (Tor), *King Kelson's Bride* by Katherine Kurtz (Ace), *Brightly Burning* by Mercedes Lackey (DAW), *Silver Wolf, Black Falcon* by Dennis L. McKiernan (Roc), *Scion of Cyador* by L. E. Modesitt, Jr. (Tor), *Mortalis* by R. A. Salvatore (Del Rey), *The Great War: Walk in Hell* by Harry Turtledove (Del Rey), *Well of Darkness* by Margaret Weis and Tracy Hickman (Avon Eos), and *Grand Conspiracy* by Janny Wurts (HarperPrism).

Children's Fantasy

The most talked about fantasy novel for children, of course, was book #4 in the Harry Potter saga: *Harry Potter and the Goblet of Fire* by J. K. Rowling (Scholastic). It's long, involved, and darker than the previous books—none of which discouraged young Potter fans, who immediately devoured the hefty tome and then demanded more. So is the new book any good? In my opinion, yes it is. We're not talking Proust here, but Rowling is an inventive and entertaining writer; her world rings true and her characters are deepening with each installment. But if you're looking for exquisite writing in addition to magical entertainment value, then here are some other books I'd recommend above Rowling's more famous work. First of all, there are the four splendid Young Adult novels discussed in the Top Twenty: *Year of the Griffin* by Diana Wynne Jones (Greenwillow), *Beast* by Donna Jo Napoli (Atheneum), *The Sterkarm Handshake* by Susan Price (HarperCollins), and *The Amber Spyglass* by Philip Pullman (Knopf). In addition to these, try: *Kit's Wilderness* by David Almond (Delacorte), an absolutely stunning novel set in an old mining town in England. It's a gorgeously written ghost story, and packs an emotional wallop. *Innocence* by Jane Mendelsohn (Riverhead Books) was published as an adult novel (which had some reviewers shaking their heads) but it's really Young Adult fiction of the Francesca Lia Block sort—a provocative, deliciously gothic tale set in a private school in New York. *The Stones Are Hatching* by Geraldine McCaughrean (HarperCollins) is excellent Celtic fantasy that reads like a cross between Alan Garner and Greer Gilman, written by a multiple-award-winning British author and folklorist. *The Wings of Merlin* by T. A. Barron (Philomel) is the fifth volume in Barron's luminous "The Lost Years of Merlin" series—a splendid work of Arthurian fiction, deeply mythic and spiritual. For historical fantasy, I recommend *The Queen's Own Fool* by Jane Yolen and Robert J. Harris (Philomel), a fascinating novel about a female jester in the court of Mary, Queen of Scots; and *The Book of the Lion* by Michael Cadnum (Viking), a vigorous novel about Richard the Lionhearted, set in England and the Middle East.

Also of note: *The Fall* by Garth Nix (Scholastic) is the first book in the "Seventh Tower" series which this author is writing for Lucasfilms. Though not quite as fine as his stand alone work, nonetheless Nix lifts this commercial assignment above the usual fantasy clichés to create a vivid imaginary world. The kids of my acquaintance love it. They also love *The Legend of Luke* and *Lord Brocktree* by Brian Jacques (Philomel), which are books #12 and #13 in the ongoing "Redwall Epic." Okay, it's a series about sentient rodents—but actually it's pretty darn good, and Jacques manages to keep it all fresh as he churns out volume after best-selling volume. *Wolf Tower* by Tanith Lee (Dutton) is the first book in "The Claidi Journals" series, a thoroughly enjoyable fantasy adventure about a runaway serving girl, told through her diary entries. *Shiva's Fire* by Suzanne Fisher Staples (Farrar, Straus & Giroux) is the story of a young student of classical dance in India. Although Staples's prose occasionally stumbles, overall this is a marvelous book, exotic, enchanting, rooted in Indian folklore and mysticism. *Sky Rider* by Nancy Springer (Avon Tempest) is a terrific ghost story involving a troubled girl, a mysterious boy, and horses. Springer transcends the "problem novel" formula to create a truly magical story. *The Grave* by James Heneghan (Frances Foster Books/Farrar, Straus & Giroux) is a fine time-travel novel about a foster kid in modern Liverpool who ends up in nineteenth-century Ireland during the potato famine. It's a moving tale about family ties, though the ending doesn't quite convince. *Prospero's Children* by Jan Siegel (Del Rey) is another book published for adults that seems to belong on the YA shelves. It's the magical story of a brother and sister (aged twelve and sixteen, respectively) who spend the summer in a sinister, remote farmhouse in the wilds of Yorkshire. *The Watcher* by Margaret Buffie (Kids Can Press) is an odd, atmospheric book about a young girl on the cusp of adulthood, and the terrible magical Game that draws her away from the family farm. *Magic Steps* by Tamora Pierce (Scholastic) is the first volume of "The Circle Opens" series. It's another typical Pierce fantasy of magic and student mages, reasonably well-written, action-packed, and perfect for younger adolescents. *The Hidden Arrow of Maether* by Aiden Beaverson (Delacorte) is an imaginary world novel that doesn't quite manage to avoid the usual clichés, but at its best the tale is reminiscent of Patricia C. Wrede's early work. *The Wind Singer* by William Nicholson (Hyperion) is the frustrating first volume in the new "Wind on Fire Trilogy" by an accomplished writer of films. It's got some good ideas and characters but the writing here is oddly flat, while the invented world lacks internal consistency. Unless the trilogy improves with the second volume, I'd resist the beautiful Peter Sis package and give this one a miss. *After Hamelin* by Bill Richardson (Annick Press) is a reworking of the Pied Piper of Hamelin folk tale, as seen through the eyes of the single child the magical piper left behind. This one has some lovely passages, but doesn't quite hang together.

For Middle Grade readers, I recommend two tales about rats and one about bats. *I Was a Rat!* by Philip Pullman (Knopf) is a hilarious take on the "Cinderella" tale, about a scruffy boy who can't get anyone to believe he used to be a rodent. *The Christmas Rat* by Avi (Atheneum) is a moving story about a bored young boy, a mysterious Christmas visitor, and a rat in the basement. *Sunwing* by Kenneth Oppel (Simon & Schuster), the sequel to Oppel's previous novel, *Silverwing*, is the charming story of the perilous adventures of a young bat in search of his father. Also of note: *The Sooterkin* by Tom Gilling (Viking), with lovely cover art by Peter de Sève, is a winsome, best-selling Australian fantasy about a young seal baby born to a woman in a nineteenth-century penal colony. *Raphael and the Noble Task* by Catherine A. Salton (HarperCollins), illustrated by David Weitzman, is a poignant tale about a gargoyle who lives in a medieval cathedral. It's a handsome little volume, filled with snippets of medieval history, Christian folklore, and Celtic myth. *The Savage Damsel and the Dwarf* by Gerald Morris (Houghton Mifflin) is the latest book in Morris's series of humorous Arthurian tales, chock full of knights, fairies, sorceresses, and damsels who seek their own salvation. *Boots and the Seven Leaguers* by Jane Yolen (Harcourt) is billed as a "rock-and-troll" novel—a pun-filled fantasy about a teenage troll, his best friend, and kid brother. *Journey to Otherwhere* by Sherwood Smith (Random House) is the third volume in the "Voyage of the Bassett" series based on the art of James Christensen—a moving story that begins in nineteenth-century England and sails into the lands of legend, encountering a variety of multicultural mythic creatures along the way. Volume four in the series is *Thor's Hammer* by Will Shetterly (Random House), an adventurous story of three boys, the old Norse gods, and a prophecy. *Cinderellis and the Glass Hill* by Gail Carson Levine (HarperCollins), illustrated by Mark Elliott, is a short but endearing revision of the fairy tale "The Princess on the Glass Mountain."

Reprints of Classics

A number of fantasy classics were reissued in beautiful new editions last year, several of them under the direction of Peter Glassman of the Books of Wonder children's bookshop in New York. I recommend: *The Secret Garden* by Frances Hodgson Burnett, with illustrations by S. Saelig Gallagher (Books of Wonder/HarperCollins); *The Magic City* by E. Nesbit, illustrated by H. R. Millar (Books of Wonder/SeaStar Books); *Rip Van Winkle* by Washington Irving, with illustrations by Arthur Rackham (Books of Wonder/SeaStar Books); *Dracula* by Bram Stoker, illustrated by master book artist Barry Moser (Books of Wonder/HarperCollins); *The Wonderful Wizard of Oz: 100th Anniversary Edition* by L. Frank Baum, illustrated by W. W. Denslow (Books of Wonder/HarperCollins); *Glinda of Oz* by L. Frank Baum, illustrated by John R. Neill (Books of Wonder/HarperCollins); *The Annotated Wizard of Oz by L. Frank Baum: Centennial Edition*, edited and with an Introduction and Notes by Michael Patrick Hearn, illustrated by W. W. Denslow (W. W. Norton); *The Wizard of Oz by L. Frank Baum: 100th Anniversary Edition*, illustrated by Michael Hague (Henry Holt); *Bed-Knob and Broomstick* by Mary Norton (combines *The Magic*

Bed-Knob and *Bonfires and Broomsticks*), illustrated by Erik Blegvad (Odyssey/Harcourt Young Classic); *The Little Prince*, written and illustrated by Antoine de Saint-Exupéry, with a new translation from the French by Richard Howard (Harcourt); *Alice's Adventures in Wonderland: A Classic Illustrated Edition*, by Lewis Carroll, compiled by Cooper Edens (Chronicle); and *The Chronicles of Narnia* by C. S. Lewis, a new boxed set of trade paperback editions illustrated by Pauline Baynes (HarperTrophy).

Single-author Story Collections

There were several good story collections published last year that fantasy readers shouldn't miss. I particularly recommend the following: *Thirteen Phantasms* by James P. Blaylock (Edgewood Press) is a handsome edition collecting the short fiction of this marvelous writer of American magical realism. It's a reprint collection with no original fiction, but it's good to have Blaylock's distinctive tales collected into one volume. *Sister Emily's Lightship and Other Stories* by Jane Yolen (Tor) collects recent fiction by one of the best fantasists working today. For readers interested in folklore and fairy tale themes, this one is a must. *Travel Arrangements* by M. John Harrison (Gollancz, U.K.) is a gorgeous collection by a top British writer whose work continues to defy all attempts at categorization. Hovering between realism and surrealism, these stories will knock you out. *Blackwater Days* by Terry Dowling (Eidolon) is another interstitial collection falling somewhere between the horror, mystery, and fantasy genres. Two of its stories are reprinted here, which will give you an idea of its range. *Triskell Tales: 22 Years of Chapbooks* by Charles de Lint (Subterranean Press) is a weighty volume collecting the "chapbook" stories and poems published annually by de Lint's own Triskell Press. Many of these tales have already been reprinted in the author's "Newford" collections, but some of the material will be new to his readers, particularly the poetry and early works. The book is packaged with lovely cover and interior art by MaryAnn Harris. *A Dance for Emilia* by Peter S. Beagle (Roc) is a single short story published in a small, slim hardcover edition. It's a contemporary fantasy tale, thoroughly enchanting, as one expects from Beagle. *Four Stories* by Kelly Link (Jelly Ink) is a small but powerful chapbook containing four tales by one of our best short fiction writers, while *Five Forbidden Things* by Dora Knez (Small Beer Press) is a more experimental work. Both chapbooks are available from Small Beer Press, 360 Atlantic Ave, PMB 132, Brooklyn, NY 11217. Fans of experimental fiction might also want to try *Contagion and Other Stories* by Brian Evenson (Wordcraft of Oregon) and *Nymph* by Francesca Lia Block (Circlet Press). The former includes Evenson's story "Two Brothers," winner of the O. Henry Award; the latter is a collection of modern erotic vignettes with folkloric imagery.

In children's fiction, the following collections contain some memorable fantasy tales: *Mixed Magics* by Diana Wynne Jones (Collins, U.K.); *Skin and Other Stories* by Roald Dahl (Viking); *The Rose and the Beast: Fairy Tales Retold* by Francesca Lia Block (HarperCollins); and *The Rumpelstiltskin Problem* by Vivian Vande Velde (Houghton Mifflin).

You'll also find some good magical stories in the following science fiction collections: *Strange Travelers* by Gene Wolfe (Tor); *Other Voices, Other Doors* by Patrick O'Leary (Fairwood Press); *The Perseids and Other Stories* by Robert Charles Wilson (Tor); *Beluthahatchie and Other Stories* by Andy Duncan (Golden Gryphon Press); and *Moon Dogs* by Michael Swanwick (NESFA Press). The latter volume includes Swanwick's brilliant essay on fantasy, "In the Tradition," which is worth the cover price alone. On the mainstream shelves, several collections contain good stories with magical elements. (See our Honorable Mentions list in the back of this book for specific story recommendations.) I recommend: *Never Trust a Rabbit* by Jeremy Dyson (Duck Editions, U.K.); *Ice Age* by Robert Anderson (The University of Georgia Press); *The Lion in the Room Next Door* by Merilyn Simonds (Putnam); *The Coffin Master and Other Stories* by John F. Deane (The Blackstaff Press, Northern Ireland); *Essence of Camphor* by Naiyer Masud, translated from the Urdu by Muhammad Umar Memon and others (The New Press); *The Medicine Man* by Francisco Rojas González, translated from the Spanish by Robert S. Rudder and Gloria Arjona (Latin America Literary Review Press); *When the Night Bird Sings* by Joyce Sequichie Hifler (Council Oak Books); and *The Roads of My Relations* by Devon A. Mihesuah (University of Arizona Press).

The best reprint volume of last year was *The Salutation* by Sylvia Townsend Warner (Tartarus Press), first published in England in 1932. This edition contains fifteen stories, including some of Warner's classic fantasy tales, with an introduction by Claire Harman. Also of note: *Everybody Has Somebody in Heaven: Essential Jewish Tales of the Spirit by Avram Davidson*, edited by Jack Dann and Grania Davis (Devora Publishing) is the third collection of Avram Davidson's work to be issued since his death. This one reprints writings that address the author's Jewish faith—including Jewish fantasy tales (like "The Golem"), along with previously unpublished material and essays on Davidson by Eileen Gunn, Barry Malzberg, Peter S. Beagle, Lisa Goldstein and others.

Anthologies

2000 was another slim year for fantasy anthologies. The best one came from outside the genre: *Whispers from the Cotton Tree Root: Caribbean Fabulist Fiction* (Invisible Cities Press), a bold, ground-breaking volume edited by Nalo Hopkinson. I also recommend *Through the Eye of the Deer: An Anthology of Native American Women Writers*, edited by Carolyn Dunn and Carol Comfort (Aunt Lute Books), which contains some lovely mythic fiction and poetry among its realist works. Likewise, *The Fat Man from La Paz: Contemporary Fiction from Bolivia*, edited by Rosario Santos (Seven Stories Press), features a small amount of magical realism among its more mainstream offerings.

In genre, Martin H. Greenberg continues to produce "theme" anthologies at an astonishing rate, and is to be commended for providing a market for short fiction writers. The best of his anthologies last year was *My Favorite Fantasy Story* (DAW), in which eighteen popular fantasy writers (Terry Pratchett, Gene Wolfe, Charles de Lint, Andre Norton, et al.) were asked to provide their all-time favorite story by another writer. The result is an interesting blend of tales by a wide range of authors from Charles Dickens to Roger Zelazny to Barbara Kingsolver. Greenberg also published *Civil War Fantastic* (DAW) and *Spell Fantastic* (DAW), co-edited with Larry Segriff. Imaginary Worlds, a small U.K.

press, published a slim volume of original fantasy stories based on Welsh mythology, *In That Quiet Earth*, available through their Web site: www.imaginaryworlds.com. For fairy tale fans, *Black Heart, Ivory Bones* (Avon Eos) is the sixth and final volume in the series of adult fairy tale fiction I edited with Ellen Datlow; and *A Wolf at the Door* (Simon & Schuster) is an anthology based on a similar theme, this time for younger readers. Good fantasy anthologies for children: *Sherwood* is a magical volume of original Robin Hood stories edited by Jane Yolen (Philomel), and *Ribbitting Tales* is a delightful collection of "frog stories" edited by Nancy Springer and illustrated by Tony DiTerlizzi (Philomel).

Three horror anthologies contain stories that may appeal to fantasy readers as well: *Ghost Writing*, an absolutely terrific volume edited by Roger Weingarten (Invisible Cities Press); *Taps and Sighs*, a fine collection of ghostly tales edited by Peter Crowther (Subterranean Press); and *Strange Attraction: Turns of the Midnight Carnival Wheel*, based on the art of Lisa Snelling, edited by Edward E. Kramer (ShadowLands Press). The following science fiction and mixed-genre anthologies contained some notable fantasy tales: *Dark Matter: A Century of Speculative Fiction from the African Diaspora*, a first-rate collection edited by Sheree R. Thomas (Warner Aspect); *Vanishing Acts*, a strong anthology of stories about endangered species, edited by Ellen Datlow (Tor); *Imagination Fully Dilated, Volume II*, based on the art of Alan M. Clarke, edited by Elizabeth Engstom (IDF Publishing); *Nebula Awards: Showcase 2000*, edited by Gregory Benford (Harcourt); and *Such a Pretty Face*, a collection of stories about heroes of epic proportions, edited by Lee Martindale (Meisha Merlin Publishing).

Poetry

For magical poetry, the top book of the year was *The World's Wife* by Carol Ann Duffy (Faber and Faber), an extraordinary collection of poems from one of the U.K.'s best writers, many of them based on myth and folklore themes. I also highly recommend *Throwing Fire at the Sun, Water at the Moon* by Yaqui writer Anita Endrezze (University of Arizona Press), an outstanding volume of poetry and prose that draws upon Christian folklore and Native American myth to tell the story of Endrezze's family history. Also of note: *Uncommon Places: Poems of the Fantastic*, edited by Judith Kerman and Don Riggs (Mayapple Press) is an interesting collection of science fiction/fantasy poetry by the likes of Brian Aldiss, Joe Haldeman, Jane Yolen and Patrick O'Leary. *Inanna, Lady of Largest Heart* by Betty De Shong Meador (University of Texas Press) is an intriguing cycle of poems based on ancient Sumerian myth. *Thunderweavers* by Juan Felipe Herrera (University of Arizona Press) is a new sequence of bilingual poems from this Mexican writer and performance artist, incorporating Mayan myth into a powerful, heartbreaking work about violence-torn Chiapas.

Magazines

My heart is heavy as I write this section, for the world of fantasy magazines has lost one of its brightest lights with the death this year of Jenna A. Felice, co-editor with Robert K. J. Killheffer of *Century*, the excellent literary quarterly of the speculative fiction field. Her vision, energy, and spirit will be sorely missed.

Under the guidance of Killheffer and Felice, *Century* came back into print last year with a number of strong, unusual stories—including the Greer Gilman piece reprinted in this volume, and other stories listed in the Honorable Mentions section. The best *Century* story of all, however, was an interstitial work of speculative fiction that was neither science fiction nor fantasy: "The Doctrine of Color," a brilliant story about art and the art world by Kathe Koja and Carter Scholz, published in *Century's* spring edition. I recommend seeking it out.

The best market for American fantasy stories continues to be the Big Three genre magazines: *The Magazine of Fantasy & Science Fiction*, edited by Gordon Van Gelder; *Asimov's Science Fiction* magazine, edited by Gardner Dozois; and *Realms of Fantasy*, edited by Shawna McCarthy. The best British magazine for fantasy is *Interzone*, edited by David Pringle. Gordon Van Gelder is now the owner as well as the editor of *F&SF*, having left his other job (editing the science fiction list at St. Martin's Press) to buy the magazine from its long-time owner, Edward L. Ferman. Although it's sad to see Ferman leave the magazine after all his years of work for our field, *F&SF* is certainly in good hands. I wish good luck to them both.

Among the smaller magazines, I found Honorable Mention stories and poems in the following venues: *Lady Churchill's Rosebud Wristlet, Aurealis, Talebones, The Third Alternative, Amazing Stories, Adventures of Swords and Sorcery, Icarus Ascending,* and *The Magazine of Speculative Poetry. Altair* (a small journal out of Australia) and *Century* provided Best of the Year stories. Also of note: A new mixed-genre magazine was launched in Somerville, Massachusetts last year, titled *New Genre*, edited by Jeff Paris and Adam Golaski. The debut issue concentrated on horror and science fiction, but contained one surrealist fantasy. On the mainstream shelves, fiction and poetry with mythic, surrealist, or magical themes could be found in a wide variety of venues. The following magazines and journals supplied Best of the Year stories and poems: *The New Yorker, Triquarterly, Zoetrope All-Story, The Colorado Review, The Iowa Review, New England Review, Agenda, The New Advocate Magazine,* and *Hemispheres.* The following contained Honorable Mention stories and poems: *Harpers, The Atlantic Monthly, The South Carolina Review, The Louisville Review, The Malahat Review, Partisan Review, Potomac Review, Chicago Review, Connecticut Review, Southwest Review, Latin American Literature and the Arts, Chinese Literature Press, Descant, Parnassus, Pleiades, Calyx, Flyaway, Poetry East, The American Poetry Review, Tar River Poetry,* and *Persimmon.*

On the World Wide Web, I recommend SCI FICTION, at *SCIFI.COM* (www.scifi.com/scifiction) as an excellent source for speculative fiction, edited by Ellen Datlow. For reviews, essays, and publishing information on fantasy, folklore, and folk music, try: *The Green Man Review*, edited by Cat Eldridge (www.greenmanreview.com); *Rambles*, edited by Tom Knapp (www.rambles.net); *Phantastes*, edited by Staci Ann Dumoski (www.phantastes.com); and *the Sf Site*, edited by Rodger Turner (www.sfsite.com). For reviews of children's books, try *The Children's Literature Web Guide* (www.acs.ucalgary.ca/~dkbrown/index.html) and *Achuka* (www.achuka.com). For fairy tales, myths, and mythic arts, try Heidi Anne Heiner's terrific *SurLaLune Fairy Tale Pages* (http://members.aol.com /surlalune/frytales/index.htm); *Lamhfada: The Online Magazine of Myth & Story* (www.lamhfada.com); and *The Endicott Studio of Mythic Arts* (www.endicott-studio.com). For magical art from Beardsley to Rackham to Waterhouse, try *The Fairy Tale Illustration Gallery*, edited by Heidi Anne Heiner (http://surlalune.tripod.com/illustrations/index.html) and *ArtMagick*, edited by Julia Kerr (www.artmagick.com). This year, I'm instituting a "Best of the Year" mention for the writer or artist in the fantasy field with the most interesting Web site. In 2000, it was an even tie between two artists: Charles Vess for *The Green Man Press* site (www.greenmanpress.com) and Mark Wagner for *The Hearts and Bones Studio* (www.heartsandbones.com).

Art

For fans of magical art, I highly recommend *Fairies in Victorian Art* by Christopher Wood (Antique Collectors Club), a beautiful volume reproducing work by most of the major Victorian fairy painters (Dadd, Doyle, Fitzgerald, Paton, Rackham, etc.) along with a very informative text by a noted Victorian art scholar. For contemporary British fairy art, try *The Faeries' Oracle*, a deck of Tarot-style cards with art by fairy painter Brian Froud, along with a book describing the cards and their use by Jessica Macbeth (Simon & Schuster). *Fairytales* by Sulamith Wülfing reproduces the ethereal watercolor paintings of this classic European illustrator (Bluestar), and *The Book of Fairies* features recent illustrations by American artist Michael Hague (HarperCollins). Celtic scholar John Matthews has published a new edition of Malory's *Le Morte D'Arthur* (Cassell & Co., U.K.) containing new watercolor paintings by Canadian artist Anna-Marie Ferguson. Fans of Pre-Raphaelite art should take note of Debra N. Mancoff's new book on *Burne-Jones* (Pomegranate), while fans of surrealism should seek out *Magritte* by Siegfried Gohr (Abrams), and *Dalí: The Salvador Dalí Museum Collection* by Robert S. Lubar (Bulfinch Press). For contemporary work in a surrealist style, try *The Artful Dodger: Images & Reflections* by Nick Bantock (Chronicle), a book about the artist behind the *Griffin and Sabine* trilogy. *Little Lit: Folklore & Fairy Tale Funnies*, edited by Art Spiegelman and Françoise Mouly (Joanna Cotler Books/HarperCollins), is a wacky, wonderful collection of fractured fairy tale cartoon art by eleven cartoonists and book illustrators, including Kaz, Walt Kelly, David Macaulay, Barbara McClintock, and Spiegelman himself. It's a hoot. If your taste in magical art runs to commercial book illustration from the fantasy genre, try *The Frank Collection* by Jane and Howard Frank (Sterling) and *Spectrum 7: The Best in Contemporary Fantastic Art*, edited by Cathy Fenner and Arnie Fenner (Underwood Books). For classic American illustration, seek out *Maxfield Parrish & the Illustrators of the Golden Age*, a beautiful new volume by Margaret E. Wagner (Pomegranate).

Picture Books

Children's picture books provide an excellent showcase for magical art and storytelling. The following picture books came out last year, and shouldn't be missed. The best picture book of 2000, in my opinion, was *Fairy Tales* by Berlie Doherty, illustrated by Jane Ray (Candlewick Press), a splendid collection of twelve classic tales recounted by one of the field's best writers, in a sumptuously designed edition chock full of enchanting, gold-embellished art. On the other hand, *The Serpent Slayer and Other Stories of Strong Women*, adapted by Katrin Tchana and illustrated by Trina Schart Hyman (Little, Brown), is another strong contender for the "Best of the Year" designation. This exuberant oversized edition features Hyman's distinctive watercolor paintings and thirteen terrific tales gathered from cultures all around the world. Another good choice for stories involving feisty, clever heroines is *Not One Damsel in Distress: World Folktales for Strong Girls*, collected and told by Jane Yolen, illustrated by Susan Guevara (Harcourt). The stories in this edition, as recounted by Yolen, are even better than the ones in *The Serpent Slayer*, but Hyman's art gives the former volume a strong appeal, so take your pick. *The Girl Who Spun Gold* by Virginia Hamilton (Blue Sky Press/Scholastic) is a beautifully penned West Indian variant of the "Rumpelstiltskin" fairy tale, combined with masterful paintings by the team of Leo and Diane Dillon. *The Merry Pranks of Till Eulenspiegel*, adapted by Heinz Janisch and translated from the German by Anthea Bell (North-South Books), is a classic German trickster story, graced with exquisite watercolors by the Viennese artist Lizbeth Zwerger. *Rocking Horse Land and Other Classic Tales of Dolls and Toys*, compiled by Naomi Lewis (Candlewick Press), is a collection of six classic fantasy tales by the likes of Laurence Housman and E. Nesbit, wonderfully illustrated and decorated by Angela Barrett. *Me and My Cat?* written and illustrated by Satoshi Kitamura (Farrar, Straus & Giroux) does not compare, as a piece of fine art, to the other titles on this list—but this hilarious story about a boy and a cat who exchange bodies is definitely one of the year's best.

Also of note: *Cinderella*, adapted and lushly illustrated by K. Y. Craft (SeaStar Books); *Little Gold Star*, a Spanish-American version of Cinderella retold by Robert D. San Souci, delicately illustrated by Mexican artist Sergio Martinez (HarperCollins); *Big Jabe*, a retelling of an African-American folk tale by Jerdine Nolen, skillfully rendered by Kadir Nelson (Lothrop, Lee & Shepard Books); *Sky Sisters*, a story about the Northern Lights by Ojibway author Jan Bourdeau Waboose, with vivid, impressionistic art by Brian Deines (Kids Can Press, Canada); *The People With Five Fingers*, a Native Californian creation myth retold by John Bierhorst, with dashing ink-and-watercolor sketches by Robert Andrew Parker (Marshall Cavendish); *Where Have the Unicorns Gone?*, a poignant little story by Jane Yolen, richly illustrated by Ruth Sanderson (Simon & Schuster); *Nobody Rides the Unicorn*, a gentle story by Adrian Mitchell, with sweet, simple paintings by Stephen Lambert (Levine/Scholastic); *Brother Sun, Sister Moon: The Life and Stories of St. Francis* by Margaret Mayo, featuring Renaissance-flavored art by Peter Malone (Little, Brown); *The Christmas Ship*, written by Dean Morrissey, illustrated with his distinctive, Rockwell-like oil paintings (HarperCollins); and *The Magic Hill*, a rediscovered story by A. A. Milne, with sprightly illustrations by Isabel Bodor Brown (Dutton).

In addition, I recommend the following children's folktale collections: *A World Treasury of Myths, Legends, and Folktales: Stories From Six Continents* by Renata Bini, illustrated by Michael Fiodorov (Abrams); *Women of Camelot: Queens and Enchantresses at the Court of King Arthur* by Mary Hoffman, illustrated by Christina Balit (Abbeville Press); *The Fabrics of Fairytale: Stories Spun from Far and*

Wide, retold by Tanya Robyn Batt, illustrated by Rachel Griffin (Barefoot Books); *The Seven Wise Princesses*, Persian stories retold by Wafa' Tarnowska, illustrated by Nilesh Mistry (Barefoot Books); *The Barefoot Book of Brother and Sister Tales*, retold by Mary Hoffman, illustrated by Emma Shaw-Smith (Barefoot Books); *The Barefoot Book of Tropical Tales*, retold by Raouf Mama, illustrated by Deirdre Hyde (Barefoot Books); *Tales From Old Ireland*, retold by Malachy Doyle, illustrated by Niamh Sharkey (Barefoot Books); *The Names Upon the Harp: Irish Myth and Legend* by Marie Heaney, illustrated by P.J. Lynch (Levine/Scholastic); *Cats of Myth: Tales from Around the World*, adapted by Gerald & Loretta Hausman, illustrated by Leslie Baker (Simon & Schuster); and *Gods, Goddesses and Monsters: An Encyclopedia of World Mythology* by Sheila Keenan (Scholastic).

Nonfiction

Several works of nonfiction published last year will be of interest to fantasy readers and writers. The very best of them was *The Oxford Companion to Fairy Tales*, edited by Jack Zipes (Oxford University Press)—Zipes's long-awaited fairy tale encyclopedia, handsomely packaged with Dulac cover art. This volume provides a wide-ranging overview of fairy tale history, scholarship, and fairy tale motifs in all areas of the arts, including entries on modern writers of fairy tales in the fantasy genre. I must warn you that the long entry on "Fantasy Literature and Fairy Tales" is something of a disappointment—the author, Shawn Jarvis, concentrates on classic fantasy and seems unaware of the fairy tale renaissance in our field in the last two decades—but otherwise this is an excellent, useful reference volume, strongly recommended. Also recommended: *New Tales for Old: Folktales As Literary Fictions for Young Adults* by Gail de Vos and Anna E. Altmann (Libraries Unlimited). This fascinating book contains a long, insightful introduction by its editors, and then provides a guide to modern fiction, poetry, art, film, opera, and ballet making use of motifs from classic fairy tales. *Touch Magic: Fantasy, Faerie and Folklore in the Literature of Childhood* is a collection of essays by Jane Yolen—the best book you'll find on this subject, bar none. This new edition, published by August House, includes new material. *The People of the Sea: A Journey in Search of the Seal Legend* by David Thomson (Counterpoint Press) is a new edition of this gorgeous Celtic classic about Irish life, folklore, and legends of the seal people, with an introduction from Seamus Heaney. It was one of my favorite books of last year, and I can't recommend it highly enough. *Fairytale in the Ancient World* by Graham Anderson (Routledge) is an interesting study looking at fairy tale motifs in texts from the classical period. Folklore fans should also be sure not to miss the special "Fairy Tale Liberation—Thirty Years Later" issue of *Marvels and Tales: Journal of Fairy Tale Studies* (Wayne State University Press), which contains good articles by Lewis C. Seifert, Elizabeth Wanning Harries, and others.

Also of note: *J. R. R. Tolkien*, a collection of essays edited by Harold Bloom, published as part of his Modern Critical Views series (Chelsea House), is a disappointment. If you're looking for Tolkien scholarship, save your money for two better volumes: *J. R. R. Tolkien and His Literary Resonances: Views of Middle-earth*, edited by George Clark and Daniel Timmons, and *Tolkien's Legendarium: Essays on the History of Middle-earth,* edited by Verlyn Flieger and Carl F. Hostetter, both published by Greenwood. *The C. S. Lewis Encyclopedia: A Complete Guide to His Life, Thought, and Writings* by Colin Duriez (Crossway Books) is a useful critical and biographical text; as is *Vast Alchemies* by G. Peter Winnington (Dufour Editions), a perceptive book about Mervyn Peake (author of *The Gormenghast Trilogy*). *The Element of Lavishness,* edited by Michael Steinman (Counterpoint Press), is a remarkable collection of letters exchanged between Sylvia Townsend Warner (author of *Kingdoms of Elfin, Lolly Willowes,* etc.) and William Maxwell, her editor at *The New Yorker* magazine, between 1938 and 1978. *Lord of a Visible World,* edited by S. T. Joshi and David E. Schultz (Ohio University Press) contains excerpts from the letters of H. P. Lovecraft, placed into a biographical arrangement. For Pre-Raphaelite fans: *The Pre-Raphaelites: Romance and Realism* by Laurence Des Cars (Abrams) is an informative study of the painters and poets of this Victorian movement. *Dante Gabriel Rossetti and the Game that Must Be Lost* by Jerome J. McGann (Yale University Press) is an insightful look at Rossetti's work in relation to modernism. For critical works on Christina Rossetti, author of the classic fantasy poem *Goblin Market,* try *The Afterlife of Christina Rossetti* by Alison Chapman (Palgrave) and *Christina Rossetti: Faith, Gender and Time* by Diane D'Amico (Louisiana State University Press).

Death in England: An Illustrated History, edited by Peter C. Jupp and Clare Gittings (Rutgers University Press), includes folklore and mythology in an extremely engrossing survey of the subject. *The History of Magic in the Modern Age* by Nevill Drury (Carroll & Graf) is a bit New Agey, but it's a useful volume if you want a brief overview of historical magical movements such as the "Hermetic Order of the Golden Dawn" or Aleister Crowley's "Magick of the New Aeon." *Synchronicity: Through the Eyes of Science, Myth, and the Trickster* by Allan Combs and Mark Holland (Marlowe & Company) is for anyone who ever thought physics and the tricksters of myth have a lot in common. *Symbols of the Sacred* by Louis Dupré (Eerdmans) reprints four now-classic essays on mythic symbolism. *Cassirer and Langer on Myth: An Introduction,* edited by William Schultz (Garland), is a good introduction to the ideas of these two 20th-century philosophers. *Contemporary Women's Fiction and the Fantastic* by Lucie Armitt (St. Martin's Press) looks at the themes of vampires, fairies, ghosts, etc. in fiction by Angela Carter, Margaret Atwood, Toni Morrison, Joanna Russ and others. *Mythatypes: Signatures and Signs of African/Diaspora and Black Goddesses* by Alexis Brooks De Vita (Greenwood) examines African and world myth in a literary context. For women's mythology, I also recommend *On the Trail of the Women Warriors: The Amazons in Myth and History* by Lyn Webster Wilde (St. Martin's Press). *Medusa: Solving the Mystery of the Gorgon* by Stephen R. Wilk (Oxford University Press) is a scholarly, lively, far ranging book on the Medusa legend, highly recommended.

Mythology and Folklore

2000 was another great year for collections of fairy tales, folktales, and myths. Here are the best of the ones to cross my desk in the last twelve months: *The Great Fairy Tale Tradition: From Straparola and Basile to the Brothers Grimm,* selected, translated, and edited by Jack Zipes (W. W. Norton), is a splendid collection of European fairy tales from the sixteenth through the nineteenth centuries, along with essays of fairy tale scholarship. No fairy tale aficionado's library should be missing this volume. *The World Guide to Gnomes, Fairies, Elves, and Other Little People* is a reprint of Thomas Keightley's classic nineteenth-century study of fairy mythology, repackaged with an attractive Rackham cover (Random House). *The Wisdom of Trees: Mysteries, Magic and Medicine* by Jane Gifford (Sterling) is a beautiful and informative book about the mythic lore of trees. *The Serpent's Tale*, edited by Gregory McNamee (The University of Georgia Press) is a slim yet extensive collection of tales drawn from world folklore and myth. *The Epics of Celtic Ireland* by Jean Markale, translated from the French by Jody Gladding (Inner Traditions), is a thorough volume of Irish epics from one of the best Celtic scholars working today. *Celtic Sacred Landscape* by Nigel Pennick (Thames & Hudson) is an attractive, oversized edition providing a tour of Celtic holy sites, while *Chronicle of Celtic Folk Customs* by Brian Day (Hamlyn) contains many interesting tidbits of Celtic folk belief. A *Dictionary of Nature Myths* by Tamra Andrews (Oxford University Press) is a handsome, useful reference volume. *The Sagas of the Icelanders*, edited by Ornólfur Thorsson (Viking), is a fat doorstop of a book containing eleven ancient Icelandic sagas and six shorter heroic tales, along with an introduction by Robert Kellogg and a preface by Jane Smiley. *Odyssey* is a lovely new translation of Homer's epic by Stanley Lombardo, introduced by Sheila Murnaghan (Hackett Publishing). *Mirror, Mirror: Forty Folktales for Mothers and Daughters to Share*, edited and introduced by Jane Yolen and Heidi E. Y. Stemple (Viking) is a charming collection of tales from around the world, compiled by Yolen and her daughter.

For Native American myths, I recommend: *Badger and Coyote Were Neighbors: Melville Jacobs on Northwest Indian Myths and Tales*, edited by William R. Seaburg and Pamela Amoss (Oregon State University Press); *Coyote Wisdom*, edited by J. Frank Dobie, Mody C. Boatright, and Harry H. Ransom (University of North Texas Press); *Coyote Tales*, edited by William Morgan, illustrated by Navajo artist Andrew Tsihnahjinnie (Kiva Publishing); *Basket Tales of the Grandmothers: American Indian Baskets in Myth and Legend*, compiled by William A. Turnbaugh and Sara Peabody (University of Washington Press); *A Story as Sharp as a Knife: The Classical Haida Mythtellers and Their World* by Robert Bringhurst (University of Nebraska Press); *Kokopelli: The Making of an Icon* by Ekkehart Malotki (University of Nebraska Press); and *Medicine Trail* by Melissa Jayne Fawcett (University of Arizona Press). Also take a look at *Native North America*, a good overview volume (with terrific photographs) by Larry J. Zimmerman and Brian Leigh Molyneaux (University of Oklahoma Press).

Other notable books: *Nectar and Ambrosia* by Tamra Andrews (Abc-Clio) is an encyclopedia of food in world mythology. *Tales of Kalila and Dimna* by Ramsay Wood, introduced by Doris Lessing (Inner Traditions), contains classic Indian animal fables from the Panchatantra. *Asian Mythology: Myths and Legends of China, Japan, Thailand, Malaysia and Indonesia* by Rachel Storm (Little, Brown); *Chinese Myths* by Anne Birrell (University of Texas Press); and *Mythology and Folklore in South-East Asia* by Jan Knappert (Oxford University Press) are three good reference volumes. *The Return of the Light* by Carolyn McVickar Edwards (Marlowe & Company) contains twelve tales about the winter solstice gathered from around the world. *The Eagle on the Cactus* contains traditional stories from Mexico retold by Angel Vigil (Libraries Unlimited); and *Tales of the Plumed Serpent* by Diana Ferguson (Collins and Brown) contains stories from the Axtec, Mayan, and Incan traditions. *The Sacred Art of Hunting* by James A. Swan (Willow Creek) is a paean to hunting, combining tales from myth with modern hunting stories. *Witches of the Atlantic World: A Historical Reader and Primary Sourcebook,* edited by Elaine G. Breslaw (NYU Press) provides an interesting overview of this subject, and makes a useful reference edition. *The Creatures of Celtic Myth* is a Celtic bestiary by Bob Curran, illustrated by Andrew Whitson (Blandford Press). *Hawaiian Magic & Spirituality* by Scott Cunningham (Llewellyn) has a distinctly New Age bent, but it's fascinating and contains some lovely photographs.

Music

Traditional music is of interest to many fantasy lovers because it draws on some of the same cultural roots as folktales and other folk arts. Contemporary Celtic and world beat music can be compared to contemporary fantasy fiction (by writers like Charles de Lint or Emma Bull), for artists in both fields are updating old folk themes for a modern age. There is such a wealth of traditional music available these days that we have room to mention only a handful of favorites from 2000 here, with priority given to those with magical, mystical, or storytelling elements. For more recommendations, check out *The Green Man Review* (www.greenmanreview.com) and *Rambles* (www.rambles.net), which I've found to be valuable sources for learning about new releases.

The traditional ballads of the British Isles often tell stories with magical themes (or dark and bloody ones!). For Irish songs, beautifully sung, I recommend Niamh Parsons's *In My Prime* (Green Linnet) and Susan McKeown's *Lowlands* (Green Linnet). Christina Harrison's *Lassie wi' the Lint-white Locks* (Glenanne Records) features lovely ballads from the Scottish tradition, while Connie Dover's *The Border of Heaven* (Taylor Park) presents Celtic music from the American frontier. Madrigal's *Elemental Grace* (Tidemark) contains original songs rooted in traditional themes, beautiful vocal harmonies, and a mix of rhythms from traditional to jazz. (Madrigal's song "Alchemy" is particularly recommended to fantasy fans.) Broceliande's self-titled first CD (Flowinglass Music) is another magical release featuring nice vocal harmonies, ranging from traditional ballad material to Early Music. For something a little different try *Do You Want Kilts With That?* from the Colorado rock-and-reel band Lalla Rookh (Magophonic), which contains interesting versions of the ballads "Two Sisters" and "Marrowbones." For music from Celtic bands, here are three good bands that were new to me last year: Shantalla, a group of accomplished Irish musicians with a strong self-titled debut CD (Green Linnet); Fernhill, featuring the tunes and ballads of Wales on the gorgeous CD *Whilia* (Beautiful Jo); and Colcannon, another band out of Colorado, with an infectious CD titled *Corvus* (Oxford Road Records). If you're unfamiliar with Celtic music, here's a good introductory CD: *Nua Teorainn: New Celtic Music from Green Linnett*, featuring Lúnasa, Niamh Parsons, Kíla, Patrick Street, Shantalla, June Tabor, among others. For great Celtic fiddle music, you can't go wrong with Liz Carroll's *Lost in the Loop* (Green Linnet), while for bagpipe music, I recommend Kathryn Tickell's *Debateable Lands* (Park Records), an excellent CD focusing on songs from the English-Scottish Border. Bagpipe fans should also be sure to seek out Susana Seivane's self-titled debut CD (Green Linnet), a splendid collection of tunes for the Galician bagpipe of northern Spain. For more Celtic music from Spain, try Milladoiro's *Auga de Maio* (Green Linnet). For Celtic music from Brittany, Kornog has a new self-titled release combining Breton music with the Scottish vocal tradition (Green Linnet); or else seek out the new CD from the man behind the whole Breton folk revival, Alan Stivell, playing acoustic and electric harp on *Back to Breizh* (Dreyfus).

If you like Celtic music with a modern kick, combined with rock, jazz, and world beat rhythms, I recommend the Irish band Kíla with their new release *Lemonade & Buns* (Green Linnet) and *Spin* (Celtic music with brass, of all things) from the New York band Whirligig (Prime CD). *Helter's Celtic* from Ashley MacIsaac, the demon fiddler from Cape Breton (Loggerhead), has some truly terrific tunes, but give MacIsaac's vocal numbers a miss. From Australia, Brother is back again after a long hiatus due to an auto accident. Their latest, *This Way Up* (Rhubarb), is a lovely blend of Celtic and Australian sounds. *Drunkards, Bastards and Blackguards* (Fabulous), by the Minneapolis trio The Tim Molloys, is rowdy good fun, and features new songs by Adam Stemple of Boiled in Lead.

The best music coming out of Minneapolis these days is from the Northside label, introducing Americans to the incredible folk music revival in the Scandinavian countries. Here are several new Northside releases that I particularly recommend to fantasy fans: Annbjorg Lien's *Baba Yaga*, a mystical CD titled after a classic figure from fairy tales, features contemporary music inspired by the traditional tunes of Norway. *Sjofn* from the Finnish band Gjallarhorn, is rooted in Finnish and Swedish traditions yet draws on music from around the world, combined with magical ballads beautifully sung by Jenny Wilhelms. Ranarim's *Till the Light of Day*, a CD of Early music and ancient Swedish ballads, features the exquisite vocals of two of the singers from Rosenberg 7. *Cugu* is a strange (yet wonderful) CD from Wimme, a modern singer in the Sámi yoik tradition. These chants (which traditionally ranged from shamanic incantations to commentary on daily life) have been updated with contemporary instrumentation, and are truly wild.

Other good music from around the world: Salsa Celtica's *The Great Scottish Latin Adventure* (Greentrax), salsa music with a Celtic influence, is better than it sounds, I promise. *Heaven's Dust* from Evoka (Three Degrees), an Algerian, Iranian, Italian-American trio based in Paris, is a wonderful blend of Celtic, African and Middle-Eastern inspired music with jazz and techno influences. *Antologia* by Madreus (Metro Blue), a "Best of Madreus" collection, contains stunning songs inspired by the ancient Portuguese "fado" tradition. Shafqat Ali Khan's self-titled CD (World Class Record) features eerily beautiful electro-acoustic music from the Punjabi tradition of India; while *So La Li* by Sabah Habas Mustapha & the Jugala All Stars (Omnium) is a terrific, lively CD of Javanese music based on traditional Sudanese texts. For Native American music, I recommend the latest release by the Navajo-Ute flutist R. Carlos Nakai, who teams up with Newang Khechog for a second CD of Native American and Tibetan music on *In a Distant Place* (Canyon). This time they're joined by William

Eaton on strings and Will Clipman on percussion. Also try *Crossroads* by Robert Tree Cody and Xavier Quijas Yxayotl (Canyon), which mixes indigenous music (with mythic themes) from the American Great Plains and Mexico.

Music recommendations from Charles de Lint: "In terms of strictly traditional Celtic CDs, two highlights of the year for me were *Think Before You Think* by the young group Danú (Shanachie) and *Lost in the Loop*, a brilliant fiddle CD by veteran Liz Carroll (Green Linnet). And speaking of veterans, Alan Stivell (probably best known for his recording *Renaissance of the Celtic Harp*, which ushered in the era of Celtic harp music) returned with his strongest CD in years, *Back to Breizh* (Keltia III), a wonderful mix of acoustic instrumentation, eclectic rhythms, hypnotic vocals and found sounds. *Seal Maiden* (Music for Little People) is a wonderful retelling of the classic selchie tale, done in spoken word and song, both handled more than ably by the talented ex-Solas singer, Karan Casey. She has a speaking voice as charming as her singing voice is lovely. For something completely off-the-wall and one of my favorites of the years, there's *Welcome to the Hotel Connemara* by De Dannan (Hummingbird). It's a collection of old pop tunes (Beatles, Roy Orbison, etc.) done in acoustic Celtic style that shouldn't come close to working but most definitely does. Listeners waiting for the next Loreena McKennitt CD (that's just saying she hasn't really retired as she's said she has) will enjoy *Dance to Your Shadow* by Kim Robertson, a mix of traditional and contemporary songs and tunes played on a variety of instruments with Robertson's harp and lovely voice at the fore. Kathryn Tickell (of various Northumbrian piping CDs fame) has recorded an oddball album mixing traditional wind and string instruments with brass, percussion and voice to make a blend of traditional and early music. Who knew she had such a good voice? It's called *Ensemble Mystical* (Park Records). And finally, for those on a budget, there was *Granite Years* (Cooking Vinyl), a budget-priced, two-CD set of the best of the Oysterband featuring thirty anthemic, mostly uptempo, brilliant slices of life. You should own all fourteen or so of their CDs, but if you can't, at least slip this one into your collection."

Awards

The World Fantasy Convention, an annual gathering of writers artists, publishers, and readers in the fantasy and horror fields, was held in Corpus Christi, Texas last year. The Guests of Honor were John Crowley and K.W. Jeter.

The following 2000 World Fantasy Awards (for works published in 1999) were presented at the convention: Life Achievement: Marion Zimmer Bradley and Michael Moorcock; Best Novel: *Thraxas* by Martin Scott (Orbit); Best Novella (tie): "The Tranformation of Martin Lake" by Jeff VanderMeer (*Palace Corbie 8*) and "Sky Eyes" by Laurel Winter (*F&SF*, March 1999); Best Short Story: "The Chop Girl" by Ian R. MacLeod (*Asimov's*, December 1999); Best Collection (tie): *Moonlight and Vines* by Charles de Lint (Tor) and *Reave The Just and Other Tales* by Stephen R. Donaldson (HarperCollins/Voyager 1998; Bantam Spectra); Best Anthology: *Silver Birch, Blood Moon*, edited by Ellen Datlow and Terri Windling (Avon); Best Artist: Jason Van Hollander; Special Award—Professional: Gordon Van Gelder for editing (St. Martin's Press and *F&SF*); and Special Award—Non-Professional: The British Fantasy Society. The judges for the 2000 award were Suzi Baker, W. Paul Ganey, Tim Holman, Marvin Kaye, and Meslissa Scoot.

The following 2000 Mythopoeic Awards were presented at Mythcon, an annual convention for academics, writers, and readers of fantasy literature. For Adult Literature: *Tamsin* by Peter S. Beagle; Children's Literature: *The Folk Keeper* by Franny Billingsley; Scholarship Award in Inklings Studies: *Roverandom* by J. R. R. Tolkien, edited by Christina Scull and Wayne G. Hammond; Scholarship Award in General Myth and Fantasy Studies: *Strange and Secret Peoples: Fairies and Victorian Consciousness* by Carol G. Silver. The award is judged by the members of the Mythopoeic Society.

WisCon, a convention for writers, artists publishers, readers, and academics interested in feminist and gender issues in speculative fiction is held annually in Madison Wisconsin. Charles de Lint and Jeanne Gomoll were the Guests of Honor in 2000. The winner of the James Tiptree, Jr. Memorial Award, for works exploring issues of gender, was Molly Gloss for her novel *Wild Life* (Simon & Schuster). The judges for the award were: Lisa Goldstein, Ellen Klages (chair), Helen Merrick, Donna Simone, and Jeff Smith.

The winner of the 2000 William L. Crawford Award for best first fantasy novel is *The Fox Woman* by Kij Johnson. The award was presented at the International Conference on the Fantastic in the Arts, March 23, 2001, in Fort Lauderdale, Florida.

That's an overview of the year in fantasy, now on to the stories themselves. Once again, there were stories we were unable to include in this volume but which should be considered among the year's best:

"Seventy-two Letters" by Ted Chiang, from *Vanishing Acts*.

"Floggings" by Kathryn Davis, from *Ghost Writing*.

"Nevada" by A. M. Dellamonica, from SCIFI.com Web site, October 11.

"Rare Firsts" by Paul di Filippo, from *Realms of Fantasy*, June.

"The Cash-point Oracle" by Jeremy Dyson, from *Never Trust a Rabbit*.

"Chip Crockett's Christmas Carol" by Elizabeth Hand, from SCIFI.com Web site, December 27.

"Night Life" by Nina Kiriki Hoffman, from *F&SF*, August.

"The Twelve Dancing Princesses" by Patricia A. McKillip, from A *Wolf at the Door*.

"Chanterelle" by Brian Stableford, from *Black Heart, Ivory Bones*.

"The Thief With Two Deaths" by Chris Willrich, from *F&SF*, June.

I hope you will enjoy the stories and poems chosen for this volume as much as I did. Many thanks to the authors, agents, and publishers who allowed us to reprint them here.

—T.W.
Devon, U.K. and Tucson, U.S.
2000–2001

Summation 2000: Horror

Ellen Datlow

The biggest newsmakers in the publishing world during 2000 were Stephen King and Harry Potter. The exclusive online publication of King's original novella "Riding the Bullet" brought immediate media attention and forced the outdated publishing industry at least to "take note." Although the story was given away free for several days by amazon.com and a few other sources, the central question about this event was whether its success proved that the Internet is a viable delivery system to print publishing or just a highly visible anomaly.

A few months later, King asked his fans via his official Web site about publishing a serialized story/novel called "The Plant" on the site in "5,000-word episodes" that readers would be able to download as a PDF file for free. King asked for $1 per download on the "honor system." King's open message to fans said the original story was first published as a Christmas card and that the work-in-progress was roughly 25,000 words long when he put it aside to work on other projects. The first installment came out in mid-July, and lasted several months. Publishing mavens saw the experiment as a test of the theory that advances in technology and the availability of the Net will allow authors to cut out some middle-men—publishers and bookstores—and sell directly to fans.

Although bookstores might feel threatened, the dollar per installment ploy might work into a very smart marketing move: people who won't pay $30 for a book might sample the author for $1 a download. If they like the product, they might turn into book buyers. After several months the glow faded as fewer readers continued to download the segments. King decided to put the ongoing story into abeyance. News media and the publishing industry took this as a sign of the failure of e-publishing, a rather short-sighted view.

This brings up the serious issue of Web piracy. The Science Fiction and Fantasy Writers of America has taken action against various sites that have made available downloads of members' stories and novels without permission and in some cases has managed to get the service providers to close down the sites. But they spring up elsewhere like mushrooms. What the pirates don't seem to "get" is that if you steal an artist's work without paying for it, you take away her livelihood. And if you do that, then why should the artist continue to produce?

J. K. Rowling's *Harry Potter and the Goblet of Fire*, the fourth book in the Harry Potter series, has captured the imaginations and hearts of children (and some adults) in the U.K., the U.S., and in many other countries. Of course, with success comes the inevitable backlash—Harold Bloom lashed out at the book and its supporters, denying any possibility that the series would make a lasting impression on children's literature. Who cares? And as a colleague opined, Bloom will probably be the one writing an introduction to a critical evaluation of the series in a few years.

In other news, the Book of the Month Club and the Literary Guild announced a "joint venture, 'Bookspan.'" Doubleday Direct, owner of the Literary Guild, is part of Bertelsmann and the Book-of-the-Month Club is a unit of Time-Warner. The two companies together own nearly forty book clubs, and they—including the Science Fiction Book Club (owned by Doubleday Direct)—will continue under their present names and continue to offer independent lists. This is one obvious effect of the Internet. Book clubs feel threatened as those without access to bookstores can now buy books online from their own homes instead of joining subscription book clubs. As more people become wired, book club sales may shrink even more than they already have.

America Online announced its acquisition of media giant Time-Warner, and the company announced that Michael Lynton would become president of its international division. The 40-year-old Lynton had served as chief executive officer of the Penguin Putnam Group for more than three years. Penguin's parent company, Pearson, announced that David Wan will replace Lynton, but will hold the title of president rather than chief executive. Meanwhile, President Phyllis Grann was promoted and given the chief executive title. Industry insiders say that Grann, who was the head of Putnam Berkley when Penguin bought it, handled most of the publishing responsibilities during Lynton's tenure. Wan said his top priority in his new role will be to "expand the power and reach of the Penguin brand and capitalize on the technology revolution that is transforming the way books are produced and sold."

Pearson bought the ailing Dorling Kindersley, which had reported a $41 million loss for the first half of the fiscal year of 2000 as a result of overproduction of *Star Wars* books and products. It will become part of Pearson's Penguin Group, although DK's content will be available to the group's various operating units.

Harcourt General, which includes the Harcourt trade publishing division, has been bought by Anglo-Dutch publisher Reed Elsevsier for a reported $4.5 billion in cash plus the assumption of $1.2 billion of Harcourt debt. Harcourt is the publisher of, among others, Stanislaw Lem, Ursula K. Le Guin, and the late Edward Gorey.

The assets of the troubled Carol Publishing Group were bought by Kensington Publishing Group upon being put up for sale late last year, after C. P. G. declared bankruptcy. The purchase included a backlist of more than 1500 titles and 130 unpublished works.

Stealth Press, founded by author Craig Spector, is a new publisher that intends to bypass bookstores completely by bringing out-of-print and backlist titles back into print in high quality hardcover editions and selling them directly through the Internet. The company, with longtime editor Patrick LoBrutto at the helm as Editor-in-Chief, launched November first with four releases including the first U.S. publication of the horror novel *Morningstar* by British author/screenwriter Peter Atkins (*Hellraiser, Wishmaster*); the best-selling Civil War novel, *Jim Mundy* by Robert Fowler; *Under Venus*, a literary novel by Peter Straub (*Ghost Story, Mr. X*); and *The Valkyrie Mandate* by Robert Vaughan. Stealth plans to publish four or more titles per month.

Leisure's Don D'Auria continues to prove that horror can and will sell by bringing out two mass market titles per month.

Wildside Press, published by Jon Betancourt, ramped up its publishing program by bringing out over two hundred titles in 2000. These range from new collections by Alan Rodgers, Darrell Schweitzer, and Bruce Holland Rogers, a reissue of a collection by Keith Roberts previously only published in the U.K., to a new version of *The Necronomicon* (with Owlswick Press) and a series of fantasy reprints.

Gordon Van Gelder, editor of *The Magazine of Fantasy & Science Fiction*, bought the magazine from Mercury Press and its longtime publisher and owner Edward L. Ferman. Van Gelder left his twelve-year editorial position at St. Martin's Press to devote himself fully to the magazine. He was the in-house editor of *The Year's Best Fantasy and Horror* for over eleven years and also published such authors as Kate Wilhelm, James Sallis, and Don Webb, to name just a few on his eclectic list.

Science Fiction Chronicle was bought by Warren Lapine's DNA Publications. Former publisher Andrew I. Porter continues as News Editor. The sale relieves Porter of many pressures of small press publishing, including time-consuming business details, and will allow him to concentrate on gathering, organizing and writing the news. Another goal of DNA's purchase is to ultimately increase the frequency from bimonthly to monthly, and provide a wider circulation base, with the other DNA magazines, for consumer-oriented advertising campaigns.

Editor Ed McFadden retitled his magazine *Pirate Writings* to *Fantastic Stories of the Imagination*.

Some of the magazines that stopped publishing during the year:

Science Fiction Age, edited by Scott Edelman, was folded by its publisher Sovereign Media/Homestead Publications with the May 2000 issue. According to Sovereign Media the paid circulation of *SF Age* dropped in 1999, and although it was still profitable through advertising revenue, it was decided that the magazine was draining resources and subscriptions from its more profitable sister magazine *Realms of Fantasy*. Edelman resigned from his other editorial positions at Sovereign to work as editor of the TV programming guide *Satellite Orbit* and switched jobs later in the year to take on the editorial helm of *Science Fiction Weekly*. Issue 50 of the quarterly *Marion Zimmer Bradley's Fantasy Magazine* was its last. *MZBFM* was first published in 1988 and, for its entire existence, was published by Marion Zimmer Bradley, who was also its first editor, aided by Rachel Holmen in recent years. With Bradley, who died in late 1999, went the funding for the venture.

Amazing Stories suspended publication, according to Wizards of the Coast Group publisher Johnny L. Wilson. The summer 2000 issue was its last. Although negotiations were reportedly underway to sell the magazine's assets, including material in inventory, to *Galaxy Online*, a sale seemed unlikely once

Galaxy Online's editor-in-chief Ben Bova resigned and the site itself disappeared. *Amazing Stories* was the first science fiction magazine, founded in April 1926 by Hugo Gernsback. It has undergone numerous changes, suspensions, and reincarnations over the decades; it would be remarkable and sad if it did not arise again.

Also discontinued were *The Writer's Network Newsletter, Prisoners of the Night, Pulp Eternity, Deadbolt, Midnight Hour, Bloodsongs* and *Implosion* (the latter two published by Implosion Publishing), the respected *Masters of Terror* Web site, *Dread, Sackcloth & Ashes, Peeping Tom, Nasty Piece of Work,* and *Enigmatic Tales.*

A recent appearance at the University of Pennsylvania Bookstore scheduled for Barry Hoffman, publisher of *Gauntlet* magazine and author of *Born Bad*, was canceled by university officials due to "the sensitive nature of the topics covered in the book" (evidently referring to apparent fictional suicides that occur on the campus in the book). The event was rescheduled to take place at the Kelly Writers House, which also canceled the signing and discussion event for the same reason.

One hundred stores in the Kroger supermarket chain pulled copies of Robert Devereaux's horror novel *Santa Steps Out* (Leisure Books) from its shelves following a customer complaint that he had purchased a pornographic book.

The British Fantasy Awards 2000 were announced September 10, 2000 at FantasyCon 2000, held at the Britannia Hotel, Birmingham, England.

Winners are: The Karl Edward Wagner Award: Anne McCaffrey; August Derleth Award Best Novel: *Indigo* by Graham Joyce (Michael Joseph/Pocket Books); Best Short Fiction: "White" by Tim Lebbon (MOT Press); Best Anthology: *The Mammoth Book of Best New Horror 10*, edited by Stephen Jones (Robinson); Best Collection: *Lonesome Roads* by Peter Crowther (Razorblade Press); Best Artist: Les Edwards; Best Small Press: Razorblade Press run by Darren Floyd.

Australia's 1999 Aurealis Awards were announced:

Science Fiction: Best Novel: *Teranesia* by Greg Egan (Victor Gollancz); Best Short Story: "Written in Blood" by Chris Lawson (*Asimov's SF Magazine,* June). Judges: Van Iken, Justine Larbalestier, Helen Merrick, Peter Nicholls.

Fantasy: Best Novel: *Aramaya* by Jane Routley (Avon); Best Short Story: "Whispers of the Mist Children" by Trudi Canavan (*Aurealis #23*). Judges: Jenny Blackford, Marian Foster, Norman Talbot.

Horror: Best Novel: *Foreign Devils* by Christine Harris (Random House); Best Short Story: "Atrax" by Sean Williams and Simon Brown (*New Adventures in Sci-Fi* Ticonderoga). Judges: Sylvia Kelso, Steve Paulsen, Peter Richter.

Young Adult: Best Novel: *A Dark Victory* by Dave Luckett (Omnibus); Best Short Story: No winner. Judges: Dianne DeBellis, Jonathan Strahan, Sean Williams.

Convenors' Award: *Antique Futures* by Terry Dowling (mp books). Convenors: Peter McNamara, Stephen Higgins.

The 1999 Bram Stoker Awards were presented May 13, 2000 in Denver, Colorado. Winners were: Novel: *Mr. X* by Peter Straub (Random House); First Novel: *Wither* by J. G. Passarella (Pocket); Long Fiction (Tie): "Five Days in April" by Brian A. Hopkins (*Chiaroscuro: Treatments of Light and Shade in Words,* July) and "Mad Dog Summer" by Joe R. Lansdale (999, Avon); Short

Fiction: "Aftershock" by F. Paul Wilson (*Realms of Fantasy*, December); Fiction Collection: *The Nightmare Chronicles* by Douglas Clegg (Leisure Books); Anthology: *999: New Stories of Horror and Suspense*, edited by Al Sarrantonio (Avon); Nonfiction: *DarkEcho Newsletter*, written and edited by Paula Guran; Illustrated Narrative: *Sandman: The Dream Hunters* by Neil Gaiman (DC); Screenplay: *The Sixth Sense* by M. Night Shyamalan (Hollywood Films/ Spyglass); Work for Young Readers: *Harry Potter and the Prisoner of Azkaban* by J. K. Rowling (Bloomsbury, U.K.; Levine/Scholastic, U.S.); Other Media: *I Have No Mouth and I Must Scream* by Harlan Ellison (Dove Audio); Lifetime Achievement Award: Edward Gorey, Charles L. Grant; Specialty Press Award: Ash-Tree Press, Christopher & Barbara Roden.

International Horror Guild Awards, given at the World Horror Convention in Denver: Novel: Stewart O'Nan, *A Prayer for the Dying* (Henry Holt); First Novel: Michael Cisco, *The Divinity Student* (Buzzcity); Long Fiction: Lucius Shepard, "Crocodile Rock," *The Magazine Of Fantasy & Science Fiction*, Oct/Nov 1999; Short Fiction: Gemma Files, "The Emperor's Old Bones," *Northern Frights 5*; Collection: Douglas Clegg, *The Nightmare Chronicles* (Leisure); Anthology: Richard Chizmar and William Schafer, eds., *Subterranean Gallery* (Subterranean); Nonfiction: Neil Barron, ed., *Fantasy and Horror: A Critical and Historical Guide to Literature, Illustration, Film, TV, Radio, and the Internet* (Scarecrow Press); Graphic Story: Axel Alonso and Joan Hilty, eds., *Flinch #1–7* (Vertigo/DC); Artist: Charles Burns; Film: *Stir of Echoes* (directed and written by David Koepp, based on a novel by Richard Matheson); Publication: *DarkEcho* (Paula Guran, publisher/editor); Television Show: *The Storm of the Century* (written by Stephen King, directed by Craig Baxley); Living Legend Award: Richard Matheson; Special Award: Don D'Auria for Leisure Books' ambitious mass market horror series; Grandmaster Award: Harlan Ellison.

Novels

Word Made Flesh by Jack O'Connell (HarperCollins/Flamingo) is this talented author's darkest and most complex novel. The grisly opening scene brutally lays out the stakes in a mystery that engulfs an ex-cop in the strange, fictional New England factory town of Quinsigamond. The ex-cop's former lover works for one of the most vicious crime lords in town while she pursues her obsession with Wormland, an experimental farm, and its creator—a man who went mad during the process and who slaughtered his family a century before. The story of the monstrous destruction of an eastern European ghetto runs throughout the book, told by a man being driven mad by his own memory and guilt. The book is an elegant and savage story of atrocity and remembrance—the power of stories to preserve the past.

Perdido Street Station by China Miéville (Macmillan, U.K.) is the second novel by this talented Briton. Although *King Rat* was good, it hardly prepared the reader for the brilliance of the author's lovingly rendered imaginary city of New Crobuzon in the world of Bas-Lag, and its denizens. A rogue scientist is hired by a Garuda, a humanoid with wings, who has had his wings sawn off by his own people in punishment for the commission of a terrible crime. The Garuda wants the scientist to help him to fly again. In order to research flight, the scientist puts out a call for any kind of winged creatures, eggs, or pupae. He is given a stolen pupa, which becomes a terrifying creature that mesmerizes then sucks its victims dry, leaving them gibbering idiots. The creature is just one of four brought into the city by a crime boss, who milks them for a drug that they manufacture. The novel is overtly, but not intrusively political, and so jammed full of sights and sounds that occasionally they overwhelm. But this combination of fantasy, dark fantasy, science fiction, and horror provides a fine ride into the fantastic.

Run by Douglas E. Winter (Alfred A. Knopf) is a speeding first novel of suspense with the unique voice of a gunrunner who works for a gun supplier, who has been almost like a father to him. But what seems to be a simple job turns into a complicated maze of conspiracy and betrayal. Its non-stop action makes the book compulsively readable.

Saving Elijah by Fran Dorf (Putnam) is an unnerving story about coping with the illness and death of a child. A child psychologist waits outside the hospital ward where her five-year-old son lies in a mysterious coma. When she follows the music she hears, she encounters a swaggering, guitar-playing ghost/demon who claims he can save her son. The price—her occasional possession by the phantom. When the boy miraculously recovers, the mother feels that she owes the demon, allowing her family and work to deteriorate as others question her sanity. Although the supernatural is a presence in the novel it takes a back seat to the drama of the family.

Indigo by Graham Joyce (Pocket Books) is less obviously supernatural than the author's previous works but no less effective. A man is called upon to handle the aftermath of his rarely seen father's unexpected death. The father was charming, rich, powerful, and had a way with women. He was also obsessed with searching for the color indigo, which supposedly could promote invisibility in the true believer. His quest signifies "Mystery" and the "Unknown." The son is a former policeman, so he is perfectly chosen to execute his father's wishes.

House of Leaves by Mark Z. Danielewski (Pantheon) is a fascinating puzzle of a first novel. A disaffected young man discovers a hulking, unshaped manuscript in a dead blind man's apartment and takes it upon himself to read and annotate it. The manuscript chronicles a family's move to a house in Virginia and what they find there. Undeniably a horror story about a haunted house and about the telling of the tale about a haunted house, what could be a clichéd tale is transmuted into metafiction with footnotes, letters from mad mothers and architectural drawings. The germ of the novel is that haunted house, and it is genuinely frightening.

Demolition Angel by Robert Crais (Doubleday) is a departure from the author's Elvis Cole novels. This one is about a former bomb squad technician with the L. A. police whose life has been shattered by the bomb that killed her lover/partner three years earlier and almost finished her off. Now she's caught up in the search for an arrogant and very efficient bomber who seems to want to snuff out the best bomb technicians in the country. This is a fascinating study of some of those who make bombs—their personalities, their obsessions.

The Indifference of Heaven by Gary A. Braunbeck (Obsidian Press) is this respected short story writer's first novel and it's a good one. A rising newscaster's life is torn apart when his pregnant wife dies of complications from premature labor. He is driven to despair by grief and guilt and from there the novel moves into Jonathan Carroll territory, albeit even darker.

Darwin's Blade by Dan Simmons (Morrow) is a lively mystery about an accident investigator who is drawn into vicious chicanery by a widespread insurance scam in California. The best parts of the novel are the investigators' gleeful and gruesome descriptions of "accidents." They are terrific at gleaning clues in Sherlockian fashion from the aftermath of huge car smash-ups.

Novel Listings

Demon Circle by Dan Schmidt (Leisure); *Fetish* by Tara Moss (HarperCollins, Australia); *The Schoonermaster's Dance* by Alan Gould (HarperCollins, Australia); *Under the Skin* by Michael Faber (Harcourt); *When Darkness Falls* by Shannon Drake (Zebra Books); *Canyons* by P. D. Cacek (Tor); *Ghost Written* by David Mitchell (Random House); *Shirker* by Chad Taylor (Walker); *Spontaneous* by Diane Wagman (L.A. Weekly Books); *Panic Snap* by Laura Reese (St. Martin's Press); *Blood of My Blood* by Karen Taylor (Pinnacle); *Blood* by Joseph Glass (Simon & Schuster); *Darkspawn* by Lois Tilton (Hawk Publishing); *Raveling* by Peter Moore Smith (Little, Brown); *The Dark House* by John Sedgwick (HarperCollins); *Period* by Dennis Cooper (Grove Press); *The Fig Eater* by Jody Shields (Little, Brown); *Last Things* by Jenny Offill (Farrar, Straus & Giroux); *Birdman* by Mo Hayder (Doubleday); *Lost Girls* by Andrew Pyper (Delacorte); *Ghost Moon* by Karen Robards (Delacorte); *Merrick* by Anne Rice (Knopf); *The Hell Screens* by Alvi Lu (Four Walls Eight Windows); *Daughters of the Moon* by Joseph Curtin (Pinnacle); *The Debt Collector* by Lynn Hightower (Delacorte); *Deviant Ways* by Chris Mooney (Pocket); *Blood to Blood* by Elaine Bergstrom (Ace); *Murcheston: The Wolf's Tale* by David Holland (Forge); *Quenched* by Mary Ann Mitchell (Leisure); *The Deepest Water* by Kate Wilhelm (St. Martin's Press); *The Spirit of the Family* by Josephine Boyle (Severn House); *Fatalis* by Jeff Rovin (St. Martin's Press); *Adam's Fall* by Sean Desmond (St. Martin's Press); *Vampire's Waltz* by Thomas Staab (Crazy Wolf Publishing); *Shadows Bend* by David Barbour and Richard Raleigh (Ace); *Lady Crymsyn* by P. N. Elrod (Ace); *Magnificat* by Chelsea Quinn Yarbro (Hidden Knowledge); *Worse than Death* by Sherry Gottlieb (Forge); *Gothique* by Kyle Marffin (Design Image); *The Vampire's Assistant* by Darren Shan (HarperCollins, Australia); *A Face Without a Heart* by Rick R. Reed (Design Image); *Full Moon–Bloody Moon* by Lee Driver (Full Moon Publishing); *From a Past Life: A Modern Ghost Story* by Penny Faith (Hodder & Stoughton, U.K.); *Judas Tree* by Simon Clark (NEL, U.K.); *The Puppet Show* by Patrick Redmond (Hodder & Stoughton, U.K.); *Deceased* by Tom Piccirilli (Leisure); *False Memory* by Dean Koontz (Bantam); *Don't Open Your Eyes* by Ann Halam (Dolphin, U.K.); *Mischief* by Douglas Clegg (Leisure); *Tribulations* by J. Michael Straczynski (DarkTales); *Eternal Sunset* by Sephera Giron (DarkTales); *A Darkness Inbred* by Victor Heck (DarkTales); *Clickers* by J. F. Gonzales and Mark Williams (DarkTales); *The Secret Life of Colors* by Steve Savile (DarkTales); *DeadTimes* by Yvonne Navarro (DarkTales); *Demonesque* by Steven Lee Climer (DarkTales); *Soul Temple* by Steven Lee Climer (DarkTales); *Ghost of the Southern Belle* by Odds Bodkin & Bernie Fuchs (Little Brown/YA); *Obsidian Butterfly* by Laurell K. Hamilton

(Ace); *Penny Dreadful* by Will Christopher Baer (Viking); *Blood Memories* by Barb Hendee (Vision Novels [Print on Demand]–1999); *Moon Rising* by Ann Victoria Roberts (Chatto & Windus, U.K.); *Hush* by Tim Lebbon and Gavin Williams (Razorblade Press, U.K.); *To Bury the Dead* by Craig Spector (HarperTorch); *The Dawning* by Hugh B. Cave (Leisure); *The Licking Valley Coon Hunters Club* by Brian A. Hopkins (Yard Dog Press); *Painkillers* by Simon Ings (Bloomsbury, U.K.); *Before I Say Goodbye* by Mary Higgins Clark (Simon & Schuster); *By Blood Possessed* by Elena Santangelo (St. Martin's Press); *A Shadow on the Wall* by Jonathan Aycliffe (Severn House, U.K.); *Lycanthropia* by Fredrick Bloxham (Robert D. Reed); *Silent Children* by Ramsey Campbell (Forge); *That's Not my Name* by Yvonne Navarro (Bantam); *Nightshade* by John Saul (Ballantine); *The Merciful Women* by Federico Andahazi, translated by Albert Manguel from the Spanish (Transworld/Doubleday, U.K.); *The Jaguar Mask* by Daniel Easterman (HarperCollins, U.K.); *Excavation* by James Rollins (HarperTorch); *Harry Potter and the Goblet of Fire* by J. K. Rowling (Levine/Scholastic); *Lowlake* by Roger Davenport (Scholastic, U.K.); *The Cunning Man* by Celia Rees (Scholastic, U.K.); *Ship of the Damned* by James F. David (Forge); *The Resurrectionists* by Kim Wilkins (HarperCollins, Australia); *Under the Overtree* by James A. Moore (Meisha Merlin); *The Mediator: Shadowland* by Jenny Carroll (Pocket Pulse); *Meh'yam* by Gloria Evans (T. Bo Publishing); *The Walking* by Bentley Little (Penguin/Signet); *The Gargoyle* by Gary Lovisi (Gryphon Books); and *Dark Within* by John Wooley (Hawk Publishing).

Anthologies

Despite the fact that some small press magazines died and *Cemetery Dance* barely published at all, short fiction is alive and thriving as evidenced by the many anthologies and collections published in 2000. By my count there were more than twice the number of original anthologies published in 2000 than there were in 1999, and about the same number of collections.

After Shocks, edited by Jeremy Lassen (Freak Press) is an all original anthology of twelve horror and dark fantasy stories set in southern California. Although few of the stories are as redolent of the region as those by Dennis Etchison or David J. Schow, some are very good. Jacket art and design is by Jeremy Lassen.

October Dreams: A Celebration of Halloween, edited by Richard Chizmar and Robert Morrish (CD Publications) is a charming 660-page compilation of non-fiction memories and short stories about what should be the horror reader's favorite holiday. Half of the fiction pieces are reprints; most of the originals are very good. Jack Ketchum's story is reprinted herein.

Imagination Fully Dilated, Volume II, edited by Elizabeth Engstrom (IFD Publishing) is a follow up to her acclaimed first collaboration with Alan M. Clark. Each story was inspired by a piece of Clark's art and several of the results are excellent. The book comes in two editions, both hardcover, containing twenty-nine stories and thirty pieces of art (twenty-four color, six monochrome). The deluxe lettered edition is leather-bound inside a felt-lined box. Accompanying the book is a matted set of the four metal plates used in the printing of one of the illustrations. The Ramsey Campbell story is reprinted herein.

Taps and Sighs, edited by Peter Crowther (Subterranean Press) is a nicely varied passel of all new ghost stories from some of the best contemporary writers on the horror scene. Although only a handful of the stories are truly frightening, many more are thoughtful, bittersweet, and moving.

Strange Attraction, edited by Edward Kramer and based on the kinetic sculptures of Lisa Snellings (ShadowLands Press) began with the excellent idea of commissioning stories about ferris wheels—to be inspired by Snellings's three-dimensional creations. Unfortunately, the idea was better than its execution—there's a disappointing sameness about many of the stories, although there are a few standouts. It comes in two editions, one a cloth limited and one leather. Both have color artwork. The deluxe leather edition is traycased and sold with a limited edition sculpture by Snellings.

Skull Full of Spurs: A Roundup of Weird Westerns, edited by Jason Bovberg and Kirk Whitham (Dark Highway Press) is an all original anthology of mostly dark tall tales inspired somewhat by *Razored Saddles*, the 1989 western gothic anthology edited by Joe R. Lansdale and Pat LoBrutto. The stories are a bit too similar, with a few exceptions. Cover jacket art is by Allen G. Douglas with interiors and back cover art by Christopher P. Nowell.

Mardi Gras Madness: Tales of Terror and Mayhem in New Orleans, edited by Martin H. Greenberg and Russell Davis (Cumberland House) contains eleven stories of varying quality about the Big Easy by Peter Crowther, Nancy Holder, and Charles de Lint, among others.

Extremes, edited by Brian A. Hopkins (Lone Wolf Publications) is a fantasy and horror anthology on the theme of faraway places, available only on CD-ROM. There are twenty stories. The attractive artwork on the cover is by Chad Savage. It's easy to use, once you download the Adobe Acrobat Reader that is part of the CD, and nicely designed. I've found that the Acrobat Reader is the ideal means for reading short stories on screen.

Dark Matter, edited by Sheree R. Thomas (Warner Books) is a cross-genre anthology of reprints and original stories by African American writers, and includes thought-provoking essays by Samuel R. Delany, Octavia E. Butler, and Walter Mosley. Delany confronts the subject of racism within the science fiction field and provides a brief historical overview of speculative fiction by African Americans. There are at least three very dark stories, including a powerful and horrific science fiction story by Steven Barnes.

F20 One, edited by Len Maynard, Mick Sims, and David J. Howe (Enigmatic Press and The British Fantasy Society) contains five fantasy or dark fantasy stories, most of them original, by British writers. The art is by Bob Covington and Dave Bezzina.

Northern Horror: Canadian Fiction Anthology, edited by Edo van Belkom (Quarry Press Fiction, Canada) is a mostly original anthology with some excellent fiction by such diverse writers (not all Canadian) as David Nickel, Kathryn Ptacek, Robert J. Sawyer, and the award-winning author/editor. While some of the stories make good use of the frozen north, others could have taken place anywhere. *Canadian Fiction* is a twice-yearly anthology of contemporary Canadian fiction.

Be Afraid!, edited by Edo van Belkom (Tundra Books) is a mostly original anthology aimed at the young adult market. Many of the fifteen stories deal with the shock of puberty and trials of adolescence, and some of the names, such as Ed Gorman and Steve Rasnic Tem, will be recognizable to the horror reader.

Another young adult horror anthology came from Australia. *Tales from the Wasteland: Stories from the Thirteenth Floor*, edited by Paul Collins (Hodder Headline, Australia) has its share of good, suspenseful stories by authors such as Robert Hood, Lucy Sussex, and Sophie Masson, but the title is pretty much a mystery to me.

Arkham's Masters of Horror, edited by Peter Ruber (Arkham House) is a wonderful overview of many of the writers published by this venerable small press publisher in its first sixty years of existence. Ruber provides a lengthy essay that attempts to shine up founder August Derleth's tarnished reputation. In addition, there are essays on each of twenty-one Arkham House authors with stories never collected previously and six never before published. One of the best is a gem by Howard Wandrei reprinted herein.

Whispered from the Grave: An Anthology of Ghostly Tales (The Design Image Group)—no editor is credited, nor is the preface signed. The book, with fourteen original ghost stories by writers such as P. D. Cacek, Tina L. Jens, Don D'Ammassa, Edo van Belkom, and others has attractive jacket art and is in the company's trademark sturdy trade paperback format.

Graven Images: Fifteen Tales of Magic and Myth, edited by Nancy Kilpatrick and Thomas S. Roche (Ace) is sort of a follow-up to *In the Shadow of the Gargoyle*. Happily, this anthology, which takes on broader themes, is much better than the earlier book. Included are fifteen stories, three of them previously published. The Kathe Koja is reprinted herein.

Brainbox: The Real Horror edited by Steve Eller (Dreams Unlimited, U.K.) is an electronic non-theme anthology easily accessed via Acrobat Reader. Some of the more noteworthy contributions are by Gary A. Braunbeck, Mehitobel Wilson, Brian A. Hopkins, and Charlee Jacob. Each story has an Afterword by the author examining the inspiration for the story.

Embraces: Dark Erotica, edited by Paula Guran was commissioned by the relatively established publisher of erotic fiction, Masquerade Press. When Masquerade stopped publishing, Venus or Vixen Press picked up the anthology. Two of the twenty stories are reprints. Some of the stories are unusual and the authors do seem to be pushing the envelope. The stories are certainly hot and include notable contributions by Stephen Dedman, Nancy Holder, and Jay Russell.

A Taste of Midnight: Vampire Erotica, edited by Cecilia Tan (Circlet Press) has eleven stories by authors including Gary Bowen and Renee M. Charles, two of them reprints.

Noirotica 3, edited by Thomas S. Roche (Black Books) finally gets it right after two volumes that contained more vignettes than stories. The newest volume has some real, honest to god storytelling but the occasional over the top erotic element sometimes undercuts the "noir" by developing ridiculous, unbelievable scenarios.

Bad News, edited by Richard Laymon (CD Publications) is a non-theme horror anthology with some good stories. The introduction by Laymon explains how he met each contributor. Dust jacket art is by Vince Natale, with design by Gail Cross.

Ghost Writing: Haunted Tales of Contemporary Writers, edited by Roger Weingarten (Invisible Cities Press) is a literate but only intermittently horrific original-and-reprint mix of ghost stories by a variety of writers better known in the mainstream. The standouts are by Bret Lott, Kathryn Harris and Peter Straub, the latter a reprint. Contributors include T. Coraghessan Boyle, Louise Erdrich, John Updike, Kathryn Harris, Nicola Griffith, and Robert Coover. Few scares with some exceptions, including Bret Lott's story reprinted herein.

Shadows and Silence, edited by Barbara and Christopher Roden (Ash-Tree Press) is the second all-original anthology of stories by contemporary writers from this Canadian press. It contains a good batch of quietly horrific stories, most but not all ghost stories. Jacket illustration, the first for the press in color, is by Jason Van Hollander. Two stories, by Glen Hirshberg and Ramsey Campbell, have been reprinted herein.

Hideous Progeny, edited by Brian Willis (Razor Blade Press) is an anthology of eighteen stories, most previously unpublished, taking off from Mary Shelley's novel *Frankenstein*. Introduction by Kim Newman; striking cover art by Chris Nurse.

Dark Terrors 5, edited by Stephen Jones and David Sutton (Gollancz, U.K.) is a giant of a book (twice the size of the previous volume in this series) and comes from a new publisher this year. It's jam-packed full of good to excellent stories running the gamut of horror and includes a powerful novella by David Case (unfortunately, too long to include here). Tanith Lee and Dennis Etchison stories are reprinted herein.

Bell, Book & Beyond: An Anthology of Witchy Tales, edited by P. D. Cacek (The Design Image Group) is an anthology of original stories by associate members of the Horror Writers Association. Few of the contributors will be familiar to readers so here's an opportunity to discover some new talent in the field of horror and dark fantasy. The organization's former president, S. P. Somtow, introduces the volume.

Queer Fear, edited by Michael Rowe (Arsenal Pulp Press) is a classy looking trade paperback of mostly original gay-themed horror stories. Some of the better known writers represented are Douglas Clegg, Brian Hodge (reprint), Michael Marano, Caitlín R. Kiernan, Nancy Kilpatrick, and Gemma Files.

Time Out Book of London Stories, Volume 2, edited by Nicholas Royle (Penguin, U.K.) contains enough stories of a dark nature or by writers recognizable to horror readers that it might be worth a look. There are some very good dark stories by Paul J. McAuley, Christopher Fowler, Kim Newman, and Conrad Williams. The McAuley is reprinted herein.

Cemetery Sonata II, edited by June Hubbard (Chameleon Publishing) contains mostly original stories taking place in cemeteries by writers such as Tina L. Jens, John Urbancik, and Dan Keohane. The production values in this trade paperback are far more professional than were those of the first volume.

Daughter of Dangerous Dames, edited by Tina L. Jens (Twilight Tales) contains thirty-nine stories and poems on the titular subject. Only a few of the stories are horror. Some of the more familiar names are Elaine Bergstrom, Chelsea Quinn Yarbro, Yvonne Navarro, Jo Fletcher, Nancy Kilpatrick, and Lois Tilton.

Twilight Tales presents Cthulhu and the Coeds, Kids & Squids, edited by Tina

L. Jens, a collection of silly mythos stories and poems, most of them published for the first time. Cover art by Rick Therrio.

Unnatural Selection, edited by Gord Rollo (LTD Books) contains mostly original (with four reprints) horror stories about extreme evolution or mutation. Among the contributors are Mort Castle, John Shirley, Nancy Kilpatrick, Brian Lumley, and Brian A. Hopkins. This e-book is scheduled for release in a print edition by Imaginary Worlds Press in August 2001.

Tessellations, edited by Jason R. Bleckly and Kain Massin (Altair Publications) is an Australian anthology of twenty stories, three of them reprints by new South Australian authors, with a foreword by Elizabeth Moon and an introduction by Sean Williams. The attractive cover art is by Margaret Anne Davies and Jennifer Etherton.

Foursight, edited by Peter Crowther (Orion/Gollancz, U.K.) is four novellas from the PS Publishing series. It includes one horror novella by Kim Newman plus novellas by Michael Marshall Smith, Graham Joyce, and James Lovegrove.

Reprint anthologies

Into the Mummy's Tomb, edited by John Richard Stephens (Berkley) includes fiction by Anne Rice, Bram Stoker, H. P. Lovecraft, and Ray Bradbury and some nonfiction pieces.

Master's Choice, Volume II: Mystery Stories by Today's Top Writers and the Masters Who Inspired Them, edited by Lawrence Block (Berkley) contains stories by Joyce Carol Oates, Edgar Allan Poe and many others.

Ghosts Across Kentucky by William Lynwood Montell (The University Press of Kentucky) presents ghost stories that he's read or been told from all kinds of people around the state of Kentucky.

The Best American Mystery Stories 2000, edited by Donald E. Westlake—Otto Penzler, series editor—(Houghton Mifflin) reprints twenty crime and suspense stories by Jeffery Deaver, Shel Silverstein, Edward Lee, and others from venues ranging from magazines such as *Zoetrope*, *Ellery Queen Mystery Magazine*, and *Playboy* to the anthology *999* and the collection *A Vaudeville of Devils*.

The World's Finest Mystery and Crime Stories: First Annual Collection, edited by Ed Gorman (Forge) is a new competitor to the Houghton Mifflin annual. It includes forty stories from the U.S. and other English-speaking lands, with tales by Mat Coward, Jeffery Deaver, Joyce Carol Oates, Ed McBain, Ian Rankin and others, culled from such diverse sources as *OWF* magazine, *Ellery Queen's Mystery Magazine*, *Subterranean Gallery*, and various other anthologies and collections.

Romantic Fairy Tales, translated and edited and with an introduction by Carol Tully (Penguin Classic) collects four key texts of the German Romantic movement: Goethe's "The Fairy Tale" (1795), Ludwig Tieck's "Eckbert the Fair" (1792), Fredrich de la Motte Fouqué's "Undine" (1811), and Clemens Brentano's "The Tale of Honest Casper and Fair Annie" (1817).

The Mammoth Book of Haunted House Stories, edited by Peter Haining (Robinson, U.K./Carroll & Graf) reprinted stories by both classic and contemporary authors such as Sir Arthur Conan Doyle, Ramsey Campbell, and Basil Copper.

Dark: Stories of Madness, Murder and the Supernatural, edited by Clint Willis (Thunder Mouth and Balliett & Fitzgerald, Inc.) has novel excerpts by Stephen King, Will Self, Patrick McGrath and Iain Banks and stories by A. M. Burrage, Robert Aickman, and Zora Neale Hurston and poetry by Robert Frost.

Writers at the Movies: Twenty-six Contemporary Authors Celebrating Twenty-six Memorable Movies, edited by Jim Shepard (HarperPerennial) includes Charles Baxter comparing Davis Grubb's novel *Night of the Hunter* with the movie made by Charles Laughton, and Stephen Dobyns writing about Fred Wiseman's documentary *Titicut Follies*.

My Favorite Horror Story, edited by Mike Baker and Martin H. Greenberg (DAW) is an interesting idea for a non-theme horror anthology. Such writers as Dennis Etchison, Stephen King, Harlan Ellison, Poppy Z. Brite, and Joyce Carol Oates choose their favorite stories and add brief introductions explaining why they chose the particular story.

Twilight Tales Presents Sort-of Scary Stories: Tales of Make-Believe for Children, edited by Tina L. Jens.

That's Ghosts for You: Thirteen Scary Stories, edited by Marianne Carus (Front Street/Cricket Books, YA). Four are originals.

And *The Mammoth Book of Best New Horror: Volume Eleven*, edited by Stephen Jones (Robinson, U.K.) has a few overlapping stories with our own volume.

Collections

Blackwater Days by Terry Dowling (Eidolon Books, Australia). Dowling has created a powerful collection of stories greater than the sum of its parts. Set at the Everton, Australia psychiatric hospital called Blackwater, the book's seven stories and four interstitial sections portray the hospital and its patients, slowly building into a satisfying climax. Two of the patients act as "psychosleuths" throughout the book and become increasingly involved in the proceedings. The book comes in a sturdy trade paperback format with a beautiful cover and interior illustrations by Shaun Tan. Two stories are reprinted herein.

A *Touch of the Creature* by Charles Beaumont (Subterranean Press) collects thirteen previously unpublished stories by a brilliant writer who died tragically young. While these recently discovered stories are perhaps not among the author's best, they are all worth reading whether they're horror stories/vignettes, tales of Hollywood, or tall tales. The book contains a preface by Beaumont's son, and an introduction by Richard Matheson. Jacket art is by Phil Parks. The book was published as a numbered limited edition of 1000 copies signed by Christopher Beaumont and a thirteen-copy lettered edition with two extra stories.

Ghost Music and Other Tales by Thomas Tessier (CD Publications) is the first collection by the talented and graceful author of such excellent novels as *Finishing Touches* and *Fogheart*. The collection has three original pieces, more vignettes than fully realized stories, but they are so good that they are exceptions to my general disappointment in the vignette form. Tessier's short stories have been published in a variety of anthologies over the years. The one characteristic they have in common is their fine writing.

Magic Terror: Seven Tales by Peter Straub (Random House) collects seven stories and novellas by the multi-award-winning author originally published between 1993 and 1998, including the award-winning "Mr. Clubb and Mr. Cuff."

Black Evening by David Morrell (CD Publications) was published on the cusp of 1999–2000 so did not get its due. While Morrell is best known for his popular thrillers *First Blood* and *The Brotherhood of the Rose*, over his career he has written some elegant and haunting short stories and novellas, including "The Beautiful Uncut Hair of Graves." Dust jacket art is by Steve Gervais, and designed by Gail Cross.

The Long Ones by Joe R. Lansdale (Necro Publications) is a collection of four novellas, one published for the first time. The new one is intended to capture the flavor of old dime novels and is an entertaining pastiche of science fiction, adventure, and horror. Lansdale has provided an afterword. The jacket illustration is by Chris Trammell and there are interior illustrations by Robert Copley.

Golden Gryphon published *High Cotton: Selected Stories of Joe R. Lansdale*, another collection of this prolific author's short stories. The stories within are those that Lansdale feels best reflect his work and include a number chosen for various "best of the year" anthologies. Lansdale provides a foreword, and an introduction to each story with a bit of background about its inception. The book sports full color cover art and a black-and-white frontispiece by J. K. Potter.

Feelings of Fear by Graham Masterton (Severn House, U.K.) is the author's fourth collection and contains twelve of his most recent short stories, including one adapted for Tony Scott's *Hunger* television series.

Sarob Press brought out four limited-printing collections of horror during 2000: *Degrees of Fear: Tales From Usher College* by contemporary author William I. I. Read, a very funny (but not scary) collection of stories featuring a hapless antiquary and his colleagues at Usher College. Five of the eight stories are original to the collection. The dust jacket art and interior art by Nick Maloret go perfectly with the stories. *"Number Ninety" and Other Ghost Stories* by B. M. Croker is volume three in the "Mistresses of the Macabre" series and gathers fifteen of the author's ghost stories from several rare collections and magazines. For most of them, this is the first time they've been reprinted in eighty years. *Not for the Night-Time* by Theo Gift (whose real name was Dorothy Henrietta Havers), volume four in the "Mistresses of the Macabre" series, is best known for her children's stories. This four-story collection was originally published in 1889. Dust jacket and interior art are by Paul Lowe. The two titles above were edited and introduced by Richard Dalby. *Echoes of Darkness* by contemporary writers L. H. Maynard & M. P. N. Sims has eight supernatural reprints and one original novella. Dust jacket and interior artwork by Iain Maynard. The dust jackets for all Sarob's titles are attractive, with black and white illustrations on glossy black backgrounds, and colored endpapers.

Tartarus Press published a number of intriguing reprint collections, like Sarob's, all with limited printings. *The Smell of Telescopes* by Rhys Hughes is the second collection by the author of *Worming the Harpy*. The stories are original, much in the way of Brian McNaughton's lauded collection, *The Throne of Bones*, published a few years ago. Quirky and fantastic and sometimes quite twisted, this is a treat for those in the mood for something utterly different. *Pan's Garden* by Algernon Blackwood brings together all of the author's supernatural nature stories in one attractive volume, with an introduction by Mike Ashley and illustrations by W. Graham Robertson, limited to 300 numbered copies. *Shapes in the Fire* by M. P. Shiel reprints this author's second collection, originally published in 1896. Shiel was influenced by Poe and was a contemporary of Wilde, Machen, Count Stenbock, Vincent O'Sullivan and Ellen Gilchrist, leading authors of the time. Introduction by Brian Stableford (revised from an earlier article). *Ringstones and Other Curious Tales* by Sarban was first published in 1951 and was the author's first publication. This new edition collects those five stories and adds an original, newly discovered "conte cruel" by the author, whose real name was John William Wall. *A Fragment of Life* by Arthur Machen prints the original, final chapter of this novella, very different from that published in the *Horlicks Magazine*. Introduction by Ray Russell. *The Green Round* by Arthur Machen is another reprinted novella. Introduction by Mark Valentine. *The Salutation* by Silvia Townsend Warner collects fifteen stories by the author. Introduction by Claire Harmon. *Oliver Onions: Ghost Stories* is over 450 pages and contains twenty-two of the author's short stories and has an introduction by Rosalie Parker. *The Lost Stradivarius* by J. Meade Falkner includes the titular supernatural novel originally published in 1895 plus two short stories previously available only in magazines, and appearing here in book form for the first time.

Horrors of the Holy: 13 Sinful, Sacrilegious, Supernatural Stories by Staci Layne Wilson (Running Free Press) contains ten originals and three reprints in a nicely designed trade paperback. Dust jacket art is by the author.

Whistling Past the Graveyard by Peter Sellers (Mosaic Press) contains thirteen crime and horror stories by this Canadian writer and editor, five of them original, about, variously, duplicitous women, innocent dupes, hitmen, private eyes, and circus freaks.

Exotic Locals by Janet Berliner and George Guthridge (Lone Wolf Publications, CD-ROM) collects ten collaborations by the authors, with an introduction by Paul Di Filippo and fascinating individual audio introductions by Berliner. I believe the stories range from 1982–2000, although there's no copyright information.

Dystopia by Richard Christian Matheson (Gauntlet Press) is an omnibus collection of over fifty stories, more than half previously uncollected and several written expressly for the book. Richard Matheson has written an introduction and Peter Straub the afterword. There are two editions: a 500-copy numbered edition, with dust jacket art by Harry Morris. All three have signed this edition. The 250-copy deluxe numbered, slipcased edition has six additional Harry O. Morris color illustrations and it is signed by fifty writers who have written introductions to individual stories.

The Third Cry to Legba and Other Invocations: The Selected Stories of Manly Wade Wellman, Volume 1, edited by John Pelan (Night Shade Books) is the first of a planned five volumes. This one contains twenty-one stories, many about the psychic investigator/adventurer John Thunstone. It includes twenty-four illustrations by Kenneth Waters.

The Shadows Beneath by Paul Finch (Enigmatic Variations) collects three stories by this British writer, two of them published here for the first time. The attractive black-and-white trade paperback is illustrated throughout by Gerald Gaubert.

Treading on the Past by Derek M. Fox (Enigmatic Variations) has four original supernatural horror stories. Introduction by Mark Chadbourn. Illustrations and cover art are by Frank Mafrici.

Bedbugs by Rick Hautala (CD Publications) is the author's first collection, with twenty-six stories from throughout his career. Matthew J. Costello provides an afterword. Dustjacket and interior art is by Glenn Chadbourne.

Tagging the Moon by S. P. Somtow (Night Shade) contains ten stories set on the dark side of L. A. by this multitalented author. One story is original to the collection, and this good-looking book has illustrations by GAK, and stark black-and-white photographs taken by the author. The dust jacket illustration and design is by John Picacio. Available in trade and limited hardcover editions.

Stoker Award winner Nancy Collins has a new short story collection, *Avenue X and Other Dark Streets* for sale under her own imprint, Scrapple Press, in conjunction with XLibris. The reprints range from weird western and dark fantasy stories to a fairy tale, noir, and horror.

Babbage Press brought out an attractive new trade paperback edition of *Lost Angels* by David J. Schow, with a new story and afterword by the author, and the original introduction by Richard Christian Matheson. The beautiful cover art is by co-publisher Lydia C. Marano.

The Death Artist by Dennis Etchison (DreamHaven) is the author's first new collection in over ten years and features twelve perfectly realized urban nightmares. The cover art, endpapers, and illustrations are by J. K. Potter.

Unforgivable Stories by Kim Newman (Pocket Books, U.K.) is a great batch of Newman's alternate history stories overlapping with some of his horror and science fiction horror. Alchemy Press/Airgedlamh Publications published *Where the Bodies are Buried,* a short collection of Kim Newman's pop culturally-conscious novellas originally published by editor Steven Jones in various anthologies. It's a really neat hardcover chapbook with an introduction by Peter Atkins, cover painting by Sylvia Starshine, and interior art by Randy Broecker. *Seven Stars* by Kim Newman (Simon & Schuster, U.K.) collects five dark fantasy stories originally published as a series of interstitial bits in last year's anthology *Dark Detectives* plus five other reprints featuring characters who are in the Seven Stars cycle.

Ghosts, Spirits, Computers, and World Machines by Gene O'Neill (Imaginary Worlds Press) is a short (50,000 words) collection of this author's work and contains eight reprints. The book has an introduction by Kim Stanley Robinson and an "outro" by Scott Edelman.

Tales of Pain and Wonder by Caitlín Kiernan (Gauntlet) is a beautifully designed and illustrated limited-edition hardcover of twenty-one stories, several of them published for the first time in 2000. Kiernan's disenfranchised waifs, depressives, and low lifes are usually sympathetic despite themselves, and her language is lovingly crafted. The book is illustrated by Richard A. Kirk, features an introduction by Douglas E. Winter, and an afterword by Peter Straub.

Shards of Darkness by E. P. Berglund (Mythos Books) is a good-looking trade paperback collection of eleven stories in the Cthulhu mythos, reprinted from such venues as *Space and Time* and *Eldritch Tales,* with notes on each story by the author, and an introduction by Robert M. Price. Cover art by D. L. Hutchinson and interior artwork by Peter Worthy.

Ghosts Who Cannot Sleep by Alan Rodgers (Wildside) is a very attractive trade paperback edition of five stories published by the author in the mid-1990s, and five original poems. The stories range from a sad tale of a junkie to an alternate history about John F. Kennedy and Lee Harvey Oswald.

Frights of Fancy by J. N. Williamson (Leisure) includes sixteen varied stories by the author, three of them original to the collection. Although the stories were all published between 1986 and 2000, the male/female dynamic often seems more at home in the 1950s when women kept house and men brought home the bacon.

Moon on the Water by Mort Castle (DarkTales) features twenty-one stories by this author whose writing career has spanned thirty years. One story is original to the collection.

Chaosium published *The Yellow Sign and Other Stories: The Complete Weird Tales of Robert W. Chambers* in a hefty (almost 650 pages), attractive trade paperback edition as part of their Call of Cthulhu series. The book is edited and introduced by S. T. Joshi.

Toybox by Al Sarrantonio (CD Publications) is a great batch of scares about things that go bump in the night. Sarrantonio is wonderful at capturing the many faces of childhood and at depicting what frightens the young. The work ranges over the past twenty years, with one previously unpublished story. Features an introduction by Joe Lansdale and an evocative dust jacket art by Alan M. Clark with jacket design by Gail Cross.

Nightscapes: Tales of the Ominous and Magical by Darrell Schweitzer (Wildside) is the author's sixth collection and contains seventeen stories reprinted from various anthologies and genre magazines. The book's wonderful cover art and design and interior spot illustrations are by Jason Van Hollander.

More Stately Mansions by John B. Rosenman (Dark Regions Press) is a late entry from 1999 collecting seven stories from 1990–1999. This trade paperback, which is illustrated throughout by Fredrik King, is a limited edition.

Contagion by Brian Evenson (Wordcraft of Oregon) is the author's third collection of odd, sometimes grotesque stories. Although published primarily in literary magazines, there is usually more than a touch of horror in his work, and the one original novella in the collection of eight stories is a doozy of a western about early barbed wire and plague.

Up, Out of the Cities that Blow Hot and Cold by Charlee Jacob (Delirium Books) is the author's second short story collection. Five of the fifteen stories are published for the first time. An introduction is provided by Tom Piccirilli, the cover design is by Colleen Crary, and interior artwork is by GAK. Limited edition.

Never Trust a Rabbit is an intriguing debut collection by Jeremy Dyson (Duckworth, U.K.). The three reprints were originally published in genre anthologies; all the other stories are published here for the first time. His work is often imbued with a slightly askew sensibility that shifts the balance from fantasy to horror but very few of his stories would be considered traditional horror. His novella "The Engine of Desire" is a knockout, despite the fact that its convolutions get a bit confusing.

Jeffrey Thomas had two collections come out in 2000. *Terror Incognita* (Delirium Books) collects several stories from small press venues and adds five original stories. All are fine, and only in comparison to the interconnected stories of

Punktown (Ministry of Whimsy) do they pale. *Punktown* is a brilliant collection of stories about a very odd place. Whether science fiction, fantasy or horror the mix works and makes this one of the best collections of the year. One of the stories from *Punktown* is reprinted herein.

City Fishing is the long overdue English language debut collection by Steve Rasnic Tem (Silver Salamander Press) and contains thirty-eight prime stories from the career of this terrifically talented, underrated writer. Four of the stories are original to the collection. Alan M. Clark is the cover artist and the author provides an introduction. Limited edition.

The Midnight Man by Stephen Laws (Silver Salamander Press) is this British author's first collection, and contains most of his short fiction, including "The Crawl." Cover art is by Frederik King and there's an introduction and notes on each story by the author. Limited edition.

Gerard Daniel Houarner's second collection *I Love You and There is Nothing You Can Do About It* (Delirium Books) has four originals and eight reprints. Introduction is by John Pelan and the artwork is by Colleen Crary.

A Haunting Beauty: Stories of the Macabre by Charles Birkin, selected by Mike Ashley (Midnight House) is the first in a projected series of volumes collecting Sir Charles Birkin's best short stories. This volume was initiated twenty years ago by the author with the assistance of Mike Ashley as a retrospective of his work, but Birkin's death in 1986 held up the marketing of the volume until recently. Included are a preface by Ashley and an introduction by Birkin.

The Corpse Light and other Tales of Terror by Dick Donovan, edited by Richard Dalby (Midnight House) was meant to be the centenary edition of this long out-of-print title but ended up coming out late, in early 2000. The book contains fourteen stories and an introduction by the editor.

The Weird O' It by Clive Pemberton (Midnight House) is one of the rarest collections of weird fiction from the early years of this century. This expanded edition features a previously uncollected tale. Introduction by John Pelan. All three titles above from Midnight House are limited, with dust jackets illustrated by Allen Koszowski.

The Vampire Master and Other Tales of Horror by Edmond Hamilton (Haffner) collects nine stories from the pulps, including four tales of supernatural horror that appeared in *Weird Tales* under the pseudonym Hugh Davidson. The introduction is by Hugh B. Cave and the afterword is a posthumously reprinted piece by Hamilton. Dust jacket art is by Jon Arfstrom, designed by Stephen Haffner. Limited edition.

The Reservoir of Dreams by Paul Bradshaw (BJM Press) collects ten stories by this British author, whose work has been published in various small press magazines since 1997. Three of the stories in this attractive 96-page perfect-bound book are reprinted from British magazines.

Sewing Shut my Eyes by Lance Olsen (FC2/Black Ice) collects nine pieces of dark, surreal satire. Illustrations by Andi Olsen.

Shoggoth Cacciatore and other Eldritch Entrees by Mark McLaughlin (Delirium Books) is a collection of short Lovecraft parodies. Six of the ten pieces are original. Poor Elder Gods—can't get no respect.

Ballymoon by Alastair G. Gunn (Enigmatic Press) is part of the Enigmatic

Variations series. The three traditional ghost stories are well written but lack suspense. The excellent black-and-white cover and interior illustrations are by Cathy Buburuz.

Twelve of Ed Gorman's crime and mystery stories are collected in *Famous Blue Raincoat* (Crippen & Landru). Gorman's short fiction often skirts the edge between mystery and horror and is always worth reading. Published in a signed, limited hardcover edition and in an unsigned trade paperback edition. A second collection, published in a mass market edition (Leisure) is *The Dark Fantastic*. It has a 2001 copyright but slipped into my home just before the new year. The seventeen stories are reprints ranging throughout the last decade (two published in 2000). Bentley Little provides the introduction.

As the Sun Goes Down by Tim Lebbon (Night Shade Books) is a perfect introduction to this talented author's short fiction. He won the British Fantasy Award for his terrific novella "White," first published as a chapbook and then reprinted in last year's volume of *The Year's Best Fanatsy and Horror*. Half of the sixteen stories in this collection are appearing for the first time, and the novella, "The Unfortunate," is another piece worthy of award notice. Although most of Lebbon's work is horror, he seems quite as comfortable writing science fiction tinged with the horrific and has occasionally been published in science fiction venues. The book is well-designed inside and out and has a beautiful jacket with art by Alan M. Clark and design by Jeremy Lassen. Ramsey Campbell provides an introduction.

Night Freight by Bill Pronzini (Leisure) with its twenty-six stories, one of them published for the first time, is a showcase for an author who crosses genres with ease. He might be better known as a writer of mysteries and historical westerns but his horror and suspense fiction is just as effective.

The Lost Bloch, Volume Two: Hell on Earth, edited by David J. Schow (Subterranean Press) continues a labor of love by Schow to explore the "missing" novels of Robert Bloch, work that was written for the pulp magazines in the 1940s and 1950s and were never before reprinted as books. This volume contains four short novels, introductions by Schow and Douglas E. Winter, and a previously unpublished interview with Bloch. Dust jacket art is by Bernie Wrightson and the cover is designed by Schow.

Gothic Fevers by Gary William Crawford (Nashville House) collects six dark fantasies illustrated by Margaret Ballif Simon.

The Vampire Stories of Nancy Kilpatrick (Mosaic Press) brings together nineteen stories published throughout the 1990s on this toothsome theme.

Winterwood and Other Hauntings by Keith Roberts (Wildside Suspense) is the first trade edition of this collection of seven ghost stories originally published in a limited hardcover edition by Morrigan Publications in the U.K. in the late 1980s.

Ash-Tree Press continued its dominance in the area of producing attractive, reasonably priced, hardcover limited editions of supernatural fiction by both contemporary authors and those long dead. The first four titles below are by contemporary authors:

Dark Matters by Terry Lamsley is the British author's third collection of supernatural tales. If subtle, supernatural stories in the tradition of M. R. James are your cup of tea, you could not do better than to read Lamsley. He has inherited the mantle and has brilliantly revitalized the form for the modern world. This new collection contains eleven stories, two of them original, one of which I've reprinted herein. Cover illustration is by Douglas Walters.

We've Been Waiting For You by John Burke with an introduction by Nicholas Royle and a foreword by John Burke is the first collection entirely devoted to Burke's "uneasy stories." Burke was the editor of the anthologies *Tales of Unease, More Tales of Unease,* and *New Tales of Unease.* Jacket art is by Jason Van Hollander.

The Lady Wore Black by Hugh B. Cave collects nineteen of his stories about cats and is simultaneously a celebration of the author's ninetieth birthday. The book has a preface by the author and an introduction by Mike Ashley. Jacket art by Paul Lowe.

Summoning Knells and Other Inventions is by A. F. Kidd, who has been active in the British small press for over twenty years, and is an avid bellringer. She has drawn on her own experiences for many of the incidents in her stories; yet another, stronger influence, the ghost stories of M. R. James, also informs and inspires many of the forty-seven tales in the collection. Introduction by the author and glossary of bell-ringing terms. Jacket art by Paul Lowe.

Reunion at Dawn and Other Uncollected Ghost Stories by H. R. Wakefield is a treasure trove of seventeen stories only recently found in the files of August Derleth. The stories were apparently meant to be published by Arkham House as a follow up to the 1961 collection *Strayers from Sheol,* and when they never appeared, it was widely assumed that Wakefield had destroyed them prior to his death in 1964. Traditional and eerie, most of them hold up rather well. Jacket art by Paul Lowe. *Phantom Perfumes and Other Shades: Memories of Ghost Stories Magazine,* edited by Mike Ashley, includes seventeen of the best tales to appear in *Ghost Stories* during its existence between 1926 and 1931. Jacket art is by Linda Dyde. *The Horror on the Stair and Other Weird Tales* by Arthur Quiller-Couch, edited by S. T. Joshi, who in his introduction discusses the author's life and times. Jacket art is by Paul Lowe. *The Cold Embrace and Other Ghost Stories* by Mary Elizabeth Braddon collects eighteen of Braddon's finest tales of the uncanny, all of which demonstrate her mastery of the form and show why she was one of the best-selling authors of her time. Includes an extensive introduction by editor Richard Dalby. Jacket art is by Jason C. Eckhardt. *In the Dark* by E. Nesbit, edited by Hugh Lamb, includes an introduction to the life of the author, best known today for her children's books. Jacket art is by Richard Lamb. *The Moonstone Mass* by Harriet Prescott Spofford, and edited by Jessica Amanda Salmonson, is by an author who wrote most of her weird tales early in life and went on to write and be known for her New England regional tales. Salmonson has collected the author's weird tales and poems in this one volume and has written an introduction, examining the life and work of Spofford. Jacket art is by Deborah McMillion-Nering. *The Secrets of Dr Taverner* by Dion Fortune, edited and with an introduction by Jack Adrian, is the third volume in Ash-Tree's Occult Detectives Library series. Fortune was a highly significant and influential figure within spiritualistic circles: a one-time member of the Order of the Golden Dawn, she left it to create another society, the Fraternity of the Inner Light, which (under another name) still exists today and which refuses to discuss her. During the 1920s and 1930s she wrote books, pamphlets, and articles about her spiritual philosophies and various sociological and sexual issues, including vegetarianism, the servant problem, and contraception. Jacket art is by Deborah McMillion-Nering.

The Ash-Tree Press Annual Macabre 2000, edited by Jack Adrian, gathers together nine stories that seem to have been forgotten by their authors, and have, in consequence, lain undisturbed in the pages of old periodicals, some for more than one hundred years. Included are "unknown" stories by E. Nesbit, S. Baring-Gould, Sax Rohmer, and Julian Hawthorne. Jacket illustration is by Rob Suggs.

Scary Rednecks and other Inbred Horrors by David Whitman and Weston Ochse (DarkTales) contains twenty-one stories by one or the other of the two authors.

Tripping the Dark Fantastic by David Bischoff (Wildside) is a collection of eight dark fantasy stories, including three original to the collection, and an introduction by Charles Sheffield.

Thank you for the Flowers by Scott Nicholson (Parkway Publishers) has thirteen stories of horror and suspense. An author's afterword tells how the stories came to be written.

Mixed-Genre Collections

Terry Bisson is known best for his humorous satire but some of his short stories are pretty brutal, including "macs" and "Incident at Oak Ridge," both reprinted in *In the Upper Room and Other Likely Stories* (Tor).

Michael Swanwick is another author not often associated with the horror field, but like Bisson, a number of his short stories contain elements of horror. Stories such as the chilling "Radiant Doors," his award-winning play, "The Dead," and "Ships," his collaboration with Jack Dann, in *Moon Dogs* (NESFA Press). A second collection by Swanwick, *Tales of Old Earth* (North Atlantic Books/Frog Ltd) has a wonderful dark fantasy published for the first time.

4 Stories by Kelly Link (Jelly Ink) is a self-published chapbook with four fantasies by this talented author. All four stories (one is in three parts) were published before.

Robert Charles Wilson's first collection, *The Perseids and other Stories* (Tor) is mostly science fiction and fantasy but a few of his stories such as "The Protocols of Consumption" and "Plato's Mirror" are darker and should be of interest to horror readers.

Beluthahatchie and Other Stories by Andy Duncan (Golden Gryphon) is a wonderful introduction to this young fantasist's short fiction. The selection is varied and includes "Saved," "From Alfano's Reliquary," the brilliant dark novella "The Executioner's Guild," and published for the first time, the terrific fantasy, "Lincoln at Frogmore."

Bruce Holland Rogers's Bram Stoker Award-winning story "The Dead Boy at Your Window" is included in his new collection *Wind Over Heaven and Other Dark Tales* (Wildside).

Blue Kansas Sky by Michael Bishop (Golden Gryphon) is this fine author's first collection since 1996. It contains four novellas, one published for the first time. Bishop's fiction ranges through science fiction, fantasy, and the occasional very dark fantasy.

The Spiral Garden by Louise Cooper (British Fantasy Society) is the British author's first collection and contains five stories, mostly fantasy. Four are reprints and the one original is a horror tale. Illustrations are by Clive Sandall and Diana Wynne Jones has written an introduction.

Meet Me at Infinity by James Tiptree, Jr. (Tor) collects previously uncollected fiction and nonfiction. This major science fiction author's work explored sexuality, gender identity, and relationships. Her work always had a dark streak to it and in her later work this comes closer to the surface.

Wrinkles at Twilight by Brian A. Hopkins (Lone Wolf Publications) is a signed and numbered limited edition CD-ROM that has an introduction by Gary Braunbeck and cover art by Alan M. Clark. Although the author is better known for his horror than his science fiction and fantasy, this is a mixture of all three genres. This is a great package of twenty-one stories, two of them collaborations, four original to the collection, plus lots of extra material like photo montages, poems, author notes, etc.

A *Saucer of Loneliness: Volume VII of the Complete Stories of Theodore Sturgeon* (North Atlantic Books) continues series editor Paul Williams' monumental task of bringing all the short fiction of this important writer of science fiction/horror/fiction back into print in attractive and sturdy hardcover books. This volume contains stories written in the autumn of 1952 to the autumn of 1953.

Barry N. Malzberg has been an underrated practitioner of the short, satirical and often dark science fiction story for many years. *In the Stone House* (Arkham House) reprints twenty-four of the author's favorites over the past fifteen years. It includes several Hugo and Nebula nominees.

Some of M. John Harrison's best work could be called fiction of unease. His fourth collection, *Travel Arrangements* (Victor Gollancz, U.K.) brings together stories from 1983–2000.

James P. Blaylock's *Thirteen Phantasms* (Edgewood Press) is the master fantasist's first collection and contains two award-winners plus fourteen other stories, including one that appeared in one of the O. Henry Award annual volumes. Although only a bit of his short fiction is dark, it's often mysterious.

Sister Emily's Lightship and other stories by Jane Yolen (Tor) collects twenty-eight stories (three original to the collection) by another master fantasist. Yolen's work runs from the whimsical to powerful lessons in darkness.

No Mercy by Pat Califia (Alyson) has eleven erotic s/m stories, some with science fiction, fantasy, or horror elements; and *The Sweet and Sour Tongue* by Leslie What (Wildside) is the debut collection of this Nebula Award-winning author. Her work combines elements of magical realism, humor, science fiction, and horror.

Poetry Collections and Anthologies

Defacing the Moon and other poems by Mike Allen (DNA Publishing) collects a cross-genre mix of this poet's work, with four poems original to the collection. Cover art and interior illustrations are by the poet.

Blood of a Black Bird by Rain Graves (Mystique Press) has an introduction by John Shirley.

Autumn Phantoms by Wendy Rathbone (Flesh & Blood Press) is illustrated throughout by such artists as Cathy Buburuz, Keith Minion, and others.

The Weird Sonneteers, edited by Keith Allen Daniels (Anamnesis Press) has weird and Lovecraftian poetry by three authors: Daniels, Jerry H. Jenkins, and Ann K. Schwader with an introduction to each work by its author.

Groping Toward the Light: Poems for Midnight and After by Darrell Schweitzer (Wildside) is an attractive book available in trade paperback and hardcover with cover illustration and interior illustrations by Jason Van Hollander.

Flowers From a Dark Star: The Selected Poetry of Charlee Jacob, edited by Bobbi Sinha-Morey (Dark Regions Press) includes four original poems by this up and coming author of prose and poetry. Illustrated by Margaret Ballif Simon.

The Complete Accursed Wives by Bruce Boston (Dark Regions Press/Talisman) collects forty poems by the author written over a period of several years. Cover art is by Margaret Baliff Simon.

A *Student of Hell* by Tom Piccirilli (Skull Job Productions) is a collection of forty poems, illustrated by several artists, with an introduction by Charlee Jacob. Signed by all the contributors.

Burial Plot in Sagittarius by Sandy DeLuca (Thievin' Kitty Publications) has an introduction by Mark McLaughlin, with cover and interior art by the author.

Results of a Preliminary Investigation of Electrochemical Properties of Some Organic Matrices by David Kopaska-Merkel (Eraserhead Press) has an introduction by W. Gregory Stewart.

Artists

The artists who work in the small press toil hard and receive too little credit (forget money). I feel it's important to recognize their good work. The following created art that I thought was noteworthy during 2000: Andrew Shorrock, Erik Wilson, Lubov, Sergey Poyarkov, Dominic Harman, Graham Billing, Adam Oehlers, Carol McLean-Carr, Mike Bohatch, Roddy Williams, David Checkley, Wendy Down, Liam Kemp, A. Wiedemann, Marge Simon, Jean-Claude Davreux, Shaun Tan, Inari Kiuri, R&D Studios, Paul Lowe, Douglas Walters, Cathy Buburuz, Rob Kirbyson, Chad Michael Ward, Steve Bidmead, Iain Maynard, Gerald Gaubert, David Grilla, Judith Huey, Suzanne Clarke, Rodger Gerberding, Joachim Luetke, Bob Hobbs, Erik M. Turnmire, Paul Swenson, Chris Whitlow, Keith Boulger, Jeff Sturgeon, Richard Whitters, James Kirkwood, Web Bryant, Lars deSouza, Steve Lines, Rob Middleton, Peter Watts, Poppy Alexander, Dave Windett, Mike Allen, Alan Hunter, Brian Coundiff, Jamie Oberschlake, Keith Minion, Margaret Anne Davies, Jennifer Etherton, GAK, BRE, MaryAnn Harris, Eric York, Dee Rimbaud, Lisa Busby, Simon Logan, Mark Roberts, Tua, and Chris Kenworthy.

Newsletters and Market Resources

Although there is no horror equivalent to the science fiction and fantasy newsmagazines *Locus* and *Science Fiction Chronicle*, there are several nonfiction publications that cater to some of the needs of the horror writer and reader. With Paula Guran's *DarkEcho* gone, the most important news source for the field is *Hellnotes*, the weekly newsletter edited by David B. Silva with Paul Olsen. *Hellnotes* provides extensive coverage of the horror field, including news in literature and film. It opens with an introductory editorial and usually has a long interview with a horror notable, short horror reviews by various people, and a view from England by Peter Crowther. *Hellnotes* is subscription based and is published 52 times a year by Phantasm Press. E-mail subscriptions are available for $21 per year ($40.00 for two years), and $55.00 a year for a hardcopy subscription ($105.00 for two years). To subscribe by credit card, go to: http://www.hellnotes.com/subscrib.htm. To subscribe by mail, send a check or money order (made out to David B. Silva) to: Hellnotes, 27780 Donkey Mine Road, Oak Run, CA 96069.

There are a number of sources for markets. *Jobs In Hell*, edited by Brian Keene, is the relative new kid on the block, having launched in 1999 with the idea of "delivering some markets to the masses and some beat downs to those who so very much deserved it to enable the working horror writer/poet/artist/etc. in a way that nobody had before." Keene is irreverent, bitchy, and passionate. A one-year/52-issue subscription to *JIH* is $20. Payments should be made to Brian Keene, NOT TO *Jobs In Hell*, and mailed to Brian Keene, 10A Ginger View Court, Cockeysville, MD 21030. Please include your email address. To order via credit card: http://www.imaginary-worlds.com/offers/jih.html. Please confirm your order with a separate e-mail.

Speculations: For Writers who want to be Read is a monthly edited, by Susan Fry and has articles about markets, on naming characters, creating aliens and the various writing workshops. It also runs interviews with various professionals. This one is aimed more at science fiction and fantasy writers than horror writers. $20 for twelve issues payable to Speculations, PMB 400, 1111 West El Camino Real #109, Sunnyvale, CA 94087–1057.

The Gila Queen's Guide to Markets, edited by Kathryn Ptacek is a content-rich newsletter, published about every six weeks and is one of the best all-around market reports, covering all kinds of fiction and nonfiction. $45 for a 10-issue subscription payable to Kathryn Ptacek, GQ HQ, P.O. Box 97, Newton, NJ 07860–0097.

Scavenger's Newsletter, edited by Janet Fox continues to cover small press markets on a monthly basis. $24 for a 12-issue subscription and $12 for a 6-issue in U.S., $23/$11.50 Canada, $29/$14.50 overseas airmail payable to Scavenger's Newsletter, 833 Main, Osage City, KS 66523–1241.

Magazines

Small press magazines come and go with amazing rapidity. It's difficult to recommend buying a subscription to those that haven't proven their longevity, but I urge readers to at least buy single issues of those that sound interesting. Unfortunately, there isn't room to mention every magazine publishing horror, so the following handful are those that I thought were the best in 2000. Surprisingly (or not) most of those that I felt had the best horror fiction in 2000 are cross-genre magazines that publish science fiction and fantasy, as well as horror:

Horror Garage, edited by Paula Guran, is a welcome new venue for short horror fiction that combines fiction with music and some movie and book coverage.

The slick-covered semi-annual's debut issue has nine very good stories (eight never before published) by some of the more familiar names in the field including Dennis Etchison, Kathe Koja, Brian Hodge, and Caitlín Kiernan. Future issues will have five or six stories per issue. Single issues available for $6.66 ($1 more for Canada, $2 for overseas orders) payable to cash, Horror Garage, P.O. Box 53, Nesconset, NY 11767.

Cemetery Dance, edited by Richard T. Chizmar, is now meant to be bi-monthly but only one issue came out during 2000. In it there were new stories by Graham Masterton, Charles Beaumont, and the conclusion to a novella by Gary A. Braunbeck. In addition, there was extensive coverage of Leisure Books, with an interview with editor Don D'Auria and an overview of the line, plus regular columns by Poppy Z. Brite, Ed Gorman, Tyson Blue, and Charles L. Grant. It gives good overall coverage of the horror field but has had an erratic publication schedule. $22.00 for six issues payable to Cemetery Dance Publications, P.O. Box 943, Abingdon, MD 21009.

Weird Tales, edited by George H. Scithers and Darrell Schweitzer, has been around in one form or another for seventy-six years and is currently on a quarterly schedule. The magazine's fiction generally provides a who's who in dark fantasy/horror with originals and reprints by Tanith Lee, William F. Nolan, Ramsey Campbell, and others. Neil Gaiman was interviewed in one issue in 2000. $16.00 for four issues payable to DNA Publications, Inc., P.O. Box 2988, Radford, VA 24143–2988.

Crime Wave 3: Burning Down the House, edited by Andy Cox, is the third issue of this excellent and beautifully designed magazine of crime fiction. The striking collage cover art is by Mike Bohatch and all the black-and-white illustrations inside by various artists (including Bohatch) are also quite good. *Crime Wave 4: Mood Indigo* had some excellent fiction, particularly a beautifully written, harrowing novelette by Marion Arnott. Again, the interior art by a variety of talented artists and cover photograph by Troy Paiva are perfect. For information in the U.S., contact Firebird Distributing (see end of summation for address).

Space and Time, the long running bi-annual small press magazine edited by Gordon Linzner, included more horror fiction and poetry than usual during 2000. Two-issue subscriptions cost $10 payable to *Space and Time*, 138 West 70th Street 4B, New York, NY 10023–4468. It's available in the U.K. through BBR Distributing.

Realms of Fantasy, edited by Shawna McCarthy, publishes a wide range of fantasy, including the occasional dark fantasy. During 2000, the magazine had more than its usual number of darker stories.

New Genre, edited by Jeff Paris and Adam Golaski, is a very attractive new bi-annual perfect-bound magazine of horror and science fiction. I'm dubious of the crossover potential of such a magazine but the first issue is promising, with excellent science fiction by A. R. Morlan and provocative horror fiction by Charlee Jacob and Paul Walther and something unclassifiable by Mark Rich. Subscriptions are $9.00 to New Genre, 25 Cutter Avenue, Somerville, MA 02144.

Eidolon's tenth anniversary issue is gorgeous, starting with its beautiful cover with art by Shaun Tan, designed by Jeremy Reston. Jeremy G. Byrne edits the

Australian quarterly. Generally a science fiction magazine, Eidolon occasionally publishes some very good fantasy and horror as well (including a story by Jack Dann, reprinted herein). Subscription rates are in Australian dollars only: $Au. 57.00 (international airmail) for four issues or $Au. 46.00 (international seamail) payable to Eidolon Publications, P.O. Box 225, North Perth, WA 6906 Australia. http://www.eidolon.net.

The other major Australian magazine is *Aurealis*, edited by Dirk Strasser and Stephen Higgins. Usually a semi-annual that features an excellent variety of science fiction and fantasy (and sometimes horror), only one issue came out in 2000. Issue #25/26 was the "next wave" issue, showcasing newer writers and it was a very good issue indeed, with some especially strong darker fiction. The illustrations are usually very good. A four-issue subscription is $Au 44.00 seamail (or $50 airmail) payable to Chimaera Publications. Credit card sales acceptable. P.O. Box 2164, Mt. Waverley, Victoria 3149, Australia. http://www.aurealis.hl.net.

On Spec, edited by the Copper Pig Writers' Society, is the major fantasy and science fiction magazine of Canada and 2000 had a very generous helping of horror. The extra large fall issue featured the fourteen prize-winning stories of the On Spec Short Story contest. A one-year subscription for this digest-sized perfect bound magazine is $18.00(U.S.) payable to On Spec, Box 4727, Edmonton, Alberta T6E 5G6, Canada.

Talebones, edited by Patrick and Honna Swenson, is an excellent quarterly mixed-genre digest-sized magazine with a generous serving of fiction, interviews and articles. Single issue $5.00. A one-year subscription is $18.00 payable to *Talebones*, 5203 Quincy Avenue SE, Auburn, WA 98092. Credit card sales acceptable.

Ghosts & Scholars, edited by Rosemary Pardoe, is an excellent bi-annual magazine devoted to continuing the M. R. James tradition of ghost stories. Its combination of original and reprinted stories, book reviews, and scholarly articles make it a must for any reader interested in the traditional ghost story. Unfortunately, Pardoe has decided to cease publication after twenty-one years, ending with issue #33 at the end of 2001. This is a great pity as this has been one of the best and most consistent venues for excellent ghost stories. For information: www.users.globalnet.co.uk/~pardos/GS.html. E-mail: pardos@globalnet.co.uk.

All Hallows: The Journal of the Ghost Story Society, edited by Barbara and Christopher Roden, is one of the best reasons to join The Ghost Story Society. This attractive, perfect-bound magazine is published thrice yearly and is only available to members. It is an excellent source of news, articles and ghostly fiction. But another good reason is the support of an organization dedicated to providing admirers of the classic ghost story with an outlet for their interest. Membership is $23.00 per year. For more information visit the Ash-Tree Press Web site or write to P.O. Box 1360 Ashcroft, BC VOK 1AO. http://www.Ash-Tree.bc.ca/gss.html.

Crypt of Cthulhu, edited by Robert M. Price, publishes fiction and nonfiction about H. P. Lovecraft and Lovecraftian themes. Although copyrighted 1999, issues #102 and #103 were not published until December 2000. The plan is to publish #104–108 every six weeks during 2001 ending with #108 in August 2001 and from then on, twice a year. $6.00 per issue + $2.00 S&H ($3.00 outside the

U.S.). Issues #102–108 are $4.50 per issue, $1.50 S&H (U.S.) + 2.00 S&H elsewhere, payable to Mythos Books, 218 Hickory Meadow Lane, Poplar Bluff, MO 63901–2160.

The Third Alternative, edited by Andy Cox, always has a cross-genre mix but #24 was pleasantly heavy on horror. The graphics are striking and the whole magazine has a professional feel to it. Also, it's chock full of reviews, a couple of mini-interviews with Joel Lane and Christopher Kenworthy and a lengthier one with Douglas Coupland. Also, in Issue #25 Alec Worley provides a useful overview of the work of the great Czech animator and surrealist Jan Svankmajer. With only four feature films—*Alice*, (his take on Lewis Carroll's *Alice*), *Faust*, *Conspirators of Pleasure*, and most recently *Otesánek* (Greedyguts)—the film-maker has not yet achieved the recognition (at least in the U.S.) that he deserves.

Century, edited by Robert K. J. Killheffer and Jenna Felice, designed by Bryan Cholfin, is back with two excellent issues of cross-genre fiction including a couple of dark tales by Robert Reed and Stewart O'Nan. It's a beautiful to look at, well-designed, perfect-bound magazine. Single copies $6.00; four issues $24.00 payable to Century Publishing, P.O. Box 150510, Brooklyn, NY 11215–0510.

In addition, *Interzone*, edited by David Pringle, and *The Magazine of Fantasy and Science Fiction*, edited by Gordon Van Gelder, published some notable horror stories.

Two important horror Webzines: *Gothic.net* (http://www.gothic.net/) and *Horror Online* (http://www.horroronline.com/). The latter is owned by Universal and is a news and review site, mostly covering movies but with book columns by horror notable Paula Guran. Gothic.net has some very good fiction on it. *SCI FICTION* (http://www.scifi.com/scifiction), the fiction area I edit for *SCIFI.COM*, also publishes the occasional horror original or classic reprint. In 2000 we published an original horror story by Kim Newman and reprints by Tom Reamy and Thomas M. Disch.

Poetry Magazines: *Frisson: Disconcerting Verse*, edited by Scott H. Urban. Single issue $2.50. $10.00 per year payable to Skull Job Productions, 1012 Pleasant Dale Drive, Wilmington, NC 28412–7617; *The Magazine of Speculative Poetry*, edited by Roger Dutcher. Single issue $5.00. $19.00 for four issues payable to MSP, P.O. Box 564, Beloit, WI 53512; *Edgar Digested Verse*, a quarterly edited by John Picinich. $2.50 per issue, $10.00 for four issues payable to John Picinich, 486 Essex Avenue, Bloomfield, NJ 07003; *Dreams and Nightmares* is edited by David Kopaska-Merkel, who continues to publish a wide variety of excellent fantasy and dark fantasy poetry as he has done since 1986. $12 for six issues ($15 outside North America) payable to David Kopaska-Merkel, 1300 Kicker Road, Tuscaloosa, AL 35404.

Nonfiction Books

The Essential Monster Movie Guide: A Century of Creature Features on Film, TV, and Video by Stephen Jones (Billboard Books), both useful and fun, has an introduction by Forrest J. Ackerman and is illustrated throughout; *Cult Movies* by Karl French and Philip French (Billboard Books) focuses on 150 films chosen by the authors as having achieved cult status. Each entry includes plot synopsis, facts about the making of the film, memorable moments, and key lines. Black-

and-white illustrations throughout; *Parasite Rex: Inside the Bizarre World of Nature's Most Dangerous Creatures* by Carl Zimmer (The Free Press) is a fascinating, horrific journey into the world of creatures that prey on other creatures; *The Two-Headed Boy and Other Medical Marvels* by Jan Bondesman (Cornell University Press) continues the author's investigation of anomalies of human development that he began with *A Cabinet of Medical Curiosities* and *The Feejee Mermaid and Other Essays in Natural and Unnatural History*. In the new book he examines historical cases of dwarfism, giantism, extreme hairiness and shows the humanity behind the strangeness; *The Bewitching of Anne Gunter* by James Sharpe (Routledge) investigates a true crime story from 1604 about the accusations and trial for witchcraft of three women in England; *The Circus Fire* by Stewart O'Nan (Doubleday) is a riveting account of the fire that broke out at a matinee performance of the Ringling Brothers and Barnum & Bailey circus on July 6, 1944 during which 167 people were killed; *Monsters from the Id: The Rise of Horror in Film in Fiction* by E. Michael Jones (Spence) posits that horror is an unconscious backlash against the Enlightenment and the evils of secular humanism; *The Strange Case of Edward Gorey* by Alexander Theroux (Fantagraphics) is a biographical essay by a longtime friend of Gorey's, with black-and-white illustrations by Gorey throughout; *Do What Thou Wilt: A Life of Aleister Crowley* by Lawrence Sutin (St. Martin's Press); *Raising the Devil: Satanism, New Religions, and the Media* by Bill Ellis (The University Press of Kentucky) reveals how the Christian Pentecostal movement, right-wing conspiracy theories, and an opportunistic media turned folk traditions into the Satanism scare of the 1980s; *The Book of Dzyan*, edited and introduced by Tim Maroney (Chaosium), the first in a series of books exploring the occult sources drawn on by H. P. Lovecraft, is a study of Madam Blavatsky's writings; *Dracula: Sense and Nonsense* by Elizabeth Miller (Desert Island Books) deflates many of the myths surrounding Bram Stoker's great creation by going back to the author's original notes and journals; *It Came From Bob's Basement: Exploring the Science Fiction and Monster Movie Archive of Bob Burns* by Bob Burns with John Michlig (Chronicle Books); *Aching for Beauty: Footbinding in China* by Wang Pin (University of Minnesota Press) argues that footbinding should not be viewed merely as a function of men's oppression of women, but rather as a phenomenon of male and female desire deeply rooted in traditional Chinese culture; *Horror of the 20th Century: An Illustrated History* by Robert Weinberg (Rizzoli) is a lavishly illustrated oversized book that begins with the birth of the Gothic novel in 1765 and covers the writers, publishers, actors, and filmmakers who have kept horror alive; *Noir Fiction: Dark Highways* by Paul Duncan (Pocket Essentials, U.K.) is a pint-sized guide that somehow manages to cram in a useful and satisfying definition of "noir," and provides an excellent introduction to the world of noir fiction by profiling some of the more important writers of the genre; *Film Noir: Films of Trust and Betrayal* by Paul Duncan (Pocket Essentials, U.K.) does the same as the above, but for the noir film; *Hershell Gordon Lewis, Godfather of Gore* by Randy Palmer (McFarland) is a profile of the man and filmmaker who made such gems as *Blood Feast* and *The Gore-Gore Girls*; *Cyborgs, Santa Claus and Satan: Science Fiction, Fantasy and Horror Films Made for Television* by Fraser A. Sherman (McFarland) begins with the first science fiction film produced for TV—1968's *Shadow on the Land*—through 1998. Illustrated with chronology and appendices and index; *The Films of John Carpenter* by John Kenneth Muir (McFarland) provides an overview of the director's career and in-depth entries for each film directed by him, from 1975's *Dark Star* to 1998's *Vampires; The Ultimate Jack the Ripper Sourcebook* by Stuart Evans (Carroll & Graf) is illustrated with 32 black-and-white photographs and has information compiled from police documents in the Scotland Yard archives, including eyewitness accounts and a selection of contemporary press reports; *Children of the Night: Of Vampires and Vampirism* by Tony Thorne (Gollancz, U.K.) covers vampires from folktale to *Buffy, the Vampire Slayer; The Ingrid Pitt Bedside Companion for Ghost Hunters* by Ingrid Pitt (B. T. Batsford/U.K.); *Ray Bradbury: A Critical Companion* by Robin Anne Reid (Greenwood Press) discusses eight of Bradbury's major works and includes an analysis of plot, setting, characters and themes; *On Writing: A Memoir of the Craft* by Stephen King (Scribner's); *The American Writer: Shaping a Nation's Mind* by Jack Cady (St. Martin's Press) is a survey of American literature. While the book concentrates on mainstream authors, it also covers work by a few science fiction writers plus H. P. Lovecraft and James Branch Cabell; *French Science Fiction, Fantasy, Horror and Pulp Fiction* by Jean-Marc L'Officier & Randy L'Officier (McFarland) is a guide to all media in French, including works from Belgium and Canada, focusing mainly on literature. With a foreword by Stephen R. Bissette; *Hauntings: The Official Peter Straub Bibliography* by Michael Collings (Overlook Connection Press) is a reference to the works of Straub including fiction, nonfiction, poetry, essays, and liner notes for jazz records and CDs. Black-and-white illustrations of the book jackets are included as well as an interview by Stanley Wiater; *Lord of a Visible World: An Autobiography in Letters* by H. P. Lovecraft (Ohio University Press) is a collection of letters, edited by David E. Schulz and S. T. Joshi, along with autobiographical excerpts of essays by Lovecraft and the text of "Some Notes on a Nonentity"; *Contributions to the Study of SF and Fantasy #92: Science and Destabilization in the Modern American Gothic: Lovecraft, Matheson, and King* by David S. Oakes (Greenwood); *The Annotated Supernatural Horror in Literature* by H. P. Lovecraft, edited by S. T. Joshi (Hippocampus Press) is the first annotated edition of this seminal work. Joshi has also provided a comprehensive bibliography of all the authors and works discussed in the text; *On the Fringe for Thirty Years: A History of Horror in the British Small Press* by David Sutton (Shadow Publishing) with an introduction by Stan Nicholls and cover art by Stephen Jones is an illustrated chapbook providing an appraisal by the author/editor, who has been active in all aspects of the field; *The Dybbuk and the Yiddish Imagination: A Haunted Reader*, edited and translated from the Yiddish by Joachim Neugroschel (Syracuse University Press); *Daphne Du Maurier: Haunted Heiress* by Nina Auerbach (University of Pennsylvania); *Gothic Radicalism: Literature, Philosophy, and Psychoanalysis in the Nineteenth Century* by Andrew Smith (St. Martin's Press); *Sixty Years of Arkham House*, edited by S. T. Joshi (Arkham House) includes a history and bibliography. Illustrations are by Allen Koszowski; *The Encyclopedia of Fantastic Film: Ali Baba to Zombies* by R. G. Young (Applause Books); *Writing Horror* by Edo van Belkom (Self-Counsel Press); *Psycho Paths: Tracking the Serial Killer Through Contemporary American Film and Fiction* by Philip L. Simpson (Southern Illinois University Press); *Fear Codex* by Bryce Stevens (Jacobyte

Books/CD-ROM) is a useful reference guide to all aspects of the Australian dark fantasy and horror scene, with brief entries on magazines, authors, illustrators, and organizations; *The Great Fairy Tale Tradition: From Straparola and Basile to the Brothers Grimm,* edited by Jack Zipes (W. W. Norton) is part of the Norton Critical Editions series. 116 fairy tales, grouped thematically, are accompanied by detailed introductions and annotations by several critics on the subject, including Zipes. Brief biographies of the storytellers and a selected bibliography are also included; *The Horror Reader,* edited by Ken Gelder (Routledge) brings together what the editor considers the best academic essays on the subject of horror since 1975, ranging from an essay by the Bulgarian, Tzvetan Todorov, that "recovers" fantasy as a literary term, to a reading of Hong Kong horror films as a reaction to the former British territory's changed political relationship with China; *The Oxford Companion to Fairy Tales* by Jack Zipes (Oxford University Press) is arranged alphabetically, and covers authors, illustrators, individual titles, and countries of origin for the fairy tales of Europe, from medieval times through Walt Disney. Sixty-seven scholars from around the world have contributed entries and there are numerous black-and-white illustrations throughout; *Cutting Edge: Art Horror and the Horrific Avant Garde* by Joan Hawkins (University of Minnesota Press) investigates the differences and relationships between avant-garde cinema and exploitation. The author proposes that the difference between the two types of cinema is that though both tend to use shocking material to explore certain themes while attempting to jolt the viewer out of complacency, exploitation, or what she calls "paracinema," maintains a more ironical distance. For example, she shows how a film such as Franju's *Eyes without a Face* can work simultaneously as an art, political, and splatter film; *Shadows in the Attic: A Guide to British Supernatural Fiction 1820–1950* by Neil Wilson (British Library Publishing) and with an introduction by Ramsey Campbell is a useful reference. It's based on the collections of the British Library, through which Neil Wilson has identified the 200 top writers active in the supernatural genre during its "golden age" from the end of the Gothic period to the birth of modern Horror. The annotated guide lists the first book appearances of significant ghost stories published between 1820 and 1950. Bibliographic details of first book appearances of stories and novels are given, with separate author and title indexes. Every work listed is accompanied by annotations and notes. Biographical information is provided on every author included, together with sources for further research and reading, biographies, critical studies, associated works and bibliographies.

Nonfiction Magazines

Video Watchdog®, edited by Tim and Donna Lucas, happily went monthly at the beginning of 2000. It's still the best magazine for up-to-date information on various cuts and variants of all kinds of movies available on video. This digest-sized magazine is always entertaining with its coverage of fantastic video and is a must for anyone interested in quirky reviews and columns. $48 for twelve issues (bulk mail), $70 first class, payable to Video Watchdog, P.O. 5283, Cincinnati, OH 45205–0283.

Gauntlet: Exploring the Limits of Free Expression is a semi-annual, published in May and November and edited by Barry Hoffman. $16 a year, payable to *Gauntlet*. The May issue in 2000 addressed problems in the comic book industry ranging from censorship to changes in distribution. The address can be found at the end of the summation.

Crime Time, edited by Barry Forshaw, is an excellent British quarterly in trade paperback format. During the year 2000 there was an extensive interview with Jack O'Connell (see my mini-review of his novel above), an overview of the writing of Cornell Woolrich, a regular column by Mike Ashley about collecting crime publications, many author profiles, an interview with Kim Newman, and an article asking Stephen Jones, Jay Russell, and Kim Newman about their contributions to the anthology, *Dark Detectives*. In addition, there are articles, columns, book and film reviews, interviews and several brief novel excerpts. *CT* provides fine coverage of the field. 30 pounds sterling for four issues payable to Crime Time Subscriptions, 18 Coleswood Road, Harpenden, Herts AL5 1EQ England. Also available from Firebird Distributing.

Specialty Press and Limited Editions

Please note that some limited editions may already be sold out by the time *The Year's Best Fantasy and Horror* is published. The publisher's Web site will usually note this. Also, there are a number of books published as limited, signed editions, which have been mentioned in other sections of this book.

Snowbound: The Record of a Theatrical Touring Party by Bram Stoker, annotated and edited by Bruce Wightman (The Desert Island Dracula Library) is a collection of fifteen stories first published in the U.K. in 1908 and never before published in the U.S.; Bram Stoker's *The Shoulder of Shasta* (The Desert Island Dracula Library), annotated and introduced by Alan Johnson, and published for the first time since 1895.

Her Misbegotten Son by Alan Rodgers (Wildside Press) is a horror novella published as a trade paperback.

Wildside Press is publishing a line of classic reprints including books by F. Marion Crawford, James Branch Cabell, Sax Rohmer, and H. Rider Haggard. The press has licensed the name "Weird Tales Library" from Weird Tales, Ltd. and brought out a reprint of "The Moon Terror" which is a legendary story from *Weird Tales* originally published in 1924, under that imprint. In addition, the press brought out *Best of Weird Tales: Novellas of 1923*, edited by Marvin Kaye & John Gregory Betancourt.

The Arthur Conan Doyle Society in conjunction with Ash-Tree Press published *The Haunted Grange of Goresthorpe* by Arthur Conan Doyle. This ghost story was originally submitted to *Blackwood's Magazine* at the end of the 1870s. Blackwood's never published it nor did they return the manuscript, and it remained in their files until the company's archives were presented to the National Library of Scotland in 1942. This is the story's first publication. The book has an introduction by Owen Dudley Edwards (Hon. President, The Arthur Conan Doyle Society), and is edited, with an afterword, by Christopher Roden (Founder, The Arthur Conan Doyle Society).

Duet for the Devil, a novel by t. Winter-Damon and Randy Chandler (Necro Publications). The introduction is by Edward Lee. Cover art is by David G. Barnett. Published in a limited hardcover edition of 100 copies and a trade paperback edition of 400 copies.

Road to Hell, the first novel by Gerard Daniel Houarner was published, also by Necro, in a limited hardcover edition of 52 copies, signed and lettered, and a signed and numbered trade paperback edition limited to 300 copies.

Subterranean Press published a variety of limited editions. First, Poppy Z. Brite's novella *Plastic Jesus,* an intriguing (but not horror) alternate history about two British musicians very much like Paul McCartney and John Lennon whose relationship changes the world. Interior illustrations are by the author and the colorful psychedelic jacket art is by Mary Fleener. Three hardcover editions: 600 signed and numbered copies, nine signed and lettered traycased copies, and a trade edition. *The Bottoms* by Joe R. Lansdale, a novel inspired by the author's novella "Mad Dog Summer." This preceded the trade edition and was typeset from the author's manuscript. before editorial changes were made. Dust jacket art is by Alan M. Clark. There is a signed, limited, slipcased edition of 400 and 26 lettered copies. Also by Lansdale, a beautifully produced, expanded version of his great novella "The Big Blow" from Douglas E. Winter's anthology *Revelations.* Dust jacket and all graphics are by Gail Cross. Three limited editions: 250 autographed numbered copies, housed in a handcrafted slipcase, with an exclusive afterword by the author; a lettered edition of only 13 copies, bound in a premium cloth, housed in a handcrafted traycase; and an unsigned hardcover trade edition, without the afterword. *Blood Dance,* a western, is part of the Lost Lansdale series. It has over a dozen full-page interior illustrations by artist Mark A. Nelson. It's published in an edition of 1,000 signed, numbered copies, and an 18-copy lettered edition bound in leather and cloth, with an original piece of the book's art bound into each traycase. Subterranean also published Bill Sheehan's accessible and thoughtful critical study of the fiction of Peter Straub, *At the Foot of the Story Tree,* in two editions—a 500-copy signed and numbered edition and 26 signed traycased copies. Dust jacket and autograph page art is by Alan M. Clark.

Fedogan and Bremer brought out two books in 2000, neither horror. *Bottled in Blond* by Hugh B. Cave is a collection of his hard-boiled Peter Kane detective stories and *Frost* by Donald Wandrei, and edited by D. H. Olson, is the first collection of the author's mystery stories.

PS publishing continued their novella chapbook program by publishing "Naming the Parts," an excellent horror novella by Tim Lebbon. Lebbon, whose novella "White" made a splash in the field in 1999, seems to have a knack for refreshing well-worn horror tropes and making them his own. Steve Rasnic Tem provides an introduction. Limited to 500 signed copies: 300 in paperback and 200 in hardcover. The jacket illustration by Alan M. Clark is too literal for its own good. The publisher also brought out two science fiction novellas with jacket art by David A. Hardy. Paul J. McAuley's "Making History" has an introduction by Michael Swanwick and Ian McDonald's "Tendéleos' Story" has an introduction by Robert Silverberg.

"The Heidelberg Cylinder" by Jonathan Carroll (Mobius New Media) is a signed and numbered limited hardcover edition of a new novella (reprinted herein) by an author who defies categorization. The beautiful dust jacket art and design is by Dave McKean. Limited to 1,000 copies.

From Gauntlet: *Hunger and Thirst* is the first novel Richard Matheson ever wrote, but it has now been published by Gauntlet for the first time, fifty years after it was written. Matheson provides a lengthy introduction explaining why the book remained unpublished for so long, as well as discussing several other aborted projects including two proposed books that were to be 2,000 pages apiece. The book is available in two states: a 750-copy signed numbered edition and a 52-copy leather-bound lettered edition, with a beveled leather traycase with the cover art inset on the traycase. It comes with a CD of Matheson reading from the book. Dust jacket art is by Harry O. Morris. *Cover,* Jack Ketchum's third novel, was originally published as a Ballantine paperback in 1987. This is its first hardcover edition. Dust jacket and interior art by Neal McPheeters. Afterword by Thomas Tessier. The book comes in two states: a 1,000-copy numbered edition signed by the author, artist, and Tessier, and a 52-copy leather-bound, traycased lettered edition that includes an additional interior illustration and a self-portrait of the author.

American Fantasy Press produced its first publication in several years as a chapbook launched at the 2000 World Horror Convention in Denver. Steve Rasnic Tem and Melanie Tem's magnificent tour de force "The Man on the Ceiling" (reprinted herein) is a thoughtful, unsettling piece of metafiction on the art of horror, what scares us, and the creative process. Limited to 500 copies, signed and numbered with cover art by J. K. Potter.

Dead Cat Bounce by Gerard Hourner (Space and Time) is a short story chapbook about a zombie cat, illustrated by GAK.

Millennium Macabre, the sixth chapbook in the Enigmatic Novella, series contains one reprinted story and two published for the first time by William Meikle with Graeme Hurry, two Scot writers. The three horror stories all feature the supernatural and one is a Cthulhu story. Attractively and appropriately illustrated by Iain Maynard.

CD Publications continued its novella series with Douglas Clegg's "Purity" and John Shirley's "Demons." "Purity" was available in two states: limited edition of 450 signed copies, and traycased lettered edition of 26 signed and lettered copies. "Demons" was available in two states: a limited edition of 450 signed and numbered copies, and a traycased lettered edition of 26 signed and lettered copies (bound in leather, with satin ribbon page marker and additional artwork).

Also from CD Publications: *Hide and Seek,* by Jack Ketchum was published by Ballantine as a paperback original in 1984, and has been out of print ever since. Ketchum wrote it as a kind of homage to the works of James M. Cain. Available in two states: limited edition of 1,000 signed copies, and traycased lettered edition of 52 signed and lettered copies (bound in leather, with satin ribbon page marker and additional full-color artwork). *Mischief* by Douglas Clegg is the hardcover edition of the novel published earlier in 2000 by Leisure in a mass market edition. The CD edition is available in two states: a limited edition of 750 signed copies, and a traycased lettered edition of 52 signed and lettered copies (bound in leather, with satin ribbon page marker and additional full-color artwork). *Mediums Rare* by Richard Matheson is a new nonfiction book focusing on Matheson's life-long interest in paranormal phenomena. In it, he dramatizes various events in psychic history. Dust jacket art is by Harry O. Morris, and the design is by Bill Walker. There is a limited edition of 600 signed and numbered copies, and a traycased lettered edition of 52 signed and lettered copies (bound in leather, with satin ribbon page marker). *You Come When I Call You*, a new novel by Douglas Clegg, is available in two states: a limited edition of 1,000 signed copies, and a traycased lettered edition of 52 signed and lettered copies. Dust jacket art is by Phil Parks. *The Traveling Vampire Show* by Richard Laymon is available in two limited editions: 1,000 signed copies, and a traycased lettered edition of 52 signed and lettered copies (bound in leather, with a satin ribbon page marker and additional full-color artwork) and also an unsigned second edition. Dust jacket art is by Alan M. Clark. *Once Upon a Halloween* by Richard Laymon is a new short novel available as a limited edition of 2,000 signed copies, and a traycased lettered edition of 52 signed and lettered copies (bound in leather, with satin ribbon page marker and additional full-color artwork). Dust jacket art is by Alan M. Clark with design by Gail Cross. *The Stickmen* by Edward Lee is a science fiction/thriller and is available in two states: a signed edition of 1,000, and a traycased lettered edition of 52 signed and lettered copies. Dust jacket and illustrated endpapers by Erik Wilson. *The Christmas Thingy* by F. Paul Wilson and illustrated by Alan M. Clark is a children's story available in three states: a trade edition, a slipcased limited edition of 350 signed and numbered copies, and a traycased lettered edition of 26 signed and lettered copies (bound in leather, with satin ribbon page marker and an original drawing by the artist either bound into the traycase or matted and framed separately).

Sims (Book One: La Causa) by F. Paul Wilson is the first of a three- or four-book series of science fiction novellas that is available in two states: a limited edition of 750 signed and numbered copies, and a traycased lettered edition of 26 signed and lettered copies (bound in leather, with satin ribbon page marker). Illustrated by Phil Parks. *Born Bad* by Barry Hoffman is available in two states: 500 signed and numbered hardcover copies with dust jacket art by Harry O. Morris, and an edition of 26 signed, lettered, and traycased copies, featuring additional Harry O. Morris artwork and a deluxe traycase, and signed by author and artist.

As part of the Perihelion Signed Limited Broadside Series, Miniature Sun Press brought out three beautiful broadsides: "The Lesions of Genetic Sin," a poem by Bruce Boston, "Hallucinating Jenny" by G. Sutton Breiding, and "Skin" by Charlee Jacob. All three are limited to 200 copies, of which 125 are signed and numbered by the author. All the collage art is by Brandon Totman.

Overlook Connection Press brought out the first hardcover edition of Kevin J. Anderson's *Resurrection, Inc.*, with introductions by David B. Silva, Janet Berliner, and Bentley Little, and dust-jacket art by Bob Eggleton. Available in three editions: a 1,500-copy signed trade edition; a 100-copy signed, sterling edition with special binding, foil embossed and slipcased; and a 52-copy lettered edition, leather-bound and foil embossed in a wood box with special endpapers and frontispiece by the artist.

DarkTales Publications published attractive, well-designed trade paperback original novels, anthologies and collections and a series of chapbooks by new and established writers such as M. Michael Straczynski, Yvonne Navarro, Mort Castle, and others. *Lifetimes of the Blood* by Adam Johnson is about an identity-changing serial killer of the centuries who is tracked down by a mysterious older man.

Mystyque Press launched with David Niall Wilson's novel *The Path of the Meteor* in a trade paperback edition featuring cover art by Lisanne Lake. Their second title is *Spinning Webs and Telling Lies*, a collection by Wilson also in trade paperback with cover art by Lake. It contains four of Wilson's Western and Native American themed stories, two collaborations with Brian A. Hopkins and a solo story from Hopkins. The books are numbered and signed by Wilson, and limited to 250 copies.

Dream Zone Publications brought out the second in its Haunted Dreams series of novellas "Death of a Valkyrie: Two Long Tales" by Peter Tennant, and a novella by Quentin S. Crisp (not the famous late bon vivant). Artwork by Sean Russell Friend.

Odds and Ends

Paper Tiger, for the past few years an imprint of the British publishing company Collins & Brown, has been producing high quality books spotlighting fantasy, dark fantasy, and science fiction artists for a number of years. Now Sterling Publishing Company is distributing them in the U.S. During 2000 there have been oversized trade paperbacks of work by Bob Eggleton (two volumes), Brom, Rodney Matthews, and Tim White and a hardcover by Anne Sudworth. What strikes me most is the variety and range of each artist's work: *Greetings from Earth* by Eggleton features work such as his dinosaur cover art for James Patrick Kelly's story "Think like a Dinosaur" in *Asimov's Science Fiction* magazine and the cover art for Brian Lumley's *Necroscope* novels. *Alien Horizons*, the second Eggleton book, has monstrous aliens among its more strictly science fiction illustrations. Nigel Suckling wrote the commentary for both books. Rodney Matthews's cartoon fantasies and surreal dark fantasies are colorful and often sly. This is a series to collect and cherish.

An Instinct for Dragons by David E. Jones (Routledge) is a fascinating book that proposes that the "dragon," a monstrous creature present in most worldwide cultures in different forms, is an amalgam of three predators that preyed on ancient humans: the eagle, the python, and the leopard.

Hans Bellmer: The Anatomy of Anxiety by Sue Taylor (MIT Press) takes a psychoanalytic approach to this artist whose most famous works of art are photographs he took of distorted and mutilated female dolls. Most scholarship to date has focused on Bellmer's work of the 1930s, especially the infamous dolls, but Taylor extends her discussion to the sexually explicit prints, drawings, paintings, and photographs he produced throughout the ensuing three decades. This dense but fascinating book includes a color frontispiece and 121 black-and-white images (eight published here for the first time), as well as appendices containing several significant texts by Bellmer previously unavailable in English. Bellmer's art is shocking and sometimes pornographic; anyone with a serious interest in the horror field should be aware of his work.

FoodChain: Encounters Between Mates, Predators, and Prey by Catherine Chalmers (Aperture) is a marvelously creepy look at nature. Gordon Grice provides a short, not-so-sweet essay and the photographer is interviewed about her work. The photographs are fascinating. Beginning with tobacco hornworm larvae eating their way out of a tomato, the photographer follows the food chain as a preying mantis then consumes one of the larvae with gusto (you can even see it cleaning its legs after the feast). Another sequence shows the mating dance of preying mantises, and in perhaps the most disturbing sequence, the birth and consumption of "pinkies" (newborn mice) by a toad and a snake.

A *Natural History of the Unnatural World* produced under the auspices of The Cryptozoological Society of London (Carroll & Brown) is a charming, straight-faced book that provides a mass of information on "the strange creatures who lurk in the dark and mysterious corners of planet Earth . . . the unusual—even mythical—creatures that populate the globe." It illustrates the field notes of scientists and explorers, far-flung reports of sightings and miscellaneous sources, with over 600 drawings and photographs of supporting evidence.

Spectrum 7: The Best in Contemporary Fantastic Art, edited by Cathy Fenner and Arnie Fenner (Underwood Press), represents some of the most striking art from the year 1999. It's both a beautiful collectible and an important survey of the state of contemporary fantasy art.

Addresses of Small Presses

American Fantasy Press, Garcia Publishing Services, P.O. Box 1059, Woodstock, IL 60098.

Arsenal Pulp Press, 103, 1014 Homer Street, Vancouver, BC V6B 2W9 Canada. www.arsenalpulp.com.

Ash-Tree Press, P.O. Box 1360, Ashcroft, BC V0K 1A0, Canada. www.Ash-Tree.bc.ca/ashtreecurrent.html.

Babbage Press, 8740 Penfield Avenue, Northridge, CA 91324. Books@babbagepress.com.

BBR Distributing, P.O. Box 625, Sheffield S1 3GY, U.K. http://www.bbr-online.com.

Chameleon Publishing, 3430 Salem Drive, Rochester Hills, MI 48306.

Dark Highway Press, 4301 Black Hawk Court, Fort Collins, CO 80526. http://www.frii.com/~bovberg/DHPress.html.

Dark Regions Press, P.O. Box 6301, Concord, CA 94524.

Dark Tales Publications, P.O. Box 675, Grandview, MO 64030. http://www.darktales.com.

Desert Island Books, 89 Park Street, Westcliff-on-Sea, Essex SSO 7PD, U.K. http://www.desertislandbooks.com.

Firebird Distributing LLC, 2030 First Street, Unit 5, Eureka, CA 95501. http://www.firebirddistributing.com.

Freak Press, 655 John Muir Dr. #417, San Francisco, CA 94132. http://www.freakpress.com.

Gauntlet Publications, 309 Powell Road, Springfield, PA 19064. http://www.gauntletpress.com.

Greenwood Publishing, 88 Post Road West, P.O. Box 5007, Westport, CT 06881. Phone: (203) 226-3571.

Haffner, 5005 Crooks Road, Suite 35, Royal Oak, MI 48073–1239. http://www.rust.net/~haffner/.

IFD Publishing, P.O. Box 40776, Eugene, OR 97404. http://www.IFDpublishing.com.

Lone Wolf Publications, 13500 SE 79th Street, Oklahoma City, OK 73150. http://www.dm.net/~bahwolf/lwp.html.

Midnight House, 4128 Woodland Park Ave. N., Seattle, WA 98103. http://www.darksidepress.com/midnight.html

Miniature Sun Press, P.O. Box 11002, Napa Valley, CA 94581. Miniaturesunpress@hotmail.com.

Mystyque Press, P.O. Box 2353, Chesapeake, VA. 23327-2353. mystyque@springmail.com.

Mythos Books, 218 Hickory Meadow Lane, Poplar Bluff, MO 63901–2160. dwynn@LDD.net.

Night Shade Books, 560 Scott #304, San Francisco, CA 94117. http://www.nightshadebooks.com.

Obsidian Press, 3839 Whitman Avenue, N. #303, Seattle, WA 98103. http://www.mmpbooks.com.

Overlook Connection Press, P.O. Box 526, Woodstock, GA 30188. http://www.overlookconnection.com.

Sarob Press, Brynderwen, 41 Forest View, Mountain Ash, Mid Glamorgan, Wales CF45 3DU U.K. http://home.freeuk.net/sarobpress.

Scrapple Press, P.O. Box 5381, Atlanta, GA 31107.

Stealth Press, 336 College Avenue, Lancaster, PA 17603. www.stealthpress.com.

Tartarus Press, Coverley House, Carlton, Leyburn, North Yorkshire, DL8 4AY, U.K.

Fantasy and Horror in the Media: 2000

Edward Bryant

Duck and Cover

Being a stodgily old-school writer myself, I'm always looking for apt metaphors embedded in public happenings, semiotic signposts suggesting directions toward probably indecipherable futures. When it comes to the element of the fantastic in pop media, I caught one of the little devils during the Academy Awards presentation back in March.

How many of you were bonding with the global viewership as Icelandic evolutionary punk rocker Björk startled the crowd in the Santa Monica Civic Auditorium by wearing her swan dress to sing "I've Seen It All," her nominated song from *Dancer in the Dark*?

It really *was* a swan dress, a short, frilly, waterfowl of a tutu creation, the strap of which came up over one shoulder terminating in a swan's head replete with beak. Host Steve Martin offered a sharp but harmless jest. On the morning after, the fashion critics were merciless, save for the *New York Times*; the observant critic there suggested that Björk was one of the few stars on hand simply being true to herself. Nothing like the Jennifer Lopez ideal of vying for Ms. Global Mammal. Before the show, Björk had bewildered the interviewers by telling them she was delighted to have starred in the critically acclaimed *Dancer in the Dark* (a fantasy film itself), but harbored no ambition ever to appear in a movie again. What, she didn't *want to be a movie star*? Then during the evening, she proceeded to wear a costume clearly out of step with what everyone else was displaying, whether sublime or tacky.

I see it as a very contemporary twist on the tale of the Ugly Duckling. That Björk wanted to affect a playful image, one highly idiosyncratic and certainly unique, is a laudable undertaking in an event representing the desperate marketing of endless pop culture icons and the interchange of billions of dollars in the new global economy.

Unsurprisingly it's increasingly difficult to market an individual in opposition to craftily constructed mass-appeal products. To be fair, it should be noted that while Björk didn't win the Oscar for her song, that statuette did go to a musical iconoclast who's been a thorn pricking conformist balloons for longer than Björk's been alive. A rather surprised Bob Dylan got the prize after a live satellite-fed performance from Sydney.

At any rate, the point I'm doggedly trying to make is that the swans of the fantastic, often derided for their peculiar appearance, are still paddling furiously among the oceanic fleets of plain brown ducks: quacking media moguls and ugly studio heads.

But the swans, bless 'em, still sneak in under the radar, sometimes even in broad daylight. Okay, so much for tortured metaphor. Now what about the real world?

Back to the Oscars, paying tribute to 2001, the year and the concept, by using a high-tech set apparently evoking a subway station of the future, and then bringing in the symbolic future, a live electronic image of Sir Arthur C. Clarke in Sri Lanka to present the award for best adapted-from-another-work screenplay. Now that *was* cool.

I'd be remiss if, in noting the winding down of the previous century and millennium, I didn't point out that The Academy Awards' final quintet for the best picture Oscar included two outright fantasy films and one fellow traveler. Not bad.

The fantasies are, of course, *Crouching Tiger, Hidden Dragon* and *Chocolat*; the almost-but-not-quite-there movie is *Gladiator*. Although comparing *Crouching Tiger, Hidden Dragon* to *Chocolat* is akin to the proverbial apples-and-oranges problem, it's inarguable that both pictures have considerable charms to offer. *Chocolat* is a good film. *Crouching Tiger* is an extraordinary one. They're similar in only one obvious way—each was presented to the audience as a general release. Something of swans in ducks' featherage. No genre labels need apply.

And while there was no qualitative equivalent of a *2001* or a *Bladerunner* over on the science fiction side of the ledger, the century still ended with a respectable bang rather than a whimper. It was a good year if not a great one.

So, Little Boy, Do You Like Gladiator Movies?

Let's get to the year's specifics.

Ang Lee is a remarkable international phenomenon. Does anyone else build quite so diverse a selection of feature films? This Taiwanese director first gained major notice with 1993's *The Wedding Banquet*, a socially astute Chinese family comedy about relationships, homosexuality, and cultural identity. Then there was 1995's *Sense and Sensibility*, a laudable entry in the recent spate of Jane Austen movies. 1997 saw an admirable adaptation of Rick Moody's novel, *The Ice Storm*. And 1999 brought *Ride With the Devil*, the adaptation of a Daniel Woodrell novel about the guerrilla border skirmishes in the American Civil War. Possibly perceived as your standard issue, garden variety historical western, the film stumbled. Box office crowds stayed away in droves. But then came *Crouching Tiger, Hidden Dragon*.

What a sensation it's turned out to be, solidly bridging the gap between art houses and suburban multiplexes. Some of that success may be because the brilliant visuals richly satisfy more conservative viewers uncertain if they want to sit through Cantonese dialog with English subtitles.

Crouching Tiger, Hidden Dragon is a nearly perfectly constructed Asian fantasy, a fable thoroughly adept at keeping eye, heart, and brain all intimately connected. Based on the novel by Wang Du Lu and set in a distant Chinese past, all the descriptive elements are suitably fantastical for a western audience. Chow Yun-Fat is the burnt-out warrior ready to give up his life's quest of avenging his murdered master, handing his sword, Green Destiny, over to security consultant (yes, it works in context) Michelle Yeoh, whose job it is to transfer the magical blade (think something along the line of Elric's runesword, Stormbringer) to Beijing for safekeeping in the house of an aging warrior. We quickly realize that Yun-Fat and Yeoh's characters' relationship is one of barely repressed love. But as warriors and professional equals, they've been too damned stuck in the traces to admit it.

In Beijing, Green Destiny is stolen by a masked bandit, the alternate identity of a young and demure noblewoman (Zhang Ziyi). The noblewoman, secretly trained to near-perfection by an older female villain (Cheng Pei Pei), is eager to evade an approaching and unwelcome arranged marriage. In the meantime she meets Yeoh's warrior woman character and the two inescapably bond.

Action swirls around the stolen sword, but not until a full sixteen minutes of exposition have elapsed from the beginning. That's not long for drama, but it's probably an eternity for martial arts fans. When the action does arrive, choreographed by master martial arts director Yuen Wo Ping (he did the flying action work in *The Matrix*), it stuns and bewitches. I'm told some fairly conservative martial arts movie purists have derided Lee's movie on grounds that the flying scenes are grossly overblown. They obviously own no poetry in their souls. The scenes here of characters bounding from ground to roof, from high tree branch to higher crown, are breathtaking, quite literally poetry in motion. It's the sort of personal locomotion that many of us viewers will recognize from our own dreams of flying.

Everything here, from the overarching story of love and revenge, and the price attendant on each, to the story-within-the-story of flirtation and escape, does more than merely work well.

Ang Lee's taken heroic fantasy, martial arts action, elements of the spaghetti western, and mixed them effortlessly into an airy confection leavened with genuine heart and emotion.

A level of complexity and achievement down, but still a marvelous achievement, is Lässe Hallstrom's faux French fantasy, *Chocolat*. This is another art house object which has drawn an enthusiastic crowd out in the open market. That shouldn't arrive as a total surprise, coming from the director of *My Life as a Dog*, *What's Eating Gilbert Grape*, and *The Cider House Rules*. It's a fairy tale and a morality piece, always balanced precariously on the razor edge of toppling over into bathos and deadly sentimentality. Robert Nelson Jacob's adaptation of the Joanne Harris novel never quite takes that fatal plunge.

Deliberately set in a chronological never-neverland somewhere in the mid- to late-twentieth century, *Chocolat* unwinds at a deliberate pace in the isolated and tiny French village of Lansquenet. It's a quiet place, administered by the supremely repressed Comte de Reynaud (Alfred Molina), a nobleman so steeped in conservative religion, he's ever unshipping a cover story about his alienated wife being off in Italy on endless vacation.

The village's entropic stillness is broken by the arrival of Juliette Binoche's free-spirited Vianne Rocher, a single mom who almost literally blows into town one day with the north wind and her daughter Anouk (Victoire Thivisol). In short order, Binoche makes the acquaintance of a troubled, aged neighbor (Dame Judi Dench), and rents from her an unoccupied patisserie. Since the village is presently suffering through a severe case of Lent, the pious Comte is incensed that anyone should be gearing up to produce pastries. Not so, Binoche assures him. The truth is even worse. She's using her arcane knowledge of herbs and spices to open a magical little shop purveying fine chocolates. In the tradition of her extraordinarily talented female forebears, Binoche creates and dispenses candies, the effects of which only *begin* with caffeine and endorphins.

Binoche's character is in the business of giving people what they need, whether they consciously realize it or not.

While the village bluenoses prudishly stew, Binoche must confront her own question of needs to be satisfied when the river gypsy Roux (Johnny Depp) arrives at the dock with a boatload of sensuality and temptation.

At the heart of both village and populace is the eternal battle between that new religion, western Christianity, and that oldtime faith, paganism. All concerned carefully keep the sweetness mixture based in milk chocolate, with just enough semi-sweet to rein in the temptation to cloy.

Chocolat's not seriously profound, but it does deliver a healthy portion of pleasure and charm. In the truest sense, it's pro-life.

Now *here's* the finest fantasy film of the year that *didn't* make it into the circle of Oscar best picture nominees. It's *O Brother, Where Art Thou?* from the ever surprising Coen brothers, Joel and Ethan. On the surface, it's a marvelously convoluted chunk of Depression-era Americana, a seriocomic piece with the emphasis on the comic. Don't be fooled. By turns sly and slapstick, *O Brother* rings changes on all manner of myths, both contemporary and ancient, and never turns cynical or mocking in the process.

The most obvious nod is to Homer's *The Odyssey*, a fact noted in the credits. Consequently the Coen brothers got an Oscar nod for best adapted screenplay(!). George Clooney makes the most of his plum role, not only being a splendid escaped convict named Ulysses Everett McGill, but evolving into a highly creditable version of Clark Gable. He's fabulous. Who would have thought it? Myths tend to be shifty critters in this movie, evolving into new images when you least expect.

When Clooney escapes a Mississippi chain gang with fellow prisoners John Turturro and indie filmmaker Tim Blake Nelson, he tells his fellows they're all bound for the Big Rock Candy Mountain if they help reclaim a million dollar booty he stashed after an armored car robbery. He's a charming and convincing liar, of course. His real goal is to regain the love of his estranged wife (Holly Hunter) and their brood of talented daughters.

On the Homeric level, the wanderers encounter everyone from a splendid trio of tunefully seductive sirens (Emmylou Harris, Allison Kraus, and Gillian Welch) to the cyclops (John Goodman playing a sociopathic Bible salesman). But the references don't stop there. The picture brings in Robert Johnson, the '30s blues giant who reputedly traded his soul to the Devil at a rural crossroads in order to gain immortal talent before dying mysteriously (probably at the irate direction of a cuckolded husband). In *O Brother* he is transformed slightly to *Tommy Johnson* for equally mysterious reasons.

Much of the picture swirls around a hotly contested state governor's contest between an old-style demagogue and a new-style reformer who's not the paragon he purports to be. One of the movie's finest set pieces is a Ku Klux Klan rally that surreally lifts shots and vocals right out of *The Wizard of Oz*. I'll only just mention the underwater segment of *Wizard's* tornado scene (to be more specific would be a criminal act of spoiling some of the script's surprises). Nods incline toward *Gone With the Wind* as well, and even, believe it or not, to perhaps the most important scene in *Moby Dick*.

The marvelous tone, not to mention the title itself, wouldn't even exist without Preston Sturges and *Sullivan's Travels*. Yes, the Coen brothers did their homework, used their imaginations, and then played on extreme talent to blend it all together. *O Brother, Where Art Thou?* is—literally—a fabulous job of re-telling, reshaping, refueling classic mythology by breathing in an invigorating and intoxicating draft of warm, hyperoxygenated air.

This is a good working definition of what people mean when they refer to an American film.

The Coen brothers' big 1984 debut splash, the noir *Blood Simple*, was re-released in 2000, by the way. This exceedingly dark suspense picture introduced Frances McDormand and featured the unutterably sinister M. Emmett Walsh as a corrupt and deadly PI. The spiffed-up version is remixed, recut, restored, and includes about five minutes of new material. Seeing it is like meeting an old and valued, if somewhat disturbed, friend.

While I'm mentioning re-releases, I should also note the new version of William Friedkin's 1973 blockbuster, *The Exorcist*. I can recall waiting in a long line in the snow, the day after Christmas, to see William Peter Blatty's bestseller-made-stomach-churner in one of Denver's premier movie palaces, now closed. Eleven minutes of new footage have been added, mostly talk, but good and useful talk. Linda Blair's performance as the possessed child is still creepy, particularly her spider-like inverted descent of the stairs in her home.

One of the great modern fantasies is how cool it is to be a writer. Well . . . okay. It *can* be, but only for a few. For most of us, it's a difficult, insecure, underpaid, lifelong Sisyphean challenge. And then there are those whose muse takes them to territories so dangerous, most of the rest of us would quail at the prospect of facing what truly endangered writers confront. This is not unknown territory for filmmakers. Angles of approach of course vary. One ambitious take on the writing down of dangerous visions can be seen in Julian Schnabel's *Before Night Falls*, a dramatic interpretation of the posthumously published memoirs of Cuban novelist Reinaldo Arenas. Schnabel was a painter before he took up film directing. His first feature, a view of Warhol protege *Basquiat*, turns out to be no one-trick pony. *Before Night Falls* is a nightmarish but inspired look at a talented gay novelist attempting to conduct his life and work with integrity and dignity inside the oppressive Castro regime. Arenas had an exceedingly difficult time smuggling his manuscripts out of prison to be published in Europe. But, it would seem, his problems were cake compared to those of another memorable writer two centuries earlier.

Philip Kaufman's *Quills*, adapted by Doug Wright from his play, stars Geoffrey Rush as the Marquis de Sade. In its own way equally powerful as a portrait of an artist chafing in prison, *Quills* is far more fanciful in its approach than *Before Night Falls*.

Kaufman and Wright begin *Quills* with a little visual jiggery-pokery to show us the Marquis interpreting the mingled sensuality and horror of a French Revolution public execution. The balance of the film moves forward in time to the Marquis' velvet imprisonment in the Charenton Asylum in the years following the Reign of Terror.

It's clear the filmmakers are pushing a fairly sympathetic view of the Marquis. He may be a monster of sexual perversion, but he's a *lovable* monster. Even his friendship with the virginal laundry maid (Kate Winslet) is not terribly sinister.

As de Sade's work continues to be set down in quill and ink, and smuggled with Winslet's help to the outside world, where sympathetic and pragmatic publishers delightedly print zillions of copies the public eats up while bluenoses whine, the French government becomes a mite testy. The Emperor Napoleon is especially pissy. He'd like simply to have the Marquis executed, but this isn't politically expedient.

So he dispatches the expert alienist, Dr. Royer-Collard (Michael Caine), to put a stop to de Sade's troublesome mischief. The good doctor arrives with new bride in tow, and immediately proves himself to be far more disturbing in his personal habits than the Marquis.

What results is an escalating battle between early 19th-century shrink and arrogant artist. In truth, the doctor proves to hold all the cards. When quills and ink are removed, the writer uses wine. When the wine goes, there's still blood. When all writing materials are vanished, tales can be written in human excrement on the walls. And that's when things start getting fairly nasty.

The cast is wonderful, including all the aforementioned plus Joaquin Phoenix as the young, idealistic cleric managing Charenton. How can art fight organized and artful repression? It really isn't a pretty picture. By turns blackly funny, hallucinogenic, and graphically brutal, *Quills* carries out the promising double meaning of its title: the organic shafts that raise up and . . . prick, that draw blood with sharp barbs.

If the history is not suitably documentary in detail, then use the Oliver Stone defense—the drama, the story, requires some considerations to be fast and loose. *Quills* is a dreamy nightmare that traffics in truths rather than strict facts.

Another fantasy that will drive literalists bonkers is Lars von Trier's *Dancer in the Dark*. What I'm talking about here is a Swedish film wherein the filmmakers attempt to create an imagined period American landscape that never really existed.

It's a tale of art and class struggle starring singer Björk in a surprisingly credible turn as a young single mother working in a hellish factory set out there somewhere in the American hinterland.

Björk's character goes through terrible travail as she's victimized by her landlord, then finds herself obliged to kill him at his own request. Brought to trial on a capital offense, the proceedings are not exactly an episode of *Arrest and Trial*, but it's fascinating to see our legal system turned into myth through alien eyes.

The real heart of *Dancer* is, of course, Björk, particularly when her character learns to take the rhythms and sounds of industrial America and transmutes them at first subtly, then vividly into vocals and choreography. It's a fine depiction of rich imagination finding a means to discover the inner music that lies dormant in anything, even horrendous factory life.

Perhaps think of the picture as a tragic working-class approach to classic MGM musicals, depicting an organic reason why dwellers in everyday life should suddenly begin moving and responding to the innate music of the environment.

In doing so, the film demonstrates again how the mind and soul of the artist can process any input, no matter how banal or mundane, and discover the imaginative soul within.

In terms of quirky fairy tale that doesn't depend on special effects in the manner of, say, a *Dungeons and Dragons*, Patrice Leconte's *Girl on the Bridge* uses math and synchronicity as an implicit means to tell the story of a nearly over-the-hill knife thrower who finds his last chance at redemption and success in the person of a suicidal young woman he rescues after she plunges into the nighttime Seine. Pop-star and actress Vanessa Paradis makes a splendid Adele, a young woman who's never had any good luck at all. Daniel Auteuil is a convincing Gabor, the stern stage performer who possesses his own challenges when it comes to good fortune.

Gabor and Adele find themselves in a peculiarly symbiotic relationship dealing with that arcane and hard-to-quantify statistical quality, luck. Think of this as a sentimental math fiction, a tale of separation and search, a topological fantasy that plays out something like a warmer and more humane π.

And then, of course, there's Ridley Scott's *Gladiator*, with Russell Crowe playing the Roman general who succeeds in war for his Caesar, then is betrayed and sent off for execution, only to end up in gladiator camp where he builds himself a final chance for vengeance. Yes, of course you've seen this plot before. And given some reasonable characters and plot machinations, it virtually always works anew.

Director Scott possesses a fine eye for image. *Gladiator* boasts plenty of spectacular imagery, whether showing no-holds-barred battle out among the barbaric Germans, or in the optically rebuilt splendor of Rome and the restored Colosseum. Though technically a historical melodrama, this is again a re-creation of an era via some creative cutting and pasting of history's facts.

But Oscars for best picture and best performance by an actor? I know I'm bucking the tide, but I don't think so. I still cling loyally, doggedly, to my memories of Kirk Douglas in Stanley Kubrick's *Spartacus*.

Requiem for a Pitch Black Cell

Here's a trio of good horror pictures, none of which was really marketed as such. This again illustrates the deceptiveness of marketing, and the potential silliness of it all.

Though she didn't win the Oscar, Ellen Burstyn deservedly received a nomination for her grueling depiction of the Mom in Darren Aronofsky's *Requiem for a Dream*. Aronofsky made waves a couple years ago with π, a terrific dark fantasy about math and Jewish mysticism.

Adapted by Aronofsky and novelist Hubert Selby, Jr., from the latter's controversial 1978 book, *Requiem* came across as no less edgy in the year 2000. Director and writer gave the talented cast a tough and unflinching script about the horrors of addiction, and utilized a level of horrific imagery that accomplished far more than simply communicating a moral.

Along with Burstyn's character toppling into the abyss of amphetamine diet pill hell, her son (Jared Leto) and the latter's girlfriend (Jennifer Connelly) find their own drug-induced dead ends. The MPAA tried to sink this one with an NC-17 rating but couldn't make it stick. The level of filmmaking here is just too high, and the moral nature of the story is inescapable. Addiction as depicted here is neither titillating nor glamorous.

Perhaps the best single jolt in the film is when Burstyn's character, strung out to nearly the end of her precarious balancing act, is stalked and attacked by a predatory . . . refrigerator. *Requiem* also includes a fine electronic score by Clint Mansell and a good acting turn by Marlon Wayans playing Jared Leto's best friend.

Director Tarsem Singh is a bright new talent comparable to his fellow Indian-American colleague, M. Night Shyamalan. Tarsem's debut feature, *The Cell*, is a darkly luminous science fiction thriller that comes across more as a horror picture. While it uses the same sort of well-honed gimmick as any number of science fiction novels (Roger Zelazny's *The Dream Master*, for one), the movie's exploration of a shrink literally entering a far-gone patient's mind in search of critical information used startling visual imagery to launch into the exploration of some legitimate moral and ethical issues.

Vincent D'Onofrio plays the nasty serial killer the cops catch early on in the story. But there are two problems. First, it's known that the killer's stuck his final young woman victim in a time-release death trap in some unknown location; and second, the killer's partitioned off in an irreversable coma. The burden then falls upon Jennifer Lopez, psychologist and experimental researcher, whose employers have developed a means of electronically transferring the mind of a therapist into the subject's unconscious. In the case of *The Cell*, the killer's mind is a visually disorienting and highly weird locale.

The film's strong points don't merely revolve around the effective visuals. Lopez's character's flirtation with one of the detectives on the case doesn't turn out in any way as stereotypical as the viewer might expect, and the nature and history of the twisted killer turns out not to be so one-sided as one might fear. Though most of the characterization is frustratingly minimalist—the writer/director tends to go along with the old adage about images and a thousand words—there's sufficient on hand to give the viewer a lingering taste of dimensionality. The dialog is crisp. But the most important aspect is that hard questions arise, and then don't get ladled easy answers.

There are rumors that the studio flinched at some of the imagery in the director's initial cut, and put down a corporate foot. If so, one can hope for restoration in some eventual director's special edition DVD.

Written and directed by David Twohy, the high concept for the U.S.–Australian *Pitch Black* might be temptingly summed up as *Alien* meets *Nightfall*. But that would be a bit unfair. When *Pitch Black* is good, it's extremely effective; when it falls down, it only plummets to the realm of solid competence.

The initial scenes are exciting enough as a futuristic interstellar transport ship crashes on a distant desert world. It's not quite the opening crash scene of *Alive*, but then no other film has done quite so well at capturing the helpless out-of-control tone of a doomed flight. Moral quandaries surface from the beginning since the pilot (Radha Mitchell) may or may not have committed an act of panic and cowardice in jettisoning some of the other passenger-carrying sections of the ship. The motley band of survivors includes a lawman, a condemned prisoner being transported to his legal doom, a few assorted crew people, an art expert, and a small band of religious zealots on a pilgrimage. Clearly the most vividly impressive survivor is the mass murderer, played with both nuance and extreme physical presence by Vin Diesel.

At first the film is an effectively gritty account of the survivors attempting to make do on a hot, parched, sandy world with few easily available resources. Then it turns out that the seemingly endless sunshine isn't quite all it's cracked up to be. Turns out that the multiple suns are coming into an infrequent alignment that will allow darkness to envelope the globe. And that's when some unspeakable nocturnal predators will appear to gobble up anything living that's proliferated during the long cycle of daylight.

At the peak of action, there's a prolonged journey across the deadly nighttime planetscape that's pretty much what you'd expect. The *unexpected* arrives as the pilot and the killer's personalities reveal some intriguingly multiple levels. *Pitch Black* ultimately succeeds as a film not so much thanks to the science fiction color and the violent action, but because it finally blossoms from having a script treating hard choices and genuine ethical decisions.

They Sometimes Bleed But They Don't Suck

What's a year without vampire flicks? 2000 saw at least three good ones, all memorable for vastly different reasons.

Back in the early 1920s, German director F. W. Murnau couldn't secure permission to film Stoker's *Dracula*, so he did what any enterprising filmmaker would do—he simply ripped off his own version of the novel and created the German expressionist masterpiece, *Nosferatu*, with relatively unknown stage actor Max Schreck effectively done up as the world's most grotesque vampire prince. Stoker's widow and the courts were not amused, and came within a fang of having all copies of *Nosferatu* destroyed. Had that happened, *Nosferatu* wouldn't have received Werner Herzog's creditable tribute in the 1979 remake, starring Klaus Kinski as the redoubtable Count. Neither would we have been treated to last year's wonderful metafictional spinoff, *Shadow of the Vampire*.

Willem Dafoe got a well deserved supporting-actor nomination for his Schreck-cum-Nosferatu role. The makeup is superb. Dafoe's acting ability carries off his performance wonderfully, though his distinctive facial features are virtually unrecognizable.

The picture's major conceit is that director Murnau craved a core of absolute realism in his fantasy construct, and so sought out and hired a real vampire to play the title character. John Malkovich, playing Murnau, generates a suitable level of whacked-out obsession for the director's persona.

Shadow of the Vampire is, by turns, both drolly comic and shockingly serious as it deals with the cold realities of art and ambition. E. Elias Merhige directs from a script by Steven Katz. A solid ensemble company, including Udo Kier, Catherine McCormack, Cary Elwes, and the ever-crazed Eddie Izzard, lends an air of manic presence to the goings-on. Some audiences will find themselves unnerved by the blend of deadpan and amusing; others, obviously, will pick up the challenge.

For something completely different, rent a copy of *The Little Vampire*. Most of us probably wouldn't have suspected director Uli Edel (*Christiane F.*) capable of jumping the traces so successfully and creating this genuinely amusing and affecting vampire fable for all ages. It comes across on the surface as a kids' film at first. But the astute viewer soon figures out there's plenty of multileveled material that can appeal to the alert of any age. If you're a fan of classic '30s film, watch for the scene playing tribute to Gable and Colbert in *It Happened One Night*.

Karey Kirkpatrick (*Chicken Run*) and Larry Wilson's script, based upon the series of children's novels by Angela Sommer Bodenburg, gives us a desperately unhappy mortal boy, *Stuart Little's* Jonathan Lipnicki, who's helplessly transported from his familiar home in Southern California to the rather bleaker landscape of contemporary Scotland. His Ugly American dad (Tommy Hinkley) has uprooted both wife and young son to accompany him as he contracts to carve a section of spectacular Caledonian countryside into a world-class golf course.

The lonely and depressed kid finds a friend one night when a bat that's blundered into his room abruptly transforms into what appears to be another boy. Of course the boy (Rollo Weeks) possesses an odd accent and even odder archaic clothing. It isn't long before our hero meets his new buddy's cute, if slightly acerbic, sister (Anna Popplewell), not to mention the parents, a wonderful pairing of Richard E. Grant and Alice Krige. Yep, they are indeed all vampires, part of an emigré crowd that fled mainland Europe three centuries before, and have successfully scrounged a food-chain niche living among mostly unsuspecting mortals in Scotland.

But now things are changing. The vampire community has an opportunity to shake their curse and regain mortal status in the near future, if they can bring a long-missing magical amulet into conjunction with an imminent celestial configuration. Naturally they need the protagonist's help. Things become even more complicated with the arrival of blundering but sinister ace vampire hunter Jim Carter.

Can't we all just live together? That's the ultimate message, of course, but the map for arriving there is gloriously tangled in both wit and affect. One of the funniest images is the vampires weaning themselves off the blood of mortal humanity and turning instead to sucking up to dairy cattle. The apparent contradiction of 300 years worth of cows turning into bovine vampires is never resolved, but the sinister lowing and the crimson eyes glowing in the dark of the dairy barn are alone worth the price of admission.

On the surface of it, the whole notion of something titled *Wes Craven Presents*

Dracula 2000 is not one to inspire confidence. An early viewer suspicion might well be that director Craven's name has been appended as a cheap and easy way of marketing a real dog of a low budget release. Have faith. Wes Craven's conscience remains clean. And the audience for *Dracula 2000* can have a hoot without a twinge of conscience.

Of course it'll help if you either have a nostalgic fondness for the classic British Hammer Films releases, or at least have some idea of what Hammer was all about. *Dracula 2000* is a very conscious tribute and light-hearted nod to Hammer, but if the referent is lost, some of the effect will evaporate as well. An unfairly abbreviated description of Hammer horror might well mention the spurting gore, the garish supersaturated Technicolor hues, the atmospheric fog and enthusiastically erotic sexuality, usually embodied in large-bosomed starlets. *Dracula 2000* has *all* that and more.

As kind of a living bridge to the old days, Christopher Plummer capably holds down a role here as Van Helsing; yes, *that* Van Helsing, Dracula's old nemesis, who in Joel Soisson's script is holding down a contemporary job as the owner of a powerful antiquities firm whose London headquarters has a very deep, extremely secure basement. Is the corporate cellar a bit Gothic in nature? You know it. It seems Van Helsing is locked in an unusual symbiotic relationship with the stashed-away Wallachian count.

The balance shifts when a gang of high-tech thieves raids the basement and hauls off what they think is an extremely valuable artifact. Little do they suspect what will leap out at them when they open the container in the cargo hold of a chartered plane on the way to New Orleans at Mardi Gras time. Timing is everything.

It's very much a reflection of the film's first scene, an echo back to the Stoker novel, the depiction of what happens to the storm-tossed vessel *Demeter* when it's conveying Dracula and his coffin from the Continent to England in the 19th century.

Part of the fun in director Patrick Lussier and producer/writer Soisson's movie is the spread of sly references to the original Stoker. Dracula's three brides are present in the New World, one of whom is *Star Trek Voyager*'s Jeri Ryan, playing a bitchy local anchorwoman before she gets her blood drained. From the classic film, Bela Lugosi's famed line, "I neffer drink . . . wine," is morphed into something more contemporary, thanks to the proliferation of Starbucks in modern America. Van Helsing's daughter Mary (Justine Waddell), who just happens to live in New Orleans, has a best friend named "Lucy Westerman," who explains to Dracula that she got her name because her mom loved the comic strip, *Peanuts.* Both our heroines wear appropriate t-shirts since each is employed by the local Virgin Megastore. Dracula is played by hunky Scottish actor Gerard Butler, who does just fine in the role, whether admitting to a reasonably clever Old Testament explanation of vampires, or using his powers of the night to execute some Hong Kong martial arts movie-style flying and fighting.

Jonny Lee Miller's the hapless hero, obliged to vacate the bloodless world of antiques when he's recruited to fight the revivified Dracula. Of course he falls for Van Helsing's daughter. Of course he's in for a world of hurt.

So was *Dracula 2000* an Academy Awards nominee? Don't be silly. It is, however, one hell of a lot of fun. Garishly amusing down to the last drop, *Dracula 2000* is a guilty pleasure no viewer should feel ashamed about admitting seeing once the lights come up.

When Mutants Are Outlawed, Only Outlaws Will Mutate

The X-Men and *Unbreakable* would make a great thematic double feature—at least if double bills still existed save at a few far-flung outdoor movie theaters.

With the big-screen franchises of *Superman* and *Batman* at least temporarily on the skids, with *Spiderman* seemingly in an endless holding pattern, and with features such as *The Punisher* released only in a few obscure video stores in Elbonia, comic book sources remain a chancy bet for film investment capitol. But what's a super hero worth if he (or she) can't occasionally break through the barriers of audience prejudice, creator silliness, and societal condescension? The Marvel Comics stable's X-Men (back in '63 when Stan Lee created them, they were the Uncanny X-Men) give it their all. Professor Charles Xavier was the master of Xavier's School for Gifted Youngsters. Comics readers quickly cottoned to the reality that the gifted youngsters were mutants, altered humans with strange and wonderful talents. And they had to live in a world they never made, a world of intolerance, fear, and prejudice against anything significantly different from the human norm.

So the book embodied the perfect mind-set to connect with every bright reader in the stands who ever worried about being the odd person out, the different one in the crowd. That made for a large and enthusiastic audience.

Film director Bryan Singer (*The Usual Suspects, Apt Pupil*) creates, with a wealth of talented help, a movie that's big, brawling, and colorful. High art? Naw. But it possesses the sort of earnest heart that carries the silly stuff through plenty of rough passages.

X-Men begins with a serious World War II German concentration camp scene in which a young boy is separated from his father and mother. The parents are packed off to die. The boy seems to have some mysterious ability to distort the heavy iron gates dividing him from the rest of his family. Not enough to accomplish his goal, but still a portentous sign for the future.

Cut to a somewhat alternate history present in which mutants are amply known to humanity. Xenophobic fear drives such politicians as Senator Robert Kelly (Bruce Davison) to push for a mutant registration act. This doesn't set well with any of the mutant population. Professor Xavier (Patrick Stewart) is still helping his school teach gifted children how to survive and develop their superhuman talents. He's aided by Jean Grey (Famke Janssen), Cyclops (James Marsden), and Storm (Halle Berry). Prof. X is pushing for a *rapprochement* between human and mutant via peaceful means. Magneto (Ian McKellen), on the other hand, is ready to use force or any other method to keep mutants on a "never again" course. Magneto remembers the Holocaust all too well. He's aided by a motley bunch including Toad (Ray Park), Sabretooth (Tyler Mane), and Mystique (Rebecca Romijn-Stamos). Wild card characters Wolverine (Hugh Jackman) and Rogue (Anna Paquin) blunder right between the adversaries.

Whether as Logan, the everyday mundane tough guy who makes his way through Canada challenging all comers in roadhouse bare-knuckles competitions, or as his alterego Wolverine, an even tougher guy with a nearly indestructible skeleton and wicked slide-out claws, Hugh Jackman is the charismatic center of the film. He steals virtually every scene he's in.

Not that the rest are any slouches. Ray Park, who played the evil Darth Maul in the last *Star Wars* movie, seems to take a true manic joy in his role as the athletically leaping Toad, with his slimy fifteen-foot tongue.

While the surface of *X-Men* is nonstop color, action, and general visual fun, the serious underlevel is the issue of how one can best serve the cause of protecting those who are "different." Subtle, it's not. But like its comic book predecessor, the film is sincere in its goal. One of its most laudable accomplishments is divulging the long-standing friendship and mutual regard in which Xavier and Magneto hold one another. They are, after all, ultimately on the same side. They simply represent polar-opposite approaches to accomplishing the same defensible goal. As in much fantasy and science fiction, the real core is discernible reality. It's the imaginative use of exaggeration that lifts the mundane into the fantastic.

In M. Night Shyamalan's *Unbreakable*, the same goal is reached via a rather different journey. The thirty-year-old writer/director's first feature, *The Sixth Sense*, was an ingeniously structured supernatural thriller that seemingly came out of nowhere and raked in nearly two-thirds of a billion dollars at the box office.

That's a hard act to beat, but Shyamalan gives it a game try. Like *The Sixth Sense*, *Unbreakable* stars Bruce Willis. This time he's a college security guard who miraculously survives a commuter train disaster that kills hundreds of others, in fact everyone else on the train. How did he manage it? What's the meaning lying beneath his miraculous survival?

His answer comes through circuitous routes, primarily by meeting Samuel L. Jackson's character, a mysterious stranger who suffers "glass bone" disease. Since childhood, he's been incredibly fragile. Indeed, when Jackson tumbles down a stadium stairs, the audience winces at the crunching destruction.

Willis's character is emotionally unready to grapple with the possibility he might be a person with superhuman powers. But Jackson's character is determined, for his own reasons, to convince him. In doing so, he reveals his own distinctive nature.

The picture lends an impeccably sincere gravity to the whole notion of superheroes and villains and what their mutual relationship can be. In doing so, it covers the same psychological landscape as *X-Men*, but without cool costumes or gaudy special effects.

In a real sense, it's a comic book movie for people who don't think they'd like a comic book movie. But it's a serious take on the whole mythos of comics, an artform that quite consciously plays on the wellsprings of our western archetypes.

Earlier I suggested pairing *Unbreakable* and *X-Men* as a double feature. Shoot, it occurs to me that one could link those two with Kevin Smith's 1997 *Chasing Amy* and *voilà*, instant one-night thematic film festival.

Feature Soup

Lord knows, there were plenty of other feature films with which to while away the time as 2000 streaked toward the new millennium. Would that one could simply extract the bits and pieces that worked well, and put them all together in a master trailer of consummate amusements.

Hollow Man remade *The Invisible Man* for the umpteenth time, but obdurately kept obsessing on the principle that absolute power would not only corrupt, it would also lead the man with the power of invisibility to spend all too much time ogling nude girls and acting in a viciously petty fashion. I suppose technically this was science fiction, but it was played as horror, as a monster movie. Poor Kevin Bacon took the unenviable title role. Fortunately for him, in much of the picture one couldn't see his face. *Hollow Man's* director, Paul Verhoeven, is an accomplished professional who should have known better. Keenan Ivory Wayans directed *Scary Movie*, an intentional parody of all the slasher flicks of the past two decades, and came up with an absolutely tasteless, utterly vulgar piece of tainted confectionary that, regardless, still had its moments of absolute hilarity. The sequence sending up *The Blair Witch Project* represented an astonishing use of special effects (I hope) snot. I laughed and laughed, and could even ignore my shame afterwards. *Scary Movie* was my guiltiest pleasure for the century. I realize I was only getting in touch with my inner fourth-grader.

In terms of interplanetary frights, Mars got visited twice during the year. In *Mission to Mars*, director Brian DePalma decides to offer homage to Stanley Kubrick rather than Alfred Hitchcock. I'm sure Mr. Hitchcock's shade is properly grateful. *Red Planet* at least has mission commander Carrie-Anne Moss lounging in orbit while her ill-fated crew of Val Kilmer, Terence Stamp, Benjamin Bratt, and others wander the Martian surface getting into trouble with ravenous bugs and such.

Satan didn't wander in solely through the re-release of *The Exorcist*; Director Harold Ramis remade Stanley Donen's 1967 *Bedazzled*. The original featured Peter Cook, Dudley Moore, and Raquel Welch. The remake has Brendan Fraser and Elizabeth Hurley. Nostalgia will win this contest every time. Regardless, in the new version of Faustian bargains and demonic seduction, Fraser, who is a terrific actor, makes a good naif, and Hurley performs creditably as a sleek, feline Satan. In Janusz Kaminski's *Lost Souls*, Winona Ryder wears entirely too much racoon eye makeup, apparently trying a shorthand visual technique for suggesting a bad-girl-gone-good as a one-time victim of demonic possession who now, as an adult, realizes that the devil's about to reincarnate into the body of Ben Chaplin. Mauro Fiore's cinematography is pretty good, but the plot still feels like *Rosemary's Baby* and *The Exorcist* put through the old Bass-O-Matic from *Saturday Night Live*. One desperately wants to like Roman Polanski's *The Ninth Gate*. After all, it's got Johnny Depp as a rare book expert on the trail of a missing volume rumored to have featured the Devil as an illustrator. After a strong beginning, something just seems to go to sleep (perhaps it's the audience) and the whole film drifts apart. It's very much too bad.

In *What Women Want*, Mel Gibson plays a bone-headed Madison Avenue stereotypical adman (actually his job is set in Chicago, but the Mad Ave. image still holds) who, after an unfortunate bathroom accident with a hairdryer, abruptly discovers he can hear the thoughts of women. What he hears is pretty fragmented, and totally unpredictable, but it gives him a leg up, as it were, on writing better commercials for a female audience. I'm not the first person to note that this film is filled with more product placement baggage than any recent film other than *Cast Away* (with its long nods to Fed Ex and Wilson). *What Women Want* displays, in fact, an entire lengthy Nike commercial right in the middle. Call it a popcorn break. Essentially this is an undemanding, facile picture that takes the lazy way out. Mel Gibson and fellow star Helen Hunt are personable enough, but most of the picture is forgettable within two hours of viewing. Since I've mentioned double features earlier in this essay, it would be interesting to pair *What Women Want* with the infinitely more astute, amusing, and entertaining film, Jenniphr Goodman's *The Tao of Steve*.

What Lies Beneath is a mainstream ghosts-and-murder tale that relies heavily on star-power, Robert Zemeckis's big-budget production pairs Harrison Ford and Michelle Pfeiffer as a long-married couple increasingly troubled when they discover their upscale lakeside house has something hideously wrong with it, at least in the supernatural sense. Wife Claire wonders if she's going insane. Husband Norman has more than a few surprises up his sinister sleeve. The big revelation is, of course, Norman's true nature; indeed, it'll shock a few audience members to see Harrison Ford attempting to look villainous. But it's actress Amber Valietta, playing the dead woman, who gets the plum scene at the end. It's a deceased character who snaffles the single most arresting visual image.

If you'd like to see a pretty fair version of a contemporary *Twilight Zone-ish* episode expanded out to feature length, rent *Frequency*. It does a good job treating time travel, time paradoxes, and the like, and all with a warm, human tone.

The big Christmas fantasy was *Dr. Seuss's How the Grinch Stole Christmas*, generally just abbreviated to *The Grinch*. As the title character, Jim Carrey endured endless hours of makeup artistry. He certainly looked just right. This is a movie intended for all ages that looks spectacular, but slogs. No spritely pace here. There seems to be an insistent chorus in the audience calling for easier access to tapes of the older TV animated version of *The Grinch*.

Outright animated features? Disney's *Dinosaur* was fine—once you got over the reality that the beasts talked in human words. *The Road to Eldorado* possesses an extraordinary blend of traditional and computer animation. It looks good, the plot and characters play reasonably well, and there's a fine ambulatory stone jaguar god. *The Emperor's New Groove* takes a peculiarly revisionist approach to South American culture and myth. But aside from that, this is a well-produced and fairly amusing feature. My favorite animation of the year, as it happens, is *Chicken Run*, with its Plasticine mastery from Peter Lord, Nick Park, and England's Aardman Animation. On one level, this is a parody of prison camp movies ranging from *The Great Escape* to *Stalag 17*. It's tempting to suggest that only the English can truly mix such a serious treatment of class oppression with outright and utter silliness. This follows the tradition of *Animal Farm* and *Monty Python*. The crew that voices the characters ranges from Mel Gibson to Miranda Richardson, and all do exceedingly well.

Finally, a few more crazed slipstream fantasies, all funny, all fairly dark. In *Nurse Betty*, Renée Zellweger's a small-town waitress in a terrible marriage, desperate for any answer to life's problems. When a couple of very bad men kill her husband in a shady deal gone haywire, her character's psyche is jogged into the persona of her most beloved soap-opera player. Road picture and psychotic episode, you gotta love it. Crank up the volume, then, and you've got *Psycho Beach Party*, directed by Robert Lee King and written by Charles Busch from his stage play. The whole movie here plays like the initial lawn scene in *Blue Velvet*—on the surface everything is placid and innocent; underneath, the hidden critters are fighting savagely to the death. *Psycho Beach Party*'s exterior is a satiric nod to the brainless beach party movies in the '60s era of the young Frankie Avalon and Annette Funicello. What's under the surfin' frenzied surface is a tangled wilderness of murder, madness, and general kinky behavior. And it's all handled with manic, even camp, enthusiasm. If a picture can be said to be wonderfully twisted, then that's the capsule description for *Psycho Beach Party*. After all, in how many other pictures can you see the male writer ably playing the role of a female investigating cop?

As long as the key word *twisted* is in mind, mention should also be made of *American Psycho*, Mary Harron's venomously witty version of Bret Easton Ellis's much-maligned bestseller. Ellis always claimed his novel was a deliberately dense satire of American consumer culture, centering its gleeful blade on an '80s sort of professional Manhattan guy who expressed himself as a serial killer. Some readers hated the Ellis approach to graphic sex and violence (obviously they were not inveterate genre horror readers); others thought Ellis should have used a scalpel in preference to a heavy cleaver. In Harron's picture, it's evident her touch is much more adroit than the original author's. Christian Bale does quite well as the killer, a young man who bends his imagination equally to savage violence and trendy interior decoration and cool lifestyle. The picture's level of surreal imagery is sufficiently pumped up, it's hard ultimately to determine what the index of total insanity truly is. A good double feature for this film would be *Fight Club*.

Finally, a splatter movie is a splatter movie is a splatter movie. Or is it? Graphic sexual and political maneuverings, betrayal and assassination, cruel mutilation of human victims and the serving up of bereaved parents' murdered children in their supper pot-pie—this may all sound pretty low-brow as entertainment. Of course it's some of the twisted attraction of William Shakespeare's probably least performed play, *Titus Andronicus*. The movie version, directed by Julie Taymor, appeared last year as *Titus*. It is, as previously mentioned not a warm and fuzzy story. The film version is gorgeously designed and shot. The script is, of course, by Mr. Shakespeare himself. In the modern tradition of redressing Shakespearean drama to refresh and sometimes to alter focus, *Titus* adopted a surreal melange of bits borrowed from a variety of historical periods. Deliberate anachronism abounds. If you saw Richard Loncraine's startling and wonderful *Richard III* in 1995, then you will be prepared for Taymore's general approach. Anthony Hopkins, as one would suspect, does quite well as the Jobesque titular character. Like the play, this film is not so much a matter for liking as it is an object of admiration.

Small Screen, Big Ambition

With so many folks investing in elaborate home theater outfits, the term "small screen" may have to be gradually phased out. But for the time being, home televisions are still smaller than the screens in suburban multiplex movie houses. And here at home, regardless of whether one's piping in programming from dish, digital cable, or old-fashioned analog (or even maybe those quaint rabbit ears you're still juicing up by balling aluminum foil around the antenna tips), the selection of science fiction, fantasy, and horror content is fairly impressive.

Let's romp quickly across the higher ground (though one viewer's high aerie may be another's swampy bottomland). Fox's *The X-Files* wound up another season, with pundits predicting its imminent end. The big change this time around was David Duchovny's scaling down his role. Agent Mulder appeared only infrequently, his role as Dana Scully's foil being ably filled by Robert Patrick (the evil cyborg in *Terminator II*). Patrick's doing a great job as tough and skeptical FBI lifer, John Doggett. *X-Files* fandom is a tough house to please, but I think Patrick's doing the job creditably. As for Scully (Gillian Anderson), much of her season's performance underscored the ticking plot device of her character's mysterious pregnancy.

When the show wrapped for the season, Duchovny laid out $25,000 to buy 340 Razor™ scooters from ⟨www.buychoice.com⟩ as gifts for the show's cast and crew. What does this portend? Who knows? This is why the series still is capable of surprise.

The Others, something of a first cousin to *The X-Files*, had a short run. This ensemble melodrama about a diverse and loose-knit gang of occult "sensitives" displayed considerable promise, but apparently didn't nail a sufficiently significant audience.

The WB's spinoff/pairing of *Buffy the Vampire Slayer* and *Angel* has worked out well. College woman Buffy doesn't have the same level of innocent charm she possessed at the beginning of the series, but the recognition of time passing and of growing maturity is a welcome breath of reality. The writing still continues to be some of the best scripting on TV. Most of the time, it's bright, sharp, funny, and non-condescending to the audience. A noble new paramilitary boyfriend, a mysterious new little sister, and a dying mom have all added a rewarding texture to the season. Perhaps the most enjoyable aspect for me has been watching Spike, the defanged (as it were) British vampire, crank up his role. Actor James Marsden is awfully good.

Lead David Boreanaz has carried the companion show *Angel* well, now that Buffy's tragic and cursed vampire first love has relocated to Southern California, starting a haphazard detective agency with invaluable aid from the onetime bitch of Sunnydale High, Cordelia Chase (Charisma Carpenter). Cordie's another character whose fictive maturity has been convincingly implemented through fairly dire plot misfortune. After a full season and part of another, *Angel*'s managed to find its sea legs.

Aaron Spelling's series *Charmed*, about the three hotty modern American witches, continues to try very hard to be as cool as *Buffy*, though never seems quite to manage the catch-up. But it has moments.

WB's *Roswell* has hung in there, sometimes skating perilously close to the chilly verge of cancellation, but has bounced back. Some have called it *Dawson's Creek* with gray skins and almond eyes, but that's a touch unkind. The series has evolved into an involving story (admittedly not to everyone's tastes) about human teens and humanoid alien teens learning to get along and to take pleasure in sharing a common world.

On USA, *La Femme Nikita* ratcheted down to the end of a final season, but audience pressure brought an order for an additional eight episodes. Most of the cast returned for the encore, and the opportunity was used to advantage by the show's creators to tighten a few more dramatic screws. Certainly TV's (deliberately) coldest and most cynical program (aside from the reality shows), this near-future melodrama of spies, counterspies, and outright terrorists has pumped a refreshingly cool draught of fresh air. But now charismatic star Peta Wilson's moving on to a new action series.

The Sci Fi Channel has gamely generated new series by the half-dozen. Among the six of them, most varieties of science fiction/fantasy programs are represented.

Lexx is your *Heavy Metaloid* science fantasy series set very far away from the here and now. Like some of the other ongoing series (others include *Farscape* and *Andromeda*), it features one honkin' big spaceship. Maybe because of its hybridized nature as a German-Canadian co-production (as good a theory as any), *Lexx* contains plenty of weirdly kinky, yet still fairly innocent, material. Protagonist Zev (Xenia Seeberg) is young, energetic, resourceful, a touch careworn, and is tragically in love with a super-android dead guy (Brian Downey). All things considered, she makes for a respectable role model.

The Invisible Man is a contemporary melodrama about a guy (Vincent Ventresca) in a government agency who can indeed be made transparent through the wonders of technology. The show's scripts fairly regularly generate some real wit, and, occasionally, a legitimate touch of irony.

Black Scorpion is, I've got to admit, pretty much an honest clone of *Batman*, save with a gender role reversal. The character named in the title (Michelle Lintel) is colorless police officer Darcy Walker in her mundane identity. But when she changes to the Black Scorpion (as her Corvette likewise morphs into a very cool set of futuristic wheels), bad guys (and girls) should watch out! As broadly as this is played, the viewer may have to take meds to be in just the right mood to watch this with maximum enjoyment. The series is a Roger Corman brainchild.

First Wave, which generates ultimately from Francis Ford Coppola's production company, is a reasonably taut series about shapeshifting aliens who zealously desire to take over our world. This last season has featured guest star Traci Elizabeth Lords as a motivated resistance sort who manages to "help" the protagonist (Sebastian Spence) by funding and organizing Raven Nation, a paramilitary group of rebels loyal and armed to the teeth. Feisty red-headed resistance fighters are never a detriment in the world of melodrama.

Rockne O'Bannon's *Farscape* is the established staple of the Sci Fi Network's series group. With an attractive cast of humans and nonhumans, great aliens courtesy of the Henson Creature Shop, and coherent stories, *Farscape* reminds me a bit of what might have happened in an alternate universe if *Star Trek* had been a tad more relaxed, and a good deal less self-important.

Even more visually striking than *Lexx* and *Farscape* is *The Secret Adventures of Jules Verne*, a series filmed in Montreal. The conceit is spelled out by the title: what if Jules Verne borrowed heavily from real-life adventures to provide the research for many of his novels? Yeah, the conceit is unlikely, but it's a heck of a lot of fun. In the context of the series, young Verne does a lot of traveling in company with Phileas Fogg (Michael Praed), an ace British Secret Service agent; Fogg's cousin Rebecca, the Service's first distaff member (Francesca

Hunt)—who could well have been Emma Peel's grandmum); and Fogg's comic manservant, Passepartout (Michel Courtemanchi). At its best, the show's writing reminds me a bit of the old *Avengers*. Or as a very European *Wild Wild West*. The visuals are lushly executed. *Jules Verne*'s collective tongue is often firmly placed in cheek. Perhaps my favorite episode has been a charismatic madman's baroque scheme to conquer Europe with armies of flying vampires powered by rocket packs.

Shows arrive and shows phase out. It's no secret that UPN's *Star Trek: Voyager* is winding down—all the season's publicity shouts that out. The only question is whether the ship and crew are going to make it back home. Want to lay a wager?

On the newer *Star Trek*–cousin front is the syndicated *Gene Roddenberry's Andromeda*, a haven for ex-Hercules, Kevin Sorbo. It's not a bad far-future, galaxy-spanning romp. Producer Robert Hewitt Wolfe (a veteran of *Deep Space Nine*) seems rightly proud of the genetically souped-up Nietzcheans, a species of human adversaries who usually resemble literate, heavily armed pro wrestlers. Filmed in eerily alien New Zealand locations, *Andromeda* achieves a respectable level of entertaining space opera. *Gene Roddenberry's Earth: Final Conflict* also continues along, sometimes oscillating wildly in terms of accomplishment.

New series for 2000, by and large, didn't fare well. Never was a show more aptly titled than NBC's *Cursed*. The show's executive producers walked early on. The brief series was not a good career move for poor Steven Weber. UPN came up with *Freedom* (hunky resistance fighters in a near-future America taken over by a fascist coup) and *Level 9* (slightly extrapolated hackers fighting computer crime).

Fox's *Freakylinks* had a good shot, but still rapidly sank from sight. Devised by the producers of *Blair Witch Project*, *Freakylinks* starred Ethan Embry as a computer whiz trying to figure out how his brother, dead for three years, has appeared apparently live and well, on a recent videotape. This series was a game attempt at crossbreeding supernatural haunts with the Internet.

Dark Angel debuted on Fox with a fair amount of muscle attached. Producers James Cameron and Charles Eglee have deep pockets and a good stock of clout. Jessica Alba works well as a genetically enhanced prototype human weapon, trying to survive as a bike messenger in a near-future Seattle. She comes across as a character with both graceful feline physicality and an endearing vulnerability. The photography is gorgeous, particularly the image ending the opening credits sequence where we see the title character sitting contemplatively on top of a damaged, graffiti-marked Seattle Space Needle as darkness falls. The whole production's a labor of quality. One might be tempted to describe the show as a (slightly) kinder, gentler *La Femme Nikita*, crossbred with a real feel of *Bladerunner* or William Gibson novels.

TV also produced some first-rate long-form works. Thanks to the Sci Fi Channel, we got another version of Frank Herbert's classic *Dune*. The new six-hour mini-series used high tech and enormous sound stages in Prague to re-create Arrakis. Producer Richard Rubinstein and writer-director John Harrison worked to give the whole production a lush otherworldly feel. It is also quite faithful to the novel. The giant sandworms rocked.

My personal favorite cable film, however, was HBO's *Xchange* from Trimark, a highly entertaining and neatly produced dark suspense movie about a relatively near future in which mind-switching technology has been reasonably perfected, only to be selfishly exploited by rapacious mega-corporations. The convoluted plot requires Stephen Baldwin and Kyle Maclachlin to alternate playing the same character after our protagonist, a morally lazy PR consultant, winds up desperately trying to recover his hijacked body. The details, the embellishments, the occasional deliberate and sardonic humor, all suggest that writer Christopher Pelham and director Allan Moyle may not be wholly unfamiliar with modern science fiction. The occasional sensual and erotic tone, the amount of sexual flesh—integral to the futuristic setting, of course—suggest the inspiration and benefits of filming in modern, worldly Montreal. Other, less fleshly, ornaments remind the viewer of prime Alfred Bester.

The Short, Short Trailer

And what will the future bring?

Some viewers are eagerly anticipating the X-Files spinoff, The Lone Gunmen. And the next Star Trek series, of course.

Others are gearing up their expectations for Eric Garcia's series adaptation on Sci Fi of his comic/mystery/science fiction novel series Anonymous Rex about an L. A. private detective who's actually a velociraptor. Honest. It works. You have to read Garcia's idiosyncratic books about evolved surviving dinosaurs who live undetected among us monkey-boy humans.

But don't discount other media than film and print. 2001 will see lines of action toys based on both Clive Barker and H. R. Giger (well, on their designs, that is). And perhaps strangest of all, a line of action figures catalyzed by Reservoir Dogs. It'll include the captive cop with the severed ear.

Now that's what weird is all about.

Comics: 2000

Seth Johnson

Another year has passed, and I've gone to the comic shop each and every of those 52 weeks in search of the best. Let's take a trip down the racks:

Transmetropolitan by Warren Ellis and Darrick Robertson (Vertigo/DC). Following the limited ongoing series format pioneered in the Vertigo line by Neil Gaiman's *Sandman*, this politically hip science fiction novel-in-progress is a surprise each and every month—it just keeps getting better and better.

Bone by Jeff Smith (Cartoon Books). Walt Kelly's *Pogo* mixed with equal doses of Tolkien and the Marx Brothers. You'll keep turning the pages as you laugh, and keep picking up new issues as an emotional epic fantasy novel unfolds.

Akiko by Mark Crilley (Sirius). The adventures of an eight-year-old girl and her friends as they travel from one fantastic alien world to another, it's still the best comic you can buy to introduce kids to the magic of comics.

Jimmy Corrigan, The Smartest Kid on Earth by Chris Ware (Pantheon Books). Some of the material in this incredible hardcover collection was first printed in Ware's irregular series from Fantagraphics, *The Acme Novelty Library*. Following the story of Jimmy Corrigan's reunion with his long-lost father, the book is certain to win Ware many new fans for his exquisitely beautiful and remarkably detailed work—even the dust jacket unfolds to reveal intricate diagrams and one of Ware's infamous cut-and-tape model kits.

Preacher by Garth Ennis and Glenn Fabry (Vertigo/DC). This series came to an end in late 2000, and months later the debate still rages: was it a modern fantasy wrapped around an exploration of religion? Was it a western, with serial killers and vampires tossed in for fun? Was it a stab at the Great American Novel in comic-book form? Perhaps it was all of the above—but it was a damn fine read.

Each of these comics has been mentioned year after year in this column—because they're some of the best. Even if you don't know where your local comic book store is, all of them have won enough fans that their publishers have collected them into trade paperback form and they can be found in general bookstores. Pick one up sometime. I promise you won't be disappointed.

Okay, enough of this column's regulars. Let's take a look at some fresh names and material.

First up, another book that you'll find in bookstores is *The Sandman Companion* (Vertigo/DC), Hy Bender's in-depth guide to the aforementioned and incredibly popular comic series written by Neil Gaiman. Bender discusses the entirety of the series with Gaiman, uncovering both hidden gems and the stories behind what might have seemed obvious, and combined with a wealth of *Sandman* miscellany, it is an essential read for any fan of the series.

For a long time I've been a fan of Tony Millionaire's *Maakies*, a surreal comic strip printed in alternative newspapers around the nation. Now Millionaire (yes, that's his real name) is finally breaking across to a wider audience with his comic from Dark Horse Comics, *The Adventures of Sock Monkey*, where model ships sail around a Victorian mansion and drunken toy crows help hunt down teacup-stealing pixies. It's a surreal world, like *Toy Story* on a steady dose of gin, but one lent a curious feeling of authenticity by Millionaire's expertly rendered work.

Dark Horse has also been wise enough to reintroduce Kazuo Koike and Goseki Kojima's *Lone Wolf and Cub* to American audiences via a twenty-two-volume collection reprinting the entirety of the series in a Japanese digest-sized, English-translated format. It hardly qualifies as "fresh material," but hopefully the reprints will bring new fans to the series, a popular Japanese import for more than twenty years.

Between his work writing for various animated programs and his popular *Milk and Cheese* strips, cartoonist Evan Dorkin somehow finds time to put out the occasional issue of *Dork*, published just as occasionally—but thankfully kept in print—by Slave Labor Graphics. There are a lot of autobiographical comics out there, but few so clearly show someone balancing atop the razor-thin wall between comedy and pathos.

I mentioned Warren Ellis's *Transmetropolitan* above, but there are several other Ellis projects worthy of note. *City of Silence* (Image), with art by Gary Irskine, shows a strong relationship to *Transmetropolitan* but abandons political satire for a wicked exploration of man's relationship with technology. The majority of *Lazarus Churchyard: The Final Cut* (Image) was published years ago in various British comics magazines, but has been long unavailable; this collection brings together the entire story of the suicidal immortal with a brand new story by Ellis and *Churchyard* artist D'Israeli. *Planetary* (Wildstorm) is an exploration of the entirety of popular fiction by Ellis and John Cassaday—successive issues slip from genre to genre but are slowly weaving together the strands of a much larger story.

Of course, Alan Moore has been exploring everything from comics history to the occult for decades, and he continues to do so in his "America's Best Comics" line. But the cream of the crop are Moore and Kevin O'Neill's *League of Extraordinary Gentlemen*, where Captain Nemo is teamed with Mina Murray, Allan Quartermain, Dr. Jekyll and the Invisible Man to defeat the evil schemes of Fu Manchu, and *Promethea*, where J. H. Williams ably illustrates Moore's exploration of the nature of myth, imagination, and magic.

Many other writers are also exploring familiar themes in some terrific comics, twisting them through a variety of lenses:

The Authority (a Wildstorm title created by Warren Ellis, Bryan Hitch and

Paul Neary but since taken over by Mark Millar and Frank Quitely) pushes the bounds of what humanity might allow of superhuman vigilantes, as a team of ultra-powered heroes slowly reshape the planet—by any means necessary, a method rightly questioned in Joe Kelly and Doug Mahnke's *Action Comics #775* (DC), "What's So Funny 'Bout Truth, Justice and the American Way?" where Superman encounters a very Authority-like team.

Popular crime comics writer Brian Michael Bendis has paired with artist Michael Avon Oeming to create *Powers* (Image), following the cases of human police detectives in a comic-book world. Alan Moore pushes that theme to an even greater extreme in *Top 10* with art by Gene Ha (America's Best Comics), where not only the cops but all the citizens in an enormous metropolis have superhuman powers.

The Marquis: Danse Macabre (Oni Press) by Guy Davis uses all of the trappings of superheroics—a costume, a secret identity, high-tech mystical gadgetry—to tell the story of a demon-hunting priest in seventeenth-century France. Conspiring with comics legend Stan Lee to create a "long-lost hero of 1950s comics," Paul Jenkins and Jae Lee uncovered the tale of *The Sentry* (Marvel), the hero so powerful everyone had to forget he ever existed.

Thunderbolts (Marvel) by Fabien Nicieza and Mark Bagley continues to tell the tale of a group of former supervillains in their attempts to go straight, while Mark Waid and Barry Kitson's *Empire* (Gorilla/Image) tells the story of what happens after a megalomanical supervillain succeeds in his scheme to take over the world.

All plumbing the mysteries of the unknown are Karl Kessel and Tom Grummett's *Section Zero* (Gorilla/Image), Tony Harris and Dusty Abell's *Lazarus 5* (DC), and Phil Amara and Guy Davis's *The Nevermen* (Dark Horse Comics), though each comic has its own twist; "Section Zero" is a government-sanctioned superhero team, the Lazarus 5 an underground cabal of occult investigators, and the Nevermen a group of two-fisted mystery men wandering a city of twisted pulp adventure.

One more must-read before we close: in 1993 Scott McCloud published *Understanding Comics* (Tundra Press, recently reprinted by Kitchen Sink Press), an attempt to deconstruct and define comics as an art form that has sparked endless debate. In 2000 McCloud returned with *Reinventing Comics* (Paradox/DC), a look at comics as an industry, exploring how the creators, the audience, and the medium might evolve in the near future. It's a less scholarly and more opinionated work, sure to spark even more debates, and definitely worthwhile reading.

If you're looking for any of the above titles, along with a lot of other great material, they should be available at your local comic shop. If you don't frequent a shop, you can find one by checking your local Yellow Pages or calling the Comic Shop Locator Service at 1-888-COMIC-BOOK.

Thanks to Westfield Comics in Madison, Wisconsin and the fine folks at FM International Distributors for their help in research and collecting materials for this year's essay.

Obituaries: 2000

James Frenkel

We've finally reached the true millennium, but in addition to the lack of cars that fly—the most attractive part of the future when I was a boy in the 1950s—neither have we discovered a way, by magic or science, to keep people from dying. And even if we could, we'd still honor those who created, with words, pictures, music, or other creative labor, works of power and imagination that inspire generations of people to create their own works, and also inspire in millions a sense of the cultural traditions from which our world draws its soul, its vitality. In a world where change seems the only constant, this is valuable, important work. If you know of the people whose names follow, share your joy in their work; if you don't know their work, seek it out—you might find your own inspiration in it.

L. **Sprague de Camp,** 92, was an important fantasy and science fiction writer for over six decades. Early in his career he wrote both solo and collaborative works, the most notable of which were solo novel *Lest Darkness Fall* and his collaborations with Fletcher Pratt, *The Incompleat Enchanter, Land of Unreason,* and other witty fantasy adventures with a political edge. Aside from his other original works, de Camp was instrumental in the revival of Robert E. Howard's Conan stories. He completed a number of them and helped Conan books get published in paperback, starting a huge Conan boom in the 1960s. He wrote many other books, including the seminal *Rogue Queen,* and a number of other fantasy inflected science fiction works, among others. He often collaborated in his later works with his wife of sixty years, **Catherine Crook de Camp,** 92, who also died this year, most notably on *Dark Valley Destiny: The Life of Robert E. Howard,* which is considered the definitive biography of Conan's creator. **Edward Gorey,** 75, was a unique artist whose style was instantly recognizable on everything he did, whether it was a book jacket and interior illustrations for dark tales, the opening and closing credits for the PBS *Mystery* series, or one of his own books. His pen-and-ink and watercolor style became so famous that the word Gorey-esque is used to describe illustration of a similar ilk. **Jean Karl,** 72, was the founder and for many years the editor-in-chief of Atheneum Books for Young Readers. She discovered a number of fine authors, fantasy and otherwise, including Patricia A. McKillip, E. L. Konigsberg (the author of *The Mixed-Up Files of Mrs. Basil E. Frankweiler*, the Newbery Award winner and others), and Patricia Wrightson. She published many wonderful fantasy and science fiction authors, including Ursula K. Le Guin, Anne McCaffrey, and Cherry Wilder, to name just a few. She also wrote her own fiction, including the dark fantasy *Beloved Benjamin's Waiting*. Books she edited won six Newbery Awards, two Caldecott Awards, one National Book Award, eight Edgar Awards, and many other honors. She also created the Aladdin mass-market imprint, and the Argo science fiction imprint at Atheneum. Everyone who worked with her knew that she had a very special talent. **Curt Siodmak,** 98, was a novelist, screenwriter, and director who wrote some groundbreaking films, including *The Wolf Man*. His career started in his native Germany, which he fled when Hitler began to actively persecute Jewish people, and he began working in Hollywood in 1937. He went on to write a number of horror films, as well as the science fiction classic, *Donovan's Brain*. **Karel Thole,** 86, was a Dutch artist renowned for decades for fantastic art on book covers throughout Europe and the United States. His work brought a unique sensibility to cover art, a marvelously evocative, sometimes sexy, always intriguing style influenced by his Flemish roots and also the surrealist tradition of artists like Max Ernst, Renè Magritte, and Salvador Dali. **Gil Kane,** 73, was one of the greatest comic book artists of the 1950s and 1960s, bringing a fresh, kinetic style of art to an industry that had become rather predictable. Reinventing "The Flash," "Green Lantern," and other superheroes, he challenged the boundaries of what could be done on a comics page, opening the way for even greater artistic experimentation in later years; he, himself, never stopped pushing the artistic envelope. **Don Martin,** 68, was an altogether different, but equally important comics artist, whose work was utterly different and completely unique within its showcase in *Mad Magazine* for more than three decades. His bizarre, ungainly people and utterly original mini-stories made him completely recognizable, whether in *Mad, Cracked,* where he moved after a falling-out with management, or in books of his original cartoons. He was a seminal influence on Gary Larson and other later off-the-wall comics artists.

Marc Davis, 86, was one of the "nine old men," of Disney's great animation team. He was responsible for creating some of the most enduring Disney characters, including Snow White, Cinderella, Sleeping Beauty, Cruella DeVil, and Tinkerbell. **Carl Barks,** 99, drew Donald Duck and other Disney Duck characters, first for films and then in comics. He was known far and wide as "the Duck Man," and his original works and prints became hugely collectible during his lifetime. **Vince Sullivan,** 88, was DC Comics's first editor. With the debut of Superman in *Action Comics* #1 and Batman in *Detective Comics* #27, Sullivan kicked off what became known as the Golden Age of American comics, and brought the world two of the most enduring icons of popular culture. Together, Superman and Batman would help to make National the top publisher in the industry, and keep it there over the years as it evolved into DC Comics. **Michael Gilbert,** 53, was an artist, art director, and author who painted covers for various science fiction/fantasy magazines, coauthored (with Andre Norton) and illustrated *Day of the Ness*, art directed *If* magazine, and was immersed in other interests as well, including the Civil War—as a re-enactor, designer of miniatures, and editor/writer for magazines. He also designed minatures of other eras.

He also worked with his wife, Sheila Gilbert, publisher of DAW Books, editorially and in art direction. A wonderful cartoonist as well, his art festooned many publications, professional and amateur, over the years. His wit and clear-eyed cynicism endeared him to all who knew him.

Penelope Fitzgerald, 83, winner of the Booker Prize, was a fine writer, whose oeuvre included some ghost stories and dark fantasy. **Emil Petaja,** 85, was a science fiction writer whose *Saga of Lost Earth* was the first of four novels based on the Finnish epic, *The Kalevala*.

Douglas Fairbanks, Jr., 90, starred in many classic adventure films, including some with fantasy themes, such as *Sinbad the Sailor*. **Sir John Gielgud,** 95, was one of the greatest stage actors of the twentieth century, and also appeared in various films, some with fantasy or horror motifs. He was especially known for his Shakespearean acting and directing, on the stage. **Jason Robards, Jr.,** 78, was a renowned stage actor who also made many films, including some with fantastic motifs. **Sir Alec Guinness,** 86, was an Acadamy Award-winning actor whose long career included a marvelous variety of comedy, drama, fantasy, and science fiction. **Billy Barty,** 76, was an actor in many films and television shows, including the film *Willow*, in which he played a wizard, and *Under the Rainbow*, in which he played a German spy. **Doug Henning,** 52, was an illusionist who brought great showmanship and considerable skills to millions via theater and television, and increased public awareness of magic considerably during his career. **George Duning,** 92, was an Oscar-nominated composer who wrote music for films and television, including various fantasies.

Rayner S. Unwin, 74, was the publisher of George Allen & Unwin, taking over after the death of his father. When he was a boy, he read *The Hobbit*, recommending that his father publish the book. It led to J. R. R. Tolkien's long career as an Unwin author. **James Allen,** 48, was the president of the Virginia Kidd Literary Agents. He worked for the agency for over thirty years, taking charge when Ms. Kidd stepped down after decades of work with some of the best-selling and most beloved authors in fantasy and science fiction, including Ursula K. Le Guin, Anne McCaffrey, Gene Wolfe, and dozens of other talented authors. **Linda Grey,** 54, was an editor and publisher, heading Dell Books as Editor-in-Chief, and Bantam Books and Ballantine Books as Publisher. She fostered the careers of many important writers, including dark fantasist John Saul, among many best-selling authors. **Dede Weil,** 56, was a friend to the field of fantastic literature. Married to Gary K. Wolfe, she was an important presence at the annual Conference on the Fantastic for a number of years, brightening and enriching the lives of all who met and were welcomed into the circle of her friendship.

John Sladek, 62, was an American writer who lived in England for twenty years. He was a marvelously unpredictable author who wrote science fiction, fantasy, and mysteries in an eclectic career. **Phyllis White,** 85, was the wife of William Anthony Parker White, better known as Anthony Boucher, writer, critic, and co-founder of *The Magazine of Fantasy & Science Fiction*. She worked for the magazine, reading the slushpile and doing the office work that kept it running; she also read for anthologies that Boucher edited, and was involved with him in the founding of the Mystery Writers of America. **Norman Kark,** 103, was a magazine editor and publisher in London, where for many years he published *London Mystery Magazine*, a quarterly digest-sized publication which included a great deal of fantasy and horror as well as crime fiction, from 1952 to 1982. **Fr. Brocard Sewell,** 87, edited *The Aylesford Review* from 1955 to 1968 and championed the work of many neglected writers, including Arthur Machen. **Guy Cullingford,** 93, was a mystery writer actually named Constance Lindsay Taylor. Her best known novel is *Post Mortem*, a mystery told from the point of view of the ghost of the murdered man. **James Matthew Barrie,** 86, a descendent of J. M. Barrie of *Peter Pan* fame, was a journalist and leading British publisher of ghost stories after World War II, in the *Ghost Book* series of anthologies. **Patricia Graverson,** 65, wrote fifteen horror novels, and was founder of the Garden State Horror Writers. **Roger Erskine Longrigg,** 70, was a British author who wrote, as "Domini Taylor," supernatural horror. **Dennis Severs,** 51, was an English eccentric—by choice, not birth—a Californian who bought a 1724 house in London, furnished its rooms in various periods ranging over 200 years, and gave tours of its electricity-less, indoor plumbing-less grandeur. **Patrick O'Brian,** 85, was famed for his Jack Aubrey/Steven Maturin novels, which were originally thought to be "Horatio Hornblower" pastiches, but which became a body of twenty books rooted more in the tradition of Jane Austen than Forester. He did write two animal fantasies—beginning as a teenager—but never acknowledged his early career until a few years before his death, when it was revealed that he had changed his name and his life story when he left his family decades earlier. **Keith Roberts,** 65, was a British science fiction writer of considerable talent. His novel *Pavane* was a memorable novel of an alternate history set in the 1960s, in which England remained Catholic, a novel both eerily evocative and powerful. **A. E. van Vogt,** 87, was a science fiction writer whose stories and novels often felt dreamlike and neared the border between science fiction and fantasy. **Don Wilcox,** 94, was a pulp writer, many of his stories science fiction or fantasy appearing in *Amazing Stories*. **March Laumer,** 76, wrote several "Oz" novels, translated others, and wrote other books besides. He was the older brother of science fiction author Keith Laumer.

Joe Mayhew, 57, was a man of many talents, but what puts him in this book is the fact that he was the person who created the position (and then filled the job himself) at the Library of Congress, of choosing science fiction and fantasy that should be acquired by the Library. He was also a cartoonist of no mean skill, winning Hugo Awards for it as a science fiction fan; he also was a published short story writer, and always a friend to those who wrote, read, and loved fantastic literature. **Andre Deutsch,** 82, was a major figure in British publishing for over fifty years, starting several companies and publishing many major authors, including some mainstream fantasy. **Frederick S. Clarke,** 51, was the founder (in 1970) and publisher of *Cinefantastique*, a durable and well produced magazine dedicated to fantasy films. **Howard Cirker,** 82, was the founder and publisher of Dover Publications, an eclectic publisher that reprinted many books in the public domain, some of them fantasy and science fiction. Dover's list also contained a variety of practical guides, and other oddments, usually in trade paperback format. **Ray Gibberd,** 52, was a director and worked for twenty years at England's Andromeda Books, a specialty bookseller. **Verna Aardema,** 88, wrote a number of children's books that used African folklore as their basis. **A. Reynolds Morse,** 85, was a bibliographer and critic of art and literature, particularly of the works of M. P. Shiel and Salvador Dali, respectively.

Roger Vadim, 72, a french filmmaker known perhaps more for his amorous affairs than his films, filmed a number of projects which dealt with fantastic subjects, including *Spirits of the Dead* (1968) and *Blood and Roses* (1960). **Anthony Gilkison,** 86, was a British filmmaker who produced, among other films, a half-dozen Algernon Blackwood short stories adapted for the screen. **Charles Gray,** 71, was a British actor best remembered as villain Ernst Blofeld in *Diamonds are Forever.* He also acted in a number of fantasy and horror films, including *The Rocky Horror Picture Show* and *The Devil Rides Out.* **Lewis Allen,** 94, was a director whose films included the classic horror film *The Uninvited* (1943), among others. **Harry W. Prichett, Sr.,** 79, created the television program "Winky Dink," one of the first children's shows to be interactive. Featuring its eponymous character getting into trouble, young viewers had to use a "magic screen" that they could put over the television screen and draw on the magic screen a way for Winky to get out of trouble. Not bad for 1954.

Steve Reeves, 74, a bodybuilder turned movie actor, became famous when he played the title role in *Hercules* (1959). That film began a spate of "sword-and-sandal" epics. **Michael Ripper,** 87, was a leading British character actor who appeared in numerous fantasy and horror films, especially Hammer films, and in many television productions as well. **John Colicos,** 71, a veteran Canadian character actor, appeared in a number of film and television productions with fantastic motifs. **Paul Bartels,** 61, was a film director and actor. Among his varied oeuvre, *Eating Raoul* may be the strangest film he directed and acted in. **Jeffrey Boam,** 53, was the screenwriter who wrote *Lost Boys,* among other fantasy films. **Marceline Day,** 91, co-starred with Lon Chaney in the 1927 silent film classic *London After Midnight.* **David Tomlinson,** 83, was a British actor best remembered for his role in *Mary Poppins.* **Sidney Hayers,** 78, was a British film and television director who worked on various horror films and many television fantasies during a long career on both sides of the Atlantic. **Andrew Faulds,** 77, was a British character actor who appeared in many 1950s and 1960s horror films. **Nancy Marchand,** 71, was a versatile actress of stage, screen, and television. **Sy Weintraub,** 76, was a film and television producer who most notably produced a number of "Tarzan" films from the late 1950s until the 1980s. **Jim Varney,** 50, was a comedian and film and TV actor best known for his character "Ernest P. Worrell," who started out in commercials and ultimately was the focus of several films.

Carmen Dillon, 91, was the first female art director in British film. She worked on a great variety of films from the 1930s through the 1970s, including many of Sir Lawrence Olivier's films, and a number of films with fantasy or horror motifs. She also trained many of the next generation of great film art directors. **Arthur Morton,** 91, was a composer, arranger, and orchestrator for over one hundred films in his long career, including many films of the fantastic. **Louis Applebaum,** 82, was also a film composer. **George Duning,** 92, was another film composer with many fantasy and science fiction film scores to his credit. **David Betherton,** 76, was an Academy Award-winning film editor who counted *On a Clear Day You Can See Forever* among his credits. **William Eckart,** 79, was a theatrical set designer who designed many major Broadway productions, and others elsewhere, from the 1950s until his death. **Eyvind Earle,** 84, was an artist who painted backgrounds for a number of Disney films, and painted for other media as well.

Dennis Gifford, 72, was a British author, collector, and comics artist who produced a number of books about film, and comics in particular. **Alfredo Alcala,** 74, was a penciler/inker for many comics at DC and Marvel Comics. He wrote and drew his own line of comics in the Philippines before starting to work for the American comics industry. His style was graceful and moody, heavily textured and dynamic. **Eliot Caplin,** 86, was a comic strip writer and playwright. He wrote for such strips as "Big Ben Bolt," "The Heart of Juliet Jones," and "Abbie 'N Slats," the latter which was passed to him by his brother, the late Al Capp.

HARLAN ELLISON

Incognita, Inc.

Harlan Ellison has published seventy-five books, winning the World Fantasy Award, the British Fantasy Award, the Mystery Writers of America Edgar Award twice, the Horror Writers Association's Bram Stoker Award five times, and the P.E.N. Award for journalism, and multiple Hugo and Nebula Awards. Although best known as a science fiction writer, he is also the author of many influential works of short fantasy fiction such as "Shatterday," "Jeffty Is Five" and, more recently, "The Man Who Rowed Christopher Columbus Ashore" and "Mefisto in Onyx." His fiction has been reprinted in Best American Short Stories *and previous volumes of* The Year's Best Fantasy and Horror. *He is also a screenwriter and media consultant, the author of books of television criticism (*The Glass Teat *and* The Other Glass Teat*), and the editor of the landmark speculative fiction anthology* Dangerous Visions. *Ellison lives in Los Angeles, California, with his wife Susan.*

"Incognita, Inc." is an elegiac story about the lands that lie "beyond the fields we know" (to borrow Dunsany's poetic designation), and the routes we take to find them. This lovely tale comes from an unusual source: it was commissioned by Hemispheres, *the inflight magazine of United Airlines.*

—T. W.

You've asked me to file the report, so that's what I'm doing. But this is also my resignation notice. It was a miserable, meanspirited job you stuck me with, and I hated even the *idea* of doing it. But I did it. I did as I was told, I suppose, because I've been with WorldSpan (formerly Black-star Holdings [Pty.] [Ltd.]) since you recruited me out of the U. of Chicago twenty years ago, and like a good obedient dog I was part of that generation between the Baby Boomers and Gen X that believed Daddy Corporation would take care of me all the way to senescence. And I *was* your good little running dog, did whatever you asked, didn't weigh the ethical freight, swallowed hard sometimes as I watched the knives go in, but I just intoned the mantra *I don't want to get involved, it ain't none of my business.* I ate those fat paychecks and never got bulimic.

But this time, oh boy *this* time it couldn't be swallowed. I particularly hated it, Howard, when you gave me the assignment and said it was apropos that *I* be the one to carry it out, seeing as how my name is Charles Trimbach. You laughed at that. You and Barry, both of you thought it was hilarious: "trim back" was a terrific play on words for such a puke job you wanted done. I couldn't swallow hard this time; it made my gorge buoyant. And the lesson I learned, if it's a lesson at all, is what prompts my resignation.

I quit, WorldSpan. Howard, Tom Jr., Kincaid, all the rest of you up on the forty-fourth floor. I'm done. Take the fat paycheck and stuff it. Done, fellahs. But I'm dogtrot trained; a lot of years; so here's my last piece of work. The report. Pardon the casual tone. But you notice: I didn't once use the eff-word.

The flight was late coming into Chicago Midway; and by the time the cab dropped me off in Old Town on the corner of N. Wells and Wieland it was coming up on late afternoon, early evening. Even with all the gentrification, it was still a sweetly raffish part of town. Jammed crisscross at the proper hemlines of Lincoln Park and the Gold Coast, what was left of Old Town still sucked up all the light and breathed back disturbing shadows. In a few more years everything between N. La Salle and Larrabee would be so squeaky clean you'd have to clear it with the condo committee to import even a tiny sinful act. But on this bitter cold February afternoon, with the blade of wind slicing in off the Lake, turning my bones to tundra, it was the old vengeful Chicago I'd grown up in.

And I got lost.

I *always* got lost in Old Town. Somewhere near Elm and Hill I turned the wrong way, got twisted, and wandered for the better part of an hour. Then, some dim memory of my childhood kicked in, and as I passed a sweep of vacant shops with the blind eyes of upstairs apartments reflecting the last tremor of setting sunlight, I saw the mouth of the dark alleyway that was my landing site. How I'd recalled it, over decades, I don't know. But there it was; and I crossed the street and stepped into dim shadowed yesterday.

There was a paper flower shoppe, and a guitar repair joint, and an antiques/ collectables store; and wedged in between the guitar emporium—with a really cherry 1947 Les Paul "Broadcaster" hanging in the fly-specked front window— and the scentless dried brayera trying to look brave like a Victorian ruined garden . . .

There was the map shop. As neat and clean and brightly painted as a little red wagon on Christmas morning. The shop of maps in which labored a man named Abner Wonacott. The old guy you had sent me to fire. Charlie Trimbach, come to "trim back" that old cartographer in a store that shouldn't have existed, but did. Maybe it always had.

In hundreds of adventure movies, there's always a map of some strange, lost land. In Muslim mythology it's Kaf, the mountain range that circles the earth. In *The Odyssey* it was Ogygia, the island where Calypso kept Odysseus a captive. If you went looking for King Kong it was "2 south, 90 east, latitudes way west of Sumatra, southwest to Skull Island." The Garden of Eden, Barsoom, Asgard and Midgard, Atlantis and Avalon, the Catacombs of Rome, Mount Olympus, Oz, Nepenthe, Lilliput, Islandia, Hi-Brasil, Lemuria.

Did you never wonder: where do these maps come from?

Who makes these maps?

By what arcane mappery do these cartographs come to be? What nameless Mercator or Henry the Navigator, what astonishing Ptolemy or Kropotkin, beat the paths to Narnia and lost Hyperborea and the Fountain of Youth?

Who, did you ever ask yourself, who? What mapmaker sat and actually drew the lines and shapes? To all those *terra incognita* venues.

One of those things no one really thinks about. You hear a story about some expedition going to Mt. Everest—"chomolungma" the Mother Goddess of the Earth—because they've got a highly reliable map of the terrain where the *yeti* mates; or Sotheby's has auctioned off for two million five a map—highly reliable—that locates El Dorado; or the Seven Cities of Cíbola; or the fabulous sunken islands of Gunnbjorn Ulfson between Iceland and Greenland; the *real* Yoknapatawpha County; the *real* Grover's Mill that changed its name and altered its city limits after that Sunday night radio broadcast on CBS in October of 1938; the *real* location of Noah's ark at seventeen thousand feet above the Aras River plain but *not* atop Mount Ararat; you hear these stories, and you may wonder for an instant . . .

Where did such a map come from?

The last survivor of a Norwegian barque. The rambling mad foot-soldier who emerged from the jungle after six months' missing. The withered septugeneric Cree sitting by the side of the road selling potions and talismans. The gypsy fortune teller. The speaking-in-tongues child who has been blind since birth.

There's always a chain of provenance—and it's always bogus. Comes to as dead an end as *terra incognita* itself. Yet the maps do exist. They come into the hands of the L. Frank Baums and the Edgar Rice Burroughses and the Ponce de Leons, the Samuel Butlers and St. Thomas Aquinases. But, do you ever ask yourself, where did *they* . . . how did *they* . . . come by these amazing—highly reliable—charts? Who draws the map that shows the entrance to the mountain where the children of Hamelin disappeared? Who describes latitude and longitude of the tropical island beyond Anacapa where Amelia Earhart came down safely and hid from the Japanese fleet? How does the singular cartographer get a highly reliable tracing of the rocky battered shore of Lemuria and the Kingdom of Prester John and the Well of Souls?

Did you ever ask that kind of question?

I never did, Howard, till that shadowy alleyway in Old Town on a bitter chill late afternoon in February.

What interior landscape I could see through the elegant gray-glass of the central pane of the ornately carved teak front door of the map shop was inchoate, indeterminate, yes, a *terra incognita*. Absolutely appropriate. The handsomely whittled wooden sign that hung by brass chains at 90° to the storefront read:

> INCOGNITA, INC.
> A. Wonacott, Prop.

I turned the bright shining gold handle of the front door, the handle in the shape of a sextant, and let the warmth from within flow out around me in the dark alley.

Then I stepped inside the curious map shop.

Understand something: I had been born and raised in Chicago, I had been away a long time, I had been married and widowed, I had a grown son and daughter who no longer needed my daily attention and who lived half a continent away, I had been a loyal corporate tool for most of my adult life, and I was solidly grounded in the pragmatic world, what they call the Real World, the continuum as received safely and sanely by those who renew their driver's licenses regularly and who watch their saturated fat intake. I do not go off on flights of fancy.

Now let me describe Incognita, Inc. to you.

All I knew was that WorldSpan had acquired this enterprise, this supposedly "mom'n'pop" shop, line-item-buried on a Schedule of Assets & Liabilities, on the second-to-the-last page of a thick sheaf of wholly owned subsidiaries of the mega-conglomerate WorldSpan had murdered in the takeover. Then had begun the pogrom, the flensing, the "de-accessioning" of properties that did not breathlessly contribute to the bottom line. The memo you e-mailed me, if you recall, Howard, used the phrase *cease and terminate this operation.*

But there had been no phone number, no fax number, no e-mail address, nothing but the shop number in a tiny commercial alleyway I couldn't find on the most detailed city map of Chicago. And so you had me fly to Old Town.

To trim back one Abner Wonacott, who apparently had been the owner and sole employee of Incognita, Inc., at this odd location, for what seemed to be—in spotty records—sixty-five years. And now I stood inside the door, and now I looked upward, and now I looked around, and now I found myself unable to grasp what I was seeing, here, inside this tiny shop.

Outside. Very small.

Inside. Vast.

I don't mean to tell you it was large. Large is the rotunda of Grand Central Station. Large is the basilica of St. Peter's Cathedral. Large is Hanging Rock in New South Wales. This was vast. Narrow, but vast. It stretched out beyond the logical, codifiable, eyesight-correct limit that Euclidean space acknowledged. The horizon line was invisible. There was no back wall to the shop. It all just stretched on out of sight, vast and deep, and going on and on till it came to a blurred point somewhere a million or so miles back there at the rear of the shop. On either side of me the walls rose straight up without break, and both walls were nothing but deep cubbyholes, hundreds of them, thousands of them, uncountable perhaps *millions* of them. Up and up and up into some sort of inexplicable ceilingless ionosphere, where clouds and chirruping creatures moved lazily. And in every cubbyhole there was a rolled map, or a group of rolled maps. Hundreds of maps, thousands of maps, uncountable perhaps . . .

And clambering all over those two walls of cubbyholes, were the tendrils of the most luxurious liana vines I've ever seen. Dark green and lustrous, the vines writhed upward and downward and from side to side, wrapping themselves about a map roll here, a pair of papyrus charts there, then extricating their tendril ends from the cubby and slithering swiftly across the face of the wall—sometimes hurling themselves full across the shop to the wall opposite—and then fled rearward, to extend their length to an unknown destination far away in the cloudy foggy misty backland of Incognita, Inc.

It was, truly, the jungle telegraph. Possibly a kind of fern FedEx. Delivery by botanical messenger.

And right in front of me, not ten steps inside the front door, was the (apparently) sole living employee of this soon-to-be-terminated establishment, Abner Wonacott. Prop.

He sat high up on a bookkeeper's stool, something hugely Dickensian in appearance, like one of those old woodcuts by "Phiz" or Cruikshank from *Dombey and Son* or *A Christmas Carol*. The desk at which he worked was a very tall slant-top, tulip stenciled with tapering legs framed with cross stretchers. The grain identified it as a very old mahogany.

He wore a full day-coat with short tails, striped trousers, wing-collar shirt with a plum-colored cravat, and a diamond stickpin glistening between the trisail lapels. He wore a pince-nez that perched securely at the bridge of his aquiline nose, his hair was thick and pure white, and it hung over his forehead with an abundant curl like a dollop of whipped cream.

His eyes were the most revelatory shade of almond I've ever seen, with very black pupils, like a pair of well-ensconced beetles frozen in hundred-million-year-old Baltic amber. It was enigmatic, trying to ascertain his age. He might have been sixty, less likely a weathered fifty, perhaps much older.

He had the kindest face ever gifted by the cruel and mostly uncaring world. He wore it without affectation.

"Excuse me," I said. "Mr. Wonacott?"

"Be with you in a spot, young man. Having a nip of a mean time with one of these isogrivs." He was working on a line, on a map he was drawing, up there on his high stool. "Grivation has never been my strong suit." He scratched quickly with the nib of a crowquill pen. "Look around. Amuse yourself. Be with you in two shakes of a lamb's tail."

I turned to look at the wall on my right. I walked across the pleasantly springy, mist-shrouded floor to the cubbyholes and marveled at what they held. Not just maps to Happy Valley and Ruritania and Lyonesse and Shangri-La; to Zothique and Ur and Erewhon and Pellucidar; but the route Verne parodied to reach the center of the Earth; a sad-looking graph locating the mass grave of the original colonists of the Lost Roanoke Colony (with a triptych map to the gravesite of Virginia Dare, first queen of the Croatan Indians); a large scroll map of "The Dark Continent" with an identifying Gothic cross marking the locale of the Elephants' Graveyard. It was somewhere near Mali.

There was a recently configured map of the shoreline of Lake Michigan indicating where to dredge to find the Bowie knife O. J. Simpson had thrown away.

"Would you like to know what our most requested item is?" I turned at his voice. He was sitting now with hands folded decently on the slant-top of the desk. I walked back to him and looked up into the kindest face in the world.

"Yes."

"Well now, you would think, wouldn't you, that it would be something like Atlantis or Camelot or an underwater configuration for Spanish treasure galleons, yes?" I smiled agreement. But no, he indicated with a waggle of a finger, "Five to one, our best seller is a personal site location map to the original *and translated into spoken English* lyrics to the song 'Louie Louie.' Isn't that remarkable?"

I stared up into his amber eyes. "Remarkable," I said, in a soft voice. "Like this shop. It's, uh, it's improbable." I felt my cheeks burning with embarrassment: "improbable." What the hell kind of a stupid word was that to use?! "It's very big. Inside."

"Oh, this is cramped quarters, I fear." He waved a hand above his head, diminishing the ascendant abyss that rose high and away over us. "You should have seen the absolutely imperial spaces accorded me when I worked for Khufu. Pyramid, it was. Very nice. And there was a canyon in Mesopo—"

I cut him off. "I've come to close you down, sir."

I couldn't help myself. I had to stop him. I felt so awful, like some sleazy server of subpoenas pretending to be an interested bypasser. "I've come from corporate headquarters to . . . I have a very generous severance check here in my . . . how is it you've worked for this company for, what is it, *sixty-five* years, can that be accurate, we don't seem to have much paperwork on all this uh . . ."

I ground to a halt. I felt just awful.

"Look," I said, "you won't remember me, but I came here, I think, once before; a long time ago; thirty-something years ago. To get a map. I'd lost something . . ."

He smiled down at me. "A bronze medal you had won, third prize in a kite-flying contest in grade school."

"Yes! Yes, that was it, exactly! You remember. I'd lost it. Your map . . ."

"To be sure. My map. It's an all-purpose item, we sell quite a lot of them. I call it the Map to Your Heart's Desire. Do you still have that medal?"

"Migod yes!" I pulled out my pocket watch, and showed him the bronze fob. "It's the only thing I've ever won in my life. Not so much as ten bucks on a lottery, but I have the bronze medal. You found it for me."

"And now you've come to put me out of business."

"Believe me, it's not my idea. They gave me this lousy job because I mentioned one day, just idly, mentioned I was from around here . . . and they thought it would be . . ."

He looked sad. "I've been expecting something like this. There was a letter from . . . what's the name of the new company that bought up the old one . . . ?"

Nowhere among the million conundra that scintillated and sang within the vast, questioning mind of the very old man who now called himself Abner Wonacott, like a heavenly chorus of inebriated lightning bugs, was there even one that wondered by whom Abner had been employed, now going on sixty-six years. If it wasn't a Pharaoh, it was a Doge, if it wasn't a Khan it was a Demiurge. The shop, and Abner under other names, had gone on for centuries. Every Friday by five P.M. the cashier's check appeared in a late post, signed in pen in an unintelligible hand, for that week's labors. Abner was only human, after all, and he did require food and shelter. And so it had been for now going on sixty-six years at this current location. Periodically, every sixteen months by rough estimation, Abner's check was nine percent greater than those that had preceded it. On his birthday—June 11 usually—and at holidaytime—he had never known if the impetus was Chanukah, Ramadan or Christmas—the check included a crisp new one hundred dollar bill as bonus. And so, without wondering, because he loved his work of a lifetime, of many lifetimes, Abner worked with serenity and satisfaction in the vast, tiny, narrow and limitless cartography shop in the shadowy, dismal, perfectly pleasant narrow alley three streets off the bustling thoroughfares of that immense metropolitan nexus that might, at other times, have been Avalon or Tyre or Carthage, might have been Marrakech or Constantinople or Vienna, but was only, in truth, for going on sixty-six years, at this location, the hamlet of Chicago.

"I will, I must say, hate to see me go. Abandoning the work to Replogle and Rand McNally will be . . . well, of course, they're very fine people, and they try to do their best, but I think they still use that silly *Here There Be Dragons* at the edge of the drop-off."

I stammered and heard myself babbling. "We, that is to say, WorldSpan, has just completed on-orbit checkout and synchronization of our three geodetic polar orbital satellites, all of which are in geosynchronous configurations 22,300 miles above the planet, all with completely automated computer-driven cartography programs." His eyes were wide as I gibbered, unable to stop myself: I'd rehearsed all this, straight from the tech memoranda, on the plane, not knowing who or what Abner Wonacott was going to be. And now I couldn't shut up. "These are electro-optical imaging satellites. We now have a multi-planar, LEO, MEO, and GEO corporate capability to provide under-an-hour mapping and geospatial products to our worldwide customers. We can 'direct-task' both an electro-optical and hyperspectral satellite to image any 100 × 100 kilometer swath on Earth. We can employ our highly refined processing algorithms which allow us to . . . levels of reflectance . . . hundreds of spectral bands . . ."

I ran down. So ashamed of myself. Just so damned, damned *ashamed* of what I'd let you make of me, Howard. I wanted to sink through the unseen, misty floor. I felt like a giant gobbet of crap. And Abner Wonacott just stared at me.

"So I am the relic from an earlier time," he said. "I seem to be, as they put it, redundant. Well, that must be it, then, of course." He slid off his high perch and put his hands on my shoulders. He was taller than I'd thought.

"What is your name, young man?"

"Charlie Trimbach, sir."

"Ah. Yes, of course, I do indeed remember the bronze medal and how you cried. Well, let me say this, Master Charles Trimbach: you are a very nice young man. You need not be so unforgiving, of yourself, and of those for whom you labor. You have turned out to be an absolutely imperial young man, and I hold no bad cess for your having come to deliver this nasty news."

I handed him the envelope containing the severance check. Though how you could pay him for what must have been hundreds of years of maps, well, I don't know, Howard; I just don't know.

He reached into a shelf beneath the slant-top of his desk, and removed a derby hat. He placed it carefully on his head at a rakish angle, took one last look around the shop—the greenery seemed to rustle a farewell—and he walked me to the door.

We stepped out into the Chicago night. It was lit by a full moon. He closed the door behind us, and turned to me as he locked up. "But with all your capacity for producing a map down to the last grain of sand in the Gobi, Charlie, the sad thing is that now and forevermore no one will be able to provide the questing customer with a route to Baskerville Hall, or Riallaro, or Nimmr in the Valley of the Sepulchre. With the closing of this little oasis, Charlie, your little civilization loses for all time to come. There is no Charta Caelestis for the improbable."

And when I turned back to see, the shop was gone. It was now a boarded-up derelict, what had once been a deli or a place where they sold banded twelve-packs of socks. Seconds.

Abner Wonacott and I walked out into the street, left the alley, and headed toward the city lights. It was terribly cold, that special awful Chicago cold that makes you think of the end of the world. He held his derby on with one hand and hunched deeper inside his jacket. I wished I'd brought a heavier topcoat. It hadn't been supposed to get this cold, this soon.

"What will you do now?" I asked him.

He shrugged. "Perhaps I'll retire somewhere nice and warm. I hear Boca is pleasant."

I wanted to cry. Just like that, so damned casually, I'd made everything go sour in the world. I fingered the bronze medal fob on my watch chain. I was a bad person, no matter what the old mapmaker said to ease my guilt. A bad person. I told him that. He smiled wryly and said, "Most of us think we're more important than we really are, Charlie. The universe isn't watching. It mostly, for the most part, doesn't care."

And at that moment, before I could wallow much more in sophomoric self-pity, a stout lady with one of those wire shopping baskets on wheels came up to us, and she looked at Abner Wonacott, the one man who could actually tell you where King Kong resided, and she said, "Excuse me, mister, is there a Domenick's around here?"

"No, not too close," he said. "There *was* an A&P for a long time, but it's gone. I think there's a Jewel Supermarket about a mile toward Lincoln Park, but . . . oh, wait a moment . . . yes, now that I recall, yes indeed there *is* a Domenick's.

"You'll have to go over three blocks that way, and then go left for two more blocks to . . ."

He paused, looked thoughtful for a moment, then reached into his inside jacket pocket and brought out a lovely fountain pen and a pad. "Here," he said, "let me draw you a map."

And all at once, the wind wasn't nearly as cold as it had been; and the night was not nearly as empty.

CLAUDIA BARBOSA NOGUEIRA

Maria de Jesus

Claudia Barbosa Nogueira is currently a Ph.D. student in comparative literature at the University of Maryland. Her writing has been published in a variety of journals, including The Southern Quarterly *and* The Berkeley Poetry Review. *Much of her work explores issues of immigration, displacement, and national and regional identification. The following magical realist tale is part of a manuscript of stories that attempt to synthesize the author's memories of her native Brazil with her imaginings of what it means to live in a place and call it home. "Maria de Jesus" first appeared in* The Colorado Review, *vol. 27, no. 2.*

—T. W.

Quilombo the bull loved windows. He would press his nose against glass and watch his reflection melt with furniture and breath. The nose ring would tap and announce to residents that a black face was staring and fuming at them. The children would cry and have nightmares, and the maids sang lullabies about windows being made of soap and water.

Quilombo knew intimate things about the people in the big house. He knew that Fernando picked his nose, knew where Dona Gloria had a triangle of moles, and he kept secrets, chewing them with his cud. He also had a deep trust in glass, his second skin—people would erupt or cry when they saw him framed on the wall, and inevitably they would flail their arms at him and sometimes let loose a flying brush or book that always bounced off the glass and landed impotent on the ground at their feet. When this happened, Quilombo would move away toward the gate he had squeezed through because servants would soon be called to escort him out to pasture.

When there weren't many people at the house, when they were off in the cities working in offices or schools, Quilombo had free rein of the windows. He would reacquaint himself with interiors and plodding around verandas and empty hammocks, would fall in love with his reflection.

Maria de Jesus would often find him flirting at the kitchen window where it was dark inside and where steam added arabesques to glass, and she'd let him stay. When no one was at the big house, she had the power to make this decision. In fact, she was glad for company, and while she made jellies and preserves and banana candy, she would talk to the bull and answer the questions she heard him ask. She'd talk about when she was a girl and how she couldn't speak until she was fourteen. She'd talk about the priest for whom she cooked and cleaned. She talked about her life before the farm, and when the bull would ask about the present and future, Maria de Jesus would pretend she hadn't heard—after all, bulls can't talk.

Maria de Jesus had come to the farm an unmarried woman and pregnant. She had also come as an elementary speaker. The priest she worked for had taught her to speak two years prior, manipulating tongue and palate with heavy fingers. He dislodged what had been impeding the flow of words, and as soon as he did, he ordered her to silence. She hadn't uttered one sound before the priest declared that she would be quiet about her abilities, that her tongue would not announce itself to the world but remain an internal organ. Maria de Jesus considered the priest a miracle worker; she could feel words building up inside her, so much so that her belly began to extend.

The priest married her to a man who was leaving the town for good.

This man was much older than she and had a temper and a love of drink. Maria de Jesus practiced her words on him complaining little by little about his dirtiness, his ungainliness and crudeness. The man would beat her into silence, and she, letting the words build up, delivered a baby boy she called Tobías.

The three lived on the farm, Tobías growing, Maria de Jesus' vocabulary growing, and the man's temper getting shorter. Maria started to long for the church where the priest would summarize all he had done at the end of the day. Now, on the farm, there was no summation from anyone—words were infrequently and only violently thrown about. Maria de Jesus developed a condition of the heart that would make her suffer the rest of her days—she began to love only that which had passed.

People who suffer from this disease are recognizable because their edges are blurry, their outlines undefined. When one interacts with them, they seem to be veiled by haze—their features muted and their voices sounding more and more like echoes. It was in this state that Maria de Jesus became pregnant again and then again.

When her children were six, three, and two, her husband disappeared. She had woken one morning, with him a lump by her side. She checked on the children, then headed to the pump to get some water. When she came back, the children were crying and the man gone. She thought nothing of it—the children cried a lot and her husband must have gone to work early. But he stayed away. When a day passed, she gave a sigh of relief. When a week passed, she began to worry and asked others if they had seen him. When a month passed, Maria de Jesus thought she was madly in love with him and would give anything to have him back.

Tobías learned he could make things disappear. He realized that by throwing pebbles at a certain angle, they'd go through the air and never land. He experimented with throwing flowers, sticks, even wooden soldiers the big-house children had left behind, and all went through a window in the air to another side no one knew about.

Tobías became famous all over the compound, and even those who believed he was just manipulating distance and vision—that it was sleight of hand—all could agree that his aim was so uncanny as to reach nowhere every time.

Tobías grew up in a special place on the farm. His advice was called for when men wanted to throw a rope around a wild horse's neck, when young women wanted to throw rings of flowers at men's feet, when kids wanted to know the best angle at which to kick a ball past Marcão. And Tobías was guaranteed the best jobs—he was the one who got to raise the levers that separated cattle in the branding corral, and the one who was picked to run the water for the veterinarian.

Maria de Jesus was too busy grieving to marvel at her son's abilities. She would sigh as she combed the lice from her children's hair and say, "It's all very well that you can make things disappear, but can you make them come back? That's the true miracle."

And so Tobías began to experiment with throwing things at angles more acute than before.

One day, when Tobías was fourteen, a cow gave birth to a five-legged calf. The calf's face was flattened, and it breathed with difficulty but determination. Its eyes shone with the fevered brilliance of a devil, and everyone agreed that this was a bad thing. The owner of the farm, summoned to see the oracle born in the middle of the morning, pulled out his revolver and aimed it at the still wet animal. Tobías ran to the animal's side, lifted it up by its front hooves, and threw it as if to give the gun a flying target. The owner aimed and fired, and the bullet lodged in a beam on the ceiling, having missed its goal entirely, the calf having vanished on its course through the air.

Two weeks later Tobías was witness to another birth, again of a five-legged calf. It had the same flattened face but was born dead, its eyes cold and hard. He wondered if it could be the same calf, if he might have been able to get it to come back. That night, he practiced with throwing his sister's near empty lipstick tube through the window in the air. He stood outside, his hands open, expecting to catch what might fall from the sky. Nothing fell. The next morning, however, he woke with a jump to find that he had a red stain on his crotch. Despite the teasing his family gave him and despite the fact that there was no wound, Tobías decided that he could make things reappear, just in a different form.

He stole his father's comb, which his mother kept next to the plaster Virgin Mary on the table, and ran outside to be where things are lighter. He again threw it out the window of air. A week later a bone was found washed up on the bank of the little creek. Maria de Jesus was certain it was her husband's and stopped chastising her son about the comb. She asked if Tobías would throw the bone for her, if he could make more of his father reappear.

So Tobías snuck into the farm owner's office where the bone was kept and threw it up so that it disappeared neatly into the night sky. Mother and son waited for months for something to come back. Every night they'd have vivid dreams of the father who bellowed at them and cursed. But nothing of flesh or consistency ever showed up. The mother asked if he was sure he had thrown it right, and Tobías said that there was nothing wrong with the throw, that the bone must have gotten stuck somewhere.

They waited a few more months and still nothing happened. Maria de Jesus grew silent and depressed. She began to mope around the farm owner's office, looking through the window for an extra bone that may have been found without any notice. She started losing weight rapidly, and Tobías began to wonder if she were doing her own disappearing trick. He tried to console her and get her to eat, but nothing worked. She was sure, she whispered, the bone had come back in her throat, that it was stopping the passage of words and food.

Tobías became desperate. He threw his mother's cooking spoon. He threw little bits of paper with writing on them that he found around the house. He threw anything that was light enough to go the distance to the other side. And things kept returning in parts. The spoon reappeared in the shape of the Big Dipper, a constellation that allowed itself to be seen in the Southern Hemisphere for a night. The bits of paper came back as a flood of birds that infested the cane fields and produced such a racket that people's ears hummed even after most of the birds were killed.

There was only one thing Tobías could think of to do, and that was to perform the most astonishing vanishing trick of all: to throw himself out the window of air and try to find his father on the other side. He kissed his mother on the forehead as she slept, told his sister and brother to take care of their mother, and stepped outside.

When Maria de Jesus woke up and found her son had gone, she quickly forgot her husband and began to grieve this new loss. But this grieving was short-lived because she began to find she had powers of her own; her silence had taught her to recognize in moments of peace that which she was missing. She found remnants of Tobías everywhere—the way the sun shone at an angle through their window slot, the way leaves fell from the tree that looked like a giant dragon, and the way dogs darted through dust devils; all such dances brought him to mind.

And all this she told the bull who watched his reflection melt with the old woman's.

LOUISE ERDRICH

Le Mooz

Louise Erdrich is one of the finest writers working in America today. She won the 1999 World Fantasy Award for her novel The Antelope Wife, *an extraordinary work of modern mythic fiction, and a National Book Critics Circle Award for her best-selling novel* Love Medicine. *Other books (for both adults and children) include* Bingo Palace, The Beet Queen, Tracks, Jacklight, The Blue Jay's Dance, Tales of Burning Love *and* The Birchbark House. *The following tender yet hilarious story, like much of Erdrich's work, draws on the author's Native American heritage. She is a member of the Turtle Mountain Band of Ojibwa, and lives with her children in Minnesota.*

"Le Mooz" comes from the January 24 issue of The New Yorker *magazine, and it is a privilege to reprint it here.*

—*T. W.*

Margaret had exhausted three husbands, and Nanapush outlived his six wives. They were old by the time they shacked up out in the deep bush. Besides, as Ojibweg in the last century's first decades, having starved and grieved, having seen prodigious loss and endured theft by agents of the government and *chimookomaanag* farmers, they were tired. You would think, at last, they'd just want simple comfort. Quiet. Companionship and sleep. But times did not go smoothly. Peace eluded them. For Nanapush and Margaret found a surprising heat in their hearts. Fierce and sudden, it sometimes eclipsed both age and anger with tenderness. Then, they made love with an amazed greed and purity that astounded them. At the same time, it was apt to burn out of control.

When this happened, they fought. Stinging flames of words blistered their tongues. Silence was worse. Beneath its slow-burning weight, their black looks singed. After a few days their minds shriveled into dead coals. Some speechless nights, they lay together like logs turned completely to ash. They were almost afraid to move, lest they sift into flakes and disintegrate. It was a young love set blazing in bodies aged and overused, and sometimes it cracked them like too much fire in an old tin stove.

To survive in their marriage, they developed many strategies. For instance, they rarely collaborated on any task. Each hunted, trapped, and fished alone. They could not agree on so little a thing as how and where to set a net. The gun, which belonged to Nanapush, was never clean when it was needed. Traps rusted. It was up to Margaret to scour the rifle barrel, smoke the steel jaws. Setting snares together was impossible, for in truth they snared themselves time and again in rude opinions and mockery over where a rabbit might jump or how to set the loop. Their avoidance only hardened them in their individual ways, and so when Margaret beached their leaky old boat one morning and jumped ashore desperate for help, there was no chance of agreement.

Margaret sometimes added little Frenchisms to her Ojibwemowin, just the way the fancy-sounding wives of the French voyageurs added, like a dash of spice, random *"le"* 's and *"la"* 's. So when she banged into the cabin screaming of "le Mooz," Nanapush woke, irritated, with reproof on his lips, as he was always pleased to find some tiny fault with his beloved.

"Le Mooz! Le Mooz!" she shouted into his face. She grabbed him by the shirt so violently that he could hear the flimsy threads part.

"Booni'ishin!" He tried to struggle from her grip, but Margaret rapidly explained to him that she had seen a moose swimming across the lake and here were their winter's provisions, easy! With this moose meat dried and stored, they would survive. "Get up, old man!" She grabbed the gun and dragged him to the boat before he'd even mentally prepared himself to hunt moose.

Nanapush pushed off with his paddle, sulking. Besides their natural inclination to disagree, it was always the case that, if one of them was particularly intrigued by some idea, the other was sure to feel the opposite way just to polarize the situation. If Nanapush asked for maple syrup with his meat, Margaret gave him wild onion. If Margaret relished a certain color of cloth, Nanapush declared that he could not look upon that blue or red—it made him mean and dizzy. When it came to sleeping on the fancy spring bed that Margaret had bought with this year's bark money, Nanapush adored the bounce while she was stingy with it, so as not to use it up. Sometimes he sat on the bed and joggled up and down when she was gone, just to spite her. For her part, once he began craftily to ask for wild onion, she figured he'd developed a taste for it and so bargained for a small jar of maple syrup, thus beginning the obvious next stage of their contradictoriness, which was that they each asked for the opposite of what they really wanted and so got what they wanted in the end. It was confusing to their friend Father Damien, but to the two of them it brought serene harmony. So, when Margaret displayed such extreme determination in the matter of the moose that morning, not only was Nanapush feeling especially lazy but he also decided that she really meant the opposite of what she cried out, and so he dawdled with his paddle and tried to tell her a joke or two. She, however, was in dead earnest.

"Paddle! Paddle for all you're worth!" she yelled.

"Break your backs, boys, or break wind!" Nanapush mocked her.

Over the summer, as it hadn't been the proper time for telling the sacred Ojibwe *adisookaanag*, Father Damien had tried to convert Nanapush by telling as many big-fish tales as he could remember, including the ones about the fish that multiplied, the fish that swallowed Jonah. Soon, Father Damien had had to reach beyond the Bible. Nanapush's favorite was the tale of the vast infernal white fish and the maddened chief who gave chase through the upper and lower regions of the earth.

"*Gitimishk!*" Margaret nearly choked in frustration, for the moose had changed direction and they were not closing in quickly enough for her liking.

"Aye, aye, *Ahabikwe!*" shouted Nanapush, lighting his pipe as she vented her fury in deep strokes. If the truth be told, he was delighted with her anger, for when she lost control like this during the day she often lost control once the sun went down also, and he was already anticipating their pleasure.

"Use that paddle or my legs are shut to you, lazy fool!" she growled.

At that, he went to work and they quickly drew alongside the moose. Margaret steadied herself, threw a loop of strong rope around its wide, spreading antlers, and then secured the rope tightly to the front of the boat, which was something of an odd canoe, having a flat, tough bottom, a good ricing boat but not all that easy to steer.

"Now," she ordered Nanapush, "now, take up the gun and shoot! Shoot!"

But Nanapush did not. He had killed a moose this way once before in his life, and he had nothing to prove. This time, he wasn't so anxious. What was happening to them was a very old story, one handed down through generations, one that had happened to his namesake, the trickster Nanabozho. He would not kill the moose quite yet. He hefted the gun and made certain that it was loaded, and then enjoyed the free ride they were receiving.

"Let's turn him around, my adorable pigeon," he cried to his lady. "Let him tow us back home. I'll shoot him once he reaches the shallow water just before our cabin."

Margaret could not help but agree that this particular plan arrived at by her lazy husband was a good one, and so, by using more rope and hauling on first one antler and then the other with all their strength, they proceeded to turn the beast and head him in the right direction. Nanapush sat back, smoking his pipe, and relaxed once they were pointed homeward. The sun was out and the air was cool, fresh. All seemed right between the two of them now. Margaret admonished him about the tangle of fishing tackle all around his seat, and there was even affection in her voice.

"You'll poke yourself," she said, "you fool." At that moment, with the meat pulling them right up to their doorstep, she did not really even care. "I'll fry the rump steaks tonight with a little maple syrup over them," she said, her mouth watering. "Old man, you're gonna eat good! Ooh," she almost cried with appreciation, "our moose is so fat!"

"He's a fine moose," Nanapush agreed passionately. "You've got an eye, *Mindimooyenh*. He's a juicy one, our moose!"

"I'll roast his ribs, cook the fat with our beans, and keep his brains in a bucket to tan that big hide! Oooh, *ishte*, my husband, the old men are going to envy the *makizinan* that I will sew for you."

"Beautiful wife!" Nanapush was overcome. "Precious sweetheart!"

As they gazed upon each other with great love, holding the rare moment of mutual agreeableness, the hooves of the moose struck the first sandbar near shore, and Margaret cried out for her husband to lift the gun and shoot.

"Not quite yet, my beloved," Nanapush said confidently, "he can drag us nearer yet!"

"Watch out! Shoot now!"

The moose was indeed approaching the shallows, but Nanapush planned in his pride to shoot the animal just as he began to pull them from the water, thereby making their task of dressing and hauling mere child's play. He got the moose in his sights and then waited as it gained purchase. The old man's feet, annoyingly, tangled in the fishing tackle he had been too lazy to put away, and he jigged, attempting to kick it aside.

"Margaret, duck!" he cried. Just as the moose lunged onto land he let blast, completely missing and totally terrifying the animal, which gave a hopping skip that seemed impossible for a thing so huge, and veered straight up the bank. Margaret, reaching back to tear the gun from her husband's hands, was bucked completely out of the boat and said later that if only her no-good man hadn't insisted on holding on to the gun she could have landed, aimed, and killed them both, as she then wished to do most intensely. Instead, as the moose tore off with the boat still securely tied by three ropes to his antlers, she was left behind screaming for the fool to jump. But he did not, and within moments the rampaging moose, with the boat bounding behind, had disappeared into the woods.

"My man is stubborn," she said, dusting off her skirt, checking to make sure that she was still in one piece, nothing broken or cut. "He will surely kill that moose!" She spoke hopefully, but inside she felt stuffed with a combination of such anxiety and rage that she did not know what to do—to try to rescue Nanapush or to chop him into pieces with the hatchet that she found herself sharpening as she listened for the second report of his gun.

Bloof!

Yes. There it was. Good thing he didn't jump out, she muttered. She began to tramp, with her carrying straps and an extra sharp knife, in the direction of the noise.

In fact, that Nanapush did not jump out of the boat had little to do with his great stubbornness or his bravery. When the moose jolted the boat up the shore, the tackle that had already wound around him flew beneath his rear as he bounced upward and three of his finest fishing hooks stuck deep into his buttocks as he landed, fastening him tight. He screeched in pain, further horrifying the animal, and struggled, driving the hooks in still deeper, until he could only hold on to the edge of the boat with one hand, gasping in agony, as with the other he attempted to raise the gun to his shoulder and kill the moose.

All the time, of course, the moose was running wildly. Pursued by this strange, heavy, screeching, banging, booming thing, it fled in dull terror through bush and slough. It ran and continued to run. Those who saw Nanapush as he passed all up and down the reservation stood a moment in fascinated shock and rubbed their eyes, then went to fetch others, so that soon the predicament of Nanapush was known and reported everywhere. By then, the moose had attained a smooth loping trot, and passed with swift ease through farmsteads and pastures, the boat flying up and then disappearing down behind. Many stopped what they were doing to gape and yell, and others ran for their rifles, but they were all too late to shoot the moose and free poor Nanapush.

One day passed. In his moose-drawn fishing boat, Nanapush toured every part of the reservation that he'd ever hunted and saw everyone that he'd ever known and then went to places that he hadn't visited since childhood. At one point, a family digging cattail roots was stunned to see the boat, the moose towing it across a slough, and a man slumped over, for by now poor Nanapush had given up and surrendered to the pain, which at least, he said later, he shared with the beast, whose rump he'd stung with bullets. The moose was heading now for the most remote parts of the reservation, where poor Nanapush was convinced he surely would die.

"Niijii," he cried out to the moose, "my brother, slow down!"

The animal flicked back an ear to catch the sound of the thing's voice, but didn't stop.

"I will kill no more!" declared Nanapush. "I now throw away my gun!" And he cast it aside, after kissing the barrel and noting well his surroundings. But as though it sensed and felt only contempt for the man's hypocrisy, the moose snorted and kept moving.

"I apologize to you," cried Nanapush, "and to all of the moose I have ever killed and to the spirit of the moose and the boss of the moose and to every moose that has lived or will ever live in the future."

As if slightly placated, the moose slowed to a walk, and Nanapush was able, finally, to snatch a few berries from the bushes they passed, to scoop up a mouthful of water from the slough, and to sleep, though by moonlight the moose still browsed and walked toward some goal, thought Nanapush, delirious with exhaustion and pain. Perhaps the next world. Perhaps this moose had been sent by the all-clever Creator to fetch Nanapush along to the spirit life in this novel way. But, just as he was imagining such a thing, the first light showed and by that ever-strengthening radiance he saw that his moose did indeed have a direction and an intention and that that object was a female moose of an uncommonly robust size, just ahead, peering over her shoulder in a way that was apparently bewitching to a male moose, for Nanapush's animal uttered a squeal of bullish intensity that he recognized as pure lust.

Nanapush, now wishing that he had aimed for the huge swinging balls of the moose, wept with exasperation.

"Should I be subjected to this? This, too? In addition to all that I have suffered?" And Nanapush cursed the moose, cursed himself, the fishhooks, and the person who so carefully and sturdily constructed the boat that would not fall apart. He cursed in English, as there are no true swear words in Ojibwemowin, and so it was Nanapush and not the Devil whom Josette Bizhieu heard passing by her remote cabin at first light, shouting all manner of unspeakable and innovative imprecations, and it was Nanapush, furthermore, who was heard howling in the deep slough grass, howling, though more dead at this point than alive, at the outrageous acts he was forced to witness there, before his nose, as the boat tipped up and the bull moose in the extremity of his passion loved the female moose with ponderous mountings and thrilling thrusts that swung Nanapush from side to side but did not succeed in dislodging him from the terrible grip of the fishhooks. No, that was not to happen. Nanapush was bound to suffer for one more day before the satisfied moose toppled over to snore and members of the rescue party Margaret had raised crept up and shot the animal stone dead in its sleep.

The moose, Margaret found, for she had brought with her a meat hatchet, had lost a distressing amount of fat and its meat was now stringy from the long flight and sour with a combination of fear and spent sex, so that in butchering it she winced and moaned and traveled far in her raging thoughts, imagining sore revenges she would exact upon her husband.

In the meantime, Father Damien, who had followed his friend as best he could in the parish touring car, was able to assist those who emerged from the bush. He drove Nanapush, raving, to Sister Hildegarde, who was adept at extracting fishhooks. At the school infirmary, she was not upset to see the bare buttocks of Nanapush sticking straight up in the air. She swabbed the area with iodine and tested the strength of her pliers. With great relief for his friend and a certain amount of pity, Father Damien tried to make him smile: "Don't be ashamed of your display. Even the Virgin Mary had two asses, one to sit upon and the other ass that bore her to Egypt."

Nanapush only nodded gloomily and gritted his teeth as Sister Hildegarde pushed the hook with the pliers until the barbed tip broke through his tough skin, then clipped the barb off and pulled out the rest of the hook.

"Is there any chance," he weakly croaked once the operation was accomplished, "that this will affect my manhood?"

"Unfortunately not," Hildegarde said.

The lovemaking skills of Nanapush, whole or damaged, were to remain untested until after his death. For Margaret took a long time punishing her husband. She ignored him, she browbeat him, and, worst of all, she cooked for him.

It was the winter of instructional beans, for every time Margaret boiled up a pot of rock-hard pellets drawn from the fifty-pound sack of beans that were their only sustenance besides the sour strings of meat, she reminded Nanapush of each brainless turning point last fall at which he should have killed the moose but did not.

"And my," she sneered then, "wasn't its meat both tender and sweet before you ran it to rags?"

She never boiled the beans quite soft enough, either, for she could will her own body to process the toughest sinew with no trouble. Nanapush, however, suffered digestive torments of a nature that soon became destructive to his health and ruined their nightly rest entirely, for that is when the great explosive winds would gather in his body. His *boogidiwinan*, which had always been manly, yet meek enough to remain under his control, overwhelmed the power of his *ojiid*, and there was nothing he could do but surrender to their whims and force. At least it was a form of revenge on Margaret, he thought, exhausted, near dawn. But at the same time he worried that she would leave him. Already, she made him sleep on a pile of skins near the door so as not to pollute her flowered mattress.

"My precious one," he sometimes begged, "can you not spare me? Boil the beans a while longer, and the moose, as well. Have pity!"

She only raised her brow, and her glare was a slice of knifelike light. Maybe she was angriest because she'd softened toward him during that moose ride across the lake, and now she was determined to punish him for her uncharacteristic lapse into tenderness. At any rate, one night she boiled the beans only long enough to soften their skins and threw in a chunk of moose that was coated with a green mold she claimed was medicinal, but which tied poor Nanapush's guts in knots.

"Eat up, old man." She banged the plate down before him. He saw that she was implacable, and then he thought back to the way he had got around the impasse of the maple syrup before, and resolved to do exactly the opposite of what he felt. And so, resigned to sacrificing this night to pain, desperate, he proceeded to loudly enjoy the beans.

" 'They are excellent, *niwiiw*, crunchy and fine! *Minopogwad!*" He wolfed them down, eager as a boy, and tore at the moldy moose as though presented with the finest morsels. "Howah! I've never eaten such a fine dish!" He rubbed his belly and smiled in false satisfaction. "*Nindebisinii*, my pretty fawn, oh, how well I'll sleep." He rolled up in his blankets by the door, then, and waited for the gas pains to tear him apart.

They did come. That night was phenomenal. Margaret was sure that the cans of grease rattled on the windowsill, and she saw a glowing stench rise around her husband, saw with her own eyes but chose to plug her ears with wax and turn to the wall, poking an airhole for herself in the mud between logs, and so she fell asleep not knowing that the symphony of sounds that disarranged papers and blew out the door by morning were her husband's last utterances.

Yes, he was dead. She found when she went to shake him awake the next morning that he was utterly lifeless. She gave a shriek then, of abysmal loss, and began to weep with sudden horror at the depth of her unforgiving nature. She kissed his face all over, patted his hands and hair. He did not look as though death had taken him, no, he looked oddly well. Although it would seem that a death of this sort would shrivel him like a spent sack and leave him wrinkled and limp, he was shut tight and swollen, his mouth a firm line and his eyes squeezed shut as though holding something in. And he was stiff as a horn where she used to love him. There was some mistake! Perhaps, thought Margaret, wild in her grief, he was only deeply asleep and she could love him back awake.

She climbed aboard and commenced to ride him until she herself collapsed, exhausted and weeping, on his still breast. It was no use. His manliness still stood straight up and although she could swear the grim smile had deepened on his face, there were no other signs of life—no breath, not the faintest heartbeat could be detected. Margaret fell beside him, senseless, and was found there disheveled and out cold so that at first Father Damien thought the two had committed a double suicide, as some old people did those hard winters. But Margaret was soon roused. The cabin was aired out. Father Damien, ravaged with the loss, held his old friend Nanapush's hand all day and allowed his own tears to flow, soaking his black gown.

And so it was. The wake and the funeral were conducted in the old way. Margaret prepared his body. She cleaned him, wrapped him in her best quilt. As there was no disguising his bone-tough hard-on, she let it stand there proudly and decided not to be ashamed of her old man's prowess. She laid him on the bed that was her pride, and bitterly regretted how she'd forced him to sleep on the floor in the cold wind by the door.

Everyone showed up that night, bringing food and even a bit of wine, but Margaret wanted nothing of their comfort. Sorrow bit deep into her lungs and the pain radiated out like the shooting rays of a star. She lost her breath. A dizzy veil fell over her. She wanted most of all to express to her husband the terrible depth of the love she felt but had been too proud, too stingy, or, she now saw, too afraid to show him while he lived. She had deprived him of such pleasure: that great horn in his pants, she knew guiltily, was there because she had denied him physical satisfaction ever since the boat ride behind the moose.

"*Nimanendam.* If only he'd come back to me, I'd make him a happy man." She blew her nose on a big white dishcloth and bowed her head. Whom would she scold? Whom would she punish? Who would suffer for Margaret Kashpaw now? What was she to do? She dropped her face into her hands and wept with uncharacteristic abandon. The whole crowd of Nanapush's friends and loved ones, packed into the house, lifted a toast to the old man and made a salute. At last, Father Damien spoke, and his speech was so eloquent that in moments the whole room was bathed in tears and sobs.

It was at that moment, in the depth of their sorrow, just at the hour when they felt the loss of Nanapush most keenly, that a great explosion occurred, a rip of sound. A vicious cloud of stink sent mourners gasping for air. As soon as the fresh winter cold had rolled into the house, however, everyone returned. Nanapush sat straight up, still wrapped in Margaret's best quilt.

"I just couldn't hold it in anymore," he said, embarrassed to find such an assembly of people around him. He proceeded, then, to drink a cup of the mourners' wine. He was unwrapped. He stretched his arms. The wine made him voluble.

"Friends," he said, "how it fills my heart to see you here. I did, indeed, visit the spirit world and there I saw my former wives, now married to other men. Quill was there, and is now making me a pair of *makizinan* beaded on the soles, to wear when I travel there for good. Friends, do not fear. On the other side of life there is plenty of food and no government agents."

Nanapush then rose from the bed and walked among the people tendering greetings and messages from their dead loved ones. At last, however, he came to Margaret, who sat in the corner frozen in shock at her husband's resurrection. "Oh, how I missed my old lady!" he cried and opened his arms to her. But just as she started forward, eager at his forgiveness, he remembered the beans, dropped his arms, and stepped back.

"No matter how I love you," he said then, "I would rather go to the spirit world than stay here and eat your cooking!"

With that, he sank to the floor quite cold and lifeless again. He was carried to the bed and wrapped in the quilt once more, but his body was closely watched for signs of revival. Nobody yet quite believed that he was gone, and it took some time—in fact, they feasted far into the night—before everyone, including poor Margaret, addled now with additional rage and shame, felt certain that he was gone. Of course, just as everyone had accepted the reality of his demise, Nanapush again jerked upright and his eyes flipped open.

"Oh, yai!" exclaimed one of the old ladies. "He lives yet!"

And although everyone well hid their irritation, it was inevitable that there were some who were impatient. "If you're dead, stay dead," someone muttered. Nobody was so heartless as to express this feeling straight out. There was just a slow but certain drifting away of people from the house and it wasn't long, indeed, before even Father Damien had left. He was thrilled to have his old friend back, but in his tactful way intuited that Margaret and Nanapush had much to mend between them and needed to be alone to do it.

Once everyone was gone, Nanapush went over to the door and put the bar down. Then he turned to his wife and spoke before she could say a word.

"I returned for one reason only, my wife. When I was gone and far away, I felt how you tried to revive me with the heat of your body. I was happy you tried to do that—my heart was full. This time when I left with harsh words on my lips about your cooking, I got a ways down the road leading to the spirit world and I just couldn't go any farther, my dear woman, because I had wronged you. I wanted to make things smooth between us. I came back to love you good."

And, between the confusion and the grief, the exhaustion and the bewilderment, Margaret hadn't the wit to do anything but go to her husband and allow all the hidden sweetness of her nature to join the fire he kindled, so that they spent together, in her spring bed, the finest and most elegantly accomplished hours that perhaps lovers ever spent on earth. And when it was over they both fell asleep, and although only Margaret woke up, her heart was at peace.

Margaret would not have Nanapush buried in the ground, but high in a tree, the old way, as Ojibweg did before the priests came. A year later, his bones and the tattered quilt were put into a box and set under a grave house just at the edge of her yard. The grave house was well built, carefully painted a spanking white, and had a small window with a shelf where Margaret always left food. Sometimes she left Nanapush a plate of ill-cooked beans because she missed his complaints, but more often she cooked his favorites, seasoned his meat with maple syrup, pampered and pitied him the way she hadn't dared in life for fear he'd get the better of her, though she wondered why that had ever mattered, now, without him in the simple quiet of her endless life.

EVE SWEETSER

Gretel in Berkeley

Eve Eliot Sweetser was raised in Minneapolis, studied Linguistics at Harvard and Berkeley, and Celtic Studies at the Université de Haute Bretagne. She is currently a faculty member in the Linguistics Department of the University of California at Berkeley, where she also teaches in the Celtic Studies Program and the Cognitive Science Program. Sweetser has published and taught on various subjects, including metaphor, cognitive approaches to syntax and semantics, and early medieval Welsh poetry. She and her husband Alex live in Berkeley with their fourteen-pound tiger cat.

In the following poem, "Gretel in Berkeley," Sweetser has updated themes from "Hansel and Gretel" and the myth of Ariadne to create a powerful meditation on the nature of memory. It was first published in the Spring 2000 issue of The Thinker: The Journal of Cognitive Science at UC-Berkeley.

—*T. W.*

The crumb trail is gone
food for the birds of time
and there is no return
to childhood—we have come
too far. From mothers' arms
to stepmothers and slaps
to witches' ovens, and then home
another way, to places not the same.

Where do they come from, then,
these paperclips?
Who dropped them one by one
along the sidewalk?
How can I
pick up these shiny frail
signposts for homeward travel—
following their trail
would I retrace whose steps
to what long-dusty backfiled memory?

I need no track
to lead me to the paper forest now.
For you
I'll let them lie.

But fellow-tracemaker,
do not rely
on scavenger-prey or gravel.
Old photos, pencil-ends, and all the Library
of links to Other Places—
beware their Janus faces.
These strewings cannot tell—
no toes or heels—which way
to home, or to the cookie house?—
they do not say.
What clues have we
but our own and each other's memory?
When visible paths
are only yarns unraveled,
set by one of us Gretels as a key
for clingers to her labyrinthine past,
where do we go for futures, at the last?

CHARLES DE LINT

Granny Weather

Charles de Lint is one of the leading writers of what some critics call "urban fantasy fiction," but which (since it's not entirely urban) can be more accurately described as modern mythic fiction. He is the author of numerous magical novels and three short story collections to date, many of them set in the common terrain of an imaginary city called Newford: Memory and Dream, Trader, Someplace to Be Flying, Dreams Underfoot, The Ivory and the Horn, *etc. His most recent works are* Triskell Tales *and* The Onion Girl *(forthcoming). In addition to writing, de Lint is a musician specializing in Celtic music, a folklorist, and a book reviewer. He lives in Ottawa, Ontario, with his wife, the artist MaryAnn Harris.*

"Granny Weather" is a brand-new Newford story, chock full of classic folklore motifs. It's another tale about Sophie Etoile (from "The Moon Is Drowning While I Sleep"), a painter with the ability to enter a mystical spirit world through the medium of dreams. The story first appeared in Imagination Fully Dilated, Volume II, *edited by Elizabeth Engstrom (IFD Publishing, Oregon)—a collection of original tales inspired by the surreal art of Alan M. Clark.*

—T. W.

My friend Jilly and I have this ongoing argument. She says there's magic, right here in this world. With all you've experienced, she asks, how can you pretend otherwise? I'm not the only one who knows you have faerie blood, Sophie, or that the Moon is your mother.

But I tell her there's a big difference between this world and the once upon a time of my dreamlands. Anything can happen in a dream. What you bring back isn't magic, it's experience, and they're not the same thing at all.

It's the last thing I expect, a bogle sitting on the end of my bed, bringing the smell of stagnant water and rotting logs into my room. He's naked, like they usually are in the swamps where I've seen them before, and ugly as phlegm. Gangly limbs, fingers and toes each with an extra joint, and he's hairless, skin black and slick as motor oil. The eyes are too big for the triangular head,

Halloween-slit eyes glowing just like there's a hot fire burning behind them. The nose lies flat against his face, like that of a pug dog, and the mouth has way too many pointed teeth in it.

I thought I was going to sleep. I guess maybe I am asleep and this time the dreamlands have taken me back into my own bedroom where this little nightmare is waiting for me. For some reason I don't feel as scared as I know I should be, though that doesn't stop me from checking out the shadows in the corners of my room to see how many little friends the bogle might have brought with him. He seems to be alone, so now I start looking for something to hit him with if he gets out of line.

"Sophie."

There's something in the sibilant tone of his voice that jumps my gaze back to him. Not innocence—these things wouldn't know innocence if it jumped up and bit them—but a sense that, whatever he's doing here, he doesn't mean me any harm. So I decide to hear him out, though I'm not saying I actually trust him. Quicks and haunts and bogles. You can't trust any of the little monsters.

"What's your name?" I ask.

I sit up, pulling the bedclothes along with me as I do. I'm wearing an oversize T-shirt as a nightie, but it doesn't feel like enough on its own. The hot coals of his gaze make me feel like I'm wearing nothing at all.

"You can call me Serth," he says after a moment's hesitation.

Not his name, I assume, but it's all I'm going to get so it'll have to do.

"So what do you want, Serth?"

"There's trouble in the fens," he tells me.

"What's that got to do with me?"

"You helped Granny Weather when we tried to drown the moon," he says.

I give a reluctant nod. It seems a long time ago, in another life.

"Now we need your help to stop her," he says.

I can't imagine a less likely scenario and tell him so.

His eyes blaze. "Even if I tell you that she's eating our children?"

And that would be bad, how? I think. Gross, certainly, but bad? Less bogle children means less bogle adults leading the unwary into the fens and drowning them.

I don't say anything, but he can read it in my face.

"Every time she eats one of us," he says, "a piece of the night goes away."

"And why is this my problem?"

"Without night, there's no day." He holds up a hand to stop me from interrupting. "Time will come to a halt."

"And?"

He glares at me. "Our world will dissolve. And once it does, the sickness will move on, spreading across the dreamlands. Eventually, even into your precious Mabon. And let me tell you, the more worlds that fall, the harder the sickness will be to defeat."

I shake my head. "Why are you coming to me? There are hundreds of you . . ." I bite my tongue before saying "little monsters." I pretend I had to clear my throat. "You people," I finish.

"You're the only one she trusts."

"And what makes that useful?" I ask.

"You can get close to her and slip a knife in between her ribs before she even suspects you mean her ill."

Somehow I doubt that, Granny Weather being who and what she is. But I've no interest in finding out anyhow.

"It's not going to happen," I tell him.

He nods. "We'll see what song you sing when the death she wakes comes creeping down Mabon's streets."

"Oh, please," I say. "This whole thing sounds like some stupid comic book."

He looks like one, too. Not the kind I grew up with—*Archie, Little Lulu*—but the kind they make nowadays where the heroes are dark and creepy and you can't tell them from the bad guys.

He glares at me. "You'll see," he says.

And then he's gone.

I'm not sure if I blinked, or woke up, but I'm alone in my room now and I appear to be awake. No bogles, though the smell of him seems to linger the way bad smells do.

I let the bedclothes fall and sit up straighter. I owe Granny Weather too much to ever think of betraying her, but I suppose I'll have to go talk to her now.

This is how it works.

I go to sleep and the next thing I know, I'm in the dreamlands. I'm still asleep, here in my apartment, my body stretched out in bed or curled up on the old sofa out on my balcony, but I'm somewhere else at the same time, transported to a place that feels just as physical and real. I've been doing it for years. It started out as daydreaming when I was a kid, then I forgot about it for the longest time until I got pulled into a dream that wouldn't let me go. After that . . . well, I don't know what made the difference, but now I go there every night, to Mabon, to the dreamlands.

Christy calls it serial dreaming, where every time you fall asleep you pick up where you left off in last night's dream, but it's more than that. What, exactly, I have no idea. I'm so used to it, I don't even think it's strange anymore. Even my friends accept it as a matter of course, which maybe tells you more about them than me.

It's funny, but Jilly, who's never even been here, has the best name for where I go. She calls it the cathedral world, because everything feels taller and bigger and brighter here. It's not that it is, only that it feels that way. It's like there's a singing inside you—in your chest, your head, your heart—and it fills you up like nothing else ever has. Only being in love comes close.

So anyway, Mabon's easy for me to reach—I kind of founded the city, though a lot of other people's dreams have built it up since—but the fairy-tale world where Granny Weather and the bogles live, that's a whole other thing. I've never gone there on my own. Granny Weather's the one who first brought me there, when she showed me how to defeat the bogles and rescue the moon.

Granny Weather. She's wizened and small, shoulders hunched over and everything about her seems dry as kindling: fingers, hair, limbs. You think she's so helpless until you look into her eyes. There you find all the mysteries of the world lying thick and dark and you realize she's much more than what she seems to be. Powerful and earthy. Formidable. The proverbial goodwife, living in her cottage, deep in an enchanted forest.

Could she be eating bogle babies? The thought brings the taste of bile to my throat. I can't imagine it. But I suppose anything's possible and if she really has taken on the role of the wicked witch in some bogle version of "Hansel and Gretel," then she must have a good reason for it. More likely, the bogle who came into my bedroom was lying. I'll only find out the truth by asking her.

At least I know a way to get to her cottage. My boyfriend Jeck originally came from that same fairy-tale world. Oh, I know what you're thinking. How pathetic can it be when your boyfriend only exists in the dreamlands. But it works for us. It's complicated, but it works.

"This is not a good idea," Jeck says. "The fens are dangerous."

We're slouched at an outdoor table in front of Johnny Brews, the coffee shop that's just down the block from the apartment we share in Mabon. Jeck's looking drop-dead gorgeous as usual, my handsome boyfriend that I can only be with in dreamland. His eyes are like no one else's I know, deep violet with long moody lashes, and his hair is as iridescent and black as a crow's wing. I reach out and brush the cowlick back from his brow.

"I know," I tell him. "And this whole business doesn't make much sense either. What makes them think I'd help them hurt Granny Weather? And that stupid story about her eating bogle babies . . ."

He gets a bit of a funny look, then.

"What?" I say. "What?"

"Maybe you don't know her as well as you think you do."

"I don't really know her at all. I only met her that one time."

He nods.

"You're not telling me she *does* eat bogle babies?"

"I just don't think it's a good idea to get involved," Jeck says.

"Except the bogle said it could affect everywhere—all the dreamlands."

Jeck sighs. "Bogles are also liars."

This was certainly true.

"And besides," he adds, "What does playing the hero ever get a person?"

"It got me you."

"Ah . . ."

And then he doesn't know what to say.

"So will you take me?" I ask. "Or at least show me the way?"

"That was never in question," he tells me.

The trick to magic is that it lies in between. In between what? It almost doesn't matter. It just has to be in between. Not blue or yellow, but green. Not sun or moon, but the light of dusk. Not river or land, but the bridge that spans the water.

So after we pay for our coffees, Jeck takes me by the hand and leads me into the alleyway that runs alongside of Johnny Brews—a narrow little lane with brick buildings rising tall on either side. A place between, you see. You can find them anywhere.

I don't notice exactly how he calls the travelling magic up, but one moment we're walking with cobblestones underfoot and the next there's damp dirt. The smell of the fens rises up around us and the city is gone. Still in the dreamlands, I know, but true dreaming's not as arbitrary as the regular kind. It takes intent and a strong will to readily move from one world to another.

Which is another way of saying, it takes magic.

We've arrived on higher ground in a grove of gnarled crack willows, boughs reaching up for the night stars, the fens around us. The grove lies about halfway between Granny Weather's cottage and the bogles' nest deep in the swamp, a lonely place. I turn to Jeck, but before I can speak, a heavy rope net drops from the boughs above and knocks us both to the ground. I can hear sibilant snickering as we try to untangle ourselves. The effort's wasted as our captors pull the net in tight, pinning us against each other, our limbs trapped between our bodies.

They're bogles, of course. Dozens of the ugly little monsters. I stare up at them from where we lie on the ground, wondering if my night visitor Serth is among them, but it's impossible to tell, they all look too much alike. Then it no longer matters. Three men, each of whom could be Jeck's twin brother, come stepping out from under the drooping boughs of the willows. I can't tell them apart, except that one of them has a small bone hanging from a thong around his neck.

The men look down at us with their dark gazes and I glance at Jeck, note the tight line of his lips. There's no love lost here, that's for sure.

"Bring them along," one of the men says.

The three of them move off. A half-dozen bogles hoist us up in the net and then, willy-nilly, we're following along behind.

I've got a hundred questions for Jeck, but now's not the time for any of them.

I never knew the bogles had actual habitations. I always pictured them living in the wet mud like newts or water snakes. And maybe most of them do, but this bunch has an old stone round tower that's half falling in on itself, perched up on a vague island of higher ground. Or maybe it belongs to Jeck's nasty kin.

See, he's related to the three men who look so much like him. They're crows, but they're also men—though nothing like the crows and ravens that Jilly likes to talk about.

"We're only blackbirds in that other world," Jeck told me once after he'd moved to Mabon. "The enchantment that lets us shift shape wasn't born in our bones and blood; it lies in the air of that otherworld. We breathe it in and we can change, but we're not even remotely related to the corbæ in your friend's stories."

That's true enough. There's nothing whimsical or charming about these brothers of his; they're just mean. I know, because I've met them before, when they were trying to drown the moon.

There's seven of them all told, including Jeck, but he's the youngest, which meant right from the start there were big things in store for him, this being a fairy-tale world and he being the seventh son and all. But he wasn't having any part of it—chucked it all and came to live in Mabon instead. Maybe that's why his brothers hate him. But while I don't really know why they've got it in for him—Jeck doesn't talk much about his family—it's not hard to figure out why they don't like me. I'm the one who rescued the moon from the watery grave that they and the bogles had prepared for her.

Even half-fallen down, the tower looms above us, old stone, water stained and overhung with vines and moss. At another time, I'd love to be here. I love old places like this. Unlike Jilly, who can call up an unfeigned interest in pretty much any place, I'm drawn primarily to these sorts of structures, buildings steeped in history. Doesn't have to be big, important bits of history; just the sense that hundreds of lives have touched a place down through the years.

The bogles take us down into the tower's basement—which is less than pleasant with its slimy stones and damp, cold air—and dump us unceremoniously on the floor. The place reeks of wet straw and old urine and my skin crawls at the thought of lying here in a bogles' toilet. It takes us a few minutes to work free from the snarls of the net, but by then this huge warped wooden door has closed us in and we hear a crossbar drop into place on the other side. A barred window set high in the wall lets in a little light, but it's not particularly comforting and the bars are too narrow for even a bird-shaped Jeck to slip through. Once we finally get the net off, we have a chance to look around a little more and realize we're not alone.

Granny Weather sits there in a corner of the room, shaking her head at the bedraggled pair we make.

"How did they trap you?" she asks. "I didn't think they'd be able to bring you back into our world against your will."

"Actually," I tell her, tugging a hand through my hair to remove bits of straw, "we found our own way."

"Whatever for?"

"They thought I might kill you for them."

It pops out of my mouth before I even realize it's going to, but Granny Weather only laughs.

"And what made you decide not to?" she asks. "You *did* decide not to, I assume."

She still looks amused, but a sudden dark light in her eyes makes me nod quickly. I tell her about Serth's unwelcome visit.

"The best lies hold a breath of the truth," she says when I'm done.

"You mean you *are* eating their babies?"

"Hardly. But an infant bogle is still an innocent, born to the dark or not, and the death of any innocent diminishes the world."

"So who is eating their babies?" I ask.

She shakes her head in exasperation. "No one. They would have told you anything to bring you across."

"I don't buy that," I say. "I can't think of a lamer reason to get me here. I've never hurt anybody in my life. Why would I start with you?"

"But it was enough to make you feel you needed to speak to me," she says.

"That's true."

"What they really wanted was for that one to bring you," she adds, pointing her chin at Jeck.

There's not much love lost between them either, though it's more on her side than Jeck's. She's never trusted him and doesn't think I should, but I don't judge anybody by their family.

He gives her a steady look. "I grew up on stories of you," is all he says.

"Yes, yes. The wicked witch in the wood. How original."

He shrugs. "If I shouldn't believe those stories, why can't you trust me?"

"Because . . ." Her voice trails off. "Because of habit," she says finally. "You're right. I can be as guilty of misjudgment as any."

"Well, I hate to break up this Hallmark moment," I say, "but don't you think we should be thinking about a way to get out of here? And what do they want with us anyway?"

"Not us," Granny Weather says and points to Jeck again. "But him. The heart of a seventh son—particularly one such as Jeck, who is the seventh son of a seventh son—is a potent ingredient for any number of spells. My guess is they plan to grind it up and feed it to the crack willow by Coffin Rock, to give it mobility and make it their brother." She shook her head. "Imagine that evil old spirit given a blackbird's wings and set loose upon the world. Bogles would be the least of our worries."

I don't even want to think about how they'll get the heart to grind it up in the first place.

I look at Jeck. "They'd do that?" I ask. "They'd cut out your heart?"

He shrugs. "We're related by blood," he says. "Not temperament. They've always had large ambitions and need a powerful ally to achieve them. When they failed to give the old willow the lightblood of a drowned moon, they would have had to look elsewhere for a gift." He placed the palm of his hand against his chest. "I can see how giving it my heart would amuse them."

I turn back to Granny Weather. "But why are we here?"

"I, because I could stop them," she says. "If they hadn't caught me off-guard and separated me from my cronebone, we wouldn't even be having this conversation. The fens would be choked with the bodies of dead bogles and blackbird brothers." She gives me a wicked grin. "I never could abide the either of them."

I was wondering how she came to be stuck here in the bogles' toilet with us.

"And you're here," she adds, "because their brother would never have returned if it hadn't been for you."

She said something along those lines a few moments ago, but it didn't really register the way it does now.

"Is this true?" I ask Jeck. "You're only here because of me?"

I get another shrug in response and feel just awful. It never even occurred to me that I was putting him in danger.

"At least escaping isn't a problem for you," Granny Weather says. "All you have to do is wake up."

I hadn't thought of that. I suppose I could have done it the moment the net dropped onto us.

I shake my head. "I'm not leaving either of you behind."

"But you must," she says. And then she tells me why.

I wake up in my bedroom and nothing feels right. It's not hard to figure out why. I'm safe, escaped from the dreamlands, while my boyfriend's lying in a bogle toilet with Granny Weather, waiting for his brothers to cut out his heart.

Then I realize that we never discussed how I'll get back to the fairy-tale world once I've collected the things that Granny Weather told me I needed to bring. And how am I even supposed to bring all that stuff over with me? When I enter the dreamlands, most of the time I can choose what I'm wearing, but I can't bring objects with me. I've tried, but unless I can imagine it in my pocket, it doesn't cross over with me. Knapsacks and purses don't work either, and this stuff Granny Weather wants me to get sure won't fit in a pocket.

So I've already screwed up, I think, until I realize that I can at least gather the objects in Mabon. That'll bring me part of the way, already into the dreamlands. And if I can't find a way over to the fairy-tale world on my own, I might be able to find someone else who can show me.

I go back to my bed and lie down again. It's already getting light outside my window and I can hear the morning traffic starting up, along with a chorus of rowdy birdsong, but I've gotten good at dropping off to sleep whenever I need to.

I wake up in Jeck's and my apartment in Mabon, already dressed for business: jeans, long-sleeved jersey, canvas jacket, sturdy walking shoes. The only concession to practicality is my digital wristwatch. I can't wear them outside of the dreamlands because when they don't stop entirely working, they tend to simply flash a random time. It's like my real-world curse. Ordinary wrist watches run backwards and all sorts of mechanical and electrical things don't work properly when I'm around. I can still remember the look on Christy's face when I tried to use his computer and crashed the harddrive just by switching it on.

I don't waste time in the apartment. Its emptiness simply drives home the fact that for every moment I'm here, Jeck's that much closer to having his heart cut out of his chest.

My first stop is the Catholic church down the street. I'm not Catholic, and I'm not even sure how much I believe in God, but when I follow Granny Weather's instructions and steal one of the votive candles—sneaking it out of the church while it's still lit, and don't think that's easy until you've tried it— the nape of my neck prickles and I know I'm waiting for lightning to strike me down dead. But it doesn't happen. Maybe the candle I bought and left in the stolen one's place evened things out in the eyes of the angels. Maybe nobody up there was paying attention.

Once outside, I blow the candle out and stow it in the pocket of my jacket, sucking at my finger where the hot wax gave me a bit of a burn.

From there I go to Kerry's Cauldron, a herb and witchery shop just down the street from Mr. Truepenny's. Kerry herself is at the counter. She's a tall, dark-haired woman, given to wearing Gypsy outfits—the Romantic kind you see in movies: low-cut white blouse, flower-print skirt, hair pushed up under a red kerchief. I've met her before, but I've never been inside her shop. It's got a wonderful smell, earthy and herby, with a touch of something feral, like a mix of deep forest loam and wild roses. Everywhere I look there are shelves of small bottles with handwritten labels, the dark glass hiding mysterious powders, dried herbs and other less identifiable things.

Kerry and I exchange pleasantries, then she asks me what I need.

"Do you, um, carry mouse hair?" I ask.

She nods. "Do you want a full pelt, a whole dried mouse, or just the loose hairs?"

I didn't expect there to be choices.

"Just the hair," I say. "I only need enough to roll into a small ball to put inside a loaf of bread."

She nods again. "Of course. You're making gifting bread."

"I guess I am."

"That's a very old recipe for favors. You don't hear much about them anymore, but I suppose that's because they don't work for everyone."

"They don't?"

My heart sinks.

Kerry shakes her head. "Not unless you're an adept or have faerie blood. So you'll be okay."

Jilly started this whole business about me having faerie blood and she's never even been to Mabon, but everybody here seems to think the same thing. I've given up arguing about it.

"Have you considered what good memory you'll offer up to the spirit of the loaf when you bake it?" she asks. "It's always good to think about that kind of thing in advance so that you don't get all rushed at the end and give away something you'll regret later."

Granny Weather had said something about keeping pleasant memories in my head while I was baking the bread, a different one for each loaf, but she didn't say why.

"What do you mean give away?" I ask.

"You don't get it back," she says. "Didn't you know that?"

I shake my head. "You really know all about this kind of thing, don't you?"

"Well, it *is* my business."

Duh.

"Don't mind me," I tell her. "I left my brain in my other jacket."

She smiles. "Do you need anything else?"

I name the other item on my list, kernels of dried Indian corn and she saves me the trip to the feed store by pulling a jar of them up from under the glass-topped display counter that stands between us. While she's packaging my order, I ask her if she knows Granny Weather.

"I'm afraid not. She sounds like an old goodwife. They all had names like that in the old days—to keep their true names private. Nowadays we just use our own, since the old naming magics have pretty much fallen by the wayside."

"So when you say goodwife," I ask, "you mean she's okay."

She turns from the table where she's measuring out my mouse hairs to give me a blank look.

"I mean, she wouldn't be a bad person," I say.

"No," Kerry tells me. "I mean like how we refer to the little people as the good neighbors as a sign of respect so that we don't get on their bad side." She pauses a moment, then adds, "Are you baking for this Granny Weather?"

I nod.

"Well, make sure you follow her instructions exactly," she says. "You don't want to annoy a goodwife."

I remember Granny Weather's bloodthirsty comment on what she'd do to the bogles and Jeck's brothers, and find myself wishing I'd let well enough alone when the bogle first showed up in my bedroom. I should have listened to Jeck. Because if I screw this up . . .

"But I'm sure you'll do fine," Kerry says as she deposits two small paper bags on the counter. "After all you—"

"Have faerie blood," I say, finishing it for her.

She smiles. "Exactly."

I wish I was as confident.

I pay for my purchases. "One last question," I say before I leave. "Do you have any tips on travelling between the dreamlands?"

"Be very clear about where it is you want to go," she says, "or you could end up anywhere."

That wasn't quite what I was hoping for.

"I was thinking more *how* to do it," I tell her.

She turns away and rummages in one of the drawers that line the wall beside her worktable. When she returns to the front counter, she places a piece of twine with a knot in it on the glass.

"Find a place in between," she says. "Do you know what I mean by that?"

I nod.

"Once you're there, keep your destination clearly in mind and untie the knot. I'm afraid it's only a one-way travelling knot. Return ones are very hard to find and much more expensive."

"That's okay," I tell her as I pay for it. "I've got somebody there to bring me back."

If we survive. If I don't screw up Granny Weather's preparations. If, if, if. I hate fairy-tale dreams.

Once I have the first loaf ready to go in the oven, I find myself stalling. What memory do I want to lose? None, of course. The better question would be, which one am I willing to lose?

I know now that it's got to be a good one. Something of significance—to me at least—or it wouldn't be a sacrifice. That's the trouble with this sort of magic, you always have to pay for it and what you pay is never something normal like putting down a few dollars and change in a store.

I stare out the kitchen window. It looks out over the backyard and from my second-floor vantage I can see almost all the way down the block, a narrow quilt of backyards. A big orange cat is crying outside of Mrs. Rowling's back door, trying to scrounge a meal. Mr. Potter is weeding his garden again—like a weed would dare make an appearance among his flowers and vegetables.

Sighing, I look back at the little piece of paper on the table in front of me. I write down on it:

The first time I sold a painting.

Then I get up and put the loaf in the oven. I think about that day, how amazing it was. I got a hundred dollars and I felt like a millionaire. Not so much because of the money, I suppose, as that it validated this crazy idea of making my living as an artist.

I start to feel a little nauseous and I sniff at the air, figuring it's the ball of mouse hair, hidden away inside the dough, but all I can smell is baking bread.

The queasiness won't go away until finally the timer on the stove goes off. I pull the baking pan out and all I've got is a black lump of a burnt loaf to show for my efforts.

I check the time in case I somehow lost track, but only an hour has passed—not nearly enough time to reduce the loaf to this. And how come I didn't even smell it burning?

Not a powerful enough memory, I decide.

After another trip to Kerry's Cauldron for more mouse hair, I try it again.

Think of something good, I tell myself. Jeck's life is at stake here.

Jeck.

I hesitate for a long moment, then write down on the paper:

The first time Jeck and I made love.

I hate this.

But then it gets worse. Where the first time I felt a little queasy, this time a stomach cramp knocks me off my chair. One moment I'm reveling in the memory of that day in the barn, the smell of the hay, that first touch, our breath mingling, the amazing intimacy I'm finding in this handsome stranger that Jeck is at the time, and the next I'm lying curled up on the floor in a fetal position ready to die, alternately burning and freezing from hot and cold flashes. In moments I'm drenched in sweat, my pulse drumming so fast I feel like my heart's going to pop out of my chest.

I feel like I'm going to faint, but that would be too easy, I guess. Instead I spend an eternity wracked with pain. When the cramps finally fade enough so that I can sit up, it's to find that it's only been ten minutes or so. I get to my feet on wobbly legs, wait for the spinning to subside, then stagger into the living room where I collapse on the couch. Drifting in and out of a daze, I almost don't hear the timer when it goes off.

The loaf is perfect and smells like heaven, never mind that there's a ball of wadded up mouse hair in the middle of it. I set it down on the counter to cool, then look at the paper I'd written my memory prompter on. I guess I was expecting to come up blank when I read the line, but the memory's still there. It just has no life left in it. All I have in my head is the plain fact of the first time Jeck and I made love, no more detailed than what I'd written down.

Well, this sucked. And I still have two more loaves to go. But then I think of Jeck and Granny Weather and put the next loaf in the oven, the one with a ball of wax from the votive candle in it.

The memory I lose this time is of that mad night that Jilly and I bonded, becoming more sisters than friends. And the cramps take me down again. If anything, they're worse than the first attack.

It takes me a long time before I can summon up the courage to put the final loaf in, the one with dried corn kernels in the center. I lose the last time I saw my dad alive. I didn't even mean to, it just popped into my head and then the cramps came and it was too late to get it back.

I end up lying on the floor of the kitchen for the full hour it takes the loaf to bake. I'm so weak when the timer goes off that I can barely get up to take the bread out of the oven. The only thing that gets me on my feet is the thought of having to go through this another time.

————

I have to sit for a couple of hours before I can do anything else. I drink some tea and nibble on soda crackers to settle my stomach, then finally pack away the loaves, what's left of the candle and some matches in a knapsack. I sling the knapsack over my shoulder and stand in the doorway between the kitchen and the living room, which is about as between as I have the energy to do. There I undo the travelling knot, careful to keep my destination clear in my mind.

I expect some new bout of cramps or sickness, but all that happens is that I end up in the middle of the herb garden that lies on the other side of the path separating the fens from Granny Weather's cottage. It's dusk, the sun just setting.

"There's spiders in that garden," she told me before I left the bogles' tower, "and their webs will keep you safe from the likes of little nightmares. Make your way there to work the spell."

Luckily, I'm not afraid of spiders.

I stay in the middle of the cobwebby garden and put the knapsack on the dirt at my feet.

Work the spell.

I'm less than happy with this whole witchy business of Granny Weather's, but there's no turning back now. If I don't go on, Jeck will die and everything I've already been through today will have been for nothing. It's not like he can wake up and be safe back home. Though sometimes I wonder about the people I meet here in the dreamlands. Do they really originate here, or are they asleep and dreaming someplace else themselves? If Jeck is, he has no memory of it, but I know I can't take that as gospel or anything. Lots of people don't know they're dreaming when they are.

I take out the candle and light it. It takes me a moment to remember which loaf goes first. The mouse hair one. I take it out of the knapsack and hold it up in both hands, facing west.

"Come," I say, repeating the words that Granny Weather told me to use. "You of the wind. I have a gift for you."

I say it three times, always facing west, but the last time, I kneel in the dirt. I don't know what to expect, who or what will come. Maybe nothing. Maybe I already screwed up. Didn't bake the loaf right. Used too many mouse hairs. Or not enough. Didn't say the words right.

Then I hear it, the slow flap of wings. It comes from the west, borne on the last rays of the setting sun, an enormous owl. When it lands on the ground in front of me, I place the loaf by its talons.

"Is this gift freely given?" a voice says.

I'm not sure if I actually hear the owl speak, or if its words are simply forming in my mind. I look at the loaf and I think of what I had to go through to bake it. It wasn't without cost to make, I think, but I suppose it is being freely given, so I nod.

The owl eats the bread far more quickly than I would have thought possible.

"I would return your kind gift with a favor," it says, those big round eyes settling their gaze on me.

I clear my throat. "Um. Granny Weather would like to get her cronebone back."

I have no idea what this is, and Granny Weather wasn't particularly forthcoming when I asked, but the owl seems to know exactly what I'm talking about.

"It shall be done."

And then it's gone, those enormous wings lifting it up into the air and away, deep into the fens. I listen to the fading whisper of them for a long moment before bringing out the second loaf, the one with the wax ball in it.

This one calls up a cloud of moths, thick as mist. Moths don't eat bread so far as I know, but this is the fairy-tale world, so I suppose anything's possible. The loaf certainly disappears quickly enough. I don't ask them for a favor. Granny Weather told me to simply tell them where their murderers are.

"Moths are spirits of the uneasy dead," she told me when I asked about that. "The ones that will come to you will be the ghosts of all of those that the bogles have led astray and drowned in the fens."

When they fly off in the same direction as the owl, I bring out the last loaf. I wonder what the corn kernels will call up. Mouse for the owl. Candle for the moths. That makes sense. Maybe this'll bring me chickens, I think. I realize I'm getting a little hysterical when that idea sets off a spate of giggling.

I catch my breath and go through the summoning for the third time.

By this point, I'm pretty much used to the unusual, but what shows up is right out of Loony Toons. There's a little outbuilding that stands behind Granny Weather's cottage. I don't know what she uses it for. To keep her wood dry, maybe for storage. I didn't realize it was a pet.

For that's what comes in response to the third summoning, an animated hut, its wooden walls creaking and cracking as the hut shifts back and forth, walking on hen's legs like in the story of Baba Yaga.

"Is this gift freely given?" it asks, like the others did, its high, cartoon voice ringing inside my head.

All I can do is nod.

It stands there, its windows looking like eyes, gaze locked on me. Finally I get up from where I'm kneeling and toss the loaf in through its open door. There's a weird chewing sound, then a small burp. I don't know whether to laugh or run.

"I would return your kind gift with a favor," it tells me.

The voice kills me. The chicken legs are bad enough, but the voice makes me feel like any minute the herbs and vegetables around me are going to pull out of the ground and start up some song and dance routine.

"Granny Weather would like her skycloak," I manage to reply.

"It hangs inside the door of her cottage."

Again there's this long pause. Then I realize that I'm supposed to go fetch the cloak. It's the only piece of clothing hanging there and seems to weigh next to nothing when I take it off the hook. I feel like I'm walking on air as I return to the herb garden, holding the cloak against my chest.

The hut's back on the ground now, like it's just a normal outbuilding. I guess the chicken legs are folded under it, out of sight. I approach its door cautiously and start to toss the cloak inside, but the cartoon voice stops me.

"The cloak should not touch the ground," the hut tells me. "Better that you carry it."

No way, I think. I'm not getting inside that thing. I can still remember the chewing sound after I tossed the loaf of bread in.

"Why do you hesitate?" it asks.

"I have this thing about stepping inside a stranger's mouth," I say.

Cartoon laughter rings in my head. The hut gives a kind of shrug. There's a creak in the wood. A cedar shingle falls off the roof.

"Then Granny Weather will have to do without her skycloak," it says. "She won't be pleased."

I think about what Kerry said about getting on the wrong side of a goodwife's temper, and sigh. Gingerly I step over the threshold. There's nothing inside. Plain wooden boards on the floor, no furnishings except for a ratty old club chair that looks like it was rescued from a dump, lopsided, the stuffing coming out of the sides.

"Sit," the hut tells me.

I don't think so.

But then the hut lurches onto its chicken legs and I go sliding across the room. I only just keep my balance and make it to the chair where I sit with the cloak bundled up on my lap. The chair doesn't move as the hut heads into the fens with a staggering walk, but it feels like my stomach does.

Oddly, I don't get sick.

Well, I tell myself. At least I don't have to find my own way back to the bogles' tower.

There seems to be a heavy mist around the tower as we approach. It's not until we're really close that I see it's not mist but a huge cloud of the white moths. Bogles are running everywhere in a panic, batting at the things with their weird extra-jointed fingers. There's already a carpet of downed moths on the wet ground, but there are so many in the air that it doesn't seem to make much difference. The moths swarm over the bogles, covering every inch of their black, oily skin, suffocating the nasty little buggers. The bogles' only defense is to submerge into the fen water, but as soon as they come up for air, the moths are waiting for them, flying into their pug noses and mouths.

Poetic justice, I guess, considering that the moths are the ghosts of the drowned victims of the bogles.

Jeck's brothers are out in the middle of this strange melée, but the moths don't seem interested in them. The brothers are trying to help the bogles, but they're not having much luck. Then one of them gives a cry. I look, just in time to see the owl drop out of the sky and tear something from around his neck. The owl rises up again, chased by six blackbirds. From its talons dangles what looks like a necklace. A little bone on a leather thong. I remember seeing it before, when they first captured us. Now I realize it must be Granny Weather's cronebone.

The blackbirds are quick, but they're like gnats compared to the owl. It bulls through them, scattering birds in a cloud of black feathers, dropping to a small window in the tower that's just above ground level. The owl slips the necklace through the bars, then flies away to a perch on a nearby tree, its job done, I guess. The blackbirds hover for a long moment. Then, screaming, they take flight.

No sooner do they go, than the tower cracks in two like a walnut, the great sides crashing down into the fens to send up tidal waves of stagnant water in which bob dead and drowning bogles. I see Jeck and Granny Weather, standing in the wreckage, unharmed. Granny Weather has her arms raised above her head, her eyes glittering with an inner fire.

The hut lurches forward until it's standing above the cracked ruin of the tower. Granny Weather's fiery gaze locks with my own.

"Give me the cloak," she says.

I toss it down.

She whips it over her shoulders and a great wind comes shrieking out of nowhere, lifting her into the sky. Seconds later, she's gone, in pursuit of the blackbirds.

I don't wait for the hut to kneel on its chicken legs. I jump down from the doorway. I look back up at my weird mount for a moment and tell it thanks before I run over to Jeck. Holding him, I offer up thanks to the moths and owl as well for the fact that he's still alive. Jeck gives me an odd look. I guess even in this fairy-tale world people don't really talk to walking huts and animals all that much.

By the time we've finished hugging, I realize that the hut's gone. I turn to see that it's almost out of sight, lurching its way back across the fens to Granny Weather's cottage. There are dead bogles everywhere, scattered on the little island and amidst the ruins of the tower, tangled up in the reeds, floating in the water. I look at their faces, wondering if Serth is among them. The white moths are dispersing; the owl's already gone. There's just us and the dead and it's all so horribly depressing.

"Let's go home," I say.

Jeck shakes his head. "Not just yet. We need to see how it ends."

I look at the carnage around us, but I realize he doesn't mean this. He means his brothers. Or maybe what's going to happen to us.

So we start slogging our way back to Granny Weather's cottage.

"What exactly is a cronebone?" I ask him as we push our way through the sedge and weeds. I've already figured out what a skycloak is from how Granny Weather took off into the air once she had it.

He nods. "Among the old goodwives, it was a way to keep their power safe from those who meant them ill. They would cut off a finger or a toe and invest the bone with their magic."

"That's too gross."

"It gets worse," he adds. "The younger they were when they did it, the more powerful the bone became. The story is that Granny Weather was three years old when she cut off her own toe to make hers."

"She did it to herself?"

"They have to do it themselves. But imagine being that young and knowing so clearly what you wanted. And being willing to do such a thing to gain it." He looks at me and picks something out of my hair. A twig. An errant leaf. "That's why you have to be so careful in your dealings with her. She is utterly focused and does nothing unless she can benefit from it."

"But she helped me rescue the moon," I say.

"Yes, but she requires the moon's light for some of her magics." He glances my way again, but his gaze slides away from mine. "I'm just saying to be careful around her and think before you speak."

"What's *that* supposed to mean?"

He gets a pained look and only shakes his head. I get the awful premonition that something really bad is going to happen.

That's another thing I hate about the fairy-tale world. Everything's oblique and anything important can only be approached in riddles. So now I know something's going to happen when we see Granny Weather again, but Jeck can't tell me what, because it's something I have to deal with without coaching or we'll have already lost.

The only thing I can know for sure is that it'll be dangerous.

Granny Weather's waiting for us by her cottage. She's disheveled and there's a wild light in her eyes. Hanging from her belt are six dead blackbirds. I glance at Jeck, but although he seems tense, I don't think it has anything to do with the fate of his brothers.

Think before I speak, he told me. I also know about the old reporter's trick, how if you keep silent the other person will feel obliged to fill that silence with something, but I have a couple of questions that are nagging at me.

"Why did the candle have to be stolen?" I ask.

Granny Weather shrugs. "Unlike the Christ man himself, the churches aren't as free with his magics."

"So the magic had to be stolen?"

She nods. I wonder what she'd think if she knew that I replaced the candle I stole with a new one that I'd paid for. It didn't seem to hurt the magic.

"And the last time I was here," I go on. "Why did you need me to rescue the moon? It seems to me you could have just done it yourself."

"The moon can be a fickle mistress," Granny Weather says. "It needed someone of her own bloodline to pull her free."

So we're back to faerie blood and Jilly's assertion that the moon was really my mother, straying into the waking world long enough to give birth to me before the fairy-tale world called her back again. I remember the face of the moon woman, sleeping there under the fen water. She had my face. But I still don't buy it. Maybe things like that can happen in the dreamlands, but not in the waking world.

"Still, we're not here to talk of old business," Granny Weather says. "I am in your debt for your rescuing of me today, and I always pay my debts. What would you ask of me?"

I feel Jeck stiffen at my side, but I don't need a warning here. I've already been through this the last time, when his brothers promised me anything in exchange for letting the moon drown. The one thing you don't do in the fairy-tale world is serve yourself. There's some moral code underlying the structure of the world, just like there is in fairy tales, and a sure way to get yourself in trouble here is to be greedy.

"Think of it as a gift," I tell her. "Freely given."

There's a long moment of silence.

Granny Weather smiles and I can't tell if she's hiding her annoyance, or if it's that I've managed to earn her respect.

"Don't come back till the next time," she says.

No sooner does she speak the last word, then we're back in our apartment in Mabon once more. The only reminder of where we've been is the stink of the fens that rises from our clothes.

I look at Jeck. "So what just happened?"

"You put yourself on equal terms with her," he said. "Because you asked for nothing in return, she's now duty-bound to leave you and anyone under your protection untouched by her magics."

"And if we hadn't?"

"We'd be hanging from her belt along with my brothers."

"So it was a good thing."

"A very good thing," he says with a smile.

I take his hand. "Come on," I tell him. "We need a long, hot shower."

Jilly loves these stories about the dreamlands. We're sitting on the old sofa out on my balcony, sharing a bottle of wine while I tell her this latest one. The window's open behind us and the nouveau flamenco playing on the stereo inside is drifting out to us. Because Jilly is here, the old mangy stray tom who lives in the alley below has actually come up onto the balcony by way of the fire escape and is letting Jilly pat him. I've been feeding him for months, but though he eats the kibbles I put out for him, we don't actually have a relationship beyond that. But then I'm not Jilly. Strays naturally gravitate to her.

"You're so lucky," she says. "Having these adventures and all."

I don't know if lucky is quite the right word. I wouldn't want to lose Mabon, but my times in the other dreamlands are never comfortable. Even though I can come back any time, simply by waking up, I don't usually remember that when I'm there. The dangers feel too real and I'm always changed when I get back. The experiences linger and become part of who I am, and that's a little disconcerting to say the least when you consider where they've taken place.

"I don't feel lucky," I tell her.

"The loaves," she says, her voice filled with sympathy.

I nod. It's not as though I've simply forgotten something. The absence of those memories are like dark holes that have been bored into my heart and they won't go away. Instead, the more time that passes since I lost them, the more I feel their absence. It's as though the rest of my memories are pulling away from these dark holes, magnifying their presence.

"I try to forget what I've gone and lost," I say, "but that just seems to make me focus on them more. It's like a heartache that gets worse instead of better."

"Then don't," Jilly says. "Don't try to forget them," she adds at my confused look. "They were taken away by magic, right? So use your own magic to deal with the loss."

"How many times do I have to tell you? I don't have faerie blood. There's no magic in me."

She only smiles. "I meant your art."

And then I understand. The art of creating something out of nothing is an act of magic. It's not only something born out of joy and love, but also out of our hurts and sorrows. And while it may not be a cure for the emotions that can assail us, it does allow us to step past the barrage of helpless sensation into other, less numbing, perspectives where it's possible to find a breathing space, and perhaps even some emotional balance.

So I get up and go into my studio, right then and there, leaving Jilly out on the balcony with the cat.

For a long moment I stand in the doorway, taking in the scent of turps and paint, then I step through, soft-soled shoes scuffling on the hardwood floor. I don't even think about what I'm doing as I squeeze paint onto my palette, put a new canvas on my easel, grab a handful of brushes. I start to lay in a loose, unformed background and I get a picture in my head of what I'm painting, a combination of my lost memories, the three of them tangled and interwoven like vines among the thorns and red berries of a hawthorn hedge.

Already, with every stroke of the brush, I can feel my anxieties lose some of their immediacy. The dark holes are still there, but I'm no longer so panicked that I think they're going to swallow me whole.

Jilly's right. It is magic, set free from the dreamlands by our imagination. Any act of creation is, from the fine arts to building a mudpie or a cat's cradle.

And if that's faerie blood, then we've all got its potential somewhere inside us, just waiting for us to call it up. Don't ever let anyone tell you different.

ELLEN STEIBER

The Shape of Things

Ellen Steiber is a writer, folklorist, and editor of children's books. She attended Carnegie Mellon University, worked in the New York publishing industry, and now lives in southern Arizona. She has published many works of fiction for children, teenagers, and adults, as well as nonfiction and poetry. Her books for young readers include The Raven Queen, Unicorn Queen, *and* Shadow of the Fox, *as well as popular mystery and "X-file" novels. Her adult stories have appeared in the* Snow White, Blood Red *anthology series,* Sirens, The Essential Bordertown, *and* The Armless Maiden.

"The Shape of Things" is a powerful coming-of-age fantasy rooted in Guatemalan folklore and shamanism. Reprinted from the April 2000 issue of The Magazine of Fantasy & Science Fiction, *this story is the first of Steiber's to appear in* The Year's Best Fantasy and Horror.

—T. W.

Nonie tells me she's going to die. "I'm going to go out soon," she says. She sounds perfectly casual, like she's telling me she's going to the store.

"You're crazy," I say.

She gives me this sad smile. "I wish. Look, I don't know how it's going to happen. Or when. I just know I'm not going to be here much longer."

Nonie is given to making dramatic pronouncements. Last year she told me that Mrs. Socorro, our tenth-grade English teacher, would pay for her sins. Mrs. Socorro got in a car accident that very weekend. Nonie had nothing to do with it. She was at some religious revival meeting her folks made her go to, but she said she had a feeling. That there was a dark aura—like a black halo—around Socorro's head, and she saw trouble coming.

Nonie can tell certain things like that. She sees things other people don't. Ever since we met, when we were five, we've played this game that Nonie made up. It's called The Shape of Things, and what you do is try to see the shapes hidden inside. Like the first day we had Socorro, she was all smiles, telling us how exciting the English language was, how we were all going to explore it together. After that first class, Nonie asked me what sort of shape I saw inside Mrs. Socorro. I thought about it, and to me she was like a bouquet of fake flowers. All bright colors but nothing real. Nonie said, "She's worse than that. Inside her there's something dark, something that got born out of anger. She keeps it hidden, but you watch—it'll be there in everything she says."

And it was. No one in our class got too excited about the English language, and Mrs. Socorro got mean. Even if she was complimenting you, there'd be this put-down inside whatever she said. It took a while before I realized that whenever I came out of her class, I felt like there was something wrong with me. Like I was dirty. For a long time what I didn't see was that the shape inside her was hatred.

Later, when I heard about Socorro's car accident, I remembered what Nonie said about the black aura around her. And because I'd had too much to drink when I heard the news, it spooked me and I tried to explain all this to my older brother Patrick. But Patrick rolled his eyes and said, "Nonie's just a drama queen with a taste for the Gothic. She couldn't tell you what was inside a cupcake without making it sound dire."

"Well, it is," I pointed out. "All those preservatives and chemicals and stuff. Eat enough cupcakes and you'll get cancer."

"You know what I mean," Patrick said.

So even though Patrick is partly right, and I don't want to encourage Nonie in all this death talk, I'm afraid I might be missing something, so I say to her, "You're not planning to off yourself, are you?"

Last year, three kids from Greenleigh, one of the schools we play in football, made some weird devil pact and then they all drank a lot of beer and shot themselves with their fathers' rifles. A lot of people have guns around here.

"No, of course I'm not going to off myself," she says. "Do I look suicidal to you?"

I look at her. Nonie's pale and skinny, with long, straight brown hair, hazel eyes, and skin that's broken out on her forehead.

"You look the same as always," I tell her.

She gazes around us. We're on the hill behind the high school, where we come to have a cigarette before going home. The hill is actually a mound of brown dirt. It used to have trees on it, but a developer razed it five years ago to put up a shopping center. The developer went bust and left us with this mound of dirt that looks down on the high school and the road into town.

"I'm going to miss this place," Nonie says. "And that's so weird. It never felt like the kind of place anyone would miss."

"Now I know you're losing your mind." I stamp out my cigarette and start down the hill.

"Cam!" she calls after me. That stops me, because Nonie's the type who never calls after anyone. She prefers you call after her. Her mother's made a lifetime career of it, not that Nonie bothers to answer. Nonie considers her mother an inferior life form.

"Okay. I give." I turn around to face her. "What's happening? Are you sick?"

"Not that I know of." She sits downs and wraps her arms around her knees. "I feel like always. School bores the hell out of me and I can't wait to get out, and then I do and everything else bores me, too."

"So . . . you're dying of boredom."

"Well, yeah, but no more than anyone else in this town." She lies down flat on her back and stares up at the sky. It's been windy all day, and the clouds are traveling fast. "What's the shape inside that big silvery one with the jagged edges?"

"A dragon," I say.

"Dragon's teeth, maybe," she agrees. "Something that shreds you." She sits up, and I notice that though she's always been thin, she looks gaunt today, her skin almost transparent. "Cam, I'm going to die. It's not something I want or something I'm planning. All I know is it's going to happen soon. I want to give you my journals," she says. "I don't want my mother to go through them when I'm dead."

That evening Nonie shows up at my house, carrying a cardboard box she can barely lift. I see her struggling with it as she comes up the walk. She has to set it down to ring the doorbell.

By this time I'm downstairs, opening the door. "What *is* that?"

"I told you," she says. "My journals."

She opens the lid and sure enough, the entire box is filled with spiral-bound notebooks. She looks around nervously. "Are you the only one home?"

"Yeah, my folks are at the town meeting, and Patrick's over at Billy Hunter's, taking apart his car." I stare at the box. "You actually filled all these notebooks?"

She grins at me. One of her front teeth is a little longer than the others. It gives her this slightly crooked grin. "Socorro always told me I was wordy. Guess she was right."

I look through the box. On the cover of each notebook Nonie's written her name, the word Journal, and the dates she started and ended her entries. The earliest one goes back to second grade.

"Nonie, if you don't want your mom to read these things, why don't you just burn 'em? That way they'll be safe forever."

She smiles when I say that. "That's a good way to think of it," she tells me.

"What?"

"Death. I'll be safe forever."

All this talk of her imminent demise is starting to creep me out. Partly 'cause she's so sure, partly 'cause she's so calm, and partly 'cause I seem to have a role to play in it.

"You're right," she says. "We should burn 'em." She gives me that loopy grin. "Think your dad will mind if we make a bonfire in your front yard?"

"You know he'd have a cardiac if he came home and saw a fire blazing away on our lawn." My father is a fire fighter. "Besides. . . ." Somehow I can't bear the idea of Nonie being gone and me having burned all her journals.

So we push the box up the stairs, and I'm just grateful I'm the only one home and don't have to explain this to anyone.

Nonie seems satisfied when we get the box under my desk. "Remember," she tells me. "No matter what my mother says, or how pathetic she seems, don't let her see these."

"I won't," I say.

"You've got to swear."

"Nonie, you're scaring me," I tell her.

"Swear it!"

So I swear to keep the journals away from her mom in the event of her death. And I make her promise to take the damn things back if she lives to be seventeen.

For a few weeks nothing calamitous or dramatic happens. Nonie and I go to school, cut as many classes as we can get away with, smoke cigarettes on the hill. She doesn't say anything more about dying, and I'm figuring it's lung cancer that will probably get us both. I also figure we still got some time on that one. I notice, though, that whenever we hang out Nonie starts humming this little tune. It's not something that you hear on the radio or in music videos.

"What is that?" I finally ask. I can't tell if it's familiar to me because I've heard her hum it so many times or because it's something I should recognize. She sings it quiet, but it's got this relentless beat, likes it's pushing something along.

"Don't know," she tells me. "But I started hearing it in my mind right around the time I realized I was going to die. So I figure it's the death song calling me."

"That's it!" I tell her. "You are giving me the willies! I don't want to hear any more about your premonitions or death chants—"

"Death *song*," she corrects me.

"Whatever. I don't want to hear about it."

She takes a last drag on her cigarette and crushes it beneath her boot. "Fair enough," she says. "I won't talk about it anymore. Talking can't change anything anyway. But I figured you knew. I figured you saw the change."

My heart is hammering now, and the hair on the back of my neck is standing straight up. "What change?"

"In my aura," she says. "There always used to be this fine blue light around me. And bit by bit, it's getting darker. Won't be long now before it goes black."

I look at her. She's got her back to the setting sun, so there's kind of a red glow in the sky behind her.

Her voice sounds surprised when she says, "You don't see it, do you?"

I shake my head. "I never could. I don't even know if all these auras you're always seeing are real."

"They're real, all right," she says so soft I can barely hear.

"So this death of yours," I try to keep my voice steady, "do you see a shape for it?" I'm imagining auto accidents, drive-by shootings, fires, movie-of-the-week hospital diseases.

She smiles. "That's the weird thing," she says. "I do. I mean, I have for a while, and it's shaped like a big cat."

That actually calms me down. There aren't any big cats in this part of the state. We don't even have a zoo. I figure for Nonie to get eaten by a big cat, she'd have to hop a plane to Central America.

She kicks at a piece of broken beer bottle on the ground. "I got a secret," she says. "For a few weeks now. Want to hear it?"

I am wondering how I ever wound up with someone who's so completely exasperating for a friend.

"I am not going to pry it out of you," I say. "Tell me if you want, or don't."

Nonie starts to laugh. "I got a boyfriend," she says, "a real, honest-to-goodness boyfriend."

Turns out Nonie's boyfriend is Miguel Alvarez. He transferred into our school late last year. No one really knows him well. Miguel not only keeps to himself, but every few weeks he up and disappears for a day. His homeroom teacher is always giving him lectures on truancy.

Miguel is not the type you'd think would go for someone as quiet as Nonie. Miguel's beautiful. He's got this thick, glossy, straight black hair that he wears down his back. He says he's part Guatemalan, part Apache, part Swedish. The Swedish is a little hard to figure, but Nonie says it accounts for why he's not fucked up about sex.

Nonie and I both did it with boys as soon as we turned sixteen. Mostly to have it done and over with. Sex is not what I'd call a big deal. Nonie's theory is that most guys our age don't really like sex, and they don't even like girls. They just like the rush and they need to be able to brag about it later.

Miguel, she says, is different. She says he's real gentle with her. Never rushes things. Loves being close after. Always makes sure she has as good a time as he does. Which is all a little surprising, considering Miguel's rep. Even the gang members in our school, the ones who carry, keep a careful, respectful distance around Miguel. I always figured he must pack some major heat of his own, but Nonie says it's not about that. It's something inside him, something they know better than to go near.

Nonie calls me up on Saturday morning and asks if I want to go to the quarry with her and Miguel. The quarry is one of the few decent things in this area. Years ago, they cut granite from the earth there. Since then it's filled up with water. Of course, there are signs posted all over, telling you it's private property, no trespassing and definitely no swimming, but it's become the generally acknowledged swimming hole anyway.

So Miguel drives us to the end of the road that leads to the quarry. He's got an old pickup truck and we sit three across the front seat, Nonie wedged in between me and Miguel, and the two of us so close that our bare thighs stick together.

It's the first time I've really hung out with Miguel. And I'm curious about him but also self-conscious. I know it's crazy, but I want Nonie's boyfriend to think I'm okay.

We climb over the padlocked fence and walk down the dirt road a ways until we reach the trail through the woods. I'm carrying a towel and wearing a bathing suit underneath my cut-offs even though it's all of seventy-four degrees out.

The trees suddenly open out onto the quarry. It always takes me by surprise. You're in thick pine trees one minute and the next, you're looking out on a pool of deep glassy water, edged by granite cliff.

"*Paraíso*," Miguel says softly.

I've had enough Spanish to know he means paradise, and while the quarry is about as scenic as things get around here, personally, I would never use that word to describe anything in this town. Besides, last year Bobby Sexton, a senior from our school, drowned in the quarry. The thing is, you're supposed to dive into the water from the highest point on the rock. It's one of those stupid dares that we all go along with, even though everyone knows that if you dive from that point and you don't hit the water just right, you hit granite. That's what happened to Bobby.

Me and Nonie and Miguel find a smooth spot on the rock that's got an oak tree arching over it. Miguel pulls a nubby, plaid blanket from his pack. Nonie stretches out on it, gazing into the branches. She's wearing cut-offs and a white camisole that rides up on her rib cage. I sit beside her, have a cigarette, and watch as Miguel cracks open a beer and carefully lets one drop fall on Nonie's bare stomach.

She doesn't react at all, not even when he licks it from her skin. I'm wondering if this is something I should be watching. But I can see she's completely at ease with him. Like she's known him forever.

Nonie closes her eyes and I open a can of soda. Miguel drinks his beer, one hand resting on her upper arm, his thumb stroking her skin. For a long time no one says anything. I listen to a fly buzzing, study the shadows in the trees, and I think I see something moving in the pines.

Miguel sees it, too. His dark eyes follow the flicker of movement. "It's hunting," he tells me softly.

"What is?"

He answers with a word in Spanish that sounds like charcoal, then says, "Don't worry. It won't come near us. Not now."

He lies down beside Nonie, soaking in the cool sun, one hand cupping her hipbone. He is so still I almost forget he's there. I'm watching Nonie, making sure that her chest continues to rise and fall, hoping that this is just a nap and not a sign of some fatal disease.

And then suddenly I start thinking about Bobby Sexton and I get really scared.

"Nonie," I say loudly. "You can't go in the water."

"Why not?" she asks.

She sits up and rubs tanning oil onto her arms. Her hair is hanging loose, hiding the side of her face.

"Because that's how it's going to happen," I say. "We're all going to dive in there. Only you won't surface. Don't you see?"

Nonie works her hair into a French braid. "I don't think so," she says calmly. "It's too cold for me to swim. That's not how it's going to happen."

"I thought you didn't know how," I say.

"I don't," she tells me. "But I know that's not the shape of it."

"Cam." Miguel's voice is drowsy. "You play this shape game, too?"

I don't answer him. Because Nonie and I have this unspoken pact to never tell anyone else about the game. Except, I realize, obviously she's told Miguel. It makes me feel funny inside. Like something got betrayed.

"Cam," she says. "I didn't tell him. Miguel just knows things."

"The way you just know things?"

She nods. It makes me feel left out, excluded from the Gifted Psychics Club.

"Well, I guess that's why you two get on," I say.

Miguel opens one sleepy eye. "*Loca* girl," he whispers.

I sort of lose it at that point. "Did you tell him?" I demanded. "And does he know that you think you're about to die?"

Miguel gets to his feet and gives me a sympathetic look.

"I'm going in," he says. He walks into the trees, vanishes in their shadows, and reemerges at the high point of the cliff. Quickly, carelessly, he arcs out over the water and enters it in a smooth, perfect dive. I hold my breath for a long moment, praying he'll surface. He does, his black hair clinging to his skin like a pelt. Nonie, her eyes closed again, doesn't watch any of this.

"We made love last night," she tells me as he begins swimming the length of the quarry. "In St. David Cemetery."

"That is so completely macabre—"

"No, it was beautiful—the gravestones were all glowing in the moonlight. And it was comforting. When I first really understood that I was going to die soon, I was so scared. And gradually that's gone away. In the cemetery with Miguel, the last of the fear left me. I felt . . . at home there."

"Well, I feel sick when you talk this way," I tell her. "I hate it! I see you and you start telling me how you won't be here much longer and—" I can't finish because my nose is running and I'm blinking back tears.

Nonie takes my hands in hers. "Listen to me, Cam," she says. "I'm not trying to scare you. I've only been telling you because I want you to know that it's not frightening for me. I want you to be okay about it, too."

"Well, I'm not." My throat is burning and the words come out ragged.

She puts her arms around me and holds me close. "You have to be," she says. "You have to be."

About a week later at three A.M. on Sunday morning, Patrick wakes me up. "The police are downstairs," he says. "They need to ask you about Nonie."

I get up, my heart locked with dread. This is it, I think. She's gone.

And she is. The police are responding to a call from her mother. Nonie went out with Miguel on Friday night. She never came back. In fact, no one can find Miguel either. The police ask me if I think they might have run away together. Or could it be another one of those crazy suicide pacts?

I tell them I don't know. They ask me where I'd look for her. And I see all the places where we used to go together—the park when we were little and mad for the swings, the vintage clothing boutique where we both bought antique silk slips, the hill behind the school. And I know they won't find her in any of those places.

Forty-eight hours later Nonie and Miguel are both officially declared missing. It comes out later that week that everything Miguel gave them was a lie. The address he gave the school was false, along with his phone number. He had no driver's license or insurance, and the state didn't have a record of his truck. His locker at school was empty. It was like Miguel Alvarez was someone we all imagined.

But Nonie . . . Nonie was real and was really gone.

Two weeks later they dragged the quarry. Nothing in the water except an old, rusted Corvette that a drunk college boy drove in there years ago.

So Nonie's mother declared that her "no-good daughter and that Spanish boy" had run away. That one day Nonie would be back, probably pregnant, and then she'd better pray for Jesus and Mary's mercy because her parents weren't going to have anything to do with her.

I was the only one who was certain Nonie was no longer alive. Until they found her body in the woods that led to the quarry. Her neck was torn open. The rest of her body was untouched.

I miss her so much. I've been screwing up in school, fighting with my folks. I keep wanting to talk to Nonie and I can't. It is months before I'm finally able to open the box with Nonie's journals in it. I start with the most recent one. It begins like this:

Today I saw Miguel for the first time. We recognized each other at once. He scared me at first—until I saw the warmth in his eyes. He took my hand, led me outside, said, "You know who I am, don't you?"

I just nodded. My voice was gone. I'd been expecting something. I just never dreamed it would be in the shape of someone as beautiful as Miguel.

"Don't worry, I will make it easy for you, *querida*," he told me. "There is nothing to fear."

We walked up to the hill behind the school and sat down in the place where Cam and I always sit. Then he said,

"In my mother's village, in Guatemala, they know that certain people are born with powers. You already know this for yourself, *querida*. They believe that when we are born into this world, there is also an animal, a *nagual*, born into the underworld, and we share the same spirit with that animal. Some people, the ones with powers—one minute they are human, the next they become their animal spirit. You understand?"

I knew what he was telling me. I said, "You have an animal inside you." I couldn't see the shape of it yet. But I sensed it there, its heart beat matching his, its strength and wariness coursing through his body.

He ran a hand down the side of my face and let me look into his eyes for what seemed a long time. I still couldn't quite see it. So he went on. He said that sometimes the *nagual* is more than *nagual*. It is *characotel*, the one who shifts shape to carry the spirits of the dying to the *Dueño de Muerte*, the God of Death. It is the *suerte*, the fate of the *characotel*, that every twenty days he or she must journey to the *Dueño* and tell him how many people are going to die.

Then he told me this story—

There was a woman characotel, and she married a man who didn't know her true nature. But he soon noticed that she was sick all the time. This was because she wasn't bringing enough spirits to the Dueño *of Death. The characoteles feed on the bones of the dead, and she wasn't getting enough of these bones. She was wasting away. The husband tried to get her to eat, to give her medicines, but she wouldn't take a thing. This made her husband very sad. Finally, a neighbor asked what was wrong; was he fighting with his wife? No, the man answered. His wife was getting weak and thin and she refused to eat with him. That is because she is a* characotel, *the neighbor said. She goes every Wednesday and Friday night to eat bones at the cemetery. You must follow her and you will see for yourself.*

So the husband did as the neighbor advised. He followed the woman at night to the cemetery. And he heard her speaking to the Dueño *of Death.*

The next morning the husband told his wife they were going to eat breakfast together. She refused, and he accused her of being a characotel. *So the characotel turned her husband into a dog. That Friday night the dog followed her to the cemetery. And the wife explained to the* Dueño *of Death that she punished her husband so that he would not tell anyone about her. The* Dueño *said that he would change the dog back into a man, but he warned the man that he would die if he told anyone what he had seen. The man agreed, but he returned home deranged, unable to work or even dress himself. The woman* characotel *soon sickened and died. The* Dueño *took her life because she was not a good worker for him. It was only after the husband told the people of his pueblo the whole story that he was cured.*

"So do you know why I told you that story?" Miguel asked.

I thought, I know why every three weeks you disappear from school . . . every twenty days the *characoteles* report to the *Dueño* of Death. But what I said was something dumb, like, "You're warning me that you'll turn me into a dog if I tell on you?"

And he said, "No. I want you to know that with my kind—it is possible to stop us."

"And then you'll die instead of me," I said.

He shrugged. "I will take my chances with the *Dueño*."

So I took his hands in mine and I looked into his eyes again. They were so dark. From another place, another time. Below us, on the road, I could hear the sounds of the traffic. But in his eyes I saw forests. I could smell the damp earth after a rain. I could hear birds calling, feel lizards scuttling along the leaves. And I could feel him moving through the trees, not as a human but as a *nagual* with the soft, rippling tread of a jaguar.

"No," I told him. "I'm not like that man in the story. I'm not frightened of you."

"*Bueno,*" he said. "Then we will have some time together before I take you."

So I am going to have time with Miguel. . . .

I read more of the journal. And I see how she snuck out of her house nearly every night to be with him. It amazes me that I never knew. I mean, I knew they were lovers. I never guessed at what he truly was. But Nonie saw the shape inside him. And he saw all that was inside her.

Nonie's very last journal entry is a short one:

Miguel says it won't be long now. And that's all right. I'm ready. Eager, even. I worry about Cam, though. I don't know how to take away her fear. But I think that maybe like the husband in Miguel's story if she is able to know the whole truth and then tell it, she will be all right.

So, Cam, if you are reading this, remember: what's inside us can take so many forms, and there is beauty even in the ones that seem most frightening. Know that when I'm gone I'll still be there for you. In certain songs. In the shadows. Whenever you see the shape of things.

—for Tania Yatskievych who gave me the seed of the story,
and Erica Swadley who set it in motion.

RAMSEY CAMPBELL

No Strings

Ramsey Campbell was presented with the World Horror Convention's Grand Master Award and the World Horror Association's Bram Stoker Award for Life Achievement in 1999. His most recent novels are The House on Nazareth Hill, The One Safe Place, Silent Children, and The Pact of the Fathers. He is currently working on The Darkest Part of the Woods. His novel, The Nameless was recently most effectively filmed in Spanish as Los Sin Nombre by Jaume Balaguero. His Web site is: http://www.herebedragons.co.uk/campbell/

According to the author, " 'No Strings' was written in most of a fortnight of August 1998 in an apartment west of Tavronitis in Crete." It was first published in Shadows and Silence, edited by Barbara Roden and Christopher Roden.

—E. D.

G ood night till tomorrow," Phil Linford said, having faded the signature tune of *Linford Till Midnight* up under his voice, "and a special good night to anyone I've been alone with." As he removed his headphones, imitated by the reverse of himself in the dark beyond the inner window, he felt as if he was unburdening himself of all the voices he'd talked to during the previous two hours. They'd been discussing the homeless, whom most of the callers had insisted on describing as beggars or worse, until Linford had declared that he respected anyone who did their best to earn their keep, to feed themselves and their dependents. He hadn't intended to condemn those who only begged, if they were capable of nothing else, but several of his listeners did with increasing viciousness. After all that, the very last caller had hoped aloud that nobody homeless had been listening. Maybe Linford oughtn't to have responded that if they were homeless they wouldn't have anywhere to plug in a radio, but he always tried to end with a joke.

There was no point in leaving listeners depressed: that wasn't the responsibility he was paid for. If he'd given them a chance to have their say and something to carry on chewing over, he'd done what was expected of him. If he wasn't doing a good job he wouldn't still be on the air. At least it wasn't television—at least he wasn't making people do no more than sit and gawk. As the second hand of the clock above the console fingered midnight he faded out his tune and gave up the station to the national network.

The news paced him as he walked through the station, killing lights. This year's second war, another famine, a seaboard devastated by a hurricane, a town buried by a volcano—no room for anything local, not even the people who'd been missing for weeks or months. In the deserted newsroom computer terminals presented their blank bulging profiles to him. Beyond the unstuffed reception desk a solitary call was flashing like a warning on the switchboard. Its glow and its insect clicking died as he padded across the plump carpet of the reception area. He was reaching for the electronic latch to let himself into the street when he faltered. Beyond the glass door, on the second of the three concrete steps to the pavement, a man was seated with his back to him.

Had he fallen asleep over the contents of his lap? He wore a black suit a size too large, above which peeked an inch of collar gleaming white as a vicar's beneath the neon streetlights, not an ensemble that benefited from being topped by a dark green baseball cap pulled as low as it would stretch on the bald neck. If he was waiting for anyone it surely couldn't be Linford, who nonetheless felt as if he had attracted the other somehow, perhaps by having left all the lights on while he was alone in the station. The news brought itself to an end with a droll anecdote about a music student who had almost managed to sell a forged manuscript before the buyer had noticed the composer's name was spelled Beathoven, and Linford eased the door open. He was on the way to opening enough of a gap to sidle through, into the stagnant July heat beneath the heavy clouds, when *Early Morning Moods* commenced with a rush of jaunty flourishes on a violin. At once the figure on the steps jerked to his feet as though tugged by invisible strings and joined in.

So he was a busker, and the contents of his lap had been a violin and its bow, but the discovery wasn't the only reason why Linford pulled the door wide. The violinist wasn't merely imitating the baroque solo from the radio, he was copying every nuance and intonation, an exact echo no more than a fraction of a second late. Linford felt as though he'd been selected to judge a talent show. "Hey, that's good," he said. "You ought—"

He had barely started speaking when the violinist dodged away with a movement that, whether intentionally or from inability, was less a dance than a series of head-to-toe wriggles that imparted a gypsy swaying to the violin and bow. Perhaps to blot out the interference Linford's voice represented, he began to play louder, though as sweetly as ever. He halted in the middle of the pedestrianized road, between the radio station and a department store lit up for the night. Linford stayed in the doorway until the broadcast melody gave way to the presenter's voice, then closed the door behind him, feeling it lock. "Well done," he called. "Listen, I wonder—"

He could only assume the musician was unable to hear him for playing. No sooner had the melody ended than it recommenced as the player moved away, as though guided by his bunch of faint shadows that gave him the appearance of not quite owning up to the possession of several extra limbs. Linford was growing frustrated with the behavior of someone he only wanted to help. "Excuse me," he said, loud enough for the plate glass across the street to fling his voice back at him. "If it's an audition you need I can get you one. No strings. No commission."

The repetition of the melody didn't falter, but the violinist halted in front of a window scattered with wire skeletons sporting flimsy clothes. When the player didn't turn to face him, Linford followed. He knew talent when he heard it, and local talent was meant to be the point of local radio, but he also didn't mind feeling like the newsman he'd been until he'd found he was better at chatting between his choices of music too old to be broadcast by anyone except him. Years of that had landed him the late-night phone-in, where he sometimes felt he made less of a difference than he had in him. Now here was his chance to make one, and he wasn't about to object if putting the violinist on the air helped his reputation too, not when his contract was due for renewal. He was almost alongside the violinist—close enough to glimpse a twitching of the pale smooth cheek, apparently in time with a mouthing that accompanied the music—when the other danced, if it could be called a dance, away from him.

Unless he was mute—no, even if he was—Linford was determined to extract some sense from him. He supposed it was possible that the musician wasn't quite right in some way, but then it occurred to him that the man might already be employed and so not in need of being discovered. "Do you play with anyone?" he called at the top of his voice.

That seemed to earn him a response. The violinist gestured ahead with his bow, so tersely that Linford heard no break in the music. If the gesture hadn't demonstrated that the player was going Linford's way, he might have sought clarification of whatever he was meant to have understood. Instead he went after the musician, not running or even trotting, since he would have felt absurd, and so not managing to come within arm's length.

The green glow of a window display—clothed dummies exhibiting price tags or challenging the passer-by to guess their worth, their blank-eyed faces immobile and rudimentary as death-masks molded by a trainee—settled on the baseball cap as the player turned along the side street that led to the car park, and the cap appeared to glisten like moss. A quarter of a mile away down the main road, Linford saw a police car crested with lights speed across a junction, the closest the traffic was allowed to approach. Of course the police could drive anywhere they liked, and their cameras were perched on roofs: one of his late-night partners in conversation had declared that these days the cameras were the nearest thing to God. While Linford felt no immediate need of them, there was surely nothing wrong with knowing you were watched. Waving a hand in front of his face to ward off a raw smell the side street had enclosed, he strode after the musician.

The street led directly into the car park, a patch of waste ground about two hundred yards square, strewn with minor chunks of rubble, empty bottles, squashed cans. Only the exit barrier and the solitary presence of Linford's Peugeot indicated that the square did any work. Department stores backed onto its near side, and to its right were restaurants whose bins must be responsible for the wafts of a raw smell. To the left a chain fence crowned with barbed wire protected a building site, while the far side was overlooked by three stories of derelict offices. The musician was prancing straight for these beneath arc-lights that set his intensified shadows scuttling about him.

He reached the building as Linford came abreast of the car. Without omitting so much as a quaver from the rapid eager melody, the violinist lifted one foot in a movement that suggested the climax of a dance and shoved the back door open. The long brownish stick of the bow jerked up as though to beckon Linford. Before he had time to call out, if indeed he felt obliged to, he saw the player vanish into a narrow oblong black as turned earth.

He rested a hand on the tepid roof of the car and told himself he'd done enough. If the musician was using the disused offices as a squat he was unlikely to be alone, and perhaps his thinness was a symptom of addiction. The prospect of encountering a roomful of drug addicts fell short of appealing to Linford. He was fishing out his keys when an abrupt silence filled the car park. The music, rendered hollow by the dark interior, had ceased in the midst of a phrase, but it hadn't entirely obscured a shrill cry from within—a cry, Linford was too sure to be able to ignore it, for help.

Five minutes—less if he surprised himself by proving to be in a condition to run—would take him back to the radio station to call the police. There might even be a phone booth in the main street that accepted coins rather than cards. Less than five minutes might be far too long for whoever needed help, and so Linford stalked across the car park, waving his arms at the offices as he raised his face to mouth for help at the featureless slate sky. He was hoping some policeman was observing him and would send reinforcements—he was hoping to hear a police car raise its voice on its way to him. He'd heard nothing but his own dwarfed isolated footsteps by the time he reached the ajar door.

Perhaps someone had planned to repaint it and given up early in the process. Those patches of old paint that weren't flaking were blistered. The largest blister had split open, and he saw an insect writhe into hiding inside the charred bulge as he dealt the door a slow kick to shove it wide. A short hall with two doors on each side led to a staircase that turned its back on itself halfway up. The widening glare from the car park pressed the darkness back toward the stairs, but only to thicken it on them and within the doorways. Since all the doors were open, he ventured as far as the nearest pair and peered quickly to either side of him.

Random shapes of light were stranded near the windows, all of which were broken. The floorboards of both rooms weren't much less rubbly than the car park. In the room to his left two rusty filing cabinets had been pulled fully open, though surely there could have been nothing to remove from them, let alone to put in. To his right a single office desk was leaning on a broken leg and grimacing with both the black rectangles that used to contain drawers. Perhaps it was his tension that rendered these sights unpleasant, or perhaps it was the raw smell. His will to intervene was failing as he began to wonder if he had really heard any sound except music—and then the cry was repeated above him. It could be a woman's voice or a man's grown shrill with terror, but there was no mistaking its words. "Help," it pleaded. "Oh God."

No more than a couple of streets away a nightclub emitted music and loud voices, followed by an outburst of the slamming of car doors. The noises made Linford feel less alone: there must be at least one bouncer outside the nightclub, within earshot of a yell. Perhaps that wasn't as reassuring as he allowed it to seem, but it let him advance to the foot of the stairs and shout into the dimness that was after all not quite dark. "Hello? What's happening up there? What's wrong?"

His first word brought the others out with it. The more of them there were, the less sure he was how advisable they might be. They were met by utter silence except for the creak of the lowest stair, on which he'd tentatively stepped. He hadn't betrayed his presence, he told himself fiercely: whoever was above him had already been aware of him, or there would have been no point to the cry for help. Nevertheless, once he seized the splintered banister it was on tiptoe that he ran upstairs. He was turning the bend when an object almost tripped him—the musician's baseball cap.

The banister emitted a groan not far short of vocal as he leaned on it to steady himself. The sound was answered by another cry of "Help" or most of it before the voice was muffled by a hand over the mouth. It came from a room at the far end of the corridor ahead. He was intensely aware of the moment, of scraps of light that clung like pale bats to the ceiling of the corridor, the rats' tails of the flexes that had held sockets for light bulbs, the blackness of the doorways that put him in mind of holes in the ground, the knowledge that this was his last chance to retreat. Instead he ran almost soundlessly up the stairs and past two rooms that a glance into each appeared to show were empty save for rubble and broken glass. Before he came abreast of the further left-hand room he knew it was where he had to go. For a moment he thought someone had hung a sign on the door.

It was a tattered office calendar dangling from a nail. Dates some weeks apart on it—the most recent almost a fortnight ago—were marked with ovals that in daytime might have looked more reddish. He was thinking that the marks couldn't be fingerprints, since they contained no lines, as he took a step into the room.

A shape lay on the area of the floor least visited by daylight, under the window amid shards of glass. A ragged curtain tied at the neck covered all of it except the head, which was so large and bald and swollen it reminded him of the moon. The features appeared to be sinking into it: the unreadably shadowed eyes and gaping whitish lips could have passed for craters, and its nostrils were doing without a nose. Despite its baldness, it was a woman's head, since Linford distinguished the outline of breasts under the curtain—indeed, enough bulk for an extra pair. The head wobbled upright to greet him, its scalp springing alight with the glare from the car park, and large hands whose white flesh was loose as oversized gloves groped out from beneath the curtain. He could see no nails on them. The foot he wasn't conscious of holding in mid-air trod on a fragile object he'd failed to notice—a violinist's bow. It snapped and pitched him forward to see more of the room.

Four desk drawers had been brought into it, one to a corner. Each drawer contained a nest of newspapers and office scrap. Around the drawers were strewn crumpled sheets of music, stained dark as though—Linford thought and then tried not to—they had been employed to wipe mouths. Whatever had occurred had apparently involved the scattering about the bare floor of enough spare bows to equip a small string orchestra. By no means anxious to understand any of the contents of the room until he was well clear of it, Linford was backing away when the violin recommenced its dance behind him.

He swung around and at once saw far too much. The violinist was as bald as the figure under the window, but despite the oddly temporary nature of the bland smooth face, particularly around the nose, it was plain that the musician was female too. The long brown stick she was passing back and forth over the instrument had never been a bow—not that one would have made a difference, since the cracked violin was stringless. The perfect imitation of the broadcast melody was streaming out of her wide toothless mouth, the interior of which was at least as white as the rest of her face. Despite her task she managed a smile, though he sensed it wasn't for him but about him. She was blocking the doorway, and the idea of going closer to her—to the smell of rawness, some of which was certainly emerging from her mouth—almost crushed his mind to nothing. He had to entice her away from the doorway, and he was struggling to will himself to retreat into the room—struggling to keep his back to it—when a voice cried "Help."

It was the cry he'd come to find: exactly the cry, and it was behind him in the room. He twisted half around and saw the shape under the window begin to cover her mouth, then let her hand fall. She must have decided there was no longer any reason to cut the repitition short. "Oh God," she added, precisely as she had done before, and rubbed her curtained stomach.

It wasn't just a trick, it was as much of an imitation as the music had been. He had to make more of an effort than he could remember ever having used to swallow the sound the realization almost forced out of his mouth. For years he'd earned his living by not letting there be more than a second of silence, but could staying absolutely quiet now save him? He was unable to think what else to do, not that he was anything like sure of being capable of silence. "Help, oh God," the curtained shape repeated, more of a demand now, and rubbed her stomach harder. The player dropped the violin and the other item, and before their clatter faded she came at Linford with a writhing movement that might have been a jubilant dance—came just far enough to continue to block his escape.

His lips trembled, his teeth chattered, and he couldn't suppress his words, however idiotic they might be. "My mistake. I only—"

"My mistake. I only." Several voices took up his protest at once, but he could see no mouths uttering it, only an agitation of the lower half of the curtain. Then two small forms crawled out from underneath, immediately followed by two more, all undisguised by any kind of covering. Their plump white bodies seemed all the more wormlike for the incompleteness of the faces on the bald heads—no more than nostrils and greedily dilated mouths. Just the same they wriggled straight to him, grabbing pointed fragments of glass. He saw the violinst press her hands over her ears, and thought that she felt some sympathy for him until he grasped that she was ensuring she didn't have to imitate whatever sound he made. The window was his only chance now: if the creature beneath it was as helpless as she seemed, if he could bear to step over or on her so as to scream from the window for somebody out there to hear—But when he screamed it was from the floor where, having expertly tripped him, the young were swarming up his legs, and he found he had no interest in the words he was screaming, especially when they were repeated in chorus to him.

JACK DANN

Marilyn

Jack Dann has written or edited over fifty books, including the international bestseller The Memory Cathedral, *which has been published in more than ten languages. His novel* The Silent *has been compared to Mark Twain's* Huckleberry Finn. *He has won the Nebula Award, the World Fantasy Award, the Australian Aurealis Award (twice), the Ditmar Award (twice), and the Premios Gilgames de Narrativa Fantastica award. He has also been honored by the Mark Twain Society. His most recent novel is* Bad Medicine. *Jack Dann lives in Melbourne, Australia, and "commutes" back and forth to Los Angeles and New York.*

Dann admits that "Marilyn" is based on "my own childhood experiences with hypnosis. I was that fourteen-year-old who conjured up—or tried to conjure up—Marilyn Monroe, and I still have a dog-eared copy of Julian Rammurti's The Fundamentals of Self-Hypnosis and Yoga: Theory, Practice, and Application." *An adaptation of "Marilyn," a substantially different take on the story, written by Dann and producer Brian Smith, has been released by the SCI-FI Channel's Seeing Ear Theatre as* Marilyn or the Monster. *The play can be found at http://www.scifi.com/set/originals/marilyn. Dann is currently working on a novel about the life of James Dean . . . after his accident. It's called* Second Chance. *And, yes, Marilyn Monroe figures as a major character in the book. "Marilyn" originally appeared in* Eidolon 29/30.*

—E. D.

I was fourteen, and she was stone white and naked and blond.

She was hazed in the pale cold light pouring in from the frost-shrouded windows of my bedroom, and I remember the dustmotes floating in the mid-afternoon sunshine, I remember the luminous living clouds of dust swirling around her great diaphanous wings, which seemed to shudder as she stepped toward the bed . . . my bed.

Those wings were white as tissue and seemed as fragile, as if they would break or crack or tear with the merest motion or gust of wind, and I remember her green-flecked eyes staring at me as she moved across my bedroom, which was filled with books and magazines and forty-five rpm records and pre-cut balsa models of World War II fighter planes (including a British Supermarine Spitfire MK XII that would be fitted with radio control) in various stages of completion, and I couldn't help myself, I looked at her breasts and at her naturally dark mat of pubic hair, and I was so terrified that I closed my eyes.

I remember, as if it had happened last month, rather than forty years ago.

It was the year that Buddy Holly, the Big Bopper, and Richie Valens were killed in a plane crash in Iowa. Alaska became the 49th State, which brought Texas down a peg, and Hawaii became the 50th. *Rio Bravo* and *Ben Hur* came out that year; Navy beat Army 43-12, and Mafia boss Joseph Barbara and forty of his "delegates" got busted at his house in Appalachian, which was about fifteen miles away from my home town in upstate New York.

I found the old book after my father died in 1987.

I was searching through the bedroom closet that he had always locked, and I was lost in the smells of cedar and old clothes—there were old leather key rings and wallets, a lifetime member Playboy card, a stiletto knife that he had taken away from me when I was sixteen, a taped envelope that contained an old black and white Polaroid photograph of a dark-haired buxom woman—certainly not my mother—wearing the skimpy outfit of a belly dancer, and there were tuxedo studs and cufflinks and silver pens and penknives, playing cards backed with photographs of nude women, white plastic collar stays of varied size, check registers, an old will in a manila envelope, letters tied with a black ribbon, expired insurance policies, a woman's red silk handkerchief, and my paperback edition of *The Fundamentals of Self-Hypnosis and Yoga: Theory, Practice, and Application* by Julian Rammurti, M.A., M.D. Its spine was broken and pages fell out as I held it open in my palm.

Dad had never told me he had taken the book. Nor had he ever told me that he had taken the stiletto.

I remember how keenly I had felt the loss of the book at the time. But that was only because it was mine . . . because it was the first book I'd found on the subject . . . and because it worked. I could find other books on yoga and hypnotism, which I did. I lived in libraries and learned clinical theories and models and techniques, and I'd even developed a flair for stage hypnotism which was the antithesis of the careful, quiet clinical process. For an instant—standing there in my father's closet, a grown man discovering the secrets of his youth, savoring the presence of the living past—I saw myself, as if in a mirror: a thin, gangly, pimply-faced boy of fourteen once again, straight brown hair greased back with pomade, red button-down shirt, collar raised, leather jacket, black pegged pants. The boy sneered into those books, indeed, as if he were looking into a mirror. A poor reflection of Elvis.

Reading . . . reading about posthypnotic suggestion and methods for creating the state of *yoganidra*. The powers of *tratakam*. Lucid Dreaming. The state of somnambulism. Hypermnesia. *Prana* and *Pranayama*. The story of the man and the bear.

I've often remembered that story of the man and the bear. It went something like this: There was a psychiatrist who was wounded in France during the Second World War. As he recuperated in a military hospital in Cornwall, he grew bored and occupied himself with a posthypnotic suggestion. He'd hypnotized himself and conjured up a great bear to provide some comic relief from the day to day boredom. All he had to do was say "Bear" and count to five and miraculously, a huge white polar bear with a long, flexible neck would stroll upright into the ward, leap about in the aisles, try to mount the nurses, frolic around the other patients, or hunch against the psychiatrist's bed and allow himself to be petted. So the bear cavorted in the mornings and afternoon, and likewise all the psychiatrist had to do was count to five and the bear would disappear. The bear had no weight, made no noise, could somersault in the air, walk on the ceiling, deftly unbutton nurses' blouses with its curved yellow claws, remove bras, and dance with any of the variously undressed doctors, nurses, patients, and visitors, who were never the wiser. The psychiatrist also conjured up the bear every night as an antidote to counting sheep, but the apparition soon began to take on a different, more ominous aspect in the dark. It became more aggressive, would not always obey commands, and when it leered, a feat the psychiatrist was certain no other bear could manage, its fangs seemed much longer than they had been during the day. So the psychiatrist mumbled "Bear," counted to five, and disappeared his ill-conceived creation.

But the bear was not so easily dismissed.

It appeared the next night, unbidden, and the next day it snapped at the nurses and bit the psychiatrist on the forearm. A warning. Although it left no marks, of course, the psychiatrist was in excruciating pain for hours.

The psychiatrist had to hypnotize himself three times to get rid of it.

Nor did that work . . . entirely; and years later, the bear would oftimes appear—a vague, threatening form in the distance—and follow the psychiatrist, who developed the disconcerting habit of always looking behind him.

So I lay on top of the prickly wool blankets of my neatly made bed and waited for Marilyn Monroe to come to me, to change me completely—change me from an awkward, pimply-faced adolescent into a full-blooded man who knew the moist secrets of women, who'd actually and really been laid, even if through the devices and snares of an altered state of consciousness known only to hypnotists and young dabblers in the arcane such as myself.

It didn't matter how I did it. What mattered was that I *did* it.

I had floated, fallen, drifted, breathed myself into the deepest, most profound state of hypnosis. I had imagined myself rowing a boat on a calm, shallow, infinite sea, every breath took me farther out upon the placid ocean, breathing in, breathing out, skiffing in smooth clockwork motion, each breath out, each breath in taking me farther, farther into a calm azure place without depth, without horizon; yet I could feel everything around me: the wool of the blanket itching my neck, the cold smoothness of the pillow case as I moved my head, the cold chill seeping in through the windows, and I saw her in that instant as I blinked open my eyes and shut them tight again. The woman who inhabited every adolescent male's dream. Walking toward me, a look of blond rapture on her painted full-lipped face—six shades of lipstick, I knew about that, Marilyn I love you, and I waited for her, waited in the dark bosom of my self-directed dream, waited for her to come upon me, slip beside me, touch me, guide me, sail me across the sea of my quickening breathing, sail me out of my virginity.

I would lose my cherry to an apparition, a ghost, a hallucination, but at thirteen, in North Leistershire, New York, population 16,000, in 1959, that was the best I could hope for.

With my eyes closed—I do believe they were closed, but perhaps they were not—I could feel her walking toward me, past the built-in, beige-painted bookshelves that housed my father's mystery collection, which he'd always kept in my room, past the door that connected to my parent's bedroom . . . walking under all the mobiles and models that floated just below the ceiling and defied gravity by mere threads; and then she was standing over me, standing beside the bed, standing beside my slippers and sneakers and cordovan dress shoes, and I *knew* that she was leaning, leaning over me now—I could hear her shallow, patient breathing and the rustling whispering of her wings, smell her overly sweet perfume mixed with a more acid, damp odor—and all I would have to do was take her in my arms, she would fall into my arms like pillows and soft toys and cushions; and all I had to do was open my eyes to see her breasts and I could raise my hands to touch them.

All I had to do was open my eyes.

I tried. I *had* to see her. I had memorized her from a hundred photographs: the mole above her swelled lips, the eyelashes heavy as cardboard, the eyelids white as chalk, the earings dangling, everything about her swollen and curved and fleshy and full of promises—

But in that instant, in that terrible instant of realization or proffered possibility, I felt everything change. I know it was my own fault, my own perverse nature, but somehow I suddenly changed the rules. Much as I desired to bring Marilyn's warm body close to my own, to enter her and lose everything I hated and instantly gain my manhood, I imagined something else instead.

In that terrifying, transforming instant I imagined that whatever I was most afraid of now stood in Marilyn's place, and I dared not open my eyes for fear of what I would see, yet I was afraid to keep them closed because it was unbearable *not* to see what was looming over me, suffocating me, watching me; and I remember the slow-motion tossing and turning and shaking, as the sea I had drifted too far upon began to rage and rise; and, in fact, I was caught between fear and desire. I could not tell how long the convulsion lasted, but once I awakened to the world of slanting sunlight and the familiar smell of bedsheets and air-freshener, I vowed never to hypnotize myself again.

After that Marilyn never came to me in my dreams, but the dark thing that I had conjured in her place shadowed me.

Like the psychiatrist who kept looking over his shoulder to check whether his great white bear was tailing him, so did I feel the presence of my apparition. But unlike the psychiatrist, who at least knew his enemy, I could only sense this manifestation of my fears. In my teens I thought of it as a monster shaped something like a bear, and I imagined its claws tapping on macadam or sidewalks, and I would turn quickly, just to check, and, of course, there would never be anything there, at least not anything untoward. Over the years, I gave up on monsters, for they, too, ceased to inhabit my dreams. My dreams had one recurrent element, and that was more an experience of synthesthesia: they would all, at one stage or another, take on the color of deep purple, yet the color would be more like damp mist, which felt thick and ominous and signaled danger, but the mist was the stuff of the world in my dreams, and it would bleed out of the sky and buildings and people—just as it would bleed out of myself—dyeing my monochrome dreams with purple fear and anxiety and uncertainty.

But I wasn't the beast entirely. Only part of it.

The dreams coalesced into reality one numbingly cold dark morning in Vietnam.

It was January 1969. We'd been stuffed into a deuce-and-a-half; one of three trucks going out of Phu Bai down south where the fighting was supposed to be heating up. Everybody was shivering, and I remember sitting perfectly still because it was warmer that way, and Joey Mantaneo was pushed against me like four o'clock on the D-train going to Brooklyn, and even in the cold he smelled like cordite and rot and piss (and that cordite smell should have alerted me that something bad was crawling toward me), and he had his war name SCARED SHITLESS painted across his flack jacket and stencilled on his helmet like he was military police, and I knew the story about how he got his name—but he was the only one in Bravo who'd never been wounded or sick, not even an infection when he cut his finger. He claimed he was a street-fighter and his gang was called "The Road Gents," even though nobody in the gang had a car, and he said he knew as much about killing before he came out here as he did after, but he always looked scared—he just had that kind of a face—and when he was green somebody said he was scared shitless and so he took that name for himself. The guy who named him was dead, but SCARED SHITLESS wasn't. Neither was BURNT COP and CALL ME WHITE, and they'd been brought up in a black bopping gang in Philadelphia called "The Flicks," whatever the hell that meant, and the rest of the guys were farmers or factory workers or mechanics—I was the only college boy, and they called me "Professor"—and they named themselves BORN TO DIE, BORN TO KILL, KILL OR BE KILLED, KILLER ANGEL, and if you believed everybody, every one of them was a stoned killer street-fighter and a drug-dealer and a hustler and a pussy-magnet, but we were all just kids. Full of piss and vinegar eight months ago, but now exhausted and sick with the shits and fungus and getting bald and everything else. And while the goddamn truck rocked and jittered in the muddy craters that was supposed to be the convoy route—I was black and blue from being thrown around in that can—everybody was singing and whistling "Reach Out, I'll Be There," and then "Mellow Yellow," and Cop and Mantaneo and Sammy Chitester were singing in falsetto, so it sounded like we had women in the chorus, and then everybody did Otis Redding's "Sittin' on the Dock of the Bay," and they were pretty good.

We sounded like a rock band without microphones coming through the storm that had kept up for days, and it seemed like the world was going to stay dark and moonlit forever; and everything was covered with leaves that blew all over like home in October, but nothing else was like home: the houses along the way that were still standing were burned and pitted from shells, and there were refugees that looked like they ought to be dead and buried walking along the road; some were wounded, and although the old people didn't seem to pay any attention to us, the rest looked at us like we were the enemy; they hated us, even though they were too afraid to say word one; and we just crashed and bounced and sang and whistled through the dark, through the rain and fog, and you would have thought you were at the south pole or something where it was twilight all the time, and then we blew out our transmission, and although a few of the guys got on the other two trucks, the rest of us marched.

We went twenty clicks before we finally bivouacked in a deserted village that wasn't far from the Citadel of Hue.

It was cold and wet and dark and I couldn't stop shivering.

Viet Cong could have been all around us, for all we could tell, even though we'd caught up with our trucks and guards were posted and the place was secured, but I didn't care about anything. None of us who'd done the marching copped guard duty, and I would have fallen asleep if I had; it was as if someone had pushed a button and all the life just went out of me. I couldn't even eat or relieve myself. I just wrapped myself up in my poncho liner and fell asleep in an empty hooch. There were bits of glass all over the floor that would sometimes catch the light like little green and yellow and orange and blue gems, the kind sold in the hobby stores along with crystals and beads, but I didn't dream about that . . . I didn't dream about jewels and beads and velvet and cold empty darkness.

I didn't dream at all.

But dreams or no dreams, we were up before first light; and our orders were to go the rest of the way, wherever that was going to be, on foot because they needed the trucks up north (where it was safe), and so we watched the deuces drive off and then we walked to paradise. That's what it looked like, anyway, and before we realized what was happening, most of us were dead. Only Joey Mantaneo and I survived, and Joey, of course, didn't even get a scratch, but he suffered later, went half-crazy with recurring nightmares; at least that was what I heard, only I can't to this day remember who I heard that from.

I didn't suffer any nightmares . . . after that I couldn't remember my dreams.

We were approaching the south bank of the Perfume River, and there were the smashed walls of what had once been beautiful French-style villas of the southern sector of Hue; and spread out before us was lush grass and fog swirling like we were walking on a carpet through clouds—the grass was deep green from all the rain, but there was a metal smell to the air; and although that mist didn't look purple, like in my childhood dreams, I sensed that this place was wrong, that it was hazy and purple and that the purple was about to bleed out from the sky and me and everyone else, but I just couldn't quite see it yet.

For all that I just said, this place was picture-perfect: a lone sampan on the river, an old man riding a bicycle up the avenue that ran along the park, for we were walking through a park. I remember breathing in and looking around, and then I saw a flash and heard an explosion, and Mantaneo screamed "Motherfuckers!" or maybe that was me, but it didn't matter because there was another explosion and I realized that I was lying flat on the ground and looking up at the sky and watching watching watching for the purple, watching waiting for the change, please God make this just a dream, and I heard a gurgling noise and a wheezing noise, and I remembered the training film I'd seen on sucking chest wounds, and I just figured my chest had been blown out and I was dying, but I didn't think "Oh my God I'm dying" or "Mamma."

Everything was still and cold and quiet as a winter morning, and Marilyn came to me, just like she did the first time.

I could smell her damp perfume and then I could feel her coming toward me and studying me like she was a doctor and I was a patient, and then she lay down on top of me, straddling me; her pale face pressed against my neck, her stiff blond hair tickling my chin and lips; and I could feel her body moving against mine, and her wings, feathered white, layers and layers of down, covered us, sheltered us, and I felt myself inside her, felt the cold ether wetness, felt myself being drawn into her, into down, into feathers, into the swirling mists of cloud, drawn into a silent, cold heaven.

Mantaneo saved my ass that day by pulling me into one of the VC's tunnels, and we hid in a dark, damp, earthy room. By all rights, we should have met up with its owner; but, as I said earlier, Mantaneo always had the right luck and never got hurt. The way I heard it later, he just waited until the VC left and somehow managed to keep me alive.

I never saw him again to thank him.

And, of course, I don't *remember* what happened.

After I came back to the World, as we called coming home in those days, I waited for Marilyn. I liked to think that she came to me every night in my dreams. But since I couldn't remember dreaming, it was moot.

My shrink told me that once I'd worked everything out and regained my health, I'd remember my dreams again. The shrink, of course, attributed everything to Post-traumatic Stress Disorder, which had become the fashionable diagnosis for everything that had happened to every grunt in 'Nam. I argued that I didn't exhibit any of the other symptoms of PTSD: diminished interest in activities, feelings of detachment from others, exaggerated startle responses, sleep disturbances, survivor guilt, memory impairment, recurrent dreams of a traumatic event, or trouble concentrating. I'd put myself through law school— memorized the Uniform Commercial Code and fifty cases a night, and I won't believe you can do *that* without concentration and a good memory. But he was not to be dissuaded. He figured that I was having nightly traumas; I just couldn't remember them.

I couldn't argue that kind of logic, so I stopped seeing him.

Eventually, of course, I started dreaming again, and I was, indeed, having recurrent dreams, but whether or not they were traumatic, I couldn't tell you because all I could remember was that they were about wings—gauzy, translucent wings that sometimes looked like feathers, sometimes like down, and sometimes like the surface of a soap bubble. I suppose I became obsessed by the very idea, obsessed with flying frogs and flying dragons and flying fish, with horseshoe bats and redwings and griffon vultures and hummingbirds, with hawk moths and wasps and hovel flies . . . and with those who like me couldn't fly. I spent hours at the botanical gardens watching the swans and remembering Marilyn's wings fanning and spreading; and I wondered, I tried to remember: were they white and feathery or were they gossamer rainbows settling around me like silken sheets, billowing, as alive as the surface of the sea?

I usually remembered them as white and feathery.

The wings of angels.

I started dating blond women—how I yearned for pale skin and white-bleached hair—and then I married a petite, dark-haired woman, may she rest in peace, and we had children and lay in bed every night, and some nights she knew I wasn't with her. I would dream pretend that she was someone else, and then for an instant the sheets would become wings.

Josiane died of ovarian cancer under cool white sheets.

I had always thought that the next time—if there were ever to be a next time—I would find myself looking at the monster that was unseen but terrifyingly present when I'd first conjured Marilyn out of an old book about hypnosis.

Every night I lived with the anticipation, with the desire and the fear—waiting for Marilyn, or the monster, Marilyn, monster; and my bones grew, my hormones changed, as did the color of my hair—from blond to brown to grey, as the years passed me through Binghamton Central High School, Broome Community College, Vietnam with its smells of cordite and damp familiar colors of fear, Hofstra University in Hempstead, Long Island, where I drove a Buick Le Sabre and wore tie-dyed T-shirts, Brooklyn Law School, clerking for Bernstein, Haversham, Lunquist, Esqs—from associate to junior to senior partner, from Brooklyn to Brooklyn Heights to Manhattan to Connecticut; marriage, children, vacations, fourteen-hour days, weekends on Fire Island, divorce, reconciliation, death, Josiane's dead, say it, admit it, there, fact, and through it all, through all the empty and disconnected nights, all that was left were desire and fear. My whole life a moment wrapped around anticipations of dreams . . . or nightmares.

Marilyn or the monster.

I did finally find them.

I'd received an invitation from my old unit to attend a reunion. It had been thirty years. I looked for Joey Mantaneo in the columns of names and addresses between the grainy photographs, but he wasn't mentioned. I was listed alphabetically, home address, home phone, business phone, just like all the other officers and noncoms and grunts. There I was, a ghost in black letter type, but Joey had disappeared.

That night I dreamed about him.

While the little black and white television blinked ghostly light into my bedroom I allowed myself to follow him, skipping around time like it was an old neighborhood, and I found him in Bayonne, New Jersey, where he was working as an electrician for the building firm of Calley & La Cross, or so I dreamed; and Joey's wife was named Louise, and he had three daughters, Marsha, Missie, and Mave, and in that dream I'd forgotten the names of my own daughters, but didn't follow that trail, lest I dwell upon how I'd failed my children and my wife, and how I—but that wasn't important; I was following Joey. I'd always be safe with Joey because he was a survivor; he survived, survived the bopping gangs and the drugs and everything else and I wouldn't let myself drift back into Vietnam, but Joey led me right back. He took me through his father's candy store and showed me how he'd grown up. He took me to Larry's Bar, which was across the street from his three bedroom apartment on Stadler Avenue, and we sat at the bar, which had a brass rail to rest your feet on, and we drank boilermakers, dropping the shot-glasses filled with Johnny Red right into the beer mugs—all the regulars had their own personal mug at Larry's. We drank three shots and beers, and I felt an overwhelming sadness as I looked at Joey, an overwhelming longing. He had lost most of his hair, had put on weight, which changed the shape of his face—took out the definition and sharp, clean good looks and replaced them with a softness that was somehow repellent; and Joey smelled bad; he was dressed in jeans and a faded shirt, and he leaned over and told me that he was still in Hue, still in Vietnam—that *we* were still in Hue— and that's when the dream broke apart.

It had been so real, as not to be a dream, although I knew that bits and pieces were wrong, that there was no company called Calley & La Cross; those were just names from the war, but Joey leaned toward me, then grabbed me by the shoulders and—

We tumbled into the VC's tunnel, back into that cold, damp morning near the Perfume River, and I was lying against the dirt wall, sitting up, while Joey pressed his hand against my chest and said, "Jesus Christ, Jesus Christ," and there were a few rays of light coming in from the entrance above, and they were golden and seemed as solid as the blades of ancient bronze swords, and I watched the dust swirling through them, swirling swirling and I remembered my room in North Leistershire, remembered lying on the bed and counting myself into a hypnotic trance, into a deep state of somnambulism, and I was fourteen and about to conjure up Marilyn out of my adolescent desires and the light pouring in through my windows, light filled with dustmotes dancing swirling, promise, everything filled with promise and—

Then Joey stopped fussing with me, and we could hear someone scraping around above. Somebody shouted *"Chew boi, chew boi,"* which meant surrender, but we could tell it was our own boys; we were all taught *Chew boi, Yuh tie len, lie day*—surrender, come out with your hands up, and then concussion, blinding light, the cracking of thunder, and then silence as my ears popped, and I felt sudden wetness all over me, sonovabitch whoever was up there couldn't wait to take prisoners, or find out who the hell we were, and I wiped my face, everything smeared with blood, Joey, Joey, Joey was all over me. I looked around, light now pouring in from the entrance that was forward and above, pouring in like mist, which swirled, turning everything to blood, and I was holding Joey's torso, but his arms and legs and head had been blown off, and I was a liar, he wasn't lucky, or maybe he was.

I closed my eyes, but the blood and light and mist could not be closed out; rather everything slowly darkened to purple, and I could feel myself tossing and shaking in slow-motion, and I remembered having convulsions before, but now it didn't matter if I closed my eyes or opened them, I'd found the monster— Joey, Joey, goddamn it, and I screamed and opened my eyes and the mist the fog cleared and I could see her, standing in the entrance that was flooded with light, pure blazing sunlight, cold winter morning light. She was moonlight white, and naked, and her eyes were drawn in black and her lips were smeared with blood and as she reached toward me, coaxing me out of the earth, her wings spread out reflexively; they were butterfly blue fans, deep azure, darkening, darkening into purple black, and they quivered, trembling to the meter of her perfectly measured pulse, and I remember.

I remember.

I whispered, "Mamma."

Just like every other grunt who thought he was about to die.

NALO HOPKINSON

Greedy Choke Puppy

Nalo Hopkinson's first novel, Brown Girl in the Ring, *won the* Warner Aspect
First Novel *contest. She followed it up with an excellent second novel,*
Midnight Robber, *and is at work on a third,* Griffone. *Her fiction has earned
her an Ontario Arts Council Foundation Award, a Locus Award, and a John
W. Campbell Award for Best New Writer. Hopkinson is also the editor of*
Whispers From the Cotton Tree Root: Caribbean Fabulist Fiction. *She grew
up in Jamaica, Trinidad, and Guyana, and now lives in Toronto, Canada.*

*"Greedy Choke Puppy" is a wicked little tale making deft use of Caribbean
myth and lore. It is reprinted from* Dark Matter: A Century of Speculative
Fiction from the African Diaspora, *edited by Sheree R. Thomas (Warner
Aspect).*

—T. W.

I see a Lagahoo last night. In the back of the house, behind the pigeon peas."
"Yes, Granny." Sitting cross-legged on the floor, Jacky leaned back against
her grandmother's knees and closed her eyes in bliss against the gentle tug
of Granny's hands braiding her hair. Jacky still enjoyed this evening ritual,
even though she was a big hard-back woman, thirty-two years next month.

The moon was shining in through the open jalousie windows, bringing the
sweet smell of Ladies-of-the-Night flowers with it. The ceiling fan beat its soothing rhythm.

"How you mean, 'Yes, Granny'? You even know what a Lagahoo is?"

"Don't you been frightening me with jumby story from since I small? Is a
donkey with gold teeth, wearing a waistcoat with a pocket watch and two pair
of tennis shoes on the hooves."

"Washekong, you mean. I never teach you to say 'tennis shoes.' "

Jacky smiled. "Yes, Granny. So, what the Lagahoo was doing in the pigeon
peas patch?"

"Just standing, looking at my window. Then he pull out he watch chain from
out he waistcoat pocket, and he look at the time, and he put the watch back,
and he bite off some pigeon peas from off one bush, and he walk away."

Jacky laughed, shaking so hard that her head pulled free of Granny's hands.

"You mean to tell me that a Lagahoo come all the way to we little house in Diego Martin, just to sample we so-so pigeon peas?" Still chuckling, she settled back against Granny's knees. Granny tugged at a hank of Jacky's hair, just a little harder than necessary.

Jacky could hear the smile in the old woman's voice. "Don't get fresh with me. You turn big woman now, Ph.D. student and thing, but is still your old nen-nen who does plait up your hair every evening, oui?"

"Yes, Granny. You know I does love to make mako 'pon you, to tease you a little."

"This ain't no joke, child. My Mammy used to say that a Lagahoo is God horse, and when you see one, somebody go dead. The last time I see one is just before your mother dead."

The two women fell silent. The memory hung in the air between them, of the badly burned body retrieved from the wreckage of the car that had gone off the road. Jacky knew that her grandmother would soon change the subject. She blamed herself for the argument that had sent Jacky's mother raging from the house in the first place. And whatever Granny didn't want to think about, she certainly wasn't going to talk about.

Granny sighed. "Well, don't fret, doux-doux. Just be careful when you go out so late at night. I couldn't stand to lose you, too."

She finished off the last braid and gently stroked Jacky's head. "All right. I finish now. Go and wrap up your head in a scarf, so the plaits will stay nice while you sleeping."

"Thank you, Granny. What I would do without you to help me make myself pretty for the gentlemen, eh?"

Granny smiled, but with a worried look on her face. "You just mind your studies. It have plenty of time to catch man."

Jacky stood and gave the old woman a kiss on one cool, soft cheek and headed toward her bedroom in search of a scarf. Behind her, she could hear Granny settling back into the faded wicker armchair, muttering distractedly to herself, "Why this Lagahoo come to bother me again, eh?"

The first time, I ain't know what was happening to me. I was younger them times there, and sweet for so, you see? Sweet like julie mango, with two ripe tot-tot on the front of my body and two ripe maami-apple behind. I only had was to walk down the street, twitching that maami-apple behind, and all the boys-them on the street corner would watch at me like them was starving, and I was food.

But I get to find out know how it is when the boys stop kissing they teeth at you so much, and start watching after a next younger thing. I get to find out that when you pass you prime, and you ain't catch no man eye, nothing ain't left for you but to get old and dry-up like cane leaf in the fire. Is just so I was feeling that night. Like something wither-up. Like something that once used to drink in the feel of the sun on it skin, but now it dead and dry, and the sun only drying it out more. And the feeling make a burning in me belly, and the burning spread out to me skin, till I couldn't take it no more. I jump up from my little bed just so in the middle of the night, and snatch off my nightie. And when I do so, my skin come with it, and drop off on the floor. Inside my skin I was just one big ball of fire, and Lord, the night air feel nice and cool on the flame! I know then I was a soucouyant, a hag-woman, like my mother before me. I know what I had was to do. When your youth start to leave you, you have to steal more from somebody who still have plenty. I fly out the window and start to search, search for a newborn baby.

"Lagahoo? You know where that word come from, ain't, Jacky?" asked Carmen Lewis, the librarian in the humanities section of the Library of the University of the West Indies. Carmen leaned back in her chair behind the information desk, legs sprawled under the bulge of her advanced pregnancy.

Carmen was a little older than Jacky. They had known each other since they were girls together at Saint Alban's Primary School. Carmen was always very interested in Jacky's research. "Is French creole for werewolf. Only we could come up with something as jokey as a were-donkey, oui? And as far as I know, it doesn't change into a human being. Why does your Granny think she saw one in the backyard?"

"You know Granny, Carmen. She sees all kinds of things, duppy and jumby and things like that. Remember the duppy stories she used to tell us when we were small, so we would be scared and mind what she said?"

Carmen laughed. "And the soucouyant, don't forget that. My mother used to tell me that one, too." She smiled a strange smile. "It didn't really frighten me, though. I always wondered what it would be like to take your skin off, leave your worries behind, and fly so free."

"Well, you sit there so and wonder. I have to keep researching this paper. The back issues come in yet?"

"Right here." Sighing with the effort of bending over, Carmen reached under the desk and pulled out a stack of slim bound volumes of *Huracan*, a Caribbean literary journal that was now out of print. A smell of wormwood and age rose from them. In the 1940s, *Huracan* had published a series of issues on folktales. Jacky hoped that these would provide her with more research material.

"Thanks, Carmen." She picked up the volumes and looked around for somewhere to sit. There was an empty private carrel, but there was also a free space at one of the large study tables. Terry was sitting there, head bent over a fat textbook. The navy blue of his shirt suited his skin, made it glow like a newly unwrapped chocolate. Jacky smiled. She went over to the desk, tapped Terry on the shoulder. "I could sit beside you, Terry?"

Startled, he looked up to see who had interrupted him. His handsome face brightened with welcome. "Uh, sure, no problem. Let me get . . ." He leapt to pull out the chair for her, overturning his own in the process. At the crash, everyone in the library looked up. "Shit." He bent over to pick up the chair. His glasses fell from his face. Pens and pencils rained from his shirt pocket.

Jacky giggled. She put her books down, retrieved Terry's glasses just before he would have stepped on them. "Here." She put the spectacles onto his face, let the warmth of her fingertips linger briefly at his temples.

Terry stepped back, sat quickly in the chair, even though it was still at an odd angle from the table. He crossed one leg over the other. "Sorry," he muttered bashfully. He bent over, reaching awkwardly for the scattered pens and pencils.

"Don't fret, Terry. You just collect yourself and come and sit back down next to me." Jacky glowed with the feeling of triumph. Half an hour of studying beside him, and she knew she'd have a date for lunch. She sat, opened a copy of *Huracan*, and read:

SOUCOUYANT/OL' HIGUE (Trinidad/Guyana)

Caribbean equivalent of the vampire myth. "Soucouyant," or "blood-sucker," derives from the French verb "sucer," to suck. "Ol' Higue" is the Guyanese creole expression for an old hag, or witch woman. The soucouyant is usually an old, evil-tempered woman who removes her skin at night, hides it, and then changes into a ball of fire. She flies through the air, searching for homes in which there are babies. She then enters the house through an open window or a keyhole, goes into the child's room, and sucks the life from its body. She may visit one child's bedside a number of times, draining a little more life each time, as the frantic parents search for a cure, and the child gets progressively weaker and finally dies. Or she may kill all at once.

The smell of the soup Granny was cooking made Jacky's mouth water. She sat at Granny's wobbly old kitchen table, tracing her fingers along a familiar stain. The wooden table had been Granny's as long as Jacky could remember. Grandpa had made the table for Granny long before Jacky was born. Diabetes had finally been the death of him. Granny had brought only the kitchen table and her clothing with her when she moved in with Jacky and her mother.

Granny looked up from the cornmeal and flour dough she was kneading. "Like you idle, doux-doux," she said. She slid the bowl of dough over to Jacky. "Make the dumplings, then, nuh?"

Jacky took the bowl over to the stove, started pulling off pieces of dough and forming it into little cakes.

"Andrew make this table for me with he own two hand," Granny said.

"I know. You tell me already."

Granny ignored her. "Forty-two years we married, and every Sunday, I chop up the cabbage for the saltfish on this same table. Forty-two years we eat Sunday morning breakfast right here so. Saltfish and cabbage with a little small-leaf thyme from the back garden, and fry dumpling and cocoa-tea. I miss he too bad. You grandaddy did full up me life, make me feel young."

Jacky kept forming the dumplings for the soup. Granny came over to the stove and stirred the large pot with her wooden spoon. She blew on the spoon, cautiously tasted some of the liquid in it, and carefully floated a whole ripe Scotch Bonnet pepper on top of the bubbling mixture. "Jacky, when you put the dumpling-them in, don't break the pepper, all right? Otherwise this soup going to make me bawl tonight for pepper."

"Mm. Ain't Mummy used to help you make soup like this on a Saturday?"

"Yes, doux-doux. Just like this." Granny hobbled back to sit at the kitchen table. Tiny graying braids were escaping the confinement of her stiff black wig. Her knobby legs looked frail in their too-beige stockings. Like so many of the old women that Jacky knew, Granny always wore stockings rolled down below the hems of her worn flower print shifts. "I thought you was going out tonight," Granny said. "With Terry."

"We break up," Jacky replied bitterly. "He say he not ready to settle down." She dipped the spoon into the soup, raised it to her mouth, spat it out when it burned her mouth. "Backside!"

Granny watched, frowning. "Greedy puppy does choke. You mother did always taste straight from the hot stove, too. I was forever telling she to take time. You come in just like she, always in a hurry. Your eyes bigger than your stomach."

Jacky sucked in an irritable breath. "Granny, Carmen have a baby boy last night. Eight pounds, four ounces. Carmen make she first baby already. I past thirty years old, and I ain't find nobody yet."

"You will find, Jacky. But you can't hurry people so. Is how long you and Terry did stepping out?"

Jacky didn't respond.

"Eh, Jacky? How long?"

"Almost a month."

"Is scarcely two weeks, Jacky, don't lie to me. The boy barely learn where to find your house, and you was pestering he to settle down already. Me and your grandfather court for two years before we went to Parson to marry we."

When Granny started like this, she could go on for hours. Sullenly, Jacky began to drop the raw dumplings one by one into the fragrant, boiling soup.

"Child, you pretty, you have flirty ways, boys always coming and looking for you. You could pick and choose until you find the right one. Love will come. But take time. Love your studies, look out for your friends-them. Love your old Granny," she ended softly.

Hot tears rolled down Jacky's cheeks. She watched the dumplings bobbing back to the surface as they cooked; little warm, yellow suns.

"A new baby," Granny mused. "I must go and visit Carmen, take she some crab and callaloo to strengthen she blood. Hospital food does make you weak, oui."

I need more time, more life. I need a baby breath. Must wait till people sleeping, though. Nobody awake to see a fireball flying up from the bedroom window.

The skin only confining me. I could feel it getting old, binding me up inside it. Sometimes I does just feel to take it off and never put it back on again, oui?

Three A.M., 'Fore day morning. Only me and the duppies going to be out this late. Up from out of the narrow bed, slip off the nightie, slip off the skin.

Oh, God, I does be so free like this! Hide the skin under the bed, and fly out the jalousie window. The night air cool, and I flying so high. I know how many people it have in each house, and who sleeping. I could feel them, skin-bag people, breathing out their life, one-one breath. I know where it have a new one, too: down on Vanderpool Lane. Yes, over here. Feel it, the new one, the baby. So much life in that little body.

Fly down low now, right against the ground. Every door have a crack, no matter how small.

Right here. Slip into the house. Turn back into a woman. Is a nasty feeling, walking around with no skin, wet flesh dripping onto the floor, but I get used to it after so many years.

Here. The baby bedroom. Hear the young breath heating up in he lungs, blowing out, wasting away. He ain't know how to use it; I go take it.

Nice baby boy, so fat. Drink, soucouyant. Suck in he warm, warm life. God, it sweet. It sweet can't done. It sweet.

No more? I drink all already? But what a way this baby dead fast!

Childbirth was once a risky thing for both mother and child. Even when they both survived the birth process, there were many unknown infectious diseases to which newborns were susceptible. Oliphant theorizes that the soucouyant lore was created in an attempt to explain infant deaths that would have seemed mysterious in more primitive times. Grieving parents could blame their loss on people who wished them ill. Women tend to have longer life spans than men, but in a superstitious age where life was hard and brief, old women in a community could seem sinister. It must have been easy to believe that the women were using sorcerous means to prolong their lives, and how better to do that than to steal the lifeblood of those who were very young?

Dozing, Jacky leaned against Granny's knees. Outside, the leaves of the julie mango tree rustled and sighed in the evening breeze. Granny tapped on Jacky's shoulder, passed her a folded section of newspaper with a column circled. Births/ Deaths. Granny took a bitter pleasure in keeping track of who she'd outlived each week. Sleepily, Jacky focused on the words on the page:

Deceased: Raymond George Lewis, 5 days old, of natural causes. Son of Michael and Carmen, Diego Martin, Port of Spain. Funeral service 5:00 P.M., November 14, Church of the Holy Redeemer.

"Jesus. Carmen's baby! But he was healthy, don't it?"
"I don't know, doux-doux. They say he just stop breathing in the night. Just so. What a sad thing. We must go to the funeral, pay we respects."

Sunlight is fatal to the soucouyant. She must be back in her skin before daylight. In fact, the best way to discover a soucouyant is to find her skin, rub the raw side with hot pepper, and replace it in its hiding place. When she tries to put it back on, the pain of the burning pepper will cause the demon to cry out and reveal herself.

Me fire belly full, oui. When a new breath fueling the fire, I does feel good, like I could never die. And then I does fly and fly, high like the moon. Time to go back home now, though.

Eh eh! Why she leave the back door cotch open? Never mind; she does be preoccupied sometimes. Maybe she just forget to close the door. Just fly in the bedroom window. I go close the door after I put on my skin again.

Ai! What itching me so? Is what happen to me skin? Ai! Lord, Lord, it burning, it burning too bad. It scratching me all over, like it have fire ants inside there. I can't stand it!

Hissing with pain, the soucouyant threw off her burning skin and stood flayed, dripping.

Calmly, Granny entered Jacky's room. Before Jacky could react, Granny picked up the Jacky-skin. She held it close to her body, threatening the skin with the sharp, wicked kitchen knife she held in her other hand. Her look was sorrowful.

"I know it was you, doux-doux. When I see the Lagahoo, I know what I have to do."

Jacky cursed and flared to fireball form. She rushed at Granny, but backed off as Granny made a feint at the skin with her knife.

"You stay right there and listen to me, Jacky. The soucouyant blood in all of we, all the women in we family."

You, too?

"Even me. We blood hot: hot for life, hot for youth. Loving does cool we down. Making life does cool we down."

Jacky raged. The ceiling blackened, began to smoke.

"I know how it go, doux-doux. When we lives empty, the hunger does turn to blood hunger. But it have plenty other kinds of loving, Jacky. Ain't I been telling you so? Love your work. Love people close to you. Love your life."

The fireball surged toward Granny. "No. Stay right there, you hear? Or I go chop this skin for you."

Granny backed out through the living room. The hissing ball of fire followed close, drawn by the precious skin in the old woman's hands.

"You never had no patience. Doux-doux, you is my life, but you can't kill so. That little child you drink, you don't hear it spirit when night come, bawling for Carmen and Michael? I does weep to hear it. I try to tell you, like I try to tell you mother: Don't be greedy."

Granny had reached the back door. The open back door. The soucouyant made a desperate feint at Granny's knife arm, searing her right side from elbow to scalp. The smell of burnt flesh and hair filled the little kitchen, but though the old lady cried out, she wouldn't drop the knife. The pain in her voice was more than physical.

"You devil!" She backed out the door into the cobalt light of early morning. Gritting her teeth, she slashed the Jacky-skin into two ragged halves and flung it into the pigeon peas patch. Jacky shrieked and turned back into her flayed self. Numbly, she picked up her skin, tried with oozing fingers to put the torn edges back together.

"You and me is the last two," Granny said. "Your mami woulda make three, but I had to kill she, too, send my own flesh and blood into the sun. Is time, doux-doux. The Lagahoo calling you."

My skin! Granny, how you could do me so? Oh, God, morning coming already? Yes, could feel it, the sun calling to the fire in me.

Jacky threw the skin down again, leapt as a fireball into the brightening air. *I going, going, where I could burn clean, burn bright, and all you could go to the Devil, oui!*

Fireball flying high to the sun, and oh, God, it burning, it burning, it burning!

Granny hobbled to the pigeon peas patch, wincing as she cradled her burnt right side. Tears trickled down her wrinkled face. She sobbed, "Why all you must break my heart so?"

Painfully, she got down to her knees beside the ruined pieces of skin and placed one hand on them. She made her hand glow red hot, igniting her granddaughter's skin. It began to burn, crinkling and curling back on itself like bacon in a pan. Granny wrinkled her nose against the smell, but kept her hand on the smoking mass until there was nothing but ashes. Her hand faded back to its normal cocoa brown. Clambering to her feet again, she looked about her in the pigeon peas patch.

"I live to see the Lagahoo two time. Next time, God horse, you better be coming for me."

DELIA SHERMAN

The Crone

Delia Sherman won the Mythopoeic Award for her historical fantasy, The
Porcelain Dove, *and has twice been short-listed for the World Fantasy Award.
Her other works include* Through a Brazen Mirror, *numerous short stories and
poems, and a forthcoming novel for children,* The Freedom Maze. *She is also
co-editor of the anthologies* The Horns of Elfland *and* The Essential
Bordertown, *and a consulting editor at Tor Books. Born in Japan, raised in
New York City, Sherman received a B.A. in English from Vassar College, and
an M.A. and Ph.D. in Renaissance Studies from Brown University. She divides
her time between New York and Boston, where she lives with fellow writer
Ellen Kushner.*

*In "The Crone," the author takes a fresh look at a figure found in fairy
tales all around the world: the old woman waiting by the side of the road. The
poem first appeared in the fairy tale anthology* Black Heart, Ivory Bones *(Avon
Books).*

—T. W.

I sit by the side of the road, comfortably planted
On a stone my buttocks have worn silky.
My garments are a peeling bark of rags,
My feet humped as roots, my hands catch
Like twigs, my hair is moss and feathers.
My eyes are a bird's eyes, bright and sharp.
I wait for sons.

They always come, sometimes twice a day
In questioning season, looking for adventure,
Fortune, fame, a magic flower, love.
Only the youngest sons will find it:
The others might as well have stopped at home
For all the good I'll do them.

It's the second sons who break my heart,
Anxious at their elder brothers' failure,

Stuck with the second-best horse, the second-best sword,
The second-best road to disaster. Often I wish
A second son would share his bread with me,
Wrap his cloak around my body, earn
The princess and the gold.

That's one wish. The second (I'm allowed three)
Is that a daughter, any daughter at all—
Youngest, oldest—seeking her fortune,
A kingdom to rule, a life to call her own
Would sit and talk with me, give me her bread
And her ear. Perhaps (third wish) she'd ask
After my kin, my home, my history.
Ah then, I'd throw off my rags and dance in the road
Young as I never was, and free.

BEN PASTOR

Achilles' Grave

Ben Pastor holds a D.Litt. from the University of Rome and an M.F.A. from Vermont College of Norwich University, where she is a professor of graduate studies. Her fiction has appeared in Alfred Hitchcock's Mystery Magazine, Ellery Queen's Mystery Magazine, and Yellow Silk. She is also a regular contributor to The Strand, and has written two mystery novels, Lumen and Liar Moon (forthcoming).

The following story is a masterful work of historical fantasy rooted in the themes of Homer's Odyssey. "Achilles' Grave" is reprinted from Ghost Writing, edited by Roger Weingarten (Invisible Cities Press, Vermont).

—T. W.

> Around them then, a great and blameless mound
> We built, the sacred host of Argive spearmen,
> Upon the jutting strand by the wide Hellespont,
> So bright a monument as to be seen by men sailing afar,
> Those who live now and those yet to be born.
> (HOMER, THE ODYSSEY, XXIV, 82–86)

The smell of the trenches rose as from rotten veins in the earth. And it wasn't so much the heat of day but the anticipated interminable length of it that made me sick with hopelessness. The broken terrain—ravines, gullies, sandy escarpments and measly bushes of wilting grass—sketched all around a planet of known yet unknown character, and the way back was not as easy as retracing my steps.

It had happened before to others, even though by now, July's end, 1915, things ought to have changed. Yet here I was, lost past the reach of my own, brought forward by the heedless impetus of the battle for Gallipoli, when after hours of bombardment we could barely hear ourselves think, and like automatons rushed forth just to escape the noise. Achi Baba, the Tree Hill, loomed before me stretching its infamous arms across the width of the peninsula. Between those rocky limbs thousands of men lay dead from the most recent attacks, and the

Turk was still entrenched at the foot of the mountain, as exhausted and dazed as we were, but not flushed out yet. Never to be.

And the loss of my patrol was not unique but soon to be unbearable, when the shock of battle should wear off me. At this hour I was still numb past the reckoning of my own wholeness—the fact that, at least, I was physically unhurt. Sitting on a rock I kept my head low to the knees and dully began to ache, not my first time for exhaustion in Gallipoli. Ears still ringing with the shrapnel fire and fusillade, at first I did not take notice of the clicking sound to my right. It was as if small rocks were misplaced and made to roll upon others, a metallic noise nearly, without echoes. There hung great weariness for killing in me, still when I looked up the nozzle of my gun followed, and it was the slender, long nozzle of another gun that met it. Our pistols fronted one another for a time through their single, dark, cyclopean eye, then the one held by the newcomer swayed briefly and swung down, to rest at the end of his arm.

His uniform was different but not alien, not really. Khaki-colored, dirt-encrusted, boots made opaque by sandy loam. Even the tropical cork helmet, though not a Wolsey, wasn't that different at all.

"No ammunition," the German said. Not regretfully but as a statement of fact, letting the useless pistol dangle from his hand as if to prove that he didn't need it to confront me.

I sought my holster also. "Same here," I said, and there wasn't much more to do in terms of hostility.

One hand in his belt, the German stood with an air of dismayed fatigue.

"I became separated from my group," I admitted. He looked around. "Lost all my men," I added.

He said nothing, but came closer. "So have I." There was blood from one of my soldiers on my clothes. "Are you wounded?" He nodded toward the stains. If my face was as chalked with dust, we must both have looked like death.

"No."

But I had a sudden great need to cry with the denial. His being here outraged me, when he was the one who had been shooting at us since daybreak. Yet he didn't look more composed than I. An aghast expression of loss stayed on his face, and I knew he was starting to mourn also, too acutely to conceal it. There came between us a revolting and anguished communion of pity for the dead, and for ourselves, who had survived them.

Meanwhile we stared at one another, looking deep for the possibility of deceit, although it didn't seem feasible that we should be playing games in the felling heat of day. Noon had rolled into an afternoon so ablaze, the crop of the earth seemed to tremble as if with inner vapors.

The German crouched, finally, hands loosely twined between parted knees. He was a young company officer, bearing a couple of long thin scars on a cheek, such as student duels afforded those days in military school. I knew the *Mensur* to be a not-so-innocent proof of a man's character. He smiled briefly in apology, his face in the shade so that his teeth stood out white as bones. "You are grieving," he said.

My first reaction was to strike him for having said it. And I could, indeed. A blow in the face and then take my chances at fighting it out with him on the rocky dirt. Would it accomplish anything? I ended up by not replying.

"We may as well be civil to each other," he said. "There's nothing else to do for now."

It was true enough. We had been shooting at each other like madmen until a moment ago, inciting our own—my Britons, his Turks—to destroy the wavy line of the adversary, and likely we had. We had killed each other's resources off. There lay the measure of shared dismay in it, I knew. This is what he meant.

"We ought to find some shade," he suggested. At that I rose, walked off and found my way to a small *nullah*, steep-sided, whose bottom promised coolness. The stench of the blown-up trenches did not get here as strongly. I could hear the calm pace of his boots following, and the small clank of stones as he began to come down too.

We sat there for a time, and as the shell-shocked numbness of the afternoon wore thin in us, grief came. It made me once more bury my head in my folded arms, and the German passed one hand across his face until the fingers rested against his mouth, looking away. He was weeping when I glanced through the corner of my eye, shoulders rigid, tears running over his hand. In his place I would have scrambled away not to expose my weakness. But there he sat, knees drawn up, going through his own helpless grief. The sharing of it embarrassed me.

"You speak English well." I threw the words in eventually, just to fill the void. He had by now composed himself and was uncorking a cloth-covered canteen. He paused and offered it to me. I refused, and he drank from it.

For a minute, perhaps, we sat with our legs cramped at the bottom of the *nullah*, flies buzzing above us, and an eerie silence that swept the broken plateau where men had died. The German made fast his canteen again, though it was pointless to replace the stopple. There was no water left in it. In excess of mine, it seemed, total control had returned to him.

"It'd be impractical to walk back now, for either one of us." He tilted the helmet forward to rest the nape of his neck on the dirt wall. "Tonight, we can."

Nothing could be opposed to that. I sat gloomily, and closed my eyes to shield them from the glare cutting like a blade upon us. Soon a rustle of paper told me the German had taken something out of his knapsack. By the repeated soft sounds I assumed it must be a book. I looked over, and he was indeed leafing through a pocket-size edition of Greek poetry.

"*The Iliad?*" I asked.

"No, no. Not *The Iliad*. *The Odyssey*." He showed me the bilingual text, Greek on one page, German on the other. Both languages were remote but not obscure to me.

So, like us, the young German officers were living the Homeric nightmare in this narrow peninsula facing the plains of Troy. I know *we* were. Homer in our pocket, we had traveled here much like Byron had, and Xerxes, the great king who sat on a throne on the highland to watch his two million bronze-clad warriors invade Europe.

"This area is what they called the Thracian Chersonesus," he volunteered.

"I know well what it is."

"What I meant is—never mind."

We sat at arm's length, myself brooding, he reading the graciously curving

Greek characters, accents afloat on the verses. Was he pragmatically killing time, or did he seriously read the poetry? And what did mill in his mind anyway? Was he planning to take me prisoner—this was more Turkish than no man's land, by all accounts—as soon as fresh troops came? And why didn't I just clamber up and go my own way, and find another *nullah* to sit in?

The truth is that I could not. Whether it was weariness of limbs or an undone laxity of the soul, there I sat, and felt I had to stay there, next to a man from the ranks of those bent on destroying us. They well nigh had, too. So what? He was right, I was grieving, but not for my men alone.

I craned my neck to see. "What part are you reading?"

"*Amph' autoisi d'epeita megan kai amymona tumbon,*" he read.

It was the verse where the building of Achilles' burial mound on the Hellespont is described.

"They raised it just across the Strait," I said. "It's bizarre, I was thinking about it this morning before the attack: *a great and blameless mound.*"

He nodded. "That's whom I'm grieving for."

"Achilles?"

"For all Achilles represents. For us. You understand."

"Yes." I did. "*This is the stone of a man dead long ago.* Christ, this is a horrible war."

He put down the book. "You see, you should let go of *The Iliad.* It's *The Odyssey* that holds the key."

"What key?"

"To grief. To the resolution of grief."

"And do you think I would miss my dead less if I read some three-thousand-year-old poetry?"

He looked away. "Of course not."

"What, then?"

"I'm thinking of the *nekuya.*"

I asked him what he meant by that, and he said, "The meeting Odysseus had with the dead."

Had he not looked so unaffected, I'd have sneered in his face. "It's nothing but a tale."

"Maybe. But I don't see why it couldn't be done."

For a fleeting moment the doubt crossed my mind that perhaps he was not in his senses. Flushed with the heat, but otherwise composed, he did not trouble himself with convincing me, and went back to reading. As for me, I stood up to climb over the *nullah*'s wall and regained the godawful plateau, run by a hot wind like an oven that opens in your face. It hissed in my ears, and the misery of the blown trenches and the dead came back to me with the stench. For an hour or more I sat on the upper crust of the land, uselessly seeking comfort in the scanty shade of a rock, so narrow it afforded no reprieve. When I looked over, I saw the German walk toward the Achi Baba with measured steps, now and then finding his way among the rubble, over the torn bundles of barbed wire. Without turning he gestured at me. "If you want water, it's this way."

We walked a stretch in silence, and before long found ourselves in a deep ravine, narrowing at the bottom into a reduced track between steep walls, fringed with vegetation.

"The spring is just to the left."

It was. We filled our canteens with icy water that trickled down and soon became lost in the heat of the ground, like a snake that slithers away. I thought of the Greeks, who gave names of swift animals to creeks and rivers. It felt good to drink.

It still amazes me why, or why at this point, I thought the true core of my grief should be admitted, one that otherwise I warded closely.

"My brother died two months ago," I said.

The German stared at me. And now that I had foolishly spoken, there was no stopping me. It was as when one starts drinking water and will not let off even though he knows the excess will make him ill. Why should I tell an enemy, I wondered. I spoke nonetheless, in a jumble of words, and ended up confessing, "Before we left England someone told him he'd die by a large river."

The German had been pouring water from the canteen on his head. He stopped. "Such was not the case, then. Not at Gallipoli."

"You forget the landing off Cape Helles. The name of his ship was *River Clyde*."

Stockstill, the German looked at me. With the sun at his back, the moist halo of short blond hair on his head reminded me of my brother. He was tall and wide-shouldered, even as my brother had been. "I am very sorry." And then, absentmindedly, "I should think you would want to speak to him again."

That carelessness sounded like blasphemy. Without warning I hit the canteen he was still holding, knocking it off his hand. It flew off far behind him. He struck me back, hard, so that I was thrown against the wet wall of the spring. He pinned me down with his boot. The Luger came out, and from the sound it made when he handled it, I realized the magazine was in it, and it was loaded. Had been loaded when he first saw me and did not shoot. Without letting go of it, he offered me his left hand to help me get up. I wriggled instead from under his relenting hold, and rose on my own, too angry to be intimidated by the pistol.

"I don't even know where he's buried, damn you!"

"But you could find out."

"You're insane."

"Do you know your way out of here and back?" He grinned. "If not, *you're* insane to be here. I know this plateau well. I can find my way back before dawn, and not be killed on a mine." Now that he had washed off the grime, his face was tanned and smooth, bearing a cruel youthfulness entirely unlike my brother. "I have been thinking of the *nekuya* for a time. And I'm going tonight. You may join me if you wish. The dead will gather."

The dead will gather. As sometimes happens, a pattern of thought is upheaved by some outwardly innocent addition to a phrase. It was what he said last that made me fling the impossibilities off, and be hopeful against hope even if it was mad.

"Going where?" I asked.

"To the slope of Achi Baba, and up its right side trail. Absurd though it sounds, it is in the strength of the sacrifice and the intent of it that the difference lies. And the place is perfect. Odysseus would like it, even, or Achilles."

I gaped. "Why would you want someone with you then, an enemy at that?"

"You are grieving hard. Your grief will also make the difference."

It was then that I started thinking of what strategic insight could be gained by climbing the mountain we had failed to take in every other way. "What guarantees do you give me that I will not be taken prisoner if I come along? Your redoubts are that way."

"I will *not* show you our redoubts, be sure. As for the rest, you will have to trust me."

I wavered, but the absurdity of the task somehow scored better than the anxiety of waiting here for the Turks to come searching for survivors. Entering the wolf's mouth was quicker and less unnerving. "I don't recall the poetry as well as you do."

He took the book out again, and put it in my hands.

"Why are *you* doing it?" I inquired.

"Because I don't think I'll get out of here, and I mean to find out when it will come. And I grieve for Achilles, of course."

"Is that all?"

"I think it's plenty."

We found a protected place to sit and read the episode where Odysseus describes to his host his sacrifice and dialogue with the dead. We pored over the text, considering the words—his knowledge of Greek was excellent—and soon I had to ask how he meant to do what he planned.

"Simple. I already set aside the things necessary."

"Down to sheep and barley?"

"Of course. And the drinks, too. The prayers are not described, but I imagine the words will come."

"And the dead?"

"And the dead."

"Just like that."

"No, not just like that. It has been long in preparation, and long in grief. This is the right time, that's all. You may come if you wish, or I will go alone."

He truly knew his way around. We went up and down the upheaved terrain, avoiding this or that expanse of land that seemed to me no more dangerous than another. We clambered into shell holes and out of them, taking in stride the horrible presence of death everywhere. Through what remained of shelled hamlets, now heaps of refuse run by meager dogs, along hastily built stacks of bodies charred to stumps, we walked, and I wondered if the dead were supposed to come as they were now, burnt or rotting under a veil of dirt.

The sun was arching down when we reached the foothill of Achi Baba.

I never thought I would get as far as this low massif, against which Britons had been battering themselves for months. Here I was, and on my way up to its sides. Before the climb we could have had a brief dinner of bully beef and tack, but chose only to drink water—in case it should make a difference to the dead, I suppose, or to our stomachs, should the dead come.

The German said we should wait until nightfall, and we did, under a light that gilded us less and less as an immaterial tongue lapping low.

"Are you really grieving for Achilles?"

The German sat on a rock, splitting measly blades of grass lengthwise with his fingers. The flimsy strips he let go between his legs to his feet. He looked over at my question as if amused by my doubts. "Yes. I always did, and I always wanted to come here."

"To Gallipoli?"

"Yes." The blades in his left hand were fragile, thin. I didn't know why I felt anxiety for them as he resumed slicing them. "Haven't you?"

"God, no."

He smiled. "So, I'm luckier than you are."

It had taken us long to reach this point because he carefully led me away from the Turkish lines, as if the confusion of the terrain were not enough to protect them. Now that the day was nearly done we began to climb. A clear glaze of topaz dressed the air, cutting out the crags above us as stenciled forms and giving us glimpses of the empty sea as we gained altitude. With night ahead of us the enterprise did not seem so absurd anymore. Certainly not ridiculous. I looked up at the forbidding goat trails that darkness began to flatten and jumble here and there, and felt apprehension instead. The German was coolly beckoning from a place where the land surged not so sheerly. We kept going up, with night adrift at us from above. Soon the fires from the Turkish camps could be seen below, to the left. I screwed my eyes for the British lines, but could not identify them in the growing shadow, and was glad of it.

The German walked securely ahead of me, soon to clamber up a rocky side that was high and more precipitous. "There isn't much to go after this," he said when I warned him that I could not keep my footing.

"I'm going down a bit," I insisted. "I don't care for heights." As I spoke, he slid down and joined the place where I crouched. "I can't very well rest here!" I protested.

"Why not? It's perfectly safe." He stood, anchoring himself somehow with his heels to roots or rock stays, careless of the crag's pendency. Only a shade of daylight remained. Still, the diminished sense of space did not help my vertigo. I dimly saw the German rummage his left front pocket and take a cigarette case out. "Do you want one?" he asked.

We smoked, and it was the most precarious smoking I ever had, flicking red points that flared as we inhaled to reveal brief sights of our faces.

"Will the dead really come?"

"Yes."

"I don't see how you can be so certain."

"We're all dead, in relative terms. Why should they not come to their own?"

"We're *not* dead, in any terms."

He flicked away the cigarette, to tumble in the windy dark. "How do you know that I am not?" But he laughed.

It was a lucid and perfectly wrought night when we reached a flat extension, adjutting from the flank of Achi Baba like a terrace. Stars garlanded the horizon and it seemed as though we were at the top of a bloody and forgotten world. Wind wrapped the mountain with the briny scent of the sea. As we climbed the last stretch, words had become slow and fewer between us.

Too far gone into them, I no longer wondered at the bizarre turn of things. My companion found his way to the wall of the ledge, looking for things, I supposed, in the luminous dark of the summer night. Low bleating indicated where the animals were kept; their weak, tender voice was archaic and familiar to my ears, because I had known the country and the mild sounds of it.

The German rejoined me, carrying something. "Honey and milk," he said, "and wine. You have the water." He put in my hand a satchel with the barley seed.

"We need a pit. Has it been dug already?"

"To your right, yes."

Some steps off, I discerned two sheep tethered to a stake. Behind them I could also see the blackness of the pit dug as a squarish trough. A chill searched my spine.

Standing or kneeling to one side of the pit, we would be facing the mountain wall, where the shadow was now perfect and uninterrupted. This hole, too small to be one grave, should be our channel to the other world? I ran between my fingers the dirt piled at its rim, wondering whether Odysseus really had dared this, if he had ever even lived. This may have been Gallipoli, but it was not 1915 anymore. Or not yet, and we were in a suspended hiatus of time.

The German stood behind me, undoing his holster.

"Do the same."

At his words something like panic took me for the part expected of me in this. He might have sensed it, because he crouched alongside me then.

"Now remember your brother," he said. "Do not just think of him: remember. It's different if you remember, the dead know. Do not pray. Remember. How you will honor him when you return to your country. Remember those plans, too."

I felt tension in his voice for the first time.

"And you?"

"I know what I have to do."

Like him, I undid the strap of the holster and laid it aside. "I'm not ready yet," I said.

He stood up. "You're confusing readiness with lack of fear."

"So I am. It amounts to the same."

He walked off and went to wait on the ledge, I presumed, where the night must have been an endless bowl of whirling stars. While he was gone I groped for his holster on the ground, found it, took out the Luger and substituted it with my empty gun, which fit perfectly in its place. Then I sat and prayed, and *remembered*.

We were unarmed and bareheaded as we brought the flask of mixed honey and milk to the pit and poured it in. Then came the wine, from an earthen bowl. I could smell its heady sweetness gulping down to the earth. Gestures were spare, ritual in their essential brevity. Some of the stars were so huge when I turned to reach for my canteen, they seemed a hand-reach away. I looked down from them and hastily went about my business, which was letting the water into the hole. It braided down like swift metal, and was gone. The German followed by widening the mouth of the satchel and sprinkling the white small barley over all. We held our breath, I know, aware of the power of night and place on us—of what circumstances made that power pulse with dread. It had been a windy evening, and it was odd that the wind should fall now, where we were most exposed to crosscurrents from the coasts. Silence grew high like a fence that enclosed us and shielded us somehow from the bitter reality beneath.

Now the German stepped back to untie the first animal, whose bleating became alarmed as he carried it over. At the pit's edge, the sheep resisted, and he had to force it down with his knee even as Odysseus must have, and Achilles when he slew the victims for Patroclus. His hand held it by the wool of the shoulder, arching its back. Skillfully he cut across the side of the sheep's neck and there was a gurgle and hiss and a warm odor of blood, sickening memory of the trenches, a useless thrashing and death. Silence was now higher than the mountain. I numbly watched and heard things happen. The German led in the second sheep and killed it. He left the carcasses draped with their heads down the pit, to drain into it. My heart felt ill.

Both of us knelt on the rocky dirt, no longer even glancing at each other. Silence climbed over the stars. The thick trench knife was now held by the German with blade downturned, even as Odysseus had, ready to plant it in the earth to keep the dead from drawing too close. I felt I could have run away long ago, but not now: the knife kept me here, and not by threat.

I had never before known of Time stretching out and magnifying itself. As if it were a folded, compacted kind of Time which is known to us and we live by, and this was the same Time but it had opened, yawned and lay flat, and incommensurable space was covered by it, so that it was an eternity gaping around us.

Bodily laxitude would have kept us kneeling for our own dead, whether or not the darkness should spew them out again.

The pit, filled with the sinister mixture and dressed by the emptying bodies of the sheep, was like a mouth that had been fed and stayed hungry, dangerously agape. And we so close to it. I was awed by the simple horror of it, as obscene a symbol as I can find even today for war and men in it—the German and myself exposed to the same dark gulf, by choice.

Would the dead come to this? The jaws of death had chewed them already. Long digested, would they be vomited out again?

How long we waited, I cannot tell. Time gaped endless, as the night glided around us and constellations wheeled above and sank behind us. Yet without moving we waited, neither one of us able to bear the thought of letting go and then regretting it forever. We had to wait. I know I did. I was past being mesmerized by the absence of sounds, or the strange presence of the man who had brought me here, still I did not quiet my mind enough to fully remember. I held the key, and stolidly toyed with it.

The past flowed back eventually as Time reached that corner of reality, even as eddies fill the bend in the river, not through my doing. But with sore thoughts of my brother it flooded me: our childhood together, hopes, war, the news of his death, and absence even of the poor knowledge of his burial place. Memory broke through like a dam, a levee of regret. An unmeasurable rush of unhappiness streamed over me, and all the while I knelt on the ledge of Tree Hill, before the bloody offering.

The pit yawned dark and sharply smelling. I was staring down at it when I heard the sudden stab of the knife in the earth. With a start I looked up.

From the opposite side of the pit, close to the ground and emerging from it as one who wades through high water or grass, a man was coming toward it. He wore a uniform, too battered to tell which. His arms were raised forward but not stretched, as if he were blindly groping for the food. My hair stood on end, my entire body bristled in the way animals cringe in fear.

He seemed as one drowned and left in the water to float supine under the surface, there and not there, blindly groping. The eyes in his face, dull, jellylike, were horribly open and as spoiled drops of milk, pupils curdled and void.

My heart had sunk so deep in the chest, I could not hear it draw blood. I was too frozen to tear myself away from the sight, as though my bones and muscles had been disconnected from one another and without structure I were lumped on the ground in a heap. My tongue clung to the roof of my mouth. Had I found the strength to shout, I'd have howled inarticulate sounds like madmen do.

"Is he your brother?"

I don't know how the German could find the courage to ask. He was still holding the knife down, like a rock hewn at my side and unwavering.

My eyes riveted to the hideous shape from the dark, I could only shake my head in denial. All I hoped for was enough energy to beg him to quit this place, but it was too late. Already it was a crowd of half-figures wading toward the pit from nothingness, pale and luminescent as the tucking of the waves at night. Here and there they swayed through one another, shuffling places. Their motions were fettered, pleading, yet hideously familiar to me. These were faces I had known. Those of my men who had died just hours ago, contorted as at the point of passing, bloodless, their clothing upheaved and stained and torn. And like cripples, from their belly down there was nothing, only the black earth from which they rose. How many could assemble in one place, it seemed incomprehensible. Shifting and fading, the faces superimposed as reflections in dark mirrors—now they were my men, now they were long-jawed Germans and Turks with big staring eyes.

And how many of them had we killed, my companion and I? How many had I sent to this swamp of darkness unthinking that I should ever see them again? It curdled my blood to think that they knew. Fear ran unchecked through me. There was no safety on this ledge, and none to be sought next to me. I could sense the revulse of the German beside me, but the knife stayed down. Whatever kept me here, it was lack of strength that rooted me.

Then I saw my brother in the fishlike pale mingle. As one in an inexorably moving throng makes out a face and it becomes the center of a now inexpressive fluidity, all other shapes lost value to me. Even fear. I found my heart again, and control of my sinews enough to kneel up.

It *was* my brother, feeling his way toward me in a tentative, halting gait. The face was his, my brother's face, though I saw now how much of his features had been expression, and how without it there was an alien cast to them—a frightening and despair-breeding estrangement, as if no longer we might know each other when we had been so close. I must have called out to him, such surge of agony seized me for seeing him there. I lunged forward and stumbled with my foot in the pit, where it sank in the squelch of blood and mixed liquids. The hand of the German reclaimed me harshly.

"Get back! You will talk to him when I let you!"

And I'd have fought his command, except that I longed to speak to my brother. I drew back. Only then the knife was pulled out of the earth, and what I witnessed next I tremble to repeat even after so many years. My brother bent over the pit and seemed to fish down with his hand to drink from it.

The German kept motionless at my side, knife resting in his lap, but I was shaking so violently, it was like a seizure that rattled the teeth in my head. Disgust and love tied slimy knots in me as I watched my brother feed from the repulsive trough. If only I had not so closely recognized the way he parted his hair, the freckles on his neck, the motion of his shoulders as he pulled up from the pit. This was no dream. Tears welled in my eyes and made him waver in my view while he looked up, mouth fouled from the drink. I found myself grasping the dirt with my hands, because I knew he would speak now.

"Why did you come here?"

I didn't see his lips part, though they must have. His face gained no expression, nor did he attempt to wipe the blood from his chin. It was his voice, the voice I knew so well, and thought I should never again hear while in this world. All reserves collapsed within me at the sound of it and I was too convulsed to speak back, but he must have known what I sought, or someone else asked for me, because, "It is by the *wadi* north of our first landing," he said. The voice was hollow as though heard through a tunnel, expressionless like the rest of him, unmoved. It was his, but now the familiar ring was gone. "You may ask the corporal, he put me there, and will remember if you tell him my tag had been blown off."

Oh, God. I could see why. There was a gaping hole in his tunic, black with blood and wide enough to have blasted life out of him. It was the sight of the wound that made his death too much for me to withstand. I cried out and stretched my hand to him across the pit. I met with nothing, my fingers met with nothing but the night air.

That was my mistake, as it had been Odysseus's. Fingering the empty space I had broken his fabric, immaterial though it may be, flimsier than web spittle. I searched with my eyes and fumbled uselessly until dejection doubled me over, because he was gone.

Not so the hazy crowd of others rising from the hard soil to draw only so close: Britons and Germans, Frenchmen, gangling Anzacs, the small, angry-looking Turks, and we facing them. But how my heart was sour by now. I felt my soul had poured itself in the pit and would be drunk by the earth, never to be returned to me. All I had meant to gain from this was over, since my brother had been swallowed back. I cared to see no more.

The shades afloat in the dark were hungry. They wanted brief sustenance and the means of speech, all of them, for all had died with unsaid things, as we likely all will. But I cared no more to witness the ghosts of their lacerated selves, flesh hanging as beggars' cloth, hair matted by the ooze of blood and brains. Fear rose and ebbed in me only because no excess can be maintained, and I had seen enough horror.

I became aware of the German again, whose stiffness was yet vigilant. Insensible to the reach of hands to him—they knew he held the power—he still warded our space by the jagged length of his knife, waiting for one more face to appear.

Slowly I tried to crawl back from him, but he held me by the arm until I resumed my slumped kneeling alongside the pit.

"Let me go," I begged. "Let me go."

"Why?"

"Let me go."

His fingers relented so that I cowered away from the hole, and at a distance crouched hiding my face in my arms, where I could weep.

Another long interval passed, until the presence he awaited came forth. I did not look, but I'm sure it was unknown to me, and I would not recall it. He must have taken the knife out then, and there followed the grim feeding into the pit and an exchange of words. All I could hear was his whispered voice, not the other's. Eyes shut behind the childish protection of my hands, I would not look over, but he did ask a question, and I caught the word *sterben*, to die, in it.

I knew that in a pale luminous curtain the dead must be facing him, and how he could speak to them with any measure of control was loathsome to me, because those bloated, hollowed faces, those gaping mouths and eyes drifting up to him should terrify him as they had me.

Let him face them alone, I cringed to myself. Shredded out of life, torn from it, let them wade to him from the hard swamp of death—my men and his alike, men we had never known, men long dead and Achilles himself, were his goodly shade able to raise itself and come bronze-clad to give answer.

When I looked up, God knows how much later, the German had replaced the knife in the soil, deep to the hilt. Across from the pit, the slow tide of the shadows pressed on and was checked, no longer wading. Pleading still, but he had no mercy on them.

There was good reason. Time was folding up again around us in the brief summer night. As a fan that closes, its creases gathered nearer and more arduous to slip through. An awareness of twilight already drew a nacred reflection on the eastern horizon. The German kept fast until the curtain of shades grew thin and faint, less and less visible, until there was nothing left beyond the pit but the bare wall of the mountain.

After he pulled back we sat as men fallen from undiscovered heights, wondering, I am sure, whether we were alive. I could not speak, and at first neither could he. His face was stark and white like a chalk stain in the fading dark— mine surely no less, judging by the way I felt.

The stars had begun to burst like bubbles in the sky when the German tucked the sheep in the hole, and began sweeping dirt on them with his hands. It amazed me that he could move.

"They ought to be skinned and burned, but there's no time."

Even his voice was efficient again. He buried the knife with the sheep and the containers, pressed the dirt over them with his boots. I still simply sat. I watched him reach for the holster belt and without check or hesitation wear it about him.

"I'll take you back to your lines," he said.

I stirred, no differently from one who is awakened and slowly gathers his wits. How cold the hours before morning were, and moist. I stood shivering, with the acute renewed knowledge that I was wearing his loaded gun, which gave me an entirely different advantage from yesterday.

"I think you will," I stammered, to which he said nothing. It was still too dark to see his expression clearly, but he must have wondered at my words. I felt drunk with fatigue, and otherwise empty inside.

All that had passed made us incapable of speaking of it, so a makeshift trite logic ruled over our motions as we set off from the ledge. The day was near breaking, an immense cosmic egg whose fracture could no longer be amazing to us after this night. Colors began to be distinguishable in it, emerging from the gray to help define shapes, distances.

My sense of balance was gone. The German had to help me find my footing down from the ledge. And it was all I could do—haltingly following him along the precipitous path, more perilous in descent, until we regained a less plunging ground and eventually the foothill. I needed to stop, but he would not let me. The way we had followed here with growing expectation and tenseness unfurled in reverse, and there was nothing left of those emotions. He drove me on, for my safety and his, giving us no time to think.

Once more we avoided trenches and redoubts, while the light of day stole upon us clear and unmarred by clouds overhead. Birds called in it. Like any other day at Gallipoli, this might have been a time to die. Shelling was likely to start any minute, we both knew: my tired steps gained machinelike sprint from the thought, while his gait drew long and easy. And comfortingly at my side was the holster, filled with its potential of death.

Past the entrenched piedmont, we trailed back the calvary through destroyed hamlets, abandoned posts, the German two steps ahead of me. His back and the nape of his neck were exposed to me, and when he turned once or twice to see if I followed, the bony and shatterable youth of his face.

We came out to the broken plateau finally, with its jumbles of twisted wire, mined fields. The sun was on the horizon. Orange red, squat, it created shadows endless and blue under rocks, tufts of grass, ourselves. Ravines and *nullahs* lay still filled with night. Whenever we passed a body we both looked away.

In absolute silence the German led, two steps ahead, bareheaded and vulnerable. I planned to undo the flap of the holster before long. In my imagination my fingers had done so many times already, sending him to join the fishlike throng of the dead, so that he should foul himself to drink blood and dirt as my brother had, were anyone ever to summon him. It was vengeance on our impiety, and my own renewed grief. I knew his mind was a captive—even as mine—of the time we had spent by the bloody pit. He could not help it any more than I could. We did not *think* of it: it was in us. And I would kill him as soon as he asked the question.

So we walked extraneous to each other, more than enemies now, myself waiting for a word, he not pronouncing it. Across the embattled ground he chose our steps for us and I accepted that choice, grudgingly, until it occurred to me that he didn't dare ask. Fear or reticence, or even just restraint, kept him from it, or canny wisdom.

And anyway, were I to kill him here and awaken echoes first and other guns right after, who should lead me back to the lines? The thought, until now secondary, came to the fore. And no solution to it. I walked with hand trembling in the belt, anxious to hurt him, impotent before my own danger and unwilling to risk my life to bring him down. Our time grew shorter like our shadows. And this is why I did what I did next, and it is unforgivable perhaps, but took the place of killing him.

"I saw nothing." I prevented his question, more calmly than I could tell the truth.

He looked back at me over his shoulder.

"There was nothing there," I added. "Just the pit and the two of us, and the dead sheep."

He turned his back to me again. His pace hesitated, then resumed the speed he had kept until now to avoid search parties and bombardment. But now he had to escape my doubt as well. I knew how fragile he must feel inside, how dazed and insecure my words must make him.

"I have seen nothing, I tell you."

He would not look at me. I was alerted that we were close to danger when he indicated to me silently what trail to take ahead. We heard Turkish voices to our left from a protected place, and came down to our hands and knees in the dust. I did not stand again until he did.

I should have killed him. Shame for lying tugged at me already, but it was done, and was less honorable than killing. I can justify myself today, and say that unless I were ready to face what I had seen, the truth was too frightening to be shared. I was not ready—would not be for years to come. What I said then was, let *him* kill his doubts for the rest of his days. My mental safety came first. Inner refusal could only feed on open denial. I saved myself thereby, in self-defense. Catching up with his pace, I lightly inquired, "And you, have you found out when you'll die?"

"I didn't ask."

I knew he had. He was aware of my game and played by the rules, without amusement. Now we were lying to each other for good. He told me in the next breath, with a neutral lack of concern, "There was no need to take my gun. You will please give it back now."

The sentence shook me from pretended apathy, because it was impossible that he should know. I had been watching him closely, and not once had he checked his holster, not even felt for it with his hand. How did he know? I swallowed hard at being discovered.

He faced me, so I handed the Luger to him, and he checked the magazine of it and then gave me back my pistol.

There was no more possibility of an exchange between us. In complete silence he brought me back to the spot where we had met, giving me a clipped indication as to the shortest way to the British line. Save for the kinder sky overhead, we could be as we had stood the day before, and nothing have happened in the meanwhile.

"Good-bye," he said, and without delay began retracing his steps until he disappeared in a depression of the upheaved earth, to emerge again but very distant, bound for the hard-held Turkish line.

It took me just over twenty minutes to negotiate my paces to our most advanced post, where I had been given up like the rest of the patrol. Hot coffee awaited me, breakfast and the clumsy congratulations of my companions. I sat and ate, letting them talk me out of distress and anger with the recited list of my lucky circumstances. The triteness of their words paled before their blindness.

"Bloody lucky, Lieutenant, that's what you are!"

"We thought you were gone for good."

"My God, old man, you come back from the dead!"

I never saw the German again. I ignore whether he survived and left Gallipoli, as we Britons did. Beaten back and unable to wrest the peninsula from the Turk, we would be evacuated within four months of that encounter, and the last thing we should see on the shore at night was the high burning piles of material we destroyed not to leave it in enemy hands. They looked like funerary pyres on the waterfront, such as the heroes of old were cremated upon, such as Achilles had been rested over, on the other side of the Hellespont, "so bright a monument as to be seen from men sailing afar."

My brother lay indeed buried by the small *wadi*, and was eventually identified by some items on him, the tag having been blown off his neck chain. But often bodies are identified with delay. Was this enough to ascribe it to what I thought I heard over the bloody pit?

Nothing so great could take place on Achi Baba. What happened that night has ever since been fashioned by me into a near perfect dream. I spent years convincing myself of it: I was young, overwrought, under the pitiless strain of a losing campaign. Who the German was and why he should take me to his sacrifice for the dead, I cannot imagine, nor do I want to.

We were deluded, I have been telling myself these many years. Many strayed off in that war to the strange no-man's-land of illusion, afterward to find their danger-fraught way back. The dead cannot be so close as to face the living by our offer of grim food, held at bay by the ancient taboo of metal: if they were, then man's existence would be at all times haunted by their silent hunger and hope to be fed.

And our intention was not pure enough for a miracle. The German wanted power over his future—myself, I sought remembrance. Could we be so self-serving in prying open the frightful chink, and be allowed in? These questions I carry with me, knowing full well that not ever again could I be brought to find out whether it can be done.

What I truly would like to hear from the German is why he did not kill me when he first saw me crumpled on the boulder, because I would have in his stead. I did not kill him only because I meant to save myself through him. It troubles me that he left me in debt, possibly twice in debt. The grudge has only grown longer with time. There's no forgiveness when those we wronged do not avail themselves of vengeance.

And it's unlikely, but were I to return to Gallipoli, the ledge on Achi Baba would be all that I wish to see once more. I'm not sure why. I shouldn't go there by night, but with the light of day it would somehow fill my soul to catch a view of the terraced edge of the mountain, and the copper-bright sea lining the Strait across from Achilles' grave.

TIA V. TRAVIS

Down Here in the Garden

Tia V. Travis lives in Northern California with her husband, writer Norman Partridge, and their four cats. Having grown up in the foothills of the Canadian Rockies, the author, like the main character in her story, which is based on the story of the ill-fated Donner Party, is all too familiar with the hazards of sub-zero temperatures.

Travis visited Donner Lake on the way home from a trip earlier this year. "It was a hot summer day and the lake was blue, tranquil, and impenetrable. I was surrounded on all sides by endless mountains and trees, a magnificent but unforgiving landscape. I imagined what it must have been like to attempt to make it through the pass in the dead of winter, struggling with broken axles, blizzards, and empty bellies. Strangely, nowhere at the interpretive center was it mentioned what some of the pioneers were forced to subsist on during that unendurable winter. The employee we talked to, despite discreet inquiries, was reluctant to discuss particulars. The most deeply moving moment was discovering a mason jar of dried beans at the memorial monument. Pinned to the jar was a drawing of a covered wagon and a smiling pioneer stick figure. Beneath this, in crayon: 'To Patty Reid, Aged 8.' A little gift from a living child to another long dead."

Travis's story "The Kiss" appeared in last year's volume of The Year's Best Fantasy and Horror. *She has a short story collection coming soon from Subterranean Press. "Down Here in the Garden" was originally published by* Horror Garage, *no. 1.*

—E. D.

"Even the wind seemed to hold its breath as the suggestion was made that were one to die, the rest might live. Then the suggestion was made that lots be cast, and whoever drew the longest slip should be the sacrifice. The slips of paper were prepared . . ."

—MARY GRAVES, SURVIVOR OF THE FORLORN HOPE,
THE DONNER PARTY, WINTER OF 1846–47

"At sunset we crossed Truckee Lake on the ice and came to the spot where we had been told we should find the emigrants. We looked all around, but no living thing but ourselves was in sight. We raised a loud hello, and then we saw a woman emerge from a hole in the snow. As we approached her, several others made their appearance in like manner, coming out of the snow. They were gaunt with famine, and I never can forget the horrible, ghastly sight they presented. The first woman spoke in a hollow voice, very much agitated, and said, 'Are you men from California, or do you come from heaven?' "

—UNNAMED MEMBER OF THE FIRST RELIEF PARTY, 1847

"Who knows what sorrows abide
In the heart of a strange lonely man?"
—FRED MCKEAN AND SHEB WOOLEY,
"THE LONELY MAN," 1961

Daren Powell sits in The Forlorn Hope outside Truckee, California, and warms his bare hands on the backs of his gloves. Despite the glowing embers in the granite fireplace, despite the crackling logs, the spicy smoke; the chill has penetrated even the deepest layers of his T-shirts, sweaters, heavy jacket; and he finds himself wrapped in the embrace of the Sierra Nevadas.

Daren's drinking partner waits at the bar for another bottle of whiskey. The last is nearly empty, the contents little more than something expedient to wash down the spit. He bottom ups his glass and stares at the dull sky beyond the windowpane, taking in the scenery as if it is nothing more than a remote, desolate postcard. Arthritic trees bent under a burden of snow . . . ragged shoulders of pines stooped against the mountains. An ice fog drifts through the pass like a slow, cold breath on the back of the neck, seeking to settle in the secret crevices, the empty places, the vast caverns of the human soul.

Whiskey burns Daren's stomach as he pours himself another shot.

Let it burn, he thinks. At least then he will feel. The last heat of life, running through his veins . . .

Outside the bar, across the empty parking lot, the highway is deserted save for the occasional intrepid SUV loaded down with the prerequisite skiing equipment. A new Saturn slides down the ice canal of Interstate 80 as if on Hans Brinker's magical silver skates. Destination: Caesar's Palace Tahoe for a weekend of discounted credit card pleasures.

Headlights cut through the dull afternoon like search lanterns, sweeping across the bleak highway. Columns of light gleam on the snow between the trees on the hills.

Daren stares at these trees, at these hills, at the mountains that lay beyond them, and takes another sip of whiskey.

He thinks about a woman.

Not *his* woman.

Not Erin, sunlight-bright as her sister's oceanfront house, where the windows reflect the sky the way a mirror reflects a face. She waits for him there, for this shipwreck of a man to wash up on the beach, a stray twist of driftwood she can sculpt into the semblance of something useful. There she is, on her sister's salmon boat on the smooth waters of the Pacific. The two of them are laughing, exuberant, as they cast their shimmering lines.

Daren lets himself exist momentarily in this vision. Lets it surround him in a warm, sunlit aura. Shell-white feet slapping across the deck. Polished toenails in search of pearls. She squints at the sky, eyes greenish-blue as the sea, and flashes a smile of welcome recognition—

And then she slips away. Her image scatters like dandelion fluff in the wind, and she leaves him here, alone, in the mountains.

Two hours earlier when he was less drunk, less depressed, less oppressed by the silence of the mountains in this late and ever later afternoon, he'd immersed his thoughts in his wife's golden caviar scent, the traces of salt she left in his senses.

No, not salt.

Something else.

Tears. No. Blood. No. Something else—

—the salty, sweaty taste of her skin. A taste he knows well, knows with eyes closed.

But now Erin—the scintillating promise of her—is replaced by the requirement of the moment.

Another woman.

A woman who flits through the unsteady trails of his mind like a strange, elusive butterfly. A woman whose presence here in the pass runs through him like a pure mountain brook. A woman who—in his mind, at least—lies forever frozen in a hard ridge of untouched snow.

There she is.

Part the branches of the trees; streaming, dripping, in the warming sun as new life begins.

Shhh, now.

She lies on her left side. She is a curved branch, the hard cracks of her spine protruding like lumps of ice. Her fingers are curled fishhooks sunk into a shroud-bed of moss. Flecks of bark, the husks of thistles, are buried deeply. Too deeply, beneath fingernails stone-white as the sky. Her lips—or so Daren imagines, in his fevered, inebriated trance—are slightly parted. Bruised. The dry ochre tint of acorn caps. Her last breath is chill smoke, a thin patina of ice rimming nostrils chapped scarlet as winter berries . . .

Her name is Robyn Corliss.

It is a name inherent to the spring, to the resurgence of life, to new beginnings. Poetically, ironically, appropriate, in the way that only life can be.

Robyn Corliss.

She lies still on the hillside, her lips silently parted.

Robyn Corliss.

She is a mystery to him.

The letters of her name tumble from the precarious edges of his mind like a handful of impenetrable runes . . . strewn down the side of a ravine. The ravine is edged with thatches of birds' nests, robins' nests lined with thistles burned to husks in the wind. He falls past the nests, past the thistles; past the pale, rooty protuberances of human hands, falls into the depths of the ravine, falls to the freezing streams far below, and he doesn't feel the thistle teeth as they tear into his body. He doesn't feel the grasping of the pale root hands, for this is only a dream, a waking dream; and the thistles, the hands, are nothing more than a collection of images, subconscious pictures, unexperienced remembrances of a woman's last moments of life . . .

Nothing more.

Robyn Corliss is thirty-four years old at the time of her death.

The articles in the Sacramento and San Francisco newspapers had been dated April 21, a little less than eight months before Daren finds himself sitting here in The Forlorn Hope. She'd been driving alone from Green River, Wyoming, to Meadow Vista, California, where she planned to meet her husband. Never before traveled through this part of the country. New territories these, Hell Hole Reservoir, Desolation Valley Wilderness, Sugar Pine Point, Donner Pass, a Second Eden . . .

. . . to some.

To many.

To none.

It would seem that at the time of Robyn Corliss's disappearance off the face of the map—December 8th of the preceding year, a day after the official closing of the road leading through the Tahoe and El Dorado National Forests—she had been ill-prepared for mountain driving in winter conditions. That she had—for undetermined reasons—deviated from the only practical course available to her: the sure thing, the main highway, the interstate. And this, on the afternoon of what would prove to be the most devastating blizzard to hit the Sierras in more than a hundred and fifty years.

Robyn Corliss's Chevrolet Beaumont—no chains on the tires (and of what use would they be, on the straight plains of Wyoming?)—had spun out of control; for a deceptive slick of ice beneath the surface layer of snow is hardly a rare occurrence in the mountains.

So—

The ice is encountered. The Beaumont skids off the through-road which had—last September, when the leaves were a prism of light and the air a promising blue—been extended west to intercept the interstate at Meadow Vista. And, if the new extension is not precisely a shorter, more direct route through the mountains, then it is—as the Department of Tourism most persuasively advertises—certainly the more *picturesque*.

The Beaumont plows directly into the embankment.

It is discovered soon after the park rangers reopen the road to the public, shortly after the second thaw of the season has revealed the chromed hulk that has hibernated all winter beneath a protective blanket of snow.

The door is open, as if the driver has just left the car for a moment—perhaps upon spotting a fleet of darting snowshoe hare in the wood; icons of winter beauty irresistible to one who has never visited the mountains in her life. Just a short delay in the itinerary before returning to the safety of a heated car. The intention being to retrace the secondary road back to the highway. And once on the highway—smooth, straight, ice-free—the driver will continue on with her dreams, her passions and pursuits; her inevitable frustrations, her depressions and defeats, her triumphs . . . her life.

Instead, the young woman's journey has ended one hundred and fifty yards northeast of her automobile on the lee side of a still sodden hill; which, on December 8th of the previous year, had been topped with an ever-deepening crust of virgin snow.

There she is.

Daren pictures her now—

Robyn Corliss.

Nutmeg brown hair gleaming in the warm, liquid glow of sunlight, sunlight that falls on the pale hollows of her cheek. She lies as if asleep beneath a stand of birch trees, the leaves of which have ripened into a tangy saffron-green.

What Robyn Corliss had intended by hiking up the steep hill in two feet of snow is anyone's guess. Perhaps she'd been attempting to make it back to the highway more than thirty miles away when the sudden storm swept her off her feet. Perhaps, with a slight concussion from the accident, she'd become disoriented, then hypothermic, in the blinding storm.

Or perhaps, as her upreaching position on the mountain hillside might suggest to the more romantically (or at least the more ambitiously) inclined, she had been in the process of climbing up to God. For surely the clouds that pass silently overhead on Donner Peak could have resembled outstretched angel wings to a freezing woman blinking snowflakes from her lashes. Angels, calling the lost ones home. . . .

Perhaps.

The temperature when Robyn Corliss freezes to death has been estimated at thirty below, with a wind chill factor ensuring exposed skin will turn to the texture of parchment in less than a minute. She's wearing a sweater and a slim dress she's bought especially for her trip at the Wal-Mart in Green River. The dress is printed with indigo irises and pink hollyhocks. Sunny yellow marigolds.

Frozen to death, while retracing her steps to the main highway . . .

Returning to civilization, to the New California.

The Western Eden, the answer to her prayers.

Instead, she's discovered uncharted territories, untried routes—

frozen to death

on a mountain that leads straight to God.

Daren turns from the window, from the scene he's rewritten thousands of times in the endless scripts of his own mind.

His drinking partner returns to the table. Lane, his name is. Daren's met him only this afternoon. He'd stepped into the bar for a drink soon after Daren himself had.

No point drinking alone, Lane had said.

No, no point at all. And really, there wasn't. Have a seat, Daren invited the stranger. Now, hours later, still here, the pale sunlight cuts the man in half as he sits.

Getting thirsty again? Lane does not await the answer before topping off Daren's drink. Lane smiles. It's a slow smile. Slow to reach eyes that are a light, clear, uncompromising gray. Gray as an overcast sky after a hard snowy sleet that drives straight through to the ground.

Daren is reminded of the salmon his wife will land on the deck of her sister's boat, a little late in the season, but why not? The fish, if they are caught, will suffocate to death. They will end their own slicing silver journeys in someone's skillet. Poached and seasoned with lemon pepper and rosemary and a little white wine . . .

. . . if they are caught. Jerked into the open air.

Lane pours himself a shot.

The man's fingernails, Daren notices, are dirty. Flecks of bark, of thistle husks . . . No, not thistle husks. Something else. *Blood*. No. A mechanic's grime. Lane is a mechanic, he's told Daren this. Repairs things—cars, engines—with his hands. Sends the travelers back on their way.

Here's to The American Dream, Lane says with a wry smile.

How deceiving, thinks Daren. *The American Dream*. But he raises his glass. Here's to

untried routes

uncharted territories—

They clink glasses.

To the American Dream. Wherever it leads.

Daren briefly meets his eyes. With their silver-gray irises, their depthless pupils, these eyes are the black-speckled bellies of salmon. Salmon still thrashing on the banks after a hard snowy sleet has just jumped them from their course. An instinctive course it is. A need to return to what has been lost. To the memory of being born.

A *hard snowy sleet, jumping them from their course, and slicing journeys that end on a plate. Far, far from home.*

That is what it is like to look into Lane's silver-gray eyes.

Then again, it's been a long time since Daren has looked into his own.

Four o'clock, Saturday afternoon.

Daren is past drunk, well past it now. And on an empty stomach, too. Doesn't seem to be doing his ulcer much good, but then, nothing does. Sour milk.

Drink up, Lane encourages. Alcohol don't freeze.

You have a point.

Lane nods. Gonna be another long, cold winter.

Outside the mercury is fifteen below, dropping steadily. Still no new snow. Just the old snow, dirty and gray as rotting gums. The wind shrieks in the trees.

Daren doesn't await a second invitation.

The glass in his hand is clear and cold, a glint of ice.

He's been sitting here in The Forlorn Hope since noon, ever since he locked up the Lake Tahoe house and hit the road. *Ten miles*. That's how far he's come since he tossed his backpack onto the passenger's seat of his old pickup. Ten miles since he'd headed west on interstate 80, theoretically toward the city of Sacramento, where he somehow still plans on spending the night in a motel. In the morning, he will head straight north on highway 8 before cutting across the 299 to the coast, drive straight into the arms of his waiting wife.

Yes, this is what he will do.

At least, that had been the strategy this morning when he'd stopped off at The Great Sierra Outdoors to say *vaya con dios* to Ingrid and Derek. It had been eight months since the newspaper articles, eight months in these mountains with his head in a bottle. That was plenty of time to decide this particular American Dream wasn't much of a dream anymore. His partners had eagerly bought out his third of the retail business.

Daren hadn't hung around at the store set back in the pines. He'd designed it to resemble a *faux* Alpine chalet, but it looked more like something off the set of *Heidi*. And just as prefabricated. Still, it was Tahoe's most popular outdoor and sporting goods store, boasting not only the very latest array of camping, hiking, skiing, snowboarding, mountain biking and mountaineering equipment, but an extensive selection of books and videos: avalanche safety, back country awareness, scenic day hikes, the basics of hypothermia prevention. The pamphlet racks were jammed with slick brochures for ski resorts, outdoor attractions, Tahoe/Reno hotels and casinos, bed and breakfasts, local maps. There—a brochure for the new extension through Tahoe and El Dorado National Forests. The cover had a photograph of a highway winding through a valley. Mountain peaks sparkled in the distance.

Untried routes . . . uncharted territories.

Daren had dropped by about eleven-thirty that morning. Ingrid was outlining the features of the new Salomon X Scream Series to a handsome male skier who'd have bought anything for the chance to hear her Norwegian accent. The accent—and the blonde hair—were sales gimmicks. Authentic gimmicks, albeit, but gimmicks.

Ingrid rang up the skis. Poles. Bindings. Chapstick. SPF 45 Sunblock. A real pro, this Nordic princess. Never missed an opening.

Derek, a twenty-something snowboarding aficionado with a superlative sense of salesmanship, was attempting to keep up with the demands of a local climbing outfit. The counter was laden with super-lightweight ropes, crampons, ascenders, titanium pulleys. Derek barely had time for a quick smile and a nod in Daren's direction before jogging off to the stockroom for a set of Advanced Base Camp Climbing packages.

Standing there on the rubber-treaded doormat in a pool of melting slush while his former partners successfully wheeled and dealed their way into the next tax bracket was beyond the realm of the depressing. It was a collision with the past, distasteful reminder of a former self. Besides, the good-byes had already been said last night over drinks and Canadian caribou steaks at The Fondue Hut; still doing business after thirty-five years on one of Tahoe's more touristy streets. It was time to leave.

It was just as well. The day had started with this ice mist drifting down through the pass. No precipitation in the immediate forecast, but a northeasterly wind stirred snow across the highway.

Leave early. Erin had urged him when they'd talked the night before.

Erin.

Ensconced in the beach house with the raucous squalling of jays on the timber deck and the breakers crashing against the rocks like the choral of Beethoven's Ninth . . .

Daren, standing in deafening silence at the front window of the house they'd just sold for a tidy profit. Neat and tidy. As if packing up the remnants of one's life in neatly labeled boxes was all that was required to leave the past behind. Lock up when you're done.

As Erin cheered and bolstered, a chattering jay herself, he said nothing. Listened mutely. Stared out at the ice-sheeted lake, a lake that shone midnight-blue in the clear, cold moonlight. If he searched—really searched—he could almost, at the very limits of his vision, discern a trail of gleaming silver footprints that traced the brittle skim of ice. A woman's footprints, the toes like silver shells . . . disappearing into the mountains.

He'd heard the lake was bottomless.

Everything will be all right, Daren, his wife reassured him. The voice of Aristotle, this one; poetics and rhetoric, a discourse in logic courtesy of AT&T's calling card. *Listen to me*, she said.

If only he could.

This will be a new start for you. For both of us. You'll see . . . you can put this to rest.

Oh, how he wants to put this to rest.

Well, the best laid plans and travel advisories . . .

All it takes is a single, decisive, last-minute swerve into the parking lot of the cedar drinking hole on the north side of the highway outside Truckee. Kill the engine. Slam the door. A friendly neon sign buzzes in the window of The Forlorn Hope. Just a little liquid fortification for the drive out of Tahoe, the drive out of Donner Pass, out of the mountains. New life, new beginning.

If only he could—

chart a new direction.

He has tried twice to call Erin at the beach house. He wants to explain that he's had a later start than he thought. Last-minute arrangements with the house, the store. Talking shop with Derek and Ingrid. Lies.

The phone rings and rings.

The two sisters are out on the boat, making a salmon run. Or perhaps his wife is reclining on the beach with a paperback propped in front of her. Danielle Steele or Dostoyevsky, depending on her passions of the moment, the crash of water on rocks, the tempests of her literary tastes. There she is. Straw sun hat. Her lips are parted slightly as she reads, and they are tinted a bright hollyhock pink, and as her lashes drift in the direction of her cheeks she looks almost, *almost*, as if she's falling asleep in the sand. It *is* Dostoyevsky. *Crime and Punishment*. Paperback descent into the damnation of humanity. It must be overcast today, for the sky has an ominous edge, the look of a prison.

Daren erases the image from his mind. Simple as swishing a stick over a sand picture.

He drains his glass to the bitter end.

Sand pictures, that's all.

The door to the bar bursts open. Daren jumps, turns his head. Someone enters, wearing a parka, bringing the smell of cold wind, diesel fuel, cough drops. Another lost traveler.

Lane has disappeared into the nothing again. No, there he is. At the bar.

Daren's head is starting to hurt, along with his stomach. He presses his forehead with the back of his hand, stares down at his gloves. He'd dropped them in the parking lot coming in here, and they'd been scattered with snowflakes. Whatever patterns, whatever destinies he may have read in the snowflakes, have melted and are no more. Looking at the pool of snowflakes is like looking at a tiny Lake Tahoe.

No. Not Lake Tahoe. Another lake. Donner Lake.

Turn left at Donner Lake. Have a nice drive.

God, he feels sick. Painful twinge in his belly. Hands, twisting. Gripping roots. Lane returns with another bottle. Just in time.

So you're heading over to Trinidad, that right?

That's right . . .

Had enough of the mountains?

Daren's attention turns momentarily to the sky on the other side of the window. Beyond the glass barrier. It stretches high into the mountains, catches there on the summits like a fish struggling on a line, finger hooks in mossy rocks . . .

Does it ever try to escape? Daren wonders. Does it ever try to twist away, to chart a new course, to continue its journey, its rightful passage through the mountains? Or does it surrender to its fate, to a life of passive captivity, like a fish suffocating on a deck, just an arm throw away from the sea?

Passive captivity . . .

Trapped in the mountains like a fish on a hook, gasping for its last breath of air.

We are all true to our natures.

It's just like going to sleep, Daren reminds himself. *Freezing to death.*

His hands tighten imperceptibly on his glass, and he stares into the depths of it as if it is a swirling snowstorm.

As long as you don't drink the life—

Daren stares at Lane. I'm sorry, what was that you said?

Lane gives him a peculiar smile. I asked if you'd tried to call your wife.

My wife—?

Erin, Lane reminds him gently. You said you had to call her.

The fragment of verse still hangs in Daren's head like strips of skin set out on a tree branch to dry. *As long as you don't drink the life, call the wife—*

Better lay off the whiskey, Powell. But he says: I tried, didn't get her. She's out on the boat with her sister.

I hear it's nice country. Up around Trinidad.

It is. Daren tries to smile, be sociable. The pain grips his stomach a moment, is gone. I think we both could use a little change of scenery, he says. But he's not sure that's true at all. He picks up his smudged glass, forgetting himself, then sets it down again. Shoves it across the table. A change of scenery. Uncharted territories. The New California . . .

Would you mind giving me directions? The young woman with hair the color of cinnamon-nutmeg asks him. She has inquisitive eyes, the slightly desperate, barely controlled smile of those who've lost their way.

I've never been through these parts, she says. It's a little colder than I expected. I thought California was all beaches! But it's beautiful . . . My husband's not due to meet me for a few days. I thought I might—

I'm sorry, Daren says, interrupting her but not impolitely so. He's trying to finish checking the invoices for the new shipment of camp stoves that has just arrived. The UPS man is awaiting his signature at the loading dock. It's Saturday after-

noon, and the store is crowded. Derek's having a problem with a return, Ingrid's off with a sore throat, and there are two customers ahead of the young woman, both of them impatient.

I'll be with you in a minute, he tells her as he verifies the credit card signature.

Oh, I'm sorry! the young woman says with an apologetic smile.

Uncharted territory, this, never been through these parts.

Daren slides a sleek new pair of BiPolar Fleece System gloves into a Great Sierra Outdoors bag. Thanks a lot, he tells the customer. Have a good one.

He turns to the next person in line. Yes, can I help you, sir? No, I'm sorry, we don't have it in stock yet. Check back early next week. The Suuinto MC-1G is one of the best global compasses on the market right now.

Does that have the built-in clinometer?

It's got everything . . .

The young woman wanders away to the store's picture window. The highway is clear today, only a little ice, and the hills have more tawny patches of dead arching grass than snow. If only the sun would come out, it might not stay cold. And the mountains are beautiful, she's never seen anything like the Sierras. This will be an adventure for her. Untried routes, uncharted territories. She has some trepidation, but it's exciting, too . . .

She spins the information rack like a roulette wheel. Learn to navigate your way by the stars. The flights of birds. Divining rods. Wagon trails.

There—

Shiny new pamphlet. Luck and fate. Destiny unfolds. The photo is of an inviting highway that leads through a deep wooded valley. Mountains peaks sparkle in the distance.

What about this one? says the young woman.

Daren's eyes flick up momentarily, then back to the slip he's filling out for the customer. He starts to write "Dec. 7" but the customer corrects him. Daren shakes his head, writes "Dec. 8."

To the young woman he says, That's supposed to be a spectacular drive. It runs right down through the Tahoe Forest, into El Dorado. Opened this fall.

Will it get me to Meadow Vista?

Sure, but take the west turnoff to the 1–80.

Where do I go from here?

Excuse me, a woman interrupts, but can you show me where your outerwear is?

Be right with you, Daren says with a nod. Sighing, he picks up a business card and writes swiftly on the back:

Drive W. on 80 to Soda Spr. Turn S at intersec., left at Donner Lake. Take first right. Take W. turnoff to Meadow Vista.

You can't miss it, he says, handing the card to the young woman.

She contemplates it a moment, then smiles at him before slipping it into her coat pocket. Thank you so much.

Not a problem. That's what we're here for. Daren smiles. Have a nice drive.

Thank you, I'm sure I will . . .

Daren turns to the next waiting customer. You were looking for outerwear? We have a sale on MountainZone—

The door clicks shut.

The store seems colder. The sun has dropped behind the mountains. The young woman has vanished into the white afternoon.

That's what we're here for, he has told her. Have a nice drive.

Untried routes. Uncharted territories . . .

It is December 8th, and the new extension Daren has just directed the woman to closed yesterday.

He knows this. Of course he knows this. It's just that he's distracted, short handed, has too much to do.

A change of scenery, Lane says. Yeah, well, I don't blame you there, friend. It can get pretty cold up here come January. Pretty lonesome, too. The wind in the trees . . . sounds just like a woman's sigh. No one there to listen, though. The Donner Party, they were all lost up here. Lost in all that snow . . . There are a hundred names for desperation.

Daren glances at the pay phone on the wall. He takes another sip of whiskey to dull the white pain building behind his forehead. It's getting late. Sacramento's a long drive in this weather and the roads aren't that great. Maybe he should try to call Erin again. No. He's way over his limit. She'd know it immediately, and he has enough to explain.

I hate to break up the party, Daren says, but I'm gonna have to get going.

He lays some bills on the table. It's been nice talking to you. Good to meet you.

Same. You taking the long trail down?

The long trail?

The 80. The long trail.

That's the one.

The interstate, while not quite as picturesque—is at least a shorter, more direct route through the mountains.

Be seein' you, Daren says.

You know it. Give my regards to Erin.

I'll do it.

Daren tries to remember, but can't, when it was he had mentioned his wife by name.

The parking lot is almost empty at this time of day. There's his pickup, a few diesels, and an old Buick on the other side of the lot. The snow is dirty, gritty, stained yellow-brown from the sour breath of exhaust. Sunlight slants through the pines on the southern slopes as he heads for the truck. The wind comes up suddenly, blows snow from the plowed drifts piled high on either side of the highway.

Man, it's getting cold. Inside the truck the air is frigid. His nostrils stick together when he breathes. He turns the key in the ignition. The engine does not turn over. He tries again. Ten minutes later he is still trying. It hasn't been cold enough to freeze the battery, not this afternoon with the sun shining. There must be something else wrong.

Yeah, fifteen years of mechanics ripping me off.

Daren gets out. The sun is sinking over the hills. A pale white glow illuminates the trees on the other side of the highway. He glares at the truck. Damn it. He doesn't know the first thing about this. Where's Erin when he needs her?

One of the rigs pulls out onto the highway toward Tahoe. Black smoke hangs in the air. It's after five: no garages open in Truckee later than that, the owners all out drinking in the bars. *Chasing the American Dream.* And tomorrow's Sunday. Small town America.

Daren's drinking partner is unlocking the door to the dilapidated old Buick.

Hey! Daren's shout echoes across the highway.

Lane glances his way. Take it easy, man, he says with a grin and a wave. He opens the Buick's door.

Wait! You said you're a mechanic—?

Lane trots across the lot, skidding on the ice. He isn't wearing gloves, and all he's got on is that jean jacket, with hooded sweatshirt underneath.

Truck die on you? Lane's breath comes out in a cold steam.

I can't get the damn thing started. It was running all right this afternoon.

Yeah, they'll do that to you. Lane raises the hood, hands already bare and red from the cold, and looks around for a few minutes.

I'm lucky you're still here, Daren says. He stands there doing nothing, feeling stupid and embarrassingly overdressed in his North Face jacket and Gore-Tex All Terrain gloves. What a joke.

While Lane bends over the engine, Daren stares out across the highway. Bare slopes, bald rock. *The sun goes down in another hour, it's going to get damn cold.*

Try 'er again, Lane calls out.

Daren does. Nothing happens. He gets out.

Lane slams down the hood with a sigh, wipes some greasy streaks on his jeans. God, his hands look cold, Daren thinks.

Lane says: I hate to tell you this, but I think you're in need of some serious parts.

What's wrong with it?

Lane shakes his head. *Mucho dinero.* Unless you got another engine in back.

Goddamn it, Daren mutters under his breath.

You know, this is just like what happened to the Donners.

Daren looks at him. What's that?

The Donner Party. Stranded, some of their wagons. Just like your truck here.

Daren smiles tersely. The Donners. Right.

It's the climate, Lane informs him. The altitude up here, makes a wagon sick through and through. The wheels contract like a man with a wrenching gut ache that won't die. Those iron tires work loose. Then the wheels. They pass over that sidling ground, they fall down and break all the spokes at the hub. It becomes a matter of *absolute necessity* that the traveler devise some means of repairing the damages. I'm quoting there, you can tell. Read that in *The Emigrants' Guide to Oregon and California.* Lanceford W. Hastings. He's the one who advertised the shortcut—

What shortcut is that? Daren says blankly.

Lane's breath streams out in cold clouds. Shortcut through Donner Pass. Of course, by the time he got around to trying it out himself, it was too late. They were done for.

Daren's aching head strains to find the relevant thread here, decides there is none. He doesn't know how much Lane has been drinking. If it's half as much as Daren has, he's probably plowed.

Listen, I don't want to put you out, but do you think you could maybe give me a lift? Which direction are you headed?

Sacramento, same as you. That's where The Donner Party were headed, too. But I could run you back to Tahoe if you want.

Daren thinks about it. He can't go back to the house tonight because the new owners are moving in. If the truck's as far gone as Lane seems to think there isn't much point in spending any money on it. It's falling apart, wasn't worth much when he bought it. Now it's just something to get him to the coast, and it's not even doing that. He lets out a frustrated sigh and thinks of Erin waiting for him at the beach house. He's having a hard time making decisions. Any decisions. Maybe he could arrange to leave the truck here until Monday, then call one of the local charities to take it off his hands. Erin could drive out and meet him in Sacramento. If Lane is headed there anyhow—

untried routes, uncharted territories . . .

Daren doesn't remember Lane mentioning anything about Sacramento in the bar.

But then you never asked. All you've been doing is brooding about your own damn self all afternoon.

I think I'll take you up on that offer, if you don't mind, Daren says. As long as you're headed toward Sacramento anyway. But I'll owe you one.

Lane smiles, a quick turn of his lips. His eyes are empty and gray as the sky.

Better get started, he says. Looks like snow.

You do any skiing? Lane asks. They're heading west on the highway in the rusted-out Buick. Tahoe Donner Basin?

I used to, Daren says distractedly. Alpine Meadows. Never did do Donner.

You might, Lane says. Might do Donner, yet. These mountains were built on human sorrow.

Daren squints out the driver's window. Sun's about packed up and gone. Days are getting shorter.

Lane's eyes are silver-gray in the pale setting sun.

Like silver-gray fish, Daren thinks abstractedly. Landscape runs past them in a silver-gray stream. *We're all fish, all of us. Swimming upstream. Uncharted courses. Fighting for our lives, a long way from home.*

Lane passes a car, eases back into his lane as if he's got all the time in the world.

It's sure pretty, this time of day, Lane says. Not quite light, not quite dark. The sun . . . see how it's still hanging in the trees. Those stands of birch, up on the hills.

Yeah, it's pretty. If you like that kind of thing. Daren's head is pounding. He can't care less about the trees.

Eliza, she sure liked that sunlight. Lane's lips curve faintly.

Eliza?

Eliza Donner. The littlest Donner. She had nothing to eat but sunlight during those long winter months. None of them did, not at first. She was just three years old, hardly more than a baby. I think of her sometimes, perched on the steps of that frozen cabin on the shores of Truckee Lake. Her hands are stiff with cold, but she's holding a dancing sunbeam on her lap. She's trapped it in her apron like a little white bird. She dashes off to show her Ma. This was in the days when they still had strength left in them. And hope. Imagine the little girl's surprise when she opens her apron and discovers there's nothing in it at all. Nothing to eat. Just an apron full of light. And not even that, now.

Lane's smile is both sadly meditative and strangely tender. It's as if this is a story he's telling about his own child. Not a child whose smile is less than dust. Daren doesn't know how to respond so he says nothing. Sits back. Watches the trees stream by. He sighs. It's definitely turning into a depressing afternoon.

They drive silently for a time, the only sound the wind whistling through the cracks in the windows. There is no heat. They have to keep the windows rolled down an inch to keep the windshield from icing up.

Lane's hands look rough and cold on the steering wheel but he doesn't seem to notice.

The skin on Daren's neck is burning cold, white as halibut, but he doesn't want to fasten the top button of his expensive North Face outershell. It wouldn't seem right somehow, not with Lane sitting there in his thin denim jacket and sweatshirt. He wonders if he should offer the man his gloves. He doesn't want to think about driving all the way to Sacramento with the windows cranked down. Has to be nearly thirty below out there. And with the wind chill . . .

Do you want to wear my gloves? he offers Lane. The steering wheel's got to be cold.

No, you keep 'em. Thanks the same.

They pass another car. The driver is a woman, her hair pale as ocean sand, the strands streaming down her back like shimmering fishing lines . . . continuing on her travels, her passions, her life.

By now, Erin and Christine will be making supper together in the kitchen. Erin tosses salad greens with expensive olive oil. A glass of white wine sits on the counter beside her. Christine poaches the salmon with lemon and a bundle of rosemary.

Slicing silver journeys that end on a plate, Daren thinks. *Far, far from home.*

It's just like going to sleep. Dying is.

There are a thousand names for desperation . . .

The two sisters are laughing, talking: men, life, sand, fish. Erin nods vigorously at something Christine has said while she grinds fresh pepper on the salad. Her hair is bleached oyster-pale. She laughs and takes a sip of wine. Put on some music, she tells Christine.

Like what?

Oh, like—

Down here in the Garden.

There's one thing left to eat

As long as you don't drink the life—

Daren can almost envision his wife through the windows of the beach house above the rocky shore, the sea a thin sliver of silver. The knife gleams as she chops a shroud-bed of herbs on the cutting block, chops right through the tip of her thumb. A spurt of blood, a little shriek—

Daren gasps, opens his eyes. He blinks back the image, still red and clear in his mind. *What in hell is wrong with him?*

Still half-drunk, that's what.

There's Donner Lake up ahead, Lane says with a gesture. That's where the settlers holed up for the winter, when they realized they weren't gonna make it through the pass.

Daren peers out the window. Nothing more than a dim outline in the falling darkness. *Why would he be thinking about Erin cutting her—*

You been out to the lake? Lane asks.

No. Daren closes his eyes wearily.

I've been out there.

Daren doesn't reply. He's thinking about The Donner Party's wagons breaking down in these mountains. *It's the altitude up here, makes a wagon sick through and through.* Nothing but canvas and the empty white sky above . . . the hand of God. Nothing but the mountains in front of them, the Great Salt Desert behind. Running out of time. Not gonna make it.

Journeys that end on a plate. Far, far from home.

Daren opens his eyes. It's dark out there. So dark.

The Buick is dirty, with fast food wrappers and drink containers littering the floor. Smell of body odor and greasy hamburgers, like Lane's been sleeping in here for the last few weeks. Threadbare woolen blanket in the back seat, and what looks like a pair of balled up dirty socks. Bundle of newspaper clippings. Something else, too. A book. The cover is threadbare, faded. Daren strains to read the title in the moonlight that pools through the windows. *The Emigrants' Guide to Oregon and California,* by Lanceford W. Hastings.

You into history? he asks Lane.

History?

The book back there. That one you were talking about . . .

There's a smile on the edges of Lane's lips, but his eyes are hard as granite. Granite on a mountain where nothing grows.

Lanceford W. Hastings. He was the one who told them to come this way. Take the shortcut, he says. Save you hundreds of miles. He'd never even tried it.

Lane is disdainful now.

The Hastings Cutoff . . . that's what you call man's arrogance in action.

Which way to go. Oh, what a dilemma. Do we go left, do we go right. . . .

The sick feeling is returning to Daren's stomach.

He never gave it a second thought before sending them on to their deaths, Lane says. Never gave it a single thought.

I—really don't know much about The Donner Party, Daren says.

Man's got to know his history.

They drive silently. The trees gray slivers in the dusk.

They look like souls, don't they. The trees. Like thin gray souls out there.

Daren rubs both thumbs against the bridge of his nose, where sweat has formed a thin sheet. Condensation on a melting glacier.

I—suppose so, he says. His gloved hands are bathed in sweat.

You have to wonder what went on in those cabins, Lane says. What they thought about. Dreamed about. I mean, when they knew there was no hope of a rescue.

Lane's driving is even, smooth.

I'll tell you what I think about, he says. But he says nothing for a half mile.

Then, as if in a strange reverie: the fine new buttons on the coat old man Donner bought at the mercantile for the trip. Shaved that sheep naked to make it. Good winter coat. You see, he'd heard it gets a mite cold in the Sierras come winter. Old George doesn't know it, but in eight months time he'll be cracking those bone buttons between his teeth, pulverizing them to powder for the calcium. No energy bars, no Gore-Tex gloves in those days. Not in those days . . . His hands tighten on the wheel. White knuckles, lumps of ice . . .

Daren closes his eyes again for a moment, balls a fist against his stomach. *Shouldn't have drank so much on an empty stomach.* He tries to remember what he's eaten today. Sunbeams. Nothing.

It's so damn cold up here in the mountains, Lane says. Ten below, twenty, thirty. No cover. Nothing to eat. The gnawing hunger starts. Passes for a while. Comes back. But there's still nothing to eat. You start thinking maybe there'll come a time you'll have to eat the rawhide laces from your snowshoes. Two days later, that doesn't seem like such a bad idea. Two days more of tramping through the snow, you're so cold, your stomach's so empty you can't think straight. Fingers frozen solid in your mittens. You think maybe you could break one off, put it in your mouth. It'd just be like sucking on an icicle. No taste to it at all. Would you say it's reasonable to cut off a baby finger to save your life? What use is a baby finger?

Daren stares at his hands, hands that are snugly protected in All-Terrain gloves, hands that seem detached. Insensible mitts. He can't feel them through the layers of insulation. If he should decide to chew on one of his thickly padded thumbs, he doubts he'd even notice the grinding motions of his teeth.

A hundred names for desperation.

You chew off your own hangnails sometimes, don't you? Lane says. Is it that much of a stretch, any real sacrifice, to eat a toe? And what if that toe were someone else's? What would you do to survive?

Daren coughs nervously. Well, I don't think I'd start by eating my snowshoes, he says. Or my fingers.

He can't for the life of him see where this conversation is leading, but he doesn't think he likes it. He's just getting carried along with it, a stick of wood in a river. He can't think straight. Walking in circles, no snowshoes. His head feels like someone has taken a hammer to it.

I mean would you eat a *man* to survive, though, Lane presses him. In the full face of God? Not much meat on a shinbone, but it'll do in a pinch. There's a barrel of salt in the wagon.

Daren stares at him. What—are you talking about?

I mean would you eat a man's heart.

His *heart*?

Lane's eyes meet Daren's in a steady gray gaze. Steady gray waters that never break the surface of ice.

No, Daren doesn't think he likes this line of questioning at all. He starts to wish he'd called a tow truck. Gone back to Tahoe. Stayed in the bar. He doesn't even know this man. Just met him in the bar in Truckee.

I—I don't know what you—

What I mean, friend, is that maybe you've already eaten a man's heart. Maybe you've eaten it and you don't know it. Chewed it up and spit it out like a blood clot on the snow.

Lane is looking intently at him now, eyes an unrelenting gray that stretch on and on with nothing to relieve them, endless gray days with no end, no relief party in sight.

Or maybe, Lane says, you didn't eat that heart yourself. Just stood by and watched while that same man got desperate enough, despairing enough, to eat his heart himself. Think of him out here, in the mountains. Everything he loves a frozen waste. The wind in the trees . . . sounds just like a woman's cries. There's no one here to listen, though.

Even the angels are lost in the snow.

There are a hundred names for desperation . . .

Lane's attention turns to the road, and he is silent.

Daren finds himself staring at the man's boots, at the scuff marks on them, worn down to the nubs. He finds himself thinking about where these boots have been all this time before he met up with the man wearing them. He thinks about what rough trails they have taken. How he's come by the frozen mud and pine needles embedded in the soles. *What trails do you walk, stranger?*

The Long Trail. I walk the Long Trail.

Lane brakes, makes a left turn off the highway onto a rough road.

Daren grips the edge of the seat. Where are we going?

Shortcut.

The Buick bounces over the icy road. There are no other vehicles out here. The woods are full of ghosts. Moon shining on slabs of snow.

Lane—

They pick up speed. Hit a bump. Something rolls out from under Daren's seat. He stares at it blankly a moment. It's a distributor cap.

They drew lots, Lane says. The Forlorn Hope did. Lots to decide which one of them they were going eat.

Daren picks up the distributor cap. Stares at it. His throat is so tight that he can barely choke out the words: Where did you—did this come from my truck?

I got something for you there in the back seat. Been using it to keep my place.

You don't even know who he is, Daren thinks. But something whispers back. *Don't you?* it whispers. *Don't you know who he is, Powell?*

Look at the book, Daren, Lane tells him. See what kind of advice that great entrepreneur Lanceford W. Hastings has for the settlers heading west. It's in there. All of it.

Lane reaches behind him and in one measured movement, dumps the book in Daren's lap.

The cover is disintegrating, a dusty brown with faded gilt letters. It smells like axle grease. Snowshoe laces. Barrel of salt. *No.* Something else—

Untried routes, uncharted territories . . .

Blackness fills in the edges of Daren's vision. He sees Robyn Corliss on a shroud-bed of moss. Her bare hands winter vegetables half-buried in the earth.

They couldn't have known it then, Lane continues dully. Could they. That the great Hastings Cutoff, the ambitious shortcut to California, had never been tried, not even by Hastings himself. And every passing afternoon the daylight grows fainter and fainter, like the last rays of dying winter light before the coffin lid is nailed shut.

Daren sees them. The wagons. They're coming out of the cold blue mountains. Thin blue shadows painted on the tops of their canvas hides, thin blue shadows as blue as winter smoke. And the wagons look like human skulls, a row of empty skulls polished clean on that white, white plain of snow. And then he sees them. The settlers. Walking dregs, more dead than alive. Men, women, children, gaunt, starving, the rank stink of human flesh and charcoal in their mouths, the gangrenous pine trees clawing at their backs, tearing their consciences to shreds.

But there was nothing to eat. There's nothing we could have done . . . You see that, can't you?

No, nothing I could have done, Daren reminds himself, but it is his wife's reasonable voice that rewinds through his thoughts.

He thinks of the woman who vanished into the white afternoon without a trace. Footsteps in the snow. Leading toward the mountains . . .

Buttons, bark, twigs, hangnails—

You've chewed off your own hangnails sometimes, haven't you?

Daren opens the book, *The Emigrants' Guide to Oregon and California.* The pages stained and brown, autumn leaves, human hide. This is a living diary, the lines within like rutted wagon trails.

Do we go left, do we go right. Or do we go straight up, to God?

The pages fall open to the rectangle of card Lane has been using to keep his place.

The Great Sierra Outdoors. Lake Tahoe.

Daren Powell, Manager.

Daren's blood turns to ice.

Where—where did you . . . His voice trails off as he turns the card over. Hasty lead pencil smudges. Hasty, hasty, Hastings . . .

Drive W. on 80 to Soda Spr. Turn S at intersec., left at Donner Lake. Take first right through to Meadow Vista.

He stares at the words. *His* words.

I found it in her coat pocket, Lane says quietly.

So quietly Daren can barely hear him.

When they brought her out of the mountains.

The hand that grips the card trembles now and he's sick, dear God, he's sick.

Lanceford W. Hastings. Lane shakes his head. There was a great writer of notes for you. An indiscriminate giver of directions. You know what his note to The Donner Party read when they found it stuck in some sage on the trail?

Daren shakes his head. Numb. He's numb. Can't think—

Two days, two nights, hard driving. Cross desert. Reach water . . .

Cross desert. Didn't take but a moment for Hastings to write that. But he didn't tell about The Great Salt Desert, how it was twice as wide as Hastings said it was, how they'd leave a third of their dying cattle, half their wagons, half their belongings back there in the desert. He didn't tell how when they came out of it they'd be covered in a layer of glittering white salt dust, tongues so swollen they don't fit in their mouths.

Daren stares at Lane. The man's expression is unreadable.

That's what comes of not being explicit, Lane says firmly. That's what comes of not being clear. People get lost out there, they can't find their way back. They rely on their guides with their lives. The ones who'll lead them through . . .

New Eden.

Promised Land.

A piece of Daren's heart is breaking off, frozen, falling into a snowy mountain stream. What can he say? That he's *sorry?* How can he say words like this to a man who has lost everything worth living for? There is nothing, nothing he can say, to wash this man's sorrow away. No river in the world deep enough.

The silence becomes a gaping ravine between them.

What is the taste of death? Salt, Blood, Loss, Hope?

Ask me what is the taste of a human heart, and it will be the same.

Ask me, friend. Ask me what it tastes like.

You should have seen the eyes of the ones that came back.

But did any of them . . . did any of them really come back? Daren wonders.

They drive on into the endless night.

Another ten miles down the highway Lane turns off the engine, the headlights. There are pine trees all around, knifed against the hills.

The two men get out of the car, stand in the crunching snow. They're in the middle of nowhere. Buried deep in the mountains.

Despite his North Face jacket, despite his All-Terrain gloves, Daren can't seem to keep his teeth from chattering. Every breath of the rare, cold air is a razor blade.

Lane is standing a ways down the highway at an unmarked spot. This is where they found her, he tells Daren. When the snow melted.

A *short delay in the itinerary,* Daren thinks. The intention being to retrace the secondary road back to the highway, to continue on with their lives, their dreams . . .

What dreams are these? There's a sour taste in his mouth, a backwash of emotion, a sick wrench in his gut.

They have no dreams.

Not the Donners, not Lane, not Daren, not any of them.

Lane's back is to Daren. He's staring up into the mountains. The air crystallizes in front of him as he breathes. Daren can't tell what he is thinking.

It is bitterly cold.

Daren is so tired. So sick. He wants to lie down in the snow. Just lie down in the snow, sleep . . . never wake up. Easier that way.

There's a cabin up there, Lane tells him. Old miner's shack up the hill from where they found my Robyn. Been there since the beginning of time.

He turns. There's a gun in his hand. It gleams silver in the moonlight.

Daren isn't at all surprised. You don't need that, he says. But it is not a plea for mercy. All the life has gone out of him.

I know it, Lane says.

I'm sorry, Daren whispers. He can't help himself. *Dear God, Lane . . .* The words fall from his lips, unreadable runes. Trailing off into nothing. *I'm so sorry, I'm so, so sorry . . .*

Lane's gray eyes are calm, dead. The salmon aren't moving. Frozen in the stream.

That makes two of us, he says.

He gestures with the gun. Let's go.

Someone has already beaten a trail through the hard rind of gleaming snow.

Daren struggles through the deep drifts, the scabby branches of twisted pines whipping his face. Following the tracks of the snowshoe hare . . . It is almost as if he has been here before. A thousand times before. Almost . . .

Lane plunges behind him through the brittle crust of snow, reciting the names of the dead. Handful of names strewn down the mountain like a scatter of bones.

Viney Graves, Miomin Pike, Loithy Donner—

All of them gone. Angels in the snow.

—*Robyn Corliss, Lane Corliss, Daren Powell*—

The man with the gun stops short.

Daren pants raggedly beside him, clutching his side.

They're at the door of the cabin now, a rough pile of logs stacked on top of each other. It's not all that far from the highway. But no one comes out here, not the rangers, not anyone. Not in the winter, when nothing lives except deep, deep within the dry brown roots.

Lane pushes in the door. Rusty hinges. No lock. No lights.

After you. Lane points with the gun.

Daren enters.

There's not much here. Four walls and a floor. A chair, a table, a bed, a lantern, kerosene. An iron cook stove, boxes of matches. Stack of new-chopped firewood piled to the ceiling in one corner. A man could live here all winter, if he had to. Live off his stamina, live off his will to survive. That's all he'd need. The will to survive.

Lane walks past Daren into the tiny room. Snow falls off his boots. Moonlight, cold and beautiful, pours in through the open door.

On the table are packages wrapped in white paper. Lane picks one up. It's small, light; almost delicate.

Pale white toes in search of pearls . . .

They labeled them, Lane tells him. The parts they ate. Each arm, each thigh. Tied them up in strips of shirts. Petticoats. Whatever they had. Just like Christmas presents. And they wrote the names of who was who on each so no one would have to eat their kinfolk.

Lane's laugh is short, rueful.

Think of it, Daren. A *world where no one would have to eat their kin.*

He sets the package gently on the table.

Still nothing moves in those pale gray eyes. The salmon have long since made the journey to someone's plate.

Daren stands frozen behind the kitchen chair. He can't seem to move.

Lane tells him, I was going to shoot you. His laugh echoes dry and hollow in the tiny shack. Just in the foot, to keep you from trying to make it back to the highway. 'Course, you're thirty miles from nowhere, and this road's been closed for a week. It's thirty below right now, dropping to forty below overnight, with no end in sight. You try to walk back in this . . . Well, let's say the chance of survival is slight, with no hope of a rescue. You stay here, you might make it. Melt snow water on the stove to drink. You could last all winter.

That is, Lane whispers, *if you want to. Only if you want to.*

Daren hears the words from a long way away.

He's thinking of a woman, a woman stumbling through a blinding snowstorm. She's trying to make it through the mountain pass, trying to make it through to him, but he's given her the wrong directions and the snow's already falling, thicker and thicker, the snowflakes are sticking to her hair, to her eyelashes, and she's swirling away from him like a snowflake in the wind.

Daren blinks back tears as he picks up the small white package labeled *erin's heart*. He cracks, breaks, falls; like chunks of ice, a river of sorrow. Still he sinks. His arms, his head, his world, sinks into the table.

erin's heart.

The red has seeped through. He presses the package to his lips, presses his wife's heart to his lips. The taste of her is just as he remembers, he'd know her with his eyes closed, and he's drinking the life through the pale white paper, drinking the river, and it washes him clean, clean.

Oh, Erin, he whispers. *I'm so sorry, so sorry* . . . But there is nothing that will wash his sorrow away, and he is carried away by the river, now, carried to the place where the salmon go . . . silver, and clean, and far away . . .

There is nothing left to do here.

Lane Corliss walks out into the night. Stands still a moment, listening to the black silence that surrounds him. Then he turns and walks.

Behind him he leaves the remains of a man. There is a heart in that man's hands. Dead and frozen. Chunk of muscle, chunk of meat. A woman's heart. Nothing more. The weight of his love in his hands.

Lane knows this weight well, for he has carried a package of his own these many months. The package is wrapped in plain white paper. It is stained dark and red as dry winter berries, and it is light as air itself. Hardly a weight at all.

He walks up the hill, through the drifts, through the trees. The cabin is a pine knot scab behind him.

There are, Lane Corliss knows, a thousand names for desperation, and a thousand ways to walk through this world. He has walked them all.

The gun drops from his hand unnoticed, is lost in the woods. He trudges on. He is tired, so tired, and it's bitterly cold here. But he knows he will make it to his destination, wherever it lies.

Untried routes, uncharted territories.

Perhaps, they will say afterward, he had been climbing up to God.

Perhaps . . . in a kinder world.

High in the mountains, it begins to snow. Lightly, at first, then . . .

> *The serpent leaves a twisted track*
> *It winds out through the snow*
> *There is no spring underneath*
> *The devil's down below.*

Down here in the Garden
There's one thing left to eat
As long as you don't drink the life
You only taste the meat.

For Brent Crosson, fellow lost traveler along the way
who would have preferred music for his song instead.

LAURENCE GOLDSTEIN

Meeting the Graiae

Laurence Goldstein is the author of three books of poetry, most recently, Cold
Reading, *and three books of literary criticism, most recently,* The American
Poet at the Movies: A Critical History, *as well as seven edited or co-edited
volumes of cultural commentary. He is professor of English at the University
of Michigan and, since 1977, editor of* Michigan Quarterly Review.

    *In "Meeting the Graiae" Goldstein revisits Greek mythology to powerful effect.
The poem first appeared in the Spring-Summer 2000 issue of* The Iowa Review
and we're pleased to be able to reprint it here as one of the year's very best.

                    —*T. W.*

Perseus speaks
. . . to press my case. Hermes had said
"Use eloquence, then violence."
All three were swan-shaped, ugly
as the spinster Gorgons they guarded,
passing their eye each to each
for quick peeks at the baffling world.
They looked easy to outwit, aunts
who trade anything for words of love.
I began with customary epithets:
"Sisters grey from your birth,
grey shadows of the elder world,
give me, not your eye or tooth,
not these remnants you share
in the holy spirit of community,
give me your vital secret. Now.
I need the address of the Nymphs
who keep the winged sandals, the cap
of invisibility, and the bag in which . . .
some enemy's head will bide its time."

They seemed to know my type: the hero
who spares them a tiny portion

of his immortality; still, they demurred
so I had to get rough, and I can.
I seized their one viscous eye
and threatened to stomp it, fling it
deep into the Tritonian lake, or eat it.
Eerie screams you can't imagine, and then
the information. I stuck the jelly
into the nearest crone's empty socket
and resumed my fabulous destiny.

And you know the rest. I slew Medusa,
stabbed to death the sea-fiend
who would have made Andromeda
its meal (she was delicious, then).
I should write my own epic deeds;
instead, past my lurid prime
I ponder the meaning of it all.
The supreme stuff of Zeus is in me
yet I feel infirm as the Graiae,
as if I were part of *their* story,
a chance adventurer, bold
but nothing extra-ordinary,
nothing they couldn't serenely outlive.
On visits to great Olympus, I'm sure
those witches entertain the gods
with *my* story, the task-oriented hunk
unworthy of a wandering eye,
one of many interruptions of their
endlessly fascinating lives, a speck
of mortal time, like a gaudy sunset.
The gods have heard it all before,
so often they lip-synch every phrase—
no text is sacred to those know-it-alls.
Yet they applaud; the story's on *me*,
boy wonder, latest has-been . . .

Yes, I do have other duties.
Send me a transcript of this interview.
I'll add it to my archive,
large enough almost for a room
in this inherited castle, grand,
richly appointed, though the kids
rarely visit, and never write.

for John Barth

ELIZABETH ENGSTROM

Riding the Black Horse

Elizabeth Engstrom is the author of seven books and over a hundred short stories, articles, and essays. Her most recent book, Word by Word—An Inspirational Look at the Craft of Writing, *is a compilation of presentations made during the annual Maui Writers Retreat and Conference. Engstrom is the director of that retreat and its Program of Continuing Education. She is the editor of* Imagination Fully Dilated *I and II. She lives with her husband and dog in the Oregon woods where she teaches the fine craft of fiction. Her Web site is: http://www.ElizabethEngstrom.com.*

"Riding the Black Horse" is a departure in tone for Engstrom. It was originally published in Horror Garage, *no. 2.*

—E. D.

The little girl sat down in the seat next to Mick, a pretty thing with long straight brown hair that shined in the dim airplane overhead reading lights. She clutched a brown-haired dolly that looked much like she did, though she was dressed in shorts and T-shirt and the doll wore a long white gown of sorts.

"Hi," Mick said. He knew that children should not talk to strangers, and that strangers should not encourage communication, but she surprised him by looking straight into his eyes and responding.

"Hi," she said. Then she looked down in a very attractive, completely unself-conscious bout of shyness.

"This will not do," her mother was saying to the flight attendant. "I need to sit next to my daughter. She's only ten, for God's sakes, this is like having her fly alone. It's worse, having her sit next to . . . next to a strange man."

The flight attendant, pushed from behind and already beginning to fray around the edges of her coif, looked at Mick. "Would you be willing to switch seats?"

"Sorry," he said. "No can do."

The mother glared. "Why not?"

He opened his inflight magazine and successfully ignored her.

The little girl tugged at her dolly's hair. "Put your seat belt on," Mick whispered to her. "It's going to be a bumpy ride." She smiled up at him as if they were conspirators in some as-yet-unrevealed scheme.

While the flight attendant went about begging other people to give up their seats, Mick settled in, closed his eyes and felt around his psychic arena for her aura. It was there, fresh and innocent. He loved that. He loved kids. He was going to have fun with this one. He hoped she was adult enough to have a sense of outrage like her mother's. That would be fun.

"I'm sorry, Ma'am," the flight attendant said to the mother. "I need you to take your seat."

The woman crouched down in the aisle next to the little girl. "I'm only two rows back on the aisle," she said. "I can see you. If you need anything, just turn around and I'll be there."

"I'll be okay," she said.

The mother pinned Mick with a killing stare, then went to her seat.

"I'm Mick," he said, and held out his hand.

"Monica," she said, and shook his hand in the shy, limp way that ten-year-olds do. He loved the feel of it.

"Can I buy you a drink, Monica?"

She smiled with sparkling eyes, and Mick was afraid he was falling in love.

"Gin and tonic? No, that tastes awful. Vodka martini? No, that's worse."

She started to giggle.

"Rum and coke? Beer? Wine? Or how about just a cup of coffee?"

"No, thank you," she said, and went back to straightening the doll's hair and clothes.

"What's your dolly's name?"

"Lucinda."

"Monica and Lucinda," he said. "You ought to be living in a British school for girls, having tea every day at four o'clock and making fun of the headmistress."

"I've been to England," she said.

"You have? You're a world traveler. And where are you going now?"

"To my grandmother's house. We're going to have to live there until she dies."

"And you don't want to?"

"I hate it there."

"Is your grandmother mean?"

"No, she's sick. She smells bad. My mother's the mean one."

"She looked mean to me, too. I'm glad she's not sitting with us."

Monica looked up with surprise, amazement and delight in her eyes. "Me, too," she whispered. "I was hoping the plane would crash."

"Well, then," Mick said, loosening his tie. "We've got a long flight. Let's have some fun."

"I know a game," she said, and retrieved her purple backpack from under the seat in front of her. She cast a glance behind her, at her mother, but as the seat belt sign was still on, they were safe. "My mother doesn't like me to play this game," she whispered.

"Well then, by all means," Mick said. "Let's have a go at it. I love games. I especially love games that mothers don't like."

She pulled from her pack a deck of blue Bicycle playing cards.

"Oh, good," Mick said, thinking Old Maid, Slapjack, War or on a good day maybe some Rummy. "Black Jack. Strip poker?"

"No," the girl said, but she was interrupted by the attendant coming by for drink orders.

"Let me buy you a drink," Mick said.

"I'll have what you're having," she whispered.

"I'm going to have a Bloody Mary," he said.

"Me, too."

What could it hurt? Mick thought, and ordered a double. Monica ordered water and drank it down, then held out her glass for him to mix her a drink. Oddly, Mick felt as if she had an old soul, and he could confide certain things in her. They were already sharing secrets.

"I was hoping the plane would crash, too," he said.

"Why? Is your mommy mean to you, too?"

He laughed. He liked the adult sparkle in her eye. No way was this girl ten years old. She was irresistible. "No, my wife. She divorced me and took everything. I have nothing left. No house, no books, no dog. Barely a job, and lots and lots of payments." And court dates, he thought, if he ever went back to California.

"We could probably crash this plane if we wanted to," she said.

Mick sipped his drink.

"I could just go up there and open that big door. The loss of pressure would suck me out, of course, and probably kill me instantly. But the plane would have to go down, and the funny oxygen things would dangle from the ceiling and the pilot would make an emergency landing somewhere, and with any luck, the plane would rip in half, and some hot metal would cut my mother's head clean off, leaving her body still strapped in by the seat belt."

"Keep drinking," Mick said, startled by the girl's admission, and the detail with which she had fantasized it. He liked her. Maybe they could run away together.

The girl took a swallow. "This is good," she said, and patted her pouty little lips on the napkin. "Too bad there isn't someone here that you'd like to kill."

"Just me."

"No," she said, "not you. You're nice."

"I'm not so nice," he said. "Let's play your game."

She looked around behind her again, then pulled the cards out of the cardboard case and set them on top of the tray table. "This is a good game," she said, "but you have to take it seriously."

"How seriously?"

"Dead seriously."

"It's just a game, Monica."

"Maybe. Okay. Pick a card."

"Is this a trick?"

"No. Pick a card."

He cut the cards and pulled one from the middle of the deck. "Do I show it to you?"

"Of course." She took it from him, looked at it, looked at him, frowned, looked at the card again, then sipped her drink. "This is the heart attack card."

"I'm sorry?"

"Heart attack." She showed him the seven of spades. "That's how you're going to die. Want to know when?"

Mick thought he could feel his chest beginning to seize already. "Not particularly."

"You don't look like a heart attack," she said. "You exercise, right?"

"Yeah."

"Must be in the family."

In fact, it was. Mick's father, mother and brother all died from heart disease at ages younger than he currently was.

"Hey," he said. "You pick a card."

"I already know my card."

"Yeah? What is it?"

She smirked up at him. "Plane crash. So's my mom's."

Was that a change in the engine's pitch he heard? He downed the last of his drink, and watched as she downed hers.

"This will probably be it," she said, and daintily wiped her mouth on the cocktail napkin.

The flight attendant came by and picked up the detritus of the cocktail hour, and Monica set her dolly up on the tray table.

Mick no longer wanted to play with her. He was too busy listening to the sounds inside his skin and the sounds outside the airplane's skin. His anxiety grew as the sky darkened outside and the reason for the seat belt sign remaining on became evident. Turbulence.

"Better hold on to Lucinda," he said to her.

"It won't hurt," she said. "It might be a little scary at first." She thought for a minute. "But I guess a heart attack does hurt, doesn't it? You'll die before we do. Still feeling okay?"

In fact, he wasn't. Cold sweat trickled down the side of his face and he felt as though there wasn't enough air in the plane to breathe.

He closed his eyes and listened to Monica sing to her dolly, and then the dolly was sitting on his chest, and Monica was breathing boozy tomato juice breath into his ear. "She's heavy, isn't she? Lucinda is very, very heavy."

"Help me," he squeaked out, and she laughed and bounced the dolly up and down on his chest in rhythm with his labored heartbeat.

Bum-bump. Bum-bump. Bum-bump.

"Please," he whispered. "Call the flight attendant."

"She can't help you," Monica said. "The plane is going down in a minute."

Mick tried to concentrate amid the burning pain that enveloped his left arm and chest, and the band that squeezed the breath out of him. I'm sorry, Lord, he tried to articulate clearly in his thoughts. I've not been a nice person, and I hope it isn't too late to ask for forgiveness.

An explosion of some kind rocked the plane and blew out a line of windows directly across the aisle. The lights went out. People began to scream. The plane headed down.

In the midst of the madness, Mick regained his calm. He heard Monica's mother desperately calling her name, but Monica was laughing, and he thought he'd take that sound with him to the grave and beyond.

He was a little more successful with his prayers after that, as his concentration focused on the very important task at hand. His wife, his daughters, the series of little girls he had terrorized in his past.

Monica was his just deserts, he knew. And as he fell down that black rabbit hole of unconsciousness, as the plane fell through the black sky toward obliteration, the only sound that he heard chilled him worse than death taking his pulse.

"Whee!" she said. "Whee!"

It was a sound he had made himself in the company of little girls way too often.

KATHE KOJA

At Eventide

Kathe Koja's novels include The Cipher, Skin, *and* Kink, *and her new novel,* Straydog, *will be published by Farrar, Straus & Giroux. She is the author of many short stories, several of which have appeared in best of the year anthologies. She lives with her husband, artist Rick Lieder, and her son, Aaron, in a suburb of Detroit.*

Koja is a gifted stylist. Her understated prose creates powerful images and brings to life the most unlovely of characters.

"At Eventide" was originally published in the anthology Graven Images, *edited by Nancy Kilpatrick and Thomas S. Roche.*

—E. D.

What he carried to her he carried in a red string bag. Through its mesh could be seen the gleam and tangle of new wire, a package of wood screws, a green plastic soda bottle, a braided brown coil of human hair; a wig? It could have been a wig.

To get to her he had come a long way: from a very large city through smaller cities to Eventide, not a city at all or even a town, just the nearest outpost of video store and supermarket, gas and ice and cigarettes. The man at the Stop-N-Go had directions to her place, a map he had sketched himself; he spoke as if he had been there many times: "It's just a little place really, just a couple rooms, living room and a workshop, there used to be a garage out back but she had it knocked down."

The man pointed at the handmade map; there was something wrong with his voice, cancer maybe, a sound like bones in the throat; he did not look healthy. "It's just this feeder road, all the way down?"

"That's right. Takes about an hour, hour and ten, you can be there before dark if you—"

"Do you have a phone?"

"Oh, I don't have her number. And anyway you don't call first, you just drive on down there and—"

"A phone," the man said; he had not changed his tone, he had not raised his voice but the woman sorting stock at the back of the store half-rose, gripping like a brick a cigarette carton; the man behind the counter lost his smile and "Right over there," he said, pointing past the magazine rack bright with tabloids, with *Playboy* and *Nasty Girls* and *Juggs*; he lit a cigarette while the man made his phone call, checked with a wavering glance the old Remington 870 beneath the counter.

But the man finished his call, paid for his bottled water and sunglasses, and left in a late-model pick-up, sober blue, a rental probably and, "I thought," said the woman with the cigarette cartons, "that he was going to try something."

"So did I," said the man behind the counter. The glass doors opened to let in heat and light, a little boy and his tired mother, a tropical punch Slush Puppy and a loaf of Wonder bread.

Alison, the man said into the phone. It's me.

A pause: no sound at all, no breath, no sigh; he might have been talking to the desert itself. Then: Where are you? she said. What do you want?

I want one of those boxes, he said. The ones you make. I'll bring you everything you need.

Don't come out here, she said, but without rancor; he could imagine her face, its Goya coloring, the place where her eye had been. Don't bring me anything, I can't do anything for you.

See you in an hour, the man said. An hour and ten.

He drove the feeder road to the sounds of Mozart, 40s show tunes, flashy Tex-Mex pop; he drank bottled water; his throat hurt from the air conditioning, a flayed unchanging ache. Beside him sat the string bag, bulging loose and uneven, like a body with a tumor, many tumors; like strange fruit; like a bag of gold from a fairy tale. The hair in the bag was beautiful, a thick and living bronze like the pelt of an animal, a thoroughbred, a beast prized for its fur. He had braided it carefully, with skill and a certain love, and secured it at the bottom with a small blue plastic bow. The other items in the bag he had purchased at a hardware store, just like he used to; the soda bottle he had gotten at the airport, and emptied in the men's room sink.

There was not much scenery, unless you like the desert, its lunar space, its brutal endlessness; the man did not. He was a creature of cities, of pocket parks and dull anonymous bars; of waiting rooms and holding cells; of emergency clinics; of pain. In the beige plastic box beneath the truck's front seat there were no less than eight different pain medications, some in liquid form, some in pills, some in patches; on his right bicep, now, was the vague itch of a Fentanyl patch. The doctor had warned him about driving while wearing it: *There might be some confusion,* the doctor said, *along with the sedative effect. Maybe a headache, too.*

A headache, the man had repeated; he thought it was funny. *Don't worry, doctor. I'm not going anywhere.* Two hours later he was on a plane to New Mexico. Right now the Fentanyl was working, but only just; he had an assortment of patches in various amounts—25, 50, 100 mgs—so he could mix and match them as needed, until he wouldn't need them anymore.

Now Glenn Gould played Bach, which was much better than Fentanyl. He turned down the air conditioning and turned the music up loud, dropping his hand to the bag on the seat, fingers worming slowly through the mesh to touch the hair.

They brought her what she needed, there in the workshop: they brought her her life. Plastic flowers, fraying T-shirts, rosaries made of shells and shiny gold; school pictures, wedding pictures, wedding rings, books; surprising how often there were books. Address books, diaries, romance novels, murder mysteries, Bibles; one man even brought a book he had written himself, a ruffled stack of printer paper tucked into a folding file.

Everything to do with the boxes she did herself: she bought the lumber, she had a lathe, a workbench, many kinds and colors of stain and varnish; it was important to her to do everything herself. The people did their part, by bringing the objects— the baby clothes and car keys, the whiskey bottles and Barbie dolls; the rest was up to her.

Afterward they cried, some of them, deep tears strange and bright in the desert, like water from the rock; some of them thanked her, some cursed her, some said nothing at all but took their boxes away: to burn them, pray to them, set them on a shelf for everyone to see, set them in a closet where no one could see. One woman had sold hers to an art gallery, which had started no end of problems for her, out there in the workshop, the problems imported by those who wanted to visit her, interview her, question her about the boxes and her methods, and motives, for making them. Totems, they called them, or Rorschach boxes, called her a shaman of art, a priestess, a doctor with a hammer and an "uncanny eye." They excavated her background, old pains exposed like bones; they trampled her silence, disrupted her work and worst of all they sicced the world on her, a world of the sad and the needy, the desperate, the furious and lost. In a very short time it became more than she could handle, more than anyone could handle and she thought about leaving the country, about places past the border that no one could find but in the end settled for a period of hibernation, then moved to Eventide and points south, the older, smaller workshop, the bleached and decayed garage that a man with a bull-dozer had kindly destroyed for her; she had made him a box about his granddaugh-ter, a box he had cradled as if it were the child herself. He was a generous man, he wanted to do something to repay her although "no one," he said, petting the box, "could pay for this. There ain't no money in the world to pay for this."

She took no money for the boxes, for her work; she never had. Hardly anyone could understand that: the woman who had sold hers to the gallery had gotten a surprising price but money was so far beside the point there was no point in even discussing it, if you had to ask, and so on. She had money enough to live on, the damages had bought the house, and besides she was paid already, wasn't she? paid by the doing, in the doing, paid by peace and silence and the certain knowledge of help. The boxes helped them, always: sometimes the help of comfort, sometimes the turning knife but sometimes the knife was what they needed; she never judged, she only did the work.

Right now she was working on a new box, a clean steel frame to enclose the life inside: her life; she was making a box for herself. Why? and why now? but she didn't ask that, why was the one question she never asked, not of the ones who came to her, not now of herself. It was enough to do it, to gather the items, let her hand choose between this one and that: a hair clip shaped like a feather, a tube of desert dirt, a grimy nail saved from the wrecked garage; a photo of her mother, her own name in newsprint, a hospital bracelet snipped neatly in two. A life was a mosaic, a picture made from scraps: her boxes were only pictures of that picture and whatever else they might be or become—totems, altars, fetish objets— they were lives first, a human arc in miniature, a precis of pain and wonder made of homely odds and ends.

Her head ached from the smell of varnish, from squinting in the sawdust flume, from the heat; she didn't notice. From the fragments on the table before her, the box was coming into life.

He thought about her as he drove. The Fentanyl seemed to relax him, stretch his memories like taffy, warm and ropy, pull at his brain without tearing it, as the pain so often did. Sometimes the pain made him do strange things: once he had tried to drink boiling water, once he had flung himself out of a moving cab. Once he woke blinking on a restaurant floor, something hard jammed in his mouth, an EMS tech above him: *'Bout swallowed his tongue*, the tech said to the restaurant manager, who stood watching with sweat on his face. *People think that's just a figure of speech, you know, but they wrong.*

He had been wrong himself, a time or two: about his own stamina, the state of his health; about *her*, certainly. He had thought she would die easily; she had not died at all. He had thought she could not see him, but even with one eye she picked him out of a line-up, identified him in the courtroom, that long finger pointing, accusing, dismissing all in one gesture, wrist arched like a bull- fighter's before he places the killing blade, like a dancer's *en pointe*, poised to force truth out of air and bone: with that finger she said who he was and every- thing he was not, *mene, mene, tekel, upharsin.* It was possible to admire such certainty.

And she spared herself nothing; he admired her for that, too. Every day in the courtroom, before the pictures the prosecutor displayed: terrible Polaroids, all gristle and ooze, police tape and matted hair but she looked, she listened care- fully to everything that was said and when the foreman said *guilty* she listened to that, too; by then the rest of her hair had come in, just dark brown down at first but it grew back as lush as before. Beautiful hair . . . it was what he had noticed first about her, in the bar, the Blue Monkey, filled with art school stu- dents and smoke, the smell of cheap lager, he had tried to buy her a drink but *No thanks*, she had said, and turned away. Not one of the students, one of his usual prey, she was there and not there at the same time, just as she was in his workshop later, there to the wire and the scalping knife, not-there to the need in his eyes.

In the end he had gotten nothing from her; and he admired her for that, too.

When he saw the article in the magazine—pure chance, really, just a half- hour's numb distraction, *Bright Horizons* in the doctor's office, one of the doc- tors, he could no longer tell them apart—he felt in his heart an unaccustomed emotion: gratitude. Cleaved from him as the others had been, relegated to the jail of memory but there she was, alive and working in the desert, in a workshop filled with tools that—did she realize?—he himself might have used, working in silence and diligence on that which brought peace to herself and pure release to others; they were practically colleagues, though he knew she would have resisted the comparison, she was a good one for resisting. The one who got away.

He took the magazine home with him; the next day he bought a map of New Mexico and a new recording of Glenn Gould.

She would have been afraid if it were possible, but fear was not something she carried; it had been stripped from her, scalped from her, in that room with the stuttering overheads, the loud piano music and the wire. Once the worst has happened, you lose the place where the fear begins; what's left is only scar tissue, like old surgery, like the dead pink socket of her eye. She did not wait for him, check the roads anxiously for him, call the police on him; the police had done her precious little good last time, they were only good for cleaning up and she could clean up on her own, now, here in the workshop, here where the light fell empty, hard and perfect, where she cut with her X-Acto knife a tiny scrolling segment from a brand-new Gideon Bible: blessed are the merciful, for they shall obtain mercy.

Her hand did not shake as she used the knife; the light made her brown hair glow.

The man at the Stop-N-Go gave good directions: already he could see the workshop building, the place where the garage had been. He wondered how many people had driven up this road as he did, heart high, carrying what they needed, what they wanted her to use; he wondered how many had been in pain as he was in pain; he wondered what she said to them, what she might say to him now. Again he felt that wash of gratitude, that odd embodied glee; then the pain stirred in him like a serpent, and he had to clench his teeth to hold the road.

When he had pulled up beside her workshop, he paused in the dust his car had raised to peel off the used patch and apply a fresh one; a small one, one of the 25 mgs. He did not want to be drowsy, or distracted; he did not want sedation to dilute what they would do.

He looked like her memories, the old bad dreams, yet he did not; in the end he could have been anyone, any aging tourist with false new sunglasses and a sick man's careful gait, come in hope and sorrow to her door; in his hand he held a red string bag, she could see some of what was inside. She stood in the doorway waiting, the X-Acto knife in her palm; she did not wish he would go away, or that he had not come, wishing was a vice she had abandoned long ago and anyway the light here could burn any wish to powder, it was one of the desert's greatest gifts. The other one was solitude; and now they were alone.

"Alison," he said. "You're looking good."

She said nothing. A dry breeze took the dust his car had conjured; the air was clear again. She said nothing.

"I brought some things," he said, raising the bag so she could see: the wires, the bottle, the hair; her hair. "For the box, I mean. . . . I read about it in a magazine, about you, I mean."

Those magazines: like a breadcrumb trail, would he have found her without one? wanted to find her, made the effort on his own? Like the past to the present, one step leading always to another and the past rose in her now, another kind of cloud: she did not fight it but let it rise, knew it would settle again as the dust had settled; and it did. He was still watching her. He still had both his eyes, but other things were wrong with him, his voice for one, and the way he walked, as if stepping directly onto broken glass and, "You don't ask me," he said, "how I got out."

"I don't care," she said. "You can't do anything to me."

"I don't want to. What I want," gesturing with the bag, his shadow reaching for her as he moved, "is for you to make a box for me. Like you do for other people. Make a box of my life, Alison."

No answer; she stood watching him as she had watched him in the courtroom. The breeze lifted her hair, as if in reassurance; he came closer; she did not move.

"I'm dying," he said. "I should have been dead already. I have to wear this," touching the patch on his arm, "to even stand here talking, you can't imagine the pain I'm in."

Yes I can, she thought.

"Make me a box," as he raised the bag to eye-level: fruit, tumor, sack of gold, she saw its weight in the way he held it, saw him start as she took the bag from him, red string damp with sweat from his grip and, "I told you on the phone," she said. "I can't do anything for you." She set the bag on the ground; her voice was tired. "You'd better go away now. Go home, or wherever you live. Just go away."

"Remember my workshop?" he said; now there was glass in his voice, glass and the sound of the pain, whatever was in that patch wasn't working anymore: grotesque, that sound, like a gargoyle's voice, like the voice of whatever was eating him up. "Remember what I told you there? Because of me you can do this, Alison, because of what I did, what I *gave* you. . . . Now it's your turn to give to me."

"I can't give you anything," she said. Behind her her workshop stood solid, door frame like a box frame, holding, enclosing her life: the life she had made, piece by piece, scrap by scrap, pain and love and wonder, the boxes, the desert and he before her now was just the bad-dream man, less real than a dream, than the shadow he made on the ground: he was nothing to her, nothing and, "I can't make something from nothing," she said, "don't you get it? All you have is what you took from other people, you don't have anything I can *use*."

His mouth moved, jaw up and down like a ventriloquist dummy's: because he wanted to speak, but couldn't? because of the pain? which pain? and, "Here," she said: not because she was merciful, not because she wanted to do good for him but because she was making a box, because it was her box she reached out with her long strong fingers, reached with the X-Acto knife and cut some threads from the bag, red string, thin and sinuous as veins and, "I'll keep these," she said, and closed her hand around them, said nothing as he looked at her, kept looking through the sunglasses, he took the sunglasses off and, "I'm *dying*," he said finally, his voice all glass now, a glass organ pressed to a shuddering chord but she was already turning, red threads in her palm, closing the door between them so he was left in the sun, the dying sun; night comes quickly in the desert; she wondered if he knew that.

He banged on the door, not long or fiercely; a little later she heard the truck start up again, saw its headlights, heard it leave but by then she had already called the state police: a sober courtesy, a good citizen's compunction because her mind was busy elsewhere, was on the table with the bracelet and the varnish, the Gideon Bible and the red strings from the bag. She worked until a trooper came out to question her, then worked again when he had gone: her fingers calm on the knife and the glue gun, on the strong steel frame of the box. When she slept that night she dreamed of the desert, of long roads and empty skies, her workshop in its center lit up like a burning jewel; as she dreamed her good eye roved beneath its lid, like a moon behind the clouds.

In the morning paper it explained how, and where, they had found him, and what had happened to him when they did, but she didn't see it, she was too far even from Eventide to get the paper anymore. The trooper stopped by that afternoon, to check on how she was doing; she told him she was doing fine.

"That man's dead," he said, "stone dead. You don't have to worry about him."

"Thank you," she said. "Thank you for coming." In the box the red strings stretched from top to bottom, from the bent garage nail to the hospital bracelet, the Bible verse to the Polaroid, like roads marked on a map to show the way.

TERRY DOWLING

The Saltimbanques

Australian writer Terry Dowling is no stranger to the pages of The Year's
Best Fantasy and Horror, *but this is the first time his fiction has appeared
as a fantasy selection in the book. The following tale, like the one chosen
by Ellen Datlow elsewhere in this volume, comes from Dowling's excellent
new collection of linked stories,* Blackwater Days *(Eidolon Press, Western
Australia). Dowling is also the author of* Rynosseros, Blue Tyson, Twilight
Beach, An Intimate Knowledge of the Night, The Man Who Lost Red,
Antique Futures, *and short stories published in a variety of anthologies and
journals.*

*"The Saltimbanques" is a haunting tale of modern magic, Australian myth,
and the painful process of maturation. It's a stunning piece, and we're very
pleased to be able to publish it here.*

—T. W.

For Danny Truswell, his world changed forever that day in 1962 exactly one
week before he turned fourteen; a hot dusty day in Reardon, one of those
blistering Australian summer days just after Christmas when the air shim-
mers into haze in every direction and the trees hang and it seems no one
is out on the streets.

He followed his usual summer holiday routine, got his chores done early, then
planned ways to lie low till about 4 P.M. when the sun was far enough down the
sky for life to ease back toward normal.

"Normal" was hardly the right term with Danny's Dad taking a rig across the
top of Australia and not due back for six days, and his Mum away in Dubbo
visiting a sick sister. Danny was having his meals with Kenny's folks and sleeping over.

"Lying low" was hardly the right term either, for Danny and Kenny (and
sometimes Annie), like most other kids, rarely managed to do the sensible thing.
It was summer holidays, after all. And Danny liked to think they had something
of an advantage over the others. They had the chart.

When you saw Reardon from the air with its dozen streets and eighty or so
houses (population 434), its two pubs, two churches, community hall, school

and library, the co-op up by the railhead near the railway station, the sheds and silos, the clumps of trees following a creek pretty well dry for a half of any year, it looked like so many clustered flecks of gray and silver set in a large, mottled red tile, with a splotchy line of dullest green winding across it (the creek with its eucalypts) and a thinner silver hairline dividing the top third (the railway line).

That was the view framed on the office wall of Hendist's Stock and Station Agents. An even larger version, two yards on a side, hung over the saloon bar of the Stockman Hotel, the red sweeping out as if Reardon was a colony on the planet Mars.

But a third such aerial shot, left over from the same 1956 International Geophysical Year shoot, tattered, faded and almost forgotten, was pinned to the wall of a deserted shed at the back of the Woke property, and that's where Kenny Woke, Danny Truswell and "Sometimes" Annie Hendist had their clubhouse and planned which properties to visit, which parts of the creek to try. It gave them an overview, a sense of the town as finite and just *a* place on the land, not *the* place. Horizontal vistas somehow locked you in too much, were too real, too irresistible to allow that other kind of perspective.

The Reardon Rangers, as they called themselves, were lucky. There'd been six of them in the group originally, but Cathy's folks had moved the family down to Dubbo, and Billy Mack and Keith Spicer, just a year before, had gotten too grown up, they reckoned, for that sort of clubhouse stuff.

Annie Hendist though, curiously, had stayed around. She was already fourteen, a long-legged brunette, disturbingly female, and while her mind often seemed on other things, she'd surprise the boys by dropping in and tagging along just as it used to be. Sometimes it'd be for cricket or soccer with other kids, sometimes on one of their Ranger expeditions.

That was how it came to be three not two on that momentous Thursday. The boys were so glad to see her again (awkward as well; they were at *that* age) when she appeared in the doorway in her shorts, striped T-shirt and old sandshoes. She looked so grown-up and knowing that they made it her turn, let her point to a destination on their aerial "chart."

Barrack Creek. Dusty and dry until five weeks after the rains in the north when, with all the impact of a miracle, it flooded just like that. But mostly dry and dead, just seeming cool because of the river gums and occasional scrappy willows, because there was shade that wasn't made by blazing, overheated iron and canvas and old boards.

She pointed to a spot close to where the creek, the train tracks and the dirt highway almost came together, creek and road curving in and curving away again, the tracks dividing them.

"How about there?" she said in that calculatedly artless way that had Danny and Kenny swapping looks.

"Roger that," Kenny said, as he so often did, a misuse of old World War II lingo.

Danny grabbed his Dad's army surplus canteen. "Fine with me."

If it had just been the two of them, Danny and Kenny would've been laughing and joking, pushing and shoving, saying goofy things, making a big deal of it. With Annie along they kept it simple, sensing that there was something fragile, special and fleeting in Annie being there. You couldn't talk it, could barely even grasp what it was, but they all knew, which had made Mr. Jarvie's words at school for the past two years so much more thrilling and embarrassing.

"Here's Kenny and Danny. Now where is Annie?" Mr. Jarvie would say. And when Dan retorted (fairly he'd thought) that Annie was only with them some-times, that naturally became part of the refrain. "Here's Kenny and Danny and Sometimes Annie," Jarvie would say when they came in, which had the other kids sniggering and sing-songing it too. Kids can be cruel, but how often their cues came from adults enjoying a different kind of humor.

Sometimes Annie it was from then on. In fact Kenny even said "Roger that!" the very first day, because he figured everyone had to have a nickname.

They were a good mile from town when they realized they probably should've picked somewhere closer. The heat was relentless. The land shimmered in every direction; the railway tracks blazed up at the sun as if just freshly poured and still molten; the highway stretched off into the burring of haze, a crusty deserted ribbon. The trees along Barrack Creek danced as if they might vanish at any moment.

When they finally did reach the bank, they found the scant shade barely helped. Leaning against the trunks of the larger river gums, they looked out at the flat stretch of creek-bed, rippling with heat, set with the shifting, black and gray shapes of old tree trunks left by past flash-flooding, set to the mindless sawing of insects, then began moving along to where the trees were thickest.

That's when they saw that someone had set up camp right near the creek. Three drab buses were parked under the thickest stand of river gums, all with roof-racks packed high with bundles and boxes lashed down every which way. No cars were visible, just three old buses, one with its dusty windows catching bits of sun, the second with the windows of the back half painted over, the third all riveted metal with no windows at all that they could tell, just the front windscreen glinting dully.

"Who's that, y'reckon?" Kenny asked, and got no answer. It was so quiet that his words seemed way too loud. Danny and Annie didn't want to speak.

They moved closer, edging along the opposite side to the visitors, slipping from tree to tree.

No one was about. The buses had to be like ovens inside, especially the third one, but Danny couldn't see anyone lying underneath them or leaning against tree trunks. The occupants were in town or off somewhere else, visiting one of the properties maybe. *Inside* only if they were crazy.

There wasn't a lot of mystery in Reardon, so sometimes you made it up. You told other kids stories about the bunyip that lived in Barrack Creek (you knew someone who knew someone who'd actually *seen* it); or the "bore woman" who appeared around the clanking windmills and poisoned the water and sometimes stole children to drown in one of the artesian dams; or the *min-min* lights you saw flickering over the railway tracks after midnight, sometimes dancing along the creek. But this was the real thing, a real mystery, nothing like the box Mr. Jarvie had put on his desk and asked them to write about, what it might contain. Here were three genuine "mystery boxes," made only more mysterious by the faded letters Danny could make out on the sides of at least two of the vehicles.

"There are words," he said.

Kenny agreed. "Roger that."

Annie turned on him. "Enough of the 'Roger that,' will you, Kenny?"

Kenny blinked at her. "Roger. Right. But there *are* words. Can you read 'em?"

None of them could. The buses were angled wrong and too dusty. They discussed moving closer, trying to make out what the words said, but even sneaking out to hide behind one of the bigger logs left by past floodwater still meant crossing the creek-bed in plain view, and, though they didn't say it, none of them wanted to do that right then.

It was just so quiet, so eerie, with insects sawing away in the scraps of grass, the tides of heat rolling along the creek and those dark windows glinting.

If only there was movement, someone visible, maybe a dog about. But it was all heat shimmer and unexpected strangeness.

"Know what?" Kenny said. "We oughta come back later an' spy on 'em. What d'you say? Come back after tea?"

Dan and Annie agreed to it, then all gladly turned and headed back toward the shimmering spill of dirty quicksilver that was Reardon.

It took no effort for Kenny to get his Mum to serve them all an early tea. Monday's leftovers made it easy. The three of them were back at the clubhouse soon after six, killing time till it got darker by testing their flashlights and locating the little caravan of buses on the chart.

"Right here, I reckon," Danny said.

Kenny leaned in close. "Roger that. Er, sorry, Annie."

"It's okay, Ken," Annie said, leaning in to see as well, which had Dan suddenly, totally aware of her, of her dark hair and how much her skin smelled of heat and summer. He could've gone crazy on it right then, but just kept pointing at the map, trying to ignore her arm pressing on his, most of all the alarming stirring in his loins, suddenly there, determined not to goof off like Kenny did whenever Annie came too close. He wanted her to like him. He liked her being close.

Then, when the air had cooled by twenty degrees and the sky was a rich, deepening blue, with stars pushing through and a scrap of a moon showing, they set off again, striking out pretty well in a straight line to where they figured the camp ought to be.

This time there were people. The kids smelled the smoke from a cookfire and heard voices well before they could make out the welcoming flicker of the fire itself and see the cheery, calmer points of hurricane lanterns. There were tents set up now too, two of them, large and square, and four people at least, then five, laughing and joking just like people anywhere. Six, Dan counted when someone else stepped from one of the buses: four men, two women.

Without discussing it, Annie moved down onto the creek. The boys followed, moved out to halfway where she was hiding behind an old log and hunkered down next to her.

In a whisper, Annie spelled out the words on the side of the bus nearest the fire. "S-A-L-T-I-M-B-A-N—now what's that? Oh yeah—Q-U-E-S. There's a 'The.' The Saltimbanques, it seems like."

"The Salt in Banks?" Danny said, even as Kenny spoke too.

"Salting Banks? What's that?"

"The name of our carnival," a man's voice answered, right near them.

Kenny yipped in fright. Danny's heart caught in his throat. Someone was there on the creek-bed close by.

"It's French," the voice continued. "I'm Berty Green. Why don't you come over an' say hello?"

The fire, the lanterns, the fact that there were two women—more importantly that Berty, whoever he was, had started walking on ahead—made it seem okay. They were just carny folk camping along the road, tired from driving in the heat.

"Let's go," Kenny said.

Dan and Annie exchanged a half-seen glittering glance, and the three of them followed Berty up into the camp.

Framed above and around by flickering tree-forms in the firelight, warmly lit by yellow lamplight and walled in by the sides of one bus and one of the tents, to Dan it was like walking onto the stage of the Community Hall back in town to do a play, or peering through the eye-hole of a diorama at some painting by that guy Mr. Jarvie liked, Breughal. Updated, sure. Australianized, yes, but just odd and interesting people caught in the middle of being easy among themselves. Yet not altogether *his* people.

And there was Berty, fully visible now and quite a sight himself, a short dusty-looking man with a sharp face, his chin and forehead pulling back from his nose like some cartoon figure who'd stood too long in a scorching westerly.

But there was hardly time to take it all in properly because Berty Green was introducing them.

"Some kids from town dropped by to pay their respects. Don't reckon I caught your names, kids."

"Danny."

"Kenny."

"Annie."

Berty gave a deep bow, then gestured at his companions. "Right you are. And here we have Jeffrey, Gwen, Walter, Haunted Jack, May and Robert."

There were nods, smiles, salutes, quick looks at the boys, longer looks at Annie from all of them, not just the men. Danny couldn't be sure who was who, but it didn't seem important just then.

"Take a seat! Take a seat!" Berty cried. "Gwen, pour our guests some tea, will you? Later we'll take you in to see Mr. Hasso."

"Mr. who?" Kenny asked.

Berty grinned. "Mr. Hasso. Our ringmaster, our maitre'd. The boss. He's been shut away all day doin' his calculations."

"All day?" Danny said. "Not in the bus without windows?"

"Oh, not in there," Berty answered. "That's our darkwagon. We only go in there on special occasions. His office is in the back o' that one." He pointed to the bus with the closed-off back half. The painted-over panes glowed with dim yellow light.

"All day?" Kenny echoed. "He would've fried to a crisp in there today."

Berty laughed. "You'n me maybe. Not our Mr. Hasso. He's a bit of a lizard that way. Likes it warm."

Gwen handed them tin cups of steaming billy tea, sweetened with condensed milk, stirred with a eucalypt twig.

"What are Saltimbanques?" Annie asked, blowing and sipping.

"That depends," Berty replied. "Going traditional now, we're showfolk, mountebanks, jugglers, acrobats, harlequins, ballerinas and buffoons."

"Clowns?" Kenny asked, missing some of the words.

"Inevitably, Kenny," Berty said. "Ask any juggler who drops his balls."

"Or any ballerina past the point of doing pointe," one of the others said, laughing. Walter, Danny thought it was.

"We're all just clowns if the figures aren't right," Gwen said, sitting by the fire again. "How's the tea?"

"Great."

"Beaut."

"Terrific, thank you."

Berty got up. "How 'bout you set your cups down awhile and we'll pay a call on Mr. Hasso?"

Danny was glad to, if only to get away from the indulgent gaze of the others around the fire. He didn't much like adults having jokes at his expense. Mr. Jarvie was bad enough.

Berty led them between the tents toward the middle bus. There was only the dull yellow glow from the back section, but Berty switched on a front cabin light as they climbed in, illuminating bench seats, a fixed table, some fitted cupboards. A door in the wall halfway down its length had a plaque with the name *Bernard Hasso* on it.

"There. Let's see if he's taking visitors." And Berty winked at them as if they knew a lot more about Bernard Hasso's ways than they let on.

He knocked lightly at the door. "Mr. Hasso? We've some young visitors from town come callin'."

There was no reply that Danny could hear, but Berty smiled at them and turned the handle, opening the door on an office that took up the whole back half of the bus.

There were bookshelves and charts along the walls, all aglow in the light of two paraffin lamps, and a big desk at the far end littered with papers, maps, lists of calculations. Bernard Hasso sat grinning at them with a pen in his hand, a large blacksmith of a man in a grimy sweat-stained shirt and dark pants. Where Berty Green had sharp features, Bernard Hasso had craggy ones, his eyes set deep under heavy black brows and above a full black mustache. It was as if a gypsy and lion-tamer had been blended with one of those dark mysterious Egyptians from either version of *The Mummy*—the 1932 original or the recent 1959 remake Hank Burgess had shown with it as a midnight double at the Lyceum in town only a month back (surely one of the weirdest choices for a double-feature ever). The smile was amiable enough, but his eyes glittered approvingly at Annie in a way Danny didn't like—the same way the others had looked at her, all except Berty. Hanging on the plywood wall behind the man's chair was a framed picture: a painting of circus figures caught while performing or rehearsing.

"So, kids. What's the verdict? What d'you think of us so far?"

"We haven't seen much yet, Mr. Hasso," Kenny said, eager as a puppy.

Bernard Hasso nodded and set down his pen. "Not much to see yet, I'm afraid. We don't play many towns during the summer."

"Don't see any animals," Kenny rattled on, clearly on automatic.

"Oh, animals come and go. We don't go in for animal acts too much. Not too much."

And Berty Green sniggered.

"You're Saltimbanques," Annie said, as if identifying a rare breed.

"Why yes, Miss—er?"

"Annie. This is Kenny and Danny."

"Miss Annie, yes." He gave glancing nods at the boys, turned his deep-set, black eyes on her again. "That's exactly what we are. Not your usual troupe of wandering players certainly. Saltimbanques every one!" He indicated the framed print on the wall behind him. "Picasso, 1905. *Family of Saltimbanques*. From his pink or rose period. The name is from the Italian *saltimbanco*, coined in 1646 from *saltare*, to leap, *in*, on, *banco*, bench. Leap-on-benches, yessir. Mountebanks, yes, charlatans and quacksalvers—another marvelous word, from the Dutch *kwakzalver*. Ignorant pretenders. Quacks. That's us."

"Do you do magic?" Kenny asked.

Berty Green sniggered again and sat on a bench seat near the door.

"Why yes, Master Kenny. Sometimes we do." Bernard Hasso patted the papers on his desk. "When the planets are right and the wind blows a certain way. Sometimes it just flows out of the land. Real magic, yessir. A fickle thing though sometimes, just like the favors of pretty young ladies."

"You sure made yourselves disappear today," Annie said, with more pluck, Dan thought, than this Mr. Hasso expected. There was something going on that Dan didn't entirely understand.

Bernard Hasso frowned, even as his eyes widened and his big smile came back. "Ah, Berty, hear that? Our young friends called earlier. We were remiss."

"Couldn't see anyone," Dan said, feeling annoyed yet curious. Something *was* going on. Adult stuff, but not like with Mr. Jarvie.

The ringmaster nodded. "Off getting supplies probably."

"Sometimes there's a bunyip here in Barrack Creek," Kenny said, determined not to be left out.

"That so, Master Kenny? What sort?"

"I dunno. You got bunyips?"

"Sometimes. Bunyips are easy." Bernard Hasso's dark eyes twinkled and glittered under his heavy brows, and Kenny looked puzzled, as if not sure if the man were making fun of him or not.

"We should be going, Mr. Hasso," Annie said, and it struck Dan that she needed to be the one to say it, that he had just been sort of drifting there in this stuffy, closed part of the bus while some other level of exchange had been going on. He wished he could've re-run everything they'd said, but it was too late now.

"Yeah, we should," he heard himself say, just to be out of there.

Dan wasn't really sure why he had to go back that night. A lot of it had to do with Annie, with how Mr. Hasso and the troupe had looked at her, with wanting to both keep her safe and impress her. It was just something he had to do.

He didn't stay at Kenny's long. He told Mrs. Woke that there were some chores he'd forgotten to get done like he'd promised but that he'd be back later, that Kenny should expect him in their front verandah sleepout as usual. At 10:12

P.M. he was pedaling out of town on his bike, riding without a light, using what moonlight there was, heading to where the creek and the highway bowed together, the silver tracks cutting between.

Dan figured he didn't have to tell anyone he'd done it, maybe Annie later on. He hurried along under a vast field of stars, watching meteors streaking down, now and then looking back at Reardon where it made its neat huddle of yellow light in the greater darkness.

Reaching the closest point to the creek, he left his bike just off the road and moved carefully across to where he figured the buses were. The camp was quiet, with a lantern burning and the fire low. The two tents were dark amid the long hulks of the buses. The only other light came from the back of the second bus where Mr. Hasso was probably still working on his mysterious calculations.

The odd thing was that no one slept in the open as you'd expect on such a mild night, arranged about the fire like you did when you camped out. Maybe they were in the third bus, the closed-up one Berty had called the "darkwagon," sleeping or practicing tricks away from prying eyes.

Dan had intended just to look them over again from the safety of darkness, to maybe eavesdrop on conversations and gather more information about the group, but mainly just to get a better feel for the whole thing, to make up for being so out of it in Mr. Hasso's office.

It was seeing the dim yellow glow from the second bus that made him cross the creek-bed and go among the darkened shapes. He'd say he'd lost a ring or something if anyone caught him, say he'd come back looking for it, though that would mean he'd have to be using the torch he had in his back pocket, the last thing he wanted to do.

He made it to the second bus, stood beneath the yellow panes, heard the muffled murmur of voices within. But the windows were closed and Danny couldn't make out words. It was infuriating.

Then the office door opened and Bernard Hasso and Berty Green emerged into the front of the bus.

"I want it brought up first thing," Mr. Hasso was saying. "Take Walter and Jack. We've got a little over eighteen hours. Mr. Atterling's party will be here at seven o'clock."

"Right," Berty said (Dan almost expected him to say 'Roger that!').

"And I've reconsidered. Tomorrow you will take the mantacycle into town, drum up some local business. We might as well be seen to be earning our way in case folks get to talking."

"Right you are, Mr. Hasso. Good night."

"Good night, Berty."

Bernard Hasso went back into his office and closed the door. Berty clambered out of the second bus and headed for the darkwagon.

Danny stood as motionless as possible, vividly aware of his heart pounding, of the torch stuck in his back pocket, of a stone in his left shoe, of how perspiration had to be making his forehead shine in the moonlight through the trees. But Berty passed obliviously by, climbed into the closed-in bus and shut the door behind him. Only then did Danny cross the intervening space and stand beside that third dark vehicle with its faded legend: *The Saltimbanques*, snaking in the darkness—an incantation to the night and all its silence.

It was *too* quiet. There were insect sounds, the usual clicks and chirrups, but absolute silence from the bus, no footsteps, no voices. But it didn't *feel* like the silence of seven sleeping people, rather more like the silence of people standing, waiting inside till he had gone away so they could resume what they'd been doing before. He imagined them there, eyes wide but catching no light whatsoever, the sighted but unseeing eyes of the living trapped in caves, buried in tombs, caught in air pockets in the holds of sunken ships.

Danny moved away as silently as he could, crept back across the creek, taking care to avoid any logs, reached his bike and hurried back to town, finally joining Kenny in their sleepout.

"You sure took your time," Kenny said drowsily as Danny climbed into bed.

"You know what it's like, Kenny. Sometimes you just get caught up."

"Roger that," Kenny said, and slipped off into sleep again.

Danny lay staring at the night, watching the stars move around the sky. When he slept at last, he dreamed he was being chased by a terrible creature called a mantacycle with Berty Green perched on its back. Bernard Hasso sat to one side working on his calculations.

Danny had meant to wake early to go spy on the camp and see what it was Berty and the others had to bring up for Mr. Hasso first thing, but when Kenny roused him at 8:06 he knew it would be too late for that.

But Annie called by the clubhouse at 9 o'clock and Dan made sure the three of them were at the northwestern end of town, maybe two hundred yards out, when Berty Green came pedaling in from the direction of the creek.

The mantacycle was quite a sight, a tall four-wheeled contraption at least six feet high and six feet square at the base and tapering in, as rusty and weird-looking as an old torture machine, with arms and overhangs and a dozen flags snaking out from as many flagpoles set into the tube-metal frame, all long, faded pennons: blue, orange, red and purple, curling out behind. The whole thing was like the skeleton of a pyramid hauled up from the bottom of the ocean, and Berty was as extraordinary a sight, bent over the pedals on a small saddle seat, elbows out, legs pumping furiously in the early heat, his long, tattered dust-coat flaring behind him. He was wearing a wide-brimmed hat set with corks on strings—no, not corks—set with dancing, swinging, bleached-white things: bird skulls, Danny saw when the mantacycle got closer.

Seeing what they were, Danny realized the little man's name was probably Birdy Green, not Berty. Somehow it just tipped everything further over into strange.

"Mornin' to you, kids!" he called when he recognized them, breathing hard and letting the tall vehicle roll to a stop, its four pumped-up tires making their gritty tearing sound on the hot road surface. "You were a big hit with Mr. Hasso last night, I have to tell ya. He figured, what the hell, let's put on a show anyway! Seven o'clock tonight. Five bob admission. Go tell your friends!"

"Roger that!" Kenny cried as Berty—Birdy!—set to pedaling again, and ran off to follow the machine into town, as if there was anything else happening in Reardon this Friday night that might stop folks being available.

In a strange way, standing there in the road with the dust settling around them was the first time Dan had ever felt truly alone with Annie. They watched

Birdy ride off with Kenny scrambling back and forth like some native runner in a Jungle Jim movie and the silence just grew up around them, the sense of being together.

"I went back there last night, Annie," he said, expecting her to act annoyed and disappointed.

"So did I," she said.

You could have knocked Danny over. "You what? When? What did you see?" So much for protecting her.

"I went real late. Around midnight, I guess. That Mr. Hasso was so creepy, Dan. I just wanted to see the place again."

"See anything?"

"Nope. When did you go?"

Danny told her, describing what he'd heard and felt, growing more and more uneasy at the thought of Annie crouching there in the dark watching the buses and the tents. "What do we do?" he said finally.

Annie shrugged. "I'm just really glad you're here, Dan."

"Me too," Danny said. "That you're here, I mean." And they started walking back toward town.

Birdy Green and his 'Frying' Machine, as townsfolk cheerfully called it (it was ten A.M. and already ninety-three degrees) were a definite hit. Locals bought him beers, shouted him an early lunch, offered to give him a tow back. By the time he was pedaling out of town at 11:48, he had two dozen kids straggling along behind like he was some latter-day Pied Piper doing a practice run. Kenny was one of them.

The kids straggled back ten minutes later, dusty and exhausted, and the day settled into its most terrible phase, the heat lending everything its dreamlike shimmer for what Hank Burgess called the "wait-out."

"Whatcha doin' after wait-out?" Hank would say from behind the bar at the Stockman Hotel, asking any number of patrons staring up at the big aerial shot of the town as if expecting some trace of Birdy's carnival to suddenly appear like stigmata or a face on a shroud.

"Dunno," most said as usual, though more and more added, "Might give the circus a look-see" and "Yeah, might give the circus a go."

Pete Byles would invariably correct whoever said it. "Ain't a circus, you blokes."

"Must be," someone would invariably answer. "Seen one clown already."

And round it would go, all through the blazing afternoon.

Annie's mum ran the pub's kitchen, so Danny heard part of it when the three Rangers dropped by so Annie could get permission to go see the show. You always remembered to check in when money was involved.

Now that they had a legitimate reason to visit the carnival (and since Kenny was seeing himself as something of a self-appointed sidekick to Birdy Green), the three Rangers went out to the campsite around six P.M. this time riding their bikes along the highway and leaving them by the road near where it bowed in to meet the railway line.

They were rather surprised to see two tents set up on the flat hard ground this side of the creek, both warmly lit, one quite large and unusually long, the other smaller and square and placed a few feet away from the bigger one like an afterthought.

No one was about so they looked into the large one first, saw twenty hurricane lamps set on as many supports, warm and welcoming, and lots of benches set up down the far end. All it was really was a large empty space. There was no bunting or posters, no attempt at decoration at all. When they peered into the smaller tent, they saw nothing but one of the bigger, darker logs from the creek. It seemed to swallow the light from the eight lanterns hanging on the uprights. Maybe that's what Birdy had had to carry up.

"Hey, they've got a chain on it!" Kenny said, and laughed. "Maybe they're worried someone'll steal it."

Kenny was right. Around one gnarled length of snapped-off root was an iron ring, with a short chain leading to a spike driven into the hard ground.

"Maybe they're going to turn it into an elephant!" Dan said, more to ease his nerves, he realized, than because he thought it was funny.

Kenny laughed though. "Roger that! Sorry, Annie. Say, why don't we go find Birdy?"

It wasn't a bad idea, Dan thought, given the little man's good humor toward them earlier in the day, and it gave them a reason to cross the creek-bed and go among the buses again, which Danny found was what he wanted to do.

But when they reached the camp, Birdy was nowhere to be seen, which made Danny think of the closed darkwagon and the silence there. The only sign of life was Mr. Hasso sitting on the doorsill of the second bus puffing on a pipe.

"Right on time," he said, knocking the pipe against the lowest step to empty it, then getting up. "Come on in awhile. It's almost showtime."

Dan had reservations about going into Mr. Hasso's office again, but at the same time wanted to test himself after what had happened the previous night. He followed Annie and Kenny and was soon standing before the ringmaster's big desk, littered as before with charts and pages of figures.

But now there was a different picture on the plywood wall behind where Bernard Hasso was once again seated. Smaller than the Picasso, almost a foot on a side, it showed a washed-out gray landscape under a lowering sky, with shapes like polished river pebbles scattered about, dull and metallic-looking, some set on their ends, some more geometric than others, those in the fore-ground rising up in columns like those limestone shapes you read about, stalag-mites. Among the clustering and spill of gray and white forms were a few touches of color, here a drab yellow stone, there an ocher one, there a pale red trapezoidal shape, but there was only one distinctive focus in the whole moody scene, a rectangular patch of red on the left side, like a window or door or even a mirror in a worn, rolled, leaden frame.

Dan was about to mention it when Mr. Hasso clapped his big hands together and grinned at them, his eyes flashing under dark brows.

"Now you see us at our best!" he said. "This is our emergent phase."

Their what? Danny didn't understand what that could mean.

"And the tents over there?" Annie asked. "All part of your calculations?"

"Exactly so, Annie. Position is crucial. Always crucial. What do they say? Time, place and identity: that's what it's all about. You kids won't know it but the layout of Reardon configures to the sacred geometry of the Vesica—quite by accident, mind you, purest chance, sweetest serendipity. A circle, a square, a triangle, a rhombus, a hexagram and polygons all tipped in together."

"Is that good?" Kenny asked.

"Oh surely it is, Kenny. Very much so. And just there where the road bends in to the creek with the tracks between, we have a most wonderful confirmation of Bruno Taut's *Stadtkrone*, can you believe it? If only I could convey even a fraction of what it means to us, the theosophical blend of ley-line traditions and geomantic corridors with the *axis urbis* of imperial Rome. The cityline. Cities built along lines of force. The ancient scemb lines. No wonder all these crackpot doctrines sprang up, spring up and will forever do so. How else to interpret the truth? But I do forget myself, going on like this. Kenny, Birdy says you were a great help today. How would you like to assist him with his final preparations now?"

"That'd be great! We didn't see him around though."

"Oh, you'll find him, I'm sure. Off you go. You'll see your friends again when the show starts."

"Hey, Roger that!" Kenny cried as he left the office. "See ya!"

Danny heard him clamber out of the bus, heard a dwindling, somehow disturbing, "Hey, Birdy! Hey, Birdy, wait up!"

Now Mr. Hasso's smile changed, or rather changed at the eyes, which glittered full of unreadable emotion.

"You changed the picture," Danny said, partly to relieve the tension, the dreadful awkwardness he felt, partly out of determination to stay with it this time no matter what happened.

"I did. We always do. Yves Tanguy, 1954. *The Saltimbanques*. What do you think of it, Danny?"

"It's strange. I prefer the other one."

"The Picasso. You do? Tell me what you see in this one."

Danny studied the strangely lit plain, the clustered eroded shapes and spires in the foreground, the scattered ones farther out, the dramatic patch of red in its frame.

"It's like things waiting for other things to arrive."

"And when they do?" Mr. Hasso's voice was rich, his words lulling, soothing. Danny concentrated on the shapes, partly wishing Annie would chip in, partly wanting to impress her and hide the fact that he was truly and deeply afraid.

"I don't know. They change. They grow."

"I see. And the patch of red?"

Danny knew he'd be asked that. "Energy. Force. Or something has scratched through the surface. Made a door maybe. Something showing through under the gray. Peeking through."

"Mr. Jarvie never knew what a smart student he had, did he, Dan? Now tell me: did you find your ring?"

"My what?"

"Last night when you came back to pay us a visit. Did you find your ring?"

Danny felt the clutch of panic, pulled back from the picture, from Mr. Hasso's incredible voice and eyes and saw that Annie wasn't standing next to him.

"Where's Annie?" he cried. "What have you done with Annie?"

"You didn't hear her? She said she had to—you know—use our convenience."

Danny didn't believe him for a moment. "And where's that?"

Bernard Hasso gestured casually. "Back over there a ways. She'll only be a minute."

"Mr. Hasso, what's going on?"

"What do you feel is happening, Danny Truswell?"

"I didn't tell you my last name!"

"Birdy picked it up in town." An answer for everything.

Did not, Danny wanted to shout right into his face, tried to recollect what else he had to remember, something Mr. Hasso had just now said. He was forgetting again. Forgetting to notice things. Like Annie going off, leaving the office. She couldn't have. Wouldn't have. Then how . . . ?

"I asked what you feel is happening, Dan," Mr. Hasso said, snaring him again with that way he had, killing thoughts by imposing others.

"Something's pushing through," Danny answered.

"Almost right. Almost got it. Now forget the red bit."

How could he? Danny stared at the picture, just couldn't help it.

"Something's getting nearer."

"Now that's really got it!" Bernard Hasso said, seeming genuinely pleased. "Slouching toward Reardon to be born. Something very pure. A network of energy, Dan. Moving across the land, traveling in lines. Lines of force. Spotlights of magic. Some of us know how to plot 'em, track 'em, use 'em. We travel the grid. Sometimes we follow, sometimes we wait for them to catch us up. It's what gives history its buzz and fizz, Danny, me pure boy! Shamans and wizards! Smart old codgers figurin' out the conjunctions. Merlin having a good day. Sacerdotes and mages, seers, sibyls and sorcerers all waiting for auspicious windows of opportunity, knowing how to play the game. Oh, it's an art, I tell ya!"

Dan tried to imagine lines of force, thought of moving spotlights of magic, and something else.

I didn't tell him my last name.

"It's supernatural then!" he managed to say.

"No, it's not! That's precisely *not* what it is. Once your so-called supernatural manifests itself then it's *natural* don't you see? *Part* of nature. This isn't nonsense about mummies responding to ancient curses. This is things happening as they always happen whether we notice them or not. It's like forgetting to notice gravity because it's always there, or what the Moon's tidal pull does to your body, or negative ions from thunderstorms. This isn't quackery, Dan. Not this! We travel the grid, flexing muscles most of us never get to try, meeting lots of different people, looking for those who think the same way we do, keeping an eye out for apprentices, too, though we're very picky there. Taking turns in trying to pass it on."

Dan was hearing yet not hearing, snared by the smooth round stones, the shadowy sky, the clustering shapes.

"Now Mr. Atterling is a politician, see, and this show's really being put on for him. He's one of those secret-handshake Freemason mystic types too, you see, Danny, but he doesn't know how to use it. So it'll do us all good to keep him careful and in his place, in awe of the way it is. Make 'im think it's us. Pay to get bits of it. But for us, for me, it has to be pure, Danny, you do understand that? It's important you do."

Danny understood stones and sky and a shadowy distance, disturbing weights, curves and edges, a comforting patch of red. Though he did hear, part of him did.

"Whatever happens, Dan," Mr. Hasso was saying, kindly enough it seemed, "it's all for a good cause. Now you run along and find your friends."

Danny stumbled from the office, blinking, shaking his head, trying to fathom what it had all been, nearly fell out of the bus.

Spotlights of magic. Moving. Getting closer.

The carnival following them.

These Saltimbanques.

The spotlights.

The lanterns. Dan noticed the lamps hanging in the trees, hanging from the buses, lighting the tents across the way, noticed how the words on the long bus sides seemed brighter, richer, firmer. So magical.

The Saltimbanques.

Performing in spotlights. Moving about. What *had* Mr. Hasso said?

Kenny was there then, grinning, excited, seeming too young all of a sudden, just too too young.

"Danny, hi!"

"You seen Annie, Ken?"

Kenny shrugged and grinned. "Think I saw her over at the big tent. Lots of people are arrivin'. You're getting sweet on her, Dan!"

"Hey, she's a Ranger too! Just want to know where she is."

Kenny's grin became a leer. "Whatever you say. But ain't that closed-up bus weird?"

"Sure is. Why, do you reckon?"

Again Kenny shrugged. "Dunno. Just don't like goin' near it. It's real quiet. Spooky."

Like someone's waiting in there, Danny thought. Listening. "You keep clear of it, Kenny, okay?"

"Don't have to tell me. See you at the show."

"See you."

By the time Danny reached the big tent, there were well over two hundred people either crowded on the makeshift benches at the far end or standing along the sides, talking and laughing, poking good-natured fun at the modest set-up. Dan hurried to join them, unable to see Annie in the crowd but sure she'd be there waiting for the show to get underway. After what Kenny had said, he was sort of glad she didn't come over to join him, though another part of him wished she would.

He'd just squeezed in between two kids he knew on one of the front benches when he noticed the four serious-looking men in crumpled dark suits seated further along the row: no doubt Mr. Arterling and his party. They were definitely from out of town and were clearly impatient; one of the men kept looking at his watch and muttering to his companions.

When Bernard Hasso entered the tent, it was without a fanfare of any kind. He just strode in looking appropriately splendid in black tails and top-hat, carrying a glossy ebony cane with a silver ferrule at one end and a faceted crystal knob at the other. It glittered and shone in the lamplight.

The chatter subsided immediately. People were grinning. This was more like it.

There ought to be a spotlight, Danny thought, seeing the ringmaster standing before them all. *He looks good but he should be standing in a spotlight.*

"Ladies and gentlemen, boys and girls," Bernard Hasso said in his rich and wonderful voice. "Welcome, one and all! We are The Saltimbanques. Nature's clowns and mountebanks. We have traveled the highways and byways of Australia to be here tonight, to offer an entertainment to the good folk of Reardon. The time is right for magic and merriment once again!"

And he held his arms wide, the crystal knob of his cane twinkling with lamp-light. There was no fanfare, but there was a sense of one as the performers ran into the tent: Walter, Haunted Jack and Gwen to the left, Robert, May and Jeffrey to the right, all wearing loose, brightly colored bodysuits, stitched all over with shapes and signs like Danny drew with his compass set at school, arcs intersected by straight lines.

All but Mr. Hasso himself ran down the length of the tent to shake hands with members of the audience, then, after pinching cheeks and tweaking noses and pulling colored kerchiefs from the pockets of some of the children, they all rushed back to form up around Bernard Hasso near the entrance.

"Here it comes!" the ringmaster cried, and began twirling his cane, making a Catherine Wheel of flashing light as his troupe began making a human pyramid to one side, Haunted Jack supporting the other six as they climbed aloft to compose themselves in a very impressive display.

Something was wrong about it though, Danny realized. He had done a bit of balancing at school, and this looked like it should topple over any second. But there was Haunted Jack holding them all, and now raising his left leg, supporting the whole thing, *and* going up on his toes.

And—was Dan really seeing it?—now raising his right leg, so the whole pattern of human forms was just hanging in the air, all strobed by the dazzling twirl of Mr. Hasso's cane.

It couldn't be.

Everyone was leaning forward trying to be sure of what they were seeing.

That's when Danny noticed how close and warm it was, and that the air smelled of woodsmoke and resin and something else. He kept blinking and sniffing to make sure of what was going on.

These hardly appeared to be the same people as the night before. They all seemed taller, stronger, not so much younger as more, well . . . in control, focused, powerful. They radiated confidence and energy.

And just how had the hovering pyramid been dismantled? For now Haunted Jack balanced Walter and an improbably nimble and alluring Gwen more skillfully than he'd seemed capable of, sitting around the campfire that first night. Robert was juggling twenty balls with casual recklessness, an almost disdainful smirk on his face. May and Jeffrey strode about on stilts, seemed to fall, would catch one another, then go teetering and tottering toward those standing along the sides at that end of the tent before steadying themselves and staggering back the other way. Now Birdy made his appearance, running about in his long coat and bird-skull hat and flinging buckets of confetti over the laughing onlookers.

At first glance, apart from the opening pyramid, the acts weren't anything special, though if you did look close, you started to notice things, how every now and then May and Jeffrey would lean too far over on their stilts yet not fall, or how one of Robert's hands would lift to wave at someone in the crowd or mop his brow without disturbing the steady flow of the balls. Even when Birdy substituted warm perfumed water for the confetti, the audience responded with delight.

There was a drunkenness, a euphoria surrounding everything. The air became heavier, smokier, dimmer. The lanterns had haloes. The resin smell was stronger than ever. People were still blinking and squinting to be sure of what was going on, but no one complained, no little kids cried, no one got up to leave. It was as if they were in the presence of magic and knew it, and all wanted part of it.

And the players came ever closer as the evening progressed, moving from the far end of the tent toward the benches.

Spotlights of magic.

Danny found himself remembering bits of what Mr. Hasso had said. Something about moving points of energy.

The performers were getting nearer. Soon they'd be clambering over the benches.

No, Danny realized. The show would end first. The smaller tent was next-door—*in a straight line to this one!*

What was it Mr. Hasso had said about ley-lines and the *urbis axis?* Cities built in lines?

More to the point, why would he have told him?

There was no time to consider it further, for once again Mr. Hasso had his arms raised, and his voice was rumbling in the silence.

"Our final treat, ladies and gentlemen, boys and girls, is in the tent next door. Yes, the Barrack Creek Bunyip itself! But it's one at a time, I'm afraid, bunyips being nocturnal and shy creatures when a crowd's around."

Muttering and exchanging uncertain smiles, the townsfolk filed out of the long tent and formed a queue outside the smaller one. Just as Mr. Hasso had stipulated, one person was allowed in at a time, to emerge a short while later blinking, with looks of puzzlement on their faces as if not quite sure what they'd seen.

"Keep it short, folks!" Robert kept saying from his place by the entrance. "There's lots of people so keep it short!"

"What did you see? What did you see?" younger kids were calling, eager for their turns, but it was clear that those who'd been inside didn't know what to say and just went off looking bewildered and smiling sheepishly to join relatives and friends.

Danny held back, hoping to see Annie, to share as much of the experience together as Robert made possible.

"You there! Danny!" Robert called. "You wanna see the bunyip or not? You'll need to be quick. Show's over in a few minutes."

Danny pushed into the tent, smelled resin almost immediately, saw the lamps had haloes, saw the log over by the tent's far wall. Someone had moved it; the chain was stretched at full length. That was all.

"Too bad, kiddo," Robert said, right behind him. "Too late, I reckon. Maybe next time."

Danny was glad to be out of there, was relieved to see Kenny right in front of him, a few feet away; noticed too, over near the large tent, Mr. Hasso shaking hands with the men in Mr. Atterling's party. They no longer looked bored or impatient but were smiling and nodding as they started walking back toward their car.

"Did you see it, Danny?" Kenny asked. "The bunyip, did ya?"

"I missed it. What did you see?"

Kenny frowned and got a silly grin on his face. "I dunno. Hard to describe it really. But it was real neat."

That's when Mr. Hasso came over. "Right then, Dan. Thought Kenny might like to help Birdy and the others strike the tents while you and me walk a bit and continue our discussion from before."

And before Kenny could express his pleasure at being a carny roustabout, Danny got in with it first. "Roger that!"

Kenny stared at him in amazement, unable to believe what he'd heard.

Mr. Hasso slapped Dan on the shoulder. "That's the way! Never know when you can use twice the pure!"

Danny looked straight at Kenny. "Roger that, too, Mr. Hasso!"

And they walked off, leaving Kenny Woke staring after them in confusion and disbelief.

Moments later, Mr. Hasso and Danny had left the others and were moving along the creek-bed. Almost all the townsfolk had gone, walking or driving back to town. A few headlights could still be seen heading off to distant properties, and if anyone noticed three bikes left by the highway they would've paid no mind. It was summer holidays, barely ten P.M., and with the days so hot, kids stayed up till all hours.

All Danny could hear apart from their footsteps and the occasional insect sound were members of the troupe calling to one another as they brought down the tents. The voices faded with distance.

"Twice the pure, Dan," Bernard Hasso said, guiding him with a hand on his shoulder. "That's the way. Still workin' on that part of it—why that kind of sacrifice is the best way to go, why sacrifice is necessary at all really. Like to think it's like the Indians killing a buffalo, you know, making an offering to the Buffalo Spirit. Then there's the alchemical angle, reconciling the opposites, and the geomantic tradition. There's just so much to know. But, hey, so long as it works, I say. What d'you reckon, Dan? Ah, but here we are."

Another tent stood in the middle of the creek, square and dark in the thin moonlight.

"In you go, boy," Mr. Hasso said. "Don't keep her waiting." And he lit the single hurricane lamp hanging on its wire hook, illuminating the only two things inside.

One of them was Annie Hendist, sitting in the middle of the dirt floor, bound hand and foot, a hankie tied in her mouth. The other was a large black tree-trunk, hooked and broken, shaped by some past flooding, just lying there. The tent had been set up around it.

In line with the other tents, Danny knew.

He hurried across to Annie, pulled the hankie from between her teeth and started freeing her while Mr. Hasso took the lantern outside with him and began lacing the tent flaps together behind him. "Won't keep you long," he said, then the lamp was extinguished, plunging them into darkness, and Dan heard footsteps moving away.

"Oh, Dan!" Annie said, grabbing his arm, standing close. "I've been so scared!"

"What happened?" Dan was vividly aware of her.

"I—I'm not sure. One moment I was in the bus with you and Mr. Hasso. Then they'd brought me here. I was so terrified, Dan. They just left me here. I didn't know what they'd do."

"It's okay, Annie. You're safe now. It's okay now." *So* aware of her.

She continued gripping his arm. He could feel her breath on his cheek. "Do you know what's goin' on, Dan?" she asked.

He didn't. He did. He tried to think back, almost had it. It was gone, then bits slipped back again.

"It's something about spotlights of energy. Moving in lines. They follow them." He was surprised to hear himself saying it. "Go from place to place, keeping up. They use it, Annie."

"For what?"

"Everything. Their performance. They were so different, so—changed. And that long tent, remember? Everyone was down one end. Their performance got closer and closer. Then it moved to the bunyip tent."

"The what tent?"

"The smaller tent. The one with the log chained down." And Danny went silent a moment. "Like this one."

Annie's eyes twinkled in the dimness. "This one isn't chained."

"I know."

They peered off to where the hooked, torn silhouette of the old log showed against the moonlit east side of the tent.

"How long we got?" Annie asked him.

"I lose track of time whenever I'm with Hasso. An hour or two. I don't know how long it takes. Let's try to get out of here."

The sturdy canvas walls had been spiked through brass eyelets on the ground outside; the lacing on the flaps was knotted outside as well. The central and corner uprights were simply too thick and too well planted to break or dislodge, and repeated running against the tent's sides seemed to have no effect at all.

They were standing by the entrance, trying to work the lacing rope so the knot was nearer, when they heard it.

Barely heard it, for it was the softest wrenching, the slightest sound of twisting.

They stared at each other, then at the shape.

And saw one of the snapped-off roots at the top move, twist.

The log was alive.

They could hear it creaking as it lifted slightly, testing the life it had, then heard a scrape, and another. There were a few pounding heartbeats of silence, then a third scrape, this time louder, harsher as it gouged the ground where it lay, made with the determination of something *discovering* itself alive, filled with the desperate chance to live again as something so new.

Annie grabbed Danny by both arms this time.

"You believing all this, Dan?" she said. Such an odd question now.

"Of course."

"He wants us 'cause we're pure, Danny. That's what he told me. You know what that means?"

"Yeah. Sure. Course I do."

"And are you?"

"What? Me? Yes. Of course. You?" He would never have dreamed of asking it. That sort of directness was four, six, ten years in his future at least.

"You know it. Quickly. Take off your shorts!"

Perhaps it was what they did then, perhaps it was Kenny arriving in time, perhaps the enlivening energy simply moved on, but Kenny Woke *was* suddenly there, stirred from his hero-worship of Birdy Green by Danny using *his* signature line like that—a sailor's SOS, a flyer's Mayday, a carny's Hey Rube!—fumbling at the tent rope, undoing the flaps, never noticing how Danny and Annie checked their clothing as they left the tent.

It all remained so dreamlike and uncertain, what happened in those few days, what Mr. Jarvie later described as "smoke and mirrors" when school started back, just "so much hypnosis and hallucination."

The heat and the sameness of the days soon wore it down all the more. Blokes at the bar of the Stockman Hotel stopped peering into the aerial shot of Reardon, began looking at their beers again as they talked, and when Danny reminded people (even Kenny) about the carnival that had played out near Barrack Creek, they said, "Oh yeah," as if it had happened years ago not weeks, but sure, of course they remembered it. But what else could you expect in a land where the heat doomed normal folk to the limbo of wait-out, blurred grain trucks and silos into dragons, burred every lonely windmill into Don Quixote tilting at himself?

And just like that, Annie went off to stay with her aunt in Mildura for a while, which was no big deal, she'd done it often enough before, but she didn't say good-bye and it just pushed the whole thing further across into unreality and lack of proper consequence.

Then Mr. Hasso's letter came.

Dear Daniel,

We pay our price too. Forfeit things like families. Something to do with the energy. May says, probably where the notion of changelings comes from down through the ages. But no Dannys, Kennys or Annies for The Saltimbanque unless we borrow, find apprentices however we can. Where else do you think we come from? It's the other thing we do. You didn't disappoint us, Dan. The magic passed through you. The child will always be drawn to magic.

For that, our heartfelt thanks.

Bernard Hasso

PS: The "bunyip" was just to motivate, you understand. Excuse the theatrics.

For a moment Danny actually thought the "child" reference was to him, but the postscript stole that in an instant. There was only one thought then, a question, desperate, bittersweet and somehow extending his whole life out into something infinitely, ultimately beyond Reardon.

Had she known all along?

In the space it took to read the few dozen words, Danny learned two crucial things, vital to learn at any age but so powerful to have at fourteen: that you always had to grant unlimited possibility, and that happy endings were as fleeting as you let them be. If not protected, they vanished out of lives like the bunyips along Barrack Creek.

JANET McADAMS

The Monster of Childhood

Janet McAdams, a poet of mixed Scottish, Irish, and Creek ancestry, grew up in Alabama, received an M.F.A. in creative writing from the University of Alabama, and a Ph.D. in comparative literature from Emory University. Presently, she teaches literature and creative writing at the University of Oklahoma. Her poetry has appeared in TriQuarterly, The North American Review, Poetry, Many Mountains Moving, Nimrod, Columbia, The Women's Review of Books, The Atlanta Review, The Crab Orchard Review, *and the anthology* Outsiders: Poems About Rebels, Renegades and Exiles.

"The Monster of Childhood" is a potent poem about childhood fear, and the stories that grow from it. It comes from McAdams's recent poetry collection The Island of Lost Luggage *(University of Arizona Press).*

—*T. W.*

In the house of your childhood, the blue monster
leaned over the iron railing and the red one hid,
the way monsters hide, in the space beneath the bed.
All night they gobbled the air you tried to breathe.
They shed dust bunnies, they groaned, their nails
grew long and yellow, as they tapped out
camp songs, lullabies—all night they tapped:
Make New Friends. The Farmer in the Dell.

I am not the mother, the father, the sister in this story.
I am not: Djinn, Mage, Fairy Godmother, Sorcerer.
Only the monsters are real in this story. They sweat

blue and red over the boy in the narrow bed.
I would chase the blue one with an owl feather duster.
I would tell the red one, Off With You!
there are other boys to bother.

But let's call this memoir, and say in this memoir,
and say, if you listen, a door is
creaking open. There's the sound of glass breaking,

a wooden soldier drumming, a stuffed bear's
thud and tumble. Vines climb the wall
that leads to your window, but there is no escape
through the wooden wardrobe, no secret
world below, no key, no underground tunnel.

The wind outside is a real wind, not pretend.
In it, the trees of childhood make a terrible sound.

GAVIN J. GRANT AND KELLY LINK

Ship, Sea, Mountain, Sky

Gavin J. Grant was born and raised in Scotland, and now lives in Brooklyn, New York. He edits and publishes the small press 'zine, Lady Churchill's Rosebud Wristlet, *and works for BookSense.com, the independent bookstore online portal. His writing has been published in* Altair, Aberrations, The Urban Pantheist, *and online at SCIFI.COM.*

Kelly Link, who also lives in Brooklyn, has published short fiction in Century, Asimov's, Event Horizon, A Wolf at the Door, *and other venues, winning the 1998 James Tiptree, Jr. Award and the 1999 World Fantasy Award. Her work has appeared three previous times in* The Year's Best Fantasy and Horror, *and has been collected in* Stranger Things Happen *(Small Beer Press).*

"Ship, Sea, Mountain, Sky" is a superb work of "imaginary world" fiction, creating, in just a few pages, a whole society steeped in myth and art, weighted by ancient traditions. The story comes from Altair 6/7, *a small journal published in Blackwood, South Australia.*

—T. W.

Father told us a story from a long time ago, when we lived by the sea. He said, "We were boatbuilders for the dead."

In my family the oldest child learned the skills from their mother or father. The boats had to be sturdy enough to go far out to sea, yet light enough to burn well. Then the northerners came and killed many of us so we moved, left the sea and our boats behind us and came to these mountains where we had to find a new path for the dead.

Our village is in a high valley where we grow most of what we need. We herd the mountain sheep and spin their rough, silky wool. We grow flax. We tend orchards. And up beyond the village, up through the orchards, a half-day's walk with a bier, is the burial place.

Father has been drinking salt wine. Now he is asleep. At mother's burial today I could see that this story is true. It is indeed a ship that we build for the dead.

I have done this, I have built ships, since I was a child. My shoulders are big from chopping and carrying wood, and my hands are hard. The other children— even my brothers and sisters—were always a little afraid of me. But there is one in the village who returns my looks and sometimes exchanges a few words with me, so I do not expect to be always lonely. It is a solitary job, but it carries respect.

Yesterday we built the fireship for my mother. Today we carried her body up to the burial ground. We all watched as father lit the pyre and it began to burn. We did not stay long, for the ship is the same as the ones that went to sea. It is a beautiful thing but it burns quickly. Soon enough the birds and animals would come to pick at her bones.

Up there my strength was needed, for father did not want to leave. He has failed fast since mother died. Two days ago as we chopped wood and gathered certain flowers and herbs, I considered what to take, what to leave for my next trip, which I cannot but feel will be soon. I have been considering all that I know, asking him for that which might fill the gaps in my knowledge. I lament what is unknown to me, what will pass with his passing.

My mother's family were sailors. Before I was born my grandparents were lost in a storm. They were fishers and traders, sometimes traveling for months at a time, only returning to the mountains a few times a year. We heard a rumor of the storm, up in the mountains. Everybody hoped that they might come into land in some distant unknown port. Eventually my mother and father began work on their only sea-going ship. They carried it all the way down to the ocean and launched it. It was a tiny thing, they said, that moved quickly beyond the surf, the flames burning fiercely. After that they turned their back on the sea. They came back to the mountains.

So our cupboards are oddly bare. We have my father's father's skullcup, my father's mother's jewelry and we have wedding masks from both. But on my mother's side we are missing a generation.

Each carving tells a story.

Here is a man and a woman sailing away to sea. Their arms are raised. They are waving good-bye to us. Their faces are not sad. They are expectant, hopeful. Skinny waves and dog-faced sea serpents curl around the prow of the boat. The ship is heavy with goods. Wind curls down out of the sky, filling the sails. At the further edges of the carving, the sea is rougher. Waves are larger. The sky is black and presses down, until it falls and tangles against the water. The boat will catch her like a knot on a comb. Their bodies will never be found.

As the sun set tonight we had the last feast for my mother. Many stories were told. This was my father's:

I was just a boy. I had a tuft of hair on each shoulder. I had bruises all over from running into doorways, chairs and tables. I had bruises from adults who'd caught me knocking over this, breaking that, running into this person, tripping up that. I had these feet, these legs that stuck out. I thought that I was smaller than I was.

Her family were sailors. So I didn't know them well, or her either. I'd been to the market for my mother and my arms were full of my purchases. I went around a corner at top speed as usual and ran right over her. The food went one way, my shoes came off and I fell on my face. I jumped straight up again. A girl was sitting down in the alley. She had long black hair, tied up in knots like a pirate queen. She was laughing so hard she didn't bother to stand up.

I wasn't just clumsy, I was rude. "You should watch where you're going," I said. I started gathering up my packages. A packet of spice had split—I tried to scoop up the stuff in my hands, and sneezed. All I had in my hand was dirt.

I grabbed up the rest of my purchases. When I was ready to go she was standing in my way. She had a frown on her face. Shake your heads! I was young, and maybe not so bright . . .

She was holding one wrist lightly as though it hurt. Still, she didn't speak. I was in a hurry. I tried to brush past her.

Many of you know this story, but not from her lips. You, my own children, have laughed at me for not fighting back, but I tell you now, I did! And I was more than fairly beaten. She was a sailor's child. She knew how to fight. When I was once again gathering my belongings, crying and snottering to myself, she left.

I got home and received no pity, for the spice I'd lost was expensive and necessary. I didn't tell anyone what had happened because I thought it was my fight. I thought I would get her back soon enough.

Of course I was mistaken. The next time I saw her I was walking along the river path and she was coming down to swim. She had long wide shoulders. Her wrist was in a cloth and wood splint. I still had bruises. "Hello, you," she said and she smiled at me. "Do you swim?"

In the water I was almost graceful. But she was like a swan.

Father would not sleep in the bed he had shared with my mother. Instead we made up a pallet for him beside the fire. Tonight he fell asleep easily.

I went out and met my particular friend under the salt tree. My friend sat, back against the trunk, and I lay my head down in that cradle the legs and the pelvis make for children and lovers. My friend combed my hair with a twig, and I closed my eyes. I could hear the little foxes that live up in the tree. Early, before it got light, I picked up a piece of wood, and because it had a good shape in my hand, I took it inside.

Father woke at dawn. I was back in my bed, and I stayed there for a while, listening to him move around the kitchen. I went out and bought fresh bread from Payta, who this once would have liked a few minutes of conversation. But my heart was still at home.

My father and I ate slowly, not speaking. We were listening to the house. I am accustomed to silence, but this silence was not comfortable. We did not fit inside it yet. It was a new kind of silence. My mother was not singing. We didn't hear her broom sweeping out the hearth. She didn't call my name, tell me to fetch in new kindling, or ask my father if he was going to shave, or did he mind looking like a bear all day, and why hadn't he laid out a plate for her at the table? As hard as we were listening, we could not hear her.

Inside the house it was too large, and outside it was too small. The path began right outside our garden. It went up through the orchards, away from the town. We fetched our tool sacks and headed up the mountain. As we approached the burning ground we heard the animals—the salt foxes and the other scavengers—scattering into the undergrowth. The birds flew away complaining.

The fireship had disappeared leaving only a few charred stakes. The spices, oils and flowers were all gone and I was relieved. I hadn't fully trusted our work of the day before. We did everything the way we always had although I deferred to my father and let him do tasks that in recent years I had begun doing. I watched discreetly while I worked on the slower, cooler fire that would consume all the ship's remnants. He neither stumbled nor made a mistake. I hoped I would be able to do the same for him some day. I hoped he would never have to do this for me.

He took the skull and limbs from the torso. The corpse was in the usual state: pulled at, blackened and burnt, mostly unrecognizable. He freed the ribs taking the slim struts from the loose structure of the body. Something had eaten the heart.

The cradle of the pelvis was next. I lifted my own small axe but Father shook his head. With his sharpest knife and axe he brought the pelvis free from the surrounding muscles and joints that held it in place. I had finished the fire and began to help him place the bones in a circle around the edge of the clearing. The spine we left in the center of the circle.

Some bones would disappear in the wind or be carried away for their marrow, and the rest we would collect after a full month had passed.

The skull went at the highest point, the wings of the shoulder blades on either side. The ribs, now individually separated made the top semi-circle, then came the arms, hands, legs, down to the bottom of the circle where the feet lay on each side of the pelvis, exactly below the skull.

When we finished we were bloody, gray from smoke and ash, cold, filthy, hungry, sick and sadder perhaps than we had ever been.

When we reached the village, that evening, by tradition someone was there to bathe us, help us and feed us once we could eat. But this night, even with the hottest water, the gentlest soaps, the warmest towels, it was bitter. On this night, it is the family of the dead that cares for us. My brothers and sisters tried their hardest. We ate the vegetable dishes that are all we can ever manage on this night and drank a lot of wine. There were more stories, more tears, always more to drink. They made up beds for us beside the fire, but all night I dreamed I was up there in the circle past the orchards. The little salt foxes gnawed on my bones.

It rained every day. Sunrise was no more than a shift from dark to light gray. My imagination would not leave my mother's corpse. Birds looked balefully from trees, unwilling to fly. In a time when my father was most in need of companionship everyone was surly and without words. People came to visit us, but my father looked at them as if he was surprised. He looked at them as if they had already died and he had taken their bodies up to the burning grounds. He looked at them as if he were measuring them. When he looked at them, they shuddered and made their excuses and left.

After a week he began clearing mother's possessions from the house. He gave most of her clothes to other families, and then there were days when I walked through the village, and thought I saw her, walking toward me, or away from me, or sitting in other people's houses, beside windows.

My father offered me the choice of her books and I took as many as I could. The others went to my brothers and sisters. The house, which no longer fit us, now seemed embarrassed and shabby, stripped of my mother's bits and pieces. The kitchen was the only room that didn't seem to change. Perhaps because my mother never liked to cook. Now I sat in the kitchen and whittled.

Everyone in the village carves something. In the summer when the ships come, the traders and sailors buy what they like. The sailors buy good luck charms: dolphins and crows; and cats with their tails curved around their feet; women, smiling, lying on their backs with their legs open.

We carve combs and tops and sea chests for sailors to take home to their wives and husbands and children. We carve little ships and skulls and potbellied devils. I was carving a salt fox, with a finger bone in its mouth. About the time I finished that fox, my father went to the family's glass-doored cabinet and took out my great-grandparents' bones, for mother was the last in the family to have known them: the skulls, so carefully looked after all these years; the rib hairpins and chopsticks; the worry beads mother had fashioned from the toe bones; the earrings; the drumsticks; both pelvic masks.

Once a trader had come to a wedding. When he saw the masks, he became very excited. He offered to pay an extraordinary sum, but of course there was no one in the village who would take his money. Perhaps at first he didn't realize what it was he was trying to buy. My father took him aside. They talked, and the trader shook his head a great deal. He laughed, I think, because he was embarrassed or shocked. I don't think he was a bad man, or a greedy man. He just wasn't very smart. He bought a carving from me, a small woman with round buttocks, curled up and lying on her side. Where her hair fell down over her face the wood was paler. You couldn't help touching her there.

Today only children made their way through the rain to see. Everyone knew what father must be doing that day. The mood in the village was somber and dark; only the children seemed immune to it. I brought them into the house and gave them sticky sweets. I answered a few questions. Many were seeing the rites for the first time.

Father placed all the bones on the big workbench. The questions died away and a boy and a girl edged forward to the bench. Hyrach and Triel, not the oldest but the least shy, the leaders of this group. All of the children here had family cabinets and histories at home but children rarely got to touch them. These were histories that grew more fragile with age and use. At the end of the month my mother's bones would come back to our house until my father, my siblings and I died. It hurt to think what short time they would reside here. The bones would hardly have time to grow brittle. My mother had not lived to see any grandchildren.

My brothers and sisters were there too. They watched the children play, gently at first and then more energetically. They played throw-the-bones, sang songs and chants that they had heard older children, adults sing. My brothers and sisters sang along. The children invented new games, beat the drum bones in time to a new song about a skeleton, a wedding, and a salt tree. They sang the chorus over and over again. They were waiting for the next thing that would happen.

A bone slipped, perhaps, on a toss and flew toward father. He plucked it from the air and signaled that they were to step back again. I took a small pestle and mortar, gathered a few larger tools from around the room and placed them all beside the bones on the workbench.

The work itself is as quick and violent as any child would wish. Father took the skulls and larger bones and without talking I began on the smaller bones, again inverting our recent habits. I knew that father didn't want to do any fine work.

I took up an awl and the children watched for a minute until father picked up one of the old stone hammers. Everyone took another step back as he warmed up, slowly whirling it in the air. The oohs and aahs lifted him a little from his torpor, and he began to put on a show the way he had done when I was a child. He whirled the hammer this way and that; the stone glittered as it twisted and danced, swung up, down, approached the table and was pulled away with a flick of the wrist. I tapped and ground away as happy as the children to watch father as he pretended to slip or to lose the hammer, eliciting more scared and excited cries. Perhaps the children didn't see but I did—there was a loud bang! and while the children screamed there was another bang! The hammer had gone right through the thin skulls and hit the table. He stopped and the fragments were gathered by willing hands. One of my sisters, Maura, was crying a little. But she was laughing too.

Now the rhythm of the work was easier and he quickly went through the skulls, the pelvic wedding masks, the larger bones even as I carefully broke up the small carved finger bones, the toes.

As he worked I couldn't help but notice how slight he was. He'd never been a big man but his carriage had made him seem so. Now the arch of his shoulders, the arc of his collarbones was apparent no matter what he wore. His shoulders hitched like the kite I had flown as a child, like the crossbar, bent and near to breaking in the current of the wind. I pictured the bones pressing so close to the skin, imagined the burning, cutting and shaping. Then, after all who had known him had gone, the breaking, shattering and spreading back onto the land. He looked up and met my eyes. I think he knew what I was seeing. He had seen others that same way.

He lay the vertebrae down in a line and took up two small iron hammers. I prepared my own accompaniment. He pulverized the bones in a delicate interweaving of strokes that I counterpointed with small notes on the remaining digits. Then it was over. The children shouted and helped sweep up the dust and shards. A rainy day like this was as good as any other so we made an informal procession to the nearest fields, my brothers and sisters trailing after us, their hands full. We spread the white fragments, the fine bleached flakes and dust among the crops. Then the children left us and we went home.

Then it seemed for him it was just a matter of waiting. At night I rubbed his aching shoulders, touched the warm skin of his arms, tried to stay away from the scars and pits where his bones were already stiff. I was haunted by that thin arc of his shoulders so rigid and formal, so weak, holding up against the daylight. He was waiting for the month to go by until he could collect her bones. Sometimes when I came in from walking or buying food I thought he waited only to die.

My younger brothers and sisters had visited, even stayed for a couple of nights during our mother's quick illness and after her death. Now they had returned to their own farms. I, the oldest and strangest, still unmarried, lived alone with my grieving father. I worked on other woodcarvings—a fat baby boy nestled inside a pumpkin, two girls kissing. I continued looking after father although he never said much. He left his own woodwork untouched.

The month passed, the rain stopped and we collected my mother's clean white bones. One femur was gone and one humerus had been badly chewed by a wild dog or a wolf. I had prepared the workshop so that it was ready for the last part of our work. When we returned I made tea and began the first rough filing of the ribs.

Father started straightway on the fine filigree work, working for hours on end without rest. When he stopped late that evening my eyes burned with tiredness. We ate by dim candlelight: he drank more tea but hardly touched the soup I had made before he went to sleep. The next day and the next were the same. He put everything he had into his work. He slept and ate less and less, and I saw this and knew that he would die soon.

Mother's skullcup has ever since been held up as the most beautiful in living memory. He told story after story around it: our history by the sea; our one bloody war; the long journey south to the hot lands and a new sea; the retracing of our steps up to these cool mountains; life in the mountains. All our tales: his own stories, mother's, ours, everyone's. Our history was written on the book of her bones.

I stopped doing anything else but the most simple preparatory work on the bones, left it to him to find the tool, the tale, the sculpture, the stories and the form. He made no mistakes, wasted nothing.

I have them all with me now. They have been drawn and copied in many forms although never by me. Long ago I trained my eldest daughter and recently I helped as she trained her eldest son. All of us have held up my mother's skullcup, worn the jewelry my father shaped from the bones. On my wedding day I wore my mother's pelvic mask. My spouse wore a more traditional one from a great-grandparent but it was mine that caught the eye.

It caught the light, ground and polished as it is to a grain that beggars belief. Father did what had never been done before, turned the pelvic bone around and carved it into a winged mask that suggests something no one can quite describe. When my granddaughter told us that soon she would marry it was my mother's mask she asked to wear.

I am the last of my siblings although I was the oldest. A strange thing. But so it goes in this strange time when we are visited by those who say they have come from across the southern ocean.

Soon, when I die, since I am the last of my family to have known my parents, my daughter and son will enact the mountain rites on my mother's beautiful bones. And my father's. He finished the wedding mask and went to bed and I remember it still how I could not wake him the next morning.

GLEN HIRSHBERG

Mr. Dark's Carnival

Glen Hirshberg's fiction and articles have appeared in magazines, journals, and alternative newspapers across North America, including All Hallows, Quarto, Edging West, Seattle Weekly, *and* L.A. Weekly, *where he is a regular contributor. He has just completed his first novel,* The Snowman's Children, *and is now at work on a second novel and a series of location-driven ghost stories. He writes and teaches in Los Angeles.*

Inspired by one cathartic night of haunted-house hunting in Montana in the frigid fall of 1989, "Mr. Dark's Carnival" made its print debut in Ash-Tree Press's Shadows and Silence *anthology, edited by Barbara and Christopher Roden. The story is one of several that Glen Hirshberg tells his students every Halloween, and he dedicates this final version to them.*

—E. D.

The Montanan is both humbled and exalted by this blazing glory filling his world, yet so quickly dead.

JOSEPH KINSEY HOWARD

S o the first question, really," I said, leaning on my lectern and looking over the heads of my students at the twilight creeping off the plains into campus, "is, does anyone know anyone who has actually been there?"

Hands went up instantly, as they always do. For a few moments, I let the hands hang in the air, start to wilt under the fluorescent light, while I watched the seniors on the roof of Powell House dorm across the quad drape the traditional black bunting down the side of the building, covering all the windows. By the time I got outside, I knew, there would be straw corpses strewn all over campus and papier mâché skeletons swinging in the trees. Few, if any, of the students who hung them there would have any cognizance of the decidedly sinister historical resonance of their actions.

"Right," I said, and returned my attention to my Freshman Seminar on Eastern Montana History. It was the one undergraduate class I still taught each year. It was the one class I would never give up. "Primary-source accounts only, please."

"Meaning stuff written at the time?" said the perpetually confused Robert Hayright from the front row.

"That is indeed one correct definition of a primary source, Mr. Hayright. But in this case, I mean only interviews you have conducted or overheard yourself. No stories about third parties."

Two-thirds of the hands dropped to their respective desktops.

"Right. Let's eliminate parents and grandparents, now, who, over the centuries, have summoned and employed all sorts of bogeymen to keep their children careful as they exit the safeties of home."

Most of the rest of the hands went down.

"High school chums, of course, because the whole game in high school, especially Eastern Montana high school, is to have been somewhere your classmates haven't, isn't it? To have seen and known the world?"

"I have a question, Professor R." said Tricia Corwyn from the front row, crossing her stockinged legs under her silky skirt and pursing her too-red mouth. Around her, helpless freshman boys squirmed in their seats. The note of flirtation in her tone wasn't for me, I knew. It was a habit, quite possibly permanent, and it made me sad. It has taken most of a century to excise most of the rote machismo from Montana's sons. Maybe next century, we can go to work on the scars that machismo has left on its daughters.

"If we eliminate secondhand accounts, parents, and high school friends, who's left who could tell us about it?"

"My dear," I said, "you have the makings of a historian. That's a terrific question."

I watched Tricia smile, trot out that string of studiously whitened teeth like a row of groomed show-horses, and abruptly I stood up straight, allowed myself a single internal head-shake. My dear. The most paternalistic and subtle weapon of diminution in the Montana teacher's arsenal.

I nodded. "That's so good a question that I'm going to dodge it for the time being." A few members of the class were still alert or polite enough to smile. I saw the astonishing white hair of Robin Mills, the Humanities Department secretary, form in the doorway of my classroom like a cumulus cloud, but I ignored her for the time being. "Let me ask this. How many of you know anyone—once again, primary sources only, please—who claims to have worked there?"

This time, a single hand went up. That's one more than I've ever had go up before.

"Mr. Hayright?" I said.

"My dog," he said, and the class exploded into laughter. But Robert Hayright continued. "It's true."

"Your dog told you this?"

"My dog Droopy disappeared on Halloween night three years ago. The next morning, a neighbor brought him home and told my dad a man in a clown suit had brought her to their door at six in the morning and said, 'Thank you for the dog, he's been at Mr. Dark's.'"

Mr. Hayright's classmates erupted again, but I didn't join them. The clown suit was interesting, I thought. A completely new addition to the myth.

"So let's see," I said gently. "Counting your father, your neighbor, and the clown"—this brought on more laughter, though I was not mocking Robert Hay-right—"your story is, at best, thirdhand."

"Not counting the dog," said Robert Hayright, and he grinned, too. I smiled, if only because, for once, everyone was laughing with him.

In the doorway, Robin Mills cleared her throat, and the mass of white hair rippled. "Professor Roemer?"

"Surely this can wait, Ms. Mills," I said.

"Professor, it's Brian Tidrow."

I scowled. I couldn't help it. "Whatever he's got can definitely wait."

Instead of speaking, Robin Mills mouthed the rest. She did it three times, although I understood her the second time.

"That fucker," I muttered, but not quietly enough, and my students stopped laughing and stared. I ignored them. "Does Kate know?" I asked Robin.

"No one's seen her yet."

"Find her. Find her now. Tell her I'll be there soon."

For a second, Robin lingered in the doorway. I don't know if she expected comfort or company or just more reaction, but I wasn't planning on giving her any. Brian Tidrow had finally committed the supreme act of havoc-wreaking he'd been threatening for years. He would get no more reaction from me, ever. I glared at Robin until she ducked her head, turned from the door.

"What was that, Professor R.?" Tricia asked.

I avoided thinking about Kate. By the time Robin located her for me, class would be over, and I'd be on my way. "You will notice, my young scholars, that I didn't even ask if any of you have been there. I have lived in Clarkston all my life, except for my eight years of university and graduate work. My parents lived here all their lives. My grandparents came from Germany right before the First World War and never left until their deaths. In all that time, not a single member of my family has ever encountered anyone who has actually, personally, been. Ever. And that leads us to the most alarming, the most discomforting question of all. Is it possible that Mr. Dark's Carnival—the inspiration for all our Halloween festivities, the most celebrated attraction or event in the history of Clarkston, Montana—never really existed?"

As always, that question took just a moment to land. It floated through the room for a few seconds like an alka-seltzer tablet dropped into a glass. And then it began to fizz.

"Wait," said one of the boys near Tricia.

"Oh my God, no way," said Tricia, her blue eyes bright as they blazed through boy after boy.

Robert Hayright shook his head. "That's wrong. You're wrong, Professor. I know it."

I put my hand up, but the fizzing continued a while longer. When it had quieted at last, I started to smile, thought of Brian Tidrow with his great-grandfather's Winchester rifle gripped in his teeth, and shuddered. Goddamn him, I thought. I refused to offer him any additional respect simply because he'd finally had the stupidity—he'd probably have called it guts—to go and do it.

"What do you know, Mr. Hayright?"

"I know there was a Carnival in 1926. It was out in the fallow fields by where the Gulf Station at the edge of town is now."

"How do you know that?"

"We studied it in high school. There were newspaper reports. Primary sources." He glanced up at me to see if I'd stop him, then went on. "Three people died of fright, including a policeman sent to investigate all the screaming."

"There was another in 1943," I said quietly, to the suddenly silent room, as the icy twilight permeated the windows and seeped into the corners like floodwater. "That one was in particularly poor taste. Reportedly, it was haunted by dozens of people outfitted as dead soldiers. Upset a lot of parents whose sons were currently overseas.

"In 1978, there were no less than three so-called Mr. Dark's Carnivals rumored around town, though two of them were meant for small children and the third turned out to be a dance. I'm not saying no one has ever called their haunted house Mr. Dark's Carnival." But as to the existence of the horrifying original . . ." I waved my hand, started to smile, sighed instead. "The fact is that every year, we build our haunted houses and collect our children and head out to cover as much of our fair miniature city as we can, hoping for that supreme horrifying experience. That haunted house that will detonate our bowels, grind our chattering teeth to rubble, and blast us out the other side shaken and giggling and alive. That Mr. Dark's Carnival that we've been told, all our lives, might just be out there, on some unnamed street, in some unexpected and unexplored corner."

For the next fifteen minutes, students hurled questions about the most persistent and ubiquitous elements of the myth—the tickets that had to be given to you or found somewhere, the ever-changing locations, the reputed deaths-by-terror. Most years, I let this part of the discussion go as long as it would, because I enjoyed hearing the variations on the legend, and the students enjoyed having the legend exploded. But this year, feeling increasingly disturbed that Robin had not floated back into the door to say she'd found Kate, and unable to shake the picture I'd formed of Brian Tidrow's last moments on Earth, I ticked off my myth-destroying points in mere minutes.

How many unexplored corners were there, exactly, in a town barely eleven miles square and 145 years old? How many new locations could there be? If tickets had to be found or given, who did the hiding and giving? Given the elaborate nature of the illusions attributed to Mr. Dark's, where were all the workers necessary to perpetuate them?

Finally, Tricia once again asked the most significant remaining question. "Was there even a Mr. Dark?" she said.

"Oh yes," I said, even more quietly, and the class froze once more. "And there are reasons, indeed, why this story has attached itself to him."

It was at that moment, of course, that Robin Mills finally rematerialized. How not surprising, I thought, indulging just a little selfish fury, that Brian Tidrow's farewell gesture should destroy my favorite moment of the teaching year. The only thing that even came close was the day I marched into my Graduate Seminar, laid a map detailing the progress of cattle introduction onto the Open Range over another showing the path of buffalo depletion, and proved, or at least suggested, that despite all our best efforts and a hundred years of imprecise historical accounting, it was anthrax, not white men, that killed the buffalo.

Outside, gray lines of snow began to drag themselves over the ground like the fringe on a giant, smothering carpet. The clouds hung heavy and low, and the first unmistakable winter wind gnawed and whined at the windows. I thought of Kate, and forgot about anger, forgot about my teaching and my love for Halloween. I started to ache.

"Scholars, I apologize," I said. "There has been a personal crisis in the Humanities Department, and I need to tend to it immediately. So we will have to continue this discussion on Monday."

"What about Mr. Dark?" Robert Hayright whined, sounding almost angry. I didn't blame him. My class had been the most popular Freshman elective for most of a decade, primarily because of the lecture I gave each year on this date.

I began to slide the notes I never used into my backpack, watched Robert Hayright slouch in his seat while Tricia rose in front of him. "Who knows?" I said, catching Robin Mills's agitated tapping against the doorframe of my room with a pen. "Perhaps one of you will find a strip of paper tacked to a tree trunk tonight, and pick it up, and stare at it in disbelief. And you'll find the real Mr. Dark. And on Monday, you'll be able to tell me just how wrong I've been. All right, I see you, Ms. Mills."

"Sorry, Professor," I heard her say. "Didn't even know what I was doing."

"Have a recommendation?" Tricia asked as the class began to file out. She was leaning forward over my desk, too close to me. Habit, again.

"About what, Ms. Corwyn?" I continued putting away papers but avoided brushing her sweater with my arm.

"Haunted houses we shouldn't miss? Particularly good streets? I hear they're going to have monsters in the river."

Startled, I looked up, found myself submerged in those too-blue eyes. "No one's done that for years," I said, and the last of my anger sank into sadness, though none of it was for Brian Tidrow. Other people have Christmas or High Holidays, and families to share them with. I have Halloween, and these kids. This year, I would have neither. "You'll have to tell me all about it."

"I will," she said. "Thanks for the great class."

Seconds later, they were gone, and all the energy in the room went with them, and I was just another academia-ghost, my skin sporting that translucent, sickly fluorescent-tan, my hair succumbing to the color-leaching chalk dust and dead air. I wanted to see Kate. I wanted to help her fight through this. For the first time in my life, I wanted Halloween to be over.

"Where is she?" I said to Robin Mills.

"Your place," she said, with no trace of the contempt she might otherwise have attached to that statement. "She called from there. She was apparently the one who found him, Professor."

"Goddamn Brian Tidrow," I said. "Goddamn him to hell." I started past Robin. I saw her start to register shock, because that's the emotion recommended, I guess, in the judgmental and Officious Department Secretary Handbook for such comments and situations.

But then she said, "Tell Kate we're all thinking of her. Tell her to come see me Monday, or whenever she wants."

I turned, smiled, realized that I'd worked near, if not exactly with, this person for fourteen years, and that it was time I got over myself. "I will," I told her. "Thanks."

Seconds later, I was strolling through the deepening dark across campus. In the trees, paper men danced and spun on the frigid wind. I heard whooping sounds from the row of fraternity houses at the campus's south end, scurrying feet as students raced excitedly for their assigned posts in haunted houses or collected dates for the evening tour through town. Underneath it all, I heard the ceaseless, sucking emptiness of the prairie, slowly pulling this town piece by piece and person by person back into the sea of cheatgrass and oblivion.

By the time I turned onto Winslow Street and left campus, the cold had clawed inside my insufficient fall windbreaker, and I could feel it climbing down my bones toward the dead center of me. The little kids were out already, racing down sidewalks lined with lit pumpkins in paper bags that glowed a glorious, leering orange. I saw a green-skinned zombie shiver up from a pile of dead leaves in the corner of a lawn and grab for two bewinged little girls who giggled and fled. The zombie watched them and smiled and shivered backward and drew the leaves over himself again. He would be there all night, I knew. He would hold his smile in longer when the older kids came, grab a little more forcefully. He'd be frozen half-through when he got home, and full of civic pride. In some towns, the neighbors force you to keep your yard tidy. In others, you're expected to show up in church, or help out at the Foodbank or on Clean the River-Beaches Day. In Clarkston, you participate in Halloween.

A half-mile from campus, the houses spread out onto their lots, and the paths marked by the paper-bag pumpkins disappeared. But the festivities continued. Even the Country Club haunted its golf course every year and opened it to the entire town, though they taped tarpaulins down on the grass. At this hour, though, with full-dark not yet fallen, these streets were relatively silent. The scares out here, it was understood, were for older kids. The zombies in the leafpiles sometimes held onto you if they caught you. I stopped just a moment outside Dean Harry Piltner's house and stood in the strings of snow. As usual, Harry had constructed a long, knee-high crawl-through maze of straw that zig-zagged back and forth across his yard. I'd once asked him where he got the wolf spiders and finger-sized roaches he occasionally set free in there to scurry and hunt and, usually, die by squishing at the hands of some screaming teen. He just smiled in response and kept his Halloween secret to himself, like any good Clarkstonian. The homemade brownies his wife left at the exit of the maze were the best anyone I knew had ever tasted.

The Blackroot River bisects Clarkston five different times as it bends back and forth through town, creating miniature peninsulas. My house, a turn-of-the-century A-frame built by one of the railroad masterminds of the Land Grab that brought homesteaders to the Open Range and, very nearly, civil war to the plains, rides the point of Purviston, the town's easternmost peninsula, like the smoke-stack on a steamtrain. As I crossed the footbridge that led directly to my door, I scanned my house for lights, but saw none. Either Kate had left, or she was sitting in the dark. I suspected the latter. In moments of personal and profes-sional crisis, Kate clung to the shadows. Otherwise, she'd never have come to Montana for her graduate work, leaving offers from four Ivies in her wake.

For just a moment, in the center of the bridge, I stopped to listen to the river. Already, its gurgle had an ugly rasp. By Thanksgiving, it would be frozen, and the streets would tuck themselves into their winter hibernation under a perpetual blanket of snow. I glanced back toward town, saw orange lights winking through the dark and heard a small child's scream erupt in the air like the call of a hunting osprey.

"You missed all the good stuff, Brian," I mumbled, surprising myself. I hadn't known I was thinking of him.

Even after I unlocked the door, it took me a few seconds to realize Kate was there, hunched on the couch by the bay window overlooking the river. She had the blue blanket my mother had knitted me, years and years ago, wrapped around her waist, and her long brown hair draped on her shoulders like a shawl. In sunlight, Kate's oddly sunken brown eyes made her look as though she never quite got enough sleep. In the half-light, the shadows lent color to her wan skin, and her eyes seemed to creep forward, and she became an astonishingly beautiful woman. At least, she became one to me.

"Hey," I said, started toward her, felt just a flicker of the old uncertainty. I've long since got over my guilt about dating Kate; student of mine or not, she's all of six years younger, with more of an academic pedigree than I ever had and no reason whatsoever to let me exploit her, or to exploit me. But I was eleven years without a significant relationship before Kate—Clarkston is a tiny, tiny place, the University tinier still, and I was born reticent, anyway—and even after two years, I've yet to regain my confidence completely.

This night, Kate did nothing to make it easy for me. She stared out the window. The window was closed, but the snow seemed to have seeped into the room somehow. I imagined I could see it winking near her ears like a cloud of will-o'-the-wisps, about to spirit her away. Stepping quickly to the couch, I dropped down beside her. She started to cry quietly. I sat and held her hand sometimes and let her.

"He wasn't even a good friend," Kate murmured, after a long, long while.

I touched her hair. "No. He wasn't."

"Too unreliable. Too wrapped up in his own pathetic problems."

"He was sick, Kate. He didn't have a choice."

For the first time that night, she turned and looked at me. The depth of her eye-cavities made it seem as if I was peering into a cave. The effect always made me want to crawl in there with her. She smiled, and I felt like laughing but didn't.

"This is a reversal," she said.

"Don't get me wrong, Kate-O. I wish he'd never come here. I wish you'd never known him. You or anyone else in the damn department, because he had that mopey, haunted intensity that all you grad students flock to like bees to pollen, and then you spread it, and then everybody's mopey and haunted."

Kate laughed, and this time, the laugh inside me slipped out.

"He was a good historian," she said, returning the squeeze of my hand now.

"He was a promising historian. You're a good one. You do the research first, then have your insights."

Without warning, she was crying again, whether for Brian Tidrow or her mother, also dead by suicide more than twenty years before, or her vindictive father, or something else entirely, I didn't know.

This time, the crying spell lasted over an hour. I listened to her breath sputter and her voice murmur and choke, watched Halloween night settle over Clarkston. The snow thickened, gathering itself on the dead grass and in the cracks on the pavement. Even through the closed windows, shouts and screams and bursts of organ music reached us from across the river. "I stepped in some of his hair," Kate mumbled at one point, and I winced and squeezed her hand as she shook. I'd forgotten she'd found him.

It was at least eight and maybe later when Kate looked up at me. The shaking in her shoulders had stilled just a little. But what she said was, "This could go on all night, David. You should go."

I blinked, startled, not sure how to answer. "Go where? This is my home. And also where I want to be."

"It's Halloween. The best day of your life, remember?"

The sentimental response proved irresistible. I hadn't had many opportunities to try one, after all. "I've had other best days, lately," I said. Then I blushed, grinned like a six-year-old, and Kate burst out laughing.

"Go haunted-housing. Come back with stories."

"Come with me."

Instantly, her smile vanished. "I've seen my dead person for the day, thanks. Oh, fuck, David." Her face crumpled again. I reached for her hand, but she shook it off. "Really," she snapped, and I jerked back. "I want you to go. I want to be alone."

"Kate, I want to be with you."

"You are with me," she said, still snapping.

For a long moment, we stared at each other. Then I picked my coat off the chair where I'd draped it and stood. I started to ask if she was sure, but she was. And I, quite frankly, was relieved, in all sorts of ways. I knew that I'd done what I could and that my actions had been noted. I knew that Kate loved me.

And I knew, in that instant, that I wasn't going to miss Halloween after all.

"I'll bring you back a brownie," I said.

"God, you're not going to crawl through Piltner's maze, are you?"

I just stood there.

"You're an eight-year-old, David."

"I'll check back in an hour. I won't be gone long."

"All right," Kate said, but she was already withdrawing into her crouch with her gaze aimed out the window.

I opened my door, stepped outside, and the cold jumped me. It had teeth and claws, and the way it tore at my skin had me checking my coatfront for rips. "Jesus," I said, started to turn back inside for gloves and scarf, thought better of it. I didn't want to be gone long, anyway. And I didn't want to disturb Kate now. Shoving my hands in my pockets and blinking my watering eyes, I drove forward into the dark.

Because I had my head down, I didn't see the thing on the footbridge until I was almost on top of it. I gasped, jerked to a stop.

At first, I took it for a newspaper blown open. Then the wind kicked up, and the edges lifted like wings but the paper itself stayed put, and I realized there was something underneath it holding it in place. A half step closer, and I thought I could see a head-shaped shadow lying in the larger, deeper shadow of the overhanging poplar trees like . . . well, like a head in a pool of blood.

Goddamn Brian Tidrow, I thought, and started forward. The man lay straight across the bridge, in the dead center of it, with his head against one railing and his feet dangling over the river on the far side. I've often wondered where all the homeless people in Clarkston come from, and why they stay. I never recognize any of them—they're no one I ever knew—despite my years of living here. And the climate can't be conducive to life on the street. Maybe the citizenry are generous, or the food at the shelters is good, or else the plains loom like the roiling oceans of nothing they are and obliterate hopes of safe passage.

This man, I decided, was sleeping or stone drunk. You'd have to be drunk to sleep in this spot, with the wind crawling over you. The only movement as I approached was the fluttering of the newspaper. The only sounds came from the river below and the town beyond.

"Hey man," I said softly. "You all right?"

The newspaper fluttered. The river hissed. The man lay still. I thought about going home to call the police. I had nothing against the poor guy sleeping on my bridge, but jail would be warmer. Kate wanted me gone, though. And sometimes, I thought, with the fatuous logic of the comfortable, there are better things to be than warm. I planted one foot, lifted the other so that I was straddling the man, and he sat up.

It was the hand he snarled in the belt of my coat, I think, that kept me from leaping straight over the railing. Clumps of curly black hair flew from his scalp like strips of shredded steel wool. His lips were white-blue with cold, his eyes so bloodshot that the red seemed to have overrun the irises and pooled in the pupils.

For several seconds, he held me there, and I held my breath, and nothing moved. He wasn't looking at me, but beyond me, past my hip at the trees and the riverbank. The intensity of his stare made me want to whirl around, but I couldn't rip my gaze from his face.

Finally, I managed to gulp some air into my lungs, and the cold shocked them out of paralysis. I coughed. The man gripped my coat, stared behind me, said nothing.

"What?" I finally said.

The hand at my waist did not relax. The direction of the gaze didn't change.

"Are you cold? Can I—" I looked down and saw the crumple of black paper pressed between the man's palm and my stomach. A whole new shudder rippled through me, drawn from a long-forgotten childhood reservoir. Blind Pew, and the Black Spot, and the Admiral Benbow Inn. Until dark, Pew told Billy Bones, on the day of Billy Bones's death. They'll come at dark.

I put my hand on the paper, which turned out to be surprisingly heavy. Construction paper. Instantly, the homeless man's hand ricocheted back to his side as though I'd triggered a catapult. The whole body beneath me spasmed backward into prone position, and the newspaper snapped into place around him. Uncrumpling the construction paper, still shuddering, I stepped back and looked at what I'd been given.

"Oh," I said. Then I said it again. Then I turned and raced for home.

Kate was still crouched by the window when I burst in. She didn't look up to ask what I'd forgotten. She looked only a little more conscious than the man on the bridge had. I marched straight to her anyway.

"Look," I said, and held the construction paper toward her. "Kate, I'm serious, look."

Her sigh came from way down inside her. Slowly, she took the paper from me, tilted it toward the light coming in the window. She read it twice. Then she stood up. The blanket stayed wrapped around her waist.

"God, David, we have to go," she said. "I'll get my coat."

"I'm going to marry this woman," I said aloud to the window as Kate stepped toward the closet. By the time she returned to me, buttoning her heaviest black overcoat around her, her movements had regained most of their usual speed and grace.

"You have to understand," I told her, touching her hair with the back of my hand. Her face still looked wan, but her eyes were bright. "This won't be my first Mr. Dark's Carnival."

"What do you mean? You don't even believe it's real."

"I've been given tickets on three previous occasions. Twice, I followed the directions on them and wound up at a frat party. Little Halloween prank from my students. The third time, I wound up at a very fine haunted house indeed, right here in Purviston, not five hundred feet from this door. Unfortunately, I happened to recognize Harry Piltner's stoop under a Cerberus costume right at the doorway, and because I'm a jerk, I said, Do I get a brownie, Har? And Harry kicked me."

"So why are we going?" Kate said, shepherding me toward the door.

"Get gloves. Hat, too. It's unbelievably cold."

We were outside now, and Kate threw her head back and stood a moment in the chill. She didn't even have her coat all the way buttoned.

"You're insane," I said, jamming my gloved hands into my pockets and hunching against the snap of the wind. "We're going, first of all, because someone went to a lot of trouble to get me these. Get somebody these, anyway. And they did it with Clarkston Halloween style, so I can't ignore it. Secondly, even if it's a frat party, the beer'll be good."

"Oh, right. You don't even drink."

I held the door of my rusty red 1986 Volvo open for her, kissed the top of her head as she bent to climb in. "You're freezing," I said, "put on your damn hat."

"Thirdly?" she said, and smiled up at me. She was even more excited than I had to admit I was.

"Thirdly, I had a feeling you'd come, in spite of everything."

Her smile widened.

"And fourthly, Kate dear," I said, nodded, and looked toward the bridge, which was empty. Purviston tickets distributed, I thought. I wondered where the homeless man would lay himself and his newspaper next. "Fourthly, one just never knows. Does one? I don't, anyway." I snapped her door shut, got in my side.

The car took four cranks of the ignition key, but it did start. It always starts. "Where to?" I said, gesturing toward the black construction paper in Kate's lap.

On it, in gray-white chalk, was a map of Clarkston with a white dotted line snaking through it and the words MR. DARK'S CARNIVAL WELCOMES YOU underneath. No skull and crossbones this time, and no come-if-you-dare warning. A classier prank, at the very least, I thought.

"Get to Winslow," Kate said, without looking down at the paper. "Take it south, all the way out of town."

To my relief, she sounded excited. Exhausted, wrecked, but excited. I threw the car's heater on, blasting us both with frigid air, and grunted. Kate stared out the window at the dark.

By now, even the streets of Purviston were alive with costumed revelers. A group of rubber-masked teens came hurtling down the sidewalk from the direction of Harry Piltner's, their wigs and winter coats caked with straw, hands flashing all over themselves in search of bugs that had probably long since dropped off. I smiled.

In town, the activity level seemed just slightly lower than usual because of the cold. By 9:30, most Halloweens, the college kids who worked the little-kid haunted houses had been released from scare-duty, and they clustered around parked cars or outside the Rangehand pub downtown and blasted hip-hop and waited for midnight, when the frat parties began in earnest and continued until the police shut them down. But this night, the trick-of-treaters had long since retreated indoors, and the partiers had stayed in their dorms, and the only people out were the heartiest Clarkstonians, tracing their habitual routes from one fright-sight to the next.

In a matter of minutes, we were out of town. At the two-mile mark, the last streetlamp stuck out of the prairie like a flag left by a lunar expedition, and then we were in darkness.

"Still know where we're going?" I said.

"Says seven miles."

"Air's getting warm."

Kate didn't answer. Snow glittered on the asphalt and the endless stunted grass all around us, as though the sky itself had shattered on the ground. The Eastern Montana plains on a snowlit night are limitless as deep space and just as empty.

After a minute or so, Kate shifted in her seat. She spoke slowly, softly. She sounded barely awake, and most likely she was after the day she'd had, and now the warming car, the chattering road, the silence. "Tell me again what you think you know, David Roemer, about Albert Aloysius Dark?"

Instantly, the last of my classroom lecture leapt to my lips. "Delighted you asked. Thought I wasn't going to get to tell anyone this year."

Kate smiled.

"Judge Albert Aloysius Dark. Born God-knows-where, educated God-knows-where, because that's the first intriguing thing about him, isn't it? There's no record of him in this state—it was a territory then, of course—before his appointment to the Bench in September 1877. In fact, there's no record of him anywhere."

"You mean you haven't found records of him yet?"

"You're not the only competent researcher in this Volvo, O Barely-Speaking-

Woman. And I'll thank you to remember the Civil War, and its prodigious though little-noted effects on the record keeping of our fair cities and towns."

Kate nodded. "Go on."

"For eight years after his appointment as ranking barrister in this desolate region, Judge Dark maintained a consistently moderate record. Right up until Christmas Eve, 1885. That ni—"

"Turn here," Kate said, and I jammed on the brakes, dragged the car to a stop, and stared.

"Turn where?"

"Back up."

I looked over my shoulder into the black, snow-streaked nothing. "Maybe the map's upside down."

Kate grinned! "Just back up, idiot."

I tapped the brake pedal, held it down so that my taillights illuminated the blackness. And there, fifteen feet or so behind the car, limned in red paint of some sort, were two tire ruts, snaking between two decrepit prairie shrubs and away into the grass. Way down in my stomach, something twitched. Nervousness. Uneasiness, maybe. Disbelief. Hope. If this was a prank, or an imitation, it was the best yet. And if it wasn't a prank . . .

"How the hell did you know that was there?"

"The map."

"But how did you see it?"

"I was looking for it. David, let's go." Kate looked at me. Her face was still red, but whether from crying or excitement, I couldn't tell.

Backing us up, I paused just a moment at the lip of the path. I cracked my window, and the whistling silence sucked at our little bubble of life inside the car.

"What are you thinking?" Kate said softly.

"Little Big Horn. The Donner Party. Fifteen or twenty other examples of overconfident white people overestimating their power over the West."

"This really could be it, David. Couldn't it?"

"It really could be something."

Kate smiled. I smiled back. Then I pushed my foot on the gas, and we were off the highway, jiggling over the dirt.

"How far?" I mumbled.

Kate glanced down at the map. "Three miles, maybe." I groaned. "Christmas Eve, 1885," she said.

I watched the grass disappear under our tires, the snow that seemed to float on ground so flat and featureless that it didn't even really seem to be there. "On Christmas Eve, at approximately 8:45 P.M., a group of local ranchers calling themselves the Guardians of Right appeared at the door of Judge Dark's rather lavish creekside home—it was destroyed by fire, incidentally, in 1956, and is now buried under the high school football stadium—and demanded entrance. With them, the Guardians had brought a Chinese homesteader who'd been hitched to a wagon with his feet bound and made to hop all the way from his claim two miles outside of town."

"How do we know this?" Kate asked.

"Primary source, my dear. The judge himself kept an impressively detailed notebook. The Guardians demanded immediate entry, a trial right then and there, and a hanging verdict. And Judge Dark, inexplicably, showed the men into his living room, then called his wife down to act as court reporter and witness. The prosecution case lasted ten minutes, and involved somewhat circumstantial but undeniably incriminating evidence of the theft of foodstores and two horses. There was no defense, seeing as how the homesteader in question did not speak English and couldn't even stand because the bones in his feet and ankles had been smashed during his trip to the Judge's door. The guilty verdict and death sentence apparently came so fast that even the Guardians were startled to silence. The Judge makes specific and rather self-satisfied note of this effect.

"What the Judge actually said next, I cannot tell you. But I can tell you what he wrote. And I can tell you that word for word: 'I attached a single condition: that the prisoner be hanged by no hand but my own, and that he stay this night, his last on this Earth, in my home, under my care.' This was assented to, and the stunned Guardians left. And on Christmas morning, in front of over a hundred witnesses in what was then the town square, Judge Albert Dark wheeled the homesteader to a poplar tree, strung a rope around his neck, positioned him in a sort of crouch in the back of a wagon, and executed him, cleanly and quickly. No one yelled 3-7-77."

"What does that mean, by the way?"

"No one knows, really," I said. "None of the original Virginia Beach vigilantes ever said. They just left those numbers pinned to their victims. Anyway, the homesteader, by every account, said not a word, and made no sound. But he did look up, right as the wagon fled him and the rope bit into his neck. Two of the four published accounts claim he was smiling. Kate, what the hell is that?"

But I could tell what it was. It was a kid. In pajamas.

He was barefoot in the grass, straddling the tire-ruts with one arm stretched perfectly perpendicular to his shoulders, pointing off into the blackness. His skin glowed white in the headlight beams, as though the snow had somehow sunk inside it. He had short blond hair that stuck straight up from his scalp. His pajamas had zebras on them.

I hit the brakes, started to slow.

"God," Kate said, as we rolled to a stop fifteen feet from the kid. "How old do you think he is?"

"How cold do you think he is?" I muttered, staring at the kid's feet.

He was about as tall as the top of my windshield. I rolled down my window, leaned out, but the child made no move toward the car, and he didn't lower his arm. For a second, it occurred to me that he was an astoundingly realistic scarecrow. But he wasn't. I could see his lips, blue with cold, twitch when the prairie wind whipped across them.

"Are you all right?" I called. The child didn't move.

Then, abruptly, I smiled. I hadn't even got to this latest Mr. Dark's Carnival, and already it had me pleading with the ghouls, trying to get them to break and speak to me. The bubble of nervous excitement in my gut swelled.

"Follow the yellow brick road," I said, and turned in the direction the child had pointed.

There were other tire-tracks, I noted, all around us. I took an absurd amount of comfort in the fact that we weren't the first car out here. I drove slowly, letting the prairie drum against the underside of the car like a choppy sea against the hull of a sailboat. Except for the dirt we stirred, nothing moved.

"How many did Judge Dark hang?" Kate asked, though her eyes, too, were straining forward into the void.

"Four, that we know of, between 1885 and statehood, when he drops from the official record as abruptly as he appeared. In each case, he allowed a local vigilante group to bring suspects to a lightning-trial, convicted the suspects, then kept them all night in his home, where one assumes he served as confessor and last-meal chef or possibly something completely different, and then performed the killing the next morning. He was apparently a master-executioner, because, according to the *Plains-Ledger,* not a single one of his charges so much as danced. And none of them said a word before they went to their makers."

"Look," said Kate, but I'd already seen.

Drawing the car forward, I pulled into a space between two pick-up trucks and switched off the ignition. There were six other vehicles arrayed around us in a makeshift parking lot. Of the drivers and passengers, I saw no trace. I looked at Kate. We listened to the snow scuttle over the roof of the Volvo. Beyond the impromptu circle of cars, the prairie grass roiled in the raging wind.

Suddenly, Kate smiled again, and the red in her lips spread up her cheeks. "Thank you for coming to get me," she said.

"Thank you for coming along, my love."

Kate blew me a kiss. She jerked the door handle down, still smiling, and—gently, as though easing into water—climbed into the night. I bumped my own door open and joined her. We stood at the hood of the car and stared around us.

There was no sound except the wind and the knocking grass. No child in pajamas appeared to point us the right way. I jammed my hands into my pocket as the cold gnawed at my wrists like a spectral and very hungry wolf.

"There," I said.

"I see it," said Kate.

It was just a glow, barely brighter than the moonlight on the snow all around us. Distances are hard enough to gauge on the plains even in broad daylight. But given the limited visibility, I decided it couldn't be more than a half-mile away, straight out from the highway into the grass. We set out walking.

It was an illusion, of course, that the dark got darker as soon as we left the circle of cars. Nevertheless, I could feel the Eastern Montana night sweep over our heads on enormous wings. I could feel its weight up there, and its talons. I kept my head down and walked. Kate walked beside me, the sleeve of her coat brushing rhythmically, repeatedly, against my own. We'd gone maybe three hundred yards when both of us looked up and saw the house.

It loomed out of the prairie shadows, black in the moonlight, inexplicable as the monolith in *2001.* The glow we saw came from a lone floodlight buried in the grass and aimed at the white fence surrounding the structure. As we got closer, I saw that the building wasn't black but barn-red, single-storied and rectangular and long. In the yard demarcated by the fence, people-shaped figures glided back and forth.

"If it was nothing else but this," I said, staring at the tableaux before me, "I think I'd be satisfied."

"It's like something out of a painting," Kate said, and that stopped me. The chill that flooded my mouth seemed to have come from inside rather than out.

For a second, I couldn't place the source of my discomfort. I looked at the structure. I looked at the floating figures, just beginning to acquire distinct faces from this distance. I looked at the fence, and then I had it.

Because it wasn't a fence. And the scene didn't remind me of a painting, but of a photograph. The one on page 212 of the *Freshman Seminar on Montana History* text I'd penned, to be exact, that showed the stacks of jumbled buffalo skeletons littering the plains during the years the Federal Government paid the most desperate or ghastly Montanans to shoot every bison they could find and export the bones downriver.

I started to speak, had to wet my lips, tried again. "There, um, been any recently reported mass-murders of oxen in the vicinity?"

Kate turned, her brow furrowed. "What?"

"Take a good gander at that fence, my dear."

She took her gander. Then she said, "Ooh. That can't be real."

"One hopes not. One hopes there is a large placard pasted over the entry reassuring us that No Animals Were Harmed or Mistreated During Creation of this Madhouse. But one is disturbed."

"Come on," Kate said, and on we went.

Up close, the bones looked a little less real, if only because they were reassuringly clean. Somehow, I'd been expecting bits of gristle to be hanging from them like party streamers. The four figures gliding back and forth in the house's mock garden were all young women, and they all wore long, white nightgowns that flowed down their forms like liquid moonlight. They were bare-armed, black-haired, and they might have been sisters. Certainly, they all had the same porcelain skin pallor, the same slightly upturned noses, the same half-smiles on their red-black lips. I found the sight of them slightly disappointing. After everything that had come so far, this seemed too familiar a horror-movie image, and something of a failure of imagination.

The mound of bones—up close, it was more hedge than fence—had one opening off to the right side of the house. Crouching beside the opening, staring straight past us at the eternity of nothing beyond, was another child. This one wore a green overcoat belted at the waist. He had jet-black hair that made his skin look bleached of features, like a face in a photographic negative. He, too, was barefoot.

When Kate and I moved toward the opening in the bones, the child suddenly shivered upright and stepped in front of us. We waited for him to speak, but of course he didn't. He didn't move, either.

"Now what?" I finally said.

The nightgown-wraiths weren't the only people in the yard, I could see now. There were other people with plain old Montana-pale skin and good winter jackets and gloves and scarves. Hauntees. Maybe eight of them, milling about.

Slowly, still looking beyond us—just like the man on the bridge, I realized, and wondered if this particular Mr. Dark ran an extended and brilliantly effective training program for his employees—the gatekeeper child raised his arm, palm upward, and held it toward us.

"Blood?" I muttered to Kate. "Cheeze-its? What does he want?"

After a long moment, Kate dipped her hand into her coat pocket and withdrew the black construction paper. "Ticket," she said happily.

"Oh yeah. Wouldn't want any party-crashers," I said, but I moved forward with Kate as she placed the folded paper in the child's hand.

"Burr," she said as she touched him. "Honey, you're freezing."

"It's not so bad," said the child, and my mouth flew open and my knees locked. I'd got used to the lack of response.

Kate maintained her poise better than I did. She glanced at me, then back at the child. Then she nodded. "You're right. It isn't." Taking my glove in her hand, she drew me forward through the bone-hedge into the yard.

We'd taken all of three steps when one of the winter coat-wrapped figures threw back the flaps of its red wool cap and squeaked, "Professor R.!" at me.

I blinked, glanced at Kate, back at the person flouncing toward me. "Um," I said. I run into students every time I leave my house in Clarkston. But somehow, for no good reason, I'd forgotten it was possible tonight. I blushed. "Hello, Ms. Corwyn."

"And who's this?" said Tricia, completely unaffected.

My blush deepened, and I felt a flicker of annoyance. Surely, at age forty-one, after seventeen years in the classroom, I'd stopped being embarrassed about the gaps that existed between my teaching self and my home self. But that didn't mean I'd found a way to bridge or even explain them. I don't know anyone who has. "This is Kate," I finally answered.

I turned to Kate for a smile, a gently mocking putdown, something. But the expression on her face had sagged. She looked at me, and she seemed so tired, all of the sudden, and I knew Brian Tidrow had floated up over her shoulder. It wouldn't be the last time, I thought.

"Okay," she said, and wandered away into the garden. I had no idea what she meant.

"Hmmm," said Tricia.

Instantly, with Kate out of earshot, I was Professor-David once more. "You just keep those fast-developing observational skills to yourself," I said and smiled with my mouth closed. A teacherly smile.

"Is this unbelievable or what? This corpse crawled up out of the river and gave me a map."

"A corpse."

"All white. I don't even know how long he was down there, because I sure didn't see him. Robert and I were walking along the bank in Poplar Park and suddenly this . . . thing wriggled up out of the water at our feet. He was stark naked except for a Speedo. Robert almost flew up the nearest tree."

I went right past the corpse. A Speedo-wearing corpse in a half-frozen river did not seem so very strange on a Clarkston Halloween night. At least, not this Clarkston Halloween night. "Robert," I said. "Robert Hayright?"

"Yeah," said Tricia. "Why?"

I felt my jaw start to drop, clamped it shut. Annoyance flared in me, though

I had no idea why. I needed to go to Kate. And I wanted to get lost in the marvelous atmosphere of this haunted house. But I couldn't quite wade out of Tricia's blue eyes yet. And I couldn't get comfortable with the way she floated through the world. I'd met people like her before, of course. A few. The ones born with brain, face, self-confidence, everything, gliding on their own private seas, remote and mesmerizing as lighted yachts as they drift among the teeming rest of us, struggling in our leaky johnboats from one shore we can't remember toward another we'll never know.

"How did that happen?" I said.

Tricia shrugged. "Robert? He asked."

Good for both of you, I almost said, decided that was beyond condescending. "I have to go find Kate."

"Don't miss the booth. It's weird as hell. Professor R., do you think this is it? The real Mr. Dark's?"

I studied her cold-flushed, happy, markless face. And my annoyance transformed into sadness, still and deep. "I think it may be our Mr. Dark's, Tricia. I think this may be as close as we'll ever get." Not until I was several steps away did it occur to me to wonder where Robert Hayright was.

In the back left corner of the backyard of the house stood a game-booth draped in red and yellow carnival bunting. Kate stood to the left of it, but she wasn't playing whatever game the booth offered. She was looking at the prairie outside the bone-hedge. Despite her presence here tonight, I knew, excising Brian Tidrow from her would take years.

I was fifteen feet away, closing fast, when two of the nightgown-girls appeared on either side of Kate, took her arms, and spun her, gently, toward the house. I hurried forward.

"Wait," I called.

"Move it, come on," Kate answered, turning her head toward me but letting the nightgown-girls lead her. The spirit of the evening seemed to have seized her once more. "I think it's our turn, David."

They were guiding her around the side of the structure toward the front door. Like all haunted houses, I surmised, Mr. Dark's could only accommodate a few guests at a time. Then the illusions had to be reset, the trap-doors and lunging scarecrow-monsters propped back on their springs, the fog machines reloaded. I had just about caught up when a third nightgown-girl drifted directly into my path, held up a warning hand like a school crossing guard, and stopped me.

"No, no," I said. "I'm with her. I came with her." I stepped to the side, and the nightgown-girl stepped with me. Her bare feet made cracking sounds in the snow-caked grass, left half-formed impressions. Her hand remained extended, blocking me. For several seconds, we stared at one another.

"They've been doing that since I got here," said Tricia, walking up next to me. "No one gets to go in with the person they came with."

"Forget that," I said, ignoring Tricia, watching Kate. The nightgown-clad guides on either side of her still held loosely to her arms, but they'd stopped walking, allowed her to turn around.

Kate's eyes were hooded in shadow. I couldn't tell if she was steeling herself, or enjoying the whole thing, or resigned, or what. All she said was, "It's okay. It'll be fun."

"I came here with you," I said. "I want to go through it with you."

"Guess there are still at least a few things we don't get to go through together," said Kate. Then she smiled another of those wide, blooming smiles, but she aimed it at Tricia. "Take care of our guy. See you out the other side, David."

She stepped forward, surprising even the guides, I think. The one on the left lost her hold on Kate's arm. The house had a white front door with a giant, ear-shaped brass handle that flashed in the icy moonlight. Kate closed her hand over it, glanced back one more time. She was still smiling. Then the door was open, and the blackness inside seemed to spill, for just a second, into the lawn. The door closed, and Kate was gone.

"It's not even fair," Tricia said. "I've been here longer than you guys."

"How long have you been here, anyway?" I muttered, unable to pry my eyes from the door. The dark in there had seemed almost solid; I half-thought it had left an impression, a formless, fading mark on the snow.

"Half an hour, maybe? There doesn't seem to be an order, though. They just come and get you. They got Robert maybe fifteen minutes ago."

"They make you go alone?"

"Some people. Some get to go in groups of two or three. Just not anyone you came here with. Think that's part of the plan? A way of making you uncomfortable or something?"

If it was, I thought, it was working. "Show me the game-booth," I said, mostly because I didn't like standing staring at the door. And somehow, I suspected I wouldn't be summoned as long as I did so.

I had my hands in my pockets, my arms tucked in tight at my sides because I thought Tricia might take my elbow or something, and I didn't want her to. But she just flicked her red-hatted head in the direction of the backyard, smiled at me, and walked off. I followed, watching the house, listening for screaming, but there was none. There was no sound at all. Other people, I thought, must have gone in before Kate and joined her to form a group, because there were only four or five hauntees left in the yard now.

A long, folding table lined the back of the first game-booth, and on the table sat a row of foot-high stuffed elephants, all crouched back on their haunches with their trunks in the air. The elephants seemed disconcerting only in their ordinariness. Once again, I was confronted with the contradictions of this place, the completely unique and elaborately controlled atmosphere and the utterly prosaic imagery. Surely, finding and playing this particular game deserved more significant reward.

Leaning against the table, smoking a cigarette, stood a gray-haired, stooped old man in a cloak. He had his chin tilted back, his eyes aimed at the roof of the booth. For a second, I thought he might be impersonating the stuffed elephants, and I started to smile. The old man lowered rheumy, red-gray eyes, and looked at me, then Tricia. "Only one play per traveler," he said, his voice more smoke than sound.

"I'm not playing," said Tricia, cheerful as ever. "He is."

"Oh," said the old man, and dropped his cigarette to his feet where it hissed in the grass. "Spin the wheel," he said to me. "Test your fate."

The wheel sat on another folding table that ran along the front of the booth, looking as though it had been ripped from a "Life" gameboard and enlarged. It was made of white plastic, roughly three feet in diameter. Positioned underneath the indicator was a circular piece of black construction paper. There was a single wedge of red paper taped over the black, at roughly high noon, with white lettering on it. The lettering read, SPINNER WINS ELEPHANT. There was lettering on the much larger black section of the circle, too. It said, DEALER LOSES HAND.

"I won Robert an elephant," Tricia told me.

I put my fingers on the wheel, jerked them back. The spinner wasn't plastic; it was bone. And freezing.

"Jesus Christ," I said.

"Oops," said Tricia, laughing happily to herself. "Forgot to mention that, didn't I?"

The gray man was no longer looking at us. He was looking beyond us. Remembering his training, I supposed. I put my hand back on the spinner, glanced at Tricia, thought of Kate, and spun the wheel.

Around and around it whirred. It made no sound. The indicator circled the grid, glided to a stop deep in the black.

"No elephant for me," I said.

With a sigh, the old man dropped his arm on the table in front of me. With his other hand, he withdrew a hacksaw from inside his coat, sighed again, shrugged. Then he drove the hacksaw straight down into his wrist, straight through it into the table, where it vibrated a few seconds in the frozen wood.

"Holy fuck," said Tricia, and flew backward.

I stared at the hand on the table, severed now, a single, long tendon dangling from it like a tongue. The old man was staring at the hand, too. Mouth working, I took a step back. It had happened so fast that I couldn't quite grasp it yet. But there was no blood. No blood. Exquisitely realistic tendon, but no blood.

"You're awfully good," I said to the man.

He nodded, lifted a garbage bag from under the table, and swept the severed hand into it. Then he retreated to the back of the booth, placed a fresh cigarette between his lips, wiggled the stump-arm into a pocket in the cloak, and reassumed his position.

"Oh my God," Tricia said, and now she did grab my arm, held onto it, went on laughing. Her laughter was irresistible, infectious, like a tickle. I felt myself burst into a smile.

We stayed arm in arm, watching the carnival booth, waiting to see what happened when the next "traveler," as the man had called us, came to play. I at least wanted to see if the gray man had new fake hands in his cloak and could attach them without turning away and blocking our vision. But a scant minute later, the nightgown ghosts appeared, one on either side of us.

"Finally," Tricia breathed.

"You're sure you're up for this?" I asked, feeling almost giddy, now. I couldn't wait to tell Kate about the booth. I couldn't wait to find her again. Besides, teasing Tricia was as irresistible as laughing with her.

Of course, she was better at teasing. "I've got my big, bad Prof," she said, squeezed my arm, and I blushed, and she looked at me, and we let the nightgown ghosts lead us back around the long, red house toward the white door, the waiting dark.

I had two wild, ridiculous thoughts as I was lead up the stoop. The first was that I'd just met Judge Albert Aloysius Dark, that he'd found the fountain of youth somewhere and decided to spend his eternity huddled away on the plains, plotting yearly appearances with selected friends. The faintly sick, perpetually bored Santa Claus of Halloween. The second thought I said aloud.

"Where's the exit?" I said.

"What?" said Tricia.

"You said Robert went in, what, twenty minutes ago now? Where did he come out?"

"I thought of that."

"Did you think of an answer?"

Tricia grinned. "After you, Professor R."

One last time, I considered the possibility that this was all a hoax, the best ever perpetrated, at least on me. God, even Brian Tidrow could be a hoax, I thought, and glanced at Tricia's face. Her red mouth hung open just a little, and her blue eyes were bright. Either I was having a far greater effect on her than I could have imagined, or this was no joke. None she was in on, anyway.

I took the handle, which, to my relief, felt like a door handle, and shoved. The door didn't creak, but swung smoothly back. I glanced over my shoulder and gasped and stumbled forward, dragging Tricia behind me. The nightgown ghosts had been right on top of us, brushing against our backs. One of them smiled blankly at me now, put her hand on the handle, pulled. "If you close . . . the door," I hummed to myself. "The night could last . . . forever." An eerie, irresistible song, from forever ago.

For a minute, maybe more, we just stood in the dark. I kept waiting for my eyes to adjust, but there was nothing to adjust to. This was blackness and silence, plain and simple. My ears almost stretched off my head, searching out sounds of people scrambling into place, spring-triggers being set. Then they searched for just plain breathing, the tap of snow against outside shingles, anything at all. But there was nothing. Stepping into that foyer was like stepping into a coffin. Worse, actually. It was like stepping completely out of the world.

"Professor R.?" I heard Tricia whisper. Somehow, I'd lost her elbow in the stumble, but I felt her hand crawl up my sleeve now, take hold of me.

"Right here," I said, though I was at least as happy to hear and feel her as she must have been me. I found myself hoping, desperately, that Kate had been allowed some sort of group to go through this with. The idea of her standing here this long, with Brian Tidrow's blown-apart head leering from under her eyelids, was more than I could bear.

The house's first overture was a touch. It was so subtle that I mistook it, for a moment, for Tricia's breath near my cheek. But then I realized I could feel it on my hands, too, a gentle, intermittent rushing of air. The first warm anything I'd encountered since the car heater.

It did feel like breath, though. As though there were dozens of people crouched right up against us, just breathing.

"Hey," I said, because even as I'd had that thought, I knew it wasn't true. Because I realized I could see, just a little. Something, somewhere, was casting a faint, green glow. I glanced toward Tricia, saw her outline.

Tricia glanced back at me. "I can see you," she said.

"Feel better?" I said.

"Nope." Even in that little light, I could see her teeth.

"Smart girl."

We were in a sort of hangar-style chamber, long and wide and empty. There was a doorway, however, fifteen feet away on the left. The glow came from there. The little puffs of air came from everywhere, but the glow was on the left.

I tugged Tricia's arm, and we started that way. Nothing dropped out of the ceiling. Nothing moved at all. As we approached the opening, I noted the crawling pace we adopted. Walking a haunted house properly is a lot like making love, I'd decided years ago. Maximum enjoyment requires concentration, the patience to allow for moments of electric, teasing agony, a suspension of disbelief in your own boundaries, and most of all, a willingness to pay attention.

Despite my yearly visits to every spook-joint in Clarkston, I hadn't paid so much attention since high school. In spite and because of everything, I smiled.

We stepped into a hallway which ran ahead for fifty feet or so and then jogged to the right.

"See, they understand, these people," I said. "You don't need fog. You don't need rubber hatchets in your head and things lunging out and grabbing your hair. You just need the dark and the silence and some imagination and—"

"No lectures, Professor," said Tricia.

My smile widened unconsciously. "But lecturing makes me feel better."

"Exactly," said Tricia, and I could see her eyes flashing. Her concentration on this moment was total. She led me forward, and I let her.

We'd gone perhaps fifteen feet when my foot hit the floor and sank, and I jerked it back. I hadn't sunk far, but I didn't like the squishiness where wood or cement should have been. I'd seen and felt and imagined too many bones tonight. I thought of a baby's skull, the soft spot, and shuddered. I lifted my foot again, put it down to the left of where I'd put it before. It sank again.

"Is this carpet?" Tricia asked.

"No idea."

"Feels gross."

"And you didn't even know Brian Tidrow."

"What?"

"Just walk, Tricia. Let's walk."

It was like I'd imagined stepping onto the moors would be, as a child, after I'd been read my first story with quicksand in it. For weeks I'd been terrified of walking in the grass. I'd had such total, unwavering faith, until then, in the ground.

Sometimes, our feet hit solid surface. Sometimes, the surface gave, depressing downward a little. This might not even be an intended effect, I decided. This could just be old, rotting wood. I didn't believe it, though.

As soon as we reached the spot where the passageway veered, the glow became a full-fledged spill of light from another doorway ten yards ahead. Without a word, we turned that way, crept forward. The floor beneath us became solid again. The rushes of air diminished, then disappeared altogether. But there were other sounds, now. Rustlings from down the hall, and a sort of drip-and-slosh from nowhere in particular. If the night had been warmer, I'd have assumed that ice was melting off the roof outside.

No sound came from the room with the doorway, though. We reached it side by side, turned toward it together, and Tricia said "Oh" and started to giggle and stopped. The effect was delayed on me, too, because the whole thing had been so studiously constructed to look real, rather than ghoulish.

On the ceiling in the center of the room, right where a light fixture should have been, a shining metal hook glinted in the seemingly sourceless green light. From the hook, not swinging, hung a slightly pudgy African American boy, maybe eight years old. The noose around his neck appeared to have bitten straight through his skin into his muscles and veins, which you could just see, little red tangles in yellow twists of twine. His tongue didn't bulge and it wasn't blue. It just drooped out the side of his lips in a peculiarly childlike way, like the untucked tail of a shirt. The boy's bare feet were at least half a yard off the floor.

A movie theater-style red rope barred Tricia and me from entering the room. But we stood a while, waiting for the kid to blink, yell "Boo," jerk forward, do any of those comforting haunted house things. But he didn't. He just hung.

Back down the hall, I heard the thud of boot on floor. I looked that way, saw a person-shaped bulk detach itself from the massing shadows and step toward us.

"Time to go, I think," I said.

"Professor R.?" Tricia said. For the first time in my experience of her, she sounded like a teenage girl.

"Let's just keep walking." I'm not sure which of us took the other's hand. "Just imagine the stories we're going to be telling on Monday."

"Monday?" said Tricia. "Shit, I'm calling everyone I've ever met as soon as I get home."

Twenty steps ahead, the passageway ended in a T. To the right, we could see one more strip of light, flickering and yellow, down near the floor this time, so we went that way. Soon, we realized we were approaching a plain wooden door, pulled most of the way shut. My least favorite door position. At least when a door is completely closed, you assume that nothing will come out to you. I heard footfall again, glanced back, saw the person-shaped shadow reach the T in the hallway and turn in our direction. Whoever he was moved just slightly more slowly than we did. But he kept coming.

We were a few feet from the door when the grunting began. For a single second, simply because we'd heard virtually nothing since we entered, it startled me. Then I started to smile. The grunt was distinctly human. Human-playing-ape.

"Oooh," It went. "Oooh-oooh."

I started to say something to Tricia and finally noticed the pajama child cloaked in the black shadows near the door. As soon as I saw him, he took a step forward. He was a bit older than the hanging boy, with long hair that lay in a black, wriggling mass on his shoulders and made his head look encased in snakes. It could have been a wig. His pajamas were yellow and baggy.

"Watch the gorilla," he said flatly, pushed the door open just a bit more, and stepped back into the shadows, his movements as precise and mechanical as the robot-pirates' at Disneyland.

"I don't like gorillas," said Tricia.

"Now, have you ever taken the time to sit down and talk to one?" I said, and she elbowed me in the ribs. The pressure of my coat against me reminded me that I wasn't warm. The house had not been heated, apparently.

Right as we reached the door, I saw the cage on the other side of it, and for the third time experienced a flicker of disappointment. The cage had been dug into the wall, lit by torches that guttered in sconces. In the cage, "ooh-oohing," was a tallish person in an old and painfully obvious gorilla suit.

"Okay," I said, and started forward, pushing the door all the way back. The gorilla-guy lunged at his bars, jammed one rubber arm through at us, grunted. My pride was up. I stared right into his eyes, tugged Tricia beside me, strolled past. When the second gorilla dropped on us from behind, I flew fifteen feet down the hall and shouted. Tricia screamed. Then both of us whirled, stunned, laughing.

The second gorilla stood in the passageway, hunched, huge, panting. He did not go "ooh." His skin still didn't look quite real, but it didn't look rubber, either. Mostly, it looked unhealthy, clinging in strips to whoever was underneath there like black, dessicated mummy-wrapping.

"Classic misdirection," I panted. "That guy was just sitting there on the wall, if we'd looked, see? But they got us focused on the one in the cage."

"You're doing it again, Professor."

"That's because that scared me shitless, Tricia."

"I noticed."

The door behind the gorillas creaked. Something else was pushing through. The shadow that had been herding us along, I suspected.

"Time to go," said Tricia, pulling me forward, and we continued down the hall.

We walked twenty paces, then twenty more. I began to wonder just how big this house was. It hadn't looked forty paces long, in any direction, from the outside. Nevertheless, we'd gone nearly one hundred before we hit the stairwell.

The architects of this funhouse had thoughtfully provided a single torch, licking the wall at eye-level, to alert passers-by that they could plunge to their deaths here. Maybe this house had been built out on the prairie because we were outside the jurisdiction of Clarkston's increasingly specific and stringent haunted-house safety code.

"We in the right place?" Tricia said.

I thought about that. "The only way to know for sure is to wait and make sure the big thing behind us catches up."

"Or we could go downstairs."

The stairs were cement, but ten steps down, the walls lost their comforting wooden skin, became dirt. Ahead was a floor, or at least a landing, and the stairwell banked to the left into total darkness.

I stopped, listened, hissed for Tricia to stop too. For the second time, and much more loudly now, I heard the dripping, sloshing sound. It came from ahead of us.

"Maybe we are going the wrong way," I said.

"I don't think so," Tricia murmured, her eyes raised above my head, and I whirled and saw the shadow-shape fill the doorway. Whatever it was wore a black cowl, complete with hood, and it was big. Six-and-a-half feet tall, at least. I couldn't see its face.

But it was carrying a gavel.

"Okay," I said. "Down, Tricia."

Down we went. The shape stayed where it was until we reached the landing, then took a single step after us. Tricia reached the landing first.

"What's down there?" I called, catching up.

"More stairs," said Tricia, and the torch behind us went out with a whisper. "Fuck."

"Let's go. Forward is homeward."

"Arm, please, Professor R."

I gave her my arm. We started down. Five steps. Ten. Down, down, down. Every few seconds, we heard a single creak behind us, as the Judge-thing in the cowl pursued at its leisurely pace.

From deep inside me, a laugh swelled. I felt it crest in the back of my throat, break into the open air.

"Oh my God, shut up," said Tricia.

But I kept on laughing. Truly, I thought, this was the best I'd ever seen. Then my foot plunged ankle deep into water, and I shouted and teetered backward.

"GROSS!" Tricia yelled, and she fell back beside me, shaking her leg, and we lay together on the steps.

A stair somewhere above us creaked.

"Kate hates puddles," I said, trying to imagine her coming through this. Suddenly, I had no laughter left. I was just overwhelmingly tired. And Brian Tidrow was dead. I hadn't liked him. I liked his being dead even less.

"What if they just lead everyone down here and drown them?" Tricia murmured.

"That would lower my overall rating of the experience," I said, trying to rouse myself to push ahead. How much longer, really, could all this be?

"We could be walking in a sewer."

"There aren't many people out here, though. So the amount of actual sewage—"

"Shut up, Professor R.," said Tricia. But she laughed, or at least expelled the air she'd been clutching in her teeth.

I got up. Tricia got up, too, and the stairs above us creaked. But there was no light to see by. Gritting my teeth, I stepped straight down into the wet, tugging Tricia behind me. The floor underneath was solid, anyway. Tricia moaned as her ankles sank, but she didn't say anything. We started forward.

Mostly, for the first few feet, I was listening. I wanted to hear where the water we disturbed rolled into a wall, thought maybe I could judge the size of this tunnel, space, whatever it was. But I couldn't really tell. I heard more stairs creaking.

"Tell me this is water," Tricia whispered.

"Hadn't even thought of that. Thanks, Tricia." I shuddered. I was whispering, too.

We'd gone another fifteen steps when overhead lights burst to life, blinding us, and shut off just as quickly, igniting fireworks on my retina. I stopped hard, the water sloshed, the disturbed dark flapped and fluttered around us.

"Now what?" Tricia said.

"Let's see if that happens again. Maybe we can see where we are."

We waited maybe a minute, which felt like twenty. Nothing happened. Shrugging, I tugged Tricia's arm, took a step, and the lights bloomed, held just a split second longer this time, and died.

"Hmmm," I said, and started forward again.

Five steps later, the water got deeper. It happened in a quick, slipping slope, and we were up to our knees, then nearly our waists. I continued to insist to myself that it was water. At least it wasn't cold. If anything, it was a little too warm.

This time when the lights flashed, they stayed on a good five seconds. My pupils telescoped, my brain locked, I got just a glimpse of wooden walls to the sides, another staircase less than fifty feet ahead, leading up. Then the dark slammed down.

"Okay. Exit ho," I said, and felt the first bump against my leg. "Uh-oh."

"What?" said Tricia.

"Just walk."

"Hey," Tricia said, and then, "JESUS. There's something——"

"Walk, Tricia. Wait for the lights."

"I don't want to see."

The lights exploded. I was watching the water. I very nearly fainted into it.

Drifting on the black, rippling surface were digits. Fingers. Thumbs. Dozens of them. Hundreds. Floating like dead fish in a dynamited pond. I saw part of an ear. The lights went out.

"Professor," Tricia said, her voice very small. "Did you see—"

"Walk, Tricia. Fast."

Mercifully, the water got shallower just a few steps further on, but the things in the water swirled more thickly around us. I kept my hands locked against my chest, burrowed straight ahead. Tricia was even faster, very nearly running as we scrambled up another slope and the water-level fell toward our knees. Both of us heard the slower, steadier sloshing behind us. But when the lights came on again, neither of us glanced back.

Seconds later, we were on the stairs, breathing hard. I might have bent over and kissed the firm, dry wood beneath me except that my pants were already stuck to my legs and sopping. Walking back across the frozen prairie to the car would be fun, I thought.

But worth it. The whole damn thing had been more than worth it. I couldn't wait to grab Kate, hold her, laugh with her. I couldn't wait to start digging around town for wood-purchase and electricity records in the hopes of tracking down the creators of all this. I couldn't wait to interview Robert Hayright and everyone else who'd been here about exactly what they'd seen. For the first time in years, I felt like writing.

More than anything else, though, I felt grateful. All my life, I'd considered myself a sort of library phantom, haunting the graveyards and record-morgues of my own history without ever, somehow, materializing inside it. But I was soaking in it, now, shivering in the relentless, terrifying rush of it.

I looked up and saw the EXIT sign glowing plainly, redly, twenty steps above me.

"That's it?" Tricia said, clutching her arms against herself and holding her sopping pantlegs very still.

"Are you joking?" I answered, but I knew what she meant. I didn't want to leave. I wanted to go on being this kind of scared forever.

Except that I didn't really want the Judge-thing to catch me. So when I heard him sloshing closer, I started up the steps. I had reached the landing, halfway to the top, when the strobe light strafed us, and the pajama-people stepped out of the wall on either side of the staircase. There were two on every stair. I froze, waited, and Tricia froze behind me. None of the pajama-people moved, either.

After a few moments, I sighed. "Bummer," I said, because I knew this trick. I'd seen it in half the haunted houses I'd ever visited. True, I was impressed by the doors cleverly carved into the walls to hide all these people until we were right on top of them. But I knew what was going to happen. I would start up the stairs, and the pajama-people would produce hatchets and clubs and raise them, slowly, looking all lurchy in the spasming light, and make vague menacing motions as I made for the door.

"Ohhh," I heard Tricia moan. I also heard a slosh and then drip from below, and I knew that the Judge-shape had reached the foot of the stairs.

"Ain't no thing," I muttered, and, ignoring the wetness in my legs, started forward.

"I hate strobes," said Tricia. But I heard her start behind me.

I had my hands in my pockets. As I passed each pajama-person in turn, I glared straight into their eyes. The only thing that surprised me was that none of them produced any rubber weapons or made any sort of threatening movement. They just stood, silent as heralds in a painting of a medieval procession, and watched me go by.

Behind me, Tricia gasped, and I glanced back, and everything went to hell.

The strobe shut down, and full-blown, blazing, ordinary light flooded the space, more than enough for me to see the Judge-thing. He was standing knee-deep in the black pool of wetness we'd traversed. I couldn't see his face because of his cowl. But I could see the fingers and thumbs floating around him.

They were moving.

Dozens of them clung to the fringe of his cloak, crawled blindly up his hanging arms, wriggling. Like bees over a beekeeper, I thought wildly, and my breath flew from me, and Tricia screamed and shoved me out of the way and hurtled up the stairs and out the exit door.

Staggering, I tore my eyes from the Judge-thing, stumbled, started to follow. Still, the pajama-people made no move to hold me. Tricia had left the door half-open in her flight, and I scrambled for it, very nearly tumbling to my knees on the steps. Three steps more. Two.

Then I was out, in a sort of clearing on the prairie, slumping to my knees behind the red house.

All at once, a burst of desperate longing exploded through me. I thought it was for the house, at first, for the fact that I would never experience another like it. That the eternal Halloween search of the lifelong Clarkstonian was over for me.

And then, at last, I processed what had been so strange about Tricia's flight. Or rather, the moment just before it. When I'd turned, she was just starting to scream. But she hadn't been looking at the fingers crawling over the Judge-thing. She'd been staring into the shadows right beside her. And in her eyes had been terror, but not only terror. There had also been recognition.

And that meant I really had seen what I thought I'd seen, right at the end.

Sick, trembling, I began to shake my head back and forth, grab at the frozen grass with my fingers, but it was too late. I understood, now, or I'd begun to, at least a little. The wriggling fingers. The Judge-thing, and the nature of its power.

The barefoot pajama-boys, and the decrepit gorilla, and the reason no one had met anyone who'd worked at this particular haunted house. I didn't know how, or why. But I did know, definitively, that the plains weren't empty after all, not the way we'd thought all these years. In fact, they were overflowing, overrun with Native Americans, homesteaders, dancing girls, ranchers, Chinese, buffalo. All the murdered, restless dead.

Helplessly, I turned around to watch Kate watch me from the doorway at the top of the stairs. She hadn't been issued her pajamas yet, I guessed. Her coat was open, now, and there was no blanket around her waist, and I could finally see the hole Brian Tidrow must have blown in her stomach, just as she walked in his door, in the seconds before he'd shot his own head off.

"No," I said.

"Good-bye, David," Kate said softly, and the door swung closed as she blew me a kiss.

STACEY RICHTER

The Cavemen in the Hedges

Stacey Richter received an M.F.A. from Brown University. Her fiction has been published in GQ, Seventeen, Granta, Michigan Quarterly Review, The Greensboro Review, LIT, *and* Nerve, *and has garnered two Pushcart Prizes. Her first volume of stories,* My Date With Satan, *was published to critical acclaim in 1999. She lives, she says, "in a small pink bungalow" in Tucson, Arizona, where she writes for the* Tucson Weekly.

"The Cavemen in the Hedges" *is an odd and terrific work of contemporary fantasy. It first appeared in the Fall 2000 issue of Francis Ford Coppola's new magazine,* Zoetrope All-Story.

—T. W.

There are cavemen in the hedges again. I take the pellet gun from the rack beside the door and go out back and try to run them off. The cavemen are tough sons of bitches who are impervious to pain, but they love anything shiny, so I load the gun up with golden Mardi beads my girlfriend, Kim, keeps in a bowl on the dresser and aim toward their ankles. There are two of them, hairy and squat, grunting around inside a privet hedge I have harassed with great labor into a series of rectilinear shapes. It takes the cavemen a while to register the beads. It's said that they have poor eyesight, and of all the bull printed in the papers about the cavemen in the past few months, this at least seems to be true. They crash through the branches, doing something distasteful. Maybe they're eating garbage. After a while they notice the beads and crawl out, covered in leaves, and start loping after them. They chase them down the alley, occasionally scooping up a few and whining to each other in that high-pitched way they have when they get excited, like little kids complaining.

I take a few steps off the edge of the patio and aim toward the Andersons' lot. The cavemen scramble after the beads, their matted backs receding into the distance.

"What is it?" Kim stands behind me and touches my arm. She's been staying indoors a lot lately, working on the house, keeping to herself. She hasn't said so, but it's pretty obvious the cavemen scare her.

"A couple of furry motherfuckers."

"I think they are," she says.

"What?"

"Motherfuckers. Without taboos. It's disgusting." She shivers and heads back inside.

After scanning the treetops, I follow. There haven't been any climbers reported so far, but they are nothing if not unpredictable. Inside, I find Kim sitting on the kitchen floor, arranging our spices alphabetically. She's transferring them out of their grocery-store bottles and into nicer ones, plain glass, neatly labeled. Kim has been tirelessly arranging things for the last four years—first the contents of our apartment on Pine Avenue, then, as her interior decorating business took off, other people's places, and lately our own house, since we took the plunge and bought it together last September. She finishes with fenugreek and picks up the galanga.

I go to the living room and put on some music. It's a nice, warm Saturday and if it weren't for the cavemen, we'd probably be spending it outdoors.

"Did you lock it?"

I tell her yes. I get a beer from the fridge and watch her. She's up to Greek seasonings. Her slim back is tense under her stretchy black top. The music kicks in and we don't say much for a few minutes. The band is D.I., and they're singing: "Johnny's got a problem and it's out of control!" We used to be punk rockers, Kim and I, back in the day. Now we are homeowners. When the kids down the street throw loud parties, we immediately dial 911.

"The thing that gets me," I say, "is how puny they are."

"What do they want?" asks Kim. Her hair is springing out of its plastic clamp, and she looks like she's going to cry. "What the fuck do they want with us?"

When the cavemen first appeared, they were assumed to be homeless examples of modern man. But it soon became obvious that even the most broken-down and mentally ill homeless guy wasn't *this* hairy. Or naked, hammer-browed, and short. And they didn't rummage through garbage cans and trash piles with an insatiable desire for spherical, shiny objects, empty shampoo bottles, and foam packing peanuts.

A reporter from KUTA had a hunch and sent a paleontologist from the university out to do a little fieldwork. For some reason I was watching the local news that night, and I remember this guy—typical academic, bad haircut, bad teeth—holding something in a take-out box. He said it was *scat*. Just when you think the news can't get any more absurd, there's a guy on TV, holding a turd in his hands, telling you the hairy people scurrying around the bike paths and Dumpsters of our fair burg are probably Neanderthal, from the Middle Paleolithic period, and that they have been surviving on a diet of pizza crusts, unchewed insects, and pigeon eggs.

People started calling them cavemen, though they were both male and female and tended to live in culverts, heavy brush, and freeway underpasses, rather than caves. Or they lived wherever—they turned up in weird places. The security guard at the Ice-O-Plex heard an eerie yipping one night. He flipped on the lights and found a half dozen of them sliding around the rink like otters. At least we knew another thing about them. They loved ice.

Facts about the cavemen have been difficult to establish. It is unclear if they're protected by the law. It is unclear if they are responsible for their actions. It *has* been determined that they're a nuisance to property and a threat to themselves. They will break into cars and climb fences to gain access to swimming pools, where they drop to all fours to drink. They will snatch food out of trucks or bins and eat out of trash cans. They avoid modern man as a general rule but are becoming bolder by the hour. The university students attempting to study them have had difficulties, though they've managed to discover that the cavemen cannot be taught or tamed and are extremely difficult to contain. They're strong for their size. It's hard to hurt them but they're simple to distract. They love pink plastic figurines and all things little-girl pretty. They love pink products perfumed with synthetic woodsy or herbal scents. You can shoot at them with rubber bullets all day and they'll just stand there, scratching their asses, but if you wave a little bottle of Barbie bubble bath in front of them they'll follow you around like a dog. They do not understand deterrence. They understand desire.

Fathers, lock up your daughters.

Kim sits across from me at the table, fingering the stem of her wineglass and giving me The Look. She gets The Look whenever I confess that I'm not ready to get married yet. The Look is a peculiar expression, pained and brave, like Kim has swallowed a bee but she isn't going to let on.

"It's fine," she says. "It's not like I'm all goddamn *ready* either." I drain my glass and sigh. Tonight she's made a fennel-basil lasagna, lit candles, and scratched the price tag off the wine. Kim and I have been together for ten years, since we were twenty-three, and she's still a real firecracker, brainy, blonde, and bitchy. What I have in Kim is one of those cute little women with a swishy ponytail who cuts people off in traffic while swearing like a Marine. She's a fierce one, grinding her teeth all night long, grimly determined, though the object of her determination is usually vague or unclear. I've never wanted anyone else. And I've followed her instructions. I've nested. I mean, we bought a house together. We're co-borrowers on a thirty-year mortgage. Isn't that commitment enough?

Oh no, I can see it is not. She shoots me The Look a couple more times and begins grabbing dishes off the table and piling them in the sink. Kim wants the whole ordeal: a white dress, bridesmaids stuffed into taffeta, a soft rain of cherry blossoms. I want none of it. The whole idea of marriage makes me want to pull a dry cleaning bag over my head. I miss our punk rock days, Kim and me and our loser friends playing in bands, hawking spit at guys in BMWs, shooting drugs . . . and living in basements with anarchy tattoos poking through the rips in our clothing. Those times are gone and we've since established real credit ratings, I had the circled-A tattoo lasered off my neck, but . . . But, I feel like marriage would exterminate the last shred of the rebel in me. For some reason, I think of marriage as a living death.

Or, I don't know, maybe I'm just a typical guy, don't want to pay for the cow if I can get the milk for free.

Kim is leaning in the open doorway, gazing out at the street, sucking on a cigarette. She doesn't smoke much anymore, but every time I tell her I'm not ready she rips through a pack in a day and a half. "They'd probably ruin it anyway," she says, watching a trio of cavemen out on the street, loping along, sniffing the sidewalk. They fan out and then move back together to briefly touch one another's ragged, dirty brown fur with their noses. The one on the end, lighter-boned with small, pale breasts poking out of her chest hair, stops dead in her tracks and begins making a cooing sound at the sky. It must be a full moon. Then she squats and pees a silver puddle onto the road.

Kim stares at her. She forgets to take a drag and ash builds on the end of her cigarette. I know her; I know what she's thinking. She's picturing hordes of cavemen crashing the reception, grabbing canapés with their fists, rubbing their crotches against the floral arrangements. That would never do. She's too much of a perfectionist to ever allow that.

When I first saw the cavemen scurrying around town, I have to admit I was horrified. It was like when kids started to wear those huge pants—I couldn't get used to it, I couldn't get over the shock. But now I have hopes Kim will let the marriage idea slide for a while. For this reason I am somewhat grateful to the cavemen.

It rains for three days and the railroad underpasses flood. The washes are all running and on the news there are shots of SUVs bobbing in the current because some idiot ignored the DO NOT ENTER WHEN FLOODED sign and tried to gun it through four feet of rushing water. A lot of cavemen have been driven out of their nests and the incident level is way up. They roam around the city hungry and disoriented. We keep the doors locked at all times. Kim has a few stashes of sample-sized shampoo bottles around the house. She says she'll toss them out like trick-or-treat candy if any cavemen come around hassling her. So far, we haven't had any trouble.

Our neighbors, the Schaefers, haven't been so lucky. Kim invites them over for dinner one night, even though she knows I can't stand them. The Schaefers are those lonely, New Age hippies who are always staggering toward us with eager, too-friendly looks on their faces, arms outstretched, like they're going to grab our necks and start sucking. I beg Kim not to invite them, but at this stage in the game she seems to relish annoying me. They arrive dressed in gauzy robes. It turns out Winsome has made us a hammock out of hemp in a grasping attempt to secure our friendship. I tell her it's terrific and take it into the spare room where I stuff it in a closet, fully aware that by morning all of our coats are going to smell like bongwater.

When I return, everyone is sipping wine in the living room while the storm wets down the windows. Winsome is describing how she found a dead cavebaby in their backyard.

"It must not have been there for long," she says, her huge, oil-on-velvet eyes welling up with tears, "because it just looked like it was sleeping, and it wasn't very stiff. Its mother had wrapped it in tinsel, like for Christmas."

"Ick," says Kim. "How can you cry for those things?"

"It looked so vulnerable." Winsome leans forward and touches Kim's knee. "I sensed it had a spirit. I mean, they're human or proto-human or whatever."

"I don't care," says Kim, "I think they're disgusting."

"Isn't that kind of judgmental?"

"I think we should try to understand them," chimes in Evan, smoothing down his smock—every inch the soulful, sandal-wearing, sensitive man. "In a sense, they're *us*. If we understood why that female caveman wrapped her baby in tinsel, perhaps we'd know a little more about ourselves."

"I don't see why people can't just say 'cavewoman,' " snaps Kim. " 'Female caveman' is weird, like 'male nurse.' Besides, they are *not* us. We're supposed to have won. You know, survival of the fittest."

"It might be that it's time we expanded our definition of 'humanity,' " intones Evan. "It might be that it's time we welcome all creatures on planet Earth."

I'm so incredibly annoyed by Evan that I have to go into the bathroom and splash cold water on my face. When I get back, Kim has herded the Schaefers into the dining room, where she proceeds to serve us a deluxe vegetarian feast: little kabobs of tofu skewered along with baby turnips, green beans, rice, and steamed leaf of something or other. Everything is lovely, symmetrical, and delicious, as always. The house looks great. Kim has cleaned and polished and organized the contents of each room until it's like living in a furniture store. The Schaefers praise everything and Kim grumbles her thanks. The thing about Kim is she's a wonderful cook, a great creator of ambiance, but she has a habit of getting annoyed with her guests, as if no one could ever be grateful enough for her efforts. We drain a couple more bottles of wine and after a while I notice that Kim has become fed up with the Schaefers too. She starts giving them The Look.

"Seriously," she begins, "do you two even like being married?"

They exchange a glance.

"No, c'mon, really. It's overrated, right?" Kim pulls the hair off her face and I can see how flushed she is, how infuriated. "I think all that crap about biological clocks and baby lust, it's all sexist propaganda meant to keep women in line."

"Well, I haven't noticed any conspiracy," offers Winsome checking everyone's face to make sure she's not somehow being disagreeable. "I think marriage is just part of the journey."

"Ha," says Kim. "Ha ha ha." She leans across the table, swaying slightly. "I know," she pronounces, "that you don't believe that hippie shit. I can tell," she whispers, "how fucking lost you really are."

Then she stands, picks up her glass, and weaves toward the back door. "I have to go check the basement."

We stare at the space where Kim was for a while. Winsome is blinking rapidly and Evan keeps clearing his throat. I explain we have an unfinished basement that's been known to fill with water when it rains, and that the only entrance to it is outside in the yard, and that Kim probably wants to make sure that everything's okay down there. They nod vigorously. I can tell they're itching to purify our home with sticks of burning sage.

While Kim is gone I take them into the living room and show them my collection of LPs. I pull out my rare purple vinyl X-Ray Specs record, and after considering this for a while, Winsome informs me that purple is a healing color. We hear a couple of bangs under the house. I toy with the idea of checking on Kim, but then I recall the early days of our courtship, before all this house-beautiful crap, when Kim used to hang out the window of my 1956 hearse, which was also purple, and scream "Anarchy now!" and "Destroy!" while lobbing rocks through smoked glass windows into corporate lobbies. It's difficult to worry about a girl like that.

It doesn't take long for the Schaefers and me to run out of small talk. I have no idea how to get them to go home; social transitions are Kim's jurisdiction. We sit there nodding at each other like idiots until Kim finally straggles back inside. She's muddy, soaked to the bone, and strangely jolly. She says there's about a foot of water in the basement and that she was walking around in there and it's like a big honking wading pool. She giggles. The Schaefers stare with horror at the puddle spreading around her feet onto our nice oak floors. I put my arm around her and kiss her hair. She smells like wet dog.

I come home from work a few days later and find Kim unloading a Toys "Я" Us bag. I notice a diamond tiara/necklace set with huge, divorcée-sized fake jewels stuck to a panel of pink cardboard. Again, she seems happy, which is odd for Kim. In fact, she's taken to singing around the house in this new style where she doesn't sing actual words, she goes "nar nar nar" like some demented little kid. It drives me crazy, in particular when the game is on, so I tell her to fucking please cut it out. She glares at me and storms off into the backyard. I let her pout for a while, but I'm in the mood to make an effort, so I eventually go out and find her standing on a chair, hanging over the hedge, gazing at the alley. I lean in beside her and see a caveman shambling off with a red bandana tied around his neck, like a puppy.

"That's weird."

"Look at his butt."

I look. There's a big blob of pink bubble gum stuck in his fur.

"God," says Kim, "isn't that pitiful?"

I ask her what we're having for dinner. She looks at me blankly and says I don't know, what are we having for dinner. I tell her I'll cook, and when I get back from picking up the pizza she's nowhere to be found. I walk from one empty room to another while the hairs on my arms start to tingle. I have to say, there's a peculiar feeling building in the household. Things are in a state of slight disarray. There's a candy bar wrapper on the coffee table, and the bag from the toy store is on the kitchen floor. I yell Kim's name. When she doesn't appear I turn on the TV and eat a few slices straight from the box. For some reason that starts to bother me, so I get up and get a plate, silverware, and a paper napkin. Kim walks in a little while later. She's wet from the waist down and all flushed, as if she's been doing calisthenics.

"I was bailing out the basement!" she says, with great verve, like basement bailing is a terrific new sport. Her hair is tangled around her head and she's sucking on a strand of it. She is smiling away. She says: "I'm worried about letting all that water just stand down there!"

But she doesn't look worried.

On the news one night, a psychic with a flashlight shining up under his chin explains there's a time portal in the condemned Pizza Hut by the freeway. Though the mayor whines he wasn't elected to buckle to the whim of every nutbar with an opinion, there are televised protests featuring people shaking placards proclaiming the Pizza Hut ground zero of unnatural evil, and finally they just bulldoze it to shut everyone up. A while after that, the incident levels start to drop. It seems that the cavemen are thinning out. They are not brainy enough for our world, and they can't stop extinguishing themselves. They tumble into swimming pools and drown. They walk through plate glass windows and sever their arteries. They fall asleep under eighteen-wheelers and wander onto runways and get mauled by pit bulls.

It looks like we're the dominant species after all; rock smashes scissors, *Homo sapiens* kicks *Homo sapiens neanderthalensis*'s ass.

As the caveman population drops, the ominous feeling around town begins to lift. You can feel it in the air: women jog by themselves instead of in pairs. People barbecue large cuts of meat at dusk. The cavemen, it seems, are thinning out everywhere except around our house. I come home from work and walk through the living room and peek out the back window just in time to see a tough, furry leg disappear through a hole in the hedge. The hole is new. When I go outside and kick around in the landscaping, I find neat little stashes of rhinestones and fake pearls, Barbie shoes, and folded squares of foil wrapping paper. They can't see that well, but have the ears of a dog and flee as soon as I rustle the window shades. One time, though, I peel back the shade silently and catch a pair skipping in circles around the clothesline. One of them is gripping something purple and hairy, and when I go out there later I find a soiled My Little Pony doll on the ground. They are not living up to their reputation as club-swinging brutes. More than anything, they resemble feral little girls.

Also, our house has become an unbelievable mess. Kim walks through the door and drops the mail on the coffee table, where it remains for days until I remove it. There are panties on the bathroom floor and water glasses on top of the television and scraps of food on the kitchen counter. I ask Kim what's going on and she just says she's sick of that anal constant-housekeeping-bullshit, and if I want it clean, I can clean it myself. She looks straight at me and says this, without flinching, without any signs of deference or anger or subtle backing away that had always let me know, in nonverbal but gratifying ways, that I had the upper hand in the relationship. She tosses an orange peel on the table before marching outside and descending into the basement.

I stand there in the kitchen, which smells like sour milk, shaking my head and trying to face up to the increasingly obvious fact that my girlfriend of ten years is having an affair, and that her lover is a Neanderthal man from the Pleistocene epoch. They rendezvous in our moldy, water-stained basement where he takes her on the cement floor beneath a canopy of spiderwebs, grunting over her with his animal-like body, or perhaps behind her, so that when she comes back inside there are thick, dark hairs stuck all over her shirt and she smells like a cross between some musky, woodland animal gland and Herbal Essences shampoo. Furthermore, she's stopped shaving her legs.

The next day, I duck out of the office claiming I have a doctor's appointment and zip back home around noon. I open the door with my key and creep inside. I don't know what I'm looking for. I think I half expect to find Kim in bed with one of those things, and that he'll pop up and start "trying to reason" with me in a British accent. What I find instead is an empty house. Kim's car is gone. I poke around, stepping over mounds of dirty clothes, then head out back and take the stairs to the basement. When I pull the door open, the first thing to hit me is the smell of mold and earth. I pace from one side to the other and shine my flashlight around, but I don't see anything suspicious, just an old metal weight-lifting bench with a plastic bucket sitting on top. Maybe, I think, I'm making this whole thing up in my head. Maybe Kim just goes down there because she needs some time to herself.

But then on my way out, I spot something. On the concrete wall beside the door, several feet up, my flashlight picks out a pattern of crude lines. They appear to have been made with charcoal or maybe some type of crayon. When I take a few steps back, I can see it's a drawing, a cave painting of some sort. It's red and black with the occasional pom-pom of dripping orange that looks like it was made by someone who doesn't understand spray paint.

I stand there for two or three minutes trying to figure out what the painting is about, then spend another fifteen trying to convince myself my interpretation is wrong. The picture shows half a dozen cars in a V-shaped formation bearing down on a group of cavemen. The cavemen's flailing limbs suggest flight or panic; obviously, they're in danger of being flattened by the cars. Above them, sketched in a swift, forceful manner, floats a huge, God-like figure with very long arms. One arm cradles the fleeing cavemen while the other blocks the cars. This figure is flowing and graceful and has a big ponytail sprouting from the top of her head. Of course, it's meant to be Kim. Who else?

I go upstairs and sit at the kitchen table, elbowing away half a moldy cantaloupe, and hold my head in my hands. I was hoping it was nothing—a casual flirtation at most—but a guy who makes a cave painting for a girl is probably in love with the girl. And girls love to be loved, even high-strung ones like Kim. I admit I'm hurt, but my hurt switches to anger and my anger to resolve. I can fight this thing. I can win her back. I know her; I know what to do.

I put on rubber gloves and start cleaning everything, thoroughly and with strong-smelling products; the way Kim likes things cleaned. I do the laundry and iron our shirts and line everything up neatly in the closet. I get down on my knees and wipe the baseboards, then up on a chair to dust the lightbulbs. I pull a long clot of hair out of the drain. There's a picture of us in Mexico in a silver frame on top of the medicine cabinet. I pick it up and think: that is my woman! It's civilization versus base instinct, and I vow to deploy the strongest weapon at my disposal: my evolutionary superior traits. I will use my patience, my facility with machinery and tools, my complex problem-solving skills. I will bathe often and floss my teeth. I will cook with gas.

A little after five Kim walks in and drops the mail on the coffee table. She looks around the house, at the gleaming neatness, smiling slightly and going "nar nar nar" to the tune of "Nobody Does It Better." I stand there in my cleanest suit with my arms hanging at my sides and gaze at her, in her little professional outfit, pretty and sexy in an I-don't-know-it-but-I-do way, clutching her black purse, her hair pulled back with one of those fabric hair things.

"God, I can't believe you cleaned," she says, and walks through the kitchen and out of the house into the yard and slams the basement door behind her.

———

Kim is so happy. The worst part is she's so disgustingly happy and I could never make her happy all by myself and I don't particularly like her this way. For a couple of weeks she walks around in a delirious haze. She spins around on the porch with her head thrown back and comments on the shape of the clouds. She asks why haven't I bothered to take in the pretty, pretty sunset, all blue and gold. Like I fucking care, I say, forgetting my pledge to be civil. It's as though someone has dumped a bottle of pancake syrup over her head—she has no nastiness left, no edge, no resentment. Her hair is hanging loose and she has dirty feet and bad breath. She smiles all the time. This is not the girl I originally took up with.

Of course, I'm heartsick; I'm torn up inside. Even so, I do my best to act all patient and evolutionarily superior. I keep the house clean enough to lick. I start to cook elaborate meals the minute I get home from work. I groom myself until I'm sleek as a goddamn seal. I aim for a Fred Astaire/James Bond hybrid: smooth, sophisticated, oozing suaveness around the collar and cuffs—the kind of guy who would never fart in front of a woman, at least not audibly. She has a big, inarticulate lug already. I want to provide her with an option.

Kim takes it all for granted, coming and going as she pleases, wandering away from the house without explanation, hanging out in the basement with the door locked and brushing off my questions about what the hell she's doing down there, and with whom. She doesn't listen when I talk to her and eats standing in front of the refrigerator with the door open, yelling between bites that it's time for me to go to the store and get more milk. One evening I watch her polish off a plate of appetizers I have made for her, melon balls wrapped in prosciutto, downing them one after another like airline peanuts. When she's finished, she unbuttons the top button of her pants and ambles out the door and lets it slam without so much as a glance back at me. Without so much as a thank you.

I trot out after her, figuring it's about time I give her a suave, patient lecture, but I'm not fast enough and she slams the basement door in my face. I pound and scream for a while before giving up and going up into the yard to wait. The night is very still. There's a full moon and the hedges glow silver on the top and then fade to blue at the bottom. I get a glass of iced tea and pull a chair off the patio, thinking to myself that she can't stay down there forever. I think about how maybe I'll catch the caveguy when he comes out too. Maybe I can tie on an apron and offer them both baby wieners on a toothpick.

After a while I hear a rustling in the hedges. At that moment I'm too miserable to be aware of the specifics of what's going on around me, so I'm startled as hell when a cavegirl pops out of the hedge, backlit in the moonlight, and begins walking toward me with a slow, hesitant gate. I sit there, taking shallow breaths, not sure whether or not I should be afraid. She has a low brow and a tucked, abbreviated chin, like Don Knotts's, but her limbs are long and sinewy. When she gets closer I see that she looks a lot stronger than a human woman does, and of course she's naked. Her breasts are like perfect human pinup breasts with bunny fur growing all over them. I can't unstick my eyes from them as they bob toward me, moving closer, until they come to a stop less than an arm's length from my chin. They are simultaneously furry and plump and I really want to bite them. But not hard.

She leans in closer. I hold very still as she reaches out with a leathery hand and begins to stroke my lapel. She lowers her head to my neck and sniffs. On the exhale I discover that cavegirl breath smells just like moss. She prods me a few times with her fingertips; after she's had enough of that she just rubs the fabric of my suit and sniffs my neck while sort of kneading me rhythmically, like a purring cat. It's pretty obvious she likes my suit—a shiny sharkskin number I've hauled out of the back of the closet in the interest of wooing Kim—and I guess she likes my cologne too. For a minute I feel special and chosen, but then it occurs to me that there's something sleazy and impersonal about her attention. I'm probably just a giant, shiny, sandalwood-scented object to her. The moon is behind her so I can't see her that clearly, but then she shifts and I get a better view of her face and I realize she's young. Really young. I feel like a creep for wanting to feel her up, more because she's about fourteen than because she's a Neanderthal.

She swings a leg over and settles her rump onto my thigh, lap-dance-style.

I say: "Whoa there. Jailbait."

The cavegirl leaps up like she's spring-loaded. She stops a few feet away and stares at me. I stare back. She tilts her head from side to side in puzzlement. The moon shines down. I reach into my glass and draw out a crescent-shaped piece of ice, moving with aching slowness, and offer it to her on a flat palm. She considers this ice cube for a good long time. I hold my arm as still as possible while freezing water trickles off my elbow and my muscles start to seize. Then, after a few false lunges, she snatches it from my hand.

"Nar," she says. Just that. Then she darts back into the hedge with her prize.

I remain in the moonlight for a while, shaking with excitement. I feel almost high. It's like I've touched a wild animal; I've communicated with it—an animal that's somehow human, somehow like me. I'm totally giddy.

This is probably how it was with Kim and her guy when they first met.

I guess I'm a complete failure with every category of female because the cavegirl does not come back. Even worse, Kim continues to treat me like I'm invisible. It's painfully clear that my strategy of suaveness isn't working. So I say screw evolution. What's it ever done for me? I go out drinking with the guys and allow the house to return to a state of nature. The plates in the sink turn brown. I shower every other day, every third. Kim and I go days without speaking to each other. By this time there are hardly any cavemen left around town; the count is running at one or two dozen. I go to the bars and everyone is lounging with their drinks, all relaxed and relieved that the cavemen aren't really an issue anymore, while I continue to stew in my own miserable interspecies soap opera. I don't even want to talk to anyone about it. What could I say? Hey buddy, did I mention my girlfriend has thrown me over for the Missing Link? It's humiliating.

One hungover afternoon I decide to skip the bars and come straight home from the office. Kim, naturally, is not around, though this barely registers. I've lost interest in tracking her whereabouts. But when I go into the kitchen, I catch sight of her through the window, standing outside, leaning against the chinaberry tree. It looks like she's sick or something. She's trying to hold herself up but keeps doubling over anyway. I go outside and find her braced against the tree, sobbing from deep in her belly while a string of snot swings from her nose. She's pale and spongy and smudged with dirt and I get the feeling she's been standing there crying all afternoon. She's clutching something. A red bandana. So it was him. The one with gum on his butt.

"Where is he?"

"He's gone," she whispers, and gives me a sad, dramatic, mini-series smile. "They're all gone."

Her sobs begin anew. I pat her on the back.

So she's curled over crying and I'm patting her thinking well, well; now that the other boyfriend is gone she's all mine again. Immediately I'm looking forward to putting the whole caveman ordeal behind us and having a regular life like we had before. I see all sorts of normal activities looming in the distance like a mirage, including things we always made fun of, like procreating and playing golf. She blows her nose in the bandana. I put my arm around her. She doesn't shake it off.

I should wait I know, I should go slow; but I can see the opening, the niche all vacant and waiting for me. I feel absolutely compelled to exploit it right away, before some other guy does. I turn to Kim and say: "Babe, let's just forget about this whole caveman thing and go back to the way it was before. I'm willing to forgive you. Let's have a normal life without any weird creatures in it, okay?"

She's still hiccuping and wiping her nose but I observe a knot of tension building in her shoulders, the little wrinkles of a glare starting around the edge of her eyes. I realize I'm in grave danger of eliciting The Look. It dawns on me that my strategy is a failure and I'd better think fast. So I bow to the inevitable. I've always known I couldn't put it off forever.

I take a deep breath and drop to one knee and tell her I love her and I can't live without her and beg her to marry me while kissing her hand. She's hiccuping and trying to pull her hand away, but in the back of my mind I'm convinced that this is going to work and of course she'll say yes. I've never made an effort like this before; I've only told her I love her two or three times total, in my life. It's inconceivable that this effort won't be rewarded. Plus, I know her. She lives for this. This is exactly what she wants.

I look up at her from my kneeling position. Her hair is greasy and her face is smeared with dirt and snot, but she's stopped crying. I see that she has created a new Look. It involves a shaking of the head while simultaneously pushing the lips outward, like she's crushed a wasp between her teeth and is about to spit it out. It's a look of pity, pity mixed with superiority; pity mixed with superiority and blended with dislike.

"I don't want a normal life without any creatures in it," Kim says, her voice ragged from crying, but contemptuous nonetheless. "I want an extraordinary life, with everything in it."

The Look fades. She brings her dirty, snotty face to mine and kisses me on the forehead and turns and walks away, leaving me on my knees. I stumble into the house after her. I can smell a trail of scent where she's passed by, cinnamon and sweat and fabric softener, but though I run through the house after her, and out into the street, I don't see her anywhere, not all night. Not the night after that. Never again.

———

Some psychic with a towel on his head says the cavemen passed through his drive-through palm reading joint on their way back to the Pleistocene epoch, and I finally go over and ask him if he saw Kim with them. He has me write him a check and then says, Oh *yeah*, I did see her! She was at the front of this line of female cavemen and she was all festooned with beads and tinsel, like she was some sort of goddess! He says it in this bullshit way, but after some reflection I decide even charlatans may see strange and wondrous things, as we all had during the time the cavemen were with us, and then report them so that they sound like a totally improbable lie.

It's bizarre, the way time changes things. Now that the cavemen are gone, it seems obvious that their arrival was the kind of astonishing event people measure their entire lives by; and now that Kim is gone it seems clear that she was astonishing too, regal and proud, like she's represented in the cave painting. I once thought of her as sort of a burden, a pain-in-the-ass responsibility, but now I think of her as the one good thing I had in my life, an intense woman with great reserves of strength, forever vanished.

Or, I don't know; maybe I'm just a typical guy, don't know what I have until it walks out on me.

I've been trying to get over her, but I can't stop wallowing in it. One night we hold a drum circle on the site of the old Pizza Hut, and I swear that after this night, I'll force myself to stop thinking about her. This drum circle is the largest yet, maybe a couple of hundred people milling around, having the kind of conversations people have these days—you know, they were annoyed and frightened by the cavemen when they were here, but now that they're gone they just want them back, they want that weird, vivid feeling, the newness of the primitive world, et cetera. My job is to tend the fire. There's a six-foot pyramid of split pine in the middle of the circle, ready to go. At the signal I throw on a match. The wood is soaked in lighter fluid and goes up with a whoosh. Everyone starts to bang on their drums, or garbage can lids, or whatever percussive dingus they've dragged along, while I stand there poking the flames, periodically squirting in plumes of lighter fluid, as the participants wail and drum and cry and dance.

We are supposedly honoring the cavemen with this activity, but in truth no one ever saw the cavemen making fires or dancing or playing any sort of musical instrument. Apparently the original Neanderthal did these things; they also ate one another's brains and worshipped the skulls of bears, though no one seems anxious to resurrect these particular hobbies. Still, I admit I get kind of into it. Standing there in the middle, sweating, with the sound of the drumming surrounding me while the fire crackles and pops, it's easy to zone out. For a moment I imagine what it might be like to live in an uncivilized haze of sweat and hunger and fear and desire, to never plan, to never speak or think in words—but then the smell of lighter fluid snaps me back to how artificial this whole drum circle is, how prearranged and ignited with gas.

Later, when the fire has burned out, some New Age hardcores roll around in the ashes and pray for the cavemen to come back, our savage brothers, our hairy predecessors, et cetera, but of course they don't come back. Those guys look stupid, covered in ash. When the sun comes up, everyone straggles away. I get into my hatchback and listen to bad news on the radio as I drive home.

CAROL ANN DUFFY

Circe and Little Red-Cap

Carol Ann Duffy was born in Glasgow, Scotland, grew up in Stafford, England, and attended the University of Liverpool. She currently lives in Liverpool, where she lectures on poetry for the Writing School at Manchester Metropolitan University. Her many publications include The Other Country, Mean Time, *and* Penguin Selected Poems, *and two children's collections:* Meeting Midnight *and* Rumplestiltskin and Other Grimm Tales. *She has won the Whitbread Prize, the Forward Prize, and is a fellow of the Royal Society of Literature.*

The two poems that follow come from Duffy's latest collection, The World's Wife *(Faber and Faber), which we highly recommend. "Circe" was also published in the March 2000 issue of* Harper's Magazine.

—*E. D. and T. W.*

Circe

I'm fond, nereids and nymphs, unlike some, of the pig,
of the tusker, the snout, the boar and the swine.
One way or another, all pigs have been mine—
under my thumb, the bristling, salty skin of their backs,
in my nostrils here, their yobby, porky colognes.
I'm familiar with hogs and runts, their percussion of oinks
and grunts, their squeals. I've stood with a pail of swill
at dusk, at the creaky gate of the sty,
tasting the sweaty, spicy air, the moon
like a lemon popped in the mouth of the sky.
But I want to begin with a recipe from abroad

which uses the cheek—and the tongue in cheek
at that. Lay two pig's cheeks, with the tongue,
in a dish, and strew it well over with salt
and cloves. Remember the skills of the tongue—
to lick, to lap, to loosen, lubricate, to lie
in the soft pouch of the face—and how each pig's face

was uniquely itself, as many handsome as plain,
the cowardly face, the brave, the comical, noble,
sly or wise, the cruel, the kind, but all of them,
nymphs, with those piggy eyes. Season with mace.

Well-cleaned pig's ears should be blanched, singed, tossed
in a pot, boiled, kept hot, scraped, served, garnished
with thyme. Look at that simmering lug, at that ear,
did it listen, ever, to you, to your prayers and rhymes,
to the chimes of your voice, singing and clear? Mash
the potatoes, nymph, open the beer. Now to the brains,
to the trotters, shoulders, chops, to the sweetmeats slipped
from the slit, bulging, vulnerable bag of the balls.
When the heart of a pig has hardened, dice it small.

Little Red-Cap

At childhood's end, the houses petered out
into playing fields, the factory, allotments
kept, like mistresses, by kneeling married men,
the silent railway line, the hermit's caravan,
till you came at last to the edge of the woods.
It was there that I first clapped eyes on the wolf.

He stood in a clearing, reading his verse out loud
in his wolfy drawl, a paperback in his hairy paw,
red wine staining his bearded jaw. What big ears
he had! What big eyes he had! What teeth!
In the interval, I made quite sure he spotted me,
sweet sixteen, never been, babe, waif, and bought me a drink,

my first. You might ask why. Here's why. Poetry.
The wolf, I knew, would lead me deep into the woods,
away from home, to a dark tangled thorny place
lit by the eyes of owls. I crawled in his wake,
my stockings ripped to shreds, scraps of red from my blazer
snagged on twig and branch, murder clues. I lost both shoes

but got there, wolf's lair, better beware. Lesson one that night,
breath of the wolf in my ear, was the love poem.
I clung till dawn to his thrashing fur, for
what little girl doesn't dearly love a wolf?
Then I slid from between his heavy matted paws
and went in search of a living bird—white dove—

which flew, straight, from my hands to his open mouth.
One bite, dead. How nice, breakfast in bed, he said,
licking his chops. As soon as he slept, I crept to the back
of the lair, where a whole wall was crimson, gold, aglow with books.

Words, words were truly alive on the tongue, in the head,
warm, beating, frantic, winged; music and blood.

But then I was young—and it took ten years
in the woods to tell that a mushroom
stoppers the mouth of a buried corpse, that birds
are the uttered thoughts of trees, that a greying wolf
howls the same old song at the moon, year in, year out,
season after season, same rhyme, same reason. I took an axe

to a willow to see how it wept. I took an axe to a salmon
to see how it leapt. I took an axe to the wolf
as he slept, one chop, scrotum to throat, and saw
the glistening, virgin white of my grandmother's bones.
I filled his old belly with stones. I stitched him up.
Out of the forest I come with my flowers, singing, all alone.

TERRY DOWLING

Basic Black

Terry Dowling is Australia's most honored writer of science fiction, fantasy and horror. He is author of Rynosseros, Blue Tyson, Twilight Beach, Wormwood, The Man Who Lost Red, An Intimate Knowledge of the Night, Antique Futures: The Best of Terry Dowling, *and co-editor of* Mortal Fire: Best Australian SF *and* The Essential Ellison. *Dowling's stories have appeared in such magazines and Webzines as* Omega Science Digest, Australian Short Stories, Aphelion, Eidolon, Aurealis, The Magazine of Fantasy & Science Fiction, Interzone, Ténèbres, Ikarie, *and* Event Horizon, *and anthologies as diverse as* Dreaming Down Under, Centaurus: The Best of Australian Science Fiction, Alien Shores, The Oxford Book of Australian Ghost Stories, *and* The Year's Best Australian Science Fiction and Fantasy. *His stories have been reprinted several times in* The Year's Best Fantasy and Horror *and the late Karl Edward Wagner's* The Year's Best Horror.

"Basic Black," from Blackwater Days, *his collection of linked stories set around the Blackwater Psychiatric Hospital at Everton, near Sydney, is a look at true and considered evil and features a rather different sort of serial killer.*
—E. D.

Once there'd been a small tea-shop in Cowell Street owned by a Mrs. Christensen, filled with lace, wooden furniture and blue and white Delft china; and when it had gotten too much for the old lady to run and was closing down, Dan Truswell had bought a cup and saucer set as a souvenir, a reminder that it had been there for its six precious years. His morning ritual was to fill the cup with Russian Caravan tea, open the French doors, take it onto the terrace, and sit drinking while looking out over the grounds to the small lake that probably gave Blackwater Psychiatric Hospital its name.

Everyone respected this particular ritual of Dan's. Phones rang elsewhere but never the one on the desk behind him. No one knocked at the door. It was to Harry Badman's credit that he intruded on Dan Truswell's reverie in a gradual way, as something served up by the landscape of green lawns, sprawling Moreton Bay figs, willows, soughing pines. He moved around the lake from the carpark, came walking across the grass, a growing point of imperfection in that peaceful scene.

It was so delicately done by the balding, middle-aged detective in the dark-gray suit that Dan accepted it with good grace.

"I wondered when you'd get here, Harry."

"What's that? You knew I was coming?"

"Got you. Truswell one. Badman nil. Thanks for the soft entry."

Harry Badman grinned briefly, sat in one of the chairs. "I need your help, Dan."

"Officially?"

"It's getting to that. Garson's on investigative support but it's an escalated and complex crime scene. We'll probably need to call you in officially."

"Then it'll have to come from Garson through Sheehan. You know that."

"It will. We're in the face-saving stage right now. Being seen to be doing everything possible. Your name came up."

"From Bill Sheehan?"

"From Sheehan, yes."

"And you're anticipating. Okay. It's the Mr. Tuesday killings. Not even a population of twenty million and suddenly we're turning up people like Jenko and this guy."

"Yes. Can I give you the files? Have you run up a profile?"

"To match with Garson's?"

Harry nodded. "Can't hurt."

"Sure. Leave the files. You want to give me a summary?"

"Is there coffee?"

"Tea. Russian Caravan."

"Ugh! But in a mug, okay, not one of those dinky little cups."

Dan had to smile. "I'll ring for the maid."

"You got a maid?"

"Truswell two. Badman nil," Dan said, then he went to find a mug, a chipped one if possible.

By the time Harry had his mug of scrounged instant coffee and Dan his steaming refill, reality was firmly in place again. There were patients wandering the grounds now, and Dan had reminded himself what it meant for Harry to have driven up from Sydney *without* phoning first, that since it was a Saturday, he'd probably done it unofficially and without Sheehan's recommendation or Garson's knowledge.

Harry placed his pocket recorder on the table and set it going.

"You've been following the Mr. Tuesday thing?" he asked.

"What's in the media. What is it—eight break-ins now, the sixteen victims all professional couples without children? The first two were burglaries only, the couples just left tied up; the next six involved murder as well, with extensive mutilation, ritual acts, a pronounced psychosexual element, a much more developed MO and crime scene. I'm sure you're holding back a lot and releasing false details to cut down on the crank calls and wrong leads but how am I doing?"

"Fine, Dan."

"So what are your verifications?"

"One, two or all of three questions. Why the feces patterns on the walls, why the black candles around the bodies, why the axe mutilations."

"So, no feces, no candles and no axe wounds."

"Right. This is worse than the Harbourside killings, Dan, if that can be said. Because of the escalating MO. Stranger than the Rain Eyes thing in April."

"If *that* can be said. You've got me, Harry. Tell me what you have."

Harry Badman took out his notebook, flipped several pages.

"The Hamiltons and the Drewes were woken at gunpoint and restrained, like you said, using handcuffs and duct tape. There was no attempt to abuse the victims, just a systematic, highly organized robbery. Security systems were neutralized. Occupants dealt with. No perp residues—hairs, fibers; no chance of DNA profiling. Then with the Haines we have a dramatically altered crime scene. The same with the Burtons, the O'Neills, the Davies and the Billingtons. Now it's murder, and now the bodies are mutilated as well, subjected to prolonged torture before death and some quite elaborate post-mortem abuse. Now there's semen over the bodies and in body orifices."

"Signs of genital penetration for that?"

"Inconclusive. Objects are left in the bodies afterward. But there's semen."

"Much of it?"

"Enough to suggest a prolonged time-frame."

"Or it's brought to the crime scene."

Harry grunted, grimaced. "Yeah, well. We're not finding the victims soon enough to know either way."

"Okay. But there's no shit, no candles, no axe injuries."

"No. We have evidence of multiple razor and needle wounds, other puncture wounds, piano wire through the eyes into the brain as probable cause of death in at least four instances that we can tell. We have cutting but no hacking. We have dislocated shoulders, broken ribs, burn wounds from acid, electrocution and direct flame."

"Like you say, prolonged and highly organized. But no fiber or hair trace?"

"Only from the victims or friends visiting prior to the crimes. None for a perpetrator. Only semen DNA."

"Which gives?"

"Caucasian male. Probably late twenties, early thirties. The good old Anglo norm."

Dan sat back, watched the sunny grounds, the lake twinkling now, the day being made, rising up, following its own escalating MO, a developing life scene. Another time he might have enjoyed the fancy. Not now.

"Difficult for Garson," he said. "It's almost as if the intruder staged the straight burglaries, then yielded to his real purpose. Couldn't hold it back."

Harry nodded. "We've allowed misdirection, everything staged so the crime appears other than it really is, but it just doesn't seem likely. Two crimes, no evident signature, barely any acknowledgment of the first two couples lying helpless in their bedrooms, then this sudden attention, sustained cruelty, overt control and marked sexual rituals."

"Or that's the staging," Dan said. "Our original profile was correct and now he's playing with us."

"You don't believe that."

"No, I don't. But these things need to be said. I'm wondering about a precipitating stressor that caused the MO change and what it could be. Maybe there's an accomplice."

"What we've been saying too. The nature of the crime scene, the acts carried out, don't suggest it though. Too personal. Too, well, intimate."

Dan nodded. "Maybe the burglar partner has gone. Left his pal to finish up."

"Yeah, well Garson's people considered that too. It'd leave you very vulnerable though, wouldn't it? Implicated in murder after such care. Hardly what the original two cases suggest."

"You think Garson will call me in on this? I'd like to meet him."

"Sheehan would like you to. Give us a week."

"Going by the dates on these files, you'll probably have another case by then."

"Yeah, well, that's why I'm here. It isn't my call—"

"But you want me to profile him anyway. So you can match it with what Garson has given."

"So we can catch this sicko, Dan. You really helped us with Jenko. Rain Eyes too, whatever that was. Please. Just read the cases. See what you come up with."

"Where will you be?"

Harry glanced around. "Down the end of the terrace, I think."

"Sorry, Harry. I've got commitments. Wait at the Sorrento in town. I'll phone around four."

"Thanks. Do I use the front door?"

"Why don't you take the lake? Finish what you started."

"Always going for closure. Thanks, Dan."

Sitting in his office between one and two, Dan read the files; didn't re-read anything right then, just kept going to get a sense of the perpetrator, the mission, the "why" motivating the "who." He scanned the meager forensic data. Mail order handcuffs. Hardware store duct tape. Three footprints, seven partials, all Size 9, deep enough to suggest a weight and height but a common enough shoe tread. No fingerprints. No fibers or hairs. No pubic hairs despite what seemed to be repeated ejaculation.

It was as Harry had said: the first two couples surprised in bed, handcuffed, bound and abandoned, their homes very efficiently ransacked, none of the victims questioned during the burglaries, asked where valuables were hidden, made to give combinations or PIN numbers.

Maybe that marked a critical phase in his operations. He didn't dare consult his captives lest it trigger his other appetite, his real mission, so carefully held in check. Often psychopaths depersonalized their victims, even when the nature and intensity of subsequent abuses suggested some vital personal connection. His casual, almost incidental depersonalization had shifted critically, dynamically, with the Haines—couple number three—became refined with the Burtons, O'Neills, Davies and Billingtons. Now blood, semen or urine were being injected into body parts, nipples were being pierced and burnt and cut away, genital openings were being horribly filled, heated needles and wire were being slipped up into the brains of struggling, dying people who knew they were dying, who had passed through increments of suffering into that state of profound self-awareness where, more than anything, they now *wanted* to die.

And the deaths! By wire, by makeshift lobotomy, by suffocation (plastic bags, tape, cling wrap), by internal bleeding, ruptured organs. By too much agony.

Dan's face set into a grim mask. The phone rang five times; he ignored it. Twice someone knocked. He didn't answer. At 2:45, after three passes through the material, he put down the folder, sat staring out at the grounds, at the tawny light, the wonderful greens and blues flecked with white-clad patients and staff moving to and from the lake. The day was generously there: golden, gilding, changing, gradually winding down, filled with creatures and things perfectly designed for it. His earlier thought again, welcomed, snatched in and savored: a developed life scene. Filled with things meant to use it. A symbiosis.

And despite the conflicting data, the standard profiles used and re-used because the recurring anomalies and disorders of human behavior *did* make for patterns and standards, he believed he had something Harry Badman could use.

But first he needed distance, something to push it all aside. Half-aware of what he was doing, he walked across to his floor-to-ceiling bookshelves, took down two volumes. Part of him knew he *was* choosing, looking for a correlative, an analogue for what this might very well be.

He read awhile, then went over what he would say. As always when profiling, he tried not to let a particular interpretation have precedence because of its novelty or how elegantly it fit available data. All likely alternatives had to be considered equally—*any* possibility supported by indicated behavior, then matched with known antecedents.

Finally he phoned Harry.

Sitting in a corner booth in the bar of the Sorrento with Harry's pocket recorder going, Dan gave what he had.

"Say there's a second perpetrator," he said.

"An accomplice with him at the crime scene?"

"No, *not* with him. Someone who comes in afterward and does the actual killing, the ritualized posing of the bodies. I should say *staging* of the bodies, but it probably is his thing."

"Go on."

"Harry, the Hamiltons and the Drewes were restrained and their houses burgled. There was no attempt to abuse the victims, just a systematic, highly organized robbery. Then we have the dramatic escalation, as you say, signs of ritualized, obsessive-compulsive behavior, yes, still highly organized."

"Didn't you say it could be staged to mislead rather than posed?"

"I did. But the time taken to torture and kill a number of victims, to carry out the post-mortem mutilation, to masturbate over each of them, is the factor. Let me talk this through. Once the Hamiltons and the Drewes were made captive, the intruder showed no interest in them at all, though that would be what is usually called a precipitating stressor. From the Haines' break-in, we get a dynamically changed crime scene; suddenly the ritual behavior is in place, the people are being killed and posed and used for some apparent post-mortem gratification. The MO has not only changed from burglary to murder, it has acquired the signature of definite psychopathy."

"But *two* people, Dan. You know what Garson will say. The killer was probably timid at first, guilty, ashamed, deliberately concealing his real purpose behind a more 'respectable' crime. Rehearsing the next phase. A trial run, a verification, then off he goes."

"And that's possible, Harry, but I can't really believe he would be capable of managing that kind of control *twice*. Once barely. Twice no. Remember, this is his *real* purpose; it commands enormous psychic energy; it fulfils and defines him. Think of the dynamics involved. You've gone to the trouble of arranging a difficult, high-risk act. You've carried our surveillance, neutralized security, eliminated the major risks one by one. He had them helpless. He didn't linger. Surely some sign of the signature would emerge, some trace."

"Maybe he jerked off in the yard."

"Maybe he did. I'm not trying to sell you anything conclusive here yet; just something you can take to Sheehan. All I'm saying is we've gone from highly organized, garden variety burglaries to highly organized psychopathic murders. If it's staging, why bother? It actually draws a more intensive allocation of police resources. Why would he want that? So, like you say, the killer has finally progressed into his real purpose for doing the crimes, or he's staging things for the fun of it, heaven knows why, or he has a psychopathic accomplice (a very risky proposition for him, and extremely unlikely), or we have a very well organized psychopath adding his signature to existing events—what in fact become crimes of opportunity for him."

Harry made a few more notes. "He doesn't create the enabling event, just knows about them somehow and takes advantage of them?"

"Correct. Like a parasite feeding off a host."

"Forgive me, Dan, but that seems as unlikely as his having an accomplice. Garson would—"

"Harry, why is it so unlikely? We accept accountants who work for corporations for years just so they can use their position of trust to embezzle when the occasion arises. We say they've gone bad, yielded to temptation, but we know from experience that some part of them has planned or at least considered it from the start. We know of corrupt police preying on existing systems, riding piggyback on the criminal networks of others. Take politicians. Nixon, for heaven's sake! That's preying on systems."

"It seems, well . . . so complex."

"What? Like tapeworms in the intestine or those mites on the backs of fleas? Lice on birds? The blueprint for piggybacking *is* everywhere in nature. It's a refinement, a niche."

"So how can we know?"

"First, let's allow that it's a possibility. Then we consider a way he can know the system he preys upon."

"Any ideas on that?"

"Not yet. But take the absence of forensic clues. Mail order handcuffs and hardware store duct tape. Three complete footprints and seven partials, all the same size and suggested body weight. No fingerprints, no hairs of fibers. No DNA trace before the semen gave us young Caucasian male. But no pubic hair with the masturbation."

"Suggesting?"

"The semen is brought to the scene or he's wearing a bodysuit so only his penis is exposed when needed."

"Go on."

"Our piggyback killer has knowledge of his—I guess host *is* the word—his host's MO, details like what he wears, shoe size, weight. Maybe he can judge these things just from seeing his host up close. Semen aside, neither man leaves anything we can sample DNA from. That means gloves, mask or hood, but like I say, care and organization in everything he does. Control is a big part of this, Harry, though I suspect it probably goes beyond that. The fact that he's able to exploit another's *MO*, make it his, add his signature."

"He'll stop if we find the host?"

"No. He'll find a new host or maybe graduate to doing it all himself, though it seems he likes the piggybacking side of it. Maybe it overcomes an initial nervousness and reticence or a residual morality, though I doubt it. He can do it because someone else is doing it."

"That's quite a leap, Dan. You can torture and kill because someone else is breaking and entering."

"We don't have the killer's psychopathology yet, Harry, but again it's what's known as a precipitating stressor. Something in this man's makeup makes the piggybacking important, even crucial—"

"Or he's imitating the whole thing."

"It may allow a suspension of moral behavior; it may be because of a fear to act."

"Or it may be part of the ritual."

"Exactly."

"So what's the profile, Dan?"

"I'm tempted to go with a lot of the standards. Anglo Saxon male. Well above average intelligence, between twenty-three and thirty-five, with low self-esteem and poor social skills, but with a deep-seated conviction of superiority, that he's better than others. Probably lives with an older parent or sibling or at least in the sphere of the care of one. His disorder may have begun with abuse in childhood. He'll probably drive a van of some sort, dark in color, well-maintained. He's not successful with women. Part of his ritual shows the need for control."

Harry nodded at the classic configuration. "His victims are already restrained. Unable to move or speak. In the first two break-ins, blindfolded as well."

"Which normally would be perfect for his needs. They're already depersonalized, already negated as people with identities and rights. They're objects he can legitimately use, even endow with a form of higher self. But none of the corpses were blindfolded, Harry. He wanted these poor wretches to see what was happening."

"So, not transforming them by these rituals?"

"I don't think so."

"Is there more?"

"Poor school record. Underachiever, probably because he felt he was too good for the usual systems of assessment. Probably no army record. Even if a measure of electronic surveillance wasn't suggested by the piggyback MO, I'd say he was in electronics or computers as a career or a hobby. A technician."

"Explains the van. Should I run this by Garson and his people? Some of it's very close to what he gave."

"Not yet, Harry. I don't want to tread on any toes here. Suggest the double perpetrator idea to Sheehan; he knows we're friends."

"Hm. Say you're right. If you were Intruder One and you read about your victims being murdered *after* you were there, wouldn't you give it away?"

"I would. You would. So who wouldn't? What sort of person?"

"You don't think it ruins your theory?"

"It's just a theory, Harry. It stands or falls with the evidence. But stay with me now. Why might it continue?"

"Tell me."

"No. I've got my view on this. You tell me."

"It might be part of how the stolen goods are fenced. Which we're working on."

"My thinking too. Say our Handler has some hold over Intruder One—old debts, blackmail, threats to kin or loved ones. Maybe he just pays well."

Harry snorted. "Not too well, going by what's being taken. Moderate hauls. But you think Handler is Intruder Two? Sets it up, knows the venue, knows One's time-frame. He goes in afterward?"

"Not necessarily. Actually I'd say no. Someone who runs a fence operation, say behind a storefront pawnshop or one of those used goods, cash converter places, is organized in a different way. He's got different priorities."

"Generally. Takes all kinds."

"Always generally. Stop doing that. What do you have on that side of it?"

"Pretty well nothing. The hauls just aren't that great. Mostly available cash. Watches. Stuff you can sell in pubs. Some feature items were taken from four of the locations—jewelry, art pieces, smaller luxury goods—but nothing insured or registered has surfaced. Like I say, all cash-down stuff anyway."

"You got a list of likely operations?"

"Yeah, but Dan, it's Sydney."

"But you've thought about it lots."

"We've been asking for transaction logs, looking at new inventory, seeing if any of the victims' names appear. That's how they could be selected: by being former clients."

"But obvious, Harry. Our intruder—let's say intruders—could just be following likely cars to likely suburb and street locales. Noting absence of children and pets. Using his job as a technician as a cover."

"We're asking around about that. What service calls have been made and such."

"So we're back to my earlier notion. The thefts are just as they were originally. What does that suggest?"

"I hate it when you do this. What do you mean? The robberies are occurring the same as before. Jewelry. Smaller objects."

"But now he's torturing them. Now they'd be pleading, gladly giving combinations and PIN numbers, anything to get him to stop. Yet no large cash withdrawals are turning up. No safes looted and left open. The thefts are *just* as they were. What does that suggest?"

"Like you say, that someone is coming in afterward."

"And could that be the *real* purpose here?"

"What?"

"Harry, he wants to have a *found* crime scene. To truly be someone else's darker, crueller shadow. Or wants the increment of terror. Think of it, you're lying there helpless, praying it's just burglary, that's all. But you've read the papers, heard the TV reports. You've heard about what's happened to the victims of other recent break-ins. You're hoping this is just a burglary. Then he goes. You feel incredible relief. You're struggling to get free and suddenly the intruder returns—or a new intruder enters. Think of the accumulated terror. You know you have no chance that it's going to be long and agonizing and there's no chance of surviving it."

"But he doesn't go for couples with children."

"Not yet anyway. And that may be part of it, Harry. If he was abused as a child, he may not want to harm a child. But he wants that despair, that sense of utter hopelessness."

"Power. Control."

"More, Harry. He wants the terrible despair. Wants them to *know* there is no chance."

"That's the sin of *accidia*. Despair. And he gets off on it, this 'accidiophile.' It gets him hot. He jerks off on it."

"Harry, I wouldn't be surprised if he's as cold as stone when he's doing it."

"But in a psychopathic frenzy, surely. There's the semen."

"Yet he's so highly organized, so methodical. I wouldn't be surprised if he's simulating psychopathic frenzy but enjoying this very calmly."

"What are you saying? A psychopath imitating psychopathic behavior that *isn't* his?"

"It may not be his semen."

"What?"

"I said before, Harry; he's smart. He may have access to a sperm bank for all we know. He's read books on serial killing. Seen the glut of movies, seen people like Dahmer, Bundy and Jenko getting attention. What if he requires more?"

"Dan, I can't even imagine that sort of person existing."

"Yes, you can, Harry. It's what we call evil."

"So you're saying it may *all* be staging? The abuses, the cruelty, the signature elements? Not posing by a revved-up psychopath feeding a desperate need, but a staged scene coolly created. Isn't there a contradiction here?"

"Yes, and I wasn't going to mention it. I have no convincing rationale for offering it. But let's say it is staging, Harry, not posing. Not someone driven to do these things, just someone *choosing* to do it, not needing, just *wanting* to do it because it is so cruel, so goddam evil?"

"But, Dan, isn't that what psychopathy is? Inappropriate affect? Critical lack of empathy?"

"Yes. But what if it is choice? No compulsion. No psychopathic obsession. No getting off on it. Just a cool-headed decision to do evil to see what it's like. Like kids pulling wings off flies."

Harry shook his head. "I can't accept the distinctions you're making. Kids learn empathy, Dan. They learn consequences and appropriate behavior. Let's say someone did this for religious reasons or to punish wrongdoers or from some twisted higher calling like they trot out in these serial killer pictures. It'd be sociopathic in an inappropriate way, hence psychopathic by definition. Many of the Nazis chose evil. Pol Pot and Krstic did. Didn't you once spend hours pointing out what it took for sociopathy to become psychopathy? I don't believe I'm hearing this."

"Then best forget you did, Harry. I always get to this point where I wonder at motive, try to push it into some existentialist extreme. We'll go with your accidiophile and the standard run I gave you. He's a clever, nasty sonofabitch and he'll strike again soon."

"What do we do?"

"I come down to Sydney just as soon as you can get me an official invite. It has to be that way."

Harry phoned with the invitation on the Tuesday.

"Sheehan wants you down here for a Thursday ten A.M. meeting, Dan, if you can make it. It's official. We're putting you up at the Sebel starting Wednesday night. Oh yes, and off the record he's the Piggyback Killer now. Sheehan and Garson are going with the idea for the time being."

"How is Garson?"

"Pissed off. Covering it well. He was Federal, remember, used to hands-on involvement. He isn't too happy about Sheehan pulling rank. But he's actually a good guy, Dan, and he wants to meet you."

"Good. It'll be good to meet him at last. What did it?"

"The official request? There's been another break-in."

"I haven't read about it."

"You won't see more than a quarter column mention for a few days. We're passing it off as unrelated."

"Your department has enough clout for that?"

"Vital for the ongoing investigation. Public safety. It'll buy a little time."

"Same MO?"

"But children this time. Two girls."

"God, I knew it."

"How did you?"

"They died before the parents, right?"

"Can't be sure yet. Seems like it though."

"Reasonably quick deaths considering? Further abuse all post-mortem?"

"Again we can't be sure. Seems like it. How can you know this, Dan?"

"He'd rather not target children per se. But it's the ultimate anguish factor for parents and he knows it. Seeing your children die. Being unable to protect the ones you love."

"But it'll get us a different public reaction, right? People won't see it as yuppie killings anymore. Accomplices and accessories will be less inclined to hide him."

"Harry, I suspect we're close to a final phase for this killer."

"Why a final phase? We figured he was just getting more reckless."

"Because it is so outrageous, like you say. You do get a different public response. But he's not reckless. He's crossed a vital line he's resisted until now. I say he'll change his MO significantly."

"To what?"

"Highway killings. Hitchhiker murders. His Handler will go with it. Still fence valuables, accept less but adapt."

"But without Intruder One?"

"I'd say so. I'd even expect a male murder victim to turn up soon. One with what's left of a healthy bank balance."

"You really believe it's this?"

"Just guessing, Harry. But if I'm right about the type, then what I'm suggesting should fit. Anything on the pawnshops?"

"A few good leads. I'll be on stakeout Wednesday night when you come in. I'll give it to you Thursday at the meeting."

"Do me a favor before that. Get me a list of the relatives of your main thirty or so fence suspects, will you? Any medical or marital backgrounds for family members."

"We're already compiling that. I'll fax it through later today."

It was alarmingly unreal, Dan found, sitting in sunny Blackwater, following safe routines while looking in on such cruelty, such callous coldbloodedness. He regretted mentioning the "dispassionate evil" notion to Harry. It had been the worst time and place, yet a crucial spin-off of his own saturation in all this—the need to find a handle on a process at all costs. He had some other conclusions, other lines of thought, but these too were facts he didn't want to share with Harry or Sheehan's people yet, let alone Garson's, though that was out of genuine professional courtesy, he liked to think. He would've expected the same.

It was the separation from the terrible events that Dan hated most, yet was at the same time grateful for—not only for perspective but just to be spared the chilling, then numbing and distracting pressure of the horrific reality. He had something Garson didn't have. Distance. Probably less distraction.

At the same time, he realized he needed to go down to Sydney just to be *appropriately* involved, to feel he was part of what he was already involved in, though he knew that the closer he got to the hands-on side of it, the harder it would be to make good judgments.

As callous as it sounded, being away from the scene helped. It was like Carla doing a crossword the other day; she had everything but one response for "pessimistic contestant." Dan had glanced at the three letters she had out of nine and immediately saw "defeatist." An obvious enough word for Carla but elusive because she'd been trying too hard. It was a bit like that here. Once you had evidence of psychopathic rather than psychotic conduct, once you had recurring patterns of behavior, whether staged or genuinely posed, you began to get a personality, began to look for a living, breathing person with opinions, choices, decisions, attitudes, favorite cuisine, and so on. It was back in the real world again.

It all came down to how Sheehan would handle Garson. Dan had the luckiest position of all: he was an adviser. Public and official pressure was on everyone else. And that single factor was why he would never go into investigative support full-time. He needed to be apart to be good at what he did.

Harry's fax gave him fifteen likelies, thirty-five highly possibles, fifty-six unlikelies fitting other criteria. Family details were included for the first fifteen. Six of the fifteen had stolen items either listed in their transaction logs or as part of current inventory.

Dan was looking the list over again in his hotel room around 7:35 that Wednesday evening, fresh from a shower after his long drive, still deciding whether to go out for dinner or have something sent up, when there was a knock at the door. No one had phoned from reception first, so Dan figured it had to be Harry checking in on his way to the stakeout.

The tall, dapper, gray-haired man at the door gave a thin smile, extended a straight, precisely composed and very well manicured hand. "Dr. Truswell? I'm David Garson. Investigative Support. I'm pleased to meet you."

"A true pleasure," Dan said, shaking hands, letting the military straight, dark-suited man walk to the middle of the room, where he turned, the lights of Sydney at his back.

"I thought it best we meet before tomorrow's meeting, Dr. Truswell, just so we're clear on how things stand."

This was possibly Dan's only chance. "Then you should know that I'm completely at your service, David. I regard it as a privilege to be able to assist by offering corroborative interpretations at this level at such a high-pressured time. I'm sure I needn't add that all public statements made by me will see me deferring to your control of this aspect of the investigations." It was a spiel Dan had planned all the way from Everton.

"Well, yes. Good. That's really it, isn't it? Keeping a unified front?" The man seemed somewhat mollified. "We just can't afford mixed signals getting out."

"I totally agree. Now that you feel some independent profiling might be useful, my suggestions will go to you direct, of course."

"Hm. Well. That's good. That's very good. We can certainly use the help. I was just concerned that we'd be dividing our efforts."

"Of course. But it's best for everyone that I'm part of your team."

Garson was much happier, Dan could see. They were closer now to a first-name basis on both sides.

"I've just boiled the jug, David. Can I make you tea or coffee?"

"Yes. Yes, tea please. White. Two sugars. Thank you, Daniel. I really just needed to have an understanding before tomorrow. These killings have got us, well, at our wits' end."

Dan set out cups. "It's been terrible, yes. Harry would've told you I insisted any suggestions from me go straight to your office."

"He did, yes. I was glad to get them. It was just the unified front business that was concerning me. How Sheehan might see it at this vital stage."

"Of course. So how close are you?" Dan was careful to say "you" not "we."

David Garson sat down at last, gazed out at the lights of the city.

"We hope to have something in the next two days if these pawnshop stakeouts pay off. Will you be tabling anything tomorrow?"

And there it was. The real concern. Anything offered when Sheehan asked for new leads and suggestions. Garson's final test.

Dan handed him his tea. He'd known Garson would be a tea drinker. "Nothing that wouldn't be better coming from you. Sheehan knows Harry and I are friends. He knew I'd be profiling anyway; it's just something we do when there are cases like this. He quizzed Harry about it, said the task force would welcome whatever profiles I worked up." A handy lie. Everyone would be glad of it. "Harry's on stakeout tonight, but I would've passed this onto him if he called later."

Garson nodded and sipped his tea. "You probably already know that three of the names on the master list are single proprietors with single male relatives living on the premises, one of them with a younger, single, male sibling employed by an electronics repair company. It's promising."

Dan felt a little bit baited but decided to risk it. "And that's the trouble, David. Piggyback seems to be changing his MO. Killing those children. It's time to move on."

"You think he'll kill his brother?"

This was more like it: a smooth, no-nonsense exchange. Dan gave a bit more, watching for the slightest telltale signs that giving counsel was being seen as intruding. "I don't think there's necessarily a brother in the first place. Piggyback is very highly organized; a parasite preying on a highly organized host. I think he'll anticipate our strategies. Efforts to purge him out."

Garson frowned, sipped his tea. "But tell me how the evidence supports it. More to the point, what motivation would there be for a burglar to remain active? He can't help but be implicated as an accomplice. A willing accessory, for that matter."

Dan removed his glasses, saw the city blur into a coronation glitter. "It doesn't go against type but it's very high risk, I agree. Especially in view of the escalation of these crimes. The children being killed." He was being careful again. So careful.

"What's your interpretation?"

"What I'd go with?" Jung had supposedly begun each of his many dream analyses by saying "*I know nothing about this dream.*" Dan made himself say a similar reminder to himself: that there were *always* other ways of seeing. "A psychopath provides the agent for the handler. May have discovered an existing operation and exploited it. The question remains: how does he induce two people to take such risks if they're not willing?"

Garson gave a decisive nod. "He uses fear."

"We agree, David. Rather than look for pawnshop owners with a male sibling or son living on the premises, I feel we should be targeting operators who have siblings or offspring gone missing."

Garson smiled for the first time. "Hostages, yes. Good, Daniel! We must tell Harry and Sheehan. I take your point with good cause. I went with Ross and Benton when Sheehan first authorized the pawnshop calls, just to get a feel of the set-up. One of the top fifteen listed, Rollerson, has a teenage daughter, Benton told us. She wasn't there when we went in, which wasn't significant then. Ross asked how she was, and Rollerson said she'd gone on a camping holiday to Queensland with friends."

"But possibly taken, yes."

"He could've been lying, but he was hostile to questioning anyway. Ross and Benton had been there before for one thing and another."

"Do you know if he lives on the premises? If there's a flat upstairs? Room for one? Piggyback could be renting."

"It's in Newton. A pretty large building. I'd say he does live on the premises. And it's large enough for flats, yes."

"Items from the burglaries have turned up there?"

Garson nodded. "Possibly smokescreen, but it's promising. Listen, I should call this in, get some surveillance organized." He stood. "You're probably tired, Daniel, but you're welcome to come along if I can get the go-ahead."

"You phone. I'll change."

"Are you licensed for a weapon?"

Dan laughed. "Sorry. Toothless in Gaza, I'm afraid."

Garson gave only a cursory smile, and Dan deeply regretted the comment. Some of the victims had been brutally bitten, others had had their teeth removed. He excused himself and went to change in the bathroom, heard Garson giving details, sounding officious and commanding, speaking with the voice of a man used to considerable personal power but now under stress.

"They'll meet us," Garson told him. "This could be it."

They crossed the City in Garson's Saab, both men alert and focused yet—both admitted when they got in the car—feeling curiously dissociated too. Like in wartime, there was the separation from reality: hours and days of nothing, then everything in split seconds. Dan was surprised to learn that for Garson, as for himself, it had all been so separate, that even he needed the clinical detachment to remain effective. But Garson had seen *all* the crime scene photographs, not just the careful selection Dan had been allowed by Sheehan. He knew more graphically, more wholly, what they were working with, how phrases like "acid burn" and "forced dental extraction" came horrifically alive.

"I keep thinking of the extent of the cruelty," Dan said, testing Garson's affect. This man had the career experience, the international reputation. Dan had a handful of effective profiles, two of them e-mail consultations for cases on the other side of the world. He was really just coming to the attention of the likes of Sheehan.

"He's cold and spiteful," Garson replied. "You've seen the files."

"But not all the images."

Garson nodded slowly. "No one should be brought to the point where they crave death."

Dan watched the streets and shops, the flow of people and the traffic, deliberately didn't look at his controlled but exhausted, newfound colleague. "What do you make of the avoidance of children till now?"

Garson kept his attention on the road. "I'm not sure it has been planned avoidance, Daniel, but I do think it substantiates what you said back at the hotel. I think he's found an existing system and exploited it. He's refining his art. Turning it into what he wants."

"Not sympathetic identification with children until now?"

"Frankly, no. I think you may be looking for a redeeming feature. I'm quite happy about arguing this part of it before Sheehan tomorrow, but if we don't catch him, I think from now on there'll be more child victims."

Dan didn't need to argue it; he had to live up to his words earlier and be seen to belong to the same team. But Garson's next question rocked him.

"Do you believe in evil, Daniel?"

"That someone can be evil? Why, yes. I do."

"What about good *and* evil? Someone capable of both?"

And there it was! His own earlier hypothetical with Harry served up to him. Coincidence? Probably inevitable under the circumstances.

"The horns of a familiar dilemma. I'd have to say impossible. The possibility of the latter negates the former." Dan realized he believed it.

"Go on."

"Taking the present case?"

"Since you mention it, yes."

Dan spoke so carefully. "Committing deeds like these shows an essential lack of empathy." Exactly Harry's words to him. "Inappropriate affect. And that indicates sociopathic and psychopathic personality."

"Illness or attitude?" It was so quickly asked.

"Statistically? Attitude. It's chosen behavior."

"Dangerous ground."

"It certainly is."

"No redeeming features?"

What was Garson's point? Dan wondered. "Ultimately none. Anything resembling such would be in service to the psychopathy. Like Hitler patting dogs, painting watercolors, being fond of children. The psychopathy is still in place."

"Machiavelli telling his master how to treat powerful friends."

Dan refused to be drawn further on it. "I'd need to read up on Machiavelli."

"You should. One wonders if advising a powerful head of state to be ruthless like that was just a way of being psychopathic by proxy. Discrepancies in the evidence aside, what gave you the piggyback/parasite idea? I know I resisted it at first."

"Telling you what you already know: humans establish systems. People prey on systems, the things other people do. I read up on parasites in nature, the mites on fleas, under the scales of fish. The lice on birds, for heaven's sake, where the bird *becomes* the world, the *raison d'etre*. The louse has no concept of flight or the aerodynamics involved. It hides in the warmth, seeing everything in terms of its needs. The bird is aware of the louse only as one of the hazards of its reality."

"And we are aware of both," Garson said.

"Yes. And grant that detachment, that pleasure in knowing. Allow the superior intelligence and cunning of this Intruder Two; grant that one of the greatest human needs is to give a life meaning, to make self meaningful, and there is both dynamic motivation and dynamic reward."

"So we have a Machiavelli, a Leonardo da Vinci of pyschopaths. I really must apologize for not bringing you in sooner, Daniel. You are every bit as good as Harry and Sheehan said. Do you think we will catch him?"

"It's hard to say. He's exploiting a niche. He would probably say he's the natural product of a system. What concerns me now, David, is that if we are even partway right about his intelligence, his detachment and control, then he will be modeling our reality as closely as we're attempting to model his."

They parked on King Street in Newtown very close to the Rollerson address. Garson used his mobile to call Dispatch, gave position and intention, then they walked past several storefronts toward Rollerson's establishment on the corner.

"Rollerson suspects nothing," Garson said. "We'll meet Ross and Benton around back. Burford, Pike, Lewis and Tunny have already gone in. Harry and his group will be in through the front door here in about ten minutes. You want to go in or not?"

"I'd like to."

"Good. Come on."

They passed windows filled with brightly lit merchandise arranged behind sturdy security grills, turned into the side street and moved down the northern side of the building to the laneway at the rear. The two detectives were near an outside staircase leading up to a first-floor landing.

"They're inside, sir," one said. "Door's open. Hewins and Clarke are with them now too."

"Thanks, Cliff." Garson produced his revolver and headed up the stairs.

Dan followed, suddenly wishing he did have a weapon as well.

The landing gave onto a hallway with four doors on the right, two on the left, and one facing them at the far end.

"Rollerson's at the end," Garson said. "Over the shop. Piggyback's probably next to it on the right."

Dan saw no sign of the six officers who had gone in ahead. "Where are Sheehan's people?" he asked in a whisper.

"Inside I'd say. The place is supposed to have been secured."

"Does that mean they've got him? It's so quiet."

Garson frowned but didn't answer.

As they were passing the first door, Dan found he was holding back. "We should wait," he said.

It seemed to trigger something in Garson. "They said it was secure." And he strode boldly down the dim hallway, stood frowning at the last door on the right, gun raised. To Dan's astonishment, he drew back his leg and kicked the door in, then disappeared inside.

Dan stood stunned, hardly believing the speed with which it had happened, that a door could kick in so easily. He rushed back to the landing to call Ross and Benton, but the back lane was deserted. The detectives had gone.

There was silence, near-silence with busy King Street beyond, but bizarre dislocation, all sense of expected sequence shattered.

This is how it must feel! Dan realized. Madness. Panic. Phobos and Deimos. Things gone alarmingly, fantastically awry.

But he'd *seen* them! Ross and Benton. Seen system and order. Pattern, procedure and expectation all confirmed. He'd seen Garson dislocate his stereotype in one act, leaning back, leg raised, striking. The door slamming in. No one coming out to see what the disturbance was. The traffic and far-off people sounds all vague and secondary. Unreal now. Too unreal.

Dan hesitated at the point of a terror he'd never felt before—a naked, personal terror—but had to know. Before he quite realized it, he was plunging down the hallway to the final right-hand door; found himself staring into a large living-room, dim and cluttered. A single standard lamp cast a mean yellow light on someone's careful disarray.

No sign of him. Not Garson, not anyone. Just cupboards, shelves, equipment. Technical stuff. Leads and wires, gutted electrical units. Hints of what looked like surveillance tech. That much expected. He saw another door, half open.

Dan felt the madness pounding, blood pumping through his chest and skull, felt the need to go yet stay and know. He entered the apartment, crossed to the half-open door, pushed it back, saw two coffins side by side on the floor, their raw wooden lids closed but perforated with air-holes, thank God. Saw the closet door open and the black bodysuit hanging there, leather or rubber but close-fitting. Dead black. *Death* black. Saw other equipment near it.

Intruder Two. The makings. The outer makings.

Heard voices then, deeper in: people talking, arguing. A voice raised in a shout, a gargled cry. Silence. Real silence.

Dan ran, pushed back another door, slammed it back, rushed down the short hall to a bedroom.

Garson was there, standing next to a body lying on the bed, a dead male, Caucasian, yes, but older than their profiled type, lying in his own blood.

"David." Dan managed that one word, staring from the military-straight man with the gun in one hand and a bloody knife in the other to the body spread and lifeless on the bed. He was staring even as Garson turned and started to walk out.

"Who is that?" Dan asked, indicating the figure on the bed. "Intruder One or Two?"

"Intruder Two."

"You're Intruder One!"

Garson half-turned his head, gave a quick sharp smile. "Sorry. No. You didn't take it far enough. Follow me."

"Garson, what do you mean?"

"Follow me."

"Where's Harry?"

"I have no idea. Wherever he's stakeout, I should think."

"But—"

"Follow me!"

Dan did so, horrified, fascinated in spite of himself, returned with him to the second room.

"In the first coffin," Garson said, "there's the man he milked for his semen. Caucasian. Your given age range. In the second is Rollerson's daughter."

"Alive?"

"They'll recover. Follow me."

Again Dan did so, followed Garson across the living room till they were out in the hall, then onto the landing above the steps and the deserted yard.

No, not deserted. There was a car in the lane now. Garson's Saab.

As Garson went down the steps, Dan was still sorting shredded realities. "Ross! Benton!" he cried.

"Sorry," Garson called back. "Just two helpers hired to play a part. The real thing you should be asking yourself, Daniel, is why I wanted you here for this. This is my hunt, after all."

"For God's sake, why?"

"Because you got so close. You will appreciate what this is."

"Garson, wait!"

The man opened the rear door of the car and smiled. "You did well with your insights into parasites and systems, Daniel, but you needed to take it one step further. I'm not David Garson."

STEVE RASNIC TEM AND MELANIE TEM

The Man on the Ceiling

Steve Rasnic Tem's stories have been published in numerous anthologies, including MetaHorror, Forbidden Acts, Dark Terrors 3, The Best New Horror, *and earlier volumes of* The Year's Best Fantasy and Horror, *as well as in various magazines. His first English language collection,* City Fishing, *was recently published by Silver Salamander Press. His latest short story collection is* The Far Side of the Lake, *available from Ash-Tree Press. He has a novel coming out in 2002 from Subterranean Press called* The Book of Days.

Melanie Tem's nine published novels include Revenant, Wilding, Black River, The Tides, *and the Stoker Award-winning* Prodigal. Leisure *will publish* Slain *in the Spring of 2002 and an as yet untitled book in 2003.*

Among her several dozen published short stories are recent sales to Extremes2, The Mammoth Book of Vampire Stories by Women, *and* Museum of Horrors. *She and her husband, Steve Rasnic Tem, live in Denver. They have four children and three grandchildren.* ·

"The Man on the Ceiling" was published as a chapbook by American Fantasy. *And it is true.*

—E. D.

Everything we're about to tell you is true.

Don't ask me if I mean that "literally." I know about the literal. The literal has failed miserably to explain the things I've really needed explanations for. The things in your dreams, the things in your head, don't know from literal. And yet that's where most of us live: in our dreams, in our heads. The stories there, those fables and fairytales, are our *lives*. Ever since I was a little boy I wanted to find out the *names* of the mysterious characters who lived in those stories. The heroes, the demons, and the angels. Once I named them, then I knew I would be one step closer to understanding them. Once I named them, they would be *real*.

When Melanie and I were married we chose this name, TEM. A gypsy word meaning "country," and also the name of an ancient Egyptian deity who created the world and everything in it by naming the world and everything in it, who created its own divine self by naming itself, part by part. Tem became the name for our relationship, that undiscovered country which had always existed inside us both, but had never been real until we met.

Much of our life together has been concerned with this naming. Naming of things, places, and mysterious, shadowy characters. Naming of each other and of what is between us. Making it real.

The most disturbing thing about the figures of horror fiction for me is a particular kind of vagueness in their form. However clearly an author might paint some terrifying figure, if this character truly resonates, if it reflects some essential terror within the human animal, then our mind refuses to fix it into a concrete form. The faces of our real terrors shift and warp the closer they come to us: the werewolf becomes an elderly man on our block becomes the local butcher becomes an uncle we remember coming down for the Christmas holidays when we were five. The face of horror freezes but briefly, and as quickly as we jot down its details, it is something else again.

Melanie used to wake me in the middle of the night to tell me there was a man in our bedroom window, or a man on the ceiling.

I had my doubts, but being a good husband I checked the windows and I checked the ceiling and I attempted to reassure. We had been through this enough times that I had plenty of reason to believe that she would not be reassured no matter what I said. Still I made the attempt each time, giving her overly reasonable explanations concerning the way the light had been broken up by the wind-blown branches outside, or how the ceiling light fixture might be mistaken for a man's head by a person waking suddenly from a restless sleep or an intense dream.

Sometimes my careful explanations irritated her enormously. Still mostly asleep, she would wonder aloud why I couldn't see the man on the ceiling. Was I playing games with her? Trying to placate her when I knew the awful truth?

In fact, despite my attempts at reason, I believed in the man on the ceiling. I always had.

As a child I was a persistent liar. I lied slyly, I lied innocently, and I lied enthusiastically. I lied out of confusion and I lied out of a profound disappointment. One of my more elaborate lies took shape during the 1960 presidential election. While the rest of the country was debating the relative merits of Kennedy and Nixon, I was explaining to my friends how I had been half of a pair of Siamese twins, and how my brother had tragically died during the separation.

This was, perhaps, my most heartfelt lie to date, because in telling this tale I found myself grieving over the loss of my brother, my twin. I had created my first believable character, and my character had hurt me.

Later I came to recognize that about that time (I was ten), the self I had been was dying, and that I was slowly becoming the twin who had died and gone off to some other, better fiction.

Many of my lies since then, the ones I have been paid for, have been about such secret, tragic twins and their other lives. The lives we dream about, and only half-remember after the first shock of day.

So how could *I*, of all people, doubt the existence of the man on the ceiling?

My first husband did not believe in the man on the ceiling.

At least, he said he didn't. He said he never saw him. Never had night terrors. Never saw the molecules moving in the trunks of trees and felt the distances among the pieces of himself.

I think he did, though, and was too afraid to name what he saw. I think he believed that if he didn't name it it wouldn't be real. And so, I think, the man on the ceiling got him a long time ago.

Back then, it was usually a snake I would see, crawling across the ceiling, dropping down to loop around my bed. I'd wake up and there would still be a snake—huge, vivid, sinuous, utterly mesmerizing. I'd cry out. I'd call for help. After my first husband had grudgingly come in a few times and hadn't been able to reassure me that there was no snake on the ceiling, he just quit coming.

Steve always comes. Usually, he's already there beside me.

One night a man really did climb in my bedroom window. Really did sit on the edge of my bed, really did mutter incoherently and fumble in the bedclothes, really did look surprised and confused when I sat up and screamed. I guess he thought I was someone else. He left, stumbling, by the same second-story window. I chased him across the room, had the tail of his denim jacket in my hands. But I let him go because I couldn't imagine what I'd do next if I caught him.

By the time I went downstairs and told my first husband, there was no sign of the intruder. By the time the police came, there was no evidence, and I certainly could never have identified him. I couldn't even describe him in any useful way: dark, featureless. Muttering nonsense. As confused as I was. Clearly not meaning me any harm, or any good, either. Not meaning me anything. He thought I was someone else. I wasn't afraid of him. He didn't change my life. He wasn't the man on the ceiling.

I don't think anybody then believed that a man had come in my window in the middle of the night and gone away again.

Steve would have believed me.

Yes, I would have believed her. I've come to believe in the reality of all of Melanie's characters. And I believe in the man on the ceiling with all my heart.

For one evening this man on the ceiling climbed slowly down out of the darkness and out of the dream of our marriage and took one of our children away. And changed our lives forever.

Awake.

Someone in the room.

Asleep. Dreaming.

Someone in the room.

Someone in the room. Someone by the bed. Reaching to touch me but not touching me yet.

I put out my hand and Steve is beside me, solid, breathing steadily. I press myself to him, not wanting to wake him but needing to be close to him enough that I'm selfishly willing to risk it. I can feel his heartbeat through the blanket and sheet, through both our pajamas and both our flesh, through the waking or the dream. He's very warm. If he were dead, if he were the ghostly figure standing by the bed trying to touch me but not touching me, his body heat wouldn't radiate into me like this, wouldn't comfort me. It comforts me intensely.

Someone calls me. I hear only the voice, the tone of voice, and not the name it uses.

Awake. Painful tingling of nerve endings, heart pumping so wildly it hurts. Our golden cat Cinnabar—who often sleeps on my chest and eases some of the fear away by her purring, her small weight, her small radiant body heat, by the sheer miraculous contact with some other living creature who remains fundamentally alien while we touch so surely—moves away now. Moves first onto the mound of Steve's hip, but he doesn't like her on top of him and in his sleep he makes an irritable stirring motion that tips her off. Cinnabar gives an answering irritable trill and jumps off the bed.

Someone calling me. The door, always cracked so I can hear the kids if they cough or call, open wider now, yellow wash from the hall light across the new forest-green carpet of our bedroom, which we've remodeled to be like a forest cave just for the two of us, a sanctuary. A figure in the yellow light, small and shadowy, not calling me now.

Neither asleep nor awake. A middle-of-the-night state of consciousness that isn't hypnagogic, either. Meta-wakefulness. Meta-sleep. Aware now of things that are always there, but in daylight are obscured by thoughts and plans, judgments and impressions, words and worries and obligations and sensations, and at night by dreams.

Someone in the room.

Someone by the bed.

Someone coming to get me. I'm too afraid to open my eyes, and too aroused to go back to sleep.

But we've made it our job, Melanie and I, to open our eyes and see who's there. To find who's there and to name who's there. In our life together, we seem to seek it out. Our children, when they become our children, already know the man on the ceiling. Maybe all children do, at some primal level, but ours know him consciously, have already faced him down, and teach us how to do that, too.

We go toward the voice by the door, the shape in the room. Not so much to find the vampires and the werewolves who have been seen so many times before—who are safe to find because no one really believes in them anymore anyway—but to find the hidden figures who lurk in our house and other houses like ours: the boy with the head vigorously shaking nonono, the boy who appears and disappears in the midst of a cluttered bedroom, the little dead girl who controls her family with her wishes and lies, the little boy driven by his dad on a hunting trip down into the darkest heart of the city, and the man who hangs suspended from the ceiling waiting for just the right opportunity to climb down like a message from the eternal. To find the demons. To find the angels.

Sometimes we find these figures right in our own home, infiltrating our life together, standing over the beds of our children.

"Mom?"

A child. My child. Calling me, "Mom." A name so precious I never get used to it, emblematic of the joy and terror of this impossible relationship every time one of them says it. Which is often.

"Mom? I had a bad dream."

It's Joe. Who came to us a year and a half ago an unruly, intensely imaginative child so terrified of being abandoned again that he's only very recently been willing to say he loves me. He called me "Mom" right away, but he wouldn't say he loved me.

If you love someone, they leave you. But if you don't love someone, they leave you, too. So your choice isn't between loving and losing but only between loving and not loving.

This is the first time Joe has ever come for me in the middle of the night, the first time he's been willing to test our insistence that that's what parents are here for, although I think he has nightmares a lot.

I slide out of bed and pick him up. He's so small. He holds himself upright, won't snuggle against me, and his wide blue eyes are staring off somewhere, not at me. But his hand is on my shoulder and he lets me put him in my lap in the rocking chair, and he tells me about his dream. About a dog that died and came back to life. Joe loves animals. About Dad and me dying. Himself dying. Anthony dying.

Joe, who never knew Anthony, dreams about Anthony dying. Mourns Anthony. This connection seems wonderful to me, and a little frightening.

Joe's man on the ceiling already has a name, for Joe's dream is also about how his birthparents hurt him. Left him. He doesn't say it, maybe he's not old enough to name it, but when I suggest that he must have felt then that he was going to die, that they were going to kill him, he nods vigorously, thumb in his mouth. And when I point out that he didn't die, that he's still alive and he can play with the cats and dogs and dig in the mudhole and learn to read chapter books and go to the moon someday, his eyes get very big and he nods vigorously and then he snuggles against my shoulder. I hold my breath for this transcendent moment. Joe falls asleep in my lap.

I am wide awake now, holding my sleeping little boy in my lap and rocking, rocking. Shadows move on the ceiling. The man on the ceiling is there. He's always there. And I understand, in a way I don't fully understand and will have lost most of by morning, that he gave me this moment, too.

I was never afraid of dying, before. But that changed after the man on the ceiling came down. Now I see his shadow imprinted in my skin, like a brand, and I think about dying.

That doesn't mean I'm unhappy, or that the shadow cast by the man on the ceiling is a shadow of depression. I can't stand people without a sense of humor, nor can I tolerate this sort of morbid fascination with the ways and colorings of death that shows itself even among people who say they enjoy my work. I never believed that horror fiction was simply about morbid fascinations. I find that attitude stupid and dull.

The man on the ceiling gives my life an edge. He makes me uneasy; he makes me grieve. And yet he also fills me with awe for what is possible. He shames me with his glimpses into the darkness of human cruelty, and he shocks me when

I see bits of my own face in his. He encourages a reverence when I contemplate the inevitability of my own death. And he shakes me with anger, pity, and fear.

The man on the ceiling makes it mean that much more when my daughter's fever breaks, when my son smiles sleepily up at me in the morning and sticks out his tongue.

So I wasn't surprised when one night, late, two A.M. or so, after I'd stayed up reading, I began to feel a change in the air of the house, as if something were being added, or something were being taken away.

Our cat Cinnabar uncurled and lifted her head, her snout wrinkling as if to test the air. Then her head turned slowly atop her body, and her yellow eyes became silver as she made this long, motionless stare into the darkness beyond our bedroom door. Poised. Transfixed.

I glanced down at Melanie sleeping beside me. I could see Cinnabar's claws piercing the sheet and yet Melanie did not wake up. I leaned over her then to see if I could convince myself that she was breathing. Melanie breathes so shallowly during sleep that half the time I can't tell that she's breathing at all. So it isn't at all unusual to find me poised over her like this during the middle of the night, like some anxious and aging gargoyle, waiting to see the rise and fall of the covers to let me know that she is still alive. I don't know if this is normal behavior or not—I've never really discussed it with anyone before. But no matter how often I watch my wife like this, and wait, no matter how often I see that yes, she is breathing, I still find myself considering what I would do, how I would feel, if that miraculous breathing did stop. Every time I worry myself with this imagined routine of failed attempts to revive her, to put the breathing back in, of frantic late night calls to anyone who might listen, begging them to tell me what I should do to put the breathing back in. It would be my fault, of course, because I had been watching. I should have watched her more carefully. I should have known exactly what to do.

During these ruminations I become intensely aware of how ephemeral we are. Sometimes I think we're all little more than a ghost of a memory, our flesh a poor joke.

I also become painfully aware of how, even for me when I'm acting the part of the writer, the right words to express just how much I love Melanie are so hard to come by.

At that point, the man on the ceiling stuck his head through our bedroom door and looked right at me. He turned then, looking at Melanie's near-motionless form—and I saw how thin he was, like a silhouette cut from black construction paper. Then he pulled his head back into the darkness again and disappeared.

I eased out of bed, trying not to awaken Melanie. Cinnabar raised her back and took a swipe at me with her paw. I moved toward the doorway, taking one last look back at the bed. Cinnabar stared at me as if she couldn't believe I was actually doing this, as though I were crazy.

For I intended to follow the man on the ceiling and find out where he was going. I couldn't take him lightly. I already knew some of what he was capable of. So I followed him that night, as I have followed him every night since, in and out of shadow, through dreams and memories of dreams, down the back-steps and up into the attic, past the fitful or peaceful sleep of my children, through daily encounters with death, forgiveness, and love.

Usually he is this shadow I've described, a silhouette clipped out of the dark, a shadow of a shadow. But these are merely the aspects I'm normally willing to face. Sometimes as he glides from darkness into light and back into darkness again, as he steps and drifts through the night rooms and corridors of our house, I glimpse his figure from other angles: a mouth suddenly fleshed out and full of teeth, eyes like the devil's eyes, like my own father's eyes, a hairy fist with coarse fingers, a jawbone with my own beard attached.

And sometimes his changes are more elaborate: he sprouts needle teeth, razor fingers, or a mouth like a swirling metal funnel.

The man on the ceiling casts shadows of flesh, and sometimes the shadows take on a life of their own.

Many years later, the snake returned. I was very awake. I'd been offered pain-killers and tranquilizers to produce the undead state which often passes for grieving but is not. I refused them. I wanted to be awake. The coils of the snake dropped down from the ceiling and rose from the floor—oozing, slithering, until I was entirely encased. The skin molted and molted again into my own skin. The flesh was supple around my own flesh. The color of the world from inside the coils of the snake was a growing, soothing green.

"Safe," hissed the snake all around me. "You are safe."

Everything we're telling you here is true.

Each night as I follow the man on the ceiling into the various rooms of my children and watch him as he stands over them, touches them, kisses their cheeks with his black ribbon tongue, I imagine what he must be doing to them, what transformations he might be orchestrating in their dreams.

I imagine him creeping up to my youngest daughter's bed, reaching out his narrow black fingers and like a razor they enter her skull so that he can change things there, move things around, plant ideas that might sprout—deadly or heal-ing—in years to come. She is seven years old, and an artist. Already her pictures are thoughtful and detailed and she's not afraid of taking risks: cats shaped like hearts, people with feathers for hair, roses made entirely of concentric arcs. Does the man on the ceiling have anything to do with this?

I imagine him crawling into bed with my youngest son, whispering things into my son's ear, and suddenly my son's sweet character has changed forever.

I imagine him climbing the attic stairs and passing through the door to my teenage daughter's bedroom without making a sound, slipping over her sleeping form so gradually it's as if a car's headlights had passed and the shadows in the room had shifted and now the man from the ceiling is kissing my daughter and infecting her with a yearning she'll never be rid of.

I imagine him flying out of the house altogether, leaving behind a shadow of his shadow who is no less dangerous than he is, flying away from our house to find our troubled oldest son, filling his head with thoughts he won't be able to control, filling his brain with hallucinations he won't have to induce, imprisoning him forever where he is now imprisoned.

I imagine the young man who is not quite our son and is far more than our friend, who lives much of the time in some other reality, who wants so desperately to believe himself alien, chosen, destined to change the world by sheer virtue of the fact that he is so lonely. He hears voices—I wonder if the voices in his head help him ignore his man on the ceiling, or if they are the voices of the man on the ceiling.

Every night since that first night the man on the ceiling climbed down, I have followed him all evening like this: in my dreams, or sitting up in bed, or resting in a chair, or poised in front of a computer screen typing obsessively, waiting for him to reveal himself through my words.

Our teenage daughter has night terrors. I suspect she always has. When she came to us a tiny and terrified seven-year-old, I think the terrors were everywhere, day and night.

Now she's sixteen, and she's still afraid of many things. Her strength, her wisdom beyond her years, is in going toward what frightens her. I watch her do that, and I am amazed. She worries, for instance, about serial killers, and so she's read every book she could find about Ted Bundy, every article about Jeffrey Dahmer, read and re-read every book. She's afraid of death, partly because it's seductive, and so she wants to be a mortician or a forensic photographer—get inside death, see what makes a dead body dead, record the evidence. Go as close to the fear as you can. Go as close to the monster. Know it. Claim it. Name it. Take it in.

She's afraid of love, and so she falls in love. Often and deeply.

Her night terrors now most often take the form of a faceless lady who stands by her bed and intends to kill her, tries to steal her breath the way they used to say cats would do if you let them near the crib. The lady doesn't disappear even when our daughter wakes herself up, sits up in bed and turns on the light.

Our daughter wanted something alive to sleep with. The cats betrayed her, wouldn't be confined to her room. So we got her a dog. Ezra was abandoned, too, or lost and never found, and he's far more worried than she is, which I don't think she thought possible. He sleeps with her. He sleeps under her covers. He would sleep on her pillow, covering her face, if she'd let him, and she would let him if she could breathe.

She says the lady hasn't come once since Ezra has been here.

I don't know if Ezra will keep the night terrors away forever. But, if she trusts him, he'll let her know whether the lady is real. That's no small gift.

Our daughter is afraid of many things, and saddened by many things. She accepts pain better than most people, takes in pain. I think that now her challenge, her adventure, is to learn to accept happiness. That's scary.

So maybe the lady at the end of her bed doesn't intend to kill her after all. Maybe she intends to teach her how to take in happiness.

Which is, I guess, a kind of death.

I know that the lady beside my daughter's bed is real, but this is not something I have yet chosen to share with my daughter. I have seen this lady in my own night terrors when I was a teenager, just as I saw the devil in my bedroom one night in the form of a giant goat, six feet tall at the shoulder. I sat up in my bed and stared at its great, humanoid, blood-shot eyes and watched as the goat's body disappeared slowly, one layer of hair and skin at a time, leaving those giant human eyes, the eyes of the devil, suspended in mid-air where they remained for several minutes while I gasped for a scream that would not come.

I had night terrors for years until I began experimenting with dream control and learned to extend myself directly into a dream where I could rearrange its pieces and have things happen the way I wanted them to happen. Sometimes when I write now it almost seems as if I'm in the midst of this extended night terror and I'm frantically using powers of the imagination I'm not even sure belong to me to arrange the pieces and make everything turn out the way it should, or at least the way I think it was meant to be.

I might wonder if the man on the ceiling is just another night terror. If so I should have the necessary tools to stop him in his tracks, or at least to divert him.

But I've followed the man on the ceiling night after night. I've seen what he does to my wife and children. And he's already carried one of our children away.

Remember what I said in the beginning. Everything we're telling you here is true.

I follow the man on the ceiling around the attic of our house, my flashlight burning off pieces of his body which grow back as soon as he moves beyond the beam. I chase him down three flights of stairs into our basement where he hides in the laundry. My hands turn into frantic paddles which scatter the clothes and I'm already thinking about how I'm going to explain the mess to Melanie in the morning when he slips like a pool of oil under my feet and out to other corners of the basement where my children keep their toys. I imagine the edge of his cheek in an oversized doll, his amazingly sharp fingers under the hoods of my son's Matchbox cars.

But the man on the ceiling is a story and I know something about stories. One day I know I will figure out just what this man on the ceiling is "about." He's a character in the dream of our lives and as a character I know he can be changed or killed.

It always makes me cranky to be asked what a story is "about," or who my characters "are." If I could tell you, I wouldn't have to write them.

Often I write about people I don't understand, ways of being in the world that baffle me. I want to know how people make sense of things, what they say to themselves, how they live. How they name themselves to themselves.

Because life is hard. Even when it's wonderful, even when it's beautiful— which it is a lot of the time—it's *hard*. Sometimes I don't know how any of us makes it through the day. Or the night.

The world has in it: children who are hurt or killed by their parents, who would say they do it out of love. Children whose beloved fathers, uncles, brothers, cousins, mothers love them, too, fall in love with them, say anything we do to each other's bodies is okay because we love each other, but don't tell anybody because then I'll go to jail and then I won't love you anymore.

Perverted love.

The world also has in it: children whose only chance to grow up is in prison, because they're afraid to trust love on the outside. Children who die, no matter how much you love them.

Impotent love.

And the world also has in it: werewolves, whose unclaimed rage transforms them into something not human but also not inhuman (modern psychiatry sometimes finds the bestial "alter" in the multiple personality). Vampires, whose need to *experience* is so unbridled that they suck other people dry and are still not satisfied. Zombies, the chronically insulated, people who will not feel anything because they will not feel pain. Ghosts.

I write in order to understand these things. I write dark fantasy because it helps me see how to live in a world with monsters.

But one day last week, transferring at a crowded and cold downtown bus stop, late as usual, I was searching irritably in my purse for my bus pass, which was not there, and then for no reason and certainly without conscious intent my gaze abruptly lifted and followed the upswept lines of the pearly glass building across the street, up, up, into the Colorado-blue sky, and it was *beautiful*. It was transcendently beautiful. An epiphany. A momentary breakthrough into the dimension of the divine.

That's why I write, too. To stay available for breakthroughs into the dimension of the divine. Which happen in this world all the time.

I think I always write about love.

I married Melanie because she uses words like "divine" and "transcendent" in everyday conversation. I love that about her. It scares me, and it embarrasses me sometimes, but still I love that about her. I was a secretive and frightened male, perhaps like most males, when I met her. And now sometimes even I will use a word like "transcendent." I'm still working on "divine."

And *sometimes* I write about love. Certainly I love all my characters, miserable lot though they may be. (Another writer once asked me why I wrote about "nebbishes." I told him I wanted to write about "the common man.") Sometimes I even love the man on the ceiling, as much as I hate him, because of all the things he enables me to see. Each evening, carrying my flashlight, I follow him through all the dark rooms of my life. He doesn't need a light because he has learned these rooms so well and because he carries his own light; if you'll look at him carefully you'll notice that his grin glows in the night. I follow him because I need to understand him. I follow him because he always has something new to show me.

One night I followed him into a far corner of our attic. Apparently this was where he slept when he wasn't clinging to our ceiling or prowling our children's rooms. He had made himself a nest out of old photos chewed up and their emulsions spit out into a paste to hold together bits of outgrown clothing and the gutted stuffings of our children's discarded dolls and teddy bears. He lay curled up, his great dark sides heaving.

I flashed the light on him. And then I saw his wings.

They were patchwork affairs, the separate sections molded out of burnt newspaper, ancient lingerie, metal road signs and fish nets, stitched together with shoelaces and Bubble Yum, glued and veined with tears, soot, and ash. The man on the ceiling turned his obsidian head and blew me a kiss of smoke.

I stood perfectly still with the light in my hand growing dimmer as he drained away its brightness. So the man on the ceiling was in fact an angel, a messenger between our worldly selves and—yes, I'll say it—the divine. And it bothered me that I hadn't recognized his angelic nature before. I should have known, because aren't ghosts nothing more than angels with wings of memory, and vampires angels with wings of blood?

Everything we're trying to tell you here is true.

And there are all kinds of truths to tell. There's the true story about how the man, the angel, on the ceiling killed my mother, and what I did with her body. There's the story about how my teenage daughter fell in love with the man on the ceiling and ran away with him and we didn't see her for weeks. There's the story about how I tried to *become* the man on the ceiling in order to understand him and ended up terrorizing my own children.

There are so many true stories to tell. So many possibilities.

There are so many stories to tell. I could tell this story:

Melanie smiled at the toddler standing up backwards in the seat in front of her. He wasn't holding onto anything, and his mouth rested dangerously on the metal bar across the back of the seat. His mother couldn't have been much more than seventeen, from what Melanie could see of her pug-nosed, rouged and sparkly-eye-shadowed, elaborately poufed profile; Melanie was hoping it was his big sister until she heard him call her, "Mama."

"Mama," he kept saying. "Mama. Mama." The girl ignored him. His prattle got increasingly louder and shriller until everyone on the bus was looking at him, except his mother, who had her head turned as far away from him as she could. She was cracking her gum.

The sunset was lovely, peach and purple and gray, made more lovely by the streaks of dirt on the bus windows and by the contrasting bright white dots of headlights and bright red dots of tail lights moving everywhere under it. When they passed slowly over the Valley Highway, Melanie saw that the lights were exquisite, and hardly moving at all.

"Mama! Mama! Ma*ma!*" The child swiveled clumsily toward his mother and reached out both hands for her just as the driver hit the brakes. The little boy toppled sideways and hit his mouth on the metal bar. A small spot of blood appeared on his lower lip. There was a moment of stunned silence from the child; his mother—still staring off away from him, earphones over her ears, still popping her gum rhythmically—obviously hadn't noticed what had happened.

Then he shrieked. At last disturbed, she whirled on him furiously, an epithet halfway out of her child-vamp mouth, but when she saw the blood on her son's face she collapsed into near-hysteria. Although she did hold him and wipe at his face with her long-nailed fingertips, it was clear that she didn't know what to do.

Melanie considered handing her a tissue, lecturing her about child safety, even—ridiculously—calling social services. But here was her stop. Fuming, she followed the lady with the shoulder-length white hair down the steps and out into the evening, which was tinted peach and purple and gray from the sunset of however dubious origin and, no less prettily, red and white from the Safeway sign.

———

The man on the ceiling laughs at me as he remains always just out of the reach of my understanding, floating above me on his layered wings, telling me about how, someday, everyone I love is going to die and how, after I die, no one is going to remember me no matter how much I write, how much I shamelessly reveal, brushing his sharp fingers against the wallpaper and leaving deep gouges in the walls. He rakes back the curtains and shows me the sky: peach and purple and gray like the colors of his eyes when he opens them, like the colors of his mouth, the colors of his tongue when he laughs even more loudly and heads for the open door of one of my children's rooms.

The white-haired woman was always on this bus. Always wore the same ankle-length red coat when it was cold enough to wear any coat at all. Grim-faced and always frowning, but with that crystalline hair falling softly over her shoulders. They always got off at the same stop, waited at the intersection for the light to change, walked together a block and a half until the lady turned into the Spanish-style stucco apartment building that had once been a church—it still had "Jesus Is the Light of the World" inscribed in an arc over one doorway and a pretty enclosed courtyard overlooked by tall windows shaped as if to hold stained glass. At that point, Melanie's house was still two blocks away, and she always just kept walking. She and the white-haired lady had never exchanged a word. Maybe someday she'd think how to start a conversation. Not tonight.

Tonight, like most nights, she just wanted to be *home*. Safe and patently loved in the hubbub of her family. Often, disbelieving, she would count to herself the number of discrete living creatures whose lives she shared, and she loved the changing totals: tonight it was Steve, and five kids, four cats, three dogs, even twenty-three plants. Exhausted from work, she could almost always count on being revitalized when she went home.

The man on the ceiling turns and screams at me. He screams until I feel my flesh beginning to shred. The man on the ceiling puts his razor-sharp fingers into my joints and twists and I clench my fists and bite the insides of my lips trying not to scream. The man on the ceiling grins and grins and grins. He sticks both hands into my belly and pulls out my organs and offers to tell me how long I have to live.

I tell him I don't want to know, and then he offers to tell me how long Melanie is going to live, how long each of my children is going to live.

The man on the ceiling crawls into my belly through the hole he has made and curls up inside himself to become a cancer resting against my spinal column. I can no longer walk and I fall to the ground.

The man on the ceiling rises into my throat and I can no longer speak. The man on the ceiling floats into my skull and I can no longer dream.

The man on the ceiling crawls out of my head, his sharp black heels piercing my tongue as he steps out of my mouth.

The man on the ceiling starts devouring our furniture a piece at a time, beating his great conglomerate wings in orgasmic frenzy, releasing tiny gifts of decay into the air.

How might I explain why supposedly good people could imagine such things? How might I explain how I could feel such passion for my wife and children, or for the simplest acts of living, when such creatures travel in packs through my dreams?

It is because the man on the ceiling is a true story that I find life infinitely interesting. It is because of such dark, transcendent angels in each of our houses that we are able to love. Because we must. Because it is all there is.

Daffodils were blooming around the porch of the little yellow house set down away from the sidewalk. Melanie stopped, amazed. They had not been there yesterday. Their scent lasted all the way to the corner.

She was so *lucky*. One year Steve had given her a five-foot-long, three-foot-high Valentine showing a huge flock of penguins, all of them alike, and out of the crowd two of them with pink hearts above their heads, and the caption: "I'm so glad we found each other." It was, of course, a miracle.

She crossed the street and entered her own block. The sunset was paling now, and the light was silvery down the street. A trick of the light made it look as though the hill on which her house sat was flattened. Melanie smiled and wondered what Matilda McCollum, who'd had the house built in 1898 and had the hill constructed so it would be grander than her sister's otherwise identical house across the way, would say to that. A huge, solid, sprawling, red-brick Victorian rooted in Engelmann ivy so expansive as to be just this side of overgrown, the house was majestic on its hill. Grand. Unshakable. Matilda had been right.

The man on the ceiling opens his mouth and begins eating the wall by the staircase. First he has to taste it. He rests the dark holes that have been drilled into his face for nostrils against the brittle flocked wallpaper and sniffs out decades worth of noise, conversation, and prayers. Then he slips his teeth over the edges and pulls it away from the wall, shoveling the crackling paper into his dark maw with fingers curved into claws. Tiny trains of silverfish drift down the exposed wall before the man on the ceiling devours them as well, then his abrasive tongue scoops out the crumbling plaster from the wooden lathe and minutes later he has started on the framing itself.

I watch as he sups on the dream of my life, powerless to stop him. Suddenly I am sixteen again and this life I have written for myself is all ahead of me, and impossibly out of reach.

Melanie was looking left at the catalpa tree between the sidewalk and the street, worrying as she did every spring that this time it really would never leaf out and she would discover that it was dead, had died over the winter and she hadn't known, had in fact always been secretly dead, when she turned right to go up the steps to her house. Stumbled. Almost fell. There were no steps. There was no hill.

She looked up. There was no house.

And she knew there never had been.

There never had been a family. She had never had children. She had somehow made up: sweet troubled Christopher, Mark who heard voices and saw the molecules dancing in tree trunks and most of the time was glad, Veronica of the magnificent chestnut hair and heart bursting painfully with love, Anthony whose laughter had been like seashells, Joe for whom the world was an endless adventure, Gabriella who knew how to go inside herself and knew to tell you what she was doing there: "I be calm."

She'd made up the golden cat Cinnabar, who would come to purr on her chest and ease the pain away. She'd made up the hoya plant that sent out improbable white flowers off a leafless woody stem too far into the dining room. She'd made up the rainbows on the kitchen walls from the prisms she hung in the south window.

She'd made up Steve.

There had never been love.

There had never been a miracle.

Angels. Our lives are filled with angels.

The man on the ceiling smiles in the midst of the emptiness, his wings beating heavily against the clouds, his teeth the color of the cold I am feeling now. Melanie used to worry so much when I went out late at night for milk, or ice cream for the both of us, that I'd need to call her from a phone booth if I thought I'd be longer than the forty-five minutes it took for her anxiety and her fantasies about all that can happen to people to kick in. Sometimes she fantasized about the police showing up at the door to let her know about the terrible accident I'd had, or sometimes I just didn't come back—I got the milk or the ice cream and I just kept on going.

I can't say that I was always helpful. Sometimes I'd tell her I *had* to come home because the ice cream would melt if I didn't get it into the freezer right away. I'm not sure that was very reassuring.

What I tried not to think about was what if I never could find my way home, what if things weren't as I'd left them. What if everything had changed? One night I got lost along the southern edge of the city after a late night movie and wandered for an hour or so convinced that my worst fantasies had come true.

The man on the ceiling smiles and begins devouring my dream of the sky.

A wise man asks me, when I've told him this story of my vanishing home again, "And then what?"

I glare at him. He's supposed to understand me. "What do you mean?"

"And then what happens? After you discover that your house and your family have disappeared?"

"Not disappeared," I point out irritably. "Have never existed."

"Yes. Have never existed. And then what happens?"

I've never thought of that. The never-having-existed seems final enough, awful enough. I can't think of anything to say, so I don't say anything, hoping he will. But he's wise, and he knows how to use silence. He just sits there, being calm, until finally I say, "I don't know."

"Maybe it would be interesting to find out," he suggests.

So we try. He eases me into a light trance; I'm eager and highly suggestible, and I trust this man, so my consciousness alters easily. He guides me through the fantasy again and again, using my own words and some of his own. But every time I stop at the point where I come home and there isn't any home. The point where I look up and my life, my love, isn't there. Has never existed.

I don't know what happens next. I can't imagine what happens next. Do I die? Does the man on the ceiling take me into his house? Does he fly away with me into an endless sky? Does he help me create another life, another miracle?

That's why I write. To find out what happens next.

So what happens next? This might happen:

After the man on the ceiling devours my life I imagine it back again: I fill in the walls, the doorways, the empty rooms with colors and furnishings different from, but similar to, the ones I imagine to have been there before. Our lives are full of angels of all kinds. So I call on some of those other angels to get my life back.

I write myself a life, and it is very different from the one I had before, and yet very much the same. I make different mistakes from the ones I made with my children before. I love Melanie the same way I did before. Different wonderful things happen. The same sad, wonderful events recur.

The man on the ceiling just smiles at me and makes of these new imaginings his dessert. So what happens next? In a different kind of story I might take out a machete and chop him into little bits of shadow. Or I might blast him into daylight with a machine gun. Or I might douse him with lighter fluid and set him on fire.

But I don't write those kinds of stories.

And besides, the man on the ceiling is a necessary angel.

There are so many truths to tell. There are so many different lives I could dream for myself.

What happens next?

There are so many stories to tell. I could tell this story:

The man from the ceiling was waiting for Melanie behind the fence (an ugly, bare, chain link and chicken wire fence, not the black wrought iron fence plaited with rosebushes that she'd made up), where her home had never existed. He beckoned to her. He called her by name, his own special name for her, a name she never got used to no matter how often he said it, which was often. He reached for her, trying to touch her but not quite touching.

She could have turned and run away from him. He wouldn't have chased her down. His arms wouldn't have telescoped long and impossibly jointed to capture her at the end of the block. His teeth wouldn't have pushed themselves out of his mouth in gigantic segmented fangs to cut her off at the knees, to bite her head off. He wouldn't have sucked her blood.

But he'd have kept calling her, using his special name for her. And he'd have scaled her windows, dropped down from her roof, crawled across her ceiling again that night, and every night for the rest of her life.

So Melanie went toward him. Held out her arms.

There are so many different dreams. That one was Melanie's. This one is mine:

I sit down at the kitchen table. The man on the ceiling lies on my plate, collapsed and folded up neatly in the center. I slice him into hundreds of oily little pieces which I put into my mouth one small morsel at a time. I bite through his patchwork wings. I gnaw on his inky heart. I chew his long, narrow fingers well. I make of him my daily meal of darkness.

There are so many stories to tell.

And all of the stories are true.

We wait for whatever happens next.
  We stay available.
  We name it to make it real.

It was hard for us to write this piece.
  For one thing, we write differently. My stories tend more toward magical realism, Steve's more toward surrealism. Realism, in both cases, but we argued over form: "This isn't a story! It doesn't have a plot!"

"What do you want from a plot? Important things happen, and it *does* move from A to B."
  In our fiction, Melanie's monsters usually are ultimately either vanquished or accepted, while at the end of my stories you often find out that the darkness in one form or another lives on and on. There's no escaping it, and I question whether you should try to escape it in the first place.

In life, our respective monsters often behave in the reverse. Steve accepts his; I'm afraid of mine. Since words can only approximate both the monsters and the vanquishment, we wrote each other worried notes in the margins of this story.

"I don't know if we can really use the word 'divine.' "

"If someone looked inside your dreams, would they really see only darkness?"

It was hard for us to write this piece.
  "This upsets me," Melanie would say.

Steve would nod. "Maybe we can't do this."
  "Oh, we have to." I'd insist. "We've gone too far to stop now. I want to see what happens."
  This piece is about writing and horror and fear and about love. We're utterly separate from each other, of course, yet there's a country we share, a rich and wonderful place, a *divine* place, and we create it by naming *all* of its parts, *all* of the angels and *all* of the demons who live there with us.

What happens next?
  There are so many stories to tell.
  We could tell another story:

TERRY LAMSLEY

Climbing Down from Heaven

Terry Lamsley spent most of his childhood in the south of England but has been living in Buxton, in Derbyshire, where many of his stories are set, for almost twenty years. He works with disturbed adolescents and their families. His stories have been published in All Hallows, Cemetery Dance, Ghosts & Scholars, Midnight Never Comes, Dark Terrors: The Gollancz Book of Horror, *and* Lethal Kisses *and have been reprinted in* Best New Horror *and* The Year's Best Fantasy and Horror. *His self-published collection* Under the Crust, *was nominated for the World Fantasy Award and the title novella won the award in 1994. Ash-Tree Press reprinted* Under the Crust *and his two subsequent collections,* Conference With the Dead *and* Dark Matters, *the latter of which supplied this strange tale.*

—E. D.

> It's all this smell of cooped-up angels
> Worries me.
> CHRISTOPHER FRY
> A SLEEP OF PRISONERS

While she was up in her room making her bed Millie noticed she had not replaced the cover on the lens of her telescope the previous night. The sky had been particularly clear and God alone knew what time it had been when she had finally managed to turn away from her contemplation of the heavens. She must have been exhausted, or in some kind of star-struck trance, when she had finally gone to bed, as she had no recollection of climbing in between the sheets. She flicked, with the tip of a tissue, the few motes of dust she imagined might have settled on the lens during the few hours it had been exposed, took up the lens cover, and carefully screwed it in place. Normally, when not in use, she kept the telescope shrouded under a silky black sheet, but the forecast was for clear skies for the night to come, and she hoped to be able to take advantage of this dark window of opportunity.

Also, it pleased her, occasionally, to leave the thing uncovered. The matt black metal tube set on its gray tripod had sculptural qualities that appealed to her, and that aroused welcome, if somewhat melancholy, thoughts of her father. The telescope, along with a half dozen star-charts he had drawn for her when she had been very little, were all she had to remember him by: indeed, these items, along with a couple of monochromatic snapshots of the man, now in the possession of Millie's sister, and taken by the unsteady hand of their mother on a cheap camera, were pretty much all that remained to prove he had existed. He had died alone and abroad a long time ago.

"It brings the stars down very close, Millie," he had explained, when he had first allowed her to use the telescope. She had been so tiny at the time she had had to stand on tiptoe to see through the eyepiece. As her father showed her how to focus, he said, "When you've had a good look at whatever star interests you most, and you've seen enough, it goes back up into its place in the sky again as soon as you take your eye away from the lens." When she witnessed the effects of magnification this appeared to be true and made sense to Millie, and for years she was under the impression that she could tamper with the fabric of the universe, pluck the stars down out of the heavens at will, trap them in the tube of the instrument for inspection, and send them back to their rightful place in the vault of heaven as soon as she got bored with them. Sometimes, in those far-off days, as she gazed up through the telescope, she had, to her distress, experienced a reversal of this sensation, and felt as though she had been wrenched up off the earth into the sky to be closer to the stars. It alarmed her greatly to find herself drawn so suddenly into the remote, black emptiness where she then found herself, but release was easily and instantly achievable: she had only to close her eyes, or take a step backward, to bring herself down to earth again. And occasionally she felt very peculiar and uncomfortable indeed, because she wondered if she was looking up through the telescope at the stars, or if they were looking down (or up) the instrument at her.

Later, when at school she had been given a better understanding of the scientific principles involved, she had felt foolish and been angry with her father for deceiving her about something so fundamental, but by that time he was not around to defend what must, at the time, have seemed to him to be nothing more than a harmless and amusing fantasy.

Millie sighed and patted the top of the telescope affectionately as though it were a dozing pet. To keep the instrument out of the possibly harmful rays of glaring sunlight streaming into the room she pulled it further back from the window through which it had been aimed and, as she did so, noticed movement in the garden of the house next door. That, in itself, was highly unusual.

A large van was parked close to the front gate and a team of overalled men was unloading it. There was a great deal of activity, but it was hard to see exactly what was going on through the branches of the intervening trees. After a while myopic Millie pulled up a chair, took the cap off the lens of the telescope again, swung its barrel down and around, made a few further adjustments, and squinted through it with her right eye.

What she was then able to see kept her intrigued for hours, until it was time to prepare the evening meal.

———

Harriet placed her briefcase carefully in the center of a table near the front door as soon as she got back from work, nodded to her sister, poured herself a neat, but modest, gin, and sat a while in silent contemplation of the day's events. Millie had no way of telling, from her expressionless face and closed eyes, if Harriet was pleased with herself and the way things had gone or not, and she knew better than to ask. Instead, she broke the silence with a statement of fact that she considered to be of significance to them both.

"Someone has moved in next door at last."

Harriet cocked an eye at her.

"A *man*," Millie added.

"Single?"

"There was no sign of a wife."

"What's he like?"

"Not like Ruggles."

Mr. and Mrs. Ruggles had been their previous neighbors. They had thrown frequent, long, tumultuous parties, with live bands playing on their patio. Their children had run wild. The police had raided the house a number of times. In the end, Mrs. Ruggles had died of a drug overdose and Mr. Ruggles removed what was left of his large family to Spain. Their over-priced house had been empty for more than two years.

"Did you get a chance to meet him?" Harriet asked.

"I only saw him from the window, while men were unloading various vans."

"Is his furniture good?"

"Couldn't say. He didn't have much, and everything was in boxes."

"*Everything?*"

"In cardboard boxes. He must have bought new things straight from the shops."

"How peculiar."

"Oh, except for a huge mirror. Antique, I think, with an ornate gold frame. That was delivered last of all."

"Sounds as though he may be a bit—eccentric," Harriet said, with an edge of distaste.

"He was smartly dressed."

"Hmm." Harriet was unconvinced. "I suppose that's something. More than could have been said about Ruggles. But what about the mirror? Sounds as though it might be valuable. You'd have thought he'd have taken more care to protect it. The sort of thing most likely to get damaged when you're moving house."

"True," Millie agreed, "but, as far as I could see, the delivery men treated it with *particular* care. Our new neighbor made sure of that." She glanced up as the fingers of the clock on the wall marked the hour. "Your meal's ready now, Harriet," she announced dutifully.

"And I'm ready for it," Harriet said, climbing eagerly out of her chair.

Next morning, Millie had little appetite for breakfast. It was one of her two volunteering days, when she helped deliver lunch and comfort to housebound pensioners in the area, and this prospect made her apprehensive. She had recently become a volunteer helper because she thought by doing so she might meet interesting people and perhaps make friends with them. It hadn't worked out like that. She had met people as lonely and isolated as herself, and had not felt at ease in their company. She persisted, however, and kept up the "good work" as Harriet called it, because she felt any company was better than none, and she feared that, otherwise, she would become a hermit, with her sister providing her only contact with the human race.

Fifteen years earlier, when they had been in their late teens, the two very different-looking women, presently ignoring each other across the breakfast table, had often been mistaken for identical twins, though there was three years difference in their ages. Then, they had had similarly attractive, though not beautiful, and rather expressionless, faces, elegant figures, and identical masses of fair, unruly hair. Emotionally, too, they had been very close. They had seemed, to outsiders, somehow to share a single life, and some who knew them at that time found the intensity of their mutual dependence downright disturbing. They were considered cool and unapproachable and, some said, selfish and arrogant. Hardly anyone who knew the sisters at that time was aware of the childhood traumas that had welded the two girls so closely together.

On Millie's ninth birthday, when Harriet had been just six, their father told them he could no longer stand the company of their increasingly mad mother, and left them for good. They never saw him again. One afternoon a month later their mother sat and drank half a bottle of whiskey in front of them, kissed them both on the tops of their heads, then ran out into the garden and shut herself in the garage. The two girls, watching through the window, waited for her to return. Very soon there was a soft explosion, they saw smoke surging out from under the garage door, and the wooden building erupted into flames. Their mother had poured petrol over her head and flicked a lighter.

Millie and Harriet spent the rest of their childhood with foster parents—kindly people who loved and cared for them, but who never really understood how deeply they had been damaged, and who therefore never made any effort to render them whole and independent of each other.

Shortly after Millie was nineteen the sisters suffered a double bereavement when their foster parents drowned while on a boating holiday on the Norfolk Broads. Alone in the world again, the girls had to find some way to support themselves. In this, Harriet had been successful. She had the confidence and good fortune to get herself a job at an Estate Agency, and was swiftly promoted. At first Millie tried, and failed, to emulate her younger sister; then, perhaps due to her total lack of success, she became increasingly ill. Afflicted with various obscure complaints, she shriveled and aged, while Harriet became plump and prosperous. Though they stayed together, in as much as they continued to live together, they drifted far apart in many other ways.

Millie was by far the older of the two in appearance. Already, in her mid-thirties, she had some of the fragile, edgy manners of an old maid, while Harriet had the dapper air of a still quite young and rising executive.

"I'd like more coffee," Harriet announced quietly, without looking up from the documents on the table beside her empty breakfast plate. "And more toast."

Millie, the kept woman, promptly slid out of her chair. As she flitted about in the kitchen, filling her sister's order, half-remembered scraps from the edges of her dreams of the previous night flashed swiftly through her mind like subliminal messages—she caught glimpses of a man stepping back and forth, now making small but urgent motions with his upraised hand . . .

She turned on the radio to drive him away until the toast was done, and she could return to the company of her sister.

Harriet left for work at 8:35 and, as always, Millie drifted from room to room, obliterating the small signs of disorder left by her sister—used ashtrays, an out-of-place gin bottle and a couple of glasses, a clumsily folded copy of yesterday's newspaper—then cleared the remains of their meal and washed the dishes. All this took less than an hour, leaving her with twice that length of time to fill before she was to be collected and taken off on her do-gooding rounds.

She drifted upstairs to make the beds and took a disapproving look at the new neighbor's garden through her telescope. During the last two years it had become a chaotic wilderness. When the Ruggleses had been in residence they had at least kept their grounds in some kind of order. Since their departure everything had run wild.

At last, spurred on by the sight of this vegetative anarchy, Millie spent the rest of the empty period that morning mowing her own lawn, keenly shaving the short bright spears of newly sprouted emerald green grass down almost level with the soil.

Because two members of the team of volunteers were sick, Millie and her companion didn't finish their duties, distributing food and encouragement to the old and infirm, until after four in the afternoon. Normally, she was back home by two.

She was aware, as she walked up the front path to her house, of fresh and powerful scents in the air. New mown grass, of course, and other more pungent, sappy smells of cut wood and the darker aroma of recently turned soil. Following her nose, she crossed the lawn toward the tall hedge that divided and concealed her garden from her neighbor's, that had been such a blessing during the time of the Ruggleses' occupancy. It had not kept the young members of the family out, and even some of the adult guests had broken through from time to time, but it had shielded her and Harriet from the worst scenes of depravity they were sure were being enacted in the Ruggleses' grounds.

Because the Ruggles children had chosen a favorite place to break into the two sisters' garden, one bush in the hedge had been snapped off and finally uprooted, leaving a gap. Millie had replaced it with a new plant that had not prospered, so it was still possible to see into the garden next door through a narrow space in the hedge. She peered through it now, searching for the source of the rich scents, and saw, to her astonishment, that a large part of the new-comer's garden had been completely re-landscaped that day. During the com-paratively brief period she had been absent, the place had been transformed. The garden had been given a completely new layout and planted with flowers, shrubs, and even trees. Whole areas of soil had been dug over, turf had been neatly laid, and crazy-paved pathways had been set down to connect the various plots. It looked slightly unreal, like an exhibition at a horticultural show. She looked up at the house beyond the metamorphosed garden and saw a figure standing in one of the uncurtained upper story windows. It was the new owner of the house, and he was watching her, she was sure. Embarrassed, she was about to move away when the man lifted one hand to his shoulder, in an imperious gesture that Millie assumed meant he wanted her to remain where she was. Then he stepped back and vanished.

Obligingly, Millie waited until he emerged from somewhere at the back of the house and made his way swiftly toward her around the edges of one of the newly planted flower beds. Millie's first impression was that, close up and in profile, he was an ugly man. He had a big, forward-thrusting chin, a high forehead with a receding hairline, and a broken nose with a dent about an inch from its tip. When he swung around toward her she could see his broad mouth, square face, and dark, alarming eyes. Smiling rather fixedly, he strode the last few yards toward her.

"Eden H. Wychammer," he announced. "Pleased to meet you."

Wondering about the "H," Millie accepted the offered hand. She felt her fingers gripped slightly, then discarded. When she didn't respond to his verbal advance at once he turned up the intensity of his smile a few notches and said, "And you are . . . ?", increasing the confusion Millie always felt when confronted by someone new.

"Miss Malcolm," Millie squawked hastily, aware of her lack of suavity.

Eden H. Wychammer, who was the same height as Millie, tilted back his head and stared down his nose at her, as though this information was not enough. Millie saw that the line of his nose curved slightly to the left, but didn't look nearly as damaged as it did from the side. She noticed his lips were glossy and shiny, as though he had been eating oily food.

"*Millicent* Malcolm, that is," she said, over loudly, into the tight silence that had come between them. "I live here with my sister Harriet."

"I believe I saw your sister this morning, driving off in a blue Porsche."

"She works in the city."

"You are single women?"

"Yes."

"You both keep very busy?"

"My sister has a full life, but I have no employment," Millie said primly. Had he been spying on them already?

It seemed he had.

"You don't seem to waste a moment of your time however," Wychammer protested. "I saw you at work in your garden earlier, then you were whisked off somewhere as soon as you'd finished." When he saw Millie's expression, he said, "I couldn't help noticing. I was looking out for the landscape designer's team, which was due here first thing to do my garden. There was a hold-up. They were late."

Glad of the opportunity to turn the conversation away from herself and her circumstances, Millie looked beyond her neighbor and said, "They've done a remarkable job. The place was a jungle. I wouldn't have thought it possible to do so much in so short a time."

Wychammer turned to admire his garden. "You get what you pay for."

"It's odd that I saw no sign of anyone at work," Millie said.

Wychammer gave Millie a look that she thought may have been slightly contemptuous and said, "They are very—discreet."

"Very," Millie agreed. "Anyway, the new plants look healthy."

"Hand-picked from the best nurseries."

"It's impressive. It will look extremely beautiful when it matures."

"It's a start, nothing more," Wychammer said modestly, and his face took on a faraway, oddly tragic look.

Millie apologized for the state of the hedge between them, which on her side had grown spiky and unruly, and badly needed clipping. Wychammer offered to lend her his state-of-the-art trimmer, the use of which she accepted as a gesture of good neighborliness, though she was nervous of machines. He went to the house to fetch the thing, returned, and demonstrated how simple it was to operate. The device, that made a sharp, silvery sound as it cut, was, Millie had to admit, efficient, safe, and easy to handle.

Millie was forced to make her excuses and leave Mr. Wychammer. She had Harriet's evening meal to prepare, she explained.

"I look forward to meeting your sister," Wychammer said as they parted. "Perhaps the pair of you would like to call around sometime . . . ?" He held his head back and peered down his nose at her again. Millie found herself looking into his flared nostrils. She smiled inanely, then hurried away, holding the trimmer in her arms like a baby.

Wychammer watched her retreating figure for a few moments, nodded to himself once, then slid back through the gap into his own grounds.

"You mean you are quite happy to go there on your own?" Millie said.

Harriet, looking plump but elegant in her working clothes, crossed her legs, sat back in her chair, and sipped her gin. "Why not, if you won't come with me? He's not an ogre is he?"

"I shouldn't think so," Millie admitted.

"He didn't ogle your body with greedy, lustful eyes?"

"Not at all, no."

"Then I should be safe enough."

"I don't doubt your safety, Harriet," Millie said. "It isn't that. But I didn't find him an easy man to talk to."

"He was awkward?"

"The opposite. Very smooth. But rather distant. He made me feel uncomfortable."

"He sounds interesting, anyway. Is he good looking?"

"His appearance is striking, but not handsome."

"How old would you say he is?"

"Hard to say. Something makes me think he's older than he looks."

Harriet got up out of her seat and stretched. "And how old does he look?"

"Oh, about our age."

"I wonder what he does for a living."

"No idea. He is well off, though." Millie told Harriet about the miraculous metamorphosis of their neighbor's garden. "I saw no sign of gardeners and their equipment, or vans delivering plants. He said the workmen had been "discreet," but they must have been more than that. More like invisible."

Harriet was not particularly impressed. "Transformations of that kind take place all the time nowadays," she said. "I see them frequently in my line of work, when clients buy new homes. The world's changing faster than you imagine, Mill."

Millie gave her sister a pale, unhappy smile.

"Well," Harriet said, "it was right and polite of him to ask us round, and I don't see why I shouldn't take up the invitation at once; go and introduce myself, and take a look at him. Sure you won't come?"

"I'll stay and watch TV, if you don't mind. I've had a hard day."

Harriet snorted at this, but made no further comment. Minutes later, Millie heard her leave the house.

Millie was not in the habit of waiting up for her sister, who occasionally sought evening entertainment in Sheffield, more than twenty miles away, and was sometimes back very late. That evening, however, she found herself starting to listen out for Harriet's return at around ten o'clock, just an hour and a half after she had set out to call on their neighbor. Millie turned the volume on the TV down low, the better to hear the sound of a key turning in the front door; then, a little later, she suddenly switched the set off in the middle of a program she regularly watched, and sat for a long time, pensive and totally still, in the perfect silence of the house. Perhaps she dozed off, because when she next looked at the clock it read 23:45. This was not late for Harriet, but it was for Millie, who was normally in bed by eleven. She went to the kitchen, poured herself a glass of milk, then went upstairs and peered through her telescope at the house next door. She was surprised to see that lights were on in a number of rooms. None of the windows had been curtained yet: doors stood wide open, so Millie could penetrate deep into parts of the building. There was little obvious sign of occupancy, as all the rooms seemed empty, except for one on the ground floor at the front, where she could see dozens of the featureless boxes that had arrived with the house's new owner, stacked almost ceiling high over most of the floor. Harriet and Mr. Wychammer were nowhere to be seen, and Millie detected no movement anywhere in the house.

At last, reluctantly, she went to bed, turned off the light, and prepared to sleep, but soon found she could not. When she shut her eyes, parts of Mr. Wychammer's face hung on top of each other in her mind in alarming disorder. The man's nostrils, without the rest of his nose, were at the top of the heap, his eyes were at the bottom, and in between hung his oil-slicked lips, which seemed to be mouthing words she could not hear. At first, she made some effort to understand what was being said, but then thought better of it. She decided she didn't want to know. At this rejection, the topsy-turvy face began to fade and, at last, flicked out, leaving her with an empty, anxious feeling.

Her bedside clock showed 01:17 when she gave up trying to sleep, and made her way back down to the kitchen. As she passed the window she had looked through earlier, she noticed all the lights were still blazing in the house next door.

"Good God, Millie, what are you doing up at this time?"

Millie opened her eyes and saw her sister's face looming in front of her.

"I came down for something to eat." Millie indicated toward a half-eaten sandwich on a plate on the table beside her.

"That's most unlike you. I thought you were dead."

Millie felt caught out. "Sorry."

"You weren't waiting up for me, were you?"

'Of course not. I went to bed ages ago.' Millie touched the top of her nightdress under her dressing gown, as though presenting it as evidence. Millie noticed, now that she was fully awake, that her sister looked preoccupied. Her eyes were bright with some inner satisfaction. Elation, even.

As she made a pot of tea for them both, Millie asked Harriet for her impression of their new neighbor.

"Remarkable person," Harriet said. "A one-off. Never met anyone remotely like him."

"You approve, then?"

"*Approve?* I don't know what you mean by that. He's very interesting. And I like his attitude. So positive, enthusiastic."

"He certainly did seem that," Millie concurred. "I suppose he's more your sort of person than mine."

"You didn't like him, did you?"

"Not really."

"I found him fascinating."

This was strong talk from Harriet. Millie wondered if her sister was in love. "And not at all *eccentric?*" she asked, emphasizing the word Harriet had uttered with distaste during an earlier conversation on the subject.

Harriet gave her a sharp look, pursed her lips, and shook her head. "He is *unique*, if you like, but there's nothing wrong with that, is there?" she challenged. "After all, it wouldn't do for us all to be the same."

Millie, to her sister's annoyance, dared to smile at the banality of this ancient wisdom. For a while, they sipped their tea in silence.

As they climbed the stairs together, Millie tried Harriet with another question. "Did you find out what he does?"

"From his conversation, he's an expert in a number of things. He's very wide ranging. The type all sorts of people would go to for help."

"Do you mean he's some kind of guru?"

'Not in the pejorative sense, no. But he has written a few guide books.'

Millie stopped at the top of the stairs. "*Guide* books?"

"You know," Harriet said rather vaguely, as she moved toward her bedroom door. "Self help—personal development, that sort of thing."

It occurred to Millie that some kind of religious fanatic might have moved in next door.

It was almost three in the morning when Millie climbed into bed for the second time. Harriet had been with Mr. Wychammer for nearly six hours! A lot could have gone on between them in that time.

This thought, and others associated with it, meant Millie had a restless time of it for the remainder of the night.

Next morning, using Wychammer's clippers, Millie cut the long hedge around her garden in a couple of hours, a task that normally took all day. She had no idea how the machine worked, but she was naturally incurious about such things and assumed that, if Wychammer was half as clever as Harriet thought he was, he may well have invented it himself. When she had gathered up the severed twigs and leaves into a heap for a future bonfire she considered returning the clippers to their owner, but found she was disinclined to confront the man again so soon. After a moment of indecision, she carried the tool indoors and stored it away in a safe place.

The remainder of the day she fidgeted about the house doing nothing of consequence. All that evening she expected Harriet, who was still palpably glowing with the heat of her new preoccupation, to make some excuse to revisit Wychammer, but she never actually got to the point of doing so. She didn't even mention his name, which was a frustration to Millie, because there were a number of questions she wanted to ask about the man, though she was reluctant to raise the subject herself. The matter that most intrigued her was that, as far as she could see (she'd taken a peep through her telescope as soon as it had grown dark), though he kept lights burning all night in almost every room, their neighbor had done nothing to furnish the place, and had not, as far as she could tell, even begun to unpack any of his boxes.

Harriet, obviously feeling the effects of the previous late night, went to bed earlier than usual, and Millie did likewise. As she closed her eyes, she had a vision of her sister tiptoeing out of the house in the small hours to some tryst with Wychammer, but dismissed the notion as preposterous.

"I'm just slipping out for a while," Harriet announced, in an exaggeratedly casual way, halfway through the following evening. She had put on one of her most expensive and attractive dresses, not the sort of thing she would wear if she intended taking a crepuscular stroll down the local lanes.

"Will you be long?" Millie inquired.

"Not sure."

"I see."

"Don't wait up for me."

"Of course not," Millie protested, as if to do so would be to commit a crime.

Nevertheless, she lay awake a long time that night. Harriet had not returned when she fell asleep.

A horrible dream lingered on in Millie's mind long into the following day. In it, she had found herself in a vast ruined church-like building. She had spent some time trying to find a way out, but all the doors were held shut by heaps of broken masonry. Part of the roof, and much of the upper structure of the walls, had fallen, and well-established plants grew out of the many heaps of rubble. Millie, following her instinct for tidiness, began to trim back this wild growth with Mr. Wychammer's clippers, which she discovered she had brought with her. She stuck to this task for some time, but seemed to have made little difference to the general appearance of the place, and was beginning to experience a familiar sense of failure, when she heard a sound above her head, and looked up.

A rope had been lowered through one of the many circular holes in the roof, and Wychammer himself was climbing nimbly down it. Behind him followed Harriet, and Millie saw at once that her sister was terrified. Millie knew the reason for this: Harriet was extremely afraid of heights. Also, Harriet was shivering, because she was wearing just her underclothing, one of the brief, exotic sets she wore for certain special occasions, and the atmosphere inside the ancient building had, during the last few moments, gone icy cold.

When Wychammer reached the ground he nodded politely toward Millie, stepped back, and shouted advice to Harriet, telling her where to put her feet and hands. Harriet was so scared, she could hardly move at all, and Millie witnessed her agonizingly slow descent with painful concern. When, after what seemed a very long time, Harriet had almost reached the ground, Wychammer reached up, took hold of her leg, and told her to drop into his arms.

Millie grew furious at this, and screamed at Wychammer to take his hands off her sister but, if he heard her, he ignored her. When he was more or less carrying Harriet, he stared back up the rope, and Millie, doing likewise, saw that someone else was descending through the gap in the roof. It had gone much darker and it was impossible to see exactly what manner of being had now come into the "church." It was dressed in some long, loose garment that flapped around it like huge wings. It seemed to flow down and around the hanging rope in a violent, determined way—so much so that the lower few yards of the rope began to flick and crack around Wychammer and Harriet like a whip. To avoid this possible danger Wychammer began to carry Harriet toward one end of the building where, Millie realized, an altar had been prepared. When the person descending behind them detached itself from the ladder, he or she went in pursuit of them, and Millie followed after.

Some kind of ceremony took place then. It didn't look quite like a wedding, though it involved a ring. Someone, somewhere, began to chant. Millie, standing rooted to the spot behind the bulk of the third person to come down the rope, could make no sense of what was happening or being said. She called out to Harriet a number of times, but all three of the celebrants ignored her totally.

When the ring was produced, Harriet, her whole body shuddering with cold, shakily held out the middle finger of her left hand, and the person in front of Millie attempted to slip on the ring. It was obvious at once to Millie that it was too small, and she began thumping the back of the figure closest to her, protesting aloud that the ring would never fit. Nobody took any notice of her.

When Wychammer saw there was a problem with the ring, he took hold of it and began wrenching it down hard on Harriet's finger. The other person encouraged and assisted him.

Harriet cried out, but made no effort to remove her hand, even when beads of blood began to appear on the tip of her finger. Wychammer and the other person pushed and tugged even harder at the ring. By the time they had forced it into place, they had stripped Harriet's finger of skin to the bottom of the middle joint.

Blood began to flow down Harriet's uplifted arm to her elbow, from where it dripped to the floor. The figure that had been last down the rope reached for a little stone bottle chained around its neck, unstoppered it, and stooped to collect the falling blood. When the bottle was full the figure rose again, turned toward Millie for the first time, and held out its arms toward her.

As he moved his head up the hood fell back, but before she could see the person's face, Millie started running. She found she was heading toward a huge mirror lying flat on the floor, the surface of which rippled like water. Without hesitation she took a frantic dive into it, and moments later found herself thrashing around in the sticky-damp sheets of her sweat-soaked bed.

The impression made on Millie by the dream was so strong it still haunted her when she was preparing to set out to do her second session of voluntary work later that morning. She was eager to get out of the house and have something to do to occupy her mind. When the doorbell rang, she assumed the woman who picked her up and took her to work had come a little early, and hurried thankfully to the door.

Mr. Wychammer was standing on the step, clutching a thick book to his chest. Millie did not step back to let him in, as he seemed to expect her to. After dryly wishing Millie a good morning, Wychammer said. "Perhaps your sister told you to expect me?" in a way that suggested he realized Harriet had done nothing of the kind.

"No," Millie said, resisting an urge to close the door firmly in his face, to shut out the creature of her nightmare.

"I trust the instrument I lent you was of some use?" he said ingratiatingly.

"It was very effective, thank you."

"I have in my possession many other contraptions I could put at your disposal. Time- and energy-savers of various kinds to assist you in your daily work. You have only to ask."

Millie thought of the little catalogues that came unbidden through the letter box every few weeks, that offered dozens of unlikely and gimmicky household devices for sale by mail, and sniffed dismissively.

Wychammer looked uncomfortable holding the heavy book. "I told your sister I'd bring this round," he explained. "She must have forgotten to mention it."

"She doesn't read books."

"I assure you, Harriet expressed an interest in this one."

Not many people, Millie reflected, got on first name terms with her sister so quickly, in just a few days. She pointed to the table near the door, where Harriet placed her briefcase when she returned from work. "Put it there, please."

Wychammer edged past her, deposited the book, and looked around. He stepped forward to peer at a painting hanging on the wall. After stooping to give it a close inspection he gave a nod of approval, murmured, "Charming," and moved further down the hall to scrutinize another picture.

"He's in now," Millie thought. "How am I going to get him out?"

"You have nice things," Wychammer observed. "Are you a collector?"

"Everything is Harriet's. She owns the house and all it contains. I am totally dependent on her. I have no income. Never have had." Millie fancied she sounded sad and foolish.

"So I believe," Wychammer said.

Millie felt betrayed. Harriet had been talking to him about her. What else had she said?

The doorbell rang again. Wychammer turned toward the source of the sound with a look of resentment, as though the mellow chime pained his ears.

"I'm afraid I must ask you to leave," Millie said with relief. "Someone's come to take me away."

Wychammer didn't bother to hide his dissatisfaction. "That's unfortunate. I was beginning to enjoy our talk. I must call around again, sometime."

Millie failed to encourage this suggestion as she let her friend into the house. Moments later the two women followed Wychammer down the garden path.

"Who's your friend?" whispered Millie's companion.

"*Not* a friend, Jenny," Millie insisted. "A new neighbor."

"What a slimy looking sod," Jenny said.

"Is that how he strikes you?" Millie was delighted with her companion's acuity.

"I wouldn't want him living next to me. I'd move."

Millie found she wanted to laugh. "My sister seems to have become very fond of him."

"More fool her," Jenny said. Millie went straight to Wychammer's book when she returned home that afternoon, opened it, and riffled through the pages. It was called A *Place for Everyone*, and subtitled, *And Everyone in their Place* by Professor E. H. Wychammer.

"Professor of what?" Millie asked herself.

The blurb on the inside flap of the dust-jacket was enthusiastic in the extreme. "Polymath Professor Wychammer's cornucopia of advice and information is indispensable to anyone wishing to rise and prosper in today's demanding and stressful world," it proclaimed, after listing the man's virtues at length. Much more pompous, portentous nonsense followed.

A surge of irritation suffused Millie's mind. She felt furiously angry with the book and slammed it shut with both hands. The dull thump it made in the empty house reminded her briefly of the quiet explosion she had heard in the garage at the moment of her mother's self destruction, an event she recalled at least once every day.

Hastily, with an expression of sharp distaste distorting her features, she replaced the book and left it for Harriet to discover.

II

A week passed. The level of the gin in Harriet's bottle no longer sank at the rate of an inch a day, Millie noticed. Previously, for many years, measuring out her two or three evening tipples with clinical precision, as though they were fortifying medicine, Harriet had drunk a bottle of Gordon's in seven days. This abrupt adoption of abstinence was only the most obvious outward evidence of the changes in Harriet's life. For Millie, who knew her better than she knew herself, there were plenty of more subtle signs that her sister was going through some inner alteration. *Conversion* was the word Millie found most fitting to describe, in her own mind, this metamorphosis.

The sight of Harriet sitting at the dinner table long after the evening meal was over, poring over Wychammer's wretched book, and scribbling notes in a note-pad she had bought specially for the purpose, drove Millie to despair. At first, Harriet had attempted to get her sister to share her enthusiasm for the man and his work, but Millie's instinctive and, to Harriet, unreasonable rejection of both, was total. They came to the point where Millie shuddered at the mere mention of Wychammer's name, and she begged her sister to talk of something else.

Millie no longer felt secure in Harriet's house. She was losing her interest in star-gazing and only used her telescope to spy on her next-door neighbor. Worse still, she found she was becoming afraid of the dark, and subject to night fears. At first, she thought her dreams, most of which were visited by Wychammer in some guise or another, were the cause of this unease, even though she could only remember snatches of them. But in a couple of weeks she wasn't dreaming much because she was hardly sleeping, and spent the nights twisting in her bed, listening for Harriet's footsteps on the stairs.

It was Millie's volunteering day again, and she had never been so glad to get out of the house. She decided to confront her sister that evening about her relationship with Wychammer: she would talk to Harriet, even if Harriet wouldn't talk to her.

When it came to it, however, she noticed, to her surprise, that Harriet appeared to be sickly and off-color, and took pity on her. Like the coat of an out-of-condition cat, Harriet's dyed black hair looked dull and dank, and clung to her scalp. Her eyes had lost the extra brightness that had been noticeable recently, and she seemed awkward and out of sorts. Millie imagined her sister had even lost some weight.

By then, Millie was in the habit of scuttling upstairs at all times of the day to take a look at the property next door. Just before serving the evening meal she couldn't resist sneaking off again to her telescope. Through it, she was surprised to see a number of people in Wychammer's garden, wandering about casually, as though it were a public park. Some of them were even picnicking. The last rays of a lurid sunset were fading fast. Millie thought they would soon feel the chill, sitting there on the grass in the gathering dusk.

After dinner Harriet glanced up sharply from time to time and stared at the curtained windows. There seemed to be a lot of traffic on the normally quiet road outside the house, and car doors banged somewhere nearby. At each slam Harriet started and winced, as though her nerves were frazzled. At last, driven by curiosity, Millie left her, went up again to the first floor, and again peered through the telescope.

There were lights shining all through Wychammer's house. Strings of multi-colored bulbs, like Christmas decorations, hung in the newly planted trees along the front drive and in various places in the garden. In their bright illumination it was possible to count twenty or more cars parked nose to tail on the drive. Many more stretched along the road beyond. Others were arriving all the time. Their drivers sneaked past slowly, searching for parking space. Two large coaches pulled up outside Harriet's house as Millie watched. Streams of people disembarked and followed each other through Wychammer's front door, which stood welcomingly open. None of the passengers had any kind of luggage, Millie noticed, so presumably they had come for a meeting of short duration, or possibly some kind of party. The latter explanation of their presence seemed unlikely, as all Wychammer's guests were dressed rather formally, in dark, somber clothes. Millie did not get the impression they had come to let their hair down: they looked a sober, serious lot. Once inside the house they made their way purposefully toward particular rooms where they stood waiting patiently, not drifting about like party-goers. They acted as though they were under instructions. Millie saw Wychammer enter a couple of rooms, address a few words to the crowds there assembled, then quickly leave. It was obvious he was completely in charge of whatever was taking place.

Noises from the floor below alerted Millie to the fact that Harriet was leaving the house. Moments later she saw her sister, a slightly hunched and ungainly figure, like someone escaping furtively from a long, uncomfortable confinement, almost running along the drive toward the neighboring house. Millie could hear the crunch of her feet on the gravel. Harriet paused for a moment when she reached Wychammer's door step, straightened up, turned to take one glance behind her, as though to satisfy herself that she had not been followed, then marched deliberately into the building.

After a while Millie noticed that no more cars were arriving. Everything had gone still and quiet.

Then all the lights in the garden went out, and the front door of Wychammer's house slammed shut.

Millie was unable to witness what happened next, however, because the windows of the next door building gradually became opaque, as though the place was filling with steam. This phenomenon, more than anything else she had seen, greatly disturbed her. She shuddered and became afraid for her sister. And, she realized, for herself.

She remained where she was for a long time, gazing out but seeing nothing, her mind full of a multiplicity of apprehensions that demanded all her attention.

Next morning, Millie couldn't remember getting into bed. She had slept well, but too heavily. Her brain felt stodgy. She looked at the clock beside her and saw it was quite early, before seven.

She got up, looked out of the window, saw that all the vehicles that had been parked outside the night before had gone, then went and tapped on her sister's bedroom door. After a few long seconds of silence a voice she hardly recognized as Harriet's called out, "What do you want?"

For a moment Millie was speechless, because her sister sounded so strange. Her voice was high and constricted, like a record played a little too fast, and heard through a damaged speaker. Millie wanted to open the door but dared not without being invited to do so. Harriet was fanatical about protecting her own private space.

At last, Millie found herself telling a lie. "I wondered if you had called out to me," she said. "Something must have woken me early, and I couldn't think what else it could have been."

"I didn't hear anything."

"I'm sorry if I disturbed you."

"Perhaps you had a bad dream."

Millie was grateful for this possibility. Briefly, she wondered if the events of the past couple of weeks, since the arrival of their new neighbor, had all been merely a bad dream, but the sound of her sister's voice when she spoke again was enough to shatter this hope.

"Millie," Harriet said, "I'm—hurt. Fetch the first-aid box and leave it outside my door."

"Hurt!" Millie yelped, appalled. "How?"

"It's not serious. But I need a bandage."

Millie almost grabbed the door handle to force an entry into the room, but restrained herself. "I'll call a doctor."

"No," Harriet snapped. "I can manage on my own," she added. "Just do as I say. *Please*." There was more than pain in her voice, Millie realized, there was a note of embarrassment, humiliation even. She was begging.

"I'll get what you want," Millie said, and ran downstairs.

At first she couldn't remember where the first-aid box was stored. It took her a couple of minutes to locate it in the back of a little-used cupboard in the kitchen. In front of it on the shelf lay the hedge clipper that Wychammer had lent her, that she had also forgotten about, and should have returned. The shock of this discovery was almost sickening, as though she had come across something organic that had been left a long time to rot. The strange shining machine looked sinister as a human skull which, she realized, to some extent, it did resemble. She could not, at that moment, have brought herself to touch it. Avoiding even looking at it, she reached above it for the handle of the red box marked with a white cross, lifted it out, and ran with it to her sister's room. She knocked on the door and said, "I've got it."

"Leave it, Millie," Harriet said. "Go away. I'll bring it in myself."

"Harriet," Millie said, finding herself suddenly in tears. "What have you done? What's happened to you?"

"I don't want to talk about it." Harriet said.

Millie had always felt she was unable to do enough for her sister, who supported her with every material thing she needed in life, and was too independent to require much, except loyalty, in return. "But Harriet, I want to help you," she said miserably. "Please tell me what I can do."

"Go away," Harriet repeated.

Millie realized her sister was now standing close to her, just behind the door. The door opened a crack.

"Millie." Harriet's voice now had a wheedling tone. "You've done all you can. Thank you. Now leave me alone. Do what you normally do. Make breakfast."

Millie fled. Behind her, she heard Harriet step onto the landing and take the first-aid box into her room. When the door had closed behind Harriet, Millie stopped and looked back. Something glistened on the polished wooden floor. She retraced her steps and saw it was a little pool of blood, about an inch in diameter. She reached for some tissues in the pocket of her dressing-gown, stooped down, and blotted up the blood.

Inside her room Harriet cried out, presumably with pain.

Harriet came down for breakfast at the usual time and took her place at the table without speaking. Millie had her back to her when she entered the room, and found a number of unnecessary, but time consuming, things to do before she felt she could turn to face her sister. When they did finally confront each other, Millie was relieved to see that Harriet's features, at least, bore no signs of damage. Her expression was hard and tight, however. She looked ill, and the smile she attempted did not succeed. It was not until Harriet began to try to eat the food in front of her that Millie realized her sister only had the use of her right hand. The left one was resting on her lap, out of sight below the edge of the table. After disposing of her cereal in silence, Harriet came to a halt when she started to try to deal with bacon and eggs. She pushed the full plate away from her little way, then drank some of her coffee slowly, with exaggerated calmness, as though nothing was amiss.

Millie said, "Did you find what you needed?"

"In the first-aid box? Yes. Everything was in place. It's hardly ever been used."

"And your wound? I take it you've hurt your other hand?"

Harriet nodded, and lifted her almost empty cup to her lips, perhaps in an attempt to avoid having to make any further comment.

Millie wasn't going to let her get away with that. "Did the—accident—happen at our neighbor's house?" she asked. "I saw you going in there. I happened to be looking out of a window. . . ."

"Did I say anything about an accident?" Almost wearily, as though she was tired and her arm was heavy, Harriet lifted her left hand and placed it on the table beside her plate. Her fingers were bandaged inexpertly together. Only her thumb and the lower part of the back of her hand were visible.

"I assumed . . ." Millie's voice died on her.

Harriet shook her head. "Not an accident," she said.

Millie stared at the bandaged hand. Blood was seeping through the gauze at the tip of the fingers. She said, "Harriet, are you not going to tell me anything about what's happened?"

Harriet shook her head, got up, went into the hall, and picked up her briefcase.

Millie said, "Surely you are not going into work like that?"

"Why not?"

"You don't intend driving with your hand in that condition?"

For a moment Harriet looked nonplussed, as though the possible difficulty of doing this had not occurred to her. After a moment's deliberation, she dismissed the problems, "I'll manage," she said. "Don't worry."

As soon as Harriet had gone, Millie went to the cupboard where she had found the first-aid box and pulled out Wychammer's clipping machine. She stood inspecting the peculiar object for some minutes, turning it over and over in her hands absent-mindedly, as though her thoughts were on other things. Then she made up her mind, and left the house with the thing under her arm. She strode across the garden to the gap in the hedge that separated the grounds of the two houses and slipped through quickly. Becoming apprehensive as soon as her feet were on Wychammer's land, she forced herself forward through the recently planted shrubs and bushes, that were now thickly leaved and, in some cases, covered in blossom, as though they had been rooted there for years, then followed the mossy, seemingly ancient, but actually modern, crazy-paved pathway that wound around toward the side of the house. When she was within fifteen feet of the nearest window, Millie took advantage of the cover offered by a trellis of intertwined roses, and came to a halt. She peered around one end of the trellis so she could see through the window into the house. She was surprised to see that the window's wooden frame was very rotten, with most of the paint peeled off. It was hard to believe that the structure of the house had degenerated so much in two years since the Ruggleses had left. The room beyond the window was, as far as she could see, empty. There was an emerald green carpet on the floor, but no furniture of any kind anywhere. She realized that if she walked a few yards, to the far end of the trellis, she would get an even better view into another nearby window. She made her way toward it, keeping her head well down.

This room was not empty. A large, gilt-framed mirror, some six feet high by eight wide, rested against the opposite wall. The floor was covered with midnight blue carpet, and on this carpet danced Mr. Wychammer. He was swooping backward and forward with his hands held out in front of him, working his fingers all the while, bending them into complex shapes, as though sending messages to his own image in elaborate sign language. The image in the mirror was darker than the reality it imperfectly copied, and it took a few moments for Millie to realize that the reflection of Mr. Wychammer in the mirror was not mimicking his actions in an exact reverse copy of his movements, but had a life of its own. It did its own, slightly different, more lethargic dance. And the two of them *were* communicating somehow. Information of some kind was passing from one to the other. They were conversing.

Millie's hands, still clutching the machine, began to tremble. She realized Wychammer was not just a charismatic, powerful, dangerous, possibly evil man. She had underestimated him—he was much more than that.

The creature that was not quite a reflection wore clothes similar to Wychammer's, but its hands were hidden in long, wide sleeves and its head was partially covered by an antiquated looking headpiece that flopped down around its ears, and over the upper part of its face, like a cowl. Millie studied the half-concealed face and saw that it wasn't quite the same as Wychammer's because, as far as she could tell, the features were unmarked, the nose unbroken. It was more conventionally handsome, appealing even, and could have been Wychammer's younger brother.

With a final rather clumsy, windmilling gesture of its arms the figure in the mirror jerked to a halt and leaned sharply forward from the waist. Millie realized it was looking straight at her, that it could see her. Better, perhaps, than she could see it, because, without realizing, in an attempt to get a better look at the creature, she had stepped out from concealment behind the trellis. The second "Wychammer" stretched out a hand toward her and she saw the tip of a pointing finger emerge from a sleeve and reach forward toward the surface of the glass. At this, Wychammer himself, who had had his back toward Millie, turned casually around and stared blankly at her. His arms, caught in mid-gesture, held out beside him, could have expressed welcome or surprise, but in fact he seemed quite unperturbed to find Millie gazing back at him.

The second figure, that seemed more interested in her, stepped sluggishly forward until it was very close to the mirror. When he was standing just inches behind the glass, he opened his mouth and Millie saw he had many sharp little teeth. Crouching, giving her a slackjawed smile, he made movements that suggested to Millie that he was going to leap through the mirror and window toward her. She suspected he could do that; could pass through both sheets of glass without breaking either. She was about to turn and run when the thing made a sudden, possibly aggressive gesture toward her and, acting without thought of the consequences, she lifted Wychammer's machine above her head with both hands and flung it with all her strength toward the face of the grinning figure.

Then she ran. Behind her the window shattered: a noise that gave her a brief feeling of elation, and seemed to make running easier. She hurtled forward in a straight line toward the gap in the hedge, trampling through flower-beds, and kicking aside any plants that got in her way. She stumbled, but did not stop until she reached her own front door. Once there, as she searched for her key, she looked back the way she had come and saw she had not been followed.

Millie sat for some hours in her favorite chair, thinking a great deal but moving not at all, waiting for her sister. Harriet returned looking sicker than ever. She sneaked into the house at three in the afternoon and locked herself in her room without saying a word to Millie. Millie put food and drink outside her door, but this was a wasted gesture. Harriet did not respond in any way.

Millie left the door of her room open when she went to bed, so she would hear if Harriet started to move about, but she was not disturbed: the house remained silent that night.

Nevertheless, Harriet was nowhere to be found next morning.

Millie searched the house, furiously cursing Wychammer as she did so, then went to the kitchen. She jerked open the cutlery draw, pulled out a six-inch knife with a pointed blade that she used to prepare vegetables, and made it safe by wrapping it in a number of paper towels. Feeling ashamed and afraid, she hid the knife in the side pocket of her slacks. This almost certainly foolhardy action had slowed her down, and taken the edge off her anger. She now felt in better possession of herself. She marched out of the house and crossed the ground toward the house next door with determination and a sense of purpose, though in fact she had no idea what she was going to do or say to Wychammer if she could find him. She thought this time he might have gone, taking Harriet with him.

Wychammer must have seen her coming, because he was sauntering toward her as she slipped through the gap in the hedge. When she stood in front of him he held his head slightly up and back, as he had done during their first meeting. Again, he looked down his nose at her, giving the impression he was glaring down at her from a great height. Both remained still and silent for some moments. Millie was glad to find she was easily able to give him back as hard a stare as he gave her.

At last Millie said, "You know why I'm here. Take me to her."

Wychammer seemed to be expecting this instruction. He nodded and, without further comment, led her down an unfurnished, untidy hallway littered with discarded, screwed-up scraps of paper that she guessed were discarded leaflets of some kind. Wychammer kicked at some of these and sent them bowling along ahead of him, as a happy, heedless child might have done. There was other rubbish strewn about and, in a number of places, stains on the floor that could have been vomit or dried blood. The interior of the house was in uniformly poor condition. The air was full of unpleasant and, to Millie, unidentifiable smells. They went through a number of rooms, some of them scattered with now-empty cardboard boxes, until they came to the one where Wychammer had been when she had spied on him from the garden. She knew this because the window she had smashed had been hastily boarded up with wooden slats, and the huge mirror still rested against one of the walls. Otherwise, it was a featureless space, like all the others she had passed through in the house. As with those other rooms there was not a single item of furniture to be seen—not so much as a chair to sit on.

"What have you done with her?" Millie demanded, when Wychammer came to a halt close to the mirror. Her voice, echoing in the emptiness, sounded less confident now, and had a wheedling edge.

Wychammer said. "You'll soon see. I'll fetch her."

He walked toward the mirror, stooped down below the level of the top of the frame, which must have been a little less than six feet high, and stepped through the glass.

Millie gasped, and put her hand to her gaping mouth, but she had known what was about to happen as soon as Wychammer had turned away from her.

After some moments of trepidation, she went closer to the mirror and stared at the reflection of the room she was in. Her own image was not reproduced there. The only figure she could see was Wychammer, retreating toward the door through which they had entered together.

Less than a minute later Wychammer and Harriet appeared at the door in the reflection in the mirror and passed through it. Instinctively, Millie turned to glance behind her at the actual doorway, which was empty.

Somewhere, wherever he really was, Wychammer laughed softly.

Harriet looked pale, tired, wounded. She had lost much of the extra weight she had carried for years but this had not improved her appearance. She resembled a recuperating invalid: someone who had been half-starved and bedridden for weeks. Her hair was plastered flat against her skull and her chalky skin glistened with sweat. Without the fastidiously applied make-up she normally wore, her face looked flat, her features undefined.

Millie spoke her sister's name once querulously, but found she had nothing else to say. The sight of Harriet horrified her into silence.

Wychammer stretched his arm across Harriet's back in a familiar gesture and hugged her close to him. Harriet allowed herself to be mauled in this way and continued to regard Millie with empty, unresponsive eyes.

"Your sister has been very concerned about your welfare, Harriet," Wychammer said at last. "Please say something to calm her fears."

Harriet's body jerked slightly. The sides of her almost white lips parted slightly. She made clicking sounds in her throat before she said, "Don't trouble yourself about me. I don't need you anymore, Millie."

Harriet held up her right hand and unwound the bandage on her middle finger to reveal a bloody stump. The top joint had been severed.

Millie stared at the stump, then turned toward Wychammer, who nodded gravely.

"It was done at my request," he said, "but voluntarily."

"Why?"

"As a token of commitment."

"In return for what?"

"My patronage and protection," Wychammer said. "And a place by my side. Obviously."

"And are you happy with that bargain, Harriet?" Millie asked irritably. She was exasperated because she knew what the answer to the question would be.

"I want nothing else. There is nothing else for me now."

"You may have given yourself up," Millie said, "but what about me? How am I to live?"

At this, Wychammer let go of Harriet and said, "Other arrangements have been made for you."

He stepped through the mirror into the room where Millie was standing, leaving Harriet on the other side.

Millie heard his soft steps getting closer to her, and remembered that she was not altogether powerless. She turned to face him, sliding her hand into her pocket as she did so to grasp the handle of the knife she had brought with her. Millie wondered if she was strong enough to thrust the knife deep enough into his chest to reach his heart. She knew she could, and would, act. She longed for the sight of the creature's blood. Only physical frailty could let her down. The way to do it, she decided, was to lunge upward and force the blade in under his ribs.

Wychammer was watching her face curiously, and with some amusement. He had stopped three feet away from Millie, who needed him closer. She had wrapped the blade of the knife too well and found that, to withdraw it, she would first have to partly unravel its paper sheath. In doing so, fumbling in the tight space of her pocket, she ran her fingers against the blade. At first, the sensation was more alarming than painful, but even so, she was unable to re-press a yelp of distress that Wychammer misinterpreted as a cry of despair. He started to speak, perhaps to offer some kind of perverse consolation, and stepped toward her, until Millie judged he was close enough. She had the knife in her grasp now.

The sight of Millie's clenched fist as it arced up toward him was the first warning Wychammer had that he was being attacked. He made no effort to avoid the blow but swung his right hand around with such speed that, for a fraction of a second, it was invisible, then grabbed Millie's wrist and twisted it once. Millie shrieked, and dropped the knife. Wychammer stooped, caught the weapon by the handle before it hit the ground, and withdrew with it back into the mirror. Millie, driven to a fury beyond reason by Wychammer's contemptuous treatment of her, and the pain he had inflicted, threw herself after him.

The man in the mirror had half turned back toward her as she smashed against the silvered glass, which cracked from top to bottom, but did not shatter. Millie, who had not doubted she would be able to pass through as easily as her enemy had, bounced back like a migrating bird that had flown full tilt against a window pane, and collapsed on the floor. Stunned, she remained in that position until a slight sound alerted her to the possibility of further danger, and she pulled herself up and looked back at the mirror.

Wychammer was standing very close on the other side of the glass, reaching up with both hands toward the back of the upper section of the mirror's thick, heavy frame. His feet were wide apart, his knees slightly bent, his chest thrust forward. Millie understood what he was straining so hard to achieve when the top of the mirror began to dip toward her. As she tried to scuttle back away from it on her hands and knees she heard Wychammer give a wordless shout. Very soon after, the mirror smashed down on top of her.

The intensity of the subsequent pain mercifully drew her away into unconsciousness.

The sound of her own whimpering was the first thing Millie was able to identify when consciousness returned. She lay absolutely still for some time while she reconstructed the events that had led to her being where she now was. She realized she was lying face down on a filthy, stinking carpet covered with fragments of broken glass. She hauled herself up a little way from the ground and forced the top half of her body around into something like a sitting position. As she did so various sharp, agonizing sensations below her knees made her gasp.

The room she was in was darker than it had been, but she was just able to see that she was situated in the center of the frame of the shattered mirror. She lay down then, feeling exhausted and defeated. On her back, finding herself, perforce, gazing upward, she saw there was a mark like an uneven black disc on the ceiling directly above her. Its outline wavered slightly, as though her eyes were unable to keep it in focus.

She stared harder, trying to give greater definition to the dark shape but, as she did so, it seemed to move smoothly up, away from her. It sank into the ceiling and soon Millie found she was looking into a vertical tunnel, about five feet in width, that was stretching further and further away. The far end of it became increasingly dark. When, after perhaps ten minutes, this most remote part had become utterly black, one or two tiny dots of silvery light appeared, as though pinpricks had been made in its surface. Other light emerged in that vicinity, unevenly spaced, and shining with unequal brilliance. Millie watched this process in stunned wonder, realizing gradually that what she could see was a section of the sky, but not a part that she recognized.

Millie knew all about the stars. Her father had taught her to identify the major constellations and she had never forgotten those first lessons. She tried now to make sense of the circle of sky above her and fit it into what she knew of the layout of the universe, but was unable to do so. The spread of stars above shone in a different sky to the one she had studied in her childhood.

Awed and alarmed by this revelation, Millie forced herself to look away and tried to take stock of her immediate situation. What little light there was in the room seemed to be merely that of the stars that must have been shining down from a very remote part of the universe. She could just make out the outline of her hand when she held it, fingers outstretched, above her face. Some sensation, mostly of cold, had returned to her body that had been, for a while, insensate. She could hear nothing at all, not even the sound of her own breathing, but there was a curious taste in her mouth, and she was aware of a particularly foul smell in the air around her, that seemed somehow to be associated with the taste.

There was a tiny sound in the air above her, like the silky hissing of a snake. Up above her face something that had been descending slowly and unseen toward her came to a halt a foot or so away from her forehead. She reached up to touch it and realized that a thick rope was dangling down from the hole in the ceiling. She took hold of the rope with both hands and began to tug at it, passing hand over hand twice in order to pull herself partially upright. Hanging onto the rope like a drowning mariner who had been thrown a line, she wondered if, were the rope to be withdrawn, she would have the strength to keep a hold of it while she was lifted up into the unfamiliar section of heaven above, and decided, with absolute certainty, that she had not. If she were borne up, she would fall off very soon, and perhaps increase her injuries when she tumbled back into the frame down on earth.

Millie leaned back, already exhausted, and was about to let go of the rope's end when it seemed to come alive in her hand and was twitched violently out of her grasp.

There was a pause then, while the rope hovered, quite still again, above her head, for what could have been seconds or hours—her perception of the passing of time seemed to have deserted her, or become deranged. Then the tip of the rope started moving again, swaying swiftly from side to side, like the tail of an impatient dog.

It was fascinating, hypnotic, snake-like, the rope.

Its movements captured all Millie's attention, absorbed her completely in her semi-conscious state, and it was only very slowly and vaguely that the gesticulations of the rope became meaningful and significant. Gradually, however, she understood that someone was clambering toward her, climbing down from heaven. She could even, she fancied, make out, against the alien pattern of the stars, the outline of a fluidly mobile figure, dressed in some loose outfit, or in tattered rags, and still a long way above her, clinging to the rope.

After an unmeasurable expanse of time, she realized who was descending.

Who it had to be.

As she waited to receive him, to *welcome* him, now, she tried to move into a posture from which she could greet him and meet him face to face. To her great distress, as she forced herself to struggle from one cramped position to another, she was aware that the stench she had previously noticed in the air around her became stronger and more pungent, until it became thick enough almost to encase her and hinder her movements.

Nevertheless, she continued to twist listlessly about until at last, overwhelmed by exhaustion that it was an exquisite pleasure to succumb to, she gave up all effort and became still.

The rope continued to snap and sway above her motionless head. And motionless Millie was to remain until someone came to claim her.

He dropped nimbly down from the rope's end and took a brief look down at what was left of Millie. Then, slowly, scrupulously missing nothing, he gathered together, bit by bit, all there was of her. He threw the pieces into a sack made of skin he always carried with him beneath his robes, tied it tight at the neck, and swung the sack over his shoulder.

After refreshing himself from a little bottle chained around his neck, he carried Millie away to join her sister, who was waiting for her in the place they had both come from.

Where their mother still looked down at the petrol she had poured over her head and body.

Where their father still gazed up at the sky.

And where the stars look neither up nor down at anyone.

JACK CADY

Jeremiah

It is a pleasure to welcome Jack Cady back to the pages of The Year's Best
Fantasy and Horror, *particularly with a story as fine as the one that follows.
Like much of Cady's work, "Jeremiah" is set in contemporary rural America,
exploring the magic of community, communication, inspiration, and redemption.
Cady, whose work often has a subtle and distinctly American magical realist
bent, is the author of many novels and collections including* The Off Season,
Inagehi, Burning and Other Stories, The Night We Buried Road Dog, *and*
The Man Who Could Make Things Vanish. *He has also recently published
a nonfiction work,* The American Writer. *Cady has lived and worked all over
the United States, but currently makes his home in the Pacific Northwest.*

"Jeremiah" is reprinted from the September issue of The Magazine of
Fantasy & Science Fiction.

—*T. W.*

At the meeting of two secondary roads, Hell-Fer-Certain Church stands
like faded rag-tags left over from a cosmic yard sale. This once quiet
country church, with a single bell in the steeple, has virginal white paint
decorated with psychedelic shades of pink and orange and green; those
colors mixing with hard yellows and blues positive as bullhorns. For a short time
in the past this abandoned church was used by a commune.

In the tower beside the cracked bell dangles a loudspeaker that once broadcast
rock music, or called faithful flower-folk to seek renunciation of a world too
weird for young imaginings. Then the speaker died, insulation burned away, the
whole business one gigantic short circuit as sea wind wailed across the wires.

And the vivid paint, itself, faded before the wind and eternal rain that washes
this northwest Washington coast. Those of us who once congregated at the
church have dispersed, some to cemeteries to doze among worms, some to
boardrooms of corporations. And some, of course, have stayed in the neighborhood, too inept, or stoned, or unimaginative to leave; although in dark and mist-
ridden hours we sometimes recall young dreams.

Then, lately, the church added one more perturbed voice to its long history.

A new preacher drifted here from dingy urban streets. In the uncut grass of the front yard a reader-board began carrying messages. It advised passersby to atone, although around here folks show little in the way of serious transgression. They cheat at cards, sometimes, or drive drunk, or sleep with their neighbors' wives or husbands; and most shoot deer out of season. On the grand scale of things worth atoning, they don't have much to offer.

But the reader-board insisted that, without atonement, the wages of sin are one-way tickets to a medieval hell, ghastly, complete, and decorated with every anguish imagined by demonic zeal; seas of endless fire, the howl of demons, sacramental violence in the hands of an angry God.

And fire, we find—be it sacramental or not—has become part of our story.

On Sundays the new preacher stood in the doorway. Jeremiah is as faded as the faded paint on his church. His black suit and string tie are frayed, his white shirts are the only white shirts left in the county, and his sod-busting shoe-tops are barely brushed by frayed cuffs of pants a bit too short, having been "taken up" a time or two. He needed no loudspeaker or bullhorn as he stood preaching in the wind. When it comes to messages like "Woe Betide," Jeremiah had the appearance, vision, and voice of an old-time prophet predicting celestial flames and wails of lost souls—no amplification needed.

There are, in this valley, some who view Jeremiah and sneer. A few others value Sunday morning services. Many are too busy or drunk to care. Some are outright displeased. Rather than tell all opinions about Jeremiah, or lack of them, a cross-section of comments by some of the valley's main players seems appropriate:

Mac, skinny, balding, and fiftyish, runs Mac's Bar and was first to see Jeremiah arrive: "As long as he stays on his side of the road I treasure the jerk. There's a certain amusement factor."

Debbie, who is an artist, a barfly, a fading beauty, and thoughtful: "I've tried a lot of this-and-that in my time, but I never molested a preacher. Have I been missing something?"

Pop, gray and wiry and always sober, is a small-time pool and poker hustler: "Seems like he works purty hard for blamed little in the collection plate."

Sarah's religious beliefs, like her tie-dyed clothes, have followed currents of popular style. Through the years she has embraced Hari Krishna, the Pope, Buddha, Siddhartha, Mohammed, and Karl Jung, while mostly wearing Mother Hubbard styles. "It's the Lord's blessing has sent Jeremiah to us. Praise the Lord. Praise him!"

Not many people live here anymore. One of the secondary roads that meet at the church corner leads up from the sea. At the harbor are abandoned docks and fishing sheds where ghosts drift through fog-ridden afternoons. The buildings are huge, like a town abandoned by giants. Ghosts glide through mist, whisper like voices of mist, fade into mist when approached. We've gotten used to them. The ghosts threaten no one, except they seem so sad, the sadness of ghosts.

The other road leads through a flat valley where empty farmhouses lean into sea winds that rumble from the western coast. The houses are ramshackle. Shakes on roofs have blown away, and broken windows welcome the scouring wind. They are, themselves, ghosts; ghost houses that daily remind us of mournful matters; symbols of abandonment and failed plans.

What was once a valley of small dairy farms has been purchased farm-by-farm, and built into one huge corporation farm worked by only a few men. Our farms once had names: River View, Heather Hill, and a dozen others.

Now, cattle are bred, no longer for milk, but as blocks of meat. The valley has become a source of supply for a hamburger kingdom, a franchise that ships product to fast food joints in Seattle, Yokohama, and maybe, even, Beirut. The cattle, well adapted to wind that roughs their heavy coats, grow thick on hormones and valley grass. Then they are trucked to slaughter.

Across the road from Hell-Fer-Certain stands an old post office little larger than a postage stamp. Weathered benches in front of the post office serve loafers, or people waiting for a bus to Seattle. A country store stands next to the post office. Mac's Bar stands next to the store. If you visit the bar on a Saturday or Sunday night you'll swear this valley holds every old pickup truck in the world. People congregate at the bar to forget they are survivors of a failed place. No one farms anymore. No one fishes.

One important thing happens on Sunday night, and it draws the Sunday crowd. Cattle get restless as headlights and marker lights of trucks appear on two-lane macadam. The trucks, twenty or more, arrive in groups of two or three. They pull possum-belly trailers built like double-deckers so as to haul more beef. The truckers will not load live cattle until Monday morning, but by Sunday night the cattle already know something stinks. The beasts become uneasy. The cattle, bred for meat and not for brains, still have survival instincts. The herds cluster together, each beast jostling toward the middle of the herd where there is an illusion of safety. Bawling carries on the winds. The entire valley fills with sounds of terror.

Folks swear it's Jeremiah's preaching riles the cattle, but we know it isn't so. As trucks roll in, Sunday nights turn into Jeremiah's busy time. He stands before Hell-Fer-Certain and preaches above the wind. His string tie flutters like a banner, and his white and uncut hair is whirled by wind that carries the bawling of bovine fear.

With no place to go, and a twelve-hour layover, truck drivers drift to the bar and buy rounds. They're good enough lads, but they have steady employment and that gets resented. They generally come through the doorway of Mac's bent like fishhooks beneath the flood of prophecy coming from across the road. Jeremiah puts the fear of God in them. Plus, truck-driving builds a mighty thirst in a man. It's that combination causes them to stand so many drinks.

This, then, is the place we live. It is not the best place, not the worst, but it's ours; a small and slightly drunken spot on the Lord's green earth. It was never, until Jeremiah and Mac got into it, a place where anything titanic seemed likely. Then Jeremiah confounded Mac's hopes. He crossed the road.

It began on one of those rare August afternoons when mist blows away, sun covers the valley grass, and hides of cattle turn glossy with light. The macadam road dries from wet black to luminous gray. A few early drinkers stay away from Mac's, vowing not to get fuzzy until the return of ugly weather.

Mac busied himself stocking beer cases behind his polished oak bar. Polished mirrors behind the bar reflected a clutter of chairs and tables around a small dance floor. The mirrors pictured colorful beer signs, brushed pool tables, dart boards, and restroom doors that in early afternoons stand open to air out the stench of disinfectant. Either a reflection in the mirrors, or a silhouette in the sun-brightened doorway caused Mac to look up.

"Praise the Lord," said the silhouette. Then Jeremiah moved out of sunlight and into the shadow of the bar.

"All I needed," Mac said as if talking to himself, "was . . . ," and he squinted at Jeremiah, "this," and he squinted harder. Mac's balding dome shone like a small light in the shadowed bar. Although he's thin, he's muscular. At the time most of the working muscles were in his jaw. "You're a bad dream," Mac told Jeremiah. "You're the butt end of a bad joke. You're turnip pie. You're first cousin to a used-car salesman, and what's worse, you're in my bar."

Jeremiah looked around the joint, which stood empty except for Debbie, the artist-barfly. Debbie looked Jeremiah over with her blue and smiling eyes, brushed long hair back with one hand, and gave a practiced and seductive smile that went nowhere; although it would have worked on a truck driver.

"A customer is a customer," Jeremiah said, and he did not sound particularly righteous. "And it appears that you could use one." He stepped to the bar like a man with experience. "Soft drink," he said. "Water chaser." Seen beneath barlight, Jeremiah turned from a cartoon preacher into a real person. His face looked older than his body. His hair, not silver but white, hung beside wrinkled cheeks, pouchy eyelids, and a mouth that sagged a little on the right side; a mouth that had preached too many adjectives, or else the mouth of a man who had suffered a slight stroke. He looked at Debbie. "A woman as well found as yourself could make a success if she cleaned up her act." Jeremiah commandeered a barstool, pushed a dollar onto the bar, and sat.

"You want something," Mac told him. "What?"

"We'll get to it," Jeremiah said, "and for your own good I will shortly get to you." He slowly turned to look over the bar. "It will be a quiet afternoon." Beyond the windows a beat-up pickup pulled away from the post office. Across the road Hell-Fer-Certain Church stood in faded psychedelic colors.

"I believe in evolution," Debbie said, her interest suddenly piqued.

"Who doesn't," Jeremiah told her, "except that it didn't produce humans. It only produced Charles Darwin. You may wish to think about that."

Debbie, thoroughly confused, now found herself thoroughly fascinated. She tried to think.

Mac, on the other hand, was not confused. After all, Mac is a bartender. "You talk like a man who is sane," he told Jeremiah, "so what's your hustle?" Mac looked through the front windows at the church. He seemed to be remembering the loud prophecy, the dogmatic hollering, the Sunday nights of wind and truck engines and sermons. "You don't talk the way you should." Mac's voice sounded lame.

"It's a problem preachers have," Jeremiah told him. "The words we use are old, time-worn, water-smooth, and even, sometimes, decapitated. Our traditions are ancient, as are the symbols; crosses and lambs and towers of wrath. Plus, in today's world the volume on everything has been cranked higher. Would you pay attention to a quietly delivered message?"

Mac hesitated, wiped the counter with a bar rag, and seemed to remember younger days, days when people actually thought that they were thinking. "You just busted your own argument," Mac said. "I never paid attention before, but I'm hearing you now."

"In that case," Jeremiah told him, "we may proceed with your salvation, and possibly my own." His voice sounded firm, advisory, nearly scolding.

Medieval hells of fire and brimstone, according to Jeremiah, were problematic ("I honor the tradition.") but Hell, itself, was certain, either in this world or the next. "All versions of hell get boring, because even anguish wears out sooner or later. I care nothing for it."

Debbie looked at her small glass of chablis, pushed it two or three inches away from her, and sat more sad than confused. Debbie is not a bad artist, and she might have been great. These days she paints cute pictures for sale to tourists. Things happen. Life happens.

"Don't get me started talkin'." Mac's tone of voice said the opposite of his words. Mac used to be a thinker, but few abstractions ever make it to a bar. Bartending causes rust on the brain.

"Which is why my main interest is atonement, thus redemption." Jeremiah sipped at his soft drink, looked at the label on the can, and gave an honest but crooked grin from his sagging mouth. "This stuff is not exactly sacramental."

"It's such a pretty day," Debbie said, "it's such a pretty day." She retrieved her small purse from the bar, walked to the doorway, and stood framed in sunlight. Then she stepped into sunlight. She walked away, not briskly, but like one enchanted by a stroll in the sun.

"Handsome woman," said Jeremiah.

"Lost customer," said Mac.

"We'll speak again, and soon," Jeremiah promised. "Between then and now you may wish to ponder a question. How many differences, if any, are there between a preacher and a bartender?" He stood, gave a backward wave as he walked to the doorway, and stepped into sunlight. His shabby suit and clod-hopper shoes made him look like a distinguished bum, or an itinerant living on the bare edge of respectability.

The fabulous weather did not last. Mist rolled in from the coast. It was followed by rain. Hides of cattle turned glossy, and rain puddled in the churchyard of Hell-Fer-Certain. On next Sunday night, as trucks rolled in, Jeremiah performed like a champion, but with a different message. Anyone who paid the least attention understood that new images entered his calls for atonement. Instead of talking about lambs, he spoke of cattle. When speaking of heaven he no longer pictured streets of gold, but streets of opportunity. The image of the cross gave way to an image of the morning star. Hardly anyone gave two snips about images, but later on we would figure Jeremiah made changes in order to get Mac's attention.

And through the week, and through the next, it was Mac who changed the most, because (though no one knew it at the time) Mac tried to answer Jeremiah's question.

A good bartender is a precious sight, and Mac was always good. His instincts were quick, accurate, nearly cat-like. He knew when to be smart-mouthed, when to be glib, and when to be thoughtful. He never lost control of the bar, but now he went beyond control and even directed entertainment.

If bar talk slowed, or the pool tables stood empty, Mac resembled a school teacher introducing new subjects. Instead of baseball, used truck parts, and cattle, we found ourselves cussing and discussing local Indian legends. We talked about the fall of empires, Roman and American. We quibbled over histories of Franklin Roosevelt and Henry Ford. In only two little weeks Mac's Bar turned into an interesting place to congregate, and not simply a place to get stewed.

Conversation improved but beer-drinking slowed. Mac ran a highly enhanced bar, but made less money. For those who know him well, Mac seemed slightly confused but almost happy. Since no one around here has been really happy for a long, long time, we were confused as well.

Meanwhile, gray day followed gray day and life went on as usual. On the coast, mist cloaked the broken wharves, warehouses, and abandoned fish cannery. Ghosts whispered through mist, nearly indistinguishable from mist, we thought them ghosts of fishermen lost at sea, ghosts of fishing boats long drowned. Thus, from the coast to the fields, memories of work and order and dreams lay as sprawled as wreckage.

Those ghosts of the land, the abandoned houses, leaned before wind and seemed ready not to shriek, but groan. Cattle lined the fences beside the road. As they appeared through mist, the cattle looked ghostly; silvered black hides, pale white faces, bovine stares toward us, and toward the road that would shortly carry them to slaughter.

Then, on a Saturday afternoon when baseball should have been the topic, Mac looked across the bar, across to Hell-Fer-Certain, and said "What does he mean by atonement?"

"It's being sorry for screw-ups." Pop, our local hustler, leaned against the end of the bar nearest the pool tables. As afternoon progressed, and as beer built confidence among customers, one or another booze-hound would challenge Pop to dollar-a-game. Pop would clean the guy's clock, and his wallet. For the moment, though, Pop was free to talk. He is a short, graying man, usually taciturn.

"It's more than that," Debbie said. "I can feel sorry for screw-ups any old time I want." She sipped at her wine. Her eyes squinched a little, and sorrow entered her voice. "Come to think of it, I usually want. Sorry most days: . . ." She realized she was saying too much. She saw her reflection in the bar mirror, smoothed her hair with one hand, smoothed wrinkles on the sleeve of her blouse with the other.

"It's recognizing that you're out of sync with the universe." Sarah, granny skirts and all, attends Mac's Bar on Saturday afternoons. She would be happier in a sewing circle or a book discussion group, but she doesn't own a sewing machine and we don't have a library.

"Ninety days for drunk-and-disorderly. That's atonement." Pop looked down the bar where sat at least three customers who knew all about doing ninety days. "I rest my case."

"That's only punishment," Debbie whispered. Almost no one heard her.

Jeremiah next appeared at ten A.M. on a rainy Monday. Truck engines roared as truckers slowed for the intersection of roads, then caught a gear and started building revs. The possum-belly trailers were crowded with living beef standing silent as ghosts, the animals packed together and intimidated; the trucks rolling purgatories for beasts.

Mac and Sarah and Debbie opened the bar. Or rather, Mac opened the bar while Sarah made morning coffee and Debbie loafed. Mac brushed pool tables and cleaned rest rooms. Sarah drank coffee and watched the road. Sarah, who is nobody's mother, looks like she would do for the sainted mother of us all. Her face is sweet, her hair hangs in long braids, her figure is slightly dumpy. Her hands are workworn because she lives by cleaning houses of corporation people. If Sarah has a problem, and Sarah does, it's because she's a sucker for any new trend. She keeps ideas the way other people keep goldfish. Like goldfish, the ideas swim in all directions.

When Jeremiah entered the bar, rain glistened on his black suit and dripped from ends of his white hair. Wrinkles in his face looked like channels for rain. He sniffed the morning smells of the bar, stale tobacco, the stench of disinfectant. The smell of fresh coffee seemed to draw Jeremiah. He sat beside Sarah who was, at least for the moment, one of his parishioners.

"Praise the Lord," said Sarah.

"You got that right." Jeremiah gave a couple of sniffs and asked for coffee. He hunched above his coffee cup. His black suit made him look like a raven regarding road-kill. "Although," he said to Sarah, "if we must unceasingly praise the Lord, does that mean the Lord has an inferiority complex? If the Lord needs constant praise we may be dealing with a major case of insecurity."

Mac used a narrow broom to sweep between bar and barstools. Jeremiah's question stopped him. He shook his head. "I got to wonder whose side you're on?"

"I like you more positive." Sarah's voice did not tremble, but she seemed alarmed. "The Lord is supposed to let people feel safe, and stuff . . . like, no mystery stuff."

"Thank God for mysteries." Jeremiah's voice sounded nebulous as mist, although his words did not. "Life without mystery would be life without dreams. The universe would be dull indeed." Outside, at the intersection of roads, a truck engine roared as its driver revved, then caught a higher gear.

"For instance," and Jeremiah looked at Mac, not Sarah or Debbie, "do cattle dream? Does a young heifer or steer muse beyond that next mouthful of grass? Are there great cattle-questions? Better yet, are there herd dreams? Does the herd graze according to music tuned only to bovine ears?" Jeremiah's voice seemed not exactly sad, but he certainly was not joking.

"And do ghosts dream?" Jeremiah looked into mist, at the road that leads down to the sea. "A ghost may actually be a dream. After someone dies, maybe a leftover dream stands up and walks."

"Quit scaring me," Sarah whispered. She raised workworn hands to cover her ears.

"I hope to scare you, because faith may be as productive as doubt. Doubt asks questions and faith does not." Jeremiah's voice was not kind. He paused. "Is there some dread realm where human dreams and the dreams of cattle are appreciably the same?" He looked across the road at Hell-Fer-Certain. "If so, what does that say about all of us?"

At the time Sarah didn't get it, and Mac didn't either. Knowing Mac, though, it was a lead-pipe cinch he'd catch on sooner or later. He leaned against the bar. "Bartenders and preachers have a lot going," he told Jeremiah. "Both have something to sell, both exercise control over others, both serve as handy ears for the confessions of sinners." Mac grinned like a naughty three-year-old. "Both flip a certain amount of bull, and what they sell wears off after a good night's sleep."

"I'd fault your logic if it was worth my time." Jeremiah pushed his coffee away. "Also, I asked about difference, not similarity."

"My mistake." Mac sounded like a ten-year-old kid caught stealing nickels.

"Meanwhile, suppose a ghost really is a leftover dream?" Jeremiah stood, stretched, looked through the windows at mist and rain. Then he looked at Mac with distaste, like a man regarding a favorite nephew arrested on a burglary rap. "You can think more clearly than you have."

"You know it," Mac said, "and I know it."

"When I was young," Jeremiah told him, "I wanted to change the world . . . wanted to make things better . . . figured to find a cure for common hatreds, ignorance, wanted to defeat war . . . prejudice . . ." He seemed as puzzled as Mac. He looked across the road at the fading colors of Hell-Fer-Certain. When he left the bar he walked slower than usual.

Atonement became the name of our game. Redemption became more than a word in a sermon. Our problem came because we didn't know what needed atoning. If anybody needed redemption it couldn't happen until we figured out our original foul-up.

But anyone with brains could see that Jeremiah made a bold if harsh play for the heart and soul of one man, Mac. Jeremiah seemed old as King Solomon, at least in experience, and maybe as wise. Being old, he knew he had little time left. What he'd said about wanting to change the world told us he wasn't fooling when he talked about dreams. We supposed if he couldn't change the world, he figured to change one man.

And, if Mac made less money, our local hustler, Pop, made more. As the bar became a place for interesting topics, guys stayed sober longer. Pop enjoyed a surge of prosperity because a good hustle depends on the full attention of the guy being hustled. Sober guys have longer attention spans. It was during a lull in sober conversation that an awful thing happened.

On a fog-bound afternoon when headlights on the road appeared as silver discs, and as fog muffled the sound of engines, Mac absent-mindedly drew a beer. He set it before a customer, and muttered to himself, "He's trying to figure out what happens when dreams fizzle . . . the death of dreams . . ."

Only Pop and Debbie heard. Debbie touched her wine glass, gave a dry little sob, and sat silent. Pop looked at Debbie, then at Mac. "You'd better not lay that one on the table," he whispered. "It will empty out the joint."

Mac emptied the bar, anyway. During the next hour he grew completely silent, then surly. If he was angry at himself and taking it out on customers, or his bar, or the universe, or on Jeremiah, no one could say. All we knew was that Mac was not jolly. As afternoon misted toward evening, customers stepped through the doorway into mist. By happy hour only Pop and Debbie remained. Bar neon glowed through mist like a token of sorrow, or like the subdued symbol of a small and unimportant corner of Hell.

"Everybody had big plans at one time or other." Pop murmured this, more to himself than to Debbie or Mac. "Time was when I didn't make a living with a pool cue." He looked at Mac in a kindly way, a way no one expects to see in a pool hustler. "We're gettin' old," Pop told Mac. "I guess we expected more . . ." He looked around the bar, at twirly beer lights and the green felt of pool tables. ". . . didn't expect more of the world, maybe. Expected more of ourselves."

"I'm headed home," Debbie whispered. "Art is not an illusion. I used to know that." She shrugged into her jacket and looked at the men. "Pay no attention. I don't understand it, either."

Fire struck our land during early morning hours. It drank deeply of wind, flared and flamed through mist like a maddened imp squalling in the middle of fields. It blasted the farmhouse of Indian Hill Farm.

Indian Hill's house stood ramshackle and wrecked a thousand yards from the road. As the first touch of dawn moved grayly above fields, fire towered and blew sideways, tongues of flame lapping at mist. Mist blew into the flames, mixed with flames, and steam exhaled from the very mouth of fire. Wind carried the fire, and fire flamed ascendent above wet fields. By full dawn, Indian Hill farmhouse lay as embers beneath a steady morning rain.

That first fire saddened us. Bar talk remembered people who once owned Indian Hill, their sons, daughters, cousins; even the name of their collie-shepherd mix, once known as the best cattle-herding dog in the valley. Bar talk remembered August days of cutting or baling hay, or of trucks pulling silver-colored tank trailers, making milk pick-ups at each valley farm. A drunk wrote "I miss you so goodam much," on the wall of the men's can, but Mac painted it over right away.

The cattle corporation uses the old barns to store equipment, even though the farmhouses are abandoned. The corporation brought in a bulldozer, cleaned up the burn site, and seeded it with grass. The bulldozer knocked down out-buildings. The old barn stood solitary in the middle of fields. It seemed a testament to memories.

The second fire took the house of Valley View Farm which stood behind a stubby lane, and up a little rise. That house had become a fearful thing. Because of the short lane, and the rise, the house brooded above the road like a specter. It was larger than most farmhouses, and two fanlights had once looked toward the road like colorful eyes. With abandonment the glass had been broken. The eyes stared toward the road, hollow as eyes of the blind.

This second fire was hard for us to talk away, think away, or drink away, It continued to flame in the minds of those who saw it (and most everyone did) long after rain washed ashes down the rise. The fire began just after nightfall on a Tuesday when the valley stood empty of tractor-trailers, of truckers, and re-duced by some few hundred cattle. As fire towered above the road, pickups pulled to the side, parked, and people talked or stared. Mist once more blew into flames, turned to steam, and steam blew across the road and into our faces. The stench of burning carried in the mist, but something worse walked to us.

Cattle were in the fields. Against all nature, the cattle drifted toward the fire. The herd formed a semicircle in the wind-blown mist. White faces of cattle stared through mist, were reddened by reflections from the fire. The cattle stared not at fire, but stared in ghostly illumination at the road where we stood helpless to affect events, and watched; where we spoke excitedly, or with sadness, or with but a murmur. The cattle seemed to stand as witness to our lives, their eyes blank as the blind eyes of the dying house.

The corporation bulldozed, seeded, and called the sheriff. One fire might be accidental. Two fires spelled arson. The sheriff went through motions, but couldn't see the point. After all, the houses were worthless.

"It's a trick question," Mac confided to Debbie on one of those afternoons when wind drops and fog gathers thick enough to hinder traffic. Across the road Hell-Fer-Certain stood in the fog like a ghost. "The difference between a bartender and a preacher is no difference at all."

"Because?"

"Because jobs have nothing to do with the basic guy." Mac looked around his bar like he saw it for the first time. "That preacher is not a beat-up church, and this bartender is not a bar. You got it?"

"If you came to that smart an answer," Debbie told him, "then it wasn't a trick question."

If Mac had changed, and if Jeremiah was using different images, Debbie changed as well. Although she told no one, images of fire occupied her, as did sadness. "There's a word called 'expiation,' " she said in a low voice. "I think we'll learn about it."

The third fire took Heather Hill Farm, and the fourth took River View. By then August was long past, September waning, as fall rains began in earnest. The valley filled with flame and steam. Cattle now grazed nearer the road, stood looking across fences in that dumb, animal manner that seems asking for explanation.

Then, on a night when the sky seemed to seep absolute darkness, as well as seeping rain, Debbie trudged toward the bar. Throughout the valley, as fires continued, sadness had become not only ordinary but a custom. We did not understand that it was not simply a few old houses being burned away. Symbolically, flame engulfed our history. People headed to the bar where night could not be defeated, but could be allayed. Neon signs colored our night world. Cone-lights above pool tables suggested focus and illumination. As Debbie passed the reader-board in front of Hell-Fer-Certain she sensed movement in the darkness. She gave a small, involuntary gasp.

"It's only me." Mac's voice sounded controlled, but fearful. "Pop is running the joint for an hour or two."

"You're standing in rain before a church that drives you nuts. Plus you've been acting spooky. Are you the arsonist?" Debbie hesitated, thought about fires and Mac's whereabouts. "You couldn't be unless you're setting them with a timer. You were behind the bar for two fires out of four."

Mac made a vague motion toward the church. "He is," Mac said.

"For the love of God." Jeremiah's voice came from darkness before the church. "For other loves as well."

"You're helping him?" Debbie asked Mac. She felt for a moment that she should flee. "What are you doing out here if you're not helping him?"

"Because I thought I liked the guy. Because I'm sicka selling beer. Because it isn't raining inside . . . how the hell do I know . . ." Mac's voice turned apologetic. ". . . sorry . . . I'm not sure why I'm here, but I am sure that hell is about to start popping. Look west."

Debbie turned. "You guys are scaring me. You are." In the west, like beginning sunset, a slight glow of orange showed at docks and cannery. "Mass fire, massive," Debbie whispered to herself. "If any of that goes, all of it goes."

"No water down there except what's in the ocean." Mac turned to where Jeremiah stood in darkness. "I reckon this is supposed to mean something?"

"I reckon it does." Jeremiah's voice did not sound preacherly, but grim. "Or maybe it's just a reckoning."

"Why are you doing this?" Debbie sensed Jeremiah's presence but could not find him in the darkness. Rain patted on her hooded parka. It puddled at her feet. "Everybody was getting by," she said. "Things aren't great but we were making it." She watched as the orange glow increased. "I won't cop on you," she whispered to Jeremiah, "or at least I guess I won't. But, you'd do well to have an explanation." She turned to Mac. "Everybody will be going down there pretty quick. Drive me."

Mac stood quiet, a man afraid, or maybe only indecisive. Debbie took his arm. She turned toward the darkness before the church. "Go ahead and tell me this is the will of the Lord," Debbie said to Jeremiah. "Then I'll know you're nuts." She walked toward Mac's pickup.

"Redemption by fire." Jeremiah's harsh whisper came from shadows before the church. "I don't think the Lord has much to do with it. You're an artist. Figure it out."

Immense fires, fires as big as cities burning, cast heat so huge they must warm the toes of heaven. Lesser fires, like the burning of a way of life, are localized, thus more spectacular.

By the time Mac and Debbie arrived, fire already covered docks and rose into the night through the roofs of warehouses. Sounds of burning, the crash of timbers, the roar of volcanic updrafts silenced the sounds of seawind and surf. Fire moved toward the enormous cannery as heat melted asphalt on the road between warehouses. When the road began to burn, a stench of petroleum mixed with dry smells of woodsmoke from flaming walls and floors; this while rain wept and blew across the scene, sizzled, pattered through mist.

Mac and Debbie stood halfway down a hill leading to the cannery. Heat coasted up the side of the hill and stopped their advance. Behind them, cresting the hill, headlights of old pickups pointed toward the fire as people arrived, the beams of light swallowed by fire. Firelight rose toward the scud of low-flying clouds, and black smoke crisscrossed through the light as heat mixed and churned the winds. As more and more people arrived headlights were switched off. People milled, clustered together, sought an illusion of unity, of safety. Fire swept into the broken doors of the cannery. Fire illuminated faces in the crowd. Firelight glowed orange on cheeks and hands. It glossed clothing with a sheen of red. Fire caused shadows, made eyes seem like hollows of night.

"Is this expiation?" Debbie whispered beneath the roar of fire. She watched as flame burst through the high roof of the cannery. Then, because it seemed nothing so awful could be a focus for good, she looked away, then gasped. She tried to turn, tried to look back up the hill, or at the wet and weeping heavens, or anywhere except where her gaze finally was forced to focus.

On the periphery of the fire vague movement began in blowing mist. At first the movement seemed only swirls of mist, then shapes began to coalesce. Shapes drifted like unimportant murmurs. Mist blew among them, seemed to offer substance, and the shapes became human figures drifting toward fire, unhesitating, herd-like and passive, not, after all, only the ghosts of fishermen drowned, but the ghosts of dreams summoned to the burning, dreams that like threatened beasts gave final screams, then fell into mute acceptance.

. . . and Debbie saw a young Mac bouncing a basketball while coaching kids, and a young Jeremiah standing before a mission school. Mostly, though, she saw a young woman sitting before canvas, saw the turn of a young wrist properly pointing a brush, sensing the depth of colors in the palette, saw a young woman alive with the high dreams of art; then watched the diminishing form of that young and lovely woman, a woman aspiring to creation, drift slowly, inexorably, to disappear into the roar of flames.

"I think," said Mac in a voice too husky to come from anything but tears, "that it's time to get the hell out."

"And I think," said Debbie, "that your expression is apt. But I'm not sure I like you anymore. Go back without me. I'll catch a ride." She managed to control her voice.

Climax and anticlimax. Fire swept across the scene in fountains and waves. When the cannery roof fell, machinery glowed red. Water pipes and steam pipes twisted, boilers stood like the crimson cauldrons of medieval hell, and people gradually stopped exclaiming, because nothing, it seems, can be remarkable forever. People climbed in their trucks, turned around, and told themselves and each other that what they really needed was a drink. The show was over, the festivities ended, a way of life had passed and no one even knew it.

Debbie, riding four-to-a-cab in a rickety pickup, looked beyond headlights and into mist. She felt slugged in the stomach. A glow stood in the sky.

To those who arrived from the destruction of the cannery, Hell-Fer-Certain Church burned as an afterthought. Flame lighted the inside of the church, and stained glass windows pictured scenes from Bible stories. Stained glass gradually fell away as heat melted lead, turned glass to powder when fire burst through to rise along the outside of the building. Psychedelic colors of pink and orange and green twisted beneath flame, turned brown, turned gray, and fell to ash. Fire roared to the top of the steeple where wind caused it to wave as a hellish flag. When the cracked bell and the broken loudspeaker fell from the steeple, only Debbie gave it more than passing thought.

As emotionally exhausted people drifted toward the bar, Debbie found she did not want a drink, did not want company, but did want to wring an explanation out of Jeremiah. And Jeremiah, it turned out, was not to be found.

Debbie looked toward Mac's bar, saw the glow of barlight, heard the loud voices of people with little information and large opinions. She turned back to the church and watched the last flames die to yellow flickers above coals. The flames licked feebly at mist, and Debbie became conscious that in the fields beyond Hell-Fer-Certain, herds lined the fences; cattle, white-faced, ghostly in the illumination from dying flames, and mute.

We woke, next day, bewildered. Dullness spread across the valley. It invaded our lives, or rather, seeped into our lives. We lived in a place where dreams had died, a world of rain and cattle and embers. It was a world stripped of sense, stripped even of ghosts, and we began to understand that hell need not be spectacular, only dull. At least that seemed true.

Debbie watched, wept, thought, and recorded in her journal this history of our destroyed world. With the eyes of an artist she watched herself in mirrors, saw drawn features, the high and accented cheekbones of age, the ravages, not of time, but of loss, and she despised Jeremiah. She listened as hatred flared among us, hot hatred because people wanted someone to blame. As guesses turned to rumor, then to conviction, it became obvious that it was Jeremiah who dealt in flame. People cursed his name. Men sought for him throughout the valley, and swore vengeance.

Our destroyed world, what had it been? Abandoned farms, abandoned fishery, and dregs of memory that recalled honest lives and loves. Many of us had come to this place in search of spiritual amity, of community; but all of that died long before the fires.

"But," Debbie said to Mac on a gray morning before the bar opened, "how much of this sits on our own shoulders?"

Mac, who since the fires had remained largely silent, did not answer. Debbie turned from him and watched Sarah, because Sarah's shock seemed deepest, bone-breaking deep. Sarah made coffee and muttered Bible-text about King Nebuchadnezzar who God changed to a beast ". . . that you shall be driven from among men, and your dwelling shall be with beasts of the field; you shall be made to eat grass like an ox, and you shall be wet with the dew of heaven. . . ." and then Sarah's voice whispered gabble, as though she spoke in tongues.

"The sumbitch rubbed our noses in our own lives." Mac moved like a tired man after a twelve-hour shift. Gray light crowded against windows of the bar in the same way that, beyond the burned church, cattle crowded fences. Mac picked up a broom, looked at it like he could not understand its use, then leaned it against the bar. He sat on a barstool and waited for coffee.

". . . and he was driven from among men, and did eat grass as oxen, and his body was wet with the dew of heaven, till his hairs were grown like eagles' *feathers*, and his nails like birds' *claws* . . ." Sarah's voice trembled with fear or ecstasy, and Debbie could not say which.

"That preacher drove himself," Mac said to Sarah, as if they were holding a normal conversation, "and he's driving us right now because he was serious, and we only think we are." He turned back to Debbie. "He's not in the fields. He's ashes. He's across the road right now, ashes in his burned church. I watched him set the fire. I walked away. He didn't." Mac turned back to Sarah. "He's preaching right now, if you listen you can hear . . . what do you hear? . . . or, maybe it's the voice out of the whirlwind . . . like in the book of Job."

It seemed to Debbie that, if Mac were not exhausted, he would be nearly as hysteric as Sarah. "I hear nothing from across the road," she said, "and if he chose to burn it's his expiation, not ours." Even though she detested Jeremiah, her mind filled with sorrow. Then she felt guilty without knowing why. And then, she felt something she could not at first understand. She had not felt joy in many a year.

She began to understand a little. Her first understanding was that she no longer despised Jeremiah. She fell silent. Listening. It seemed to her that from the fields came a sense of movement, the herd movement of cattle; and from the coast, echoes of screams.

"You're right about one thing," she told Mac. "He rubbed our noses in our own lives. Even if he's ashes, he's still doing it because nobody's leaving town. We're all still standing here, and we're unreal. We're staring over fences."

"The dreams were real," Mac whispered. "We're the husks of dreams." He looked across the road where white-faced cattle stood in mist. At the intersection of roads trucks slowed. An engine roared as a tractor-trailer driver caught a higher gear. Another engine roared. "Why did the guy do his own atonement and leave us holding the bag?"

"That's a cop-out," Debbie told him. "Dream new dreams and quit blaming the other guy." Debbie paused, alive in the knowledge that Jeremiah had failed with Mac but had succeeded with her. Jeremiah had forced them to hate him, had sickened them, so that they must rebel against their lives or die. He had fought that they might once more learn to love. There were many arts, and many roads to them. Maybe Jeremiah had been traveling a road of art, and not religion.

Debbie yearned to comfort Mac and Sarah, and yet she knew that would be wrong. She felt, in some harsh way, ordained. She watched Mac and saw that her words were going nowhere. But, Mac, being Mac, would think about them, so maybe later . . . and then Debbie made her voice stern, nearly punishing, and hoped it would not break with compassion.

"The world is full of gurus," she told Sarah above the roar of truck engines. "Find another one. Lacking that, you may want to consider a question."

JANE YOLEN

Three Questions

Jane Yolen divides her time between homes in western Massachusetts and St. Andrews, Scotland. Although best known as the multi-award-winning author of children's books and original fairy tales (for which she has been called "the Hans Christian Andersen of America"), she has also written several gorgeous magical novels for adult readers, edited numerous anthologies and folklore collections, and published her poetry in journals and books for both children and adults.

The following poem, about language and storytelling, comes from pages of The New Advocate *magazine.*

—T. W.

1. In a technological society, why care about literature?

> Do you suppose that God, sitting
> At a heavenly desk, papers piled
> On stars, on planets, on nebulas,
> On galaxies, on far horizons,
> The bureaucratic litter of eternity,
> Worries about literature?
>   Of course,
> Though He calls it story,
> That back end of history,
> Herstory, mystory, yourstory, ourstory,
> The sum and summation,
> The ad and ad nauseum,
> The fabulation of human talents,
>   The course
> We humans run.

2. What is literature for anyway?

> Anyway you look at it,
> Literature is Life,

Or so say the critics
Who are the handmaidens of story,
The spearcarriers, the secondaries,
The walk-ons, the also-rans,
The cameo bit part players
Who, like God, hand us the Word
From which the world is remade.
But the storyteller sets the globe spinning
With the breath of life.
Turn a page, turn a world.
Call me Ishmael, call me Huck,
Call me Valjean, or Peter Rabbit,
Call me down the rabbit hole,
And I will come falling, flying, floating,
      Fearless,
Drinking deep from a borrowed cup of courage.

3. Can literature be a tool for tackling the planet's problems?

Let us consider the wheel,
The water mill, steam engine,
Jet propulsion, computer chip.

Let us consider the stick,
The shovel, hoe, harrow,
The tractor, the combine.

Let us consider the slingshot,
The sword, rifle, cannon,
The H-bomb, the smart bomb.

Let us consider the word.
Let us consider
      the book.

IAN RODWELL AND STEVE DUFFY

The Penny Drops

Ian Rodwell and Steve Duffy met at the University of East Anglia in Norwich during the autumn of 1982. These days Steve lives and works in North Wales; he's written stories in a variety of genres and, in 1988, Ash-Tree Press published a collection of his M. R. James pastiches, The Night Comes On. *He's also had tales of the uncanny appear in anthologies such as* Midnight Never Comes, Shadows and Silence, *and* The Year's Best Fantasy and Horror, Twelfth Annual Collection, *and in magazines including* Ghosts & Scholars *and* All Hallows.

Ian works in London for a global law firm, but still lives in East Anglia, the location for most of his and Steve's stories of the Five Quarters. They share many interests—a love of unruly guitar music, out-of-season seaside resorts, and 1970s sitcoms, and an abiding hatred of Manchester United FC—but still after eighteen years remain deeply divided on one crucial question: the merits, actual or merely alleged, of traditional English ale. . . .

This is, according to the authors, "the second in a series of linked tales of the Five Quarters, an unofficial East Anglian drinking club whose five members meet on or around each quarter-day to socialize and spin tales of varying height. The previous meeting saw one of the five, the bookseller Mr. Gliddon, regale the company with an eerie reminiscence of his youthful travels in Provence; here, we join the Quarters on the occasion of their next encounter, late in the following March. Most of the names and locations in this story have been altered at the insistence of Mr. Scaife, a solicitor and a naturally cautious man to boot; for the rest, we must trust the sound and normally unimpeachable character of Mr. May." The story was originally published in Ghosts & Scholars *number 30.*

—E. D.

Though no one would ever call him a particularly overbearing man, Mr. Ashworth was capable, when the occasion demanded, of getting his own way. Spring had brought around both the next meeting of the Five Quarters, and his own turn in its "chair"—this latter circumstance granting him the right to set the time and place of the Society's quarterly rendezvous. On the principle that a change is as good as a rest, he had suggested that they forgo, just this once, their usual milieu of saloon bar and snug, and spend their afternoon in more invigorating surroundings. Why not a brisk walk, he encouraged, along the beach at Nestburgh; a fish supper, drinks at the Lighthouse and Compass, and then home? After all, the Society's only real business was to allow its five members to socialize (or to *mardle*, as the local Norfolk expression has it) in an environment safely removed from the demands of office, bank, and shop. Such business, insisted Mr. Ashworth, could be conducted as well in the bracing open air as in the congenial back bar, thus blending with the spice of variety a piquant element of novelty.

The ensuing vote was on the whole satisfactory, if in one quarter somewhat acrimonious, the motion being eventually carried four-to-one. The four, we now encounter striding out along the shingle beach that curls northwards from the Suffolk town of Nestburgh, the fifth meanders some twenty yards to the rear, all the time maintaining a loud barrage of complaint and invective that cuts effortlessly across the keen wind buffeting in from the slate-grey sea.

Mr. Wilde—the inevitable dissenter—was not happy, and made his feelings known at every opportunity. At last, after a distance of a mile or so, Messrs. Gliddon, Ashworth, Scaife, and May, whose votes had of course won the day, called a halt and waited impatiently for their tardy colleague to catch up. With an ill-tempered blow from his stick, Wilde sent a hapless plastic jerrycan spinning into the foam at the water's edge and came puffing and panting up alongside them. "We turn around this instant," he threatened, with a particularly malevolent glance in Ashworth's direction, "or you'll have a dead man to carry back to Nestburgh, and it'll be murder."

"Oh really, Wilde," Scaife chastized his fellow-Quarter, "if I didn't know you were only malingering, I'd book you in to the old folk's home myself. You should keep in better shape, you know." And with an especially (for Wilde) infuriating smirk of self-satisfaction, he patted a waist trimly honed, even in advancing middle age, by semi-competitive tennis and semi-vegetarian diet.

"Yes, buck up, Wilde," enthused Ashworth, "just to that far headland, see? Beyond those groynes—it's only another mile at the most."

"Ashworth," spluttered Wilde, in the midst of a peculiarly refulgent coughing fit, "have you taken leave of your senses? Every mile along this damnable beach is a mile further away from the Lighthouse and Compass—that's a mile away from the best-kept cellar this side of Southwold, in case you're wondering why on earth I've as much as deigned to go along with this stupid bloody pantomime in the first place. Now if you think I'm prepared to endure even a yard more of this filthy linear wasteland . . ."

As Scaife prepared to counterattack with the figures for alcohol-induced coronaries among the sedentary over-sixties, Gliddon raised his hand in placation. "Compromise, gentlemen, blessed compromise? We rest here for half an hour or so, enjoying the prospect and the bracing air, then amble back to Nestburgh at our leisure—and . . . ," quickly anticipating the grumble of complaint already forming deep in Wilde's congested chest, ". . . in the meantime, might I suggest that we refresh ourselves with *these?*" Very carefully he unslung a small canvas knapsack from his shoulder. Laying it on the shingle bank and unbuckling its flap, he proceeded to extract, like some especially convivial conjuror, a half-bottle of London gin, a half of single malt, assorted mixers, a wide-mouth thermos filled with ice cubes, a Tupperware box of thin-sliced lemons, and five stout stacking tumblers. Certainly no magician ever delighted his audience more thoroughly. Even Wilde, the storm clouds on his brow fading in an instant, beamed, "My dear Gliddon: always the man of surprises, eh? This of course alters things entirely," and with a contented "hurrumph," he flopped his not inconsiderable bulk onto the shingle beside the makeshift bar.

As Gliddon set to mixing the drinks and Ashworth rubbed his hands together like an unctuous vicar, Scaife and May followed Wilde's example; the former meticulously inspecting the beach for undesirable flotsam before gingerly sitting down, while the latter perched gawkily atop an old and battered shooting-stick, for all the world like some odd wax-jacketed albatross. Soon the Quarters found themselves deep in familiar conversations: if there were disagreements, then they were trivial and signified little, for as Mr. Wilde was fond of saying, a day without an argument is like a soup without the salt.

"One of my favorite views, this," confided Scaife a little later, as Gliddon uncapped his assorted bottles for the second (or more probably the third) time. "Sky, sea, the empty beach disappearing into the horizon . . . I daresay I'm an Anglian at heart. Always reminds me of that story I once read—Gliddon, you'll know the one, you recommended it to me—set in Felixstowe, wasn't it? There was one part, just before dusk; it was on a lonely beach, like this, and the protagonist, who's taken something he shouldn't have from some tomb or burial-ground or other, turns back to see someone—or should I say something—following him, but always keeping the same distance, just far enough away for him not to be able to see who or what it is. Very effective image, that, I think."

"Oh, for goodness sake," expostulated Wilde, "some of us have barely recovered from Gliddon's unbelievable outpourings last Christmas. Really, can we not talk about something else, please?"

"Yes, I remember the one," enthused Ashworth, blithely ignoring the complaints of his friend, the eternal rationalist. "M. R. James, I think: didn't it have something to do with a whistle?"

"Oh, I see, a supernatural whistle, was it, Ashworth?" rejoined Wilde, never the one to concede the conversational high ground. "That'd come in handy: perhaps you could use it to summon up that black dog of yours?"

Ashworth, who had at the last meeting made a rather ill-judged admission to the effect that he had once seen Black Shuck (or thought he had, or couldn't really be quite sure), blushed to the roots of his thin fair hair and murmured, "No need to rake that up, Wilde, no need at all."

"Well, what am I to do?" reasoned Wilde with an air of injured innocence. "I have one colleague obsessed with devil dogs, another gibbering about malevolent whistles—and poor old Gliddon, well, the less said about *that* the better. Which only leaves," he continued, twisting round on the shingle, "our dear friend May. Tell me, is there anything hereabouts," Wilde waved his hand expansively, taking in Nestburgh on one horizon and the beach receding into low cliffs on the other, "to engender mortal terror in your sturdy Northallerton soul? A possessed herring-gull, perhaps, or maybe a phantasmal prophylactic come in on the tide?"

The look that crossed May's face was hard to categorize; if Wilde missed its significance, it was not lost on Mr. Gliddon at least. In his usual taciturn manner (ascribed by some to his north-country upbringing, though I of course refrain from judgment), the surveyor held a finger in the air as if to test the wind, then pointed slowly and wordlessly back in the direction of Nestburgh.

"What's that?" questioned Wilde, a touch nonplussed at his friend's reaction and straining his eyes back along the beach. "What are you pointing at, man— lighthouse, beach-huts, car-park, snack van . . . ?" he frailed off in no little confusion. "Dear God, May, I know the hot dogs in those places are supposed to be like nothing on earth, but I never heard them called infernal by anyone who really meant it!"

"I wouldn't know about that," said May calmly. "I was pointing at the pier, as it happens."

"The pier?" echoed Ashworth.

"That's right;" May nodded his head. "Now, you know me; I'm fairly level headed and there's not much scares me." His colleagues nodded, remembering two-fisted tales of May's "no prisoners" approach as captain of his University's rugby club. "But you could pay me a king's ransom this minute, and I wouldn't set foot on that, or any other, pier."

Which naturally provoked the question, why? At first the various pleas for elucidation were firmly but politely declined by the smiling May. Only gradually did he began to give ground, driven at least in part, I guess, by a dogged desire to annoy Wilde (now throwing pebbles at the plastic jerrycan bobbing in the surf and tut-tutting at the reprehensible turn the conversation had taken) by prolonging his separation from the bibulous delights of the Lighthouse and Compass, and with an anecdote tailor-made to provoke his skeptical nature to apoplexy. And so it was, as the sea rasped mournfully against the shingle of the lonely beach and the skies to landward of our five friends began to show the first faint rouging of sunset, that May, crouched seablown on his shooting-stick, told the following story.

Go back to 1986—the height of the property boom, all wide-boys in BMWs with their pinstripes and Filofaxes. It was as mad round Suffolk as anywhere back then; the price of land was going through the roof, and I was doing as well as any of the competition in Brampton, at least. Still, I was a long way off the big league, which was why I was especially pleased one day when I got a phone call from a Bosco Arnold, the MD at Red Manor Properties, the big London firm. About seventeen, he sounded: yah, yah, yah, proper little upwardly mobile professional. You had to laugh, really.

Mind you, Red Manor were the real thing—they had their finger in God knows how many pies, construction and redevelopment and so on. I wondered what they'd want with me, until Arnold told me that I'd been recommended by old Dougie Pearson, who was the other prop in my College team—bless his size twelve boots! He was at Halston's by then, a rather swanky firm of surveyors in the City; they were Red Manor's usual agents, but on this particular bit of business it was felt a local man would be handier—cheaper, too, I daresay, but still it was nice of Dougie, and I felt I owed him one.

It seemed that Red Manor were negotiating an option on the seafront up at Hemsley, on the north Norfolk coast. Do any of you know the place? You might remember the pier at least—broken clean in two by the great storms of fifty-three, and never mended since. The plan was to slap a monorail between the two halves, landward to seaward, tidy up the broken ends a bit, and redevelop it as a "marine-side leisure experience": nightclub, video-game arcade, sushi bar, the works. This was where I came in. You see, they needed someone to give the old pier the once-over—nothing too detailed at first, just to find out whether or not it was likely to fall down on them before they turned a profit on it. If there were no major structural defects, they'd go on to commission a full survey and unleash the legal johnnies. Was I interested?

Certainly I was. Young Bosco was over the moon, and said I was to start ASAP: Red Manor would have the documentation—legal bumph, most of it—sent by courier, and his PA would book an appointment with a Mr. Williamson, the Borough Solicitor at Hemsley, for me to pick up the keys. And with that, he was gone.

Well, well. Red Manor Developments, eh? This would be a story worth telling down the lodge on Monday night, at least. But there was something else behind my on-the-spot acceptance. The pier at Hemsley, I thought: Good Lord. It must have been over thirty years since I was last there. Second week in August every year, my father used to drive us all down to the Norfolk coast for the holidays, to Hemsley more often than not. Luxurious it wasn't—a back-street boarding house with me and my two sisters squeezed into a single attic room—and the budget didn't run to extravagance, exactly; but all through those long, dragging July days (remember, eh, Ashworth, when you thought the holidays would never come?) we looked forward to the candy floss and donkey rides the way some folk look to Mecca. It would be nice to see Hemsley again, I thought; interesting, at the very least.

Well, Flash Harry was as good as his word, and later that day an imposing little bundle arrived by dispatch. Attached to the front was a word-processed note which read: "Williamson at Hemsley Town Hall—11:30 tomorrow. Go for the jugular: B. A." As I sifted through the junk—leases, charge deeds, and all the rest of it—a plan began to form. Normally, with an assignment like this I'd drive there and back the same day. But no; why not take the opportunity to have a good look at the old place again? Well, the more I thought about it, the better the plan seemed. Sheila (this was before her illness, you understand) was up visiting relatives in Cleveland, and the prospect of becoming Microwave Man for a week didn't exactly appeal. I could book into an hotel—nothing too fancy, no point in going overboard on the old expenses—carry out the survey and write the report up in the evening. I imagined a nice quiet out-of-season residents' lounge, antimacassars on the armchair, grandmother clock ticking away, view of the esplanade from a big bow-window . . . it wouldn't be Mon Repos on Gasworks Lane this time, at any rate. Helen, my secretary, could type everything up the next morning and the couriers would have it in Arnold's hands by the afternoon. A God-given opportunity to show those London types just what a small, provincial outfit could do!

So, the next morning found me cruising slowly along Hemsley promenade in the old Rover. It was a proper Norfolk March day, bright and windy, warm enough when the sun was out but every passing cloud had you reaching for a jacket or a sweater fairly sharpish. I was keeping an eye out for a likely hotel—nothing much open till the Easter break, seemed to be the consensus—but all the time I was glancing over at the pier on the far side of the esplanade, the twin turrets at the landward end, the farther length marooned a couple of hundred yards out in the dishwater North Sea. Just as I'd resigned myself to a day-visit after all, I spotted what struck me as a passable two-star establishment, The El Morocco, with a "Vacancies" sign hanging outside.

Not too shabby: there was a nasty crack in the pebble-dash that said "subsidence" straight off, and the whole thing would have been none the worse for a lick of paint; but perhaps you only notice these things if you're a surveyor. It was sound enough in a down-at-heels Edwardian way, but the views at least promised to be exhilarating and, best of all, it was clearly open for business. The reception was reassuring: it bore the classic hallmark of any decent, small hotel—the subtle blend of beeswax polish and essence of English breakfast. But where was the rest of the great British seaside experience: the tasteful sepia prints of turn-of-the-century Hemsley, the back-issues of *Country Life* and *Punch*, the handwritten sign saying DOORS LOCKED AT TEN-THIRTY—NO BATHS AFTER EIGHT? Instead, there were hand-tinted lithographs of Marrakech and the *souk* at Algiers, no aspidistra or mother-in-law's-tongue, but a sheaf of white lilies in a pot fashioned to represent a human skull. Very unorthodox; very un-Hemsley!

I was about to ring the bell when the owner appeared from some back room. He was a curious figure. If I had to describe him, I'd take a leaf from Gliddon's book and call him *louche*; I don't think there's an English word that covers it exactly. He wore a frayed Tattersall check shirt, the top two buttons of which he chose to leave undone, revealing a rather vibrant paisley silk neckerchief underneath. His complexion tended towards the grey and pallid, and wasn't helped by his day's growth of beard and his tired, bloodshot eyes: he looked a bit like Lilli Marlene after a hard night with the garrison, if you get my drift. But despite his dishevelled appearance I still couldn't help warming to the fellow. He had a lopsided grin and a tangled shock of fair hair drawn rakishly over his forehead; he'd have seemed far less out of place on the verandah at Raffles' in Singapore, or in the Parade Bar in Tangiers, and I couldn't help but wonder how he'd ended up in dear old Hemsley.

We shook hands and introduced ourselves; his name was Mr. Anthony. "Were you noticing my ring?" he inquired, in a dignified drawling tone. "The stone is somewhat unusual; it is an exceptionally fine specimen of the girasole, though of course you may know it better as the fire-opal. A coquettish little fellow—see how he gleams in the light?" Now, how could you not like someone who came out with a line like that? After the usual exchange of pleasantries, and having secured a room for the night, I mentioned that few of my proprietor's fellow hoteliers seemed to be properly open yet.

"Oh, I am a hardy perennial in a field of shrinking violets," he confided, loosening his r's in the Continental fashion. "I thrive on the right sort of company, and I find the trade is steady if not over-plentiful." He took an unfiltered

Camel from its packet on the reception desk and lit it with all the self-possession of a man who'd sooner beg leave to take in oxygen than ask permission to smoke. "But, tell me," he consulted the freshly signed register, "Mr. May, what brings you to Hemsley—not the crabbing or shrimping, I venture?"

"Actually, I'm here on business, Mr. Anthony," I said, and his eyes rolled in encouragement; "I'm meant to be surveying the old pier."

"Goodness, the pier, hey?" he smiled, savoring the smoke from his cigarette as if it were the perfume of Paradise. "Quite the man for controversy, then?"

Of the two of us, controversy seemed more in his line. "I'm sorry?" I said.

"*Frightful* rumors," he went on, "flying around town for weeks like little swallows; and like most rumors they seem to grow in extravagance with each telling. They're going to renovate the pier; demolish it; replace it with one a mile long; transform it into a multi-entertainment complex—we'll end up with a most spectacular palace of sin if they're all to be believed. All in all," he added, favoring me with an outrageous wink, "I can't think why such an enticing prospect should engender such hostility. Of course, pleasure is my speciality, so to speak, but one would think my fellow hoteliers might be glad of the change as well. After all, it's not as if the pier in its present state is particularly attractive; quite the opposite, in fact. But to read some of the letters to the local rag, anyone would think they were trying to turn the thing into a veritable *seraglio!*"

"Oh, you know the Norfolk siege mentality," I faltered; "they're hardly great lovers of change hereabouts at the best of times. Why, look at that business last year down at Yarmouth . . ." At that moment I caught sight of the clock behind the reception. "Good gracious, I do apologize, Mr. Anthony, but I must dash. I'm due at the council offices by half-past: we must continue our little chat later on this evening."

"So soon," sighed Mr. Anthony with amused equanimity; "no, don't worry about your bag, I will take it up later. If you take a left at the front door, and then left again, you will find yourself at the headquarters of the forces of reaction within five minutes, no less."

Following my landlord's directions, I was reassured to see that Hemsley had changed very little over the past thirty years. There were the usual offenders— the Golden Nugget, the Eldorado, the Fun-o-Rama, all nasal bingo and squalling video games—but underneath it all there was still the plain old turn-of-the-century watering-place, making its few graceful concessions to the holidaymakers that were growing grey with it.

There was more to complain about at the Town Hall. I'd been expecting some formidable Edwardian edifice, bedecked in ornate curlicues and mock-heraldic inscriptions, which would have been tasteless and bad enough. But even bad taste is better than no taste at all; and when I came across a two-story shoebox built in the style I can only describe as early Legoland—red tubular railings all over it and scuffed black rubber tiles underfoot—I was hard put to decide whether it was the council offices or the town car park.

The office of Mr. Williamson left something to the imagination; namely, walls. The borough solicitor was apparently not considered sufficiently important to merit his own room; instead, he was partitioned away by some hessian screening from the rest of the open-plan upstairs. The clatter of word-processors and dot-matrix printers interrupted our conversation as we sat and sipped our self-service machine coffee—at least, it had said coffee on the label, though Bisto was more my guess. Through it all, Mr. Williamson maintained an air of perfect poise; a small, round, finickity man in a dark off-the-peg three-piece. Aware of my own rather workaday appearance (but then, Williamson wasn't about to go clambering over some dilapidated old pier, was he?), I tried to be at my most professional and precise.

To do him justice, Mr. Williamson was quite friendly, and he quickly took me through the assorted keys: security fences for either end of the pier, funhouse, and all the rest of the refreshment stalls, et cetera. He explained that a local fisherman, Mr. Polstead, had been retained to row me across to the farther end of the pier; all I'd need to do would be to let him know when I was ready and the boat would be along. Practicalities concluded, I was keen to make a start, but Williamson was obviously loath to release me without a brief canter through his favorite topic.

"Yes," he purred, leaning back in his swivel-chair, with a second cup of coffee in one hand and a musty digestive from the office packet ready to dunk in the other, "the devolution of title in this case is fascinating, absolutely fascinating." To him, maybe; but, eager to court good relations with the "other" side, I listened with half an ear, trying to smile encouragingly at all the right places.

Now, if I remember anything of what he said, it seems that ownership of foreshore land is normally vested in the Crown—that right, Scaife?—but, by virtue of Hemsley's allegiance to the Royalist cause, and more particularly its bloodthirsty defiance of the Roundheads during the great siege back in the Civil War, Charles II granted the foreshore, and the various rights appurtenant thereunto, absolutely to the town *in perpetuo*, shortly following the Restoration. Thus in 1887 the Council were at liberty to grant a lease of ninety-nine years to the Hemsley and District Pleasure Pier Company, at a premium of four hundred pounds and a peppercorn rent thereafter. All well and good, I would have thought, but Williamson was having none of it. "Would you believe," he went on, becoming so indignant that the wetted end of his biscuit fell off unnoticed into the coffee cup, "the fool of a clerk, although providing for the day-to-day upkeep and maintenance of a pier, failed to make any explicit provisions regarding extraordinary damages or Acts of God? Which meant, of course," he continued, shaking his head at the ineptitude of the unfortunate clerk, "that when the pier was breached in the winter storms of fifty-three, the tenant company was under no legal obligation to reinstate or make good!"

"Goodness, how appalling," I ventured, wondering why Mr. Williamson was inclined to take the oversight so very personally.

"Quite! The Company, of course, were quite happy to pocket the insurance monies—the pier had not been a particularly successful commercial concern since before the War—and leave the structure to fall into further disrepair. The Council could do nothing . . ."

"Until," I chimed in, eager to hurry things along, "this January when the lease ended and you were able to regain possession. Well," I added jovially, "you must have been delighted when my client submitted his proposal?"

My comment—innocent enough—seemed to cause Williamson some confusion, and his reply was cautious, hesitant even.

"Oh yes, rather. Yes, indeed. The . . . um . . . the County Council was, of course, very pleased."

"And the Town Council?" I prompted, intrigued by Williamson's sudden discomposure and rather curious as to its cause.

"Well," again the solicitor seemed to be selecting his words with care; "this is to go no further, Mr. May, but as you can appreciate the Council is bound to reflect the wishes of the local people—and, to be absolutely honest with you, there is a good deal of opposition to any redevelopment of the pier, however tasteful or well-intentioned. Of course, in my professional capacity I must remain neutral, but I can appreciate—and I put it no stronger—the view in some quarters that the pier has, in its current condition, a certain—how do they put it?—a certain melancholic charm, shall we say, which proves quite an attraction for a type of visitor less inclined to seek out pleasure at every opportunity. To don the gown and wig of the Devil's own advocate, Mr. Arnold's offer is certainly an excellent one: but would the town be best served by trying to emulate our more commercial coastal cousins? Might we not lose more in the bargain than we gained? A mere thought, Mr. May, a mere thought."

Through this little smoke-screen he was throwing out I could sense Mr. Williamson's assurance returning. For the life of me, though, I couldn't see the attraction of a rusting ruin on the sea-front to any type of visitor, however bent on avoiding pleasure he or she might be, and I reckoned there was more to this let-well-enough-alone point of view than the solicitor was prepared to let on. More might have come of it, but Mr. Williamson suddenly remembered an important meeting of the Refuse and Sanitation Committee or somesuch, which naturally required his urgent attendance. Of course, I know when there's a door being shut—especially when my foot's in the way—so with a final handshake, I promised to return the keys the following morning and was on the point of leaving when Williamson, with the over-casual manner of someone trying to disguise a nagging preoccupation as a mere inconsequentiality, remarked, "Oh, and Mr. May, just a thought? Best be finished by dark. I don't believe the electrics on the far section of the pier are working, you see, and I'd hate to have you clambering around in the dark—Health and Safety and all that, ha-ha!"

"Thanks, but I've brought a lantern," I said sweetly, and took my leave.

As I fetched my kit-bag from the boot of the car outside the El Morocco I tried to fathom out the attitude of the Town Solicitor. In all my years of business I had yet to meet a vendor's representative so ambivalent about the prospect of a deal; perhaps, I thought, with all my professional cynicism, there was some shady local consortium with its own designs on the pier—a consortium with which, maybe, Mr. Williamson was not wholly unconnected? Still waters run deep, especially in the local politics of a place like Hemsley. By the time I had crossed the esplanade and headed off towards the pier, I was half convinced that I'd hit upon the truth of the matter, and I was wondering how much of my suspicions I could legitimately transmit back to young me-laddo Bosco at Red Manor. But that was later; now I had a job to do.

If you know Hemsley, you might remember there's a small jetty just to the north of the pier, where the fishermen work on their boats. Several of them broke off from their nets to scrutinize me; one waved vigorously and shouted out something indecipherable in the freshening breeze. "Mr. Polstead, I presume," I muttered to myself and waved back in greeting before turning to the pier.

The landward end, first. The fence across the entrance was covered in graffiti'd signs warning of unsafe planking, shaky stanchions, and all manner of other hazards for which the Council loftily disclaimed responsibility. The padlock opened easily and I stepped through onto the pier, wondering what manner of decrepitude would confront me. But my fears were pretty much unfounded: as I trod carefully over the worn salt-scoured boards, on the look-out for any rotten patches, I thought matters might have been much worse, all things considered. Given the exposure and lack of maintenance, the surface seemed remarkably robust. Yes, to be sure, the odd section of planking would need replacing, but it was in much better condition than I had anticipated, much better. Next, I lowered myself down the various service ladders that ran below, to take a look at the stanchions and the ribbing. Balanced precariously over the scummy grey foam, dictaphone clenched firmly in my free hand, I searched diligently for signs of metal distress, corrosion or fatigue. But, again, I was amazed at the overall soundness of the structure. "You've got yourself a bargain, Mr. Arnold," I muttered into the dictaphone, and tutted to myself at the transparency of Mr. Williamson's little stratagem. I clambered back up onto the decking, the first part of my inspection over, and shut the gates up before waving and hollering to Mr. Polstead by the jetty. With a parting jest to his cronies and a gruff "halloo" to me, the fisherman helped me down into a small dinghy and began to row steadily and unhurriedly towards the far section.

As we covered the short distance, I looked up and ahead along the length of the sundered pier, not with the eyes of the dispassionate surveyor but as one meeting up with an old friend, now raddled by age and ill health, after many years' separation. No hurdy-gurdies or winkle stalls now; no rows and rows of deck chairs bearing snoring black-clad grannies, clutching cannonball handbags to their chests; no hordes of screaming children, spades and buckets in their sticky candy-floss hands. Just an expanse of bare, wind-lashed boards, and the odd herring gull circling overhead, suspiciously monitoring my every move.

"All in order?" asked Mr. Polstead, breaking my reverie. Not knowing whether he belonged to the lotus-eaters of Mr. Anthony's camp (but rather doubting it), or to the *sic-transit-gloria* school of Mr. Williamson, my reply was suitably noncommittal. Given the strength of local opinion, I certainly wasn't about to drop my own two-penn'orth into the Hemsley rumour mill if I could possibly help it. Polstead, for his part, seemed happy enough with my bland and innocuous reply—though I was surprised when, after helping me out onto the builders' ladder tied to the foot of the broken pier-end, he stayed put in the boat, and made as if to row straight off again.

"Aren't you coming up?" I asked, thinking an hour or so's poke around the place might give him something of an inside track in the local pier debate.

"No, no," he said, face pulled down into a frown; "no, I best be off. Few things to sort out before the evening catch. But you'll be right enough up there, I should think. Just give us a flash of that light o' yours when you've all done and I'll be out presently." And with that, he was gone; rowing back to the jetty with a vigor that up to now had been markedly absent from his stroke.

With a shrug I climbed up on the marooned end of the pier and looked about me, suddenly aware of the sheer loneliness of the place. The forlorn remains of coconut-shies and rifle-ranges, not to mention the squat rotunda of the Funhouse looming at the furthermost end, combined to emphasize the air of neglect and abandonment; it was as if these ghosts of happier and more lively times made the present desolation even more poignant.

Dismissing these somber thoughts, I quickly set to work again, aware of the ever-advancing time. There was still an hour or two of daylight left, and I wanted to make the most of it: I didn't fancy the prospect of dangling under the boards with my lantern in one hand, my dictaphone in the other, and nothing left over to hang on with—especially in the keen wind, more noticeable in this exposed spot. Basically, I wanted to be no longer than was strictly necessary, and to get back on terra firma before dark.

I made pretty rapid progress; eventually, as I stretched my back after a particularly cramped examination of the old boiler room, I realized that there was only one part of the survey left: the Funhouse. There'd be light enough inside, though, with any luck: in the boiler room I'd found an electric generator with a spoonful of petrol left in it, and managed to start it up after about ten minutes' mad cranking.

As I walked up to the wooden rotunda, its glass front pock-marked with broken panes, I pulled up short with a sharp gasp of surprise. There seemed to be a small figure, a dwarf or a midget perhaps, crouching by the Funhouse door—was I not alone on the pier? Well, I realized my mistake in no time, though my embarrassment was none the less for having gone unobserved. The ominous figure was merely a kiddies' automaton, a Jolly Jack Tar still on his plinth after thirty years' buffeting from the wind and rain. In fact, I thought I recognized him from my childhood visits, for all his cloth sailor's jacket was pecked ragged by the gulls and stained by the sharp salt air. He wouldn't have recognized me so easily, perhaps, especially as his eyes, once bright blue, had faded with the years to blind white orbs. As I scrambled in my pocket for the Funhouse key, I was struck by a thought. Chuckling to myself, I pulled out a tuppenny bit and, with little hope or expectation of any outcome, pushed it into the machine's rusty slot. Nothing: I began to unlock the Funhouse door, glad that inflation had put the extravagance within my reach—tuppence would have been a lot to pay for nothing, when I was last here! However, Jack still had a surprise for me: from deep within his plinth came a rumble which slowly developed into the wheezing clank of old cogs and levers coming back to life. Then, with a jolt that made me jump like a startled hare, the sailor's head flung back; his jaw dropped to release a volley of ear-splitting cackles, and his arms sawed at chest-height, brushing the lapels of my coat as if to buttonhole me like that other Ancient Mariner.

I was delighted, not to say amazed, that the machine should still work after so long; and for a while I enjoyed the spectacle, the shaking figure convulsed in mirth at its own peculiar private joke, body rocking back and forth on its box as the black-bearded head nodded in time to the guffaws, blank eyes rolling weirdly in their sockets. But, as the seconds passed, I couldn't help but think that, strange as it sounds, the laughter was, well, rather unpleasant—*knowing*, if you see what I mean—especially since it seemed to continue for far longer than my cash donation strictly merited. But, at last, with a final gasp and a clunk, the figure slumped back into silence and I walked through the door and into the Funhouse, ears ringing from my unconventional welcome.

It was like shedding thirty years in an instant. Immediately, long-forgotten images from my childhood crowded around me. The large glass windows, those that remained intact, were muckier than you'd believe possible, but there were still odd glimmers coming through the cracks by which to see things. I could just about make out the little shut-off room at the center of the rotunda, that used to be off-limits to the youngsters; hopefully there'd be electric lighting in there, or it'd be a lantern job. I tried the switches by the door: here and there, the odd bulb responded and the Funhouse emerged from near-dark into a shadowy half-light, as far in as the door through to the Tea-Rooms on the farther side. In a sudden burst of light-headedness, I rummaged through my pockets for more twopennies and for the next ten minutes the professional man gave way to the boy of ten. What the Butler Saw, The Lucky Dip, Wheel of Fortune, Test Your Strength—I played them all, every single one of them that still played and wasn't broken or rusted fast. But, and you can interpret this as you like, it wasn't long before I experienced a weird sense of anticlimax. Maybe the past is never quite as you remember it—maybe those famous spectacles aren't so much rose-tinted as dusty and fingered with grease, so they refract the past into odd and misleading patterns. Perhaps there's always a kind of cheating involved with the Funhouses of this world, and we're always left dissatisfied; even when we're tiny children, led away in tears at the end of the too-long, too-hot afternoon.

It wasn't any one big let-down that left me feeling this way. It was more a combination of things, trifling on the face of it; little, inconsequential circumstances. The arm-wrestling game, with its big muscular hand reaching out as if it might grab you and never relinquish its grip: I tried it, and it exerted a pressure that was more than a match for me, the old prop-forward—it would have pulled the arm off any youngster, surely. Then there was the crane in the Lucky Dip, that whirled round heedless of my hand on the controls, and smashed against the glass of its case like the claw of some mad trapped thing. And as for the Wheel of Fortune, the particularly trite message it delivered seemed to sum up the prevailing mood of bathos and unfulfilment. "An Unexpected Encounter": well, yes, quite.

So, unaccountably depressed, I left aside the attractions and started back to work, finding as before the basic structure to be fundamentally good despite some superficial and inevitable damage from the elements. There was, however, one thing that puzzled me. The dust on one or two of the remaining panes of glass was smudged from the inside, almost as if someone had been trying to clear a space to look out. Kids rowing out to the pier-end, I concluded; probably an unlocked door behind the Tea-Rooms. I made a mental note to check this after finishing with the Funhouse—there was just the inner, central room left now; the room I'd never entered, not even as a boy.

Now—do you remember the sheer, irresistible attraction of the one thing your parents forbade you to do? For some it was climbing a particular tree, or riding their bike on a busy road; but, for me, it was that secret room in the Funhouse. During our last but one visit to Hemsley there wasn't a day I didn't pester my father relentlessly for permission to go inside it. He didn't really approve of the amusements, though—if you think I'm a typical Yorkshire misery-guts, you should have seen him—and his answer was always a curt "No, you're not old enough, ask me again next year." So I was stuck with the rest of the smaller boys that crowded around the little room and its curtained-off entrance, desperately peering past elbows and craning over shoulders to catch a glimpse inside. I knew there were games in there; big boys' games, that were weird and wonderful and forbidden to the likes of me, and I'd have sold my soul to get in and have a go.

Anyway, the following year, as soon as we'd unloaded the old Austin Seven, I dragged my father off along the pier to the Funhouse. This was it—after a year of waiting, I was now old enough for my very own rite of passage. I could barely contain my excitement as we rushed past the Jolly Jack Tar, the Strong-arm and all the other amusements through to the middle of the rotunda and the darkened room.

But imagine my distress when we found the way cut off by a hurdle and a large, hand-written CLOSED sign pinned to it. I wasn't a demonstrative child— far from it—so the floods of tears that accompanied the discovery forced my father, not usually one to challenge authority, to investigate further. He asked the girl in the change-booth how long it would be before the room was reopened. She looked at him without enthusiasm, as if he'd asked her for a run-down of her vital measurements. With obvious disdain, she said, "Oh, I don't know; probably next week some time," and resumed her manicure.

"That's all right," replied my father, "we'll come back, then; tell me, what day is it due to be fixed?" With this latest, Dad might as well have been proposing to sell her to the white-slavers. With eyes raised to the ceiling and a muttered, "I'll get Mr. Hedgecock," she disappeared, to return a minute or so later with a sweaty, weaselly little man in overalls. He repeated the cashier's story, but after strenuous cross-examination from my father (who, once roused to make a fuss, took pride in carrying on to the bitter end), he finally conceded, "Well, sir, it's this way: there's been complaints, you see, complaints, yes. All very unpleasant, you understand—Council matter, nothing to do with me as such."

"Nothing to do with you? And we've come all this way to spend our hard-earned money in this so-called resort of yours? Well, I don't think that's good enough, do you?" retorted my father, and the two of them went on to argue the toss for five minutes or so. At the end of it, obviously desperate to get rid of us, Hedgecock finally pushed a small bag of change into my father's hands and in a whining, wheedling manner said, "Look—here you go. Compliments of the manager, sir. Hate to see the young nipper disappointed and all that, but there really is nothing more to tell. Next year, now, we'll have something even better to play—you mark my words if we don't." And with that, he scuttled off to his den at the back of the rotunda.

Well, of course, next year, thanks to the great storm of '53, never came. But now, I thought, it was time at last . . . I pulled aside the blackout curtain, which fell rottenly from its rungs in a heap at my feet; took a breath to brace myself, and went into the secret room.

If there was electricity inside, there were no bulbs. I had to switch my lantern on to see, and the powerful beam picked over five or six shrouded hulks clustered round the central pillar, dust-sheets thrown over them thirty years ago; half-a-dozen sleeping beauties waiting for their prince to come and wake them. The first one I uncovered was a Haunted House: one of those wonderfully macabre old tableaux you never seem to see at the seaside amusements nowadays. A machine such as this, you might never see in all your life, perhaps.

I reached into my pocket and my fingers closed around my final twopenny bit. Fair enough: I slotted it home but with a brusque clunk the coin was ejected. I tried it again, and again, but each time the coin was spat out with contempt. Typical, I thought: it would be this machine—the pick of the bunch—that was too sensitive to be fooled by decimal coinage. "What you need," I said to myself half-aloud, "is an old penny." Then, of course, it came to me. The change-booth. Cursing my obtuseness, I dodged out to the mouldering old kiosk and scrabbled through the muck and dust on the counter. At first I thought I was out of luck: apart from a rolled-up copy of the *Picture Post* that might have seen service as a fly-swatter in times gone by, and an old mug half-filled with some revolting tar-like substance, there was nothing to be seen, and certainly no spare change in the empty half-moon wooden drawers below. Driven to desperation, I pulled out all the drawers one by one, feeling round where the light couldn't reach, until against all odds, at the back of the very last drawer, my fingers closed around a couple of coins: two old pennies. Leaving one behind on the counter, I rushed back to the inner room and its Haunted House and pushed my coin into the slot, all fingers and thumbs with anticipation. And what happened?

Nothing. The excitement slowly drained from me and the years fell back on my shoulders. I was no longer that eager ten-year-old in amongst the big boys; I was a surveyor covered in filth and seagull-muck, feeding pennies into a dead machine. With a sigh, I reached down for my dictaphone to record the last of my observations on the Funhouse. I was raising it to my lips with Record pressed down when, clunk, the machinery came whirring into motion. An eerie music-box tune, horribly rusty and askew, started up: the Haunted House, after thirty years of silence, was about to play.

What's that, Gliddon; what did it look like? Well. Imagine a glass case, four foot by two, in which there sits a large, beautifully scaled town house, the sort of thing a successful merchant or an old Dutch burgher might have owned in Rotterdam or King's Lynn, with lots of small yellow celluloid windows in its front prospect. It's dark, but you can just make out a small, cloaked figure, made to scale, standing by the door. It wasn't there before, when first you looked; it might have appeared out of thin air. It's got on one of those floppy, plumed cavalier hats, that obscures its head and face—I wish I'd been able to see its face, in retrospect. Nothing much happens for a minute, just the cracked off-center music, and then the game—is it a game? I don't know what to call it—begins.

Flickering lights appear at one or two of the windows, tiny bulbs pretending to be candles, and the whole tableau is suddenly suffused in a sickly faint green light—it's hard to describe, but have you ever seen the strange phosphorescence that sometimes lingers over marshes—will o' the wisp, it's called, or corpse candles, up in Yorkshire? No? Well, maybe that's just as well. Now, slowly the figure comes to life—perhaps it's the clockwork, but it seems to have a creeping action, coming forward a bit at a time, as if it was having difficulty in moving. As if it had been still for too long; more than thirty years, even.

Its head twists from side to side; it might be searching for something, you'd rather not think about what, for you know it's a nasty little homunculus even if you can't see its face. The door pops opens, and there's a little squeal from the hinges. Through it goes, and slowly, up the stairs; you can see it every now and again through the candle-lit windows. There's something round its face that gleams; you can't see what, it moves out of view just as you think you've got it.

There's a room at the top of the house: through the window you see a bed, with drapes along the sides and a little bulb-lantern guttering on the table beside it. The drapes pull partway back with a mechanical jerk, and there's a young girl asleep in the bed. Out in the corridor, the figure reaches the door to the chamber and hesitates. You watch, through the warped yellow windows; you rather wish that the game would end there; that the figure would retreat down the stairs, its purpose unfulfilled. But of course, it doesn't.

On the contrary, it creeps into the room; and then, a mere pace or so from the sleeping girl, it stops, and the music stops with it. Slowly, the figure stretches out its hands—though I don't know if I can call them that because, well, hands have fingers, don't they?—and again for a second you get that sense of a glinting to its face, though you still can't properly see it. Then, ever so quickly, it just dives the short distance to the bed in a horrible sort of scuttling glide. At the same instant, the young girl comes bolt upright and sees the figure almost upon her. She screams—the machine screams—as if every nightmare imaginable had come true in that instant. I don't know how they managed that scream—it's like nothing that came before it, nothing you ever heard. The homunculus, its arms raised high above its head, falls upon its victim and, at that moment, all the lights in the great house are extinguished. As the last echoes of that final, desperate shriek die in the darkness of the inner room, your eyes, readjusting to the gloom, see the cloaked figure back in its original position by the door—see it vanish into the ground, and you've had your penny's-worth. The game is over.

That's what it was like, Gliddon. Not so pleasant, eh? To tell you the truth it made me feel quite sick, and I didn't wonder that the weaselly Mr. Hedgecock had received complaints. They were lucky the whole Funhouse wasn't closed down, if you ask me. I picked up my lantern and went outside for a breath or two of fresh air, and was sorely tempted to finish the job there and then; call it an afternoon. But good sense (all right, Wilde, Yorkshire stubbornness) soon returned—was I really going to abandon a survey, and one for Red Manor Developments at that, because of a rather disagreeable children's entertainment? Well, no, I wasn't; but as I made my final inspection, the light now fading around me, I didn't stand on ceremonies, if you get my drift. I doubt fifteen minutes had passed before I showed a light for Mr. Polstead—SOS, I flashed; it was the only Morse I knew.

I don't remember much about the row back to land. Polstead was as uncommunicative as before and really I was in no mood to humor him. Once, I thought I could hear Jolly Jack Tar laughing from back on the pier, though of course it must have been the gulls. Sometimes they sound like laughter, don't they; or like children screaming? Once more on dry land, I gave Polstead a couple of bob for a drink, and stopped off for one myself, before I went back to the hotel for dinner. I didn't much care for the pub: it was modern inside, too dark to really see what you were doing, and I noticed that it seemed to be the rendezvous for some of Hemsley's shadier characters, slouching in the ill-lit recesses of the booths. God knows what sort of iffy transactions were going on back there, I thought. There was one bloke in particular—you couldn't make out hardly anything of him, just a silhouette against the deep blue neon light—that for some reason struck me as being particularly disreputable. He had the booth to himself, and I didn't see him get up or take a drink once all the time I was there; he was just slumped up against a wall, rocking slightly from side to side. Very suspicious.

Back at the El Morocco that evening, I was still restless, not really myself. Perhaps thinking about my childhood had done it; it happens that way sometimes, as you get older. Mr. Anthony himself had prepared dinner—"A morsel, Mr. May, a mere morsel. I'm afraid the chef and I have recently come to an irrevocable parting of the ways; a great, great pity, but if there is one thing I cannot stand it is truculence . . ."—but I'm afraid I only toyed with the food, good though it was. (I wonder whether another guest would have taken umbrage at couscous and stuffed aubergine for dinner in a Hemsley hotel, by the way?) I was sufficiently mindful of my manners to apologize for my half-cleared plate, but Anthony dismissed me with a casual wave of the hand—"Not at all—the Fainting Imam is, perhaps, an acquired taste, a fact I am inclined to forget. It derives its name from the reaction of the Imam upon its first appearance at his table—what an exquisitely attuned palate he must have possessed, to respond in so theatrically gratifying a manner! Perhaps I shall have it cold tomorrow, for breakfast; after all, it is a sin to waste a well-stuffed aubergine." Trying to suppress a smile, I retired to the lounge to start composing my report on the day's work.

With a brandy at my side, I sat in the very armchair I had imagined, antimacassars and all, with the obligatory views out over the lamp-lit promenade. I even got the report written, or most of it, though towards the end I began to feel even more restless and irritable. From time to time I broke off from my work and stared out through the window. I could see someone out on the esplanade, standing across the road in the dark space between the sickly yellow streetlights. Perhaps he was waiting for a bus, with his rain-hat, was it, and his rubber cape on; but the bus never came, and he waited there still. Just stood there in the shadows with his absurd hat pulled down across his face, staring over at the hotel. "Damned gawpers," I muttered, and closed the curtains. But I still wasn't comfortable: would you believe it, I ended up by moving that armchair back into the middle of the room, away from the window. This was satisfactory enough for thirty minutes or so; but not long afterwards I started to get the peculiar sensation that someone was reading over my shoulder; something I simply cannot bear. Of course there was no-one there (yes, Scaife, I did look); but knowing there's no-one there does you no good, if you still get that creepy feeling between your shoulder-blades.

Back to the report, however—I rewound my dictaphone tape to the beginning and played through the greater part of my running notes, and everything went to back up my initial impression. The pier was in astoundingly good condition considering, and would, with the addition of young Bosco's monorail contraption, adequately support any developments Red Manor had planned. That was money in the bank for me, and I set aside my pen with a sense of relief at around elevenish. Dear old Anthony had kept a respectful distance all evening while I worked, but now he brought me a nightcap and talked entertainingly of his past adventures: a restaurant in Tangiers, a rooming-house in the Patpong quarter of Bangkok—it was a cosmopolitan and varied CV, no doubt about it, and it should have landed him somewhere a little livelier than Hemsley in his declining years. And apart from that, chatting to Anthony took my mind off the business of the window.

"The twin banes of my existence: chefs and policemen," pronounced Anthony, at the conclusion of one of his exorbitant tales. "Brothers under the skin, you see; brutish, small-minded functionaries, wholly incapable of appreciating the artistic temperament, the whimsical caprice of idle fancy—but I fear the sea air has tired you, Mr. May. You are wilting, the flesh is weak. Or perhaps I am the culprit—I abase myself before you; I beg forgiveness. *Que je suis desolée!*"

"No—please, it's just that I've had a rather tiring day of it," I protested, struggling to swallow the yawns that cracked my jaw. "And this peculiar liqueur of yours is a good deal more potent than it tastes—I think I'd better go up now, or you'll end up carrying me."

"What an amusing notion," said Anthony appraisingly. "Any particular time in the morning?" Well, I remembered I had to drop the keys off first thing with Williamson, so I asked Anthony for a shout around half-past-seven and made my way upstairs.

The bathroom at the El Morocco was tucked away at the end of a passage, as if sharing Anthony's fastidiousness toward the baser functions. Since there were no other guests I had it to myself, and I consequently allowed myself the luxury of a good long soak in the tidemarked old bath. I'd only had time for a quick shower before the evening meal. The last of the pier's grime came away in the relaxing foam, and I ran some more hot in with my toes as I slid to almost submerging-point. I was probably halfway asleep—though far from all the way, don't think that—when I noticed that the door seemed to be open: the door I thought I'd locked, when I first came into the bathroom.

The plastic shower curtains, which I'd pulled to on getting into the bath to stop the splashes, were green and only partly translucent: still I could see a thin slice of light from the corridor showing in the door crack, reflecting softly on the seagreen tiles inside. Between the door and the light seemed to be a figure, waiting to come in. I thought at first it was Anthony, and I called out, "Shut the door, there's a good chap: I'm just getting out now." It hadn't struck me that he would be using the same bathroom—I'd imagined there'd be one in his private quarters, wherever they were. Obviously, if I was keeping him waiting, it was a shame—but I did think he might have knocked.

No reply; but the figure moved into the room, and now I saw that it was actually a good foot shorter than Anthony. Also, there was something about its head—what looked almost like horns at first, till I realised it was wearing a hat; a wide-brimmed hat, that curled upwards on one side, down at the other. My first thought was of the person waiting by the bus-stop on the esplanade, whose bus had never come—that was bizarre enough, but straight away another figure replaced it in my mind's eye. A figure from earlier on in the afternoon; only that was unthinkable, and it was then I started to worry.

"Who's that?" I called out, louder than before. The figure paused, and then came further into the room. There was something about its motion horribly reminiscent of that other I was so anxious to forget; the jerking movements, the turnings of the head, the odd gleam—that couldn't be its eyes? Surely not. Or I hoped not, at any rate. Living things don't have eyes like that; nothing has.

I was actually quite scared now: no sense in not admitting it. The intruder came up to the chair on which my clothes were heaped, and brushed against it, knocking it over. On to the floor went all my stuff, and the fall must have activated the playback button on my dictaphone, which I'd left in my jacket pocket, because now I heard, faint and tinny, the tape begin to play. The figure stopped, and seemed to listen: I listened too, goosepimples all over, and heard my own voice reeling off measurements and observations, with the wind in the girders of the pier moaning somewhere faraway off in the background. Then there was a blip on the tape, where I'd pressed Stop earlier on, and the next thing that came on nearly finished me off.

Remember back in the Funhouse, how I said I'd pressed Record on the dictaphone just as the Haunted House began to come to life? Well, I must have kept my finger down, because there was the music-box tune playing on the tape, all cracked and menacing. Hearing that was the worst thing in the world, because it brought it all back a hundredfold—I had no doubt at all now as to what was on the other side of the curtains, and what it would do when the music stopped. I didn't stop to wonder whether it was possible, or whether I was mad, or asleep and dreaming it all—any more than you'd stop to think "this can't be happening to me," when your car wheels go out from under you on the ice, and you're skidding across into the oncoming traffic. The dictaphone reeled on, and the thing waited, not moving at all, and I knew that I had to try and get out of its range before the tune was finished, or . . . you know what.

I drew my legs up under me, flexing my knees and resting my weight on the pads of my feet. There was a non-slip rubber bath-mat—God bless Mr. Anthony!—which might give me some purchase, and stop me from going headlong on the wet porcelain. I looked about for something I might use as a weapon, but there was nothing—a few toiletries in plastic bottles, nothing made of glass that I could smash and use an edge of. There was a long plastic back-scrubbing brush in a suction-cup caddy: I tried it surreptitiously, but there was no weight to it, and I couldn't help but remember those thin, cruel claws on the haunted-house creature. It would never be a fair fight—all I could hope to do was flee.

The music took me by surprise when it stopped—in between bars, just like that—and my grip on the side of the bath slipped, so that I fell backwards with a great slop of water. The thing started at the noise, and immediately raised its arms. As it began to dart forwards, I squealed like a stuck pig and thrashed my way up and out of the bath, scrabbling at the flimsy plastic curtain as the figure launched itself at the place where my head had been just a second ago.

I never actually saw it in the end. The curtain bellied in where the thing dived forward, and the trailing edge was wrapped around it by my crazy burst for freedom, out of the bath and onto the linoleum. I brushed against something as I cleared the sill of the bath; it was alive and clutching, and just the feel of it through the curtain turned my blood to water. I didn't look back: I scuttled my way on hands and knees out through the open door, and was halfway along the corridor when strong hands grasped me on the shoulders. Again I screamed, before I realized that it was Mr. Anthony: Mr. Anthony, in a flamboyant peacock wrap, staring at me as if I'd completely lost my wits, which I suppose for the moment I had.

I told him there was an intruder, that I'd been attacked while in the bathtub:

later on I ended up telling him everything, but just then there was only one thing on my mind. He heard me out, and lent me the towel over his arm to cover myself, and then naturally we went back into the bathroom. There was a great big rent in the shower-curtain, and it was hanging half-off its pole, and everything was topsy-turvy—but there was no intruder, no homunculus, and so it looked like I had some explaining to do. He let me dry myself off, though I asked him to stay in the room with me all the while; we went then to his quarters on the first floor back, and I spilled the lot, without any shame or embarrassment. He was a good listener, not interrupting me or asking pointless questions, when I had finished, he lit another cigarette from the stub of his last and inhaled with a deep and thoughtful breath.

"I dare say," he said, his voice low and soothing, "most people would put all this down to a kind of waking dream—long hours, fatigue, an over-stimulated imagination. That would, of course, be the rational thing to say: the prosaic, matter-of-fact explanation. No?" I shook my head in mute stubbornness, and he smiled, reflectively. "Quite so; no. I think not. I am, as the popular saying has it, a man of the world—which, if it is to mean anything, means that I am more than usually aware of what may properly be said to belong to this world, and what may not. During my years of roaming I have tried to keep at all times an open mind, and as a consequence I have witnessed many things—some of them calculated to stretch the credulity of a less receptive man to the limit. There are even now vignettes that present themselves to the memory: certain passages in a little ruined temple in the foothills of the Atlas mountains, with the drums of Bou Jeloud throbbing through the firelight, and the shadow-figures writhing in time with the wild Corybantic rhythms; a strange and dreadful feast in the backroom of a Laotian brothel, a shrilly crying monkey held down on its worn marble slab while the servants sharpened their long steel knives, and the diners looked on impassively in their robes . . . Strange, the infinite complications of the human mind, hey?"

"But tonight—in the bathroom—you didn't see . . ." I couldn't go on.

"I came running when I heard the scream," said Mr. Anthony, returning with a little shudder to the present, "by which time you were already in the corridor. I venture to suppose that you were not without reason in cutting short your ablutions in such a fashion. You see, despite my somewhat raffish aspect I am in many ways a trusting soul: my nature is not that of doubting Thomas. I prefer to think that, if I were to be placed in such a position, I should believe without seeing, like the apostle whom it is said Jesus loved best."

Enough of that night: after we'd done talking, I spent what was left of it in Anthony's own bed, while he made shift on the chaise-longue in his sitting-room. I didn't sleep a wink, what with thinking of the pier, and the haunted house, and all the business later on, in the bathroom. As soon as it was light, I got dressed and tiptoed out past my sleeping host. I wandered aimlessly around the town for an hour or so, watching it wake up to another dull out-of-season day, till I eventually took refuge in a small back-street cafe. I ordered coffee and toast, and tried to gather my senses together: you see, there was something I needed to do.

I ripped up the report I had composed the evening before and left it on the tray to be thrown away with the rest of the rubbish. Then, amongst the tomato-shaped sauce bottles and greasy plates, I roughed out a second draft; one in which I condemned the Hemsley pier as "structurally unsound," "grossly unstable" and "constituting a definite danger to the public." Don't touch it with a bargepole, was my advice to Bosco Arnold & Co. Professionally, of course, it was hugely unethical; went contrary to the interests of the client, could have ended my career, etc., etc. But, you see, I had to consider the wider picture—the world outside the Surveyor's Disciplinary Committee, that the R.C.S. Code of Practice doesn't touch. Writing it off as a derelict was the only way I could make anyone understand that whatever its physical appearance, the Hemsley pier was rotten to its foundations and should be left well, well alone.

That done, I called round at the council offices to drop off my keys with Mr. Williamson. Perhaps I wasn't looking quite my best, because he made me sit down in his own swivel-chair, and actually paid for a cup of gravy for me from the coffee-machine. I put it down to a spot of the old trouble—stomach disorder, blah blah blah—and if he thought that was just the usual euphemism for a night on the town in wild old Hemsley, then he did me the favor of not showing it.

We talked about nothing—about the weather, just like two old colleagues. We agreed that spring was a little late this year, and it had been a disappointing March, all in all. We certainly hoped it would pick up for the Easter weekend; going away, was I? No; quite so. See to the garden, ha-ha. Oh, and yes—might he trouble me for the, the, er? He took back the keys without showing any special concern; or so he thought. If I hadn't been so under the weather I'd have found it quite exquisite, how on edge he was; how desperate not to let his curiosity get the better of his discretion. It was only when I was getting up to leave that he weakened at last: "Do forgive me, Mr. May—it's not the done thing I know— rather a breach of etiquette and all that . . ." He paused, twisting his fingers in a cat's-cradle of embarrassment and indecision, "but is there any indication you can give, any pointers, no matter how general, you can provide regarding . . ."

"Regarding yesterday's survey and my recommendations to Red Manor?" I had to put him out of his misery, poor old idiot. My normal reaction would have been a brusque refusal, what Wilde would call my native Yorkshire impoliteness, but this particular morning? Suddenly I was very tired, and all I wanted to do was go home and forget about Hemsley, Red Manor, and the whole damned kit and caboodle of them.

"Well, let me put it this way, Mr. Williamson," I said: "I don't think the Town Council will be disappointed. As far as I'm concerned, that pier is fit for just one thing; the bottom of the sea."

Williamson mumbled something—it sounded remarkably like "Thank God"— and then smiled. "Thank you, Mr. May; I appreciate your frankness. The County Council will be sorry, of course; but it's probably for the best, I think, probably for the best."

On that note we shook hands; just two old business partners, as I say, with the dirty deed well and truly done.

May rose to his feet, flexed his long legs against their stiffness and readjusted his wax jacket against the freshening wind. "So, Wilde. There you have it—local man goes bonkers, eh? What do you make of that?"

Wilde's reply would doubtless have been illuminating, not to say libelous in the extreme and possibly fatally injurious to the continued good-fellowship of the Five Quarters. Sadly, however, a floating lemon-pip in the dregs of his gin chose that moment to go down the wrong way and reduced him to a bout of unlovely spluttering and choking; and so it was left to Ashworth to respond.

"May, tell me, is the pier still standing? I mean, if so, wouldn't some kind of warning be in order—Scaife, you're the legal man . . ."

"Some kind of warning?" choked Wilde in hoarse incredulity, finally regaining the power of speech. "Warning against mischief-making Yorkshire tykes, you mean. Look at him, smirking away there—he made it all up—go on, look me in the eyes and tell me that's not the most God-almighty pack of fibs you've ever told in all your life, May. Come on—you're pulling our legs, trying to go one better than Gliddon there, admit it!"

Smiling a little, May shook his head. "Can't do that, Wilde," he said; "it was all just as I described, every last detail." Gliddon looked at him for a long moment and nodded, once; an understanding seemed to pass between the two of them, which was not lost on the rest of the Quarters.

"I don't believe this," said Wilde, exophthalmic in disbelief: "I really don't. What are you trying to tell us? Hulking great Mauler May of the Front Row, and the kiddies' slot machine that put the wind up him? Accosted in the bathroom, running around hotel corridors in the altogether with this, this drawling semi-degenerate straight out of the brothels of Bangkok—I bet they've never heard about *that* at the lodge on a Monday night, have they? Kept that bit quiet, I bet!"

"I wonder he bothers to tell it at all, Wilde," said Scaife quietly, "if that's the best you can come up with. You're supposed to be his friend, you know."

Thus chastened, Wilde subsided a little, and Scaife went on: "As for a warning, Ashworth—no need. What was left of old Hemsley pier went down for good in the '87 hurricane—maybe you weren't so far out in that second report after all, May, because there's certainly nothing left of it now bar a few stanchions sticking out at low tide."

"Act of God," said the surveyor, gazing back down along the beach towards Nestburgh and its own thumb of a pier, stubby and inelegant; "you can't legislate for things like that. Come; it's getting on, and we've got the walk back into town yet."

A queer sense of anti-climax lay heavy in the air on the way back, and there was little talk among the party. Once ensconced in the snug of the Lighthouse and Compass, the Quarters revived in spirits somewhat, and on returning to the corner table with a round of drinks, May nudged Wilde's plump and tweedy shoulder with a hard elbow. "You know, it strikes me I didn't quite finish telling you everything back on the beach: there's one more thing to add, if you want to hear it."

"Well, I suppose we might as well have the rest of the farrago," said Wilde heavily, wiping the spillings from his pint glass on the beer-mat before him. "Try and keep your elbows to yourself in the telling of it, there's a good chap; the suit's only just back from the cleaner's, and I don't know what they put in this mild, but it stains like the devil." May chuckled maliciously, and took up his tale again.

"You know I moved offices a year or so ago? Well, I was packing up all my files when I came across a bundle of old professional journals—the kind of thing you stuff into a drawer intending to read, and then promptly forget about. But you know how it is when you get rooting through a pile of that stuff—I started reading one, and then another, and an hour or so had passed when I stumbled across an obituary notice; it was for a surveyor named Radlett, based over in Dereham.

"Well, it's never pleasant to hear of a death in the profession; but, to tell you the truth, I'd had some dealings with this Radlett, and I wasn't too impressed. Typical old-school Brylcreem boy, he was; do anything if the money's right— just the sort that gives us all a bad name among the public. Not that I expected to read anything like that in the obit, of course! We're all angels once we're dead, and I was sure I was going to learn how well respected old Radlett was, and how much he did for charity, and how the Pope was putting the canonization through in time for Christmas, and so on. I skim-read the piece, just to confirm my prejudices, until I saw the words "Hemsley" and then "pier"; after that, I started to read it a bit more carefully.

"Now, after Red Manor turned down the option on the pier—and before the '87 hurricane rather put paid to things—it seems that one or two other developers had begun to sniff around, and apparently this Radlett had gone there, just as I had, to carry out a survey. The similarity ends there, though—they found old Radders dead in his hotel bed in the Seabreeze, the morning after he'd done his survey and been out to the pier. You only get the sanitized version in the obituary, of course, but it went on to say that despite initial suspicions, death was finally attributed to a heart attack.

"This is where I began to feel uneasy, and I think you know why. 'Despite initial suspicions, despite initial suspicions . . .' I just couldn't get that phrase out of my mind. So in the end I decided to go ahead and ring someone I knew on the local force; very reliable officer, name of DCI French . . ."

"Thank goodness for the dear old lodge, eh, May?" interrupted Wilde spitefully. "No, no, don't elaborate, old chap; hate you to have your tongue pulled out at the root or your liver fed to the ravens, or whatever it is they do to *informers*. Tell me, is he any good on having speeding endorsements wiped, on your license? I might get you to put me forward, if you don't think I'd bring the tone down."

"I was going to say," rejoined May, his voice for once tinged with a hint of exasperation, "that I'd once done some cut-price surveying for Sarah French and she was all too keen to return the favor. Well, she rang me back a few days later, and I went to work with all the fabled Yorkshire charm—you can ask Wilde about that, eh? Oops, sorry, Wilde—look, you've split that pint all down your shirt-front, you clumsy beast.

"Luckily, Sarah came up with the goods. I won't bore you with the details, but it seemed the whole Radlett business was a bit irregular—that the authorities had more or less agreed to disagree, and had swept things under the carpet that didn't quite chime with the eventual verdict. You know the way situations like that are dealt with, out in the real world away from the crime-shows on the telly. Hunches and intuition are all very well, and so is going out on a limb against the advice of your superiors; but it does leave you out in the cold a bit, come promotion time, and for every brilliant Sherlock Holmes there's a hundred plodding Inspector Lestrades, if you catch my meaning.

"The fact was, Radlett's room had been in a hell of a mess when they found him in the morning. Bedside table upturned, lamp broken, sheets and blankets rucked up on the floor—all the classic signs of a struggle, not to mention our old friend Foul Play. Then there was the state of the body: now what do you think they saw on it, when they looked to see if he was still breathing?"

Scaife and Gliddon muttered noncommittally; Ashworth was noticeably paler than either of them, but managed to ask, "W—what?"

"Marks, is what, Ashworth; livid red marks, on the neck."

"Like hands," ventured Mr. Gliddon intently, "the pressure of fingers?"

May paused, rather in the manner of a card player preparing to play his trump. "Hands, yes . . . but fingers? Well, let's put it this way: if they were fingers you could be sure of one thing at least—whoever it was didn't bite his nails." He gestured with his own fingertips, sketching long extravagant claws beyond his own neatly-trimmed cuticles.

"Yes, but what did the coroner say at the inquest?" cut in Wilde, engrossed despite himself.

"Ah," continued May, "now this is interesting. The police on the spot made their own notes: marks and contusions on the neck, classic peri-mortem bruising pattern, defensive wounding, all very suspicious—but they weren't medically trained, couldn't possibly give an opinion, have to wait until the autopsy, etc., etc. But when they get poor Radlett on the slab, a few hours later, guess what? No marks, no bruises: nothing but the usual lividity, and a couple of burst blood vessels in the eyes. So, the scene-of-crime reports went out of the window: death was due to a heart attack, plain and simple. Which wasn't too mysterious, after all: old country surveyor, bit overweight, more than a bit out of condition, slap in the danger zone. Ask any insurance company. And the staff in the Seabreeze had said he'd appeared a bit out of sorts the evening before—they thought he'd been overdoing it, out on the pier. His own doctor gave evidence that he was treating Radlett for angina and high blood pressure, and he was very receptive to the heart-attack idea. So, there was nothing more to investigate, and the file was closed."

"But the room, the struggle?" questioned Scaife, enthralled. "Didn't that set off any warning bells?"

"No, no, not really: spasms caused by coronary failure was the official story. It does happen; but I get the impression a lot of people on the Hemsley force weren't too keen to go along with it in this particular instance. And what about those marks? Well, they never did explain them away—still haven't. Sarah French had actually talked to one of the officers at the scene, and he was still swearing blind that he'd seen what he'd seen, and no one was going to shake him, and so on. Apparently, his Inspector had him in and said, all right son, no one's saying you didn't see these marks; just don't go round shooting your mouth off about it, there's a good boy. Now about that promotion . . . and that was the end of it, as far as the police were concerned.

"So," concluded May, carefully unwrapping a Henri Wintermans, "that was what DCI French had to say. I know it goes to round off the story a bit, but really I wish I hadn't asked, what with the fresh light it throws on things."

"Good Lord, May," breathed Ashworth, his face a study in puzzlement and trepidation, "this is remarkable, quite remarkable! So you're quite convinced, in your own mind; you really think this Radlett was killed by—by whatever it was that came after you in the bathroom that night?"

"I have no idea, Ashworth: I really don't think about it that often, or I try not to, at least. But I can't help thinking about what he got up to on the old pier—in fact, I'd give a packet of money to know just one thing."

"And what's that?" said Gliddon softly.

May smiled. "Well, it's silly, really—but I often wonder whatever became of the second penny there in the change booth, that worked the Haunted House."

BRET LOTT

The Train, the Lake, the Bridge

Originally from Los Angeles, Bret Lott graduated in 1981 from California State University at Long Beach. In 1984, he received an M.F.A. from the University of Massachusetts, Amherst, where he studied writing under the late James Baldwin. He teaches at the College of Charleston in South Carolina, where he is writer-in-residence and a professor of English. He is the author of several novels including The Hunt Club, Dead Low Tide, *and* Jewel, *two collections of short fiction,* A Dream of Old Leaves *and* How to Get Home, *and a memoir,* Fathers, Sons and Brothers.

"The Train, the Lake, the Bridge" was originally published in Ghost Writing: Haunted Tales of Contemporary Writers *edited by Roger Weingarten.*

—E. D.

We save this story for only the darkest winter nights, the thickest snows, when we know we cannot dig out for a few days, and so are guaranteed each other's company.

Sure, there are plenty of stories we pass back and forth among us. There is the story of Elder Hosmer, dead these one hundred years, and the Hosmer place, about the light that passes from window to window early midsummer mornings. There is the story of the Indian, one of King Philip's men, and how he screams certain evenings from the top of Greenscott Hill, his foot snapped in a saw-toothed bear trap generations ago. And there is the Provost (maybe he set the trap the Indian was caught in, we often speculate) and the story of how he walks our creeks and streams autumn nights, his wife's scalp in one hand, his own bloodied hatchet in the other. These are all stories we tell indiscriminately when we are hunting, rifles crooked in our arms as we stand before a blazing campfire at dawn, or walking home nights after town meeting, or after large suppers.

But the story of the train is irrefutable. It happened. We were there, three boys, but boys with enough sense and enough fear to know when not to tamper with the truth. It was the truth that frightened us the most.

As was often our habit during the Great Depression, and as we still do today, our families had gathered together for dinner. It was a night much like this, a night of snow, and by 10:30 there was no chance of anyone leaving. There had not been much snow that winter, not until that night, but there had been bitter cold, and Shatney Lake had already frozen clear and thick. We were assured of having nothing to do the next day: no work, no school, only the giant task of digging ourselves out, and even then there would be no hurry. The snow was there to stay, and we had no idea when it would let up. We started to bunk down for the night, the men and boys in the front room and kitchen, the women and girls in the bedrooms. We boys settled into our quilts and blankets and waited for the stories our fathers used to tell. They did not fail us. There was nothing more pleasant back then than to be warm, full, and have a frightening story in our heads before falling off to sleep.

And, like every night, we waited for the last train through, a train that made no stop in our small town, but which we counted on every night to rock us gently to sleep, the rhythm of the boxcars like the soft roll of thunder in a summer storm. The train came by, and we closed our eyes, imagining we were on it, riding the rails to destinations unknown, the train rolling along the ridge and slowly curving toward deep, frozen Shatney Lake, then crossing the old trestle, disappearing until the next night, when we would imagine the same things all over again.

But as soon as the rocking of the boxcars disappeared, there came a scream of metal on metal that seemed to last hours, as though Satan had wanted to wake the world on that peaceful night. The scream shuddered up and down the valley until surely every household within four miles had been awakened.

We got up and looked out the windows but could see little, the snow was falling so heavily. Something had happened, we all knew, something terrible. Our fathers decided to go have a look, but our mothers decided otherwise. They would not let the men outside, not in that storm, not in that cold, not in that snow. While they argued the point, we boys climbed out the kitchen window. We were going whether our fathers did or not. We waded through the snow up to the crest of the ridge and to the tracks.

Once there, we looked back to the house and saw a faint yellow glow from one of the windows. All else was white, save for the tracks cleared of snow by the train only a few minutes before. Our fathers would be out there soon, we knew, either to find out what happened or to take us home.

From the crest we could see nothing around us, but we knew the track from summer days, following it out to Shatney and the bluffs, walking the gravel and rock bare-footed, skipping every other creosoted tie. The tracks slowly curved to the lake, and once there on those hot days we would climb down somewhere on the old trestle, drop our fishing lines in, and spend the rest of the day. But these thoughts were far away. We wanted to find out what in God's world had happened.

We reached the lake and stopped dead. There in the white darkness we saw the broken timber of the trestle and the twisted rail torn from the edge of the bluff overlooking Shatney. Had the snow been falling any more heavily, had it drifted any more, had we not been looking where we placed each step, the three of us would have stepped off the edge and fallen to the ice forty feet below.

Look, one of us said, pointing off into the snow. He was pointing down. There was something dark there on the lake. We climbed a few feet down onto the ice-covered rocks and stared hard into the swirling, blowing snow. There was something huge and dark and awful down there, something that took on more and more detail as we stared at it, until we realized it was a boxcar. It was a boxcar planted halfway into the ice, hammered into the lake like a spike. It was silent, a dark leviathan in a sea of white snow. We said nothing, only watched the terrible thing standing on end.

And there in the howling wind, the snow stinging our faces, our bodies shivering, the boxcar started to move, slipping slowly down, down, silently into the ice. At first the movement was imperceptible; we imagined it was our eyes or the cold or the play of the snow, but before we could say anything, the boxcar disappeared into the ice, swallowed into the lake as if it were a snake returning to its hole.

Our fathers arrived a few minutes later to find us still there on the rocks staring into the white, none of us having yet spoken a word. We said nothing on the way home, said nothing until we were back inside and near the fire. Our mothers scolded us for having gone, while our fathers looked out the windows, speaking quietly to each other. We were sent to bed after we drank some coffee, but we could not sleep. The snow continued.

The next morning was bright and clear, and the three of us, having not slept all night, watched the sun rise over the ridge. Our footprints out into the snow had long since disappeared. The snow had drifted so that it took us a good hour just to clear a path from the house to the barn. We fed the horses, which stood in the darkness of the barn, their breath shooting from their mouths like great clouds.

We came out of the barn and saw that our fathers were leaving for the trestle, snowshoes on, daypacks on their backs. We came running at them, yelling and crying about wanting to go—it was our right, we reasoned, as we had been the first ones there and had seen the last boxcar slip into the ice. In the morning light, the sun banging up off the new snow, the awfulness of that huge black car was wearing off, and the idea of that sunken train in the lake seemed more like an adventure. It was a novelty, something out of the ordinary. We wanted to go down there and look again. They decided to let us go.

Damage to the trestle was greater than we had seen the night before. The bridge had fallen from the bluffs to midlake, and the wooden structure looked like some great animal bowing down on its knees. Ice had collected on all the crossbeams and had broken many of the struts in half. We figured that when the engine first moved out onto the trestle, the added weight then broke in two the already ice-laden crossbeams. The engine and the cars following it had fallen in line into the lake.

We stood at the top of the bluff and looked off to where we had seen the boxcar the night before. All that was left to indicate anything had happened at all, that anything had ever been near the lake surface last night, was a sunken area of snow about thirty feet off the edge of the rocks and a little to the right of the bridge. Snow had covered the skim of ice which had already formed in the hole.

Suddenly we heard a whistle blast break clean across the valley, carried across the snow. We turned from the lake to see an engine coming around the last curve before the lake, moving slowly, the prow scraping snow from the tracks as it moved along. The railroad people had arrived.

Only two men had been aboard the wreck, the maintenance supervisor told us. The supervisor was a clean-shaven man and wore blue overalls and shiny black boots. He had on a wool cap and a heavy coat slick with machine oil. Two engineers, he told us, and four empty boxcars coming down from Canada. He told us they had known for a long time that this bridge was a hazard, and that sooner or later the worst was bound to happen, and that they were going to have to close the route anyway, what with the Depression and all. He said it was a terrible shame that it had happened at all, and that it had been these two men in particular. We looked at him for a few moments, then looked at each other.

Then the supervisor broke out several shovels from inside the cab and asked if we didn't mind giving him and his assistant a hand down there on the ice. Railroad policy, he told us, demanded that all accidents be verified, and he had an idea that if we dug away some of the snow from the ice he might be able to verify the engine number, just to make double sure the right train had gone down. The right wives had to be notified of their husbands' demises, the supervisor said.

We took the shovels, as did our fathers, and climbed down the rocks onto the ice. The lake had been frozen a month or so, and we had no fear the ice would not support us. It seemed a foot thick.

We started clearing, keeping a safe distance from the hole where the train had entered. We dug into the snow, clearing an area where the supervisor imagined the engine must have been resting, but all we could see through the ice was the cold dark water below. No train. He had us dig in a wider area, enlarging the borders of the original area, and then we stopped digging again. He saw nothing. He asked that we clear a little larger area, nearer the hole, and we did. Our fathers shoveled snow with less and less enthusiasm, but we boys thought it great fun, and with each request of the supervisor dug even more furiously. Still there was no sign of the train.

After an hour and a half of digging, our fathers quit, saying that the railroad should be damned for sending out good men on a dangerous bridge in the first place. Down on his knees, his hands cupped around his eyes, the supervisor was oblivious and only stared down into the ice.

And then he screamed.

He stood up quickly, and slipped on the ice, then tried to stand up again.

"What is it?" we asked. "What is it?"

But before he could answer, if indeed he had ever had any intention of answering, we looked down to where he had been searching and saw a man under the ice, frozen, gray, his arms out to either side in perfect silence.

He wore blue jeans and a red and black plaid jacket. He had no face, only a blurred gray area where we expected to see his face.

We all stood there on the ice, none of us moving any closer to what was there under the supervisor. He still screamed and slipped on the ice, calling for our help, for anyone's help. He could not move from his spot above the frozen man.

Then they appeared, first one, then three, then five, all around us, beneath the ice. It took a moment, and then we recognized these men.

They were hoboes, bums catching rides on a southbound train, the same men who hung out of empty cars on summer days and hooted at us fishing from the trestle below them. But these men below us did not move and kept floating to the ice like swimmers seeking air. They appeared from nowhere, and we could not keep them from coming, a dozen, twenty, thirty of them, all bobbing to the surface in different positions, some curled up like stillborn animals, others stretched out straight. They wore overalls and caps and flannel shirts and coats, but none had faces, only the blurred, undefined patches above their shoulders. And still they came.

We tried to run on the ice, to get away, but slipped and fell over one another, falling to the ice, our faces meeting the formless faces of the dead. We screamed; the railroad men screamed, our fathers screamed. We struggled to make it to the snow, to get off the ice and those dead men, those derelicts who had no family except those around them, and who would never receive any burial except that which the lake had given them. We struggled to the snow, almost diving in head first when we finally made it off the ice.

And then, just as suddenly, the bodies disappeared, first one, then another, then another, all sinking back to the lake bottom and the train, their home. They seemed to peel away from one another, and fell slowly back into the blue.

We did not stay there to figure out what had happened, but moved as quickly and as silently as we could up onto the ice-covered rocks of the bluff, back onto the tracks, and home. The supervisor and his assistant climbed into the cab without a word, the shovels still down on the ice, and backed the engine along the tracks, first slowly, then faster and faster.

They were gone from the valley by the time we made it home.

The story is finished. There is silence in my living room as everyone here thinks over matters: the train, the lake, the bridge. There are no ghosts to speak of in this story, and it is precisely this fact that frightens us. We have no legends to create around this tale, no stories of old Indians or Provosts we can exaggerate. There are no ghosts, except the trestle, still torn and twisted after fifty years, a reminder of our childhood. The train stopped coming through this valley the night of the wreck and has not been back since.

We are no longer rocked off to sleep by the rolling train, but now must put ourselves to sleep, drinking warm milk, reading, or simply staying up all night, assuring ourselves we are alive in this frozen wilderness.

And there is the ghost of the lake, the silence that is taken there. There are no screams at midnight, no candlelights in windows, no blood. We no longer fish there, no longer dare even to set foot in that lake for what we know is buried there. There is only silence.

CLAUDIA ADRIÁZOLA

Buttons

Bolivian writer Claudia Adriázola was born in La Paz and graduated from the Universidad Católica Boliviana. Her short stories have appeared in various South American journals, and have been collected in Abuelas, Ángeles y Lunas, *published in La Paz in 1998.*

The following story, "Buttons," is a gentle and moving piece of magical realism reprinted from The Fat Man from La Paz: Contemporary Fiction from Bolivia, *edited by Rosario Santos (Seven Stories Press). It was translated from the Spanish by Jo Anne Engelbert, who has also translated Jorge Luis Borges, Julio Cortázar, Isabel Allende, and Jose Martí, among others.*

—T. W.

The little box lay there, almost hidden among Grandmother Mara's dresses and antique silver. The women of the family, all in black, milled about the table. Eyes still wet with tears, they were removing objects from chests and glass-doored cabinets and laying them on the table in no particular order. Delicate porcelain dolls, watch parts, a cuckoo bird, Cristobal's first clay figures, a desiccated slice of Canela's wedding cake, and a bisque angel about to take flight, though his wings had been missing for years.

Mara's daughters—Menta, Canela, and Almendra—and her granddaughter, Alba Mora, had gathered in the parlor of her house, now inhabited by her soul.

Together they remembered the time Mara woke up at midnight dying of thirst and drowsily swallowed a whole flask of holy water someone had brought from the most famous sanctuary in Yugoslavia. The next day she realized that her entire house was flooded with angels. Blue angels in the parlor, black angels in the kitchen, angels fluttering from the terrace to the entrance, angels perched on door tops, angels everywhere. A group of cherubs stroked her tousled hair as her guardian angel led her by the hand. "There's an angel on your shoulder," she would say to them, as though she were saying. "There's a fly on your sleeve." Such were the visions that they produced in Mara what she referred to as her "state of grace," a condition that lasted all her life.

The women also remembered the time Mara proved once and for all that she hadn't been joking about her vocation as an acrobat, how she had qualified by nimbly following the cat the entire length of the high wall that separated her property from that of Desiderio Flores. And then they recalled the Saturday when she surprised them with a real tea party for their dolls, with tiny cakes and miniature gelatin molds. They remembered the many times they had found her lying facedown on the grass, looking for four-leaf clovers. And they couldn't help laughing when somebody remembered the day Mara brushed her teeth with her brother Cristobal's burn ointment.

They reminisced about her until nightfall and continued remembering her until daybreak. They remembered her until there were no more stories nor words, nor tears nor laughter to accompany their memories. Then the three daughters retired in silence, each with the feeling that a fragment of their mother's ghost had taken residence in her own soul. At last the only one who remained in the parlor was Mara's granddaughter, Alba Mora.

With the blurred, transparent image of her grandmother Mara seated across the table from her, looking into her eyes, Alba Mora idly began to finger the items scattered there. She picked up the little box that lay half-hidden among the Spanish nougat candy, Indonesian lace, crumbs from the Last Supper, and some sheets of paper that exhaled a permanent fragrance of roses. She opened it carefully. Inside she found a profusion of buttons glazed with a delicate sepia film, like an old photograph. Clinging to some were tangled strands of the thread that once had held them to a dress. Some were split; others lacked a chip of tortoise veneer. All, without exception, were fragments of a former life.

Alba Mora picked up a silver button, its delicate filigree formed of tiny flowers intertwined with ivy. Holding it, she began to see lives and events as if she were watching a film in the town's only movie theater. Distant scenes from Grandmother Mara's life began to drift into the room, turning it into an ethereal stage set. Suddenly her mother, Canela, appeared, fifteen years younger and wearing a coat that looked more like a gown. The silver filigree buttons stood out against the dark gray cloth, closing the coat in a dangerous curve that hugged her body. Only then did Alba Mora realize that if she and her mother had been contemporaries, they would have been identical twins.

In her fine coat with its filigree buttons, Canela seemed almost unapproachable. Of all the daughters, she had always been the one most conscious of her lineage. She was the eldest, the most elegant, the one with the most lavish lace blouses imported from China, the one who liked to look down at her sisters. Canela played the piano and could make a perfect chignon with her eyes closed. And naturally, she embroidered exquisite stars and flowers on napkins and on interminable sheets of fine percale.

What no one knew was that if she went around with her nose in the air, as if her neck had been starched, always staring over people's heads, it was because she was afraid to see her eyes reflected in those of another person. And if she spent all her time baking cookies and chocolate cakes, it was because she knew no other way to while away her solitary hours.

No one would have guessed that Canela had long conversations with the plants in her flowerpots, or that she embroidered tablecloths with the secret intention of using them one day in her own home—if she had not met Rosendo Corzon, a man who, judging from the way he went through life, thought he was immortal.

Rosendo went through the street without looking beyond the end of his nose. He was always falling down wells and drains and stepping into holes in the ground. He had had splinters removed from his face with tweezers because he kept walking into trees, and had had his stomach pumped any number of times because he made a habit of eating any dreadful thing that came to hand.

It was none other than this absentminded man who succeeded in getting Canela to lower her eyes and look into his. And it was he who would share the yards and yards of cloth Canela had been embroidering all her life.

For a long time people in the town wondered how two people who were so different could ever get along. They were simply unaware that Rosendo's very absentmindedness enabled him to bypass the intricate and elaborate defenses of Canela's heart, and that this was enough for her to let her hair fall loose around her shoulders, to add slices of mango and banana to her chocolate cakes, and to plant her potted flowers outside in the garden.

Alba Mora smiled and understood more about her mother in a minute than she had ever suspected in a lifetime.

Alba touched a blossom-shaped button, and Aunt Almendra appeared, swathed in her sky-blue story. She arrived with the copper-colored braids of a young girl and the grave misfortune of having been born left-handed. So left-handed, in fact, that at school they had tried everything to cure her of that mania. But even though they encased her left hand in a fingerless glove, tied it behind her back, and punished her whenever she showed her left-handedness in public, Almendra remained faithful to her instinct, even when the school principal had the brilliant idea of sewing her left sleeve to the side of her dress.

And if Mara had not noticed that something odd was happening to her daughter—after all, the child was beginning to count everything, even the peas and grains of rice on her plate—the experiments to make her right-handed might have ended God knows where, perhaps in amputation. But at this point she set her daughter free and let her become the lovely painter and harpist whose talent would be the pride of the town.

The last button Alba Mora picked up did not have a definite shape. It looked like a mushroom lined with a little piece of brown leather. Suddenly, like an apparition, Aunt Menta materialized in the very center of the room, wearing a jacket of chestnut-brown suede and with her hair terribly mussed. If she could have done so, Menta would certainly have continued brushing her teeth with that mixture of ashes and lemon that her grandmother Violeta had used well into old age. Just as surely, she would have gone on competing with the neighborhood boys to see who could spit the farthest and carving animals out of pieces of wood with her grandfather Casiano's knife, if it had not been for the arrival in the town, on a day like any other, of a certain Don Santos Donaire, the only man capable of taming Aunt Menta's rebelliousness.

And all would have turned out well if it had not been for the sensation Santos had of sharing his life with another man, rather than with a woman. And just as suddenly as he had appeared, Santos Donaire disappeared, on a day just like any other, leaving Menta as much alone as when he met her.

After a long time a letter arrived addressed to Menta Arcani. It was from Santos Donaire, who said that if she wanted to see him again, she had to promise to change her character. She would have to swear on her father's soul and to

Saint Jude Thaddeus and Saint Catherine. Menta, who believed neither in her father nor in the saints, swore. And even though she found it degrading to weep and wait for him, and humiliating to sigh and pray for him to return, she wept and waited. And she sighed and prayed, just as her grandmother Violeta had taught her. But Santos Donaire never returned. Years later news reached her that in a well not far from town the body of a man had been found. In one hand he held a piece of wood carved into a condor, and in the other a letter addressed to Menta Arcani.

Alba Mora saw all the women in her family. All had buttons; all had fragrant names. With a clumsy hand she tore a button from her own blouse and placed it among the other buttons in the little box. Then she closed it carefully with the certainty that one day her granddaughter—Rosa, Lavanda?—would receive this family legacy and come to know her better.

At that moment she began to weep all the tears she had stored up in a lifetime. She wept for the little pieces of carved wood, for the peas and grains of rice. She wept for the holy water and the dolls' birthday party. She wept for the time she was rejected when she tried out for the choir and for the goldfish that died when she was a child. She wept, finally, because she had been holding back tears from the time of her great-grandmothers.

Then she saw Mara pass by for the last time, like a sigh of lace and sea foam. She saw her as an acrobat, floating gracefully from invisible ropes suspended from the ceiling. Accompanied by cherubin and seraphim. And with her guardian angel leading her toward eternity.

ELIZABETH HOWKINS

Snow Blindness

Elizabeth Howkins has been writing since she won an essay contest at age ten. She has taught foreign languages, worked as a bilingual counselor's assistant with Latino students, and has been an antiques dealer. Her husband is a psychiatrist, "handy for a writer," according to Howkins. She has been a prize winner of the Peterloo Poets Competition in the U.K., Merit Award winner of the Atlanta Review International Poetry Competition, and finalist of the River Oak Review and Rainer Maria Rilke Poetry Competition. Her poetry has been published in Psychopoetica, Staple, iota, Smoke, *and* Working Titles *in the U.K., and in* Americas Review, Osiris, Paris Atlantic, Lummox Journal, Yfief, The Silver Web, Frisson, The Iconoclast, *and* Medicinal Purposes *in the U.S.*

"Snow Blindness" was first published in Penny Dreadful, *issue twelve.*

—E. D.

An angel points the tip of his wing
due North like the needle of a compass
and we plod on
stepping on the hem of his shadow
into the deepening snow.

We hug our cloaks to us
like warm sparrows
pressed flat against our breasts.

The sun has packed its baggage.
Even the moon has dropped its lid.
Only our breath scratches out faint fossils
of light in the wedges of space between us.

The snow deepens and lengthens.
Perhaps we are even walking
on the tops of towns.

The lady in the rear, with a hole
in her parka sharp as a cookie-cutter star,

sings a stanza of *Amazing Grace*.
The man in the shiny red boots is falling behind.

Whatever birds there were, have long since
frozen like petals to their boughs.
The one child we brought along
has become tedious and is begging for crumbs.

Last night we ate a final few beaten biscuits.
The last of the red wine congeals like blood
in our mouths.
The wind is getting pushier by the hour.

We cannot go back.
We can only go forward.
We have already crossed that line.

The last person in the row smoothes over
our footprints with a rake.
Our hands disappear in front of us.
along with our elbows and our wrists.
The single, faint star we follow calls our bluff
puts down four aces and splutters out
and we move on blindly, into the airless room
through which the darkness takes us
into that final space
that has neither windows nor doors.

GREER GILMAN

Jack Daw's Pack

Greer Gilman is the author of one novel to date: Moonwise, *a highly unusual, controversial work of mythic fiction which won the Crawford Award for Best First Novel in 1992. It was also short-listed for both the James Tiptree, Jr. and Mythopoeic Awards, and Gilman herself was short-listed for the John W. Campbell Award for Best New Writer. As critic Michael Swanwick has noted, "In its influence,* Moonwise *was certainly the most important fantasy work of the past decade for the simple reason that it roused an entire generation of new and unknown fantasy writers to Ambition. For a year after it came out, the conventions and writers' workshops buzzed with a constant mutter of amazement. A total unknown, with her first book, had reinvented not only the substance but the language of the fantasy novel, all to the satisfaction not of the perceived marketplace but of her own inner demons."*

"Jack Daw's Pack," like Moonwise, *is a tale that comes from the twilight realm that lies in between fiction, folklore, and poetry. The author, who has recently completed her second novel, lives in Cambridge, Massachusetts. "Jack Daw's Pack" first appeared in the Winter 2000 issue of* Century *magazine.*

—T. W.

The Crow

He is met at a crossroads on a windy night, the moon in tatters and the mist unclothing stars, the way from Ask to Owlerdale: a man in black, whiteheaded, with a three-string fiddle in his pack. Or in a corner of an ale house, querulous among the cups, untallied; somehow never there for the reckoning, though you, or Hodge, or any traveller has drunk the night with him. A marish man: he speaks with a reedy lowland wauling, through his beak, as they say. He calls Cloud crowland. How you squall, he says, you moorland ravens; how you peck and pilfer. He speaks like a hoodie crow himself, all hoarse with rain, with bawling ballads in the street. Jack Daw, they call him. A witty angry man, a bitter melancholy man. He will barter; he will gull. In his pack are bacca pipes, new ones, white as bones, and snuff and coney-skins and cards. He plays for nothing, or for gold; packs, shuffles. In a game, triumphant, he plucks out the Crowd of

Bone, or Brock with her leathern cap and anvil, hammering at a fiery heart, a fallen star. (It brock, but I mended it.) Death's doxy, he calls her, thief and tinker, for she walks the moon's road with her bag, between the hedges white with souls; she takes. Here's a lap, he says, in his shawm's voice, sharp with yelling out for ale. Here's a blaze needs no bellows. Here's a bush catches birds. He mocks at fortune. The traveller in the inn forgets what cards he held, face down, discarded in the rings of ale; he forgets what gold he lost. He'd none in his pockets, yet he played it away, laid it round and shining on the sanded board, a bright array. On each is stamped a sun.

And elsewhere on that very night, late travelling the road between Cold Law and Soulsgrave Hag, no road at all but white stones glimmering, the sold sheep heavy in his purse, another Tib or Tom or Bartlemy will meet Jack Daw. He will stand at the crossroads, bawling in his windy voice, a broadside in his hand. There'll be a woodcut at the head: a hanged man on the gallantry, crows rising from the corn. Or this: a pretty drummer boy, sword drawn against the wood, and flaunting in her plumy cap. Two lovers' graves, entwined. A shipwreck, and no grave at all. You must take what he gives. Yet he will barter for his wares, and leave the heavy purse still crammed with coppers, for his fee is light. He takes only silver, the clipped coin of the moon: an hour of the night, a dream of owls. Afterwards, the traveller remembers that the three-string fiddle had a carven head, the face his own. With a cold touch at his heart, he knows that Jack Daw's fiddle wakes the dead; he sees their bones, unclad and rising, clothing with the tune. They dance. He sees his girl, left sleeping as he thought; Joan's Jack, gone for a soldier; his youngest child. Himself. They call him to the dance. He sees the sinews of the music string them, the old tunes, "Cross the Water to Babylon," "The Crowd of Bone." Longways, for as many as will, as must, they dance: clad in music, in the flowers and the flesh.

What the Crowd of Bone Sang

She is silent, Ashes, and she dances, odd one out. In the guisers' play, she bears a bag of ashes of the old year's crown to sain the hearths of the living, the hallows of the earth. The children hide from her, behind the door and in the shadow of the kist; not laughing, as they fear the Sun. Click! Clack! He knocks the old man dead, that headed him before. And tumbled by the knot of swords, he rises, flaunting in their gaze. The girl who put on Ashes with her coat of skins, who stalks them, bites her cheek and grimaces so not to laugh; she feels her power. She looks sidelong at the Sun.

They say that Ashes' mother got her gazing in her glass. *Undo*, the raven said, and so she did, undid, and saw her likeness in the stony mirror, naked as a branch of thorn. The old witch took it for herself; she cracked the glass, she broke the tree. They bled. Devouring, she bore her daughter, as the old moon bears the new, itself again; yet left hand to its right. And they do say the old one, Annis, locks her daughter in the dark of moon, winterlong and waning, and that Ashes' birth, rebirth, is spring. They say the sun is Ashes' lightborn brat. She is the shadow of the candle, the old moon's daughter and her mirror; she is tarnished with our breath and death. She's winter's runaway.

They are old who tell this.

But the girl who put on Ashes with her tattered coat walks silent, flown with night and firelight and masking. She is giddy with the wheel of stars. She sees the brands whirled upward, sees the flash of teeth, of eyes. The guisers shout and jostle. They are sharp as foxes in her nostrils: smoke and ale and eager sweat. She moves among them, nameless; she wears her silence like a cloak of night. Ah, but she can feel the power in her marrow, like a vein of stars. Her feet are nightfall. She could tuck a sleeping hare within her jacket, take a hawk's eggs from its breast. Her hand could beckon like the moon and bid a crone come dancing from the chimneynook to sweep about her and about; could call the sun to hawk at shadows, or a young man to her lap, and what he will.

And in the morning, she will lay by Ashes with her rags, and wash her face, and comb the witchknots from her hair; but Ashes in the tale goes on.

In spring, she rises from her mother Annis' dark; they call the snow-drops Ashes' Steps. The rainbow is her scarf. She dances, whirling in the April storm; she fills her hands with hailstones, green as souls. And there are some have met her, walking backward on the lyke road, that they call the white hare's trod, away from death; she leaps within the cold spring, falling, filling up the traveller's hands. She is drunken and she eats.

At May, the riddlecake, as round as the wheeling sun, is broken into shards, one marked with ashes; he that draws her share is Sun. But he was sown long since, and he's forgotten harrowing. He rises and he lies. Light work. He breaks the hallows knot of thorn; he eats the old year's bones for bread. Sun calls the stalk from the seeded earth, draws forth the green blade and the beard to swell his train. He gives the meadows green gowns. And flowers falling to his scythe lie tossed and tumbled, ah, they wither at his fiery kiss. They fall in swathes, in sweet confusion, to his company of rakes, his rade of scythesmen all in green. The hay's his dance. Vaunting, he calls the witchstone, Annis, to the dance, for mastery of the year, and wagers all his reckless gold. But he has spent his glory and must die. The barley is himself.

Ashes reaps him. By harvesting, she's sunburnt, big with light. She wears a wreath of poppyheads; her palms are gashed, they're red with garnering. They open like a cry. Her sickle fells the standing corn, the hare's last hallows, and he's gathered in her sheaf. She's three then, each and all the moon, his end: her sickle shearing and her millstone trundling round, her old black cauldron gaping for his bones.

The Harper's Lad

His hair was yellow as the broom, as ragged as the sun. A ranting lad, a spark for kindling of the year. His name was Ash. It was Unhallows, in the grey between May Eve and morning. On the hills, the fires died. He'd leapt the nine hills in a turning wheel, from dusk to dusk, and rode rantipole with witches. Ah, they'd raged, howking at the earth with long blue nails. When they shook their tangled hair, the soulstones clattered, red as blood, and eyestones, milky white and black; and birdskulls, braided through the orbits, in their nightlong hair. He was drunk with dancing. He'd another girl to meet; had lingered, waking with his blue-eyed witch. *The owl flew out, the raven in,* sang mocking in his head, like Ashes in the old play. As he slouched along the moor, he heard a hoarse voice, in windy snatches, singing. Some belantered rantsman, he thought.

"*Oh, my name it is Jack Hall, chimney sweep, chimney sweep . . .*" A crow's voice, chanting, hoarded iron in a hinge.

There were some had sung all night, thought Ash; he'd gone to other games. It was lightward, neither sun nor moon, but the grey cock's hour. He was late. He hastened toward the beck.

"*And I've candles lily white, oh, I stole them in the night, for to light me to the place where I must lie.*"

They met by the trey stone, back of Law. A fiddler from a dance, it seemed, in a broad hat and battered jacket, with his face like the back of a spade. His hair was white as barley. "Out," he cries. "D'ye call this a road?"

"Flap ower it, then, awd corbie. D'ye call that a voice?"

"Called thee."

A glance at the three-string fiddle. "Canst play us a dance on thy crowdy, catgut? Light our heels, then."

"What, is thy candle out?"

"I've a lantern to light it at."

"Of horn?"

But Ash was thinking of the blue-eyed witch, as rough as juniper, as fierce. She'd scratched him. Ash thought of the fire, how it whirled and crackled when they burned the bush; the sparks flew up like birds. The fire was embers: for a coal of juniper will burn a winter's night. Would burn a nine month at the heather's roots. Closing his eyes, he saw late-risen stars whirl round, the Flaycraw all one side afire, and rising, naked to his bones. The hanged lad in the sky. He played for the dancers in the starry hey. He played the sun to rise. But that was Hallows; they were winter stars, another turning of the wheel, and other witches. Vixens in a cage of straw. Hey up, he must be giddy drunk. Were all yon ale and randy turned his wits. But he'd a spark in him yet. And Ash thought of the dark-eyed lass who waited, like a sloethorn and a clear gold sky. A traveller. Whin. He'd best be going on. He tossed a coin to the fiddler. "Here's to thy bitch."

"And for thy pains."

They found the broadside in his jacket, after. Some said the woodcut was a high green gallows, and the harper's boy hanged dead. And others, it were nothing like: the white hare running and the hag behind. The black hare's bonny, but the white is death, they say: the moon's prey and her shadow.

Ash thrust the broadside in his pocket and went on down the road. His tousled head was bare, as yellow as the weeds called chimneysweepers, that are gold and come to dust.

Scythes and Cup

Poor Tom a' Cloud, and so he died?

His husk, an old wife says, and drinks. *Scarce bearded when he's threshed and sown.* Another, brown as autumn, broad-lapped, takes the cup; she kneads the cake. *Wha's dead? He's for thy belly, when he's risen, girl. He's drunken and he sleeps; his dreams are hallows, all a maze of light, of leaves. When's time, he'll wake wood.* And says the third, *as thrawn as frost, the youngest of the three: At dusk, at Hallows Eve, he rises, starry wi' a ceint o' light: t' Sheaf, Awd Flaycraw, clapping shadows frae th' fields of night. Yon hanged lad i' th' sky.*

And Ashes?

Ah, she mourns and she searches. And rounding wi' his child, she spins. D'ye see yon arain webs ont moor? Tom's shrouds, they call 'em. Bastards' clouts. And she may rive at Mally's thorn for shelter; owl's flown, there's none within. No hallows. So she walks barefoot and bloodfoot, and she lives on haws and rain. And moon's her coverlid, her ragged sheet.

Sheath and Knife

The girl lies waiting in the high laithe, knife in hand. Hail rattles on the slates. She cannot hear—what? Hunters. Closer still, she holds the knife, the same which cut the cord. Her breasts seep milk, unsuckled. Ah, they ache. Her blood wells, she is rust and burning; blood will draw *them.* Talons. Wings. Her mind is black and bright with fever. She would slip them, fight them, but her body clags her. It is sodden; it is burning. Sticks and carrion. The wind wauls, the rooftrees creak; below is muck and sleet and stone. She's drawn the ruined ladder up. Holed up. She stares at dark until the earth cants, until the knife's edge calls her back. Sharp across her palm: a heartline. White, then red. Her blood and milk spilled on the musty straw. That will call them, that will draw them from the dark, the tree, the bairn. But the earth starves for what she will not give it. Their voices tell her she is famine, she is hailseed, withering, the cold share in the dust.

She was Ashes. Ah, she'd flyted with them, wives and lasses, as they'd stripped her of her guising, scrubbed her, tugged the witchknots from her hair. *Cross all and keep nowt,* they'd told her, turning out the sooty pockets, folding up the tattered coat; and late and morning, privily, desperately, she'd drenched and drenched, but could not rid her belly of the seed. She's Ashes still. Still guising, in a tinker's jacket, oh, a brave lad, with her bloody hole. Caught in Ashes. Holed up. Crouching, clenching, in her darklong pain, she'd heard the shadows of the women mocking, turning out the pockets of the coat. Knife. Haws. Pebbles. Eggshells. There, the whirligig she'd cried for, that she'd broken, long years since. They hold up a skint and bloody hare. *Here's one been poaching.* Shivering, she shuts her eyes, but still she sees the brat like bruised fruit trodden in the grass, the cry between her legs. Windfall for the old ones. Ashes to ashes. His furled hand, like bracken. His blind mouth at her tit. If they'd found him there, they'd slain him, for the earth to drink. *Keep nowt.* She'd hung no rags to the hallows tree, when she'd left him. She'd not beg awd ones. And she'd nowt to give. Her hair was cut long since and burned. Her tongue was dry. But she'd wrapped him in a stolen jacket, nowt of Ashes. Twined a stranger's tawdry ring about his neck. Why? For the daws to pyke at? She's seen the crows make carrion of halfborn lambs, their stripped skulls staring from their mother's forks. On the slates, the dry rain dances, shards of Annis, shards of souls. Heel of hands against her aching eyes, until it's red, all red as foxes, and their green stench in the rain.

Coffer and Keys

At Hallows Eve, Ashes' mother hunts, unthralled from her stone. She is the wintersoul, the goddess of the high wild places, fells and springs and standing stones, the mistress of the deer. Her child's her prey.

Her mother Annis hates her, that her child (her child) is not herself. She wears her daughter at her throat in chains of ice, her blood as rings; she tears the new Sun, red with birthblood, from her daughter's side.

In winter, Ashes dies, is graved within her mother's dark.

And her bairn's shut up in Annis' kist, says an old wife, jangling her bunch of keys. *Down where she sits i' dark, and tells her hoard of souls. And he's Sun for her crown. So all t'world's cold as Law and blind as herself.* She leans and whispers. *D'ye hear her at window with her nails?* The dark-eyed children huddle by the hearth and stare at her, the old wife crouching with her cards of wool. Her shadows cross her shadows, like a creel unweaving. *Ah, but he's for Mally's lap, she haps him all in snow. It's winter and her loom is bare. Wood's her cupboard, and her walls are thorn; her bower's all unswept. Thou can't get in but she lets thee. And she's Tom Cloud's nurse. But Brock—ah, well no, Brock's death's gossip and she's keys to all locks. Will I tell ye how Brock stole him?*

Why? says the boldest.

For a bagpipe that plays of itself, says the eldest, as she rocks the babby. *Hush, ba.*

For a bellows til her blaze.

Not for Annis.

But there are some say Ashes journeys on the river of her milk, that she's the lost star from the knot of stars they call Black Annie's Necklace, or Nine Weaving, or the Clew, that rises with the fall of leaves, a web like gossamer and rain. The Nine are sisters, and they weave the green world and the other with a mingled skein of light and dark, weave soul and shroud and sail; but Ashes winds the Sun within her, that the old Moon shears.

And some say no, that Ashes is a waif on earth, and scattered with the leaves. She rocks the cradle in the midnight kitchen, where no coal nor candle is, in houses where a child has died. And some have heard her lulling in the dying embers; seen her shadow in the moonspill, in the leaf's hand at the pane.

Poppyheads

The woman in the stubble field moves slowly, searching. Her palms are creased with blood. Her tangled hair is grey. There is something that she's lost: a knife among the weeds, a stone from off her ring. Her child, she says. If you suckle at her dry breast, drink her darkness, she must speak your fortune, love and death. She once told other fates, with other lips. And still she squats among the furrows, lifting up her ragged skirts for anyone or none. She holds herself open, like an old sack in a barn. No seed within, all threshed to chaff and silence. She was Ashes. She is no one. By the sticks of the scarecrow, she crouches, scrabbling at the clodded earth and crying, "Mam. Mam, let me in!"

Sieve and Shears

There must be one called Ashes at the wren's wake, when they bring the sun. At Hallows, she is chosen. All the girls and women go with candles, lating on the hills. And if a man by chance (unchance) should see one, she will say she's catching hares, she's after birds' nests, though it rattle down with sleet and wind. They both know that she lies. Her covey are not seeking with their candles, but are sought. And one by one, the tapers dwindle, or are daunted by the wind; the last left burning is the chosen. Or they scry her in an O of water from the Ashes spring, at midnight, when the Nine are highest. They will see her tangled in their sleave of light, as naked as a branch of sloethorn, naked as the moon. And though the moon in water's shaken by their riddling hands, its shards come round and round. Then swiftly as the newfound Ashes runs, longlegged as a hare, she'll find the old coat waiting at her bed's head, stiff with soot and sweat and blood. She walks in it at Lightfast, on the longest night, the sun's birth and the dark of moon. She smutches children's faces with her blacknailed hands. And their mothers say, *Be good, or she will steal thee. Here's a penny for her bag.* Her mother's tree is hung (thou knows) with skins of children, ah, they rattle like the winter leaves, they clap their hands.

The Scarecrow

The starved lad in the cornfield shivers, crying hoarsely as the crows he flights. He claps them from the piercing green, away like cinders into Annis' ground. Clodded feet, cracked clapper, and his hair like what's o'clock, white dazzle. *Piss-a-bed*, the sheep-lads cry him. What he fears is that the Ashes child will dance among the furrows, rising to his cry. What he fears is that the crows will eat him. They will pick his pretty eyes. And he dreads his master's belt. Yet he sings at his charing. At nights, he makes the maids laugh, strutting valiant with the kern-stick, up and down. *Hunting hares?* calls Gill. *Aye, under thine apron,* he pipes, as the Sun does, guising. And they laugh and give him barley-sugar, curds and ale. *Thou's a bold chuck,* cries Nanny. *Will I show thee a bush for thy bird?* And he, flown and shining, with the foam of lambswool on his lip, *I's not catched one. But I will, come Lightfast. I'll bring stones.* How they crow! And Mall with the jug cries, *My cage is too great for thy cock robin, 'twill fly out at door.*

Now he shakes with cold and clacks his rattle, and the cold mist eats his cry. The Ashes child will rise, unsowing from the corn: a whorl of blood, a waif. Craws Annis will crouch in the hedgerow, waiting; she will pounce and tear him with her iron nails, and hang his tatters from the thorn. Jack Daw will make a fiddle of his bones. He knuckles at his stinging eyes. He wants to cry. He sings. Back and forth, he strides the headland, as the guisers do, and quavers. *My mother was burned as a witch, My father was hanged from a tree....* When he sees the hare start from the furrow, he yells, and hurls a stone.

The Hare, the Moon

The moon's love's the hare, his death is dark of moon. He is her last prey, light's body, as the midnight soul, night's Ashes, is her first: All Hallows Eve, May Eve, her A and O. In spring, the waning of her year, she hunts in green: not vivid, but a cold grey green, as pale as lichened stone; afoot, for her hunt is scattered. And she hunts by night. Where her feet have passed is white with dew. Swift and mad, the hare runs, towards hallows, to the thicket's lap, unhallowing in white. He sees the white moon tangled in her thorn. Her lap is sanctuary. He would lie there panting, with his old rough jacket torn, his blood on the branches, red as haws. But at dawn, the hey is down. The white girl rises from the tree; she dances on the hill, unknowing ruth. Yet he runs to her rising, eastward to the sky. Behind him runs his deerlegged death, his pale death. There are some now blind have seen her, all in grey as stone, grey green in moving. No another says, as red as a roe deer or the moon in slow eclipse. At dawn, she will be stone.

They are sisters, stone and thorn tree, dark and light of one moon. Annis, Malykorne. And they are rivals for the hare, his love, his death; each bears him in her lap, as child, as lover and as lyke. They wake his body and he leaps within them, quick and starkening; they bear him light. Turning, they are each the other, childing and devouring: the cauldron and the sickle and the cold bright bow. Each holds, beholds, the other in her glass. And for a space between the night and morning, they are one, the old moon in the new moon's arms, the paling of her breast. The scragged hare slips them as they clasp. He's for Brock's bag, caught kicking.

Masks

Wouldst know thy fortune? her lover says. And laughing, as his bright hair ruffles at her breath, *Ah. What's o'clock?*

Not yet, she says, low-voiced. (The stone in his ear, like the blood of its piercing. The bruised root stirring on his thigh.) *Not dawning yet. Nor moon nor sun.*

Will not it rise? he says, rounding.

And go to seed. She smiles, remembering. *Not yet. I've plucked it green.*

The Rattlebag

The boy kneels, drunken, in the barn. They hold her down for him, the moon's bitch, twisting, cursing in the filthy straw. A vixen in a trap. He holds the felly of the cartwheel, sick and shaken, in the reeling stench. Cold muck and angry flesh. Their seed in snail tracks on her body, snotted in her sootblack hair. Their blood—his own blood—in her nails. She is Ashes and holy. He fumbles, tries to turn his face. He's not thirteen. "Get it into her, mawkin!" calls the bagman, wilting. Ashes and fear. "Thinks it's to piss with." "Hey, crow-lad! Turn it up a peg." "Spit in t'hole." And the man with the daggled ribbons, his fiddle safe in straw, cries, "Flayed it's thy mam?"

The Hare, the Moon (Turned Down)

The black hare's bonny, as they sing: she lies under aprons, she's love under hedges. And she's harried to the huntsman's death, the swift undoing of his gun. But the white hare's death, they say: a maid forsaken or a child unmourned, returning from her narrow grave. A love betrayed. Her false lad will meet her on the moor at dusk, a pale thing fleeting; he will think he gives chase. But she flees him and she follows, haunting like the ghost of love. She draws him to his death. And after he will run, a shadow on the hills, a hare: the moon's prey and her shadow. Love's the black hare, but the white is death. And one's the other one, now white, now black, and he and she, uncanny as the changing moon. They say the hare lays eggs; it bears the sun within a moon. A riddle. Break it and there's nought within.

Riddles

He holds her ring up, glancing through it with his quick blue eye; and laughs, and pockets it. A riddle. What's all the world and nothing?

> O, says she, *thine heart. 'Tis for any hand. Thyself would fill it.*
> And he, *Nay, it is th' owl in thine ivy bush. It sulks by day.*
> *Aye,* says she, *and hares by night.*
> *Thy wit, all vanity and teeth.*
> *Thy grave.*
> *At midnight, then? I'll bring a spade and we'll dig for it.* His
> white teeth glimmer, ah, he knows how prettily; and daring
> her, himself (for the thorn's unchancy, and this May night
> most of all), he says, *At the ragtree?At moonrise.*

Waking Wood

Between the blackthorn and the white is called the moon's weft, as the warp is autumn, Hallows, when her chosen sleeps. He dreams of lying in her lap, within the circle of her flowering thorn; his dreams wake wood. Between the scythe and frost he's earthfast, and his visions light as leaves. He keeps the hallows of the earth. And winterlong he hangs in heaven, naked, in a chain of stars. He rises to her rimes. When Ashes hangs the blackthorn with her hail of flowers, white as sleet, as white as souls, then in that moon the barley's seeded, and the new green pricks the earth. He's scattered and reborn. As in the earth, so in the furrows of the clouds, his Sheaf is scattered, whited from the sky until he rises dawnward, dancing in his coat of sparks. He overcrows the sun; he calls the heavens to the earth to dance. And in their keep, the Nine weave for their sister's bridal, and their threads are quick, their shuttles green and airy, black and white and red as blood. They clothe her in her spring and fall. In the dark before May morn, the Flaycraw dances, harping for the Nine to rise, the thorn to flower and the fires to burn, the wakers on the hills to dance. *The hey is down,* they cry. *Craw's hanged!* They leap the fires, lightfoot; crown their revelry with green. Not sloe. The blackthorn's death and life-in-death; the white is love. The bride alone is silent, rounding with the sun.

Riddles, Turned

She looks at him though all her rings. There's mischief in her face, a glittering on teeth and under lids. *An you will, I may.*

Quickening

At quickening, the white girl rises, lighter of herself; she undoes her mother's knots. Alone of all who travel Brock's road backward, out of Annis' country, out of death, she walks it in her bones, and waking. Neither waif nor wraith nor nimbling hare, but Ashes and alone. The coin she's paid for crossing is of gold, and of her make: her winter's son. Yet she is born unknowing, out of cloud. Brock, who is Death's midwife, sains her, touches eyes, mouth, heart with rain. She haps the naked soul in earth.

All the dark months of her prisoning, in frost, in stone, her shadow's walked the earth, worn Ashes outward, souling in her tattered coat. She's kept the year alive. But on the eve of Ashes' rising, the winter changeling is undone. From hedge to hall, the women and the girls give chase, laughing, pelting at the guisers' Ashes, crying, *Thief!* Bright with mockery and thaw, they take her, torn and splattered, in the street. *What's she filched? Craw's stockings. Cat's pattens. Hey, thy awd man's pipe! And mine. And mine.* Gibing, they strip her, scrub her, tweak the tangles from her hair, the rougher for her knowing. All she's got by it—small silver or the gramarye of stars—is forfeit. All her secrets common as the rain. And they scry her, and they whisper—is it this year? From her Ashes? Is't Sun for Mally's lap? They take her coat, her crown, her silence. Naked and nameless then, she's cauled and comforted, with round cakes and a caudle of the new milk. She is named. Then with candles they wake Ashes, and with carols, waiting for the silent children and the first wet bunch of snowdrops at the door.

They say that Ashes wears the black fell of an unborn lamb; her feet are bare. She watches over birthing ewes and flights the crows that quarrel, greedy for the young lambs' eyes. Her green is wordless, though it dances in the wind; it speaks. Her cradle tongue is leaves. And where she walks grow flowers. They are white, and rooted in the darkness; they are frail and flower in the snow. It is death to bring them under a roof; but on the morn of Ashes waking, only then, her buds are seely and they must be brought within, to sain the corners of the hearth. The country people call them Drops of Ashes' Milk. She is the coming out of darkness; light from the tallow, snowdrops from the earth, Bride from the winter hillside; and from Hell, the child returned.

She is silent, Ashes; but she sings her tale. The guisers strung the fiddle with her hair, the crowd of bone. It sings its one plaint, and the unwed, unchilded, dance:

> My mother bare me in her lap,
> Turn round, the reel doth spin;
> As white the cloth she wove for me,
> As red my blood within.
> As black the heart she bore to me,
> As white the snow did fall;

As brief the thread she cut for me;
A swaddling-band, a pall.

The Ragthorn

It was lightward and no lover. Whin sat by the ragtree, casting bones. There were rings on her every finger, silver, like a frost. They caught and cast, unheeding, caught and cast. A thief, a journey by water. Sticks and crosses. All false.

The thorn was on a neb of moorland, at the meeting of two becks: a ragthorn, knotted with desires, spells for binding soul with soul and child in belly. Charms for twisting heartstrings, hemp. They were bright once and had faded, pale as winter skies. Bare twigs as yet. The sloe had flowered leafless, late; the spring was cold. In the moon-blanched heath a magpie hopped and flapped and eyed the hutchbones greedily. He scolded in his squally voice. "Good morrow, your lordship, and how is her ladyship?" called Whin. She knew him by his strut and cock: his Lady's idle huntsman, getting guads in his beak. The bird took wing. The bare bones fell. "Here's a quarrel," she said, and swept them up, and cast again. When Ash came, she would rend him, with his yellow hair. Or bind him to her, leave him. Let him dangle, damn his tongue. She'd dance a twelvemonth on his grave. Ah, but she would be his grave, his green was rooted in her earth. And she thought of his white teeth in the greeny darkness and his long and clever hands. His hair like a lapful of flowers.

Whin was long-eyed, dark and somber, with a broad disdainful mournful mouth and haughty chin. But there was mischief in her face, as there was silver glinting in her hair: nine threads, a spiderwork of frost. Her clothes were patchwork of a hundred shades of black, burnt moorland, moleskin, crows and thunder; but her scarf was gold, torn silk and floating like a rag of sunrise. Looking up, she started—even now—and then she sighed and whistled softly, through her teeth. "Yer early abroad," she said. "Or late. T'fires are out."

Down the moor came a woman, slowly, feeling with a stick, and a child before her on a leash, its harness sewn with bells. Its hair was hawkweed. When it stumbled, it rang; she jerked it upright. Whin watched in silence as the two came onward: the beggar groping with her blackshod stick, the white child glittering and jangling. They were barefoot. She was all in whitish tatters, like the hook moon, scarved about her crowblack head, and starveling, with a pipe and tabor at her side. When she felt the rags on the branches brush her face, she called, "Wha's there?"

"A traveller," said Whin. "Will you break fast wi' us?"

"Oh aye," said the beggar, with her long hands in the ribbons, harping, harping. "Gi's it here." The blind woman slung down her heavy creel and sat, her stick across her knees, and held out her palm. Whin put bread on it. "Hallows with ye," she said. The long hand twitched like a singed spider; it snatched.

"Since ye'd be casting it at daws afore t'night," said the beggar.

"Wha said I's enough for twa?" said Whin.

The beggar crammed. She wolfed with her white eyes elsewhere, as if it were something else she wanted, that she tore. Her brat hid, grimed and wary, in her skirts, and mumped a crust. "And why else wouldst thou be laiking out ont moor, like a bush wi' no bird in it?" said the beggar. "Happen he's at meat elsewhere." She listened for Whin's stiffening. And grinning fiercely through her mouthful, "D'ye think I meant craw's pudding? Lap ale?" The bluenailed hand went out again, for sausage and dried apple, which she chewed and swallowed, chewed and spat into her fledgling's mouth. "Ye'd best be packing."

Whin drank. Too late to whistle up her dog, off elsewhere. The beggar took a long swig of Whin's aleskin. As she raised her arm to wipe her mouth, her sleeve fell back; the arm was scarry, roped and crossed with long dry welts. "Will you drink of mine?" she said, mocking; and undid her jacket for the clambering child, for anyone. Her breast was white as sloethorn.

Whin was cutting sausage with her streak of knife, and whistling softly through her teeth, as if her heart were thistledown, this way and that. "... *If I was black, as I am white as the snow that falls on yon fell dyke* ..."

The child suckled warily; it burrowed. The beggar pirled its hair; she nipped and fondled, scornfully. "It fats on me. D'ye see how I am waning?" She was slender as the moon, and white; and yet no girl, thought Whin: the moon's last crescent, not her first. Her hair was crowblack in a coif of twisted rags, the green of mistletoe, and hoary lichen blues. At her waist hung a pipe of a heron's legbone and a tabor of a white hare's skin. She had been beautiful; had crazed and marred. Her eyes were clouded, white as stones. There was a blue burn on her cheek, like gunpowder, and her wolfish teeth were gapped. Yet her breast was bell heather; her hands moved like moorbirds on her small wrists. They were voices, eyes. Looking elsewhere, she called to Whin, "You there. See all and say nowt. Can ye fiddle? Prig petticoats? I c'd do wi' a mort."

Whin said, "I's suited."

"And what's thou here about?"

"Gettin birds' nests," said Whin, all innocence.

"What for, to hatch gowks?"

"Crack eggs to make crowds of."

"And what for?"

"Why, to play at craw's wake."

The beggar wried her mouth. "Tha'rt a fool."

"And what's thou after?" said Whin. "Has thy smock blown away?"

"Hares," said the beggar.

"Black or white?"

"All grey to me." The beggar set the child down, naked in its cutty shirt. "Gang off, I's empty as a beggar's budget."

"Wha's brat is thou?" said Whin to the babby.

"No one's. Cloud's," said the beggar.

"Ah," said Whin.

The beggar did up her jacket. The child sat by her petticoats with a rattle; a wren tumbled round within a clumsy cage. "Will we do now?"

"How's that?" said Whin.

"Ah," said the beggar. "I give and take. My ware is not for town." She looked sidelong. Like a snake among heather roots, her hand was in her petticoats. She found something small and breathed on it, spat and rubbed and breathed. "Here," she said to Whin, holding out a round small mirror. "Is't glass?"

"It's that." It was clouded, cold; she held it gingerly. There was earth on it, and in the carving. It was bone. She looked in it and saw another face, not hers:

a witch, a woman all in green, grey green. A harewitch. A green girl, gaunt and big with child. The beggar was listening with her crooked face. "No," said Whin. "My face is me own."

"A pretty toy," the beggar said. "An ape had worn it in his cap."

Whin turned it; she ran her thumb round the edge. Earth bleared it. There was gravedust on her hands; she dared not wipe them. She kept her voice light. There are witches on the walk, between times. If you meet them, you must parry. "Here's thieving. Does they wake when yer come and go?"

"They keep no dogs," said the beggar. "And they sleep. This?" Between her hands was a scarf like an April sky, warped with silver. It was cloud and iris, changing. It was earthstained, like the sky in water in a road, a rut. She drew it through and through her hands. A soul.

"Here's a fairing," said Whin, and shivered.

"Aye, then," said the beggar. "There's a many lads and lasses gangs to't hiring at that fair, cross river, and they bring twa pennies til their fee." Her voice grew deeper. " 'Here's fasten penny,' they says. And mistress til them, 'Can tha reap? And can tha shear?' " Her fingers found the wafted scarf; they snatched it from the air. "And then they's shorn."

Whin watched it fluttering. The scarf had changed, like brown leaves caught in ice. "That's not on every bush. Was never a hue and cry when you—?"

"Cut strings? Wha said I did?" Her fingers brushed, ah, lightly, at Whin's neck, where the gold scarf flaunted, like a rag of dawn.

Whin flinched, but flung her chin up. "I've a fancy to't drum."

"I's keeping that," said the beggar. "For't guising."

"Did yer gang wi' them? Guisers?"

"I were Ashes."

"Ah," said Whin.

The child in the heather clapped its hands, it crowed. At its jangling, the small birds rose and called. Whin looked sidelong at it, smiling through her rings. "And you getten yer apron full. Here's catching of hares."

The beggar twitched its string. "I'd liefer gang lighter."

"Cold courting at Lightfast. Find a barn?"

"Back of Law, it were, and none to hear us. It were midnight and past, and still, but for t'vixens crying out on t'fell. On clicketing, they were, and shrieked as if their blood ran green. But for t'guisers ramping. See, they'd waked at every door, they'd drank wren's death. And went to piss its health at wall. 'Up flies cock robin,' says one, 'and down wren'; and another, 'Bones to't bitches.' 'And what'll we give to't blind?' says third, and scrawns at fiddle. 'Here's straw?' they said. 'And threshed enough,' said I. But they'd a mind to dance, they'd swords. D'ye think brat's like its father sake? Is't Sun? Or has it Owler's face, all ashes? Hurchin's neb? Think it one of Jack Daw's get?"

"Nine on one?" said Whin, furious.

The stone-eyed beggar shrugged.

"Dogs."

"Boy and all," said the beggar. "They set him on." Thrub thrub went the fingers on the little drum and stopped the windless pipe. They pattered. "Happen not his brat. Nor old man's nowther. Cockfallen, he were." She leaned toward Whin's silence, secret, smiling with her wry gapped mouth. Her eyes were changeless. "But I marked 'em, aye, I marked 'em all." She drew a braid of hair from underneath her cap, undid the knot with swift sure fingers. Moving on the wind, the trees was silver, black and silver. It was wind, as full of blackness as the northwind is of snow. "There," she said. In her fingers was an earring, gold, with a dangling stone, a bloodred stone. "D'ye know its make?"

Whin sat. Her hands were knotted, rimed with rings. False, said her heart's blood. False. The black hair stirred and stirred, so much of it, like shadow. The beggar leaned toward her silence, with her scarred white throat. "Is't torn, his ear?" She flipped the earring, nimbly as a juggler, tumbling it and sliding it on and off each finger, up and down. "What will you give for't?"

The child's white hair was dazzling in her eyes, like snow, like whirling snow. Whin turned her face. "It's common enough." But the needles of the light had pierced her; she was caught and wound in hinting threads.

The beggar palmed it, pulled it from the air. "And which of nine?" she said, her white face small amid her hair, like shadow. "There was one never slept that night, nor waked after. Drowned," she said. "Wast thine? They found him in Ash Beck. They knowed him by his yellow hair, rayed out i't ice. Craws picked him, clean as stars. Or will. Or what tha will. Wouldst barley for a death?"

Her fingers pattered on the drum. "That's one. And which is thine? There's one he s'll take ship and burn. He s'll blaze i't rigging, d'ye see him fall? And ever after falling, so tha'lt see him when tha close thine eyes. That's one.

"And one s'll dance ont gallows, rant on air. Is't thine? His eyes to feed ravens, his rags to flay crows. D'ye see them rising? Brats clod stones. And sitha, there's a hedgebird wi' a bellyful of him. And not his eyes. She stands by t'gallows. D'ye see her railing? That's one.

"And one s'll be turned a hare and hunted, dogs will crack his bones. There's a pipe of his thighbone and a drum of his fell. And tha s'll play it for his ghost to dance. And there's a candle of his tallow, for to light thee to bed. With such a one, or none, or what tha will. That's one. And which is thine?" She leaned closer. "D'ye take it? Is it done?"

Whin said nothing, caught in rime.

"Is't done?" said the beggar, chanting.

"And if it's done?"

Whin's fingers found the knot of the child's leash; undid it stealthily.

"Is't done?"

"Undone and all to do," cried Whin, springing up.

The whitehaired child had slipped his lead; he whirled and jangled as he ran. His hair was flakes of light. He whirled unheeding on the moor. And childlike fell away from him, like clouds before the moon, the moon a hare, the hare a child. He lowped and whirled and ranted. Whin caught him; he was light, and turning in her blood to sun. She bore it. By its light, she saw the beggar's shadow, like a raven on the rimy earth, that hopped and jerked a shining in its neb, a glass. A *thief*! the raven cried. Whin stood, as if the cry had caught her, in the whirring of the light like wings, a storm of wings; held fast. The child was burning in her hands, becoming and becoming fire. And she herself was changing. She was stone; within her, seed on seed of crystal rimed, refracted. She was nightfall, with a keel of moon, and branching into stars. She was wood and rooted; from her branches sprang the light, the misselchild. In that shining she was eyes of leaves, and saw her old love's blood, like holly, on the snow.

The child in the embers crowed, A *thief!*

And at his cry, Whin turned and ran, but still she held him fast. Behind her, the white-eyed woman shrank and whirred; the raven in her quillied out and rose, black-nebbed and bearded, with a woman's breasts. The waters of the beck leapt white. Amid the raven's storm of hair, its face, a congeries of faces, gaped for blood. Whitebrowed and ironbeaked; but its body was a woman's, cold and perfect to the fork: that too was beaked and gaping. It was shadow, casting none. Its very breath unhallowed.

Sun. The raven cried to its rising, "She's stolen my milk!" as Whin leapt the blackrocked foaming river. Cried and withered, like a flake of ash, and all its eyes went out.

The moor was sticks and ashes; frost and fire.

Whin held a heap of embers in her hands. They sang with dying, fell and faded into ashes. They were cold. She dared not spill them. With a shrug of her sleeve, she wiped her eyes, glittering with soot and tears.

The sun had risen. Whin turned from it and turned. White. A mist, a hag wreathed round and round her, cloud cold as law. Beyond her, by the tree, she saw a white moor and a standing stone, unshaped. An iron crown was on it, driven deep with iron tangs, and rusting. There were nailholes where the eyes should be. The tree was silver, bowed beneath a shining weight of ice, in rattling shackles of glass. They cracked and glittered, falling. As she turned away, Whin saw a girl unbending from the tree, a knee as rough as bark; or nothing, wind among the rags.

And as she looked, the frost was flowering, the tree was white with bloom.

The Thief

At the moorsend guisers came, in rags, in ashes, garlanded with green. They wore their coats clapped hindside fore; and a man in petticoats swept round them with a broom. A *thief!* A *thief!* they called, and clodded earth at the ravenstone. *Craw's hanged,* they cried. They paid no heed of Whin. A boy set garlands, rakish, on its crown. A girl in green tatters stooped for the beggar's blackshod stick, flung down; she strode it and she cantered, flourishing her whip. Moonbent and moledark, Hurchin tried his bagpipe, with a melancholy wheeze and yowl and buzzing, like a cat among wasps. Ragtag and bagpipe, they ranted and crowed.

There was one among them, in and out, unseen: a smutchfaced little figure, dark and watchful, with a heavy jangling pack. A traveller by kindred: breeched and beardless, swart and badgerly of shoulders. By its small harsh voice, a woman, so Whin guessed. And dressed as Ashes in the guisers' play. She wore grey breeches and a leathern cap, a coat of black sheepskins, singed and stained about the cuffs with ashes and with blood. Her hair was shorn across the brows and braided narrowly with iron charms. The hag had grizzled it; a hand undid the years.

"Hallows wi' thee," said Brock, nodding.

"And with ye," said Whin. What river had she leapt?

"Crawes Brig," the traveller said, and crossed to meet Whin at the beckside, stone to stone. Sifting through the flinders in Whin's hands, she found a something, round and tarnished; thumbed it to a gleam. A coin. She spun it round. The one side was obliterate—an outworn face, a bird?—on the other was a rayed thing, like a little star or sun. "That'll pay for't dance," said Brock, and smiled, small and sharp as the new moon. She took a bag of craneskin from her sleeve, and held it open for the ashes. There were coins in it and bones; she drew it tight. "Undone," she said, "and all to do."

Whin bared her throat, undid her scarf and jacket to the heart; she bowed her head beneath the cord. She saw at heart a shadow of the deepless water and the pale boat riding, shrouded with her soul. Brock hung the soulbag at her throat; she marked Whin's face with ash.

Whin gazed at her. "It's your coat Ashes wears."

"Aye," said Brock. "It's lent for travelling. Way's cold in but thy bones."

Whin said, "It's bonny on this earth, this morn; I'd linger."

And Brock said, "D'ye think it's dead alone as dance?"

Whin said, "I saw yon lady's scarf, her soul; she will not dance."

"Will she not?" A wind in the quickthorn shook the silver on the trees. Whin saw a grove of girls, of sisters, woven in their dancing, scarved in light. A hey as white as hag. Nine Weaving. "She dances now," said Brock. "She's rising into dawn, and rooted; she is walking from her mother's dark, toward winter, ripening until t'moon reaps her and she lies i' dark. Plum and stone. And she'll gang heavy til she's light."

"What's she?" But Whin had seen her in the glass, and barefoot in the shards of glass.

"Left hand til her mother's right, white's black. Not waning but t'childing moon. Unwitch, unmaiden and unwise. Her mother's sister and her make. Thysel."

"Her mother?" Whin did not name Annis.

"Aye, t'awd witch got her in her glass. And keeps her." Brock looked sidelong at the stone, the hill. Whin saw it, through and through, as black as sky. It was a woman sleeping, with the hooked moon at her heart, and stars and gatherings of stars within her side. She was the fell they stood upon, her hair unwreathing in a coil of cloud.

"How—?"

"She quickens wi' herself," said Brock. "She's moon, and mews her daughter in her dark. But I've keys to all locks, and I come and go. When's time, I s'll call on witch and steal her daughter to't dance. Will yer gang wi' me?"

Whin said, "I were Ashes."

"Ah," said Brock.

The scarf was in Whin's ashy hands; she ran it through and through a ring. "It were guising at Lightfast, and he'd bright long hair. Outlandish. I were fifteen, so I went down moor with him. I never see'd his face."

"So yer gotten a bairn?"

"Me mam and her gran—they'd've ta'en him and slain him. For an Ashes child. And sown his blood wi' t'corn. And they'd bind me til them, sleep and waking, while I's light of him. And whored me after. I left him under ragthorn."

The scarf was knotted. "And I prayed no crows'd come, nor foxes. But I never stayed. I never turned til home. I's walking since."

Brock's eyes were shadowed in her hair. "And what d'ye think? Here's a woman weeping and she laps her child i't shroud; she lulls her fondling on her knee. Her nails are broken, for she's graved it with her hands. Her milk is sore. And here's an old crone wailing, that she cannot comfort them. It's winter, and her loom is bare. And here's a fondbegotten brat, and nowther clout nor cladding til his arse. Tom Cloud. And thorn's his lap. And here's a vixen and her seven cubs; she dances like a flake of fire, crying, *Blood!* There's a many tales. And which is his?"

Whin said, "I'd want him well and growed."

"And thysel?"

"Away," said Whin. "I'd not be ended in a tale."

Brock tilted her face; the small cold iron clinked and jangled. "And here's a lad roved out wi' guisers—"

"No," said Whin, struck cold.

"And which?" said Brock. "And when? It's done, and long since done, and all to do."

Whin rubbed her hands against her breeches, crumpling the stormy scarf; the ash was pale against her clothes. Her blood was branching ice. *And which is thine?* the beggar said, herself met barefoot on the road. What child was sacrifice? And who had laid her down? "He's not—He's—"

"What moon makes of him."

Whin looked where the white tree shone. "And yet she dances."

"In her turn, and with him, in her turn. She bears him in her lap."

"I'd set her free."

"It's guisers turn all tales, and wake her to't dance. There's never endings. Will tha play for us?"

"A while," said Whin.

The rout came onward, fluttering with strips of rags. They shook a knot of bloody ribbons in her face. She knew them all by part. That broad-faced shepherd with the crown of horn. The old man with the bundled swords, the stripling with his pipe and drum. Those ranting lads. The Fool. The Awd Moon, with his petticoats and broom. Herself, with the box of coins, the bag of ashes. And the lad with bright unravelled hair. He bore a pole, with a cage of thorns, ungarlanded; the crow within it swung, down-dangled by a leg, its wings clapped open, and its beak agape and stark. Whin took her scarf and tore it, waif by waif, and hung the cage with rags of sun.

Aside and smiling, then she saw the white-haired fiddler raise his bow. Brock held the silver to him, beckoning Jack Daw; she called the tune.

And there began the wheedling of a little pipe, a small drum's thud.

The Guisers

They come like hoarfrost and are gone. In their packs are dreams, lies, memories: the old moon's spectacles; a bunch of rusty keys; a baby's rattle like a wooden wren; spindles and whorls; blunt shears; a half burnt doll; a tangle of bright silks, bent nails; a tallow candle and a knife; a crowd of bone. It sings its old plaint in an outland tongue. They strung it with her hair. Or there are gold rings, chaffered at the door, for nothing, for a gnarl of ginger and a rime; cast shoes of leather. The lady left them, walking into song. 'Twas they who put the grey hawk's feather in her bed. And there's a shirt, a little slashed, once fine, but stained with hanging. They had it from his back. His eyes went to the crows; his bones dance.

If they come as guisers, you must let them in: the slouched one with her bag of ashes; the patched one with his broom of thorn. They bring the sun.

JUSTIN TUSSING

The Artificial Cloud

Justin Tussing has an M.F.A. from the Iowa Writer's Workshop, and has been a fellow at the Fine Arts Works Center in Provincetown. He is currently the director of the Iowa Young Writer's Studio, a summer program for high school students.

"The Artificial Cloud" is a lyrical fantasia that combines a distinctly modern sensibility with the language of classic turn-of-the-century fantasy. It comes from the pages of TriQuarterly, 107/108.

—T. W.

Munjoy hung in a clever, leather harness. Below him lay the whole Valley. He could see the two castles and the long wall that stood between them. Clouds slipped past like giant wet cats.

All morning Munjoy had used his spyglass to watch the girl play chess. The girl had been playing chess and losing. He thought her face was so void of emotion as to be indicative of a type of boredom reserved for the very poor and the very wealthy. She wore a brocaded dress that started, like a collar, just beneath her chin and piled around her feet; it extended down past her wrists, covering the back of her hands, concluding in loops through which she'd threaded her middle fingers. A line of buttons no bigger than a bee's eyes ran down the front of the dress. At the conclusion of each game her opponent reached across and unfastened a button; these were so closely spaced that, although they'd been playing all morning, the dress was open only as far as her clavicles. Munjoy assumed her opponent to be the King; the man dipped pieces of bread in a crock full of a black jelly; he had a mane of red hair which fell over his shoulders and he had a long beard which glistened from the jelly he'd spilled upon it. The man had ten fat, pink fingers and as many rings. This couple sat in a flagstone courtyard. All around them, Munjoy observed falcons, parrots, and egrets perched on carved, wooden stands; jesses fastened to the birds' legs were tied to their perches. The birds were universally tiny. Juveniles, thought Munjoy. A small flamingo snapped its black beak at a man who brushed its feathers with a red dye. The courtyard was in the center of a large castle. Pairs of uniformed guards protected the building's entrances.

Munjoy recorded his observations in a notebook. He wore a jumpsuit of bleached cotton that buttoned in back and which he had to be helped into. Munjoy was a dwarf and he had fingers like toes; buttons were a challenge. To maximize its camouflage, the jumpsuit had just a narrow rectangular eye slit. The loosely woven cloth allowed Munjoy to breathe, but in order to eat he had to tug the hole over his mouth.

In addition to the spyglass, notebook, and pens, Munjoy carried a long, curved, cavalry sword and some provisions: hard cheese, water, and the circular loaf of bread which was traditional, meant to symbolize that future time when his country would have dominion over the Valley. Munjoy used colored inks to differentiate between agricultural, military, and political observations.

On an autumn day in the Eastern Land, the King noticed a cloud that resembled the head of a hound his father had once owned. He had been playing chess with his consort when he looked upward in contemplation. There were many other clouds in the sky. "I name that cloud Hound's Head," he said, and then he pointed it out to the girl. When the man had finished winning the game he looked up and there was the cloud, where he had last seen it, where it stayed all afternoon (he presumed that naming it had somehow made it permanent). The most unique aspect of the cloud, the girl said, was its immutability. Neither suspected that what made the cloud remarkable was Munjoy.

Each morning, before dawn, Munjoy was strapped aboard the cloud. Each morning he was handed a brand new notebook by an engineer named Hurst, the day's date embossed in gold on the cover. He tried to make small talk with the man who maintained the cloud, but Hurst considered the dwarf simply luggage. So Munjoy situated himself in his hanging seat and, after making sure that all of his equipment was within reach, he gave the high sign with a mittened hand. Hurst launched the cloud.

Munjoy hated the mornings. The cloud gained altitude slowly, only a few hundred feet when it passed over the Town. Here Munjoy would smell the wood smoke leaking up the chimneys. He'd watch the dark, smoke-stained windows. His own house looked so empty to him. And the fact that Munjoy knew his house was empty made it much worse to him than the empty-looking houses where he knew neighbors slept. Then he was over the fields: potatoes, rye, and wheat. Approaching the Frontier, he'd see the small orange dots of the watch fires. By the time he'd passed over the Wall he would be quite high; he could see past the lowest mountain passes to other mountains with their redundant spires. Everything outside of the Valley looked cold. Then there would be a slight bump when the cloud reached the end of its tether.

Munjoy's dwarfism had given him a certain prominence. At the Harvest Festival, maiden girls would run up behind Munjoy and throw their skirts over his head, then run off shrieking. When he turned sixteen, the age at which other boys were conscripted into the Royal Guard, he started work as an ox driver at the King's granary.

The granary smelled sour—crushed rye and ox piss. The ox was named Sissy and he trudged an orbit around the building, harnessed to a long spar that turned the millstone. Munjoy followed behind with a stripped sapling that he never employed, except to scatter flies. Like a compass with a stone point, Munjoy and Sissy etched a single circle.

Then one day, when Munjoy showed for work, there was only the muddy circle where the mill had stood. The building had been dismantled and its separate parts stacked onto a pair of hay wagons.

"What's this?" Munjoy asked Hurst—the engineer stood by the loaded wagons and smoked a thin cigarette.

"Are you Munjoy?"

The dwarf nodded.

"Proclamation of the King, you've been drafted."

"To do what?"

"You can hitch your ox to one of those wagons, for a start." Hurst told Munjoy where to take the wagons.

Having only known circles, the ox had to dissect the road into a series of arcs. Munjoy felt bad for the animal. And Munjoy felt bad for himself, too. Hurst stopped them at a great domed barn, painted silver-gray, just before the talus at the base of the mountains.

"Do you swear allegiance to the King, the Sovereign, and most Just?" Hurst asked.

"I do," said Munjoy.

"When will the Western Land reign over the entire Valley?"

"It is inevitable," said Munjoy, "as long as Righteousness and Justice exist."

Then Hurst walked him into the barn.

Sometimes, as he made his observations, Munjoy imagined that there was a man beneath every cloud, an entire cloud army, and that they were united in a silent brotherhood. On such days, each cloud that passed over the mountains seemed like a triumph.

A conscientious spy, Munjoy made detailed observations. On his first flight he wrote: Military (red)

As I slipped over the boundary, I felt some anxiety, but the people seem to have taken no notice. Wise and wonderful is the King. The Wall appears to be of a width equal to its height. Twenty feet? Solid. A trench runs along the foot of the Wall and there is an earthworks studded with sharpened poles. Guard posts are located at regular intervals. A larger post (mess or command?) is connected to the outposts by a series of roofed tunnels. The roofs are thatched. There seem to be about two hundred men guarding the wall at any one time, each is equipped with a weapon, swords and hammers. I've observed individuals digging with the swords, possibly for potatoes. I've seen no ladders or ramps that might indicate an intention to surmount the Wall in the immediate future. The earthworks might disguise an attempt to tunnel beneath the Wall, but I see no movement—no pick-axes, no shovels.

Agriculture (green)

The crops have been planted. I recognize a variety of bean, clover, and tomatoes. Men, women, and children can be seen weeding the fields. I've noticed some indi-

viduals harvesting small lumps which I'd guess to be potatoes. There are shallow, square ponds which contain orange fish—a boy proceeds from one pond to the next with a wheelbarrow. He uses a shovel to scatter corn over the water. Far to the north there is a group of white animals grazing which could be sheep, goats, or possibly large fowl. They harvested their hay very early and it is moldering. Their horses are swaybacked.

Political (black)

I have located their sovereign. He sits on a patio of the castle and plays chess with a young woman. She loses each game. Their Kings sits in a sturdy leather chair—loops of rope at each corner allow posts to be inserted so that an honor guard can move him about the premises. The girl wears a dress that fastens in front with a single line of closely spaced buttons—for each game she loses she undoes a button. She has been losing for hours and the dress is open to a point just even with tops of her breasts. Men in military uniforms engage the pair in conversation for a few minutes then excuse themselves. Servants rub their King's feet with lotions and a chef comes out with ornate dishes designed to look like bird's nests, flowers, and turtles. Their King appears to be bored by everything except the girl; she appears bored with everything. Their King says something to her and she walks over beside him. He sticks his face into the opening of her dress like he's searching for a lost coin. Fortunate are we.

After his first flight, Munjoy was presented with a commendation from his King for "Services Toward the Restoration of the Valley." Munjoy's name was written in a fancy script above the King's seal and signature. The next day, the dwarf tucked the paper inside his undershirt as he was helped into his flying suit. The little man was harnessed beneath his cloud. The doors of the barn swung open and the lanterns spilled light into the dark morning. Munjoy felt essential.

Hurst approached Munjoy as he hung in the undercarriage. "We'll need to hold that paper for you," he said.

"Why?"

"In case of an accident," said Hurst, "so there can be nothing to connect you to the King."

"The tether," said Munjoy.

Hurst stuck his hand out and waited.

Munjoy passed the paper out the suit's eye slit.

As the tether paid out, Munjoy could feel Sissy's steps vibrating along the line.

The King made it his habit to wait outside the barn in his carriage so he could personally debrief Munjoy when the little man returned in the evening.

"Describe her again," said the King.

Munjoy picked up his notebook and re-read the passage: "She wears a crown of orange flowers. Miniature yellow butterflies alight on the flowers and fan her with their wings. When she moves they erupt in a cloud which stays just above her until she is still and they re-settle. For lunch she was served a platter of fingerling trout and she only ate the cheeks."

"She's magnificent," said the King. "I command you, continue."

"She is joined by her King. He wears dark woolen pants and no shirt. There are many scars on his back and chest. He stands next to her and she traces the scars with her fingertips. She talks to him for some time. A pair of servants come out and erect a privacy screen around the couple—there is no roof to this structure. They entertain one another in the customary fashion."

"He's a toad," said the King. "And a poor warrior. Of course, my skin is as free of blemishes as a baby's."

"I have no doubt," said Munjoy.

"From now on you needn't concern yourself with mundane observations. Do you understand?"

"I do." Munjoy looked at the notebook in his hands.

"Do you understand when I say, 'mundane.' "

"I understand."

"The girl," said the King. "Only watch the girl." He took the notebook from Munjoy. Then he rapped his knuckles on the wall of the carriage and the door opened; a page helped Munjoy out. Hurst waited outside. The engineer regarded Munjoy before the King summoned him.

Munjoy's observations became the property of the King and a state secret. If he wrote, as he did one day, "Today is my birthday, I am thirty-four," then that too became a secret.

When Munjoy arrived at the barn the next day, he found bushel sacks of sand attached to corners of the cloud's undercarriage. "To test the structure's capacity," Hurst informed him. "Our King is concerned whether the cloud is able to carry more precious cargoes." When the cloud was launched, the dwarf could feel Sissy's every plodding step as the animal unwound the tether. With this new weight, the cloud flew lower than before. So low that Munjoy could feel the heat of chimneys. When he passed above the Wall, from the light of the watch fires, he could see that the men on sentinel duty busied themselves with small tasks: he observed a man creating a crocheted doily and there was a man with a small knife who carved a linked chain from a solid block of wood. Out of respect for the solitary men, Munjoy didn't write these things down; the King would only view such details as weaknesses to be exploited.

There was quality to the tautness when the slack came out of the cloud's tether, almost a groaning.

All morning Munjoy glassed the patio, but there was no sign of the woman. A child swept the courtyard with a corn husk broom. Then Munjoy found her, sitting on top of a turret. A rope was wrapped around her waist and tied to a stone. She had a telescope balanced on the parapet and it pointed right at him.

The sight of the girl watching him stole his breath. With care not to lose sight of her, he moved his hand in a slow wave—she copied this gesture as if his reflection.

Munjoy saw her King appear behind her. The man watched the girl for a minute. As Munjoy watched, he reached around her and cupped his hands over her breasts. The girl spun about, startled. Her telescope tumbled end over end, until it smashed in the courtyard below. Munjoy watched the cords in the girl's throat as she yelled at the man. The man pointed into the sky and she swatted him. A servant appeared to untie the woman and escort her inside.

When the cloud began its retreat with a lurch. Munjoy thought of Sissy, of the animal's subservience to the tether's reel. He remembered the notebook and he started to fill it.

It was after sunset before the cloud could be winched into the barn. Hurst released Munjoy from the harness and told him the King waited outside in his carriage. The King had requested that Munjoy bring the notebook.

Munjoy climbed into the carriage and took a seat across from the King. He read what he had written. There was a pause once he'd finished.

"Read it again," the King said.

"She doesn't appear until noon." Munjoy followed his finger on the page. "She limps and uses a cane."

"My poor bird," said the King.

"After lunch, an attendant arrived and put up a privacy screen. The attendant cleaned a number of sores and boils which were on the girl's spine."

"What kind of a man would beat such a girl?"

"I'm not certain they are evidence of a beating," said Munjoy.

"Absolutely," said the King. "They are nothing else."

"There are certain diseases and infirmities which cause abscesses and boils."

"I've solicited your observations, not your opinions. It is my intention to bring this girl here."

"Your Majesty," said Munjoy. "First I would have to get past the Wall and then there is the Countryside. Because of the obvious problems with visibility, I have very little knowledge of night defenses. The Castle itself is well guarded and has an interior that I know nothing more of than what I've inferred, right or wrong."

"Munjoy," said the King, "You've already circumvented those obstacles. You'll pluck her straight into the sky."

Munjoy decided the King had given this idea very little thought.

"I have spoken with my engineer and I'm certain that he can solve any technical problems."

All of the freedom that Munjoy had come to associate with being above the valley evaporated. "What if she refuses my rescue?"

"She's not being rescued by a dwarf in a cloud. She's being rescued by a king. You are only the vehicle. Besides, such an exceptional woman can only have contempt for those people. I shall introduce myself to her and entreat her to come. That will be sufficient. These details are nothing for you to concern yourself with."

"I'm your servant," said Munjoy.

"Once she is my Queen, the things that you've seen will be forgotten."

Munjoy nodded his head.

"I will compose a letter for you to deliver." Then the King leaned forward and grasped Munjoy by the shoulders. "Understand, I would attach myself to that contraption, if it weren't for other duties."

Munjoy bowed.

"You're excused."

Munjoy had just finished brushing Sissy when Hurst walked into the stall. Bluebottle flies covered welts on Sissy's back; they shimmered like sequins. Munjoy hung a step-ladder on a wooden peg.

"Whoever is driving him has to lay off the whip."

"You and the animal are both in a fine mess," said Hurst.

"We are." Munjoy scratched the animal's dewlap. "He has a great disposition because he's only known kindness."

"And they took the berries off him, that kills the fight."

"He's just like us, he's only limited by who he is."

"The King is only limited by what he can imagine."

"That's the problem," said Munjoy. "It has me stuck in a cloud."

"Where no one else has ever been."

"It's quite impossible to describe."

"Can you see over the mountains?"

"I can," said Munjoy.

"What's there?"

"More mountains."

"Do you know why he chose you?" Hurst asked.

"Because I'm the smallest."

"Because you're an orphan and an outcast. If there was an accident, who would miss you?"

Munjoy made a few swipes with the brush across Sissy's deep chest.

"When I designed the cloud, I always expected I'd be the pilot," said Hurst. "Our King forbid it."

The next morning, Munjoy waited by the ox's stall to see who was handling him. A boy walked into the stall carrying a cane-handled quirt. In one hand the boy grabbed the cord that fastened to the ring in the animal's septum. He gave three quick lashes and Sissy flipped one foot after the other; the ox's hooves kneaded the soft earth.

"He's like you or me, it takes him a while to get moving in the morning," said Munjoy.

"He's going now," said the boy, laying another stripe across the animal's haunches.

"I mean you shouldn't beat him," Munjoy said, stepping in front of the boy.

The boy stood half a head higher than Munjoy; he gave a sharp tug on the rein and Sissy came to a halt.

"He's my friend," said Munjoy. "Don't mistreat him."

"You've got a job and I've got a job," said the boy. "If the King orders me to beat him, then that's what I'll do. I'd tell him nice if I could, but all he understands is the whip." With that he swatted the back of Sissy's leg and took him out of his stall.

When Munjoy approached the cloud he noticed a large reel attached to the front of his harness. Metal crank arms jutted from each side and culminated in bone T-handles. Hurst fitted the device with a cover complete with sleeves for the cranks. With the engineer's assistance, Munjoy got into his jumpsuit and, together, they got him situated in his harness. A sheepskin pad protected Munjoy's chest from the sharp edges of the brass reel.

Hurst made sure that Munjoy's arms were long enough to turn the cranks. The man flipped a lever on the reel then grabbed a wire that stuck out from beneath the cover and walked out through the barn doors. The cranks spun as the wire paid out. Munjoy was instructed to turn the handles. He turned the cranks and the device slowly retrieved the wire.

"That's just a simple tool, a mechanical advantage," said Hurst. "Let me show you what I've been putting my heart into." The engineer wheeled a lorry underneath the cloud. An object was hidden beneath a shroud. With a flourish, he yanked the sheet away.

There on the cart sprawled a giant, black eagle; it had powerful, thick shoulders that became wings which flowed into fragile feather fingers. The head was cocked to one side and its eyes were green jewels. A curved beak was clamped on a golden bit which, in turn, was connected to a bridle; reins looped over the horn of the King's finest tooled-leather saddle. A latticework of gold highlights showed the details of every overlapping feather that formed the body. Talons, sharp as knives, finished feet that were tucked beneath the body. It was the most beautiful thing Munjoy had ever seen.

Hurst attached the bird to the wire from the reel; he turned the cranks and lifted the bird off the truck. Now he stuck a key into a hole in the bird's back. The bird's wings began a slow rhythmic beating and its head tracked a lazy, side-to-side arc. "I'm going to notify the King that you can see him."

Munjoy watched the metal bird imitating flight.

"I told you he'd come up with something appropriate," said the King.

"I have no imagination," said Munjoy. He could not understand how the machine's simple movements could contain such dignity.

"There are certain people who possess Vision and for them the world holds no limits. Hurst is such a person."

"How can one world contain such wonders?" Munjoy asked as the mechanical bird surveyed the barn.

"Do you know what the most destructive emotion is?" asked the King.

"Loneliness," said Munjoy.

"Yes," said the King.

Munjoy watched the bird.

"That's why I've sent you to get her."

"She's very wonderful," said Munjoy.

"Only I could appreciate her," said the King.

"I understand."

The King removed a document from his jacket and held it before Munjoy. "Put this in the bird's mouth and, when she is by herself, lower it to her." He passed the paper to Munjoy.

"As you command," said Munjoy.

"Bring her to me." The King kissed Munjoy on the top of head.

Hurst launched the cloud into the blackness.

The black bird kept sentinel as Munjoy drifted out over the town. He could smell apple wood in the chimney smoke and he knew that the trees which hadn't produced fruit had been felled. It was late autumn.

The days had become shorter. The night sky appeared on the horizon, framed by the high mountains, like a cold portal, like something one might pass through. Munjoy lowered the mechanical bird so it skimmed over the Countryside. The sight of the bird passing over the watch fires satisfied the dwarf. Munjoy reeled the bird in, and man and machine passed over the Wall together.

Munjoy knew when he was over the Castle.

The night before, Munjoy had looked about his house for something he might bring with him on this flight, some talisman. Inside, the house was dim. It surprised him that none of his things did he remember as being given to him. He'd crawled into his bed, little more than a low nest, where a cat might choose to drop a litter. He could think of nothing that wouldn't seem a burden if he were to carry it above the Valley.

Munjoy found the girl alone on the parapet. In one hand she held the broken telescope and with the other she made a noncommittal wave, a stirring of the air. In the half-light Munjoy read the letter the King had entrusted him with: *I am the King of the Clouds. I have been watching you. I need you. Climb aboard this bird and I'll take you away with me. Together we shall live in splendor on the other side of the World.* The letter was unsigned. Munjoy took a pen out and on the bottom of the King's letter he signed his own name. Then he rolled the letter up and stuffed it in the bird's beak. He started the bird on its long descent.

Almost half an hour passed before the artificial bird neared the patio. The girl went back into the Castle. As the bird continued to descend, the real birds on the patio panicked. The little flamingo fell from its perch and flapped about upside down. A red-tailed hawk stooped on one foot and tried to remove its hood with its other talons. A gyrfalcon flew a tight circle at the end of its jesses.

Munjoy was cautious, hoping not to drop the bird all the way to the flagstones. The sunlight helped—he knew he just had to prevent the bird from reaching its shadow. When he stopped it, the girl emerged at the edge of the courtyard; she looked at the bird for a few minutes before she approached it. It seemed to Munjoy, in those moments while she stood across the courtyard, that the bird seemed greatly diminished. Munjoy realized that he'd only watched the girl from this rather awkward perspective. The girl walked across the courtyard and with a quick stab of her hand she snatched the paper from the bird's beak. As she unrolled the King's letter, Munjoy saw that the way she held it close to her face suggested she might be squinting.

Fifteen-hundred feet above her, Munjoy watched through his spy-glass as the girl lifted a leg over the bird. The King's finest saddle seemed no bigger than a milking stool beneath her. She was a giant. She clamped her legs around the bird and looked upward. Munjoy started to turn the organ grinder.

Someone must have spotted the giantess once she'd cleared the castle's walls. People gathered in the patio to point up at her. Her king was there; he shouted. A group of soldiers took to assuming different formations. Munjoy's arms burned and burned; he found himself kicking his legs in an attempt to assist in cranking the enormous reel. He wanted just to watch her, but sweat running into his eyes made him blind.

For the first time, as she was retrieved into the cloud, the giantess could see past the snow-capped spires that surrounded the Valley. In her excitement, she spurred the tail feathers; they snapped off and fell like arrows into the crowd gathered beneath her. When Munjoy heard the giantess's laugh—the first thing to reach him from the world below—it gave him new energy.

"Munjoy," she called into the belly of the cloud.

The dwarf's arms were nothing but ether and fire, still he reeled until her huge hands latched onto his ankles. The giantess's touch sent electricity through the dwarf's exhausted body.

"I'm rescued," she said.

Munjoy couldn't speak. In his labor, the suit's eye slit had slipped around and hooked over his ear. He fumbled with his clothing so he might see her. He heard the cloth tearing, and the giantess peeled the hood over his head. Munjoy huffed the air.

"You're the King of the Clouds." Her hair was wild in the wind; it pointed its curly fingers in every direction. She had hungry green eyes.

"No," said Munjoy. He thought it likely his chest would explode.

"You'll take us out of the Valley."

"I'm just Munjoy. A dwarf."

The giantess couldn't stop her hands. She tore the seams out of his jumpsuit. Her fingers were all over the little man's body.

"You shouldn't touch me."

"Why?" she asked.

"I'm bringing you across the Wall so my King can make you his wife." Munjoy closed his eyes, he could barely stand to tell her. "He has no idea you're a giant."

"We're flying over the mountains," she said.

"This is not flying. It's a machine. See the tether?" Munjoy pointed at the line leading off into the distance. "Soon we'll be reeled in just like I reeled you in."

"Look," she said, pointing at a nameless place over the mountains. "That's where we're heading."

Munjoy couldn't begin to understand what he was feeling.

"You've chosen me. We're taking a journey," she said.

The dwarf felt a chill from the sweat cooling.

"From up here you can see anything and you saw me."

"I wanted you," said Munjoy.

"You have me. I'm with you. We're together. We just have to get past these mountains."

"I wanted to share this," said Munjoy. "We can see the whole valley."

"You're wonderful. I'll be yours forever. We only need to get over those mountains." The giantess's hands had found the heat between his thighs.

"That's everything," said Munjoy.

"Exactly." The giantess had climbed from the bird, into the cloud with Munjoy. She'd wrapped herself around him. She smelled of musk and green onions.

The tether shuddered; the wind moaned over it. Munjoy thought he could feel Sissy stumble. "I don't know if we have any hope," he said.

"Save us."

Munjoy unsheathed the sword. He couldn't reach the tether.

"Let me," the giantess said, extending a spar of an arm.

———

With the tether severed, the cloud sailed toward the mountains. In this one moment there was enough time for Munjoy to imagine a world with limitless hope. They could make it out of the Valley. The girl was strong; she would protect him. It seemed that everything was possible. Sissy was free—the ox could spiral through fields of sweet clover. With the right breeze, it seemed the cloud might stay aloft forever. Then it listed. It turned on its side. Munjoy saw the girl's destiny was tangled with his own; it was obvious, irresistible, and straight down.

RAMSEY CAMPBELL

No Story in It

About "No Story in It" the author explains that the story was written around an Alan M. Clark painting—the image the protagonist proposes for his book cover: "The image let me focus ideas I'd already scattered through my notebooks for further development. I had also recently been writing a memoir of the late John Brunner for my column in Necrofile. *While there is little of John in my protagonist, I'm afraid that John—were he alive now—would have no difficulty identifying with him. Nor would far too many writers in our field as well as his."*

One of Campbell's greatest strengths is his ability to put the reader into the scene, no matter how strange and unsettling that may be. "No Story in It" is from Imagination Fully Dilated II, *edited by Elizabeth Engstrom.*

—E. D.

"Grandad."

Boswell turned from locking the front door to see Gemima running up the garden path cracked by the late September heat. Her mother April was at the tipsy gate, and April's husband Rod was climbing out of their rusty crimson Nissan. "Oh, Dad," April cried, slapping her forehead hard enough to make him wince. "You're off to London. How could we forget it was today, Rod."

Rod pursed thick lips beneath a ginger mustache broader than his otherwise schoolboyish plump face. "We must have had other things on our mind. It looks as if I'm joining you, Jack."

"You'll tell me how," Boswell said as Gemima's small hot five-year-old hand found his grasp.

"We've just learned I'm a cut-back."

"More of a set-back, will it be? I'm sure there's a demand for teachers of your experience."

"I'm afraid you're a bit out of touch with the present."

Boswell saw his daughter willing him not to take the bait. "Can we save the discussion for my return?" he said. "I've a bus and then a train to catch."

"We can run your father to the station, can't we? We want to tell him our proposal." Rod bent the passenger seat forward. "Let's keep the men together," he said.

As Boswell hauled the reluctant belt across himself he glanced up. Usually Gemima reminded him poignantly of her mother at her age—large brown eyes with high startled eyebrows, inquisitive nose, pale prim lips—but in the mirror April's face looked not much less small, just more lined. The car jerked forward, grating its innards, and the radio announced "A renewed threat of war—" before Rod switched it off. Once the car was past the worst of the potholes in the main road Boswell said "So propose."

"We wondered how you were finding life on your own," Rod said. "We thought it mightn't be the ideal situation for someone with your turn of mind."

"Rod. Dad—"

Her husband gave the mirror a look he might have aimed at a child who'd spoken out of turn in class. "Since we've all over-extended ourselves, we think the solution is to pool our resources."

"Which are those?"

"We wondered how the notion of our moving in with you might sound."

"Sounds fun," Gemima cried.

Rod's ability to imagine living with Boswell for any length of time showed how desperate he, if not April, was. "What about your own house?" Boswell said.

"There are plenty of respectable couples eager to rent these days. We'd pay you rent, of course. Surely it makes sense for all of us."

"Can I give you a decision when I'm back from London?" Boswell said, mostly to April's hopeful reflection. "Maybe you won't have to give up your house. Maybe soon I'll be able to offer you financial help."

"Christ," Rod snarled, a sound like a gnashing of teeth.

To start with the noise the car made was hardly harsher. Boswell thought the rear bumper was dragging on the road until tenement blocks jerked up in the mirror as though to seize the vehicle, which ground loudly to a halt. "Out," Rod cried in a tone poised to pounce on nonsense.

"Is this like one of your stories, Grandad?" Gemima giggled as she followed Boswell out of the car.

"No," her father said through his teeth and flung the boot open. "This is real."

Boswell responded only by going to look. The suspension had collapsed, thrusting the wheels up through the rusty arches. April took Gemima's hand, Boswell sensed not least to keep her quiet, and murmured "Oh, Rod."

Boswell was staring at the tenements. Those not boarded up were tattooed with graffiti inside and out, and he saw watchers at as many broken as unbroken windows. He thought of the parcel a fan had once given him with instructions not to open it until he was home, the present that had been one of Jean's excuses for divorcing him. "Come with me to the station," he urged, "and you can phone whoever you need to phone."

When the Aireys failed to move immediately he stretched out a hand to them and saw his shadow printed next to theirs on a wall, either half demolished or never completed, in front of the tenements. A small child holding a woman's hand, a man slouching beside them with a fist stuffed in his pocket, a second man gesturing empty-handed at them . . . The shadows seemed to blacken, the sunlight to brighten like inspiration, but that had taken no form when the approach of a taxi distracted him. His shadow roused itself as he dashed into the rubbly road to flag the taxi down. "I'll pay," he told Rod.

"Here's Jack Boswell, everyone," Quentin Sedgwick shouted. "Here's our star author. Come and meet him."

It was going to be worth it, Boswell thought. Publishing had changed since all his books were in print—indeed, since any were. Sedgwick, a tall thin young but balding man with wiry veins exposed by a singlet and shorts, had met him at Waterloo, pausing barely long enough to deliver an intense handshake before treating him to a headlong ten-minute march and a stream of enthusiasm for his work. The journey ended at a house in the midst of a crush of them resting their fronts on the pavement. At least the polished nameplate of Cassandra Press had to be visible to anyone who passed. Beyond it a hall that smelled of curried vegetables was occupied by a double-parked pair of bicycles and a steep staircase not much wider than their handlebars. "Amazing, isn't it?" Sedgwick declared. "It's like one of your early things, being able to publish from home. Except in a story of yours the computers would take over and tell us what to write."

"I don't remember writing that," Boswell said with some unsureness.

"No, I just made it up. Not bad, was it?" Sedgwick said, running upstairs. "Here's Jack Boswell, everyone . . ."

A young woman with a small pinched studded face and glistening black hair spiky as an armored fist emerged from somewhere on the ground floor as Sedgwick threw open doors to reveal two cramped rooms, each featuring a computer terminal, at one of which an even younger woman with blonde hair the length of her filmy flowered blouse was composing an advertisement. "Starts with C, ends with e," Sedgwick said of her, and of the studded woman, "Bren, like the gun. Our troubleshooter."

Boswell grinned, feeling someone should. "Just the three of you?"

"Small is sneaky, I keep telling the girls. While the big houses are being dragged down by excess personnel, we move into the market they're too cumbersome to handle. Carole, show him his page."

The publicist saved her work twice before displaying the Cassandra Press catalogue. She scrolled past the colophon, a C with a P hooked on it, and a parade of authors: Ferdy Thorn, ex-marine turned ecological warrior; Germaine Gossett, feminist fantasy writer; Torin Bergman, Scandinavia's leading magic realist . . .

"Forgive my ignorance," Boswell said, "but these are all new to me."

"They're the future." Sedgwick cleared his throat and grabbed Boswell's shoulder to lean him toward the computer. "Here's someone we all know."

BOSWELL'S BACK! the page announced in letters so large they left room only for a shout line from, Boswell remembered, the *Observer* twenty years ago— "Britain's best sf writer since Wyndham and Wells"—and a scattering of titles: *The Future Just Began, Tomorrow Was Yesterday, Wave Goodbye to Earth, Terra Spells Terror, Science Lies in Wait* . . . "It'll look better when we have covers to reproduce," Carole said. "I couldn't write much. I don't know your work."

"That's because I've been devouring it all over again, Jack. You thought you might have copies for my fair helpers, didn't you?"

"So I have," Boswell said, struggling to spring the catches of his aged briefcase.

"See what you think when you've read these. Some for you as well, Bren,"

Sedgwick said, passing out Boswell's last remaining hardcovers of several of his books. "Here's a Hugo winner, and look, this one got the Prix du Fantastique Écologique. Will you girls excuse us now? I hear the call of lunch."

They were in sight of Waterloo Station again when he seized Boswell's elbow to steer him into the Delphi, a tiny restaurant crammed with deserted tables spread with pink and white checked cloths. "This is what one of our greatest authors looks like, Nikos," Sedgwick announced. "Let's have all we can eat and a liter of your red if that's your style, Jack, to be going on with."

The massive dark-skinned variously hairy proprietor brought them a carafe without a stopper and a brace of glasses Boswell would have expected to hold water. Sedgwick filled them with wine and dealt Boswell's a vigorous clunk. "Here's to us. Here's to your legendary unpublished books."

"Not for much longer."

"What a scoop for Cassandra. I don't know which I like best, *Don't Make Me Mad* or *Only We Are Left*. Listen to this, Nikos. There are going to be so many mentally ill people they have to be given the vote and everyone's made to have one as a lodger. And a father has to seduce his daughter or the human race dies out."

"Very nice."

"Ignore him, Jack. They couldn't be anyone else but you."

"I'm glad you feel that way. You don't think they're a little too dark even for me."

"Not a shade, and certainly not for Cassandra. Wait till you read our other books."

Here Nikos brought meze, an oval plate splattered with varieties of goo. Sedgwick waited until Boswell had transferred a sample of each to his plate and tested them with a piece of lukewarm bread. "Good?"

"Most authentic," Boswell found it in himself to say.

Sedgwick emptied the carafe into their glasses and called for another. Blackened lamb chops arrived too, and prawns dried up by grilling, withered meatballs, slabs of smoked ham that could have been used to sole shoes . . . Boswell was working on a token mouthful of viciously spiced sausage when Sedgwick said, "Know how you could delight us even more?"

Boswell swallowed and had to salve his mouth with half a glassful of wine. "Tell me," he said tearfully.

"Have you enough unpublished stories for a collection?"

"I'd have to write another to bring it up to length."

"Wait till I let the girls know. Don't think they aren't excited, they were just too overwhelmed by meeting you to show it. Can you call me as soon as you have an idea for the story or the cover?"

"I think I may have both."

"You're an example to us all. Can I hear?"

"Shadows on a ruined wall. A man and woman and her child, and another man reaching out to them, I'd say in warning. Ruined tenements in the background. Everything overgrown. Even if the story isn't called *We Are Tomorrow*, the book can be."

"Shall I give you a bit of advice? Go further than you ever have before. Imagine something you couldn't believe anyone would pay you to write."

Despite the meal, Boswell felt too elated to imagine that just now. His capacity for observation seemed to have shut down too, and only an increase in the frequency of passers-by outside the window roused it. "What time is it?" he wondered, fumbling his watch upward on his thin wrist.

"Not much past five," Sedgwick said, emptying the carafe yet again. "Still lunchtime."

"Good God, if I miss my train I'll have to pay double."

"Next time we'll see about paying for your travel." Sedgwick gulped the last of the wine as he threw a credit card on the table to be collected later. "I wish you'd said you had to leave this early. I'll have Bren send copies of our books to you," he promised as Boswell panted into Waterloo, and called after him down the steps into the Underground, "Don't forget, imagine the worst. That's what we're for."

For three hours the worst surrounded Boswell. **SIX NATIONS CONTINUE RE-ARMING . . . CLIMATE CHANGES ACCELERATE, SAY SCIENTISTS . . . SUPERSTITIOUS FANATICISM ON INCREASE . . . WOMEN'S GROUPS CHALLENGE ANTI-GUN RULING . . . RALLY AGAINST COMPUTER CHIPS IN CRIMINALS ENDS IN VIOLENCE: THREE DEAD, MANY INJURED** . . . Far more commuters weren't reading the news than were: many wore headphones that leaked percussion like distant discos in the night, while the sole book to be seen was *Page Turner*, the latest Turner adventure from Midas Paperbacks, bound in either gold or silver depending, Boswell supposed, on the reader's standards. Sometimes drinking helped him create, but just now a bottle of wine from the buffet to stave off a hangover only froze in his mind the image of the present in ruins and overgrown by the future, of the shapes of a family and a figure poised to intervene printed on the remains of a wall by a flare of painful light. He had to move on from thinking of them as the Aireys and himself, or had he? One reason Jean had left him was that she'd found traces of themselves and April in nearly all his work, even where none was intended; she'd become convinced he was wishing the worst for her and her child when he'd only meant a warning, by no means mostly aimed at them. His attempts to invent characters wholly unlike them had never convinced her and hadn't improved his work either. He needn't consider her feelings now, he thought sadly. He had to write whatever felt true—the best story he had in him.

It was remaining stubbornly unformed when the train stammered into the terminus. A minibus strewn with drunks and defiant smokers deposited him at the end of his street. He assumed his house felt empty because of Rod's proposal. Jean had taken much of the furniture they hadn't passed on to April, but Boswell still had seats where he needed to sit and folding canvas chairs for visitors, and nearly all his books. He was in the kitchen, brewing coffee while he tore open the day's belated mail, when the phone rang.

He took the handful of bills and the airmail letter he'd saved for last into his workroom, where he sat on the chair April had loved spinning and picked up the receiver. "Jack Boswell."

"Jack? They're asleep."

Presumably this explained why Rod's voice was low. "Is that an event?" Boswell said.

"It is for April at the moment. She's been out all day looking for work, any work. She didn't want to tell you in case you already had too much on your mind."

"But now you have."

"I was hoping things had gone well for you today."

"I think you can do more than that."

"Believe me, I'm looking as hard as she is."

"No, I mean you can assure her when she wakes that not only do I have a publisher for my two novels and eventually a good chunk of my backlist, but they've asked me to put together a new collection too."

"Do you mind if I ask for her sake how much they're advancing you?"

"No pounds and no shillings or pence."

"You're saying they'll pay you in euros?"

"I'm saying they don't pay an advance to me or any of their authors, but they pay royalties every three months."

"I take it your agent has approved the deal."

"It's a long time since I've had one of those, and now I'll be ten percent better off. Do remember I've plenty of experience."

"I could say the same. Unfortunately it isn't always enough."

Boswell felt his son-in-law was trying to render him as insignificant as Rod believed science fiction writers ought to be. He tore open the airmail envelope with the little finger of the hand holding the receiver. "What's that?" Rod demanded.

"No panic. I'm not destroying any of my work," Boswell told him, and smoothed out the letter to read it again. "Well, this is timely. The Saskatchewan Conference on Prophetic Literature is giving me the Wendigo Award for a career devoted to envisioning the future."

"Congratulations. Will it help?"

"It certainly should, and so will the story I'm going to write. Maybe even you will be impressed. Tell April not to let things pull her down," Boswell said as he rang off, and, "Such as you" only after he had.

Boswell wakened with a hangover and an uneasy sense of some act left unperformed. The image wakened with him: small child holding woman's hand, man beside them, second man gesturing. He groped for the mug of water by the bed, only to find he'd drained it during the night. He stumbled to the bathroom and emptied himself while the cold tap filled the mug. In time he felt equal to yet another breakfast of the kind his doctor had warned him to be content with. Of course, he thought as the sound of chewed bran filled his skull, he should have called Sedgwick last night about the Wendigo Award. How early could he call? Best to wait until he'd worked on the new story. He tried as he washed up the breakfast things and the rest of the plates and utensils in the sink, but his mind seemed as paralyzed as the shadows on the wall it kept showing him. Having sat at his desk for a while in front of the wordless screen, he dialed Cassandra Press.

"Hello? Yes?"

"Is that Carole?" Since that earned him no reply, he tried "Bren?"

"It's Carole. Who is this?"

"Jack Boswell. I just wanted you to know—"

"You'll want to speak to Q. Q., it's your sci-fi man."

Sedgwick came on almost immediately, preceded by a creak of bedsprings. "Jack, you're never going to tell me you've written your story already."

"Indeed I'm not. Best to take time to get it right, don't you think? I'm calling to report they've given me the Wendigo Award."

"About time, and never more deserved. Who is it gives those again? Carole, you'll need to scribble this down. Bren, where's something to scribble with?"

"By the phone," Bren said very close, and the springs creaked.

"Reel it off, Jack."

As Boswell heard Sedgwick relay the information he grasped that he was meant to realize how close the Cassandra Press personnel were to one another. "That's capital, Jack," Sedgwick told him. "Bren will be lumping some books to the mail for you, and I think I can say Carole's going to have good news for you."

"Any clue what kind?"

"Wait and see, Jack, and we'll wait and see what your new story's about."

Boswell spent half an hour trying to write an opening line that would trick him into having started the tale, but had to acknowledge that the technique no longer worked for him. He was near to being blocked by fearing he had lost all ability to write, and so he opened the carton of books the local paper had sent him to review. *Sci-Fi on the Net*, *Create Your Own* Star Wars™ *Character*, *1000 Best Sci-Fi Videos*, *Sci-Fi from Lucas to Spielberg*, Star Wars™: *The Bluffer's Guide* . . . There wasn't a book he would have taken off a shelf, nor any appropriate to the history of science fiction in which he intended to incorporate a selection from his decades of reviews. Just now writing something other than his story might well be a trap. He donned sandals and shorts and unbuttoned his shirt as he ventured out beneath a sun that looked as fierce as the rim of a total eclipse.

All the seats of a dusty bus were occupied by pensioners, some of whom looked as bewildered as the young woman who spent the journey searching the pockets of the combat outfit she wore beneath a stained fur coat and muttering that everyone needed to be ready for the enemy. Boswell had to push his way off the bus past three grim scrawny youths bare from the waist up, who boarded the vehicle as if they planned to hijack it. He was at the end of the road where the wall had inspired him—but he hadn't reached the wall when he saw Rod's car.

It was identifiable solely by the charred number plate. The car itself was a blackened windowless hulk. He would have stalked away to call the Aireys if the vandalism hadn't made writing the new story more urgent than ever, and so he stared at the incomplete wall with a fierceness designed to revive his mind. When he no longer knew if he was staring at the bricks until the story formed or the shadows did, he turned quickly away. The shadows weren't simply cast on the wall, he thought; they were embedded in it, just as the image was embedded in his head.

He had to walk a mile homeward before the same bus showed up. Trudging the last yards to his house left him parched. He drank several glassfuls of water, and opened the drawer of his desk to gaze for reassurance or perhaps inspiration at his secret present from a fan before he dialed the Aireys' number.

"Hello?"

If it was April, something had driven her voice high. "It's only me," Boswell tentatively said.

"Grandad. Are you coming to see us?"

"Soon, I hope."

"Oh." Having done her best to hide her disappointment, she added "Good."

"What have you been doing today?"

"Reading. Dad says I have to get a head start."

"I'm glad to hear it," Boswell said, though she didn't sound as if she wanted him to be. "Is Mummy there?"

"Just Dad."

After an interval Boswell tried "Rod?"

"It's just me, right enough."

"I'm sure she didn't mean—I don't know if you've seen your car."

"I'm seeing nothing but. We still have to pay to have it scrapped."

"No other developments?"

"Jobs, are you trying to say? Not unless April's so dumbstruck with good fortune she can't phone. I was meaning to call you, though. I wasn't clear last night what plans you had with regard to us."

Rod sounded so reluctant to risk hoping that Boswell said, "There's a good chance I'll have a loan in me."

"I won't ask how much." After a pause presumably calculated to entice an answer, Rod added, "I don't need to tell you how grateful we are. How's your new story developing?"

This unique display of interest in his work only increased the pressure inside Boswell's uninspired skull. "I'm hard at work on it," he said.

"I'll tell April," Rod promised, and left Boswell with that—with hours before the screen and not a word of a tale, just shadows in searing light: child holding woman's hand, man beside, another gesturing . . . He fell asleep at his desk and jerked awake in a panic, afraid to know why his inspiration refused to take shape.

He seemed hardly to have slept in his bed when he was roused by a pounding of the front-door knocker and an incessant shrilling of the doorbell. As he staggered downstairs he imagined a raid, the country having turned overnight into a dictatorship that had set the authorities the task of arresting all subversives, not least those who saw no cause for optimism. The man on the doorstep was uniformed and gloomy about his job, but brandished a clipboard and had a carton at his feet. "Consignment for Boswell," he grumbled.

"Books from my publishers."

"Wouldn't know. Just need your autograph."

Boswell scrawled a signature rendered illegible by decades of autographs, then bore the carton to the kitchen table, where he slit its layers of tape to reveal the first Cassandra Press books he'd seen. All the covers were black as coal in a closed pit except for bony white lettering not quite askew enough for the effect to be unquestionably intentional. **GERMAINE GOSSETT,** *Women Are the Wave.* **TORIN BERGMAN,** *Oracles Arise!* **FERDY THORN,** *Fight Them Fisheries* . . . Directly inside each was the title page, and on the back of that the copyright opposite the first page of text. Ecological frugality was fine, but not if it looked unprofessional, even in uncorrected proof copies. Proofreading should take care of the multitude of printer's errors, but what of the prose? Every book, not just Torin Bergman's, read like the work of a single apprentice translator.

He abandoned a paragraph of Ferdy Thorn's blunt chunky style and sprinted to his workroom to answer the phone. "Boswell," he panted.

"Jack. How are you today?"

"I've been worse, Quentin."

"You'll be a lot better before you know. Did the books land?"

"The review copies, you mean."

"We'd be delighted if you reviewed them. That would be wonderful, wouldn't it, if Jack reviewed the books?" When this received no audible answer, he said, "Only you mustn't be kind just because they're ours, Jack. We're all in the truth business."

"Let me read them and then we'll see what's best. What I meant, though, these aren't finished books."

"They certainly should be. Sneak a glance at the last pages if you don't mind knowing the end."

"Finished in the sense of the state that'll be on sale in the shops."

"Well, yes. They're trade paperbacks. That's the book of the future."

"I know what trade paperbacks are. These—"

"Don't worry, Jack, they're just our first attempts. Wait till you see the covers Carole's done for you. Nothing grabs the eye like naïve art, especially with messages like ours."

"So," Boswell said in some desperation, "have I heard why you called?"

"You don't think we'd interrupt you at work without some real news."

"How real?"

"We've got the figures for the advance orders of your books. All the girls had to do was phone with your name and the new titles till the batteries went flat, and I don't mind telling you you're our top seller."

"What are the figures?" Boswell said, and took a deep breath.

"Nearly three hundred. Congratulations once again."

"Three hundred thousand. It's I who should be congratulating you and your team. I only ever had one book up there before. Shows publishing needs people like yourselves to shake it up." He became aware of speaking fast so that he could tell the Aireys his—no, their—good fortune, but he had to clarify one point before letting euphoria overtake him. "Or is that, don't think for a second I'm complaining if it is, but is that the total for both titles or each?"

"Actually, Jack, can I just slow you down a moment?"

"Sorry. I'm babbling. That's what a happy author sounds like. You understand why."

"I hope I do, but would you mind—I didn't quite catch what you thought I said."

"Three hundred—"

"Can I stop you there? That's the total, or just under. As you say, publishing has changed. I expect a lot of the bigger houses are doing no better with some of their books."

Boswell's innards grew hollow, then his skull. He felt his mouth drag itself into some kind of a grin as he said "Is that three hundred, sorry, nearly three hundred per title?"

"Overall, I'm afraid. We've still a few little independent shops to call, and sometimes they can surprise you."

Boswell doubted he could cope with any more surprises, but heard himself say, unbelievably, hopefully, "Did you mention *We Are Tomorrow?*"

"How could we have forgotten it?" Sedgwick's enthusiasm relented at last as he said, "I see what you're asking. Yes, the total is for all three of your books. Don't forget we've still the backlist to come, though," he added with renewed vigor.

"Good luck to it." Boswell had no idea how much bitterness was audible in that, nor in, "I'd best be getting back to work."

"We all can't wait for the new story, can we?"

Boswell had no more of an answer than he heard from anyone else. Having replaced the receiver as if it had turned to heavy metal, he stared at the uninscribed slab of the computer screen. When he'd had enough of that he trudged to stare into the open rectangular hole of the Cassandra carton. Seized by an inspiration he would have preferred not to experience, he dashed upstairs to drag on yesterday's clothes and marched unshaven out of the house.

Though the library was less than ten minutes' walk away through sunbleached streets whose desert was relieved only by patches of scrub, he'd hardly visited it for the several years he had been too depressed to enter bookshops. The library was almost worse: it lacked not just his books but practically everyone's except for paperbacks with injured spines. Some of the tables in the large white high-windowed room were occupied by newspaper readers. **MIDDLE EAST WAR DEADLINE EXPIRES . . . ONE IN TWO FAMILIES WILL BE VICTIMS OF VIOLENCE, STUDY SHOWS . . . FAMINES IMMINENT IN EUROPE . . . NO MEDICINE FOR FATAL VIRUSES** . . . Most of the tables held Internet terminals, from one of which a youth whose face was red with more than pimples was being evicted by a librarian for calling up some text that had offended the black woman at the next screen. Boswell paid for an hour at the terminal and began his search.

The only listings of any kind for Torin Bergman were the publication details of the Cassandra Press books, and the same was true of Ferdy Thorn and Germaine Gossett. When the screen told him his time was up and began to flash like lightning to alert the staff, the message and the repeated explosion of light and the headlines around him seemed to merge into a single inspiration he couldn't grasp. Only a hand laid on his shoulder made him jump up and lurch between the reluctantly automatic doors.

The sunlight took up the throbbing of the screen, or his head did. He remembered nothing of his tramp home other than that it tasted like bone. As he fumbled to unlock the front door the light grew audible, or the phone began to shrill. He managed not to snap the key and ran to snatch up the receiver. "What now?"

"It's only me, Dad. I didn't mean to bother you."

"You never could," Boswell said, though she just had by sounding close to tears. "How are you, April? How are things?"

"Not too wonderful."

"Things aren't, you mean. I'd never say you weren't."

"Both." Yet more tonelessly she said, "I went looking for computer jobs. Didn't want all the time Mummy spent showing me how things worked to go to waste. Only I didn't realize how much more there is to them now, and I even forgot what she taught me. So then I thought I'd go on a computer course to catch up."

"I'm sure that's a sound idea."

"It wasn't really. I forgot where I was going. I nearly forgot our number when I had to ring Rod to come and find me when he hasn't even got the car and leave Gemima all on her own."

Boswell was reaching deep into himself for a response when she said, "Mummy's dead, isn't she?"

Rage at everything, not least April's state, made his answer harsh. "Shot by the same freedom fighters she'd given the last of her money to in a country I'd never even heard of. She went off telling me one of us had to make a difference to the world."

"Was it years ago?"

"Not long after you were married," Boswell told her, swallowing grief.

"Oh." She seemed to have nothing else to say but, "Rod."

Boswell heard him murmuring at length before his voice attacked the phone. "Why is April upset?"

"Don't you know?"

"Forgive me. Were you about to give her some good news?"

"If only."

"You will soon, surely, once your books are selling. You know I'm no admirer of the kind of thing you write, but I'll be happy to hear of your success."

"You don't know what I write, since you've never read any of it." Aloud Boswell said only, "You won't."

"I don't think I caught that."

"Yes you did. This publisher prints as many books as there are orders, which turns out to be under three hundred."

"Maybe you should try and write the kind of thing people will pay to read."

Boswell placed the receiver with painfully controlled gentleness on the hook, then lifted it to redial. The distant bell had started to sound more like an alarm to him when it was interrupted. "Quentin Sedgwick."

"And Torin Bergman."

"Jack."

"As one fictioneer to another, are you Ferdy Thorn as well?"

Sedgwick attempted a laugh, but it didn't lighten his tone much. "Germaine Gossett too, if you must know."

"So you're nearly all of Cassandra Press."

"Not any longer."

"How's that?"

"Out," Sedgwick said with gloomy humor. "I am. The girls had all the money, and now they've seen our sales figures they've gone off to set up a gay romance publisher."

"What lets them do that?" Boswell heard himself protest.

"Trust."

Boswell could have made plenty of that, but was able to say merely, "So my books . . ."

"Must be somewhere in the future. Don't be more of a pessimist than you have to be, Jack. If I manage to revive Cassandra you know you'll be the first writer I'm in touch with," Sedgwick said, and had the grace to leave close to a minute's silence unbroken before ringing off. Boswell had no sense of how much the receiver weighed as he lowered it—no sense of anything except some rearrangement that was aching to occur inside his head. He had to know why the news about Cassandra Press felt like a completion so imminent the throbbing of light all but blinded him.

It came to him in the night, slowly. He had been unable to develop the new story because he'd understood instinctively there wasn't one. His sense of the future was sounder than ever: he'd foreseen the collapse of Cassandra Press without admitting it to himself. Ever since his last sight of the Aireys the point had been to save them—he simply hadn't understood how. Living together would only have delayed their fate. He'd needed time to interpret his vision of the shadows on the wall.

He was sure the light in the house was swifter and more intense than dawn used to be. He pushed himself away from the desk and worked aches out of his body before making his way to the bathroom. All the actions he performed there felt like stages of a purifying ritual. In the mid-morning sunlight the phone on his desk looked close to bursting into flame. He winced at the heat of it before, having grown cool in his hand, it ventured to mutter, "Hello?"

"Good morning."

"Dad? You sound happier. Are you?"

"As never. Is everyone up? Can we meet?"

"What's the occasion?"

"I want to fix an idea I had last time we met. I'll bring a camera if you can all meet me in the same place in let's say half an hour."

"We could except we haven't got a car."

"Take a cab. I'll reimburse you. It'll be worth it, I promise."

He was on his way almost as soon as he rang off. Tenements reared above his solitary march, but couldn't hinder the sun in its climb toward unbearable brightness. He watched his shadow shrink in front of him like a stain on the dusty littered concrete, and heard footsteps attempting stealth not too far behind him. Someone must have seen the camera slung from his neck. A backward glance as he crossed a deserted potholed junction showed him a youth as thin as a puppet, who halted twitching until Boswell turned away, then came after him.

A taxi sped past Boswell as he reached the street he was bound for. The Aireys were in front of the wall, close to the sooty smudge like a lingering shadow that was the only trace of their car. Gemima clung to her mother's hand while Rod stood a little apart, one fist in his hip pocket. They looked posed and uncertain why. Before anything had time to change, Boswell held up his palm to keep them still and confronted the youth who was swaggering toward him while attempting to seem aimless. Boswell lifted the camera strap over his tingling scalp. "Will you take us?" he said.

The youth faltered barely long enough to conceal an incredulous grin. He hung the camera on himself and snapped the carrying case open as Boswell moved into position, hand outstretched toward the Aireys. "Use the flash," Boswell said, suddenly afraid that otherwise there would be no shadows under the sun at the zenith—that the future might let him down after all. He'd hardly spoken when the flash went off, almost blinding its subjects to the spectacle of the youth fleeing with the camera.

Boswell had predicted this, and even that Gemima would step out a pace from beside her mother. "It's all right," he murmured, unbuttoning his jacket, "there's no film in it," and passed the gun across himself into the hand that had been waiting to be filled. Gemima was first, then April, and Rod took just another second. Boswell's peace deepened threefold as peace came to them. Nevertheless he preferred not to look at their faces as he arranged them against the bricks. He had only seen shadows before, after all.

Though the youth had vanished, they were being watched. Perhaps now the world could see the future Boswell had always seen. He clawed chunks out of the wall until wedging his arm into the gap supported him. He heard sirens beginning to howl, and wondered if the war had started. "The end," he said as best he could for the metal in his mouth. The last thing he saw was an explosion of brightness so intense he was sure it was printing their shadows on the bricks for as long as the wall stood. He even thought he smelled how green it would grow to be.

JOHN F. DEANE

A Migrant Bird

Irish storyteller and poet John F. Deane was born on Achill Island in 1943, and now lives in Dublin, where he edits the Dedalus Press. He is the founder of Poetry Ireland, the national poetry society, as well as its journal, Poetry Ireland Review. *Deane's novels, story collections, and poetry volumes include* Walking on Water; Christ, with Urban Fox; Free Range; One Man's Place; Flightlines; *and* In the Name of the Wolf. *He was awarded the O'Shaugnessy Prize for Poetry in 1998.*

"A Migrant Bird" *is a quietly magical tale, exploring a state of enchantment evoked by music and the creative process. It is reprinted from Deane's most recent collection:* The Coffin Master and Other Stories (The Blackstaff Press, Belfast, Northern Ireland).

—T. W.

The door opened and a draft of sour air hit Fonsie on the chest. He coughed his sandpaper cough and looked up from his low stool. A young man had come in, carrying what looked suspiciously like a guitar case. He wore a green baseball cap, turned peak to nape, a chunk of hair waving through the gap in front—like a crested grebe, Fonsie thought. A migrant bird, please God, for there was never a guitar stood up naked in Frankie's Hill-top Inn before. Cowshite! Fonsie said to himself, and bugger it!

The young man looked around the bar as if he had a mission. He wore a gray sweat shirt with *Up Yours* printed in purple lettering across his chest. A big brass ring was dangling from one ear. He had a small silver ring fixed in his nostril. Fonsie shuddered.

Someone had left another pint on the table in front of him, one of the Germans, probably, and he dived into its sweet black depths for consolation. He left the cream along his upper lip a while, then slowly drew his tongue through it, sighed deeply and left the glass down on the table. Fonsie, his face the gray brown of old harness leather, wore a black felt hat tilted at a challenging angle back over his head. He took a handkerchief from his breast pocket, folded it, tucked it and the tailpiece of the fiddle under his chin until everything was snug as a rabbit in its burrow. He lifted the bow and poured a long golden-liquid chord across the floor of the bar. The customers were bathed in honey.

Fonsie closed his eyes and took a deep breath. He began to play, slow-waltz time, two sharps, "Rich and Rare Were the Gems She Wore." He saw a large and generous bosom, rising and falling like a summer sea, he saw red and flowering lips, opening and closing on perfect teeth and a moist, welcoming tongue, he saw emeralds and diamonds and pearls and a tiara, rich as the lake of night that is alive with stars. He laid his head between those wondrous breasts and when he finished the tune he was resting by the hearth of a grand lord's manor.

The drinkers in the Hill-top Inn applauded noisily. Fonsie retuned his top string, twanging it close to his ear so he could savor it. The young intruder had drawn up a stool and positioned himself beside Fonsie. The old man sniffled loudly, took a long sweep from his pint, settled his fiddle again and leaped off the very edge of a high cliff into "Bonnie Katie's Irish Reel." He closed his eyes and giggled with delight. Didn't he know Katie well! Well? intimately! he would go so far as to say . . . well, didn't he chase her? round and round and round among the haycocks in Horan's lower meadows, over the bottoms, back across the lower stream, her laughter like the challenge of the skylark against a morning sky, her petticoats lifting about her till she fell, tittering and joysome, down among the shakings, and he fell beside her, his fingers skittering along the mearin's of her backbone.

When he paused he was startled by the wild clamor of applause that brought him back to the pub. He opened his eyes and there were people around him clapping their hands and smiling at him. He grinned, clumsily, and took the fiddle from under his chin. It was like taking a wedge of his jaw away, his empty mouth gaped after it, and he filled that gap with a long and cooling drag from his pint after his dry-throated chase around the meadows.

The baseball cap leaned in, suddenly: "Old man, they kept talking while you played! How can you put up with that?"

Fonsie looked at him. He was very young, though big and handsome, in a sledgehammer sort of way. "They do come here, sir, to have a pint an' a chat . . ."

"But how can they pick up the words if they keep chattering?"

"There's no words comin' from me fiddle, sir. I just plays."

Fonsie dived for refuge into his pint. He finished it but kept the glass up against his mouth and glanced at the young man. He was reaching a big hand towards Fonsie; a large silver bangle clattered against a wooden one on his wrist. It was a strong wrist, covered with soft golden down, like a migrant bird's.

"Hi!" he said. "My name is Brad Pinkleman. And yours?"

"Fonsie, Fonsie Conlon."

"Can I get you a pint?"

Fonsie nodded. Anything to be agreeable, and he had journeys yet to make, across arid grounds. He closed his eyes again and set off, a fine ashplant in his right hand, a satchel filled with boxty bread in the other, and a paper-stoppered bottle loaded with Irish whiskey. He was on "The Connaught Man's Rambles," out of Ballina and into Enniscrone, down to Sligo and beyond, to Carrick; a pause, in Dromod, for "Peggie's Wedding," and then a dash to Castlebar where he dallied a while with his "Fair Gentle Maid." He leaned forward, his lips pouting, her lips pouting too, the space between him and her not that great, and closing by the second. He put his tongue out from between his teeth and as he did so he turned the corner into the last few bars of the tune, remembered he had no teeth, shut his mouth sharply and opened his eyes.

"I see you don't move up in the positions, Fonsie."

It was Brad Pinkleman shouting into his ear, trying to be heard over the fine applause. Fonsie began his pint. The young man was drinking straight from a foreign-looking, long-necked bottle.

"No then, sir, I do shtop on this wan shtool th' whole time."

"No, no, no! I mean you don't ever move your left hand up along the neck of your instrument, kind of limits your potentialities, if you know what I mean. Second and third positions. That sort of thing. See?"

"I do jusht play, like, you know. Sir." Fonsie thought he'd lay it on a bit thick for this young genius. "Sure you do only want to be in the wan position for "Fanny Power." Fonsie chuckled and gave the migrant bird a playful dig with his knuckle-sharp elbow.

"I don't quite follow you"—and the young man lifted his bottle and took a long glug from the neck. Like a suckin' lamb, thought Fonsie. Brad began to unzip his bag and—to Fonsie's horror—a great yellow guitar was lying across his knees.

"Frankie told me I could try out a song or two, if you don't mind, of course. Might help to bring some of the younger generation into the inn, if you know what I mean?"

Fonsie was dismayed. He had played on Thursday nights, in this corner, on this stool, for over twenty years and had hardly ever missed a night. Holy Thursdays maybe, or when Christmas Day fell on a Thursday. But what could he say?

"Let Erin Remember . . ." he muttered, through his pint, a sound like stones stuttering in a mountain stream.

There was a big man standing over Fonsie, another pint extended out of the battlefield of the bar. "For you," the man shouted down at Fonsie. "Ein pound of Guinness. Und can man hear *Die Koolin*? if I please? I come from Germany, no? zis music pleases me very. *Danke. Danke schon. Und sláinte.*"

"As a Beam o'er the Face of the Waters," Fonsie mumbled, grinning; Germans! they'd soon have every house in the townland bought up and converted; migrant birds, all of them, stretching the winter season into several years. However! and he stretched out his hand for the pint.

"How's the meadows, Fonsie?" someone called to him.

"They're lyin' down, Vinnie, lyin' down. Thank God for the man that invinted the silage!"

Brad drew a chord from his guitar and it fell onto the cement floor of the bar in a million pieces of shattered glass. Fonsie took a great swipe out of his pint and felt the cool hands within him massage his troubled soul.

"Fonsie"—the young man was leaning toward him again—"what kind of an oddball name is that?"

The old man looked up at him. He was a looker, mind you, the young women would leap on him, surely. The way they never leaped on Fonsie. Except in his head, of course, when the music was flying. Brad had big candid eyes; the hands lying ready on the guitar were covered in fine, light brown hair and every second finger sported a ring.

"Alphonsus. It's short for Alphonsus. Fonsie. After the saint, you know. Saint Alphonsus."

Brad, his brown hair down over one eye, knocked another row of bottles off a high shelf and began, in a strong bass voice, to sing. His eyes remained open, following the reactions of his audience.

"Green," went the words, as Fonsie heard them, "*Green me a crew for the long voyage out, oh baby green me, green me a crew; yeah, yeah, oh baby yeah; flag me a wave for the long voyage out, oh baby lean on me.*" Then he knocked several rows of bottles off several rows of shelves, his head lowered and beating up and down to his rhythms, his lower lip clenched in his fine, calf's teeth.

"*Green me a crew for the long voyage home, oh baby green me, green me a crew; yeah, yeah, oh baby yeah; wave me a flag for the long voyage home, oh baby lean on me.*"

He has a good voice, Fonsie thought, if only he could find a song to fit into it.

When he finished, Brad seemed a little disappointed with the bemused applause that came from the crowd. But word would spread, his thews! his baby cheeks! It was between times, yet, between times in this backwash corner of the world.

"How's about you playin' 'Danny Boy', Fonsie? and maybe I can strum along?"

Strum along! Cowshite! thought Fonsie, and bugger it! Yeah! But outside himself Fonsie smiled and tucked his fiddle back under his chin.

"What key's she in?" Brad asked.

Fonsie looked down at his bow as if the long curved timber held the answer. "Two sharps," he mumbled.

"Key of D. Right, old man, let's you and me strike up a storm for these innocents!"

Fonsie lowered his fiddle, reached for his pint and took a long, relieving scoop from it. Then he began to play, his eyes closed, his body moving proudly along from glen to glen and down the mountainside. He stepped out slowly onto a late summer meadow and Danny, young and eager and foolish, preening himself in his uniform of war, marched past him and away into the future. Don't be in such a hurry away from those who know and love you, Fonsie whispered to the brightly colored back. But there was somebody at Fonsie's shoulder, moving with him as he flew into a valley all hushed and white with snow, there was a large presence, a bulked shadow keeping pace, offering to help him over stones, to open gates for him, to take his hand . . .

In sudden irritation Fonsie leaped away into the air like a black cat pounced on by a dog and came back down running toward the "Humors of Ballymanus." This was better, he was free again, racing and cavorting round a noisy market square, in and out like a frisky pup between the legs of the cattle, nipping at them, teasing the big slow beasts while he whooped and skittered with laughter. He was joined by "Paddy Haggarthy" and "Nora Creina," and together they raced and frolicked, down side-alleyways, over gurgling waterways, tripping lightly along rough tractorways, back up the slopes and into Frankie's Hill-top Inn.

A great thirst had risen again within Fonsie's chest and he finished his pint with gusto.

"Well, old man"—it was Brad again—"you could give Yehudi a master class any day!"

Fonsie presumed, because he was that kind of an old man, that this was intended as some sort of a compliment; he grinned his cave-mouth grin and licked the froth slowly from along his upper lip. He got up, stiffly, from his stool and made his way to the toilets, shouldering his way through the air thickened with congratulations.

Fonsie passed the new gents' toilet and went out into the yard where he had been going these past twenty years. He stood against the stable wall and sighed with satisfaction. The stars were beautiful overhead; there was scarcely a breath of wind. He felt a little dizzy and his chest was rough as a harrow. The world turns heavily, he thought, like an old, unoiled cartwheel. He thought he might give Frankie's a skip next Thursday night; the thought made him feel heavy as a haycock after rain.

"And if you come," he sang it quietly, "and all the flowers are dying, and I am dead . . .

He turned back toward the door of the bar. As he crossed the familiar old rutted yard he heard the shrill high call of a curlew passing west over the mountain toward the sea. He knew it well, the curlew, he knew the lovely whirring sound its wings made through the night air, he knew the loneliness and the challenge both mixed into that local, endangered cry. He raised his head toward the darkness and smiled. He could hear the young man scattering his broken bottles about the floor inside. He giggled as another air came to his mind out of the darkness: "Go Where Glory Waits Thee." "One sharp," he said aloud, "and up yours, too."

He paused again, his hand on the latch of the back door of Frankie's Hill-top Inn. "Brad!" he said to himself. "Brad. What kind of an oddball name is that?"

DONELLE R. RUWE

The Thousandth Night

Dr. Donelle Ruwe is an English professor at Fitchburg State College, Massachusetts, where she teaches British literature, Native American literature, and poetry. Her chapbook, Condiments, *won the Kinloch Rivers Award and her poetry has been published by* The Poetry Review, Sycamore Review, Poetry East, New England Review, *and other journals. She was raised in Idaho, received a Ph.D. from the University of Notre Dame, and plays bluegrass music on the side.*

"The Thousandth Night" is reprinted from the New England Review, *vol. 21, no. 2.*

—T. W.

And then Scheherezade grew desperate for a story,
for a line to spin into a dance of seven shawls to snatch
his wandering thoughts, but it was hard. He was a king
of refined tastes, and she no lovelier than a dozen others
in the harem of perfumed shoulders and delicate hips.
Barely fifteen, she soon exhausted her small stock
of family stories and parables. Modest, she would not
look into his face, had seen only this luxurious room,
and it, in the second year, began to speak—lush curtains
became shifting dunes and magic carpets, the Arabian lattice
a labyrinthine cave. She imagined magic lamps and genii,
an adventurous orphan imbued with her own voice and features—
she survived another night, and always Aladdin was freed.
In the third year of sleepless nights, she began repeating
entire motifs. She was who she was, singular, and feared
she could not hold his interest. She stopped fixing her hair.
But still he returned each night, would sit on her low pallaise,
expectant, waiting for some word or gesture. Deprived of sun,
paper, and books, on the thousandth night, when the stone
    ceiling
contracted, and the ocher walls, like listening ears, closed in,

she stopped. Her hands stroked the changeable silk of her sheets.
Perhaps this would be the gesture. Or perhaps it was silence
he'd desired all along. It no longer mattered. She'd forgotten
how to speak, was lost in admiring the shape of her hands—
how they fit her wrists, and her wrists fit her body.
What were these miraculous things? She couldn't name them.

ANDY DUNCAN

The Pottawatomie Giant

Andy Duncan has a B.A. in journalism from the University of South Carolina, an M.A. in creative writing from North Carolina State University, and an M.F.A. in fiction writing from the University of Alabama. He is also a graduate of the 1994 Clarion West writers' workshop and a frequent attendee of the Sycamore Hill Writers' Conference. His stories have been published in Starlight 1, Asimov's, Realms of Fantasy, Event Horizon, Best New Horror, and Weird Tales. They've recently been collected in the volume Beluthahatchie and Other Stories. Duncan has been short-listed for the Nebula Award, Hugo Award, International Horror Critics' Award, and John W. Campbell Award for Best New Writer. He lives in Tuscaloosa, Alabama, and teaches literature and creative writing at the University of Alabama.

"The Pottawatomie Giant" is a moving "alternate history" story about former heavyweight boxing champion Jess Willard and escape artist Harry Houdini. It comes from the fiction section of the SCIFI.COM Web site, November 1, 2000.

—T. W.

O n the afternoon of November 30, 1915, Jess Willard, for seven months the heavyweight champion of the world, crouched, hands on knees, in his Los Angeles hotel window to watch a small figure swaying like a pendulum against the side of the *Times* building three blocks away.

"Cripes!" Willard said. "How's he keep from fainting, his head down like that, huh, Lou?"

"He trains, Champ," said his manager, one haunch on the sill. "Same's you."

Training had been a dispute between the two men lately, but Willard let it go. "Cripes!" Willard said again, his mouth dry.

The street below was a solid field of hats, with an occasional parasol like a daisy, and here and there a mounted policeman statue-still and gazing up like everyone. Thousands were yelling, as if sound alone would buoy the upside-down figure writhing 150 feet above the pavement.

"Attaboy, Harry!"

"Five minutes, that's too long! Someone bring him down!"

"Five minutes, hell, I seen him do thirty."

"At least he's not underwater this time."

"At least he ain't in a milk can!"

"Look at him go! The strait-jacket's not made that can hold that boy, I tell you."

"You can do it, Harry!"

Willard himself hated crowds, but he had been drawing them all his life. One of the farm hands had caught him at age twelve toting a balky calf beneath one arm, and thereafter he couldn't go into town without people egging him on to lift things—livestock, Mr. Olsburg the banker, the log behind the fancy house. When people started offering cash money, he couldn't well refuse, having seen Mama and Papa re-count their jar at the end of every month, the stacks of old coins dull even in lamplight. So Jess Willard, at thirty-three, knew something about what physical feats earned, and what they cost. He watched this midair struggle, lost in jealousy, in sympathy, in professional admiration.

"God damn, will you look at this pop-eyed city," Lou said. "It's lousy with believers. I tell you, Champ, this fella has set a whole new standard for public miracles. When Jesus Christ Almighty comes back to town, he'll have to work his ass off to get in the newspapers at all." Lou tipped back his head, pursed his lips, and jetted cigar smoke upstairs.

"Do you *mind?*" asked the woman directly above, one of three crowding a ninth-floor window. She screwed up her face and fanned the air with her hands.

"Settle down, sister, smoke'll cure you soon enough," Lou said. He wedged the cigar back into his mouth and craned his neck to peer around Willard. "Have a heart, will you, Champ? It's like looking past Gibraltar."

"Sorry," Willard said, and withdrew a couple of inches, taking care not to bang his head on the sash. He already had banged his head crossing from the corridor to the parlor, and from the bathroom to the bedroom. Not that it hurt— no, to be hurt, Willard's head had to be hit plenty harder than that. But he'd never forgotten how the other children laughed when he hit his head walking in the door, that day the Pottawatomie County sheriff finally made him go to school. All the children but Hattie. So he took precautions outside the ring, and seethed inside each time he forgot he was six foot seven. This usually happened in hotel suites, all designed for Lou-sized men, or less. Since Havana, Willard had lived mostly in hotel suites.

Leaning from the next-door window on the left was a jowly man in a derby hat. He had been looking at Houdini only half the time, Willard the other half. Now he rasped: "Hey, buddy. Hey. Jess Willard."

Willard dreaded autograph-seekers, but Lou said a champ had to make nice. "You're the champ, now, boy," Lou kept saying, "and a champ has gotta be *seen!*"

"Yeah, that's me," Willard said.

His neighbor looked startled. Most people were, when they heard Willard's bass rumble for the first time. "I just wanted to say congratulations, Champ, for putting that nigger on the canvas where he belongs."

"I appreciate it," Willard said. He had learned this response from his father, a man too proud to say *thanks*. He tried to focus again on Houdini. The man seemed to be doing sit-ups in midair, but at a frenzied rate, jackknifing himself repeatedly. The rope above him whipped from side to side. Willard wondered how much of the activity was necessary, how much for effect.

The derby-hatted guy wasn't done. "Twenty-six rounds, damn, you taught Mr. Coon Johnson something about white men, I reckon, hah?"

Ever since Havana. Cripes. Houdini's canvas sleeves, once bound across his chest, were now bound behind him. Somehow he'd worked his arms over his head—was the man double-jointed?

"Say, how come you ain't had nothing but exhibitions since? When you gonna take on Frank Moran, huh? I know that nigger ain't taken the fight out of you. I know you ain't left your balls down in Cuba." He laughed like a bull snorting.

Willard sighed. He'd leave this one to Lou. Lou wouldn't have lasted ten seconds in the ring, but he loved a quarrel better than any boxer Willard knew.

"Balls?" Lou squawked, right on schedule. "Balls? Let me tell you something, fella."

Now Houdini's arms were free, the long canvas strap dangling. The crowd roared.

"When Moran is ready, we'll be ready, you got me?" Lou leaned out to shake his finger and nearly lost his balance. "Whoa," he said, clutching his hat. "Fella, you're, why, you're just lucky there's no ledge here. Yeah. You think he's taking it so easy, well, maybe you want to spar a few rounds with him, huh?"

Now Houdini had looped the canvas strap across the soles of his feet, and was tugging at it like a madman. More and more of his white shirt was visible. Willard resolved that when he started training again—when Lou got tired of parties and banquets and Keys to the City and let Willard go home to the gymnasium, and to Hattie—he would try this upside-down thing, if he could find rope strong enough.

"Well, how about I spar with *you*, buddy? Who the hell are you, Mr. Milksop?"

"I'm his manager, that's who I am! And let me tell you another thing . . ."

Houdini whipped off the last of the jacket and held the husk out, dangling, for all to see. Then he dropped it and flung both arms out to the side, an upside-down T. Amid the pandemonium, the jacket flew into the crowd and vanished like a ghost. Trash rained from the windows, as people dropped whatever they were holding to applaud. Willard stared as a woman's dress fluttered down to drape a lamppost. It was blue and you could see through it. Even the guy with the derby was cheering, his hands clasped overhead. "Woo hoo!" he said, his quarrel forgotten. "Woo hoo hoo!"

With a smile and a shake of his head, Lou turned his back on it all. "The wizard of ballyhoo," he said. "Too bad they can't string up *all* the Jews, eh Champ?" He patted Willard's shoulder and left the window.

As he was winched down, Houdini took inverted bows, and there was much laughter. Willard, who had neither cheered nor applauded, remained motionless at the window, tracking Houdini's descent. Someone's scented handkerchief landed on his head, and he brushed it away. He watched as the little dark-haired man in the ruffled shirt dropped headfirst into the sea that surged forward and engulfed him. His feet went last, bound at the ankles, patent-leather shoes side by side like a soldier's on review. Willard could imagine how they must shine.

———

That night, as Willard followed Lou up the curving, ever-narrowing, crimson-carpeted stairs leading to the balconies of the Los Angeles Orpheum, the muffled laughter and applause through the interior wall seemed to jeer Willard's every step, his every clumsy negotiation of a chandelier, his every flustered pause while a giggling and feathered bevy of young women flowed around his waist. Hattie didn't need feathers, being framed, in Willard's mind, by the open sky. These women needed plenty. Those going down gaped at him, chins tipping upward, until they passed; those going up turned at the next landing for a backward and downward look of frank appraisal. "We had a whole box in Sacramento," Lou muttered as he squinted from the numbers on the wall to the crumpled paper in his hand. "Shit. I guess these Los Angeles boxes is for the quality." A woman with a powder-white face puckered her lips at Willard and winked. Grunting in triumph, Lou overshot a cuspidor and threw open a door with a brown grin. "Save one of the redheads for me, willya?" Lou hissed, as Willard ducked past him into darkness.

Willard stopped to get his bearings as a dozen seated silhouettes turned to look at him. Beyond, the arched top of the stage was a tangle of golden vines. The balcony ceiling was too low. Willard shuffled forward, head down, as Lou pushed him two-handed in the small of the back. "Hello," Willard said, too loudly, and someone gasped. Then the others began to murmur hellos in return. "So good to meet you," they murmured amid a dozen outstretched hands, the male shapes half-standing, diamond rings and cufflinks sharp in the light from the stage. Willard was able to shake some hands, squeeze others; some merely stroked or patted him as he passed. "A pleasure," he kept saying. "A God's honest pleasure."

Lou made Willard sit in the middle of the front row next to Mrs. Whoever-She-Was, someone important; Lou said her name too fast. She was plump as a guinea hen and reeked of powder. Willard would have preferred the aisle. Here there was little room for his legs, his feet. Plus the seat, as usual, was too narrow. He jammed his buttocks between the slats that passed for armrests, bowing the wood outward like the sides of a firehose. As his hams sank, his jacket rode up in back. Once seated, he tried to work the jacket down, to no avail. Already his face was burning with the certainty that all eyes in the hall were focused not on the stage but on the newly hunchbacked Jess Willard. "Don't worry, he's just now begun," Mrs. Whoever whispered across Willard, to Lou. "You've hardly missed a thing."

His knees cut off the view of the stage below. He parted his knees just a little. Between them, on the varnished planks of the stage far below, Houdini patted the air to quell another round of applause. He was a short, dark, curly-haired man in a tuxedo. At his feet were a dozen scattered roses.

"Thank you, my friends, thank you," the little man said, though it sounded more like "Tank you"—a German, Willard had heard, this Houdini, or was it Austrian? Seen from this unnatural angle, nearly directly above like this, he looked dwarfish, foreshortened. He had broad shoulders, though, and no sign of a paunch beneath his cummerbund. Lou jabbed Willard in the side, glared at Willard's knees, then his face. Sighing, Willard closed his knees again.

"Ladies and gentlemen—are the ushers ready? Thank you. Ladies and gentlemen, I beg your assistance with the following part of the program. I require the services of a committee of ten. Ten good men and true, from the ranks of the audience, who are willing to join me here upon the stage and to watch closely my next performance, that all my claims be verified as accurate, that its every particular be beyond reproach."

The balcony was uncomfortably hot. Sweat rolled down Willard's torso, his neck. Mrs. Whoever opened her fan and worked up a breeze. A woman across the auditorium was staring at Willard and whispering to her husband. He could imagine. *All I can say is, you cannot trust those photographs. Look how they hide that poor man's deformities.*

"Ten good men and true. Yes, thank you, sir, your bravery speaks well for our boys in Haiti, and in Mexico." A spatter of applause. "The ushers will direct you. And you, sir, yes, thank you as well. Ladies, perhaps you could help us identify the more modest of the good men among us?" Laughter. "Yes, madam, your young man looks a likely prospect, indeed. A fine selection you have made—as have you, sir! No, madam, I fear your fair sex disqualifies you for this work. The stage can be a dangerous place."

Willard retreated to his program, to see which acts he missed because dinner with the mayor ran late. Actually, the dinner, a palm-sized chicken breast with withered greens, had been over quickly; you learned to eat fast on the farm. What took a long time was the mayor's after-dinner speech, in which he argued that athletic conditioning was the salvation of America. Willard bribed a waiter for three thick-cut bologna sandwiches, which he munched at the head table with great enjoyment, ignoring Lou. Now, looking at the Orpheum program, Willard found himself more kindly disposed toward the mayor's speech. It had spared him the "Syncopated Funsters" Bernie & Baker, Adelaide Boothby's "Novelty Songs and Travesties" (with Chas. Everdean at the piano), Selma Braatz the "Renowned Lady Juggler," and Comfort & King in "Coontown Diversions," not to mention a trick rider, a slack-wire routine, a mystery titled "Stan Stanley, The Bouncing Fellow, Assisted by His Relatives," and, most happily missed of all, The Alexander Kids, billed as "Cute, Cunning, Captivating, Clever." And crooked, thought Willard, who once had wasted a nickel on a midget act at the Pottawatomie County Fair.

"Thank you, sir. Welcome. Ladies and gentlemen, these our volunteers have my thanks. Shall they have your thanks as well?"

Without looking up from his program, Willard joined the applause.

"My friends, as I am sure you have noticed, our committee still lacks three men. But if you will indulge me, I have a suggestion. I am told that here in the house with us tonight, we have one man who is easily the equal of any three."

Lou started jabbing Willard again. "G'wan," Willard whispered. "I closed my knees, all right?"

"Knock 'em dead, Champ," Lou hissed, his face shadowed but for his grin.

Willard frowned at him, bewildered. "What?"

"Ladies and gentlemen, will you kindly join me in inviting before the footlights the current heavyweight boxing champion—*our* champion—Mr. Jess Willard!"

Willard opened his mouth to protest just as a spotlight hit him full in the face, its heat like an opened oven.

Willard turned to Lou amid the applause and said, "You didn't!"

Lou ducked his chin and batted his eyes, like a bright child done with his recitation and due a certificate.

"Ladies and gentlemen, if you are in favor of bringing Mr. Willard onto the stage, please signify with your applause."

Now the cheers and applause were deafening. Willard gaped down at the stage. Houdini stood in a semicircle of frenziedly applauding men, his arms outstretched and welcoming. He stared up at Willard with a tiny smile at the corner of his mouth, almost a smirk, his eyes as bright and shallow as the footlights. *Look what I have done for you,* he seemed to be saying. *Come and adore me.*

The hell I will, Willard thought.

No, *felt,* it was nothing so coherent as thought, it was a gut response to Lou, to the mayor, to Mrs. Whoever pressing herself up against Willard's left side in hopes of claiming a bit of the spotlight too, to Hattie more than a thousand miles away whom he should have written today but didn't, to all these row after row of stupid people, most of whom thought Willard hadn't beaten Jack Johnson at all, that Johnson had simply given up, had *floated* to the canvas, the word they kept using, *floated,* Cripes, Willard had been *standing there,* had heard the *thump* like the first melon dropped into the cart when Johnson's head had bounced against the canvas, *bounced,* for Cripes' sake, spraying sweat and spit and blood, that fat lip flapping as the head went down a second time and stayed, *floated,* they said, Willard wasn't a *real* fighter, they said, he had just *outlasted* Johnson—an hour and forty-four minutes in the Havana sun, a blister on the top of his head like a brand, Hattie still could see the scar when she parted his hair to look—*outlasted,* the papers said! Beneath the applause, Willard heard a distant *crunch* as he squeezed the armrest, and was dimly aware of a splinter in his palm as he looked down at Houdini's smirking face and realized, clearly, for the first time: *You people don't want me at all, a big shit-kicker from the prairie.*

It's Jack Johnson you want.

And you know what? You can't have him. Because I beat him, you hear? I beat him.

"No, thanks!" Willard shouted, and the applause ebbed fast, like the last grain rushing out of the silo. The sudden silence, and Houdini's startled blink, made Willard's resolve falter. "I appreciate it," he added. He was surprised by how effortlessly his voice filled the auditorium. "Go on with your act, please, sir," Willard said, even more loudly. Ignoring Lou's clutching hand, which threatened to splinter Willard's forearm as Willard had splintered the armrest, he attempted comedy: "I got a good seat for it right here." There was nervous laughter, including someone immediately behind Willard—who must have, Willard realized, an even worse view than he did.

Arms still outstretched, no trace of a smile now, Houdini called up: "Mr. Willard, I am afraid your public must insist?"

Willard shook his head and sat back, arms folded.

"Mr. Willard, these other gentlemen join me in solemnly pledging that no harm will come to you."

This comedy was more successful; guffaws broke out all over the theater.

Willard wanted to seek out all the laughers and paste them one. "Turn off that spotlight!" he yelled. "It's hot enough to roast a hog."

To Willard's amazement, the spotlight immediately snapped off, and the balcony suddenly seemed a dark, cold place.

"Come down, Mr. Willard," Houdini said, his arms now folded.

"Jesus Christ, kid," Lou hissed. "What's the idea?"

Willard shook him off and stood, jabbing one thick index finger at the stage. "Pay *me* what you're paying *them*, and I'll come down!"

Gasps and murmurs throughout the crowd. Willard was aware of some commotion behind him, movement toward the exit, the balcony door slamming closed. Fine. Let them run, the cowards.

In indignation, Houdini seemed to have swollen to twice his previous thickness. Must come in handy when you're strait-jacketed, Willard thought.

"*Mister* Willard," Houdini retorted, "I am pleased to pay you what I am paying these gentlemen—precisely *nothing*. They are here of their own free will and good sportsmanship. Will you not, upon the same terms, join them?"

"No!" Willard shouted. "I'm leaving." He turned to find his way blocked by Lou, whose slick face gleamed.

"Please, Champ, don't do this to us," Lou whispered, reaching up with both hands in what might have been an attempted embrace. Willard grabbed Lou's wrists, too tightly, and yanked his arms down. "Ah," Lou gasped.

Houdini's drone continued as he paced the stage, his eyes never leaving the balcony. "I see, ladies and gentlemen, that the champ is attempting to retreat to his corner. Mr. Willard, the bell has rung. Will you not answer? Will you not meet the challenge? For challenge it is, Mr. Willard—I, and the good people of this house, challenge you to come forward, and stand before us, like a champion. As Mr. Johnson would have."

Willard froze.

"Or would you have us, sir, doubt the authenticity of your title? Would you have us believe that our champion is unmanned by fear?"

Willard turned and leaned so far over the rail that he nearly fell. "I'll do my job in the ring, you do your job onstage," he yelled. "Go on with your act, your trickery, you faker, you four-flusher!" The audience howled. He shouted louder. "Make it look good, you fake. That's all they want—talk!" He felt his voice breaking. "Tricks and snappy dialogue! Go on, then, give 'em what they want. Talk your worthless talk! Do your lousy fake tricks!" People were standing up and yelling at him all over the theater, but he could see nothing but the little strutting figure on the stage.

"Mr. Willard."

Willard, though committed, now felt himself running out of material. "Everybody knows it's fake!"

"Mr. Willard!"

"Four-flusher!"

"Look here, *Mister* Jess Willard," Houdini intoned, his broad face impassive, silencing Willard with a pointed index finger. "I don't care what your title is or how big you are or what your reputation is or how many men you've beaten to get it. I did you a favor by asking you onto this stage, I paid you a compliment, and so has everyone in the Orpheum." The theater was silent but for the magician. Willard and those in the balcony around him were frozen. "You have the right, sir, to refuse us, to turn your back on your audience, but you have no right, sir, *no* right whatsoever, to slur my reputation, a reputation, I might add, that will long outlive yours." In the ensuing silence, Houdini seemed to notice his pointed finger for the first time. He blinked, lowered his arm, and straightened his cummerbund as he continued: "If you believe nothing else I do or say on this stage today, Mr. Willard, believe *this*, for there is no need for special powers of strength or magic when I tell you that *I can foresee your future.* Yes, sir."

Now his tone was almost conversational as he strolled toward center stage, picked up a rose, snapped its stem, and worked at affixing it to his lapel. "Believe me when I say to you that one day soon you no longer will be the heavyweight champion of the world." Satisfied by the rose, he looked up at Willard again.

"And when your name, Mr. Millard, I'm sorry, Mr. *Willard*, has become a mere footnote in the centuries-long history of the ring, everyone—*everyone*— even those who never set *foot* in a theater—will know *my* name and know that *I* never turned my back to my audience, or failed to accomplish *every* task, *every* feat, they set before me. And that, sir, is why champions come and champions go, while I will remain, now and forever, the one and only, Harry Houdini!" He flung his arms out and threw his head back a half-second before the pandemonium.

There had been twenty-five thousand people in that square in Havana, Willard had been told. He had tried not to look at them, not to think about them— that sea of snarling, squinting, sun-peeled, hateful, ugly faces. But at least all those people had been on his side.

"Go to hell, Willard!"

"Willard, you bum!"

"Willard's a willow!"

"Go to hell!"

Something hit Willard a glancing blow on the temple: a paper sack, which exploded as he snatched at it, showering the balcony with peanut shells. Willard felt he was moving slowly, as if underwater. As he registered that Mrs. Whoever, way down there somewhere, was pummeling him with her parasol—shrieking amid the din, "You bad man! You bad, bad man!"—Willard saw a gentleman's silver-handled cane spiraling lazily through the air toward his head. He ducked as the cane clattered into the far corner. Someone yelped. With one final glance at the mob, Willard turned his back on the too-inviting open space and dashed—but oh, so slowly it seemed—toward the door. People got in his way; roaring, he swept them aside, reached the door, fumbled at it. His fingers had become too slow and clumsy—numb, almost paralyzed. Bellowing something, he didn't know what, he kicked the door, which flew into the corridor in a shower of splinters. Roaring wordlessly now, Willard staggered down the staircase. He cracked his forehead on a chandelier, and yanked it one-handed out of the ceiling with a snarl, flinging it aside in a spasm of plaster and dust. His feet slipped on the lobby's marble floor, and he flailed before righting himself in front of an open-mouthed hat-check girl. Beyond the closed auditorium doors Willard could hear the crowd beginning to chant Houdini's name. Willard kicked a cuspidor as hard as he could; it sailed into a potted palm, spraying juice across the marble floor. Already feeling the first pangs of remorse, Willard staggered onto the sidewalk, into the reek of horseshit and automobiles. The doorman stepped back, eyes wide. "I ain't done nothing, Mister," he said. "I ain't done nothing." Willard growled and turned away, only to blunder into someone small and soft just behind him, nearly knocking her down. It was the hat-check girl, who yelped and clutched at his arms for balance.

"What the hell!" he said.

She righted herself, cleared her throat, and, lips pursed with determination, held out a claim ticket and a stubby pencil. "Wouldja please, huh, Mr. Willard? It won't take a sec. My grandpa says you're his favorite white man since Robert E. Lee."

Jess Willard lost the heavyweight title to Jack Dempsey on July 4, 1919, and retired from boxing soon after. When the fight money dried up, the Willards packed up Zella, Frances, Jess Junior, Enid, and Alan, left Kansas for good and settled in Los Angeles, where Willard opened a produce market at Hollywood and Afton. By day he dickered with farmers, weighed oranges, shooed flies, and swept up. Nights, he made extra money as a referee at wrestling matches. He continued to listen to boxing on the radio, and eventually to watch it on television, once the screens grew large enough to decently hold two grown men fighting. He read all the boxing news he could find in the papers, too, until holding the paper too long made his arms tremble like he was punchy, and spreading it out on the kitchen table didn't work so good either because the small print gave him a headache, and there weren't any real boxers left anyway, and thereafter it fell to his grandchildren, or his great-grandchildren, or his neighbors, or anyone else who had the time to spare, to read the sports pages aloud to him. Sometimes he listened quietly, eyes closed but huge behind his eyeglasses, his big mottled fingers drumming the antimacassar at one-second intervals, as if taking a count. Other times he was prompted to laugh, or to make a disgusted sound in the back of his throat, or to sit forward abruptly—which never failed to startle his youngest and, to his mind, prettiest great-granddaughter, whom he called "the Sprout," so that despite herself she always gasped and drew back a little, her beads clattering, her pedicured toes clenching the edge of her platform sandals—and begin telling a story of the old days, which his visitors sometimes paid attention to, and sometimes didn't, though the Sprout paid closer attention than you'd think.

One day in 1968, the Sprout read Jess Willard the latest indignant *Times* sports column about the disputed heavyweight title. Was the champ Jimmy Ellis, who had beaten Jerry Quarry on points, or was it Joe Frazier, who had knocked out Buster Mathis, or was it rightfully Muhammad Ali, who had been stripped of the title for refusing the draft, and now was banned from boxing anywhere in the United States? The columnist offered no answer to the question, but used his space to lament that boxing suddenly had become so political.

"Disputes, hell. I disputed a loss once," Willard told the Sprout. "To Joe Cox in Springfield Moe in 1911. The referee stopped the fight, then claimed I *wouldn't* fight, give the match to Cox. Said he hadn't stopped nothing. I disputed it, but didn't nothing come of it. Hell. You can't win a fight by disputing."

"I thought a fight *was* a dispute," said the Sprout, whose name was Jennifer. Taking advantage of her great-granddad's near-blindness, she had lifted the hem of her mini to examine the pear-shaped peace symbol her boyfriend had drunkenly drawn on her thigh the night before. She wondered how long it would take to wash off. "Boyfriend" was really the wrong word for Cliff, though he *was* cute, in a scraggly dirty hippie sort of way, and it wasn't like she had a parade of suitors to choose from. The only guy who seemed interested at the coffeehouse last week was some Negro, couldn't you just die, and of course she told him to buzz off. She hoped Jess never found out she'd even said so much as "Buzz off" to a Negro boy—God knows, Jess was a nut on *that* subject. Nigger this and nigger that, and don't even bring up what's his name, that Negro boxer, Johnson? But you couldn't expect better from the old guy. After all, what had they called Jess, back when—the White Hope?

"No, no, honey," Willard said, shifting his buttocks to get comfortable. He fidgeted all the time, even in his specially made chair, since he lost so much weight. "A fight in the ring, it ain't nothing *personal*."

"You're funny, Jess," Jennifer said. The old man's first name still felt awkward in her mouth, though she was determined to use it—it made her feel quite hip and adult, whereas "Popsy" made her feel three years old.

"You're funny, too," Willard said, sitting back. "Letting boys write on your leg like you was a Blue Horse tablet. Read me some more, if you ain't got nothing else to do."

"I don't," Jennifer lied.

Jess Willard died in his Los Angeles home December 15, 1968—was in that very custom-made chair, as a matter of fact, when he finally closed his eyes. He opened them to find himself in a far more uncomfortable chair, in a balcony at the Los Angeles Orpheum, in the middle of Harry Houdini's opening-night performance, November 30, 1915.

"Where you been, Champ?" Lou asked. "We ain't keeping you up, are we?"

"Ladies and gentlemen, these our volunteers have my thanks. Shall they have your thanks as well?"

Amid the applause, Lou went on: "You ought to *act* interested, at least."

"Sorry, Lou," Willard said, sitting up straight and shaking his head. Cripes, he must have nodded off. He had that nagging waking sensation of clutching to the shreds of a rich and involving dream, but no, too late, it was all gone. "I'm just tired from traveling, is all."

"My friends, as I am sure you have noticed, our committee still lacks three men. But if you will indulge me, I have a suggestion. I am told that here in the house with us tonight, we have one man who is easily the equal of any three."

Lou jabbed Willard in the side. "Knock 'em dead, Champ," he said, grinning.

For an instant, Willard didn't understand. Then he remembered. Oh yeah, an onstage appearance with Houdini—like Jack London had done in Oakland, and President Wilson in Washington. Willard leaned forward to see the stage, the magician, the committee, the scatter of roses. Lou jabbed him again and mouthed the word, "Surprise." What did he mean, surprise? they had talked about this. Hadn't they?

"And so, ladies and gentlemen, will you kindly join me in inviting before the footlights the current heavyweight boxing champion—*our* champion—Mr. Jess Willard!"

In the sudden broil of the spotlight, amid a gratifying burst of cheers and applause, Willard unhesitatingly stood—remembering, just in time, the low ceiling. Grinning, he leaned over the edge and waved to the crowd, first with the right arm, then both arms. Cheered by a capacity crowd, at the biggest Orpheum theater on the West Coast—two dollars a seat, Lou had said! Hattie never would believe this. He bet Jack Johnson never got such a reception. But he wouldn't think of Johnson just now. This was Jess Willard's night. He clasped his hands together and shook them above his head.

Laughing above the cacophony, Houdini waved and cried, "Mr. Willard, please, come down!"

"On my way," Willard called, and was out the balcony door in a flash. He loped down the stairs two at a time. Sprinting through the lobby, he winked and blew a kiss at the hat-check girl, who squealed. The doors of the auditorium opened inward before him, and he entered the arena without slowing down, into the midst of a standing ovation, hundreds of faces turned to him as he ran down the central aisle toward the stage where Houdini waited.

"Mind the stairs in the pit, Mr. Willard," Houdini said. "I don't think they were made for feet your size." Newly energized by the audience's laughter, Willard made a show of capering stiff-legged up the steps, then fairly bounded onto the stage to shake the hand of the magician—who really was a *small* man, my goodness—and then shake the hands of all the other committee members. The applause continued, but the audience began to resettle itself, and Houdini waved his hands for order.

"Please, ladies and gentlemen! Please! Your attention! Thank you. Mr. Willard, gentlemen, if you will please step back, to make room for—The Wall of Mystery!"

The audience oohed as a curtain across the back of the stage lifted to reveal an ordinary brick wall, approximately twenty feet long and ten high. As Willard watched, the wall began to turn. It was built, he saw, on a circular platform flush with the stage. The disc revolved until the wall was perpendicular to the footlights.

"The Wall of Mystery, ladies and gentlemen, is not mysterious whatsoever in its construction. Perhaps from where you are sitting you can smell the mortar freshly laid, as this wall was completed only today, by twenty veteran members, personally selected and hired at double wages by the management of this theater, of Bricklayers' Union Number Thirty-four. Gentlemen, please take a bow!"

On cue, a half-dozen graying, potbellied men in denim work clothes walked into view stage left, to bow and wave their caps and grin. Willard applauded as loudly as anyone, even put both fingers in his mouth to whistle, before the bricklayers shuffled back into their workingmen's obscurity.

"Mr. Willard, gentlemen, please approach the wall and examine it at your leisure, until each of you is fully satisfied that the wall is solid and genuine in every particular."

The committee fanned out, first approaching the wall tentatively, as if some part of it might open and swallow them. Gradually they got into the spirit of the act, pushing and kicking the wall, slamming their shoulders into it, running laps around it to make sure it began and ended where it seemed to. To the audience's delight, Willard, by far the tallest of the men, took a running jump and grabbed the top of the wall, then lifted himself so that he could peer over to the other side. The audience cheered. Willard dropped down to join his fellow committeemen, all of whom took the opportunity to shake Willard's hand again.

During all this activity, Houdini's comely attendants had rolled onstage two six-foot circular screens, one from backstage left, one from backstage right. They rolled the screens to center stage, one screen stage left of the wall, one screen stage right. Just before stepping inside the left screen, Houdini said: "Now, gentlemen, please arrange yourselves around the wall so that no part of it escapes your scrutiny." Guessing what was going to happen, Willard trotted to the other side of the wall and stood, arms folded, between the wall and the stage-right screen; he could no longer see Houdini for the wall. The other men found their own positions. Willard heard a *whoosh* that he took to be Houdini dramatically closing the screen around him. "I raise my hands above the screen like so," Houdini called, "to prove I am here. But now—I am gone!" There was another *whoosh*—the attendants opening the screen? The audience gasped and murmured. Empty, Willard presumed. The attendants trotted downstage into Willard's view, professionally balanced on their high heels, carrying between them the folded screen. At that moment the screen behind Willard went *whoosh*, and he turned to see Houdini stepping out of it, one hand on his hip, the other raised above his head in a flourish.

Surprised and elated despite himself, Willard joined in the crescendo of bravos and huzzahs.

Amid the din, Houdini trotted over to Willard, gestured for him to stoop, and whispered into his ear:

"Your turn."

His breath reeked of mint. Startled, Willard straightened up. The audience continued to cheer. Houdini winked, nodded almost imperceptibly toward the open screen he just had exited. Following Houdini's glance, Willard saw the secret of the trick, was both disappointed and delighted at its simplicity, and saw that he could do it, too. Yet he knew that to accept Houdini's offer, to walk through the wall himself, was something he neither wanted nor needed to do. He was Jess Willard, heavyweight champion of the world, if only for a season, and that was enough. He was content. He'd leave walking through walls to the professionals. He clapped one hand onto Houdini's shoulder, engulfing it, smiled and shook his head. Again almost imperceptibly, Houdini nodded, then turned to the audience, took a deep bow. Standing behind him now, feeling suddenly weary—surely the show wouldn't last much longer—Willard lifted his hands and joined the applause. Backstage to left and right, and in the catwalks directly above, he saw a cobweb of cables and pulleys against stark white brick—ugly, really, but completely invisible from the auditorium. On the highest catwalk two niggers in coveralls stood motionless, not applauding. Looking about, gaping, he was sure, like a hick, Willard told himself: Well, Jess, now you've had a taste of how it feels to be Harry Houdini. The afterthought came unbidden, as a jolt:

And Jack Johnson, too. Disconcerted, Willard turned to stare at the stage-right screen, as two of the women folded it up and carted it away.

Jennifer barely remembered her Grandma Hattie, but she felt as if she sort of knew her by now, seeing the care she had lavished for decades on these scrapbooks, and reading the neat captions Hattie had typed and placed alongside each item:

FORT WAYNE, 1912—WORKING THE BAG—KO'd J. Young in 6th on May 23 (Go JESS!)

The captions were yellowed and brittle now, tended to flutter out in bits like confetti when the albums were opened too roughly.

"I'm a good typist, Jess," Jennifer said. "I could make you some new ones."

"No, thanks," Jess said. "I like these fine."

"Where's the Johnson book?"

"Hold your horses, it's right here. There you go. I knew you'd want that one."

Jennifer was less interested in Jack Johnson per se than in the fact that one of Hattie's scrapbooks was devoted to one of her husband's most famous opponents, a man whom Jess had beaten for the title, and never met again. Jennifer suspected this scrapbook alone was as much the work of Jess as of Hattie—and the aging Jess at that, since it began with Johnson's obituaries in 1946. Hence the appeal of the Johnson scrapbook; this mysterious and aging Jess, after all, was the only one she knew. The last third of the book had no typewritten captions, and clippings that were crooked beneath their plastic. The last few pages were blank. Stuck into the back were a few torn-out and clumsily folded newspaper clippings about Muhammad Ali.

"Johnson was cool," she said, turning the brittle pages with care. "It is so cool that you got to fight him, Jess. And that you won! You must have been proud."

"I *was* proud," Willard said, reaching for another pillow to slide beneath his bony buttocks. "Still am," he added. "But I wish I had known him, too. He was an interesting man."

"He died in a car wreck, didn't he?"

"Yep."

"That's so sad." Jennifer knew about the car wreck, of course; it was all over the front of the scrapbook. She was just stalling, making noise with her mouth, while pondering whether now was the time to get Jess talking about Johnson's three wives, all of them white women, all of them *blonde* white women. Jennifer was very interested to know Jess's thoughts about that.

"You fought him in Havana because, what? You weren't allowed to fight in the United States, or something?" She asked this with great casualness, knowing Johnson was a fugitive from U.S. justice at the time, convicted of violating the Mann Act, i.e. transporting women across state lines for "immoral purposes," i.e. white slavery, i.e. sex with a white woman.

"Yeah, something like that," Jess said. He examined the ragged hem of his sweater, obviously uninclined to pursue the conversation further. God, getting an eighty-seven-old man to talk about sex was *hard.*

"I was trying to tell Carl about it, but I, uh, forgot the uh, details." She kept talking, inanely, flushed with horror. *Massive* slip-up. She never had mentioned Carl in front of Jess before, certainly not by name. Carl was three years older than she was, and worse yet, a dropout. He was also black. Not Negro, he politely insisted: black. He wanted to meet Jess, and Jennifer wanted that to happen, too—but she would have to careful about how she brought it up. Not this way! Sure, Jess might admire Jack Johnson as a fighter, but would he want his teenage great-granddaughter to date him?

"There was some rule against it, I think," Jess said, oblivious, and she closed her eyes for a second in relief. "I be doggoned but this sweater wasn't worth bringing home from the store." He glanced up. "You didn't give me this sweater, did you, Sprout?"

"No, Jess," Jennifer said. She closed the Johnson scrapbook, elated to avoid *that* conversation one more day.

"I wouldn't hurt you for nothing, you know," Jess said. "Wouldn't let no one else hurt you, neither."

She grinned, charmed. "Would you stand up for me, Jess?"

"I sure would, baby. Anybody bothers you, I'll clean his clock." He slowly punched the air with mottled fists, his eyes huge and swimming behind his glasses, and grinned a denture-taut grin. On impulse, Jennifer kissed his forehead. Resettling herself on the floor, she opened one of the safer scrapbooks. Here was her favorite photo of Jess at the produce market, hair gray beneath his paper hat. He held up to the light a Grade A white egg that he smiled at in satisfaction. Grandma Hattie had typed beneath the photo: TWO GOOD EGGS.

"One hundred and thirteen fights," Jess said. Something in his voice made Jennifer glance up. He looked suddenly morose, gazing at nothing, and Jennifer worried that she had said something to upset him; he was so moody, sometimes. "That's how many Johnson fought. More than Tunney, more than Louis. Twice as many as Marciano. Four times as many as Jeffries, as Fitzsimmons, as Gentleman Jim Corbett. And forty-four of them knockouts." He sighed and repeated, almost inaudibly, "Forty-four."

She cleared her throat, determined, and said loudly: "Hey, you want to write another letter?" About once a month, Jess dictated to her a letter to the editor, saying Ali was the champ fair and square whether people liked it or not, same as Jack Johnson had been, same as Jess Willard had been, and if people didn't like it then let them take Ali on in the ring like men. The *Times* had stopped printing the letters after the third one, but she hadn't told Jess that.

He didn't seem to have heard her. After a few seconds, though, his face brightened. "Hey," he said. "Did I ever tell you about the time I got the chance to walk through a wall?"

Relieved, she screwed up her face in mock concentration. "Well, let's see, about a hundred million billion times, but you can tell me again if you want. Do you ever wish you'd done it?"

"Nah," Jess said, leaning into the scrapbook to peer at the two good eggs. "I probably misunderstood him in the first place. He never let anybody *else* get in on the act, that I heard of. He was too big a star for that." He sat back, settled into the armchair with a sigh. "I must have misunderstood him. Anyway." He was quiet again, but smiling. "Too late now, huh?"

"I guess so," Jennifer said, slowly turning the pages, absently stroking her beads so that the strands clicked together. Beside her Jess began, gently, to snore. She suppressed a laugh: Could you believe it? Just like that, down for the count. Without realizing it, she had turned to a clipping from the *Times*, dated December 1, 1915.

TWO CHAMPIONS MEET
RING ARTIST, ESCAPE ARTIST SHAKE ON ORPHEUM STAGE

Young Jess looked pretty spiffy in his evening wear, Jennifer thought. *Spiffy*, she knew from reading the scrapbooks, had been one of Grandma Hattie's favorite words. Jess was crouched to fit into the photograph, which must have been taken from the front row. The two men looked down at the camera; at their feet a couple of footlights were visible. At the bottom edge of the photo was the blurred top of a man's head. Someone had penciled a shaky arrow from this blur and written, "Lou." The background was murky, but Jennifer could imagine a vaulted plaster ceiling, a chandelier, a curtain embroidered with intricate Oriental designs. Beneath the clipping, Grandma Hattie had typed: JESS MEETS EHRICH WEISS a.k.a. HARRY HOUDINI (1874–1926). On the facing page, Houdini's faded signature staggered across a theater program.

Even as a kid, Jennifer had been intrigued by Houdini's eyes. Although the clipping was yellowed and the photo blurred to begin with, Houdini always seemed to look right at her, *into* her. It was the same in the other photos, in the Houdini books she kept checking out of the library. He wasn't Jennifer's type, but he had great eyes.

As she looked at the clipping, she began to daydream. She was on stage, wearing a tuxedo and a top hat and tights cut up to *there*, and she pulled back a screen to reveal—who? Hmm. She wasn't sure. Maybe Carl; maybe not. Daydreaming was a sign, said the goateed guy who taught her comp class, of sensitivity, of creativity. Yeah, right. Sometimes when she was home alone—she told no one this—she put on gym shorts and went out back and boxed the air, for an hour or more at a time, until she was completely out of breath. Why, she couldn't say. Being a pacifist, she couldn't imagine hitting a *person*, no, but she sure beat hell out of the air. She really wanted to be neither a boxer nor a magician. She was a political-science major, and had her heart set on the Peace Corps. And yet, when Carl had walked into the coffeehouse that night alone, fidgeting in the doorway with an out-of-place look, considering, maybe, ducking back outside again, what did she say to him? She walked right up to Carl, bold as brass (that was another of Grandma Hattie's, BOLD AS BRASS), stuck out her chin and stuck out her hand and said, "Hi, my name is Jennifer Schumacher, and I'm the great-granddaughter of the ex-heavyweight champion of the world." Carl shook her hand and looked solemn and said, "Ali?" and people stared at them, they laughed so hard, and if *I* ever get a chance to walk through a wall, she vowed to herself as she closed the scrapbook, *I'm* taking it—so *there*.

HOWARD WANDREI

George Is All Right

Howard Wandrei, like many pulp writers, worked in several genres, but the bulk of his later fiction was for the detective pulps. Not as well known to horror readers as his brother Donald, Howard Wandrei had a keen ear for dialogue and a sharp eye for irony in human relations.

Written a number of years ago, "George Is All Right" is reprinted from Arkham's Masters of Horror, *edited by Peter Ruber.*

—E. D.

The thing about Lenin was his transcendental allegiance to just one master. It was one of those things that I do not understand; the silent, powerful, tawny Great Dane was Dr. George Parr's, and not once have I seen Parr exhibit any affection for the beast. Ordinarily I don't mind dogs, but I heartily disliked that one because I was afraid of him; whatever was wrong with Parr, besides, didn't make him the best of company; I had been thinking I'd finish the drink and call it a night and Parr would go right on drinking, morose, unreachable in his self-sufficiency.

Parr and I had a pair of stools at the bar in Scully's, down in the Village. Behind the bar hung a sign, "Ask for Scully." Ask for Scully, and any of three bartenders will be on hand to see if you want another one. It's subtler than jiggling your glass, and the next one is always as good as the last one. My knees were hiked up under the lip of the bar, and my heels were hung on the highest rung of the stool so that I'd be as far away from Lenin as possible. The picture recurs to me like a kind of second-hand nightmare even now. Accidentally I'd step on his bull-whip of a tail, or perhaps merely nudge him in passing, and that tawny thunderbolt would snap my foot off at the ankle. It was the only time I ever heard a sound out of the beast; I am a tired man; Parr himself told me it was because I am subject to violent dreams, and one of the things that keeps me from getting enough rest is Lenin's growl. He was at full length on his belly in the buttery sawdust sprinkled underfoot, and the continuous violence of the low growl occurred like a freak, spontaneous resonance of the floor itself.

Parr looked down, then at the couple approaching from the entrance near us.

A man and a woman; neither of them looked down at the dog. Lenin rose with movement that was both rigid and fluid and stood partially blocking the way, shivering with that continuous growl. It was audible only to us, but it was a perfectly horrible sound of raving animal hate. The woman was a beauty; she turned her head casually and smiled at Parr.

Parr nodded. "Down, Lenin," he said quietly. "George is all right."

Turning his head, the dog retreated only enough to keep his ugly jaws from brushing the man as he passed. Aside from the woman's real beauty, which was of the dark, voluptuous order, there was something so oddly preoccupied in the manner of both that I watched them go to one of the tables at the other end of the bar. I wanted to get another look at the man's face; they walked not as though he were escorting her but as though she was guiding him. I had an idea he was blind.

"Do you know them?" I asked.

"That was George Forth Courtney." Parr's voice was very flat. I recognized the name. A brilliant architect, Courtney had dropped out of sight some while back when he was at his best.

"And the woman?" I asked.

"My wife, Margaret." His voice was completely unemotional.

I should have kept my mouth shut.

I looked down at Lenin, too embarrassed even to apologize for my rudeness. Down on the sawdust again, Parr's hound crouched motionless, watching Courtney's back. Parr was looking at me with a malicious little smile.

"After all," he said, "you really don't know a damned thing about me, do you?"

All I could do was stutter a pithy rejoinder to the effect that few people did know a great deal about anyone. "Fathers and sons and all that," said I. Meanwhile I had given Scully the password and our drinks were being replenished. I did know that Parr had been a great surgeon, and that his name had ceased occurring in the press some while before I met him. It was none of my business why. If he had any reason for quitting his practice so young besides having plenty of money it must have been a good reason.

"That's a sage contribution," he remarked. "I suppose you think I'm decent enough, or something just as vague, and let it go at that. What would you think if I told you I killed someone?"

His eyes were narrower and bright with a kind of cold-blooded curiosity.

"I suppose you mean—" I began.

"No, I don't mean any surgical blunder," he anticipated me. "I never lost a patient during or after an operation. What do you think of that, eh? There I was, a pretty fair hand at the job of saving human lives, supposedly, and I destroyed one. It wasn't done on the operating table, either. That's what you're thinking, isn't it? No, there'd be witnesses in that case, and besides he was one of the healthiest specimens I ever saw. Well, you understand, don't you? I murdered a man."

I grinned at him like a fool because I didn't think he meant it; he meant it, all right; when I reached for my new drink I knocked it down and had to ask for Scully again. I felt disgusted with life; I didn't want to know anything about Parr's murders, but he was wound up.

"You're grinning like an idiot," he said, "so you probably don't believe me. But perhaps you'll change your mind."

"I believe you; let's talk about something else."

"No. Will you please listen?"

He was wound up.

Every summer, he said, he used to go up to Billson's with Margaret. Billson's is a few miles down from Middletown and is more a side road than a village. At the junction of the dirt road with the highway is a general store, and diagonally across the highway from it is a farmhouse. The dirt road winds for three-quarters of a mile into a wooded pocket in the hills where Parr owned the handsome house that used to be Billson's, and not far off the remodeled barn in which Billson and his wife still lived. At Parr's the road straightened out to climb a few hundred feet of hill mostly paved with an outcrop of bluish, slaty rock. Beyond Courtney's house on the shoulder of the hill the road degenerated into a series of stony, rutted undulations, debouching with a crazy downhill flourish into the paved highway which is the short route from Billson's to Middletown.

They had the little valley to themselves. Behind Parr's house were tennis courts and a pistol range. Both Courtney and himself had collections of fine weapons and as marksmen were very closely matched. Just a stroll below Parr's house Courtney, Parr, and Billson themselves had dredged out a rill and erected a concrete dam to create a fine swimming pool for the use of no one but themselves and their guests. They owned all the property between the two main roads and hunted it together for mushrooms, or periodically to clear out the big copperheads common in the locality, or the woodchucks that got into Billson's tomato vines. Halcyon days.

So much of the narrative bore a suspicious resemblance to a pattern of story I had heard, read, and written before. It was commonplace save for the fact that my friend Parr was involved in it. Commonplace for a while.

He had a precise way of speaking, and made slight, expressive movements with his hands and long, blunt-ended fingers as though he were doing things with a scalpel. He was saying, "Courtney was in love with Margaret. I could understand that because she is quite beautiful. Don't you think so?"

He was going along with such damned meticulous calm that I had no warning; I flinched, nodded as I cleared my throat so that it wasn't necessary for me to say anything. It permitted me to look in her direction; her eyes looked velvety and paid attention only to Courtney across the table from her; she was grave and lovely, wearing a popular style of dress of deepest green with a shirred bodice that accentuated the splendid conformation of her torso and breasts as it was designed to. Her red lips were of haunting shape but otherwise indescribable, moving compellingly in quiet conversation with Courtney alone. Other customers along the bar stole glances at her but she showed no awareness of the covetous stir she aroused. No doubt she was used to being beautiful.

"Courtney and I have the same name," Parr said. "George. When she spoke to either of us her inflection was exactly the same. I really had no idea of what was going on until I began thinking that she said 'George' in only one way. It had been going on all along, but until then I never—ah—"

"Tumbled."

"Yes, that's good. Tumbled. You know, it's flattering to a man to know that his wife is admired; but when she returns the interest it is something quite different. I couldn't believe that Margaret would do such a thing to me; I felt so sure that I didn't want to make myself ridiculous by asking her point-blank. And at the same time I was afraid to ask her for fear that she might admit it. We had been married about two years; I'm sure we were equally in love with each other, and I never considered the idea that I might lose her.

"You realize, I drove to New York every morning, starting at about seven-thirty. Courtney worked at all hours in his studio up there on the hill, and I never knew whether he was at Billson's or in town. After the first couple of times I never went up the hill in the morning to invite him to ride with me because I hate to wake a man up. The more sleep a man can get these days the better. Margaret used to ride in with me and spend the day in town doing one thing and another, but after a while I got so clever about shaving and making my own breakfast that I never awakened her. Are you married, Guernsey?"

I shrugged, if that meant anything to him.

"Well, I'll tell you: The most beautiful thing I have ever enjoyed was Margaret when she was asleep in the morning, with her hair spread out on the pillow in curls like black silk, and with her lips parted a little. It was a pleasure just to stand there and look at her. She used to laugh at me because I liked to watch her brush her teeth. I think," Parr said somberly, "that I loved her too much. Do you think it's a mistake to let a woman know that a man is hers absolutely? Altogether?"

"I don't know a damned thing about it. Go ahead."

Parr went on torturing himself meticulously. "To me it's an indecent idea that a woman can get satiated with love and go elsewhere. Novelty can't be so important. At any rate, I suppose it was my doing, their having whole days together, and sometimes periods of two and three days when I had to stay in town.

"One morning I met Billson. He was sitting on a rock near the garage with a rifle on his knees, waiting for a woodchuck that was eating his tomatoes. We had a hit-and-miss conversation for a while, as usual. But there was something guarded and eccentric in his manner, and it struck me that for the past several weeks he had acted as though something was bothering him more and more. It was a dirty thing for me to do but I said it spontaneously, without thinking. Just one of those devilish things that occur to a man. I said, "This is probably my last summer here, Billson, but you'll come to see me in town, won't you?"

"He looked positively scared for a minute, and then he asked me what was wrong. All I said was, 'I thought you must know about it—about Courtney and Margaret; so I'll have to leave pretty soon.'

"You see, I really wasn't sure that Courtney and Margaret were having an affair until I said that, and then I knew that it had been going on for a long while. For a moment Billson looked flabbergasted. Then he must have decided that I was pumping him, and he wasn't that kind of person. Without a word he got up from the rock and turned his back on me and walked off with his rifle on his shoulder. I can still remember the way the sun gleamed on the barrel of that rifle as he walked away on the path home. That was the last I saw of Billson, and we were good friends. It stunned me, because his silence was proof that he had observed a great deal.

"I set a trap for Courtney.

"One afternoon I left a prescription with a druggist in Middletown as a blind. I told him it was important, and that he should call me at eleven sharp and have it picked up if I was unable to do it myself before then.

"After dinner that night Courtney and I and Margaret were having cocktails down at my place. We did that a lot. Courtney was good company. After ten-thirty I pretended I was very tired and excused myself. Margaret rose, too; when Courtney had gone back up the hill Margaret and I went to bed. At eleven sharp the phone rang, and I had to go downstairs to answer it. It was only the Middletown druggist, but I told Margaret it was an emergency appendectomy, that it was a pretty bad one because it was Dr. So-and-so himself who called and he was afraid to operate. I would be gone all night, and would telephone her from New York the next day.

"The idea wasn't in the least improbable. While I was up there I got my share of emergency calls; if it was distant enough or circumstances required it I'd stay all night at the place or at some hotel rather than waste the time driving back to Billson's, then drive directly to New York in the morning.

"I went roaring up the hill past Courtney's in second gear as though in a large and hellish hurry, and tore the humps off the road beyond because he could see me until I turned into the highway to Middletown if he was looking. It was a calm night; there was no moon, but the stars were so bright and thick that the sky looked frosty. There wouldn't be any doubt of Courtney's recognizing my car from the sound of the motor, whether he got a good look at me or not.

"The light in his studio was burning when I went by. On the road to Middletown I thought of him nursing a drink, perhaps, looking down the hill and letting his mind speculate on what had sent me off in such a hurry. As the trees grew, he could see one of the bedroom windows in my place, and we could see almost the whole of his studio. I got to thinking about that, not driving very fast but not loafing either. Since Courtney's house was on an eminence, turning his lights on and off would be chancey; the signaling could be seen for quite a distance. Therefore, if there was any signaling the responsibility had to be Margaret's, and I know now that it was. There was a small bronze reading lamp in the bedroom, which was admirably suited for the purpose. They wouldn't use the telephone, or course; those country lines leak all over.

"Giving them plenty of rope I drove all the way to Middletown, picked up my prescription and started back. There was no traffic at that hour when I approached Billson's road, so I turned off my lights and gave the car just enough gas to make the rises between the highway and Courtney's. All the lights in his house were out and I thought: he's gone to bed, and what a fool's errand I've given myself.

"It was devilish hard driving by starlight. The crickets were going that night as I've never heard them before. They must have been out by the billions. The damned incessant scream of them all around made me dizzy, and I knew it was only sheer luck that had kept me on the road so far. Going past Courtney's—I could just make out the loom of it because of the silvering of starlight on the roof—I decided the game wasn't worth the candle, and feeling mighty ashamed of myself I switched the headlights on. I didn't know what I was going to say to Margaret about my unexpected return except to confess what a dismal bonehead

I had been. And she'd laugh at me, which for some sidewise reason was something to look forward to.

"Those were powerful bluish-white headlights for country driving, and Courtney staggered as though he had been hit with something solid. He had just left my house and was coming back up the hill. He kept on coming, shielding his eyes from the glare of the lights and keeping close to the wall bounding my place. It's a field stone wall, about six feet high at that point.

"Between them they must have concluded that there had been something peculiar about my behavior during the evening and the risk of the whole night was too great, but he had delayed just a few minutes too long. I had the gas pedal pressed all the way down, and was dropping the car down that hill of slate like a falling stone, straight for him. That told him for sure who I was and what was going to happen.

"He tried to reach the other side of the road, where he might have been able to climb the embankment, but I headed him off. He sprinted for the wall again, but before he could have made the top and swung over I could have done the job by sideswiping him, and he knew it. I had him. With the road like a narrow chute between hillside and wall he was hopelessly trapped. I enjoyed it," Parr stated, "because I knew he didn't want to die, and his brain must be bursting with horror.

"Just before the machine hit him he did something completely unexpected. He jumped. Not for the wall but upward, with all his might. I could see the cords of his neck stretched taut with the effort, and he had the face of a gargoyle.

"I ducked. He did just clear the bonnet of the car with that wonderful leap. He was twisting, and both his heels smashed into the windshield. The blow stretched him out straight, whipcracking him at full length against the top of the car and catapulting him into the air."

Parr snapped the stem of his empty cocktail glass without any melodrama. He did it quite deliberately as though for emphasis, and Scully gave us new drinks and picked up the casualty without batting an eye.

"The car was going so fast that I was past the driveway before I could stop. I took the flashlight from the dash compartment and went back. Courtney was lying outstretched in the middle of the road; when I played the light over him he was motionless. I went over to the wall to look at my house, and there wasn't a light on nor any sound, so I went back to Courtney. He was as dead as mutton. He was gone. I went over him from end to end, and it was remarkable that there wasn't a broken bone in his body. Not even a skull fracture as far as I could tell, but he was gone. The shock had snuffed him out."

Parr snapped his fingers. The sound cracked like a light handclap and Lenin pointed his nose up at Parr briefly.

"I picked him up and carried him around through the drive into the house. We never locked up, and I only had to haul open the screen door. There was a big sofa in the living room that I laid him out on, and except for a little bleeding at the mouth he looked as though he were merely in a deep sleep.

"A grandfather clock stood by the hall entrance to the living room, and I never was more afraid of an inanimate object than of the brass pendulum of that clock. I couldn't help looking at it. The clock-case reminded me of a coffin, and that confounded slow ticking sounded like a thing coming on step by step in wooden shoes.

"I had a sort of laboratory up there that I had made out of the old woodshed. There was a small refrigerator stocked with snakebite serum, vaccines, some junk of my own that I was experimenting with in connection with mushroom poisoning, and so on.

"I gave him a shot of adrenalin, even though he had been dead for more than five minutes. You know how it's done, don't you?"

I shook my head; I happened to catch sight of myself in the bar mirror, and I remember wondering if I always screwed my face up into that baleful expression when I was listening closely.

"A long needle is used and is inserted directly into the muscles of the left ventricle of the heart. It sounds drastic and it does no good more often than not. Nothing happens to your man; he goes on being dead, and then you quit because you *don't want* him back. Unalterable changes occur in the nervous system and the structure of the brain. There are authentic cases of men being revivified after a time nearly as long as five minutes; not very many of them live long subsequently and most of those who do survive for any great while are things. Imbeciles.

"So I quit; I hadn't succeeded in getting the least tremor of action out of Courtney. Aside from the ticking of the clock there wasn't any sound; I looked at the clock to see how long I had been a murderer, and as nearly as I could judge it was a little over twelve minutes. And there was Margaret standing just inside the doorway.

"She was in sandals and a light crepe robe, and as beautiful as something out of a dream. She was standing with her lungs fully inflated and must have been there for perhaps ten or twelve swings of that cursed clock's pendulum; the robe hung in folds as exact as though she were done in Carrara altogether. She paid no attention to me at all. I wasn't there.

"Then she let that breath go with Courtney's name. She said, '*George!*'

"Just once. It wasn't my name; it wasn't horror at what I had done, nor even a very loud cry. But it was more shattering than a scream all the same, and full of such grief and longing that I knew she was through with me completely. It gives you something to think about, doesn't it?" Parr asked gravely. "The subtle distances such a cry can reach.

"Courtney opened his eyes as she ran across the room and flung herself down on the sofa beside him. His arms went around her waist as though it was his privilege alone henceforth and Margaret—" Parr swallowed—"looked at me with the blackest hate imaginable in a human being.

"Before morning I left Billson's permanently for New York, driving down as usual. As I was turning out of Billson's road into the lower highway Lenin caught up with me. I had left him tied up on the front porch but he had snapped the leash, and I couldn't make him go back." Parr lifted his glass half an inch, brought the bottom down on the bar with a brisk tap of finality.

I looked at Parr's lean, melancholy countenance in the mirror and my own baleful one. On the floor behind us Lenin's low, raving growl started again, and I turned my head to see Margaret Parr and Courtney coming our way on their way out. This time I got a good look at Courtney's face. He was a bigger man than Parr, handsomely built, with regular, delicate features held expressionless with the composure of a saint. His hair was a gleaming warm brown and was beautifully trimmed, looking as though a woman's fingers kept its soft waviness fitted to his head.

I would have said that where Parr was interesting Courtney was arrestingly handsome. Except that Courtney's eyes with their somewhat feminine lashes were lusterless, sickeningly empty of all intelligence whatsoever. He walked like animated stone, and his skin had a marble translucency.

That one look I had was enough of that faultlessly groomed zombie. I got rid of the remainder of my drink, signaled Scully and told him to shake me up three in a line. That would do for a starter, because I told myself that the night was as good a night as any for me to spend getting fried.

As Margaret passed I breathed the subtle, exciting scent she wore again, and held a hand over my nose to keep out the throttling chill of the grave mingled with that perfume.

Beside me Parr said grimly, "Down, Lenin. Down."

SUSANNA CLARKE

Mr. Simonelli or the Fairy Widower

This story marks Susanna Clarke's fourth appearance in The Year's Best Fantasy and Horror *annual collections, which is particularly remarkable as the author only began publishing fiction in 1996. Since then, she has written tales for* Starlight, *volumes 1 & 2;* Black Swan, White Raven; Sandman: Book of Dreams; *and* A Fall of Stardust. *She lives with fellow writer Colin Greenland in Cambridge, England, and is at work on her first novel.*

Once again, Clarke cooks up a splendid fairy story reminiscent of the works of Sylvia Townsend Warner, with a pinch of Jane Austen and a dash of Charlotte Brontë thrown in for good measure. This is a wry, unusual rendition of the classic folk tale "Midwife to the Fairies," set in nineteenth-century Derbyshire. "Mr. Simonelli or the Fairy Widower" is reprinted from the anthology Black Heart, Ivory Bones (Avon Books).

—T. W.

Allhope Rectory, Derbyshire
Dec. 20th, 1811

To Mrs. Gathercole

Madam,

I shall not try your patience by a repetition of those arguments with which I earlier tried to convince you of my innocence. When I left you this afternoon I told you that it was in my power to place in your hands *written evidence* that would absolve me from every charge which you have seen fit to heap upon my head, and in fulfilment of that promise I enclose my journal. And should you discover, madam, in perusing these pages, that I have been so bold as to attempt a sketch of *your own character*, and should that portrayal prove *not entirely flattering*, then I beg you to remember that it was written as a private account and never intended for another's eyes.

You will hear no entreaties from me, madam. Write to the Bishop by all means. I would not stay your hand from any course of action which you felt proper. But one accusation I must answer: that I have acted without due respect for members of your family. It is, madam, my all too lively regard for your family that has brought me to my present curious situation.

> I remain, madam, yr. most obedient & very humble Sert.
> The Reverend Alessandro Simonelli

From the Journals of Alessandro Simonelli

Aug. 10th, 1811   Corpus Christi College, Cambridge
I am beginning to think that I must marry. I have no money, no prospects of advancement, and no friends to help me. This queer face of mine is my only capital now and must, I fear, be made to pay; John Windle has told me privately that the bookseller's widow in Jesus-lane is quite desperately in love with me, and it is common knowledge that her husband left her nearly £15 thousand. As for the lady herself, I never heard anything but praise of her. Her youth, virtue, beauty, and charity make her universally loved. But still I cannot quite make up my mind to it. I have been too long accustomed to the rigors of scholarly debate to feel much enthusiasm for *female* conversation—no more to refresh my soul in the company of Aquinas, Aristophanes, Euclid, and Avicenna, but instead to pass my hours attending to a discourse upon merits of a bonnet trimmed with coquelicot ribbons.

Aug. 11th, 1811
Dr. Prothero came smiling to my rooms this morning. "You are surprised to see me, Mr. Simonelli," he said. "We have not been such good friends lately as to wait upon each other in our rooms."

True, but whose fault is that? Prothero is the very worst sort of Cambridge scholar: loves horses and hunting more than books and scholarship; has never once given a lecture since he was made Professor, though obliged to do so by the deed of foundation every other week in term; once ate five roast mackerel at a sitting (which very nearly killed him); is drunk most mornings and *every* evening; dribbles upon his waistcoat as he nods in his chair. I believe I have made my opinion of him pretty widely known and, though I have done myself no good by my honestly, I am pleased to say that I have done him some harm.

He continued, "I bring you good news, Mr. Simonelli! You should offer me a glass of wine—indeed you should! When you hear what excellent news I have got for you, I am sure you will wish to offer me a glass of wine!" And he swung his head around like an ugly old tortoise, to see if he could catch sight of a bottle. But I have no wine, and so he went on, "I have been asked by a family in Derbyshire—friends of mine, you understand—to find them some learned gentleman to be Rector of their village. Immediately I thought of you, Mr. Simonelli! The duties of a country parson in that part of the world are not onerous. And you may judge for yourself of the health of the place, what fine air it is blessed with, when I tell you that Mr. Whitmore, the last clergyman, was ninety-three when he died. A good, kind soul, much loved by his parish, but not a scholar. Come, Mr. Simonelli! If it is agreeable to you to have a house of your own—with garden, orchard, and farm all complete—then I shall write tonight to the Gathercoles and relieve them of all their anxiety by telling them of your acceptance!"

But, though he pressed me very hard, I would not give him my answer immediately. I believe I know what he is about. He has a nephew whom he hopes to steer into my place if I leave Corpus Christi. Yet it would be wrong, I think, to refuse such an opportunity merely for the sake of spiting him.

I believe it must be either the parish or matrimony.

Sept. 9th, 1811
I was this day ordained as a priest of the Church of England. I have no doubts that my modest behavior, studiousness, and extraordinary mildness of temper make me peculiarly fitted for the life.

Sept. 15th, 1811   The George, Derby
Today I traveled by stagecoach as far as Derby. I sat outside—which cost me ten shillings and sixpence—but since it rained steadily I was at some trouble to keep my books and papers dry. My room at the George is better aired than rooms in inns generally are. I dined upon some roast woodcocks, a fricassee of turnips and apple dumplings. All excellent but not cheap and so I complained.

Sept. 16th, 1811
My first impressions were *not* encouraging. It continued to rain, and the country surrounding Allhope appeared very wild and almost uninhabited. There were steep, wooded valleys, rivers of white spurting water, outcrops of barren rock surmounted by withered oaks, bleak windswept moorland. It was, I dare say, remarkably picturesque, and might have provided an excellent model for a descriptive passage in a novel, but to me who must now live here, it spoke very eloquently of extreme seclusion and scarce society characterized by ignorant minds and uncouth manners. In two hours' walking I saw only one human habitation—a grim farmhouse with rain-darkened walls set among dark, dripping trees.

I had begun to think I must be very near to the village when I turned a corner and saw, a little way ahead of me in the rain, two figures on horseback. They had stopped by a poor cottage to speak to someone who stood just within bounds of the garden. Now I am no judge of horses, but these were quite remarkable; tall, well-formed, and shining. They tossed their heads and stamped their hooves upon the ground as if they scorned to be stood upon so base an element. One was black and one was chestnut. The chestnut, in particular, appeared to be the only bright thing in the whole of Derbyshire; it glowed like a bonfire in the gray, rainy air.

The person whom the riders addressed was an old bent man. As I drew near I heard shouts and a curse, and I saw one of the riders reach up and make a sign with his hand above the old man's head. This gesture was entirely new to me and must, I suppose, be peculiar to the natives of Derbyshire. I do not think that I ever before saw anything so expressive of contempt, and as it may be of some interest to study the customs and quaint beliefs of the people here, I append a sort of diagram or drawing to show precisely the gesture the man made.

I concluded that the riders were going away dissatisfied from their interview with the old cottager. It further occurred to me that, since I was now so close to the village, this ancient person was certainly one of my parishioners. I determined to lose no time in bringing peace where there was strife, harmony where there was discord. I quickened my steps, hailed the old man, informed him that I was the new Rector and asked him his name, which was Jemmy.

"Well, Jemmy," said I, assuming a cordial manner and accommodating my language to his uneducated condition, "what has happened here? What have you done to make the gentlemen so angry?"

He told me that the rider of the chestnut horse had a wife who had that morning been brought to bed. He and his servant had come to inquire for Jemmy's wife, Joan, who for many years had attended all the women in the neighborhood.

"Indeed?" said I in accents of mild reproof. "Then why do you keep the gentleman waiting? Where is your wife?"

He pointed to where the lane wound up the opposite hillside, to where I could just discern through the rain an ancient church and a graveyard.

"Who takes care of the women in their childbeds now?" I asked.

There were, it seemed, two executors of that office: Mr. Stubb, the apothecary in Bakewell, or Mr. Horrocks, the physician in Buxton. But both these places were two, three hours hard ride away on bad roads, and the lady was already, in Jemmy's words, "proper poorly."

To own the truth, I was a little annoyed with the gentleman on the chestnut horse who had not troubled until today to provide an attendant for his wife: an obligation which, presumably, he might have discharged at any time within the last nine months. Nevertheless I hurried after the two men and, addressing the rider of the chestnut horse, said, "Sir, my name is Simonelli. I have studied a great variety of subjects—law, divinity, medicine—at the university at Cambridge, and I have for many years maintained a correspondence with one of the most eminent physicians of the age, Mr. Matthew Baillie of Great Windmill-street in London. If it is not disagreeable to you, I shall be happy to attend your wife."

He bent upon me a countenance thin, dark, eager. His eyes were exceptionally fine and bright and their expression unusually intelligent. His black hair was his own, quite long, and tied with a black ribbon in a pigtail, rather in the manner of an old-fashioned queue wig. His age, I thought, might be between forty and fifty.

"And are you an adherent of Galenus or Paracelsus?" he said.

"Sir?" I said (for I thought he must intend the question as a joke). But then, since he continued to look at me, I said, "The ancient medical authorities whom you mention, sir, are quite outdated. All that Galen knew of anatomy he got from observing the dissections of pigs, goats, and apes. Paracelsus believed in the efficacy of magic spells and all sorts of nonsense. Indeed, sir," I said with a burst of laughter, "you might as well inquire whose cause I espoused in the Trojan War as ask me to choose between those illustrious, but thoroughly discredited, gentlemen!"

Perhaps it was wrong to laugh at him. I felt it was wrong immediately. I remembered how many enemies my superior abilities had won me at Cambridge, and I recalled my resolution to do things differently in Allhope and to bear patiently with ignorance and misinformation wherever I found it. But the gentleman only said, "Well, Dando, we have had better fortune than we looked for. A scholar, an eminent physician to attend my lady." He smiled a long thin smile which went up just one side of his dark face. "She will be full of gratitude, I have no doubt."

While he spoke I made some discoveries: to wit, that both he and his servant were amazingly dirty—I had not observed it at first because the rain had washed their faces clean. His coat, which I had taken to be of brown drugget or some such material, was revealed upon closer inspection to be of red velvet, much discolored, worn and matted with dirt and grease.

"I had intended to hoist the old woman up behind Dando," he said, "but that will scarcely do for you." He was silent a moment and then suddenly cried, "Well, what do you wait for, you sour-faced rogue . . . ?" (This startled me, but a moment later I understood that he addressed Dando.) ". . . Dismount! Help the learned doctor to the horse."

I was about to protest that I knew nothing of horses or riding but Dando had already jumped down and had somehow tipped me onto the horse's back; my feet were in the stirrups and the reins were in my hands before I knew where I was.

Now a great deal is talked in Cambridge of horses and the riding of horses and the managing of horses. A great number of the more ignorant undergraduates pride themselves upon their understanding of the subject. But I find there is nothing to it. One has merely to hold on as tight as one can: the horse, I find, does *all*.

Immense speed! Godlike speed! We turned from the highway immediately and raced through ancient woods of oak and ash and holly; dead leaves flew up, rain flew down, and the gentleman and I—like spirits of the sad, gray air—flew between! Then up, up we climbed to where the ragged gray clouds tore themselves apart like great doors opening in heaven to let us through! By moorland pools of slate-gray water, by lonely wind-shaped hawthorn trees, by broken walls of gray stones—a ruined chapel—a stream—over the hills, to a house that stood quite alone in a rain-misted valley.

It was a very ancient-looking place, the different parts of which had been built at many different times and of a great variety of materials. There were flints and stones, old silvery-gray timbers, and rose-red brick that glowed very cheerfully in the gloom. But as we drew nearer I saw that it was in a state of the utmost neglect. Doors had lost their hinges and were propped into place with stones and stuffed around with faded brown rags; windows were cracked and broken and pasted over with old paper; the roof, which was of stone tiles, showed many gaping black holes; dry, dead grasses poked up between the paving stones. It gave the house a melancholy air, particularly since it was surrounded by a moat of dark, still water that reproduced all this desolation as faithfully as any mirror.

We jumped off our horses, entered the house, and passed rapidly through a great number of rooms. I observed that the gentleman's servants (of which he appeared to have a most extraordinary number) did not come forward to welcome their master or give him news of his wife but lurked about in the shadows in the most stupid fashion imaginable.

The gentleman conducted me to the chamber where his wife lay, her only attendant a tiny old woman. This person was remarkable for several things, but chiefly for a great number of long, coarse hairs that grew upon her cheeks and resembled nothing so much in the world as porcupine quills.

The room had been darkened and the fire stoked up in accordance with the old-fashioned belief that women in childbirth require to be heated. It was abominably hot. My first action upon entering the room was to pull back the curtains and throw open the windows, but when I looked around I rather regretted having done any such thing, for the squalor of that room is not to be described.

The sheets, upon which the gentleman's wife lay, were crawling with vermin of all sorts. Pewter plates lay scattered about with rotting food upon them. And yet it was not the wretchedness of poverty. There was a most extraordinary muddle everywhere one looked. Over here a greasy apron embraced a volume of Diderot's *Enyclopédie*; over there a jeweled red velvet slipper was trapped by the lid of a warming-pan; under the bed a silver diadem was caught on the prongs of a garden-fork; on the window-ledge the dried-out corpse of some animal (I think a cat) rested its powdery head against a china-jug. A bronze-colored velvet garment (which rather resembled the robe of a Coptic pope) had been cast down on the floor in lieu of a carpet. It was embroidered all over with gold and pearls, but the threads had broken and the pearls lay scattered in the dirt. It was altogether such an extraordinary blending of magnificence and filth as I could never have conceived of, and left me entirely astonished that anyone should tolerate such slothfulness and neglect on the part of their servants.

As for the lady, poor thing, she was very young—perhaps no more than fifteen—and very thin. Her bones showed through an almost translucent skin which was stretched, tight as a drum, over her swollen belly. Although I have read a great deal upon the subject, I found it more difficult than I had imagined to make the lady attend to what I was saying. My instructions were exceptionally clear and precise, but she was weak and in pain and I could not persuade her to listen to me.

I soon discovered that the baby was lodged in a most unfortunate position. Having no forceps, I tried several times to turn it with my hand, and at the fourth attempt I succeeded. Between the hours of four and five a male child was born. I did not at first like his color. Mr. Baillie told me that newborn children are generally the color of claret; sometimes, he said, they may be as dark as port-wine, but this child was, to all intents and purposes, black. He was, however, quite remarkably strong. He gave me a great kick as I passed him to the old woman. A bruise upon my arm marks the place.

But I could not save the mother. At the end she was like a house through which a great wind rushes, making all the doors bang at their frames: death was rushing through her, and her wits came loose and banged about inside her head. She appeared to believe that she had been taken by force to a place where she was watched night and day by a hideous jailoress.

"Hush," said I. "These are very wild imaginings. Look about you. Here is good, kind . . ." I indicated the old woman with the porcupine face. ". . . who takes such excellent care of you. You are surrounded by friends. Be comforted." But she would not listen to me and called out wildly for her mother to come and take her home.

I would have given a great deal to save her. For what in the end was the result of all my exertions? One person came into this world and another left it—it seemed no very great achievement.

I began a prayer of commendation, but had not said above a dozen words when

I heard a sort of squeal. Opening one eye, I saw the old woman snatch up the baby and run from the room as fast as her legs could carry her.

I finished my prayer and, with a sigh, went to find the lady's husband. I discovered him in his library where, with an admirable show of masculine unconcern, he was reading a book. It was then about seven or eight o'clock.

I thought that it became me as a clergyman to offer some comfort and to say something of the wife he had lost, but I was prevented by my complete ignorance of everything that concerned her. Of her virtue I could say nothing at all. Of her beauty I knew little enough; I had only ever seen her with features contorted in the agonies of childbirth and of death. So I told him in plain words what had happened and finished with a short speech that sounded, even to my own ears, uncommonly like an apology for having killed his wife.

"Oh!" he said. "I dare say you did what you could."

I admired his philosophy though I confess it surprised me a little. Then I recalled that, in speaking to me, she had made several errors of grammar and had employed some dialect words and expressions. I concluded that perhaps, like many gentlemen before him, he had been enticed into an unequal marriage by blue eyes and fair hair, and that he had later come to regret it.

"A son, you say?" he said in perfect good humor. "Excellent!" And he stuck his head out of the door and called for the baby to be brought to him. A moment later Dando and the porcupine-faced nurse appeared with the child. The gentleman examined his son very minutely and declared himself delighted. Then he held the baby up and said the following words to it: "On to the shovel you must go, sir!" He gave the child a hearty shake. "And into the fire you must go, sir!" Another shake. "And under the burning coals you must go, sir!" And another shake.

I found his humor a little odd.

Then the nurse brought out a cloth and seemed to be about to wrap the baby in it.

"Oh, but I must protest, sir!" I cried. "Indeed I must!" Have you nothing cleaner to wrap the child in?"

They all looked at me in some amazement. Then the gentleman smiled and said, "What excellent eyesight you must have, Mr. Simonelli! Does not this cloth appear to you to be made of the finest, whitest linen imaginable?"

"No," said I in some irritation. "It appears to me to be a dirty rag that I would scarcely use to clean my boots!"

"Indeed?" said the gentleman in some surprise. "And Dando? Tell me, how does he strike you? Do you see the ruby buckles on his shoes? No? What of his yellow velvet coat and shining sword?"

I shook my head. (Dando, I may say, was dressed in the same quaint, old-fashioned style as his master, and looked every inch what he no doubt was—a tattered, swaggering scoundrel. He wore jackboots up to his thighs, a bunch of ragged dirty lace at his throat, and an ancient tricorne hat on his head.)

The gentleman gazed thoughtfully at me for a minute or two. "Mr. Simonelli," he said at last, "I am quite struck by your face! Those lustrous eyes! Those fine dark eyelashes! Those noble eyebrows! Every feature proclaims your close connection with my own family! Do me the kindness, if you will, of stepping before this mirror and standing at my side."

I did as he asked and, leaving aside some difference in our complexions (his as brown as beechmast, mine as white as hot-pressed paper) the resemblance was, I confess, remarkable. Everything which is odd or unsettling in my own face, I saw repeated in his: the same long eyebrows like black pen-strokes terminating in an upward flourish; the same curious slant to the eyelid which bestows upon the face an expression of sleepy arrogance; the same little black mole just below the right eye.

"Oh!" he cried. "There can be no doubt about it! What was your father's name?"

"Simonelli," I said with a smile, "evidently."

"And his place of birth?"

I hesitated. "Genoa," I said.

"What was your mother's name?"

"Frances Simon."

"And her place of birth?"

"York."

He took a scrap of paper from the table and wrote it all down. "Simon and Simonelli," he said, "that is odd." He seemed to wait for some further illumination upon the matter of my parentage. He was disappointed. "Well, no matter," he said. "Whatever the connection between us, Mr. Simonelli, I shall discover it. You have done me a great service and I had intended to pay you liberally for it, but I have no notion of relations paying for services that ought to be given freely as part of the duty that family members owe one another." He smiled his long, knowing smile. "And so I must examine the question further," he said.

So all his much-vaunted interest in my face and family came to this: he would not pay me! It made me very angry to think I could have been so taken in by him! I informed him briefly that I was the new Rector of Allhope and said that I hoped to see him in church on Sunday.

But he only smiled and said, "We are not in your parish here. This house is Allhope House, and according to ancient agreement I am the Lord of Allhope Manor, but over the years the house and village have become separated and now stand, as you see, at some distance from each other."

I had not the least idea what he was talking about. I turned to go with Dando, who was to accompany me back to the village, but at the library door I looked back and said, "It is a curious thing, sir, but you never told me your name."

"I am John Hollyshoes," said he with a smile.

Just as the door closed I could have sworn I heard the sound of a shovel being pushed into the fire and the sound of coals being raked over.

The ride back to the village was considerably less pleasant than the ride to Allhope House had been. The moonlight was all shut out by the clouds and it continued to rain, yet Dando rode as swiftly as his master, and at every moment I expected our headlong rush to end in broken necks.

A few lights appeared—the lights of a village. I got down from the black horse and turned to say something to Dando, whereupon I discovered that in that same instant of my dismounting he had caught up the reins of the black horse and was gone. I took one step and immediately fell over my trunk and parcels of books— which I presume had been left for me by Dando and which I had entirely forgot until that moment.

There seemed to be nothing close at hand but a few miserable cottages. Some distance off to the right half a dozen windows blazed with light, and their large size and regular appearance impressed me with ideas of warm rooms, supper tables, and comfortable sofas. In short they suggested the abode of a *gentleman*.

My knock was answered by a neat maidservant. I inquired whether this was Mr. Gathercole's house. She replied that *Admiral* Gathercole had drowned six years ago. Was I the new Rector?

The neat maidservant left me in the hall to go and announce me to someone or other, and I had time to look about me. The floor was of ancient stone flags, very well swept, and the bright gleam upon every oak cabinet, every walnut chest of drawers, every little table, plainly spoke of the plentiful application of beeswax and of pleasant female industry. All was cleanliness, delicacy, elegance—which was more, I discovered, than could be said for me. I was well provided with all the various stains, smears, and general dishevelments that may be acquired by walking for hours through heavy rain, galloping through thickly wooded countryside, and then toiling long and hard at a childbed and a deathbed; and in addition I had acquired a sort of veneer of black grease—the inevitable result, I fancy, of a sojourn in John Hollyshoes's house. The neat maidservant led me to a drawing-room where two ladies waited to see what sort of clergyman they had got. One rose with ponderous majesty and announced herself to be Mrs. Gathercole, the Admiral's relict. The other lady was Mrs. Edmond, the Admiral's sister.

An old-fashioned Pembroke-table had been spread with a white linen cloth for supper. And the supper was a good one. There was a dish of fricasseed chicken and another of scalloped oysters, there was apple tart, Wensleydale cheese, and a decanter of wine and glasses.

Mrs. Gathercole had my own letter, and another upon which I discerned the unappetizing scrawl of Dr. Prothero. "Simonelli is an Italian name, is it not?" asked Mrs. Gathercole.

"It is, madam, but the bearer of the name whom you see before you is an Englishman." She pressed me no further upon this point, and I was glad not to be obliged to repeat the one or two falsehoods I had already uttered that day.

She took up Dr. Prothero's letter, read aloud one or two compliments upon my learning in a somewhat doubting tone, and began to speak of the house where I was to live. She said that when a house was for many years in the care of an ancient gentleman—as was the case here—it was liable to fall into a state of some dilapidation—she feared I would have a good many repairs to make and the expense would be very great, but as I was a gentleman of independent property, she supposed I would not mind it. She ran on in this manner and I stared into the fire. I was tired to death. But as I sat there I became conscious of something having been said which was not quite right, which it was my duty to correct as soon as possible. I stirred myself to speak. "Madam," I said, "you labor under a misapprehension. I have no property."

"Money, then," she said. "Government bonds."

"No, madam. Nothing."

There was a short silence.

"Mr. Simonelli," said Mrs. Gathercole, "this is a small parish and, for the most part, poor. The living yields no more than £50 a year. It is very far from providing an income to support a gentleman. You will not have enough money to live on."

Too late I saw the perfidious Prothero's design to immure me in poverty and obscurity. But what could I do? I had no money and no illusions that my numerous enemies at Cambridge, having once got rid of me, would ever allow me to return. I sighed and said something of my modest needs.

Mrs. Gathercole gave a short, uncheerful laugh. "You may think so, Mr. Simonelli, but your wife will think very differently when she understands how little she is to have for her housekeeping expences."

"My wife, madam?" said I in some astonishment.

"You are a married man, are not you, Mr. Simonelli?"

"I, madam? No, madam!"

A silence of much longer duration.

"Well!" she said at last, "I do not know what to say. My instructions were clear enough, I think! A respectable, married man of private fortune. I cannot imagine what Prothero is thinking of. I have already refused the living of Allhope to one young man on the grounds of his unmarried state, but he at least has six hundred pounds a year."

The other lady, Mrs. Edmond, now spoke for the first time. "What troubles *me* rather more," she said, "is that Dr. Prothero appears to have sent us a scholar. Upperstone House is the only gentleman's house in the parish. With the exception of Mrs. Gathercole's own family, your parishioners will all be hill-farmers, shepherds, and tradesmen of the meanest sort. Your learning, Mr. Simonelli, will all be wasted here."

I had nothing to say, and some of the despair I felt must have showed in my face for both ladies became a little kinder. They told me that a room had been got ready for me at the Rectory, and Mrs. Edmond asked how long it had been since I had eaten. I confessed that I had had nothing since the night before. They invited me to share their supper and then watched as everything I touched—dainty china, white linen napkins—became covered with dark, greasy marks.

As the door closed behind me I heard Mrs. Edmond say, "Well, well. So that is Italian beauty! Quite remarkable. I do not think I ever saw an example of it before."

Ten o'clock, Sept. 17th, 1811

Last night complete despair! This morning perfect hope and cheerfulness! New plans constantly bubbling up in my brain! What could be more calculated to raise the spirits than a bright autumn morning with a heavy dew? Everything is rich color, intoxicating freshness, and sparkle!

I am excessively pleased with the Rectory—and hope that I may be allowed to keep it. It is an old stone house. The ceilings are low, the floor of every room is either higher or lower than the floors of neighboring rooms, and there are more gables than chimneys. It has fourteen rooms! What in the world will I do with fourteen rooms?

I discovered Mr. Whitmore's clothes in a cupboard. I had not, I confess, spared many thoughts for this old gentleman, but his clothes brought him vividly before me. Every bump and bulge of his ancient shoes betray their firm conviction that they still enclose his feet. His half-unraveled wig has not yet noticed that his poor old head is gone. The cloth of his long, pale coat is stretched and bagged, *here* to accommodate his sharp elbows, *there* to take account of the stoop of his shoulders. It was almost as if I had opened the cupboard and discovered Mr. Whitmore.

Someone calls me from the garden. . . .

Four o'clock, the same day
Jemmy—the old man I spoke to yesterday—is dead. He was found this morning outside his cottage, struck clean in two from the crown of his head to his groin. Is it possible to conceive of anything more horrible? Curiously, in all the rain we had yesterday, no one remembers seeing any lightning. The funeral will be tomorrow. He was the first person I spoke to in Allhope, and my first duty will be to bury him.

The second, and to my mind *lesser*, misfortune to have befallen the parish is that a young woman has disappeared. Dido Puddifer has not been seen since early this morning when her mother, Mrs. Glossop, went to a neighbor's house to borrow a nutmeg grater. Mrs. Glossop left Dido walking up and down in the orchard with her baby at her breast, but when she returned the baby was lying in the wet grass and Dido was gone.

I accompanied Mrs. Edmond to the cottage to pay a visit of sympathy to the family, and as we were coming back Mrs. Edmond said, "The worst of it is that she is a very pretty girl, all golden curls and soft blue eyes. I cannot help but suppose some passing scoundrel has taken a fancy to her and made her go along with him."

"But does it not seem more likely," said I, "that she went with him of her own accord? She is uneducated, illiterate, and probably never thought seriously upon ethical questions in her life."

"I do not think you quite understand," said Mrs. Edmond, "No girl ever loved home and husband more than Dido. No girl was more delighted to have a baby of her own. Dido Puddifer is a silly, giddy sort of girl, but she is also as good as gold."

"Oh!" said I, with a smile, "I daresay she was very good until today, but then, you know, temptation might never have come her way before."

But Mrs. Edmond proved quite immoveable in her prejudice in favor of Dido Puddifer and so I said no more. Besides, she soon began to speak of a much more interesting subject—my own future.

"My sister-in-law's wealth, Mr. Simonelli, causes her to overrate the needs of other people. She imagines that no one can exist upon less than seven hundred pounds a year, but you will do well enough. The living is fifty pounds a year, but the farm could be made to yield twice, thrice that amount. The first four or five years you must be frugal. I will see to it that you are supplied with milk and butter from Upperstone-farm, but by midsummer, Mr. Simonelli, you must buy a milch-cow of your own." She thought a moment. "I daresay Marjory Hollinsclough will let me have a hen or two for you."

Sept. 20th, 1811
This morning Rectory-lane was knee-deep in yellow and brown leaves. A silver rain like smoke blew across the churchyard. A dozen crows in their clerical dress of decent black were idling among the graves. They rose up to flap about me as

I came down the lane like a host of winged curates all ready to do my bidding.

There was a whisper of sounds at my back, stifled laughter, a genteel cough, and then: "Oh! Mr. Simonelli!" spoken very sweetly and rather low.

I turned.

Five young ladies; on each face I saw the same laughing eyes, the same knowing smiles, the same rain-speckled brown curls, like a strain of music taken up and repeated many different ways. There were even to my befuddled senses the same bonnets, umbrellas, muslins, ribbons, repeated in a bewildering variety of colors but all sweetly blending together, all harmonious. All that I could have asserted with any assurance at that moment was that they were all as beautiful as angels. They were grouped most fetchingly, sheltering each other from the rain with their umbrellas, and the composure and dignity of the two eldest were in no way compromised by the giggles of the two youngest.

The tallest—she who had called my name—begged my pardon. To call out to someone in the lane was very shocking, she hoped I would forgive her but, ". . . Mama has entirely neglected to introduce us and Aunt Edmond is so taken up with the business about poor Dido that . . . well, in short, Mr. Simonelli, we thought it best to lay ceremony aside and introduce ourselves. We are made bold to do it by the thought that you are to be our clergyman. The lambs ought not to fear the shepherd, ought they, Mr. Simonelli? Oh, but I have no patience with that stupid Dr. Prothero! Why did he not send you to us earlier? I hope, Mr. Simonelli, that you will not judge Allhope by this dull season!" And she dismissed with a wave of her hand the sweetest, most tranquil prospect imaginable; woods, hills, moors, and streams were all deemed entirely unworthy of my attention. "If only you had come in July or August then we might have shown you all the beauties of Derbyshire, but now I fear you will find it very dull." But her smile defied me to find any place dull where *she* was to be found. "Yet," she said, brightening, "perhaps I shall persuade Mama to give a ball. Do you like dancing, Mr. Simonelli?"

"But Aunt Edmond says that Mr. Simonelli is a scholar," said one of her sisters with the same sly smile. "Perhaps he only cares for books."

"Which books do you like best, Mr. Simonelli?" demanded a Miss Gathercole of the middle size.

"Do you sing, Mr. Simonelli?" asked the tallest Miss Gathercole.

"Do you shoot, Mr. Simonelli?" asked the smallest Miss Gathercole, only to be silenced by an older sister. "Be quiet, Kitty, or he may shoot *you*."

Then the two eldest Miss Gathercoles each took one of my arms and walked with me and introduced me to my parish. And every remark they uttered upon the village and its inhabitants betrayed their happy conviction that it contained nothing half so interesting or delightful as *themselves*.

Sept. 27th, 1811

I dined this evening at Upperstone House. Two courses. Eighteen dishes in each. Brown Soup. Mackerel. Haricot of mutton. Boiled chicken particularly good. Some excellent apple tarts. I was the only gentleman present.

Mrs. Edmond was advising me upon my farm. ". . . and when you go to buy your sheep, Mr. Simonelli, I shall accompany you. I am generally allowed to be an excellent judge of livestock."

"Indeed, madam," said I, "that is most kind, but in the meantime I have been thinking that there is no doctor nearer than Buxton, and it seems to me that I could not do better than advertise my services as a physician. I dare say you have heard reports that I attended Mrs. Hollyshoes."

"Who is Mrs. Hollyshoes?" asked Mrs. Edmond.

"The wife of the gentleman who owns Allhope House."

"I do not understand you, Mr. Simonelli. There is no Allhope House here."

"Whom do you mean, Mr. Simonelli?" asked the eldest Miss Gathercole.

I was vexed at their extraordinary ignorance but, with great patience, I gave them an account of my meeting with John Hollyshoes and my visit to Allhope House. But the more particulars I gave, the more obstinately they declared that no such person and no such house existed.

"Perhaps I have mistaken the name," I said—though I knew that I had not.

"Oh! You have certainly done that, Mr. Simonelli!" said Mrs. Gathercole.

"Perhaps it is Mr. Shaw he means," said the eldest Miss Gathercole, doubtfully.

"Or John Wheston," said Miss Marianne.

They began to discuss whom I might mean, but one by one every candidate was rejected. *This* one was too old, *that* one too young. Every gentleman for miles around was pronounced entirely incapable of fathering a child, and each suggestion only provided further dismal proofs of the general decay of the male sex in this particular part of Derbyshire.

Sept. 29th, 1811

I have discovered why Mrs. Gathercole was so anxious to have a rich, married clergyman. She fears that a poor, unmarried one would soon discovery that the quickest way to improve his fortune is to marry one of the Miss Gathercoles. Robert Yorke (the clergyman whom Mrs. Gathercole mentioned on my first evening in Allhope as having £600 a year) was refused the living because he had already shown signs of being in love with the eldest Miss Gathercole. It must therefore be particularly galling to Mrs. Gathercole that I am such a favorite with all her daughters. Each has something she is dying to learn, and naturally I am to tutor all of them: French conversation for the eldest Miss Gathercole, advanced Italian grammar for Miss Marianne, the romantic parts of British History for Henrietta, the bloodthirsty parts for Kitty, Mathematics and Poetry for Jane.

Oct. 9th, 1811

On my return from Upperstone House this morning I found Dando at the Rectory door with the two horses. He told me that his master had something of great importance and urgency to communicate to me.

John Hollyshoes was in his library as before, reading a book. Upon a dirty little table at his side there was wine in a dirty glass. "Ah! Mr. Simonelli!" he cried, jumping up. "I am very glad to see you! It seems, sir, that you have the family failing as well as the family face!"

"And what would that be?" said I.

"Why! Lying, of course! Oh, come, Mr. Simonelli! Do not look so shocked.

You are found out, sir. Your father's name was *not* Simonelli—and, to my certain knowledge, he was never at Genoa!"

A silence of some moments' duration.

"Did you know my father, sir?" said I, in some confusion.

"Oh, yes! He was my cousin."

"That is entirely impossible," said I.

"Upon the contrary," said he. "If you will take a moment to peruse this letter you will see that it is exactly as I say." And he handed me some yellowing sheets of paper.

"What your aim may be in insulting me," I cried, "I cannot pretend to guess, but I hope, sir, that you will take back those words or we shall be obliged to settle the matter *some other way*." With the utmost impatience I thrust his letter back at him, when my eye was caught by the words "the third daughter of a York linen-draper." "Wait!" I cried and snatched it back again. "My mother was the third daughter of a York linen-draper!"

"Indeed, Mr. Simonelli," said John Hollyshoes, with his long sideways smile.

The letter was addressed to John Hollyshoes and had been written at the Old Starre Inn in Stonegate, York. The writer of the letter mentioned that he was in the middle of a hasty breakfast and there were some stains as of preserves and butter. It seemed that the writer had been on his way to Allhope House to pay John Hollyshoes a visit when he had been delayed in York by a sudden passion for the third daughter of a York linen-draper. His charmer was most minutely described. I read of "a slight plumpness," "light silvery-gold curls," "eyes of a forget-me-not blue."

By all that I have ever been told by my friends, by all that I have ever seen in sketches and watercolor portraits, this was my mother! But if nothing else proved the truth of John Hollyshoes's assertion, there was the date—January 19th, 1778—nine months to the day before my own birth. The writer signed himself, "Your loving cousin, Thomas Fairwood."

"So much love," I said, reading the letter, "and yet he deserted her the very next day!"

"Oh! You must not blame him," said John Hollyshoes. "A person cannot help his disposition, you know."

"And yet," said I, "one thing puzzles me still. My mother was extremely vague upon all points concerning her seducer—she did not even know his name—yet one thing she was quite clear about. He was a foreign gentleman."

"Oh! That is easily explained," he said. "For though we have lived in this island a very long time—many thousands of years longer than its other inhabitants—yet still we hold ourselves apart and pride ourselves on being of quite other blood."

"You are Jews perhaps, sir?" said I.

"Jews?" said he. "No, indeed!"

I thought a moment. "You say my father is dead?"

"Alas, yes. After he parted from your mother, he did not in fact come to Allhope House, but was drawn away by horse races at *this* place and cock-fighting at *that* place. But some years later he wrote to me again telling me to expect him at midsummer and promising to stay with me for a good long while. This time he got no further than a village near Carlisle where he fell in love with two young women . . ."

"Two young women!" I cried in astonishment.

"Well," said John Hollyshoes. "Each was as beautiful as the other. He did not know how to choose between them. One was the daughter of a miller and the other was the daughter of a baker. He hoped to persuade them to go with him to his house in the Eildon Hills where he intended that both should live forever and have all their hearts' desire. But, alas, it did not suit these ungrateful young women to go, and the next news I had of him was that he was dead. I discovered later that the miller's daughter had sent him a message which led him to believe that she at least was on the point of relenting, and so he went to her father's mill, where the fast-running water was shaded by a rowan tree—and I pause here merely to observe that of all the trees in the greenwood the rowan is the most detestable. Both young women were waiting for him. The miller's daughter jangled a bunch of horrid rowan-berries in his face. The baker's daughter was then able to tumble him into the stream, whereupon both women rolled the millstone on top of him, pinning him to the floor of the stream. He was exceedingly strong. All my family—*our* family I should say—are exceedingly strong, exceedingly hard to kill, but the millstone lay on his chest. He was unable to rise and so, in time, he drowned."

"Good God!" I cried. "But this is dreadful! As a clergyman I cannot approve his habit of seducing young women, but as a son I must observe that in this particular instance the revenge extracted by the young women seems out of all proportion to his offense. And were these bloodthirsty young women never brought to justice?"

"Alas, no," said John Hollyshoes. "And now I must beg that we cease to speak of a subject so very unpleasant to my family feelings. Tell me instead why you fixed upon this odd notion of being Italian."

I told him how it had been my grandfather's idea. From my own dark looks and what his daughter had told him, he thought I might be Italian or Spanish. A fondness for Italian music caused him to prefer that country. Then he had taken his own name, George Alexander Simon, and fashioned out of it a name for me, Giorgio Alessandro Simonelli. I told how that excellent old gentleman had *not* cast off his daughter when she fell but had taken good care of her, provided money for attendants and a place for her to live, and how, when she died of sorrow and shame shortly after my birth, he had brought me up and had me educated.

"But what is most remarkable," said John Hollyshoes, "is that you fixed upon that city which—had Thomas Fairwood ever gone to Italy—was precisely the place to have pleased him most. Not gaudy Venice, not trumpeting Rome, not haughty Florence, but Genoa, all dark shadows and sinister echoes tumbling down to the shining sea!"

"Oh! But I chose it quite at random, I assure you."

"That," said John Hollyshoes, "has nothing to do with it. In choosing Genoa you exhibited the extraordinary penetration which has always distinguished our family. But it was your eyesight that betrayed you. Really, I was never so astonished in my life as I was when you remarked upon the one or two specks of dust which clung to the baby's wrapper."

I asked after the health of his son.

"Oh! He is well. Thank you. We have got an excellent wet-nurse—from your own parish—whose milk agrees wonderfully well with the child."

Oct. 20th, 1811

In the stable-yard at Upperstone House this morning the Miss Gathercoles were preparing for their ride. Naturally I was invited to accompany them.

"But, my dear," said Mrs. Edmond to the eldest Miss Gathercole, "you must consider that Mr. Simonelli may not ride. Not everyone rides." And she gave me a questioning look as if she would help me out of a difficulty.

"Oh!" said I, "I can ride a horse. It is of all kinds of exercise the most pleasing to me." I approached a conceited-looking gray mare, but instead of standing submissively for me to mount, this ill-mannered beast shuffled off a pace or two. I followed it—it moved away. This continued for some three or four minutes, while all the ladies of Upperstone silently observed us. Then the horse stopped suddenly and I tried to mount it, but its sides were of the most curious construction and instead of finding myself upon its back in a twinkling—as invariably happens with John Hollyshoes's horses—I got stuck halfway up.

Of course the Upperstone ladies chose to find fault with me instead of their own malformed beast, and I do not know what was more mortifying, the surprised looks of Miss Gathercole and Miss Marianne, or the undisguised merriment of Kitty.

I have considered the matter carefully and am forced to conclude that it will be a great advantage to me in such a retired spot to be able to ride whatever horses come to hand. Perhaps I can prevail upon Joseph, Mrs. Gathercole's groom, to teach me.

Nov. 4th, 1811

Today I went for a long walk in company with the five Miss Gathercoles. Sky as blue as paint, russet woods, fat white clouds like cushions—and that is the sum of all that I discovered of the landscape, for my attention was constantly being called away to the ladies themselves. "Oh! Mr. Simonelli! Would you be so kind as to do *this*?" or "Mr. Simonelli, might I trouble you do do *that*?" or "Mr. Simonelli! What is your opinion of such and such?" I was required to carry picnic-baskets, discipline unruly sketching easels, advise upon perspective, give an opinion on Mr. Coleridge's poetry, eat sweet-cake and dispense wine.

I have been reading over what I have written since my arrival here, and one thing I find quite astonishing—that I ever could have supposed that there was a strong likeness between the Miss Gathercoles. There never were five sisters so different in tastes, characters, persons, and countenances. Isabella, the eldest, is also the prettiest, the tallest, and the most elegant. Henrietta is the most romantic, Kitty the most light-hearted, and Jane is the quietest; she will sit hour after hour, dreaming over a book. Sisters come and go, battles are fought, she that is victorious sweeps from the room with a smile, she that is defeated sighs and takes up her embroidery. But Jane knows nothing of any of this—and then, quite suddenly, she will look up at me with a slow mysterious smile and I will smile back at her until I quite believe that I have joined with her in unfathomable secrets.

Marianne, the second eldest, has copper-colored hair, the exact shade of dry beech leaves, and is certainly the most exasperating of the sisters. She and I can never be in the same room for more than a quarter of an hour without beginning to quarrel about something or other.

Nov. 16th, 1811
John Windle has written me a letter to say that at High Table at Corpus Christi College on Thursday last Dr. Prothero told Dr. Considine that he pictured me in ten years' time with a worn-out slip of a wife and a long train of broken-shoed, dribble-nosed children, and that Dr. Considine had laughed so much at this that he had swallowed a great mouthful of scalding-hot giblet soup, and returned it through his nose.

Nov. 26th, 1811
No paths or roads go down to John Hollyshoes's house. His servants do not go out to farm his lands; there *is* no farm that I know of. How they all live I do not know. Today I saw a small creature—I think it was a rat—roasting over the fire in one of the rooms. Several of the servants bent over it eagerly, with pewter plates and ancient knives in their hands. Their faces were all in shadow. (It is an odd thing but, apart from Dando and the porcupine-faced nurse, I have yet to observe *any* of John Hollyshoes's servants at close quarters: they all scuttle away whenever I approach.)

John Hollyshoes is excellent company, his conversation instructive, his learning quite remarkable. He told me today that Judas Iscariot was a most skillful bee-keeper and his honey superior to any that had been produced in all the last two thousand years. I was much interested by this information, having never read or heard of it before, and I questioned him closely about it. He said that he believed he had a jar of Judas Iscariot's honey somewhere and if he could lay his hand upon it he would give it to me.

Then he began to speak of how my father's affairs had been left in great confusion at his death and how, since that time, the various rival claimants to his estate had been constantly fighting and quarreling among themselves.

"Two duels have been fought to my certain knowledge," he said, "and as a natural consequence of this, two claimants are dead. Another—whose passion to possess your father's estate was exceeded only by his passion for string quartets—was found three years ago hanging from a tree by his long silver hair, his body pierced through and through with the bows of violins, violoncellos, and violas like a musical Saint Sebastian. And only last winter an entire houseful of people was poisoned. The claimant had already run out of the house into the blizzard in her nightgown, and it was only her servants that died. Since I have made no claim upon the estate, I have escaped most of their malice—though, to own the truth, I have a better right to the property than any of them. But naturally the person with the best claim of all would be Thomas Fairwood's son. All dissension would be at an end, should a *son* arise to claim the estate." And he looked at me.

"Oh!" said I, much surprised. "But might not the fact of my illegitimacy . . . ?"

"We pay no attention to such things. Indeed with us it is more common than

not. Your father's lands, both in England and elsewhere, are scarcely less extensive than my own, and it would cost you very little trouble to procure them.
Once it was known that you had *my* support, then I dare say we would have you
settled at Rattle-heart House by next Quarter-day."

Such a stroke of good fortune, as I never dreamt of! Yet I dare not depend
upon it. But I cannot help thinking of it *constantly*! No one would enjoy vast
wealth more than I; and my feelings are not entirely selfish, for I honestly believe
that I am exactly the sort of person who *ought* to have the direction of large
estates. If I inherit, then I shall improve my land scientifically and increase its
yields three or fourfold (as I have read of other gentlemen doing). I shall observe
closely the lives of my tenants and servants and teach them to be happy. Or
perhaps I shall sell my father's estates and purchase land in Derbyshire and marry
Marianne or Isabella so that I may ride over every week to Allhope for the
purpose of inquiring most minutely into Mrs. Gathercole's affairs, and advising
her and Mrs. Edmond upon every point.

Seven o'clock in the morning, Dec. 8th, 1811
We have had no news of Dido Puddifer. I begin to think that Mrs. Edmond
and I were mistaken in fancying that she had run off with a tinker or Gypsy.
We have closely questioned farm-laborers, shepherds, and innkeepers, but no
Gypsies have been seen in the neighborhood since midsummer. I intend this
morning to pay a visit to Mrs. Glossop, Dido's mother.

Eight o'clock in the evening, the same day
What a revolution in all my hopes! From perfect happiness to perfect misery in
scarcely twelve hours. What a fool I was to dream of inheriting my father's
estate!—I might as well have contemplated taking a leasehold of a property in
Hell! And I wish that I might go to Hell now, for it would be no more than I
deserve. I have failed in my duty! I have imperiled the lives and souls of my
parishioners. My parishioners!—the very people whose preservation from all
harm ought to have been my first concern.

I paid my visit to Mrs. Glossop. I found her, poor woman, with her head in
her apron, weeping for Dido. I told her of the plan Mrs. Edmond and I had
devised to advertise in the Derby and Sheffield papers to see if we could discover
anyone who had seen or spoken to Dido.

"Oh!" said she, with a sigh, " 'twill do no good, sir, for I know very well where
she is."

"Indeed?" said I in some confusion. "Then why do you not fetch her home?"

"And so I would this instant," cried the woman, "did I not know that John
Hollyshoes has got her!"

"John Hollyshoes?" I cried in amazement.

"Yes, sir," said she. "I daresay you will not have heard of John Hollyshoes for
Mrs. Edmond does not like such things to be spoken of and scolds us for our
ignorant, superstitious ways. But we country people know John Hollyshoes very
well. He is a very powerful fairy that has lived hereabouts—oh! since the world
began, for all I know—and claims all sorts of rights over us. It is my belief that
he has got some little fairy baby at End-Of-All-Hope House—which is where

he lives—and that he needs a strong lass with plenty of good human milk to suckle it."

I cannot say that I believed her. Nor can I say that I did not. I do know that I sat in a state of the utmost shock for some time without speaking, until the poor woman forgot her own distress and grew concerned about *me*, shaking me by the shoulder and hurrying out to fetch brandy from Mrs. Edmond. When she came back with the brandy, I drank it down at one gulp and then went straight to Mrs. Gathercole's stable and asked Joseph to saddle Quaker for me. Just as I was leaving, Mrs. Edmond came out of the house to see what was the matter with me.

"No time, Mrs. Edmond! No time!" I cried, and rode away.

At John Hollyshoes's house Dando answered my knock and told me that his master was away from home.

"No matter," said I, with a confident smile, "for it is not John Hollyshoes that I have come to see, but my little cousin, the dear little sprite"—I used the word "sprite" and Dando did not contradict me—"whom I delivered seven weeks ago." Dando told me that I would find the child in a room at the end of a long hallway.

It was a great bare room that smelled of rotting wood and plaster. The walls were stained with damp and full of holes that the rats had made. In the middle of the floor was a queer-shaped wooden chair where sat a young woman. A bar of iron was fixed before her so that she could not rise, and her legs and feet were confined by manacles and rusty chains. She was holding John Hollyshoes's infant son to her breast.

"Dido?" I said.

How my heart fell when she answered me with a broad smile. "Yes, sir?"

"I am the new Rector of Allhope, Dido."

"Oh, sir! I am very glad to see you. I wish that I could rise and make you a curtsy, but you will excuse me, I am sure. The little gentleman has such an appetite this morning!"

She kissed the horrid creature and called it her angel, her doodle, and her dearie-darling-pet.

"How did you come here, Dido?" I asked.

"Oh! Mr. Hollyshoes's servants came and fetched me away one morning. And weren't they set upon my coming?" She laughed merrily. "All that a-pulling of me uphill and a-putting of me in carts! And I told them plainly that there was no need for any such nonsense. As soon as I heard of the poor little gentleman's plight," here she shook the baby and kissed it again—"I was more than willing to give him suck. No, my only misfortune, sir, in this heavenly place, is that Mr. Hollyshoes declares I must keep apart from my own sweet babe while I nurse his, and if all the angels in heaven went down upon their shining knees and begged him, he would not think any differently. Which is a pity, sir, for you know I might very easily feed two."

In proof of this point she, without the slightest embarrassment, uncovered her breasts, which to my inexperienced eye did indeed appear astonishingly replete.

She was anxious to learn who suckled her own baby. Anne Hargreaves, I told her. She was pleased at this and remarked approvingly that Nan had always had a good appetite. "Indeed, sir, I never knew a lass who loved a pudding better. Her milk is sure to be sweet and strong, do not you think so, sir?"

"Well, certainly Mrs. Edmond says that little Horatio Arthur thrives upon it. Dido, how do they treat you here?"

"Oh! sir. How can you ask such a question? Do you not see this golden chair set with diamonds and pearls? And this room with pillars of crystal and rose-colored velvet curtains? At night—you will not believe it, sir, for I did not believe it myself—I sleep on a bed with six feather mattress one atop the other and six silken pillows to my head."

I said it sounded most pleasant. And was she given enough to eat and drink?

Roast pork, plum pudding, toasted cheese, bread and dripping: there was, according to Dido Puddifer, no end to the good things to be had at End-Of-All-Hope House—and I dare say each and every one of them was in truth nothing more than the moldy crusts of bread that I saw set upon a cracked dish at her feet.

She also believed that they had given her a gown of sky-blue velvet with diamond buttons to wear, and she asked me, with a conscious smile, how I liked it.

"You look very pretty, Dido," I said, and she looked pleased. But what I really saw was the same russet-colored gown she had been wearing when they took her. It was all torn and dirty. Her hair was matted with the fairy-child's puke and her left eye was crusted with blood from a gash in her forehead. She was altogether such a sorry sight that my heart was filled with pity for her, and without thinking what I did, I licked my fingertips and cleaned her eye with my spittle.

I opened my mouth to ask if she were ever allowed out of the golden chair encrusted with diamonds and pearls, but I was prevented by the sound of a door opening behind me. I turned and saw John Hollyshoes walk in. I quite expected him to ask me what I did there, but he seemed to suspect no mischief and instead bent down to test the chains and the shackles. These were, like everything else in the house, somewhat decayed and he was right to doubt their strength. When he had finished he rose and smiled at me.

"Will you stay and take a glass of wine with me?" he said. "I have something of a rather particular nature to ask you."

We went to the library, where he poured two glasses of wine. He said, "Cousin, I have been meaning to ask you about that family of women who live upon my English estates and make themselves so important at my expense. I have forgot their name."

"Gathercole?" said I.

"Gathercole. Exactly," said he, and fell silent for a moment with a kind of thoughtful half-smile upon his dark face. "I have been a widower seven weeks now," he said, "and I do not believe I was ever so long without a wife before—not since there were women in England to be made wives of. To speak plainly, the sweets of courtship grew stale with me a long time ago and I wondered if you would be so kind as to spare me the trouble and advise me which of these women would suit me best."

"Oh!" said I. "I am quite certain that you would heartily dislike all of them!"

He laughed and put his arm around my shoulders. "Cousin," he said, "I am not so hard to please as you suppose."

"But really," said I, "I cannot advise you in the way you suggest. You must excuse me—indeed I cannot!"

"Oh? And why is that?"

"Because . . . because I intend to marry one of them myself!" I cried.

"I congratulate you, cousin. Which?"

I stared at him. "What?" I said.

"Tell me which you intend to marry and I will take another."

"Marianne!" I said. "No, wait! Isabella! That is . . ." It struck me very forcibly at that moment that I could not choose one without endangering all the others.

He laughed at that and affectionately patted my arm. "Your enthusiasm to possess Englishwomen is no more than I should have expected of Thomas Fairwood's son. But my own appetites are more moderate. One will suffice for me. I shall ride over to Allhope in a day or two and choose one young lady, which will leave four for you."

The thought of Isabella or Marianne or any of them doomed to live forever in the degradation of End-Of-All-Hope House! Oh! it is too horrible to be borne.

I have been staring in the mirror for an hour or more. I was always amazed at Cambridge how quickly people appeared to take offense at everything I said, but now I see plainly that it was not my words they hated—it was this fairy face. The dark alchemy of this face turns all my gentle human emotions into fierce fairy vices. Inside I am all despair, but this face shows only fairy scorn. My remorse becomes fairy fury and my pensiveness is turned to fairy cunning.

Dec. 9th, 1811

This morning at half past ten I made my proposals to Isabella Gathercole. She—sweet, compliant creature!—assured me that I had made her the happiest of women. But she could not at first be made to agree to a secret engagement.

"Oh!" she said. "Certainly Mama and Aunt Edmond will make all sorts of difficulties, but what will secrecy achieve? You do not know them as I do. Alas, they cannot be reasoned into an understanding of your excellent qualities. But they can be worn down. An unending stream of arguments and pleas must be employed, and the sooner it is begun, the sooner it will bring forth the happy resolution we wish for. I must be tearful; you must be heartbroken. I must get up a little illness—which will take time as I am just now in the most excellent good looks and health."

What could the mean-spirited scholars of Cambridge not learn from such a charming instructress? She argued so sweetly that I almost forgot what I was about and agreed to all her most reasonable demands. In the end I was obliged to tell her a little truth. I said that I had recently discovered that I was related to someone very rich who lived nearby and who had taken a great liking to me. I said that I hoped to inherit a great property very soon; surely it was not unreasonable to suppose that Mrs. Gathercole would look with more favor upon my suit when I was as wealthy as she?

Isabella saw the sense of this immediately and would, I think, have begun to speak again of love and so forth, only I was obliged to hurry away as I had just observed Marianne going into the breakfast-room.

Marianne was inclined to be quarrelsome at first. It was not, she said, that she did not wish to marry me. After all, she said, she must marry someone and she believed that she and I might do very well together. But why must our engagement be a secret? That, she said, seemed almost dishonorable.

"As you wish," said I. "I had thought that your affection for me might make you glad to indulge me in this one point. And besides, you know, a *secret engagement* will oblige us to speak Italian to each other constantly."

Marianne is passionately fond of Italian, particularly since none of her sisters understand a word. "Oh! Very well," she said.

In the garden at half past eleven Jane accepted my proposals by leaning up to whisper in my ear: "His face is fair as heav'n when springing buds unfold." She looked up at me with her soft secret smile and took both my hands in hers.

In the morning-room a little before midday I encountered a problem of a different sort. Henrietta assured me that a secret engagement was the very thing to please her most, but begged to be allowed to write of it to her cousin in Aberdeen. It seems that this cousin, Miss Mary Macdonald, is Henrietta's dearest friend and most regular correspondent, their ages—fifteen and a half—being exactly the same.

It was the most curious thing, she said, but the very week she had first beheld me (and instantly fallen in love with me) she had had a letter from Mary Macdonald full of *her* love for a sandy-haired Minister of the Kirk, the Reverend John McKenzie, who appeared from Mary Macdonald's many detailed descriptions of him to be almost as handsome as myself! Did I not agree with her that it was the strangest thing in the world, this curious resemblance in their situations? Her eagerness to inform Mary Macdonald immediately on all points concerning our engagement was not, I fear, unmixed with a certain rivalry, for I suspected that she was not quite sincere in hoping that Mary Macdonald's love for Mr. McKenzie might enjoy the same happy resolution as her own for me. But since I could not prevent her writing, I was obliged to agree.

In the drawing-room at three o'clock I finally came upon Kitty, who would not at first listen to anything that I had to say, but whirled around the room full of a plan to astound all the village by putting on a play in the barn at Christmas.

"You are not attending to me," said I. "Did not you hear me ask you to marry me?"

"Yes," said she, "and I have already said that I would. It is *you* who are not attending to *me*. You must advise us upon a play. Isabella wishes to be someone very beautiful who is vindicated in the last act, Marianne will not act unless she can say something in Italian, Jane cannot be made to understand anything about it so it will be best if she does not have to speak at all, Henrietta will do whatever I tell her, and, Oh! I long to be a bear! The dearest, wisest old talking bear! Who must dance—like this! And you may be either a sailor or a coachmen—it does not matter which, as we have the hat for one and the boots for the other. Now tell me, Mr. Simonelli, what plays would suit us?"

Two o'clock, Dec. 10th, 1811
In the woods between End-Of-All-Hope House and the village of Allhope.
I take out my pen, my inkpot, and this book.
"What are you doing?" whimpers Dido, all afraid.
"Writing my journal," I say.

"Now?" says she in amazement. Poor Dido! As I write she keeps up a continual lament that it will soon be dark and that the snow falls more heavily—which is I admit a great nuisance for the flakes fall upon the page and spoil the letters.

This morning my vigilant watch upon the village was rewarded. As I stood in the church-porch, hidden from all eyes by the thick growth of ivy, I saw Isabella coming down Upperstone-lane. A bitter wind passed over the village, loosening the last leaves from the trees and bringing with it a few light flakes of snow. Suddenly a spinning storm of leaves and snowflakes seemed to take possession of Upperstone-lane and John Hollyshoes was there, bowing low and smiling.

It is a measure of my firm resolution that I was able to leave her then, to leave all of them. Everything about John Hollyshoes struck fear into my heart, from the insinuating tilt of his head to the enigmatic gesture of his hands, but I had urgent business to attend to elsewhere and must trust that the Miss Gathercoles' regard for me will be strong enough to protect them.

I went straight to End-Of-All-Hope House, and the moment I appeared in the bare room at the end of the corridor, Dido cried out, "Oh, sir! Have you come to release me from this horrid place?"

"Why, Dido!" said I, much surprised. "What has happened? I thought you were quite contented."

"And so I was, sir, until you licked your finger and touched my eye. When you did that, the sight of my eye was changed. Now if I look through this eye"— she closed her left eye and looked through her right—"I am wearing a golden dress in a wonderful palace and cradling the sweetest babe that ever I beheld. But if I look through *this* eye"—she closed the right and opened her left—"I seem to be chained up in a dirty, nasty room with an ugly goblin child to nurse. But," she said hurriedly (for I was about to speak), "whichever it is, I no longer care, for I am very unhappy here and should very much like to go home."

"I am pleased to hear you say so, Dido," said I. Then, warning her not to express any surprise at anything I said or did, I put my head out of the door and called for Dando.

He was with me in an instant, bowing low.

"I have a message from your master," I said, "whom I met just now in the woods with his new bride. But, like most Englishwomen, the lady is of a somewhat nervous disposition and she has taken it into her head that End-Of-All-Hope House is a dreadful place full of horrors. So your master and I have put our heads together and concluded that the quickest way to soothe her fears is to fetch this woman"—I indicated Dido—"whom she knows well, to meet her. A familiar face is sure to put her at her ease."

I stopped and gazed, as though in expectation of something, at Dando's dark, twisted face. And he gazed back at me, perplexed.

"Well?" I cried. "What are you waiting for, blockhead? Do as I bid you! Loose the nurse's bonds so that I may quickly convey her to your master!" And then, in a fine counterfeit of one of John Hollyshoes's own fits of temper, I threatened him with everything I could think of: beatings, incarcerations, and enchantments! I swore to tell his master of his surliness. I promised that he should be put to work to untangle all the twigs in the woods and comb smooth all the grass in the meadows for insulting me and setting my authority at naught.

Dando is a clever sprite, but I am a cleverer. My story was so convincing that he soon went and fetched the key to unlock Dido's fetters, but not before he had quite worn me out with apologies and explanations and pleas for forgiveness.

When the other servants heard the news that their master's English cousin was taking the English nurse away, it seemed to stir something in their strange clouded minds and they all came out of their hiding places to crowd around us. For the first time I saw them more clearly. This was most unpleasant for me, but for Dido it was far worse. She told me afterward that through her right eye she had seen a company of ladies and gentlemen who bent upon her looks of such kindness that it made her wretched to think she was deceiving them, while through the other eye she had seen the goblin forms and faces of John Holly-shoes's servants.

There were horned heads, antlered heads, heads carapaced like insects' heads, heads as puckered and soft as a moldy orange; there were mouths pulled wide by tusks, mouths stretched out into trumpets, mouths that grinned, mouths that gaped, mouths that dribbled; there were bats' ears, cats' ears, rats' whiskers; there were ancient eyes in young faces, large, dewy eyes in old worn faces, there were eyes that winked and blinked in parts of anatomy where I had never before expected to see any eyes at all. The goblins were lodged in every part of the house: there was scarcely a crack in the wainscotting which did not harbor a staring eye, scarcely a gap in the banisters without a nose or snout poking through it. They prodded us with their horny fingers, they pulled our hair and they pinched us black and blue. Dido and I ran out of End-Of-All-Hope House, jumped up upon Quaker's back and rode away into the winter woods.

Snow fell thick and fast from a sea-green sky. The only sounds were Quaker's hooves and the jingle of Quaker's harness as he shook himself.

At first we made good progress, but then a thin mist came up and the path through the woods no longer led where it was supposed to. We rode so long and so far that—unless the woods had grown to be the size of Derbyshire and Nottinghamshire together—we must have come to the end of them, but we never did. And whichever path I chose, we were forever riding past a white gate with a smooth, dry lane beyond it—a remarkably dry lane considering the amount of snow which had fallen—and Dido asked me several times why we did not go down it. But I did not care for it. It was the most commonplace lane in the world, but a wind blew along it—a hot wind like the breath of an oven, and there was a smell as of burning flesh mixed with sulphur.

When it became clear that riding did no more than wear out ourselves and our horse, I told Dido that we must tie Quaker to a tree—which we did. Then we climbed up into the branches to await the arrival of John Hollyshoes.

Seven o'clock, the same day
Dido told me how she had always heard from her mother that red berries, such as rowan-berries, are excellent protection against fairy magic.

"There are some over there in that thicket," she said.

But she must have been looking with her enchanted eye for I saw, not red berries at all but the chestnut-colored flanks of Pandemonium, John Hollyshoes's horse.

Then the two fairies on their fairy-horses were standing before us with the white snow tumbling across them.

"Ah, cousin!" cried John Hollyshoes. "How do you do? I would shake hands with you, but you are a little out of reach up there." He looked highly delighted and as full of malice as a pudding is of plums. "I have had a very exasperating morning. It seems that the young gentlewomen have all contracted themselves to someone else—yet none will say to whom. Is that not a most extraordinary thing?"

"Most," said I.

"And now the nurse has run away." He eyed Dido sourly. "I never was so thwarted, and were I to discover the author of all my misfortunes—well, cousin, what do you suppose that I would do?"

"I have not the least idea," said I.

"I would kill him," said he. "No matter how dearly I loved him."

The ivy that grew about our tree began to shake itself and to ripple like water. At first I thought that something was trying to escape from beneath it, but then I saw that the ivy itself was moving. Strands of ivy like questing snakes rose up and wrapped themselves around my ankles and legs.

"Oh!" cried Dido in a fright, and tried to pull them off me.

The ivy did not only move; it grew. Soon my legs were lashed to the tree by fresh, young strands; they coiled around my chest and wound around the upper part of my right arm. They threatened to engulf my journal but I was careful to keep *that* out of harm's way. They did not stop until they caressed my neck, leaving me uncertain as to whether John Hollyshoes intended to strangle me or merely to pin me to the tree until I froze to death.

John Hollyshoes turned to Dando. "Are you deaf, iron-brains? Did you never hear me say that he is as accomplished a liar as you and I?" He paused to box Dando's ear. "Are you blind? Look at him! Can you not perceive the fierce fairy heart that might commit murder with indifference? Come here, unseelie elf! Let me poke some new holes in your face! Perhaps you will see better out of those!"

I waited patiently until my cousin had stopped jabbing at his servant's face with the blunt end of his whip and until Dando had ceased howling. "I am not sure," I said, "whether I could commit murder with indifference, but I am perfectly willing to try." With my free arm I turned to the page in my journal where I have described my arrival in Allhope. I leant out of the tree as far as I could (this was very easily accomplished as the ivy held me snug against the trunk) and above John Hollyshoes's head I made the curious gesture that I had seen him make over the old man's head.

We were all as still as the frozen trees, as silent as the birds in the thickets and the beasts in their holes. Suddenly John Hollyshoes burst out, "Cousin . . . !"

It was the last word he ever spoke. Pandemonium, who appeared to know very well what was about to happen, reared up and shook his master from his back, as though terrified that he too might be caught up in my spell. There was a horrible rending sound; trees shook; birds sprang, cawing, into the air. Anyone would have supposed that it was the whole world, and not merely some worthless fairy that was being torn apart. I looked down and John Hollyshoes lay in two neat halves upon the snow.

"Ha!" said I.

"Oh!" cried Dido.

Dando gave a scream which if I were to try to reproduce it by means of the English alphabet would possess more syllables than any word hitherto seen. Then he caught up Pandemonium's reins and rode off with that extraordinary speed of which I know him to be capable.

The death of John Hollyshoes had weakened the spell he had cast on the ivy, and Dido and I were able quite easily to tear it away. We rode back to Allhope, where I restored her to joyful parent, loving husband, and hungry child. My parishioners came to the cottage to load me with praises, grateful thanks, promises of future aid, etc., etc. I however was tired to death and, after making a short speech advising them to benefit from the example I had given them of courage and selflessness, I pleaded the excuse of a headache to come home.

One thing, however, has vexed me *very much*, and that is there was no time to conduct a proper examination of John Hollyshoes's body. For it occurs to me that just as Reason is seated in the brain of Man, so we Fairies may contain within ourselves some *organ of Magic*. Certainly the fairy's bisected corpse had some curious features. I append here a rough sketch and a few notes describing the ways in which Fairy anatomy appears to depart from Human anatomy. I intend to be in the woods at first light to examine the corpse more closely.

Dec. 11th, 1811

The body is gone. Dando, I suppose, has spirited it away. This is most vexatious as I had hoped to have it sent to Mr. Baillie's anatomy school in Great Windmill-street in London. I suppose that the baby in the bare room at the end of the corridor will inherit End-Of-All-Hope House and all John Hollyshoes's estates, but perhaps the loss of Dido's milk at this significant period in its life will prevent its growing up as strong in wickedness as its parent.

I have not abandoned my own hopes of inheriting my father's estate and may very well pursue my claim when I have the time. I have never heard that the possession of an extensive property in Faerie was incompatible with the duties of a priest of the Church of England—indeed I do not believe that I ever heard the subject mentioned.

Dec. 17th, 1811

I have been most villainously betrayed by the Reverend John McKenzie! I take it particularly hard since he is the person from whom—as a fellow clergyman—I might most reasonably have expected support. It appears that he is to marry the heiress to a castle and several hundred miles of bleak Scottish wilderness in Caithness. I hope there may be bogs and that John McKenzie may drown in them. Disappointed love has, I regret to say, screwed Miss Mary Macdonald up to such a pitch of anger that she has turned upon Henrietta and me. She writes to Henrietta that she is certain I am not to be trusted and she threatens to write to Mrs. Gathercole and Mrs. Edmond. Henrietta is not afraid; rather, she exults in the coming storm.

"You will protect me!" she cried, her eyes flashing with strange brilliance and her face flushed with excitement.

"My dear girl," said I, "I will be *dead*."

Dec. 20th, 1811
George Hollinsclough was here a moment ago with a message that I am to wait upon Mrs. Gathercole and Mrs. Edmond *immediately*. I take one last fond look around this room. . . .

FRANCESCA LIA BLOCK

Bones

Francesca Lia Block is one of the most popular writers of fiction for teenagers in America today, celebrated for her distinctive, incisive tales of urban fantasy noir. She is the author of Dangerous Angels, Girl Goddess #9, I Was a Teenage Fairy, Violet & Claire, *and* The Hanged Man. *Her fiction has been translated into seven languages and published around the world.*

The Rose and the Beast, Block's latest collection, is an intriguing contribution to the shelves of modern volumes retelling classic fairy tales with a contemporary twist. "Bones" is the author's take on Bluebeard, set in the hills of Los Angeles. The story is vintage Block, both edgy and poetic, and not for Children Only.

—T. W.

I dreamed of being a part of the stories—even terrifying ones, even horror stories—because at least the girls in stories were alive before they died.

My ears were always ringing from the music cranked to pain-pitch in the clubs. Cigarette smoke perfumed my hair, wove into my clothes. I took the occasional drug when it came my way. The more mind-altering the better. I had safe sex with boys I didn't know—usually pretty safe. I felt immortal, which is how you are supposed to feel when you are young, I guess, no matter what anybody older tells you. But I'm not sure I wanted immortality that much then.

I met him at a party that a girl from my work told me about. It was at this house in the hills, a small castle that some movie star had built in the fifties with turrets and balconies and balustrades. People were bringing offerings—bottles of booze and drugs and guitars and drums and paints and canvases. It was the real bohemian scene. I thought that in it I could become something else, that I could become an artist, alive. And everyone else wanted that, too; they were coming there for him.

Once he'd come into the restaurant late at night and I took his order but he didn't seem to notice me at all. I noticed him because of the color of his hair and goatee. I heard that he was this big promoter guy, managed bands, owned some clubs and galleries. A real patron of the arts, Renaissance man. Derrick Blue they called him, or just Blue. It was his house, his party, they were all making the pilgrimage for him.

It was summer and hot. I was sweating, worried my makeup would drip off. Raccoon pools of mascara and shadow around my eyes. The air had that grilled smell, meat and gasoline, that it gets in Los Angeles when the temperature soars. It was a little cooler in the house so I went in and sat on this overstuffed antique couch under some giant crimson painting of a girl's face with electric lights for her pupils, and drank my beer and watched everybody. There was a lot of posing going on, a kind of auditioning or something. More and more scantily clad girls kept coming, boys were playing music or drawing the girls or just lying back, smoking.

Derrick Blue came out after a while and he made the rounds—everybody upped the posing a little for him. I just watched. Then he came over and smiled and took my hand and looked into my eyes and how hungry I was, in every way. I was always hungry for food—blueberry pancakes and root beer floats and pizza gluey with cheese—I thought about it all the time. And other things. I'd sit around dreaming that the boys I saw at shows or at work—the boys with silver earrings and big boots—would tell me I was beautiful, take me home and feed me Thai food or omelets and undress me and make love to me all night with the palm trees whispering windsongs about a tortured, gleaming city and the moonlight like flame melting our candle bodies. And then I was hungry for him, this man who seemed to have everything, and to actually be looking at me. I didn't realize why he was looking.

He found out pretty fast that I wasn't from around there, didn't know too many people well, lived alone in a crummy hotel apartment in Korea-town, ate what I could take home from work. He knew how hungry I was. He asked everything as if he really cared and I just stared back at him and answered. He had blue eyes, so blue that they didn't dim next to his blue-dyed hair. Cold beveled eyes. They made the sweat on my temples evaporate and I felt like I was high on coke coke coke when he looked at me.

The crimson girl on the wall behind me, the girl with the open mouth and the bared teeth and the electric eyes, looked like she was smiling—until you looked closely.

Derrick Blue caught my arm as I was leaving—I was pretty drunk by then, the hillside was sliding and the flowers were blurry and glowy like in those 3-D postcards—and it was pretty late, and he said, stay. He said he wanted to talk to me, we could stay up all night talking and then have some breakfast. It was maybe two or three in the morning but the air was still hot like burning flowers. I felt sweat trickle down my ribs under my T-shirt.

We were all over his house. On the floor and the couches and tables and beds. He had music blasting from speakers everywhere and I let it take me like when I was at shows, thrashing around, losing the weight of who I was, the self-consciousness and anxiety, to the sound. He said, You're so tiny, like a doll, you look like you might break. I wanted him to break me. Part of me did. He said, I can make you whatever you want to be. I wanted him to. But what did I want to be? Maybe that was the danger.

The night was blue, like drowning in a cocktail. I tasted it bittersweet and felt the burning of ice on my skin. I reeled through the rooms of antiques and statues and huge-screen TVs and monster stereo systems and icy lights in frosted glass. If you asked me then if I would have died at that moment I might have said yes. What else was there? This was the closest thing to a story I'd ever known. Inside me it felt like nothing.

That night he told all the tales. You know, I am still grateful to him for that. I hadn't heard them since I was little. They made me feel safe. Enchanted. Alive. Charms. He said he had named himself for Bluebeard, if I hadn't guessed. He said it had become a metaphor for his whole life. He took a key from his pocket. I wasn't afraid. I couldn't quite remember the story. I felt the enchantment around us like stepping into a big blue glitter storybook with a little mirror on the cover and princesses dancing inside, dwarves and bears and talking birds. And dying girls. He said, the key, it had blood on it, remember? It was a fairy, and she couldn't get the blood off, no matter what she did. It gave her away. I knew that Bluebeard had done something terrible. I was starting to remember. When I first heard that story I couldn't understand it—why is this a fairy tale? Dead girls in a chamber, a psychotic killer with blue hair. I tried to speak but the enchantment had seeped into my mouth like choking electric blue frosting from a cake. I looked up at him. I wondered how he managed it. If anyone came looking for the women. Not if they were a bunch of lost girls without voices or love. No one would have come then.

Part of me wanted to swoon into nothing, but the other women's bones were talking. I didn't see the bones but I knew they were there, under the house. The little runaway bones of skinny, hungry girls who didn't think they were worth much—anything—so they stayed after the party was over and let Derrick Blue tell them his stories. He probably didn't even have to use much force on most of them.

I will rewrite the story of Bluebeard. The girl's brothers don't come to save her on horses, baring swords, full of power and at exactly the right moment. There are no brothers. There is no sister to call out a warning. There is only a slightly feral one-hundred-pound girl with choppy black hair, kohl-smeared eyes, torn jeans, and a pair of boots with steel toes. This girl has a little knife to slash with, a little pocket knife, and she can run. That is one thing about her—she has always been able to run. Fast. Not because she is strong or is running toward something but because she has learned to run away.

I pounded through the house, staggering down the hallways, falling down the steps. It was a hot streaky dawn full of insecticides, exhaust, flowers that could make you sick or fall in love. My battered Impala was still parked there on the side of the road and I opened it and collapsed inside. I wanted to lie down on the shredded seats and sleep and sleep.

But I thought of the bones; I could hear them singing. They needed me to write their song.

TANITH LEE

The Abortionist's Horse
(A Nightmare)

Tanith Lee lives on Britain's Sussex Weald with her husband and two cats. To date she has published more than seventy novels and collections and nearly two hundred short stories. Some of her recent and forthcoming titles include Faces Under Water, Saint Fire, A Bed of Earth, *and* Venus Preserved *(the first four volumes in the "Secret Books of Venus" series);* White as Snow *(an adult retelling of the Snow White legend); an epic fantasy duet,* Mortal Suns *and* The Immortal Moon, *plus the children's books* Islands in the Sky, *and the quartet* Wolf Tower, Wolf Star, Wolf Queen, *and* Wolf King.

Her Web site is: http://www.tanithlee.com.

About the following story, the author explains: "John Kaine, my husband, came up with the title. Both he and I tend to get titles out of thin air, frequently without a story attached. (And anyone who's seen much of my work lately, will realize that he has also given me many ideas and plotlines for stories—which, with my own stream of ideas, makes sure I am a seven-days-a-week writing factory.) This title is so threateningly pictorial that of course the story itself arrived swiftly on its heels—or hoofs." It was first published in Dark Terrors 5, *edited by Stephen Jones and David Sutton.*

—E. D.

Naine bought the house in the country because she thought it would be perfect for her future life.

At this time, her future was the core upon and about which she placed everything. She supposed that was instinctive.

The house was not huge, but interesting. Downstairs there was a large stone kitchen recently modernized, packed with units, drawers, cupboards and a double sink, with room for a washing machine, and incorporating a tall slender fridge and an electric cooker with a copper hood. The kitchen led into a small breakfast room with a bay window view of the back garden, a riot of roses, with one tall oak dominating the small lawn. At the front of the house there was also a narrow room that Naine christened the parlor. Opposite this, oddly, was the bathroom, again very modern, with a turquoise suite she would never have chosen but quite liked. Up the narrow stair there were a big linen cupboard, and three rooms, the largest of which was to be Naine's bedroom, with white curtains blowing in fresh summer winds. The two smaller rooms were of almost equal size. One would be her library and workroom. The third room also would come to have a use. It, like the larger bedroom and the parlor, faced to the front, over the lane. But there was never much, if any, traffic on the lane, which no longer led down into the village.

A housing estate had closed the lane thirty years before, but it was half a mile from the house. The village was one mile away. Now you reached it by walking a shady path that ran away behind the garden and down through the fields. A hedgerow-bordered walk, nice in any season.

The light struck Naine, spring light first, and almost summer light now, and the smells of honeysuckle and cow parsley from the lane, the garden roses, the occasional faint hint of hay and herbivorous manure blowing up the fields.

You could just hear the now and then soft rush of cars on the main road that bypassed the village. And church bells all day Sunday, sounding drowned like the ones in sunken Lyonesse.

Her Uncle Robert's death had given Naine the means for this venture. She had only slightly known him, a stiff memory of a red-brown august man handing her a lolly when she was five, or sitting on a train with the rest of the family when she was about thirteen, staring out of the window, looking sad at a bereavement.

The money was a surprise. Evidently he had had no one else he wanted to give it to.

The night of the day when she learned about her legacy there was a party to launch the book Naine had been illustrating. She had not meant to go, but, keyed up by such sudden fortune, had after all put on a red dress, and taken a taxi to the wine bar. She was high before she even entered, and five white wines completed her elevation. So, in that way, Uncle Robert's bequest was also responsible for what happened next.

At twenty-seven, Naine had slept with only two men. One had been her boyfriend at twenty-one, taken her virginity, stayed her lover for two years. The second was a relationship she had formed in Sweden for one month. In fact, they had slept together more regularly, almost every night, where with the first man she had only gone to bed with him once or twice a week, so reticent had been their competing schedules. In neither case had Naine felt very much, beyond a slight embarrassment and desire for the act to be satisfactorily over, like a test. She had read enough to pretend, she thought adequately, although her first lover had sadly said, as he left her forever to go to Leeds, "You're such a cool one." The Swede had apparently believed her sobs and cries. She knew, but only from masturbation, that orgasm existed. She had a strange, infallible fantasy which always worked for her when alone, although never when with a man. She imagined lying in a darkened room, her eyes shut, and that some presence stole toward her. She never knew what it was, but as it came closer and closer, so did she, until, at the expected first touch, climax swept through her end to end.

At the party was a handsome brash young man, who wanted to take Naine to dinner. Drunk, elevated, she accepted. They ended up at his flat in Fulham, and here she allowed him to have sex with her, rewarding his varied and enthusiastic scenario with the usual false sobs and low cries. Perhaps he did not believe in them, or was only a creature of one night, for she never heard from him or saw him again. This was no loss.

However, six weeks later, she decided she had better see a doctor. In the past her methods of contraception had been irregular, and nothing had ever occurred. It seemed to her, nonsensically but instinctively, that her lack of participation in the act removed any chance of pregnancy. This time, though, the spell had not worked.

Abortions were just legally coming into regular use. For a moment Naine considered having one. But, while believing solidly in any woman's right to have an unwanted fetus removed from her womb, Naine found she did not like the idea when applied to her own body.

Gradually, over the next month, she discovered that she began to think intensely about what was inside her, not as a thing, but as a child. She found herself speaking to it, silently, or even aloud. Sometimes she was even tempted to sing it songs and rhymes, especially those she had liked when small—"Here We Go Round the Mulberry Bush," and "Ride a Cockhorse to Banbury Cross." Absurd. Innocent. She was amused and tolerant of herself.

Presently she was sure that the new life belonged to her, or at least that she was its sponsor. With this in mind, she set about finding a house in the country where the child might be brought up away from the raucous city of its conception. The house by the lane looked so pretty at once, the cow parsley and docks standing high, the sunlight drifting on a pink rose classically at the door. When she learned there was the new hospital only two miles away in Spaleby, and besides, a telephone point in the bedroom for the pre-ordained four-in-the-morning call for an ambulance, Naine took the house. And as she stepped, its owner, in over the threshold, a wave of delight enveloped her, like the clear, spotted sunshine through the leaves.

As Naine walked up to the bus-stop by the main road, she was thinking about what a friend had said to her over the phone, the previous night. "You talk as if it didn't have a father." This had come to Naine only hours afterward. That is, its import. For it was true. Biology aside, the child was solely hers, and already Naine had begun to speak of it as feminine.

She realized friends had called her less and less, during the fortnight she had been here. In the beginning their main interest had seemed to be if she was feeling "horribly" ill—she never was. Also how she had "covered" herself. Naine had put on her dead mother's wedding ring, which was a little loose, and given the impression she and a husband were separated. Once the friends knew she was neither constantly spewing nor being witch-hunted as a wanton, they drew off. Really, were they her friends anyway? She had always tended to be solitary, and in London had gone out perhaps one night in thirty, and that probably reluctantly. She enjoyed her work, music, reading, even simply sitting in front of the TV, thinking about other things.

The bus-stop had so far been deserted when Naine twice came to it about three, for the 3:15 bus to Spaleby. Today, in time for the 1:15 bus, she saw a woman was already waiting there. She was quite an ordinary woman, bundled in a shabby coat, maybe sixty, cheerful and nosy. She turned at once to Naine.

"Hello, dear. You've timed it just right."

Naine smiled. She wondered if the woman could see the child, faintly curved under the loose cotton dress. The bulge was very small.

"You're in Number 23, aren't you?" asked the woman.

"Oh . . . yes I am."

"Thought so. Yes. I saw you the other day, hanging your washing out, as I were going down the lane."

Naine had a vague recollection of occasional travelers using the lane, on foot, between the stands of juicy plants and overhanging trees. Either they were going to the estate, or climbing over the stile, making off across the land in the opposite direction, where there were three farms, and what was still locally termed the Big House, a small, derelict and woebegone manor.

"Miss your hubby, I expect," said the woman.

Naine smiled once more. Of course she did, normal woman that she was; yes.

"Never mind. Like a lot of the women when I was a girl. The men had to go to Spaleby, didn't come back except on the Sunday. There was houses all up the lane then. Twenty-seven in all, there was. Knocked down. There's the pity. Just Number 23 left. And then modernized. My, I can remember when there wasn't even running water at 23. But you'll have all the mod cons now, I expect."

"Yes, thank you."

"I expect you've done a thing or two to the house. I shouldn't wonder if you have."

Naine sensed distinctly the nosy cheerful woman would love to come in and look at Number 23, and she, Naine, would now have to be on guard when the doorbell rang.

"I haven't done much."

"Just wait till hubby gets home. Shelves and I don't know what-all."

Naine smiled, smiled, and wished the bus would arrive. But she would anticipate Naine would sit with her, no doubt. Some excuse would have to be found. Or the guts to be rude and simply choose another seat.

Two cars went by, going too fast, were gone.

"Now the lane used to go right through to the village, in them days. There wasn't no high road here, neither. You used to hear the girls mornings, going out at four on the dot, to get to the Big House. Those that didn't live in. But the Missus didn't encourage it. She was that strict. Had to be. Then, there was always old Alice Barterlowe." The woman gave a sharp, sniggering laugh. It was an awful laugh, somehow obscene. And her eyes glittered with malice. Did Naine imagine it—she tried to decide afterward—those eyes glittering on her belly as the laugh died down. At the time Naine felt compelled to say, "Alice Barterlowe? Who was that?" It was less the cowardly compulsion to be polite than a desire to clear the laugh from the air.

"Who was *she*? Well that's funny, dear. She was a real character hereabouts. When I was a nipper that were. A real character, old Alice."

"Really."

"Oh my. She kep' herself to herself, did old Alice. But everyone knew her. Dressed like a man; an old laboring man, and rode astride. But no one said a word. You could hear her, coming down that lane, always at midnight. That was her hour. The hoofs on the lane, and you didn't look out. There goes Alice, my sister said once, when we'd been woke up, and then she put her hand over her mouth, like she shouldn't have said it. Nor she shouldn't. No one was meant to know, you see. But handy for some."

This sinister and illogical dialogue ended. The woman closed her mouth as tight as if zipped. And, before Naine could question her further—or not, perhaps—the green bus came chugging along the road.

"Old Alice Barterlowe. Oh my goodness yes. I can remember my gran telling me about her. If it was true."

It was five days later, and the chatty girl in the village shop was helping Naine load her bag with one loaf, one cabbage, four apples and a pound of sausages.

"Who was she?"

"Oh, an old les. But open about it as you like. She had a lady-friend lived with her. But she died. Alice used to dress up just like the men, and she rode this old mare. Couldn't miss her, gran said, but then you didn't often see her. You *heard* her go by."

"At midnight."

"Midnight, that's it."

"Why? Where was she going?"

"To see to the girls."

"I'm sorry?"

"Girls up the duff like."

"You mean . . . you mean pregnant?"

"She was an abortionist, was Alice."

Naine had only felt sick once, a week after she had moved in. Sitting with her feet up for half an hour had taken it right off. Now she felt as if someone was trying to push her stomach up through her mouth. She retched silently, as the chatty girl, missing it, rummaged through her till.

I will *not* be sick.

I *won't*.

The nausea sank down like an angry sea, leaving her pale as the now hideous, unforgivable slab of cheese on the counter.

"Here you are. Three pound change. Yes, old Alice, and that old horse. Half dead it looked, said my gran, but went on for years. And old les Alice was filthy. And this dirty old bag slung on the saddle. But she kept her hands clean as a whistle. And her stuff. There wasn't one girl she seen to come to harm."

"You mean—it didn't work."

"Oh it *worked*. It worked all right. They all got rid of them as wanted to, that Alice saw to. She was reliable. And not one of them got sick. A clean healthy miscarriage. Though my gran said, not one ever got in the family way after. Not even if she could by then. Not once Alice had seen to her."

On the homeward shady path between the hedges and fields, Naine went to the side and threw up easily and quickly among the clover. It was the sausages, she thought, and getting in, threw them away, dousing the bin after with TCP.

Ride a cock-horse to Banbury Cross.

To see a fine lady upon a white horse—

The rhyme went around in Naine's head as she lay sleepily waking at five in the summer morning. The light had come, and patched beautifully through her beautiful butterfly-white curtains. On a white horse, on a white horse—

And something sour was sitting waiting, invisible, unknowable, not really there.

Old Alice Barterlowe.

Well, she had done some good, surely. Poor little village girls in the days before the Pill, led on by men who wouldn't marry them, and the poor scullery maids seduced at the Big House by some snobby male relative of the strict Missus. What choice did they have but those clean strong probing fingers, the shrill hot-cold pain, the flush of blood—

Naine sat up. Don't think of it.

Ride a cock-horse, clip clop. Clip clop.

And poor old Alice, laughed at and feared, an ugly old lesbian whose lover had died. Poor old Alice, whose abortions always worked. Riding astride her ruinous old mare. Down the lane. Midnight. Clip clop. Clip clop.

Stop it.

"I'll get up, and we'll have some tea," said Naine aloud to her daughter, curled soft and safe within her.

But in the end she could not drink the tea and threw it away. A black cloud hung over the fields, and rain fell like galloping.

When Naine phoned her friends now, they could never stay very long. One had a complex dinner on and guests coming. One had to meet a boyfriend. One had an ear infection and talking on the phone made her dizzy. They all said Naine sounded tired. Was there a sort of glee in their voices? Serve her right. Not like them. If she *wanted* to get pregnant and make herself ill and mess up her life—

Naine sat in the rocker, rocking gently, talking and singing to her child. As she did so she ran her hands over and over along the hard small swelling. I feel like a smooth, ripening melon.

"There's a hole in my bucket, dear daughter, dear daughter . . ."

Naine, dozing. The sun so warm. The smell of honeysuckle. Sounds of bees. The funny nursery rhyme tapping at the brain's back, clip *clop*, clip *clop*.

Naine was dreaming. She was on the Tube in London, and it was terribly hot, and the train kept stopping, there in the dark tunnels. Everyone complained, and a man with a newspaper kept saying, "It's a fly. A fly's got in."

Naine knew she was going to be terribly late, although she was not sure for what, and this made it much worse. If only the train would come into the station, then she might have time to recollect.

"I tell you there's a fly!" the man shouted in her face. "Then do it up," said Naine, arrogantly.

She woke, her heart racing, sweat streaming down her, soaking her cotton nightdress.

Thank God it was over, and she was here, and everything was all right. Naine sat up, and pushed her pillows into a mound she could lean against.

Through the cool white curtains, a white half-moon was silkily shining. A soft rustle came from the trees as the lightest of calm night breezes passed over and over, visiting the leaves.

Naine reflected, as one sometimes does, on the power of the silliest dreams to cause panic. On its Freudian symbols—tunnels, trains, *flies*.

She stroked her belly. "Did I disturb you, darling? It's all right now." She drank some water, and softly sang, without thinking, what was tapping there in her brain, "Clip *clop*, clip *clop*. Clip *clop*, clip *clop*. Here comes the abortionist's *horse*." Then she was rigid. "Oh Christ." She got out of bed and stood in the middle of the floor. "Christ, Christ."

And then she was turning her head. It was midnight. She could see the clock. She had woken at just the proper hour. Alice Barterlowe's hour.

Clip *clop*, clip *clop* . . .

The lane, but for the breeze, was utterly silent. Up on the main road, came a gasp of speed as one of the rare nocturnal cars spun by. Across the fields, sometimes, an owl might call. But not tonight. Tonight there was no true sound at all. And certainly not—*that* sound.

All she had to do now, like a scared child, was to be brave enough to go to the window, pull back the curtain a little, and look out. There would be nothing there. Nothing at all.

It took her some minutes to be brave enough. Then, as she pulled back the curtain, she felt a hot-cold stinging pass all through her, like an electric shock. But it was only her stupid and irrational night-fear. Nothing at all was in the lane, as she had known nothing at all would be. Only the fronds of growing things, ragged and prehistoric under the moon, and the tall trees clung with shadows.

Past all the houses Alice had ridden on the slow old wreck of the horse, down the lane, and through the village. To a particular cottage, to a hidden room. In the dark, the relentless hands, the muffled cries, the sobs. And later, the black gushing away that had been a life.

Why did she do it? To get back at men? Was it only her compassion for her own beleaguered sex, in those days when women were more inferior than, supposedly, during the days of Naine?

Go away, Alice. Your time is over.

It was so silent, in the lane.

Clip *clop*, clip *clop*, clip *clop*, clip *clop*.

Here comes . . .

Naine went downstairs to the bathroom. She felt better after she had been sick. She took a jug of water and her portable radio back upstairs. A night station played her the Beatles, Pink Floyd, and even an aria by Puccini, until she fell asleep, curled tight, holding her child to her, hard, against the filmy night.

The doctor in Spaleby was pleased with Naine. He told her she was doing wonderfully, but seemed a bit tired. She must remember not to do too much. When they were seated again, he said, sympathetically, "I suppose there isn't any chance of that husband of yours turning up?"

Naine realized with a slight jolt she had been convincing enough to convince even the doctor.

"No. I don't think so."

"Some men," he said. He looked exasperated. Then he cheered up. "Never mind. You've got the best thing there."

When she was walking to the town bus-stop, Naine felt weary and heavy, for the first time. The heat seemed oppressive, and the seat for the stop was tormentingly arranged in clear burning yellow light. Two fat women already sat there, and made way for her grudgingly. She was always afraid at this point of meeting the awful, cheery, nosy woman. Because of the awful woman, Naine no longer pegged out washing, and had kept the postman waiting on her doorstep twice while she peered at him from an upstairs room, to be sure.

Somehow, to see the awful woman again would be just too much. She might start talking about Alice Barterlowe. Naine was sure that her child, in its fifth month, was generally visible by now. That would set the awful woman off, probably. *No use for old Alice, then.* No. No.

When the bus came, the journey seemed to last for a year, although it took less than half an hour. All the stops, and at every stop, some woman with a bag. And these women, though not the awful woman, might still sit beside her, might say, Oh, you're at Number 23 in the lane. The lane where the abortionist rode by at midnight on her nag.

Exhausted, Naine walked down from the main road. She made herself a jug of barley water and sipped a glass on the shady side of her garden. The grass had gone wild, was full of daisies, dandelions, nettles, purple sage and butterflies.

"I'm so happy here. It's so perfect. It's what we want. I mustn't be so silly, must I?" But neither must she ever speak her fear aloud to her child. Of all the things she could tell the child—not this, never this.

And around and around in her head, the idiotic rhyme, compounded of others that had gone wrong . . .

Clip *clop*, clip *clop*.

She must have been courageous. Alice. To live as she did, and do what she did. Especially then. It took courage *now*. Naine could recall the two girls caught kissing at school, and the ridiculous to-do there had been. Did they *know* what they were *doing*? Dirty, nasty. They had been shunned, and only forgiven when one confessed to pretending the other was a boy. They were *practicing* for men. For their proper female function and role.

Naine, of course, was properly fulfilling both. Naine must like men, obviously. Look at her condition. It was her husband who was in the wrong. She had been faithful, loving, admiring, aroused, orgasmic, conceptive, productive. But *he* had run off. Oh yes, Naine was absolutely fine.

She did not want any dinner, or supper. She would have to economize, stop buying all this food she repeatedly had to throw away.

But then, she had to eat, for the sake of the child. "I will, tomorrow, darling. Your mother won't be so silly tomorrow."

She had told the doctor she could not sleep, made the mistake of saying "I keep listening—" But he was ahead of her, thank God. "The pressure on the stomach and lungs can be a nuisance, I'm afraid. Ask Nurse to give you a leaflet. And you've only moved out here recently. I know, these noisy country nights. Foxes, badgers rustling about. Whoever said the country was quiet was mad. It took me six months to get used to it." He added that sleeping pills were not really what he would advise. Try cutting down on tea and coffee after five P.M., some herbal infusion maybe, and honey. And so on.

After the non-event of dinner, Naine watched her black-and-white eighteen-inch TV until the closedown. Then she went next door and had a bath.

She had never been quite happy with the bathroom downstairs. It could be grim later, when she was even heavier, lumbering up and down with bladder pressure, to pee. Maybe when things were settled anyway, she could move the bathroom upstairs, put the workroom here.

The child's room, the room the child would have; she had been going to paint that, and she ought to do so. Blue and pink were irrelevant. A sort of buttermilk color would be ideal. Pale curtains like her own. And both rooms facing onto the lane. It would not matter about the lane, then. By then, Naine would laugh at it, but not the way the awful woman had laughed.

Clip *clop*. Clip *clop*.

After the bath, bed. Sitting up. Reading a novel, the same line over and over, or half a page, which was like reading something in ancient Greek. And the silence. The silence waiting for the sound.

Clip *clop*.

Turn on the radio. Bad reception sometimes. Crackling. Love songs. Songs of loss. All the lovely normal women weeping for lost men, and wanting them back at any cost.

At last, eyes burning, lying down. We'll go to sleep now.

But not. The silence, between the notes of the radio. A car. A fox. The owl. The wind. Waiting . . .

Clip *clop*, clip *clop*.

It was the horse she couldn't bear. It was the horse she saw. Not old Alice in her dirty laborer's clothes, with her scrubbed hands and white nails. The horse. The horse whose hoofs were the sound that said, Here comes Alice, Alice on her horse.

Old house. Try to feel sorry for the poor old horse, as try to feel proud of courageous Alice. But no, the horse's face was long and haggard, with rusty drooping eyes, yellow, broken, blunt teeth, dribbling, unkempt. Not a sad face. An evil face. The pale horse of death.

"I'm sorry I can't sleep, baby. You sleep. You sleep and I'll sing you a lullaby. Hush-a-bye, hush-a-bye."

But the words are wrong. The words are about the white pale horse. The night-mare. The nag with the fine lady, the old lesbian. Clippity-clop—

Clip *clop* clip *clop*

Clip *clop* clip *clop*

It was coming up in her, up from her stomach, her throat, like sick. She couldn't hold it in.

"Clip clop clip clop clip clop clip clop here comes the abortionist's horse!"

And then she laughed the evil laugh, and she knew how it had trundled and limped down the lane, its hoofs clipping and clicking, carrying death to the unborn through the mid of night.

"It's my work that's the problem. I didn't realize it would be so awkward." She was explaining to the estate agent, who sat looking at her as if trying to fathom the secret. "I'll just have to sell up and get back to London. It really is a nuisance."

"Well, Mrs. Robert . . . well, we'll see what we can do."

As Naine again sat on the hot seat waiting for the bus, she thought of the train journey to London, of having nowhere to go. She had tried her friends, tentatively, to see if she could bivouac a day or two. One had not answered at all. One cut her short with a tale of personal problems. You could never intrude. One said she was so sorry, but she had decorators in. This last sounded like a lie, but probably was true. In any case, it would have to be a hotel, and the furniture would have to be stored. And then, flat-hunting five months gone, in the deep, smoky city heat. The house had been affordable down here. But London prices would allow her little scope.

It doesn't matter. I can find somewhere better after you're born. But for now. For now.

She knew she was a fool, had perhaps gone a bit crazy, as they said women did during pregnancy and the menopause. Even the kind doctor, when she had vaguely confessed to irrational anxieties, said jokingly, "I'm afraid that can be par for the course. Hormones."

To leave the house—*her* house—how she had loved it. But now. Not now.

No one came to look at the house, however. When she phoned the agents, they were evasive. It was a long way out unless you liked walking or had a car. And there had been a threat of the bus service being cut.

Day by day.

Night by night.

Over and over.

Its face.

The horse.

She was dreaming again, but even unconscious, she recognized the dream. It was delicious. So long since she had felt this tingling. This promise of pleasure. Her sexual fantasy.

She was in the darkened room. Everything was still. Yet someone approached, unseen.

They glided, behind dim floating curtains. The faint whisper of movement. And at every sound, her anticipation was increasing. In the heart of her loins, a building marvelous tension. Yes, yes. Oh come to me.

Naine, sleeping, sensed the drawing close. And now her groin thrummed, drum-taut. Waiting . . .

The shadow was there. It leaned toward her.

As her pulses escalated to their final pitch, she heard its ill-shod metal feet on the floor. A leaden midnight fell through her body and her blood was cold.

Its long horse face, primal, pathetic and cruel. The broken teeth. The rusty, rust-dripping half-blind eyes. It hung over her like a cloud, and she smelled its smell, hay and manure, stone and iron, old rain, ruinous silence, crying and sobbing, and the stink of pain and blame and bones.

The horse. It was here. It breathed into her face.

Naine woke, and the night was empty, noiseless, and then she felt the trapped and stifled pleasure, which had become a knot of spikes, and stumbling, half falling down the stairs, to the inconvenient lower bathroom, she left a trail of blood.

Here, under the harsh electric light, vomiting in the bath, heaving out to the lavatory between her thighs the reason the light the life of her life, in foam and agony and a gush of scarlet, Naine wept and giggled, choking on her horror. And all the while knowing, she had nothing to dread, would heal very well, as all Alice's girls did. Knowing, like all Alice's girls, she would never again conceive a child.

STEWART O'NAN

Endless Summer

Stewart O'Nan was born and raised in Pittsburgh and lives in Connecticut. He is the author of seven novels, including A Prayer for the Dying, The Speed Queen *(original title:* Dear Stephen King*), and most recently,* Everyday People. *He has also written* The Circus Fire, *about the fire that killed 167 people at the Ringling Bros., Barnum and Bailey Circus matinee on July 6, 1944.*

O'Nan says that "Endless Summer" was influenced by Paul Cody's very scary novel, The Stolen Child, *and, "is supposed to be—in a very strange way—a love story." It was originally published in* Century *number 6.*

—E. D.

for Paul Cody

They saw me at the lake, when I had the cast on, the one I made in the basement. They saw me messing with the trailer hitch. They came over.

"Hey," they said, "need a hand with that?"

Guys and girls both, the young ones. That's who went there.

They had long earrings like chandeliers. They had long blonde hair parted in the middle, their bright combs poking out of their cutoffs. They had muscle shirts and puka beads, they had shaved legs and baby oil for the sun.

"How'd you do that?" they said.

"How do you sail with one hand?" they said.

"Let me help you," they said.

When there were two of them, I let them fix it so the taillights worked, then I thanked them and left.

They were all leaving; that's why they were there in the parking lot. I could leave and come back and they'd be gone.

"How much can a Bug tow?" they said. "Nothing heavy, I bet."

They saw me from across the lot, putting away their blankets, their wet towels around their waists. Suits still wet and smelling of the lake. They walked out into the shallows and stood there sipping beers. The garbage was full of cans, every one of them worth a nickel. I almost wanted to stop and fill a bag.

"Thanks," I said. "It's hard with this on."

"No problem," they said.

"No sweat."

"My dad has one just like this," they said.

They had wallets, licenses, credit cards. They had keys I had to throw in the river. Rolling papers, little stone bowls. They had bubble gum. They had Lifesavers.

"How does it go together?" they asked.

"How did it come apart?"

They knelt down in front of me to see what they were doing. They had freckles from coming to the lake; they had sunburnt shoulders, and their hair was lighter than in the winter. The ends, and around the top. They smelled like lotion, they smelled hot. They wore flip-flops so you could see their toes, the hard skin of their heels.

They liked my car. They asked how old it was, if I might sell it, how much I'd ask.

"How do you shift with that?" they asked.

They lifted the two ends of the connectors. They didn't see the other set duct-taped under the tongue. They didn't know they couldn't put it together, that it was impossible. They tried to do it the regular way, like you would.

"Here's your trouble," they said.

They turned to say it, to show it was two male ends.

The parking lot was empty, everyone down at the beach. Kites in the sky. Hot dogs on the free barbecues the county put in. Charcoal smoke.

They smiled as they turned, like I didn't know. Like I was an idiot or something; so dumb I'd busted my arm. Pathetic. A little weak thing.

The lot was empty, kites in the sky.

I had the cast over my head and brought it down hard.

"Oh," they said, the bigger ones.

Or, "uh."

Nothing really interesting.

They fell across the hitch, and the first thing I did was grab them by the hair and pull them up. I could use the hand. It looked like I couldn't but I could all along.

So stupid.

I grabbed them by the hair and the back of the waistband and spun them into the car. Because I already had the door open. They saw me like that first, with the door open. Helpless. They came over to see what they could do.

Most the same age. The older ones I let go. They were young, with good skin. I liked them best that way. Blonde, tall. The boys had muscles. They were everywhere that summer, like a song on the radio you can't get away from. You start to sing it anyway.

They came from the city, or just outside of it. They lived with their parents, or with friends over the G. C. Murphy's, or they were at school for summer semester. They had IDs for work, they had chits for free drinks. They had bottle caps in their pockets. Heineken and Lowenbrau, Bud and Bud Light.

Love, love will keep us together.

They lay back in the seat when I folded it down and put a towel over them. They were breathing, they were making breathing sounds.

The lot was full, windshields all glinting in the sun. You could hear the little sound of the lake.

"Oh God," they said.

"Please," they said.

They had freckles on their chests. They had bright white tan lines. They had the red marks their suits made around their waists. Their hair was still wet from the lake, and smelled like it. They had sand there.

They got up to see what was happening and I hit them with the cast again, backhand. I didn't even have to look.

"Oh," they said again. "Uh."

The highway was empty, the fields, the barns. All of it hot. A mile away from the lake, you couldn't tell it was there, just hills.

They didn't see the dust in the mirror, didn't hear the rocks clunking in the wheel wells.

"What year is that?" they asked.

I laughed then. Me, pathetic. Weak.

"An accident," I said. "Nothing major."

"I really appreciate it," I said, and already I wanted to hit them and never stop. Right there in the lot. But I waited.

They smelled like pot, like wine, like the cheap beer from the concession stand. Old Milwaukee. Sometimes I didn't even kiss them after.

They stayed that way until I got them down to the rec room. They woke up when I opened the vinegar under their noses. I already had them tied up, their ankles to their wrists and then their necks. I could raise and lower them over the beam to make them shut up.

I didn't really need the mask; it was more for them.

"Please," they said. "Oh my God please."

They were all lying there in the sun with the waves coming in. That summer, it seemed it was always a beautiful day. The outlook for the weekend was good. They heard it in the morning, waking up to the clock radio, drinking coffee, thinking of taking Friday off. Hard to find a parking spot. They circled the lot, signaled to stake their claim.

They drove little pickups and Camaros with pinstriping. They drove their mother's old Volare with the peeling wood-grain decal. Their keychain had the name of their insurance company on it. Their key-chain had a picture of their niece.

Think of me, babe, whenever . . .

They prayed. They closed their eyes and they prayed.

They had a favorite sweater around their necks, in case it got cold later. They had a dab of mustard above their upper lip. They had a bump where the cast hit them. They had a tattoo of a moon, its eye winking just below where their tan stopped. They had gold chains that broke if you pulled on them too hard, and blue eye shadow you couldn't rub off.

"What happened to you?" they asked, like it was funny.

"You do that sailing?"

They screamed when they saw the knife.

They said, "Oh my God."

They said, "No."

The lot. The lake. A beautiful day, highs in the mid-eighties.

Some sweet-talking girl comes along . . .

They screamed.

"Be quiet," I said.

The windows were boarded over, with cinder blocks piled against them, but they didn't know that.

I lifted them up. Now I was doing all the talking.

"Shhh," I said.

"Please," I said, and they looked like all of them by then. They looked like they knew how it felt to be me, and for a second even I was sorry for them. For a second we were together there, me and them. We knew.

How I wanted to be honest then. You don't know.

I reached over and touched their hair, the two of us quiet in the still air of the basement.

"It's all right," I said. "I'm not going to hurt you."

JONATHAN CARROLL

The Heidelberg Cylinder

Jonathan Carroll is the author of a number of acclaimed novels, including
Voice of Our Shadow, Bones of the Moon, From the Teeth of Angels, After
Silence, Black Cocktail, Outside the Dog Museum, A Child Across the Sky,
Kissing the Beehive, The Marriage of Sticks, *and most recently* The Wooden
Sea. *He won the World Fantasy Award for his story* "Friend's Best Man" *and
his short fiction has been collected in* The Panic Hand. *From the publication
of his first novel* Land of Laughs, *Carroll has delighted readers with his
memorable characters and his overflowing imagination. He has the ability to
swerve unerringly between science fiction, fantasy, and horror—often in the
same piece of fiction.*

*"The Heidelberg Cylinder" was originally published by Carroll in
conjunction with Mobius Press as a limited edition hardcover chapbook.*

—*T. W. and E. D.*

It began the day our new refrigerator was delivered. A big silver thing that
looked like a miniature Airstream trailer turned on its side. But Rae loved it.
We had bought it a few days before. In January I told her as soon as my raise
comes in, you get your fridge. And I kept my promise, all six hundred and
thirty-nine dollars of it.

Two puffing deliverymen came in the pouring rain to curse and shove it into
place in our kitchen. Both guys were in big bad moods, that was plain. But no
wonder—who wants to deliver appliances in a ripping thunderstorm? When they
were finished and I'd signed the delivery papers, Rae offered coffee. That perked
them up. After they'd done stirring and sipping and settling into the chairs one
guy, "Dennis" it said on his shirt, told a strange story that got us thinking.

For the past few days while driving around making deliveries, they'd seen piles
of furniture all over town stacked in the middle of sidewalks. That didn't seem
so strange to me. But Dennis said they saw it at least ten times overall: big piles
of furniture heaped up, just sitting there unguarded usually.

"No that's not true," his partner Vito piped in. "Remember when we saw the
man and woman standing next to a pile up on Lail Avenue, arguing? They were
really fighting! Arms flying, pointing fingers at each other. It was like one had

thrown the other outta the house with all their stuff, but you couldn't tell who'd thrown who."

"Just furniture? Nothing else? No moving vans there or anything? No people guarding the stuff?"

"Nope, that's the weird part. These piles of furniture and boxes, like whole households, stacked up and no one around. Go figure."

The four of us sat there drinking coffee, thinking it over. Then Dennis said, "We saw another pile coming over here today. Remember that nice blue leather couch and TV I pointed to? Jeez, stuff looked brand new. Big screen TV . . . Just sitting out in the rain getting drenched.

"Times are tough. Maybe it's coincidence, but I hear a lotta people are being thrown out of their houses by the banks."

"All at the same time? I don't think so, partner," Vito said sarcastically to him and winked at me.

Dennis straightened up and threw him a black look. "You got a better explanation, genius?"

"Nope. Just that it's weird. Never in my life have I seen stuff that nice left out alone on the street unguarded. And so many times. In the rain? Makes the whole town look like a big yard sale."

Right then Chapter Two began but none of us knew it yet. Before anyone had a chance to say more, the doorbell rang. I looked at Rae to see if she was expecting someone. She shook her head. Who now?

I got up to answer it. A second after opening that door I wished I hadn't. Standing on my porch were two guys looking like wet seals. One glimpse and you wanted to say, "No thanks to whatever you've got," slam the door in their faces and run for cover.

Naturally they were smiling. But you know the kind—totally fake. No one smiles like that without putting too much face into it. Or they got a gun stuck in their back. These guys were wearing identical brown suits freckled dark all over with rain. Bright yellow plastic nametags were pinned on their breast pockets. White shirts with the top button buttoned but no ties. Both had bowl haircuts that made them look like monks or The Beatles gone bad. And they smelled. I'm sorry to have to say that, but they did. They smelled like they'd lived in their buttoned-up rayon shirts way way too long.

"Good morning, sir! I'm Brother Brooks and this is Brother Zin Zan."

"Brother who? You want to say all that again?" I stood back and gave them a lot of room, just in case they exploded and their crazy went all over my porch.

"Brooks and Zin Zan. Would you have a few moments to spare? It may just change your life!"

I knew where this was leading and was just about to adios them, but a thunderclap shook the house and rain came down like a tidal wave. What could I do, shove them back out in that flood? Really unhappily I asked, "You want to come in a minute?"

Their faces lit up like Yankee Stadium for a night game. "We certainly would! Thank you very much."

In for a penny, in for a pound. "Want some coffee? Looks like you could use it."

"No thank you, sir. But it's certainly kind of you to offer."

"Well, come on in." They stepped into the hall and I closed the door. They both wore black basketball sneakers with a brand name written in white on the side that I couldn't make out. I thought it was kind of strange that Bible guys would be wearing sneakers. Much less underneath a suit.

"Bill, who was it?" Rae called out.

"Brooks Brothers and Sen Sen." I couldn't resist saying. And you know what? Brooks started laughing.

"That's very funny, sir. People always make that mistake. But actually, it's Brother Brooks. And Brother Zin Zan. He's from New Zealand."

"New Zealand. Is that right? You're pretty far from home. Sorry for the mistake. Come on in."

I went first to see what would happen. When Rae and the delivery guys caught a view of who was following me, they got exactly the same look on their faces— Whaaat?

"Everybody, this is Brother Brooks and Brother Zin Zan. They say they can change our lives." I said it like I was introducing an act in Las Vegas.

Picking right up on it Dennis said, "Sounds good to me. Anything to stop delivering refrigerators!"

Rae stared at me like I'd gone nuts. Both of us hate door-to-door preachers with their ridiculous speeches and too many teeth. Her face asked, why had I let these guys in? Suddenly our house was like the dog pound—every stray in town under one roof, dripping on her carpets. I sat down but the Brothers kept standing. To my surprise, Zin Zan started talking. He had a strong accent. Then I remembered he was from New Zealand. The whole time he spoke, Brooks gave him an all-attention smile that looked as phony as a tinfoil Christmas tree.

"We represent a brotherhood called The Heidelberg Cylinder. Our avatar is a man named Beeflow."

"Beef-low?" Dennis looked at his partner and me, then wiggled his eyebrows and O'd his mouth.

"No, sir, Bee-flow. We believe we are entering the Second Diaspora. It will formally begin with the Millennium and continue for another 16,312 years."

"Sixteen thousand, you say? With or without intermissions?"

My sweet wife tried to smooth that one over. "Would you two like some juice?"

"Thank you, Ma'am, but we don't drink anything but water. Beeflow says—"

"Who's this Beeflow?"

"Our spiritual master. Chosen avatar by—"

"What's an avatar? Sounds like that new model Honda."

Brother Brooks liked that one too. He smiled and for the first time it looked real. "No sir, an avatar is an incarnation of a deity. A kind of God in human form, you could say."

"What did your Mr. Beeflow do before he became God?"

Maybe it was the way Rae said it, so respectful and serious. Or maybe because Dennis and I were watching each other when she spoke. Whatever, as soon as my wife asked her question so gently, the three of us guys cracked up. I mean big time. We laughed so hard we choked.

"He was a travel agent."

"Good career move!" I said, which brought down the house again. Except for

Rae. She FedExed me her stone face and I knew what that meant. I shut up fast.

"So what do you guys believe in? I mean, like a quick wrap-up of your religion?"

"We believe in rent control, a river view when possible, and forced air heating."

The living room got silent fast. Real silent.

"Say that again?"

"Room, sir. We believe in the just and proper distribution of room. Human space. Apartments, houses, it makes no difference. A civilized place to live."

"Geodesic domes," Zin Zan added, nodding.

"What the Hell are you talking about? I'm not following you here, Brother Brooks."

"Well sir, have you noticed all of the furniture out on the streets of the city recently? Piles of it, looking like it's waiting to be picked up?"

"We were just talking about that!"

"It is the first sign of the beginning of the Diaspora."

"What's that?"

"A Diaspora is the breaking up and scattering of a people. The forced settling of people far from their ancestral homelands."

"You mean they're being moved out?"

"Yes, exactly."

"By who? Who's moving them?"

"Satan."

I cleared my throat and snatched a quick glimpse of Rae. She gave me a look that said, "Don't make trouble with these guys." So instead of cracking wise about the Satanic Moving Company, I looked at the others to see if they were going to snap at the bait.

"All those piles of stuff out on the streets are there because the Devil's throwing people out of their houses? Why's he doin' that?"

Zin Zan picked it up. "Because Hell is filled to overflowing Sir, and Satan needs the room. He plans to re-populate the earth with the fallen."

I didn't know about the others but I was so embarrassed by the direction this conversation was taking that I could only stare at the floor and hope those Brothers would evaporate by the time I looked up again.

"So you're saying that if I was bad and die now, there's no room for me in Hell and I may end up back here living next door?" Vito said in a voice full of "you gotta be shittin' me."

My eyes still down, I heard Zin Zan's thick accent field the question. "Why do you think the world's in such bad straits, sir? New fatal diseases being discovered every day, crime the likes of which defy human imagination. How do you explain people's vast and unfailing indifference to one another?

"Because so many of them are dead. They have no souls. This has been going on for some time. The dead bring death back with them when they return to earth."

What can you say to something looney-tuney like that? I felt like taking a nap. I felt like getting up from where I was sitting, maybe or maybe not giving a wave to everyone in the room, and walking right out of there into the bedroom

and my pillow and about an hour of nighty-night. My brain felt tired and like
it had had something lousy and too heavy for lunch.

"Yeah? Well prove it, Brothers." Dennis spoke like he was spitting and said
that last word like a Black soul brother. You know, he said it "bruddas" and
there wasn't any respect in the word.

Not that it touched the Heidelberg Cylinder boys. They smiled on like two Ken
dolls on a date with Barbie. Brooks politely asked, "What do you mean, sir?"

Dennis pointed an "it's your fault" finger at him and shook it. "You know
exactly what I mean. Guys like you have been coming to my door for years,
talking about how the world's gonna end tomorrow. God's gonna kick my butt
for sinning unless I repent. Armageddon's coming so watch out! Well you know
what? Arma-geddon pretty damned sick of hearing that stuff from your like. If
you think you're so right about what you're saying, prove it. That's all—show us
it's true. You say the Devil's on earth moving dead people out of their houses?
Show me!"

Vito put a thumbs up. "I agree! Show me too!"

I kind of felt like doing it too. I myself was sick of gleamy-eyed wackos coming
to my house with their cheap pamphlets and 'God's-gonna-get-you' threats. Having the big fat nerve to tell me I'd done everything wrong with my life. And I'd
better start dancing to their tune or else. Oh yeah? How do you know; you been
watching my every move?

What I resented most was how damned sure people like this were that they
were right. Hey, maybe they were, but how could they be so convinced? I admit
I wasn't sure of anything in life, much less how His Majesty upstairs in heaven
makes things work. But at least I admit it. Listening to these dudes talk, or
others like them who'd appeared over the years with their own smudged magazines and weird smiles, God was as easy to understand as the baseball scores.

"Well?"

The not-so Righteous Brothers blinked at the same time and smiled again.
But kept their traps shut.

"Huh? Can you prove you're right? Or are you going to tell me to wait till
Judgment Day rolls around to find out?"

"Oh no sir, we can show you right now. That's not a problem." Brooks spoke
and his voice was as nice as rice. I mean he spoke like what Dennis had just
asked was the easiest favor in the world to grant. You want me to show you
Satan? You want me to open up the back of the big clock and show you how it
ticks? Follow me, sir—this way to Satan. Just like that. Simple.

"What the fuck are you guys talking about?"

Rae caught her breath hearing my word, but I couldn't help myself. I was
suddenly as hot and sizzling as a frying chicken. I didn't like where this conversation was going. And I sure didn't believe what was just said. All eyes were on
me like the kid who just farted in class. Dennis and Vito's faces said ha-ha, but
Rae's was uh-oh because she knows my temper. The Brothers were calm as usual.

"You can sit there with a straight face and say you'll show me Satan this
minute?"

"We can show you proof, sir. All the proof you'll need. We just have to go
up to Pilot Hill."

"What's on Pilot Hill?"

"The proof you want."

"What proof?"

The brothers stood up. "We can go right now. We'll give you a thousand dollars each if you're not happy with our proof."

The room went stone quiet for the second time in ten minutes.

Rae said in a wiggly voice, "A thousand dollars?"

"Oh yes, ma'am. We have no desire to waste your valuable time." Brooks reached into his pocket and pulled out a roll of bills as thick as a Big Mac. So help me God, that man's hands contained more cash than I'd ever seen one person hold, outside of a bank teller.

Vito whistled one note low and asked what I'm sure we were all wondering: "How much you got there?"

Brooks looked at his hand. "I think ten thousand dollars. How much do you have, Brother Zin Zan?"

Zin stuck out his lower lip and nodded. "Ten thousand." He patted his pocket.

"Each of you guys is carrying ten grand?" Dennis's amazed voice cracked halfway through the sentence.

"That's the way we do things in our organization, sir. We want you to be happy with your decision, one way or the other."

Vito stood right up. "Well I just made my decision—let's go!"

Dennis too. "I'm with you. Pilot Hill, here we come."

Rae looked at me and then stood up slowly. The Brothers did too. Only I stayed where I was sitting. To emphasize that fact even more I crossed my arms and went humph.

"What's the matter, Bill?"

"You know damned well what the matter is, Rae! This whole thing is nuts. The three of you are going out the door with these screwballs because they dangled some free money in front of you. Dangled but didn't give. Well how about this: I'll come too if you give me my thousand dollars right now, Brothers. Not later—this second. I'll give it back to you when we get there if I'm so convinced you're right."

"I'm fine with that, sir. It's no problem." Brooks said and without one second's hesitation peeled ten crisp new hundred-dollar bills off his Big Mac. "Here you go." He crossed the room and handed them to me.

"Hey, I want mine too if he's getting his now!"

"Me too."

"Yes, me too please." Rae said that. She is a shy, kind woman who doesn't even complain when someone big steps on her toe at the market. But now here she was wanting her thousand dollars up front just like everyone else. I was setting a bad example, but at least we were all a thousand dollars richer for it.

Then an evil thought came riding in. I looked suspiciously at the money in my hand. Maybe it was too fresh, too new? Was real money really that green? "How do we know this isn't fake? That it's not counterfeit or something?"

Brother Zin Zan was counting off hundreds while Brooks was handing Vito his share. "Oh we can stop at a bank on the way and have it checked if you like. But I guarantee you it's real."

I looked at my money like it might have something to say. This whole thing was so crazy, why shouldn't we just accept it at face value? Four thousand dollars was being handed out in that room and everyone was as cool as cucumbers about it. Like it happened to us every day and now was just the payoff hour. Rae wore a smile that was somewhere between happiness and crime.

"How do you want to go over there?"

"What do you mean?"

Dennis waved his hand around the room. "Well there's six of us. You want us all to go in your car?"

Zin Zan shook his head. "We don't have a car."

I shook mine. "We got a little Hyundai. We can barely get the two of us into it. It wouldn't know what to do with six people."

"It'd have a heart attack," Rae said, and it was like the first joke she'd made in five years.

All the guys smiled at her and I felt pretty proud to have a wisecracking wife. First she's putting out a greedy hand just like the others for a thousand dollars and now she was cracking jokes. She was suddenly a completely different woman from the one I knew, but I kind of liked it.

"Then I say we all go in the truck."

"What truck, yours? And ride in the back with the rest of the appliances?"

"Naah—you and your wife can sit up front with Dennis. Me and the Brothers will get in back."

Brooks and Zin Zan nodded to that and so did Rae. Who was I to argue? We put on our raincoats and waded out into the storm. Where I looked left and right but didn't see any furniture truck. "So where is it?"

"Right there. Right in front of you."

Right in front of me was a red truck. But on the side of it was a picture of a smiling white pig wearing a black baseball cap. The poor little guy was being roasted on a spit. Now I ask you, why would you put a baseball cap on a pig you were cooking? Even more, why would the pig be smiling while it died? Above that dumbass picture was written "Lester's Meat." Which, when you thought about it, didn't sound very appetizing either. I made myself a mental note never to buy Lester's Meat.

"That's a meat truck."

"It's my uncle's. He lets me use it to make deliveries sometimes."

"You deliver appliances in a meat truck?"

"It's been known to happen." Vito and Dennis grinned at each other like they knew something we didn't.

"This is too weird. My new refrigerator was in there up alongside a side of beef?"

"No, the truck's empty now. He only lets me use it when it's empty."

"Yeah, but is my fridge going to smell of raw meat now?"

"I'm afraid we're going to have to walk," Brooks said.

"Walk? Why?"

"Because members of the Heidelberg Cylinder are strict vegetarians. Not vegan but strict vegetarian. We don't eat anything with a face. We avoid contact with any form of meat."

"What the Hell are you talking about? You're not having contact with meat. We're going to Pilot Hill, like you wanted."

"I'm sorry, but we're not allowed contact with anything to do with meat. If there's a remnant in that truck it could contaminate us. No, it's out of the question. Brother Zin Zan and I will walk up to Pilot Hill and meet you there."

"It's three miles away. It'll take you an hour to get there! Look, I got a better idea. You guys get in the front and we'll all get in the back. I don't mind being contaminated by meat. Rae?"

She nodded. The Brothers looked at each other and shrugged that the idea was okay with them. Which is how we ended up standing inside a cold empty truck holding on for dear life while getting real intimate with the smell of fresh beef and etcetera. Then about three minutes after the ride began, the only little light bulb back there that lit anything flickered-flickered-flickered and went out. Poof—total blackness.

"Real cozy back here, huh?" Vito said from somewhere nearby in the blackness.

"I can't see a damned thing."

"Not much to see. Just a bunch of empty space."

"Bill?" Rae's voice was small, like she was far away.

"Yeah?"

"I'm scared now. I don't think I want to go."

"Why's that? You were fast enough taking their money." I threw in with a little twist-of-the-knife in my voice.

"I know, but I gotta bad feeling now."

"Why?"

"Because those men are so sure of themselves. They got pockets full of money and can give away a thousand dollars just like that to prove they're right."

"Four thousand dollars."

Vito made his whistle again. "Four thousand smackers. Did you ever carry four thousand dollars in your pocket? From the way they talked, it sounds like these guys do it every day. Kind of tempting when you think about it, you know?"

The darkness felt like it was suddenly heavier. So did the silence that followed what he'd said.

"What's your point?"

Vito tried to sound light but I heard the rats gathering on the other side of his voice. "Well, there's twenty thousand dollars sitting up there next to the driver. That's a lot of money."

"Bill—"

A hand touched me on the elbow and I assumed it was Rae's. I patted it until I realized it was too damned big for her hand and that it was Vito's instead.

I gave him a fast hard poke that couldn't have felt good. "Just what the Hell are you doing?"

"Nothing, man. Take it easy. It's dark in here, in case you didn't notice. I'm just trying to get my bearings."

"Well, get them away from me."

Why was he touching my elbow in the dark like that? And why was he making suggestions like maybe we should do something criminal about the twenty thousand dollars sitting in the Brothers' pockets at that very minute?

"Bill?"

"What Rae?" I said it pretty harshly, and angry voices are not that woman's favorite music. Sure enough, her answer came back at me like a flame-thrower.

"Don't you talk to me like that, Bill Gallatin! I don't like any of this. I want to go home. They can have their money back. I don't care. I just want to go back home now."

"Well honey, wait till we stop and they let us out. There's not much we can do till then."

"But we should be there by now. It's not that far. How come we haven't gotten there yet?"

I took a deep breath and licked my tongue back and forth across my lips, which is usually my procedure when I'm trying hard to stay calm. When I was sure I had my temper back on its leash I spoke. "I don't know why we aren't there yet, sweetheart. Pilot Hill's on the other side of town, remember. It takes a little while to get there."

"I want to get out of this truck right now; it's creepy and weird."

"Well sure it is. It's pitch black and we're standing in the back of a meat truck!"

"I don't mean that."

"Well what do you mean, Rae?" I lost my composure and my voice came out sounding damned irritated.

The next thing I know, my good wife's crying because she's scared, while at the same time I'm realizing this is all my fault, basically. I was the one who invited Brother Brooks and Zin Zan into our house not one hour ago. Before them everything was just fine—we had a new refrigerator, we were shooting the breeze with the movers, and finishing our coffee.

Before I had a chance to say anything more, the truck began slowing. Then it stopped with a jerk that sent us all flying, judging by the sound of things around me. Vito yelled "Hey!" and Rae squealed, but I was quiet because it was all I could do to stop from falling flat on my face. My mother used to say never try standing up when the bus is going around a corner. Now I had one to add to that—never try keeping your balance in the dark. You need to see stuff so you can judge angles and tilts. At that moment I couldn't see anything so I was groping out with my hands, basically reaching for whatever would have me.

Unfortunately I found something.

What's warm and furry and licks your hand in the dark? A dark that had gotten ten times darker because all of a sudden it was totally silent in there except for the sound of me being slurpy-licked by an eager tongue.

"Shit!" I yanked my hand and body back like they'd been in fire and doing so, lost my balance after touching something warm and furry. I didn't know where I was falling because it was whoa-whoa-whoa backward. But still it was away from the tongue and that was all that mattered.

I fell on my ass. One of those breath-death drops where you land bullseye on the tenderest part of your spine. It sent an atomic jolt of pain up to the tips of my ears and then shivered back down my body, gradually looking for a place to stop.

When I could breathe again around the pain, I said "Rae?" Nothing. Then I said "Vito?" Silence. Nothing but me, the dark and whatever thing had licked me.

"Mr. Gallatin? My name is Beeflow. I'll be your guide now."

———

The voice was right next to my ear. Right next to it. I was on my ass, remember. It was a nice voice—smooth and low—but without warning hearing it so close to me in that all-out darkness, know what my first thought was? The very first one?

Is it little?

Is this thing standing up, or bending down to talk into my ear? How big is it? Not what is it, or how did it suddenly get two inches from my ear. How big is it?

Then I tried sliding away from whatever it was.

"Don't be afraid."

"Get away from me! Where are the others? Rae?"

"You needn't worry; they're fine."

"Prove they're fine."

"Bill, we're fine."

"Rae?"

"Yes sweetie, don't worry. I'm in Los Angeles."

"What? Where? What?"

"Yes! I'm at the Universal Studios tour with Vito. We're about to go into the *Back to the Future* ride. I'm so excited!"

Her voice sounded like she was talking on a telephone. In her background was a lot of noise—kids shouting and laughter, some sounds I didn't recognize. Then to my amazement, I heard the bold theme song to "Back to the Future." I recognized it right away. We owned the video and would pop it in the machine pretty often because it was one of our favorites.

"Bill? We're going in now. I'll talk to you later, honey, and give you a full report. Do you have the tickets, Vito?"

"Got 'em right here."

The son of a bitch! Ever since we got married six years ago Rae and me have talked about going to L.A. and especially to the Universal Studios Tour to take that ride because we like the movie so much. Now here was some moving man I didn't even know accompanying my wife instead of me.

I was so angry at the thought that for a few seconds I forgot where I was and what had been going on.

"You see Mr. Gallatin, everything is all right. By the time your wife's ride is over, you'll know everything and the two of you will be back home again. But in the meantime she can be having the time of her life. Do something she's always wanted to do. Isn't that super? We try to make everybody happy."

"No it's not super! I was supposed to be there with her! How come Vito gets to go while I'm here with a sore ass talking to you in the dark? Who are you anyway? Can't you turn on some lights?"

"You wouldn't want that. You don't want to see me." He said it quietly and kind of to-himself sad.

"Why's that?"

It was quiet a minute. Then he said something that slammed shut every door in my head. "Do you ever look in the toilet after you go?"

"What?"

"Sneak a peek at what your body didn't want. Check to see what your stomach set free?"

"For God's sake! That's disgusting."

"Tell the truth now, son."

"You're not my doctor! Why should I tell you that? I've had enough. I want out. How do I open this door?"

"If you open it you'll see me and that will be the end for you." The tone of his voice said this is the truth—don't doubt it. "I asked about looking in the toilet because in a way that's what I am. I'm everything about yourself you don't like, Mr. Gallatin. I am the shit you look at in the toilet. Once a delicious meal, now just brown stink."

I would have laughed in his face if I could have seen it. But since it was so dark, I barked out a loud phony one to give him the same effect. "You're nuts. And why did you lick me? What was that all about?"

Now he laughed. "That wasn't me—it was your old friend Cyrus. Who's right here next to me. Remember him?"

"No. Who's Cyrus?"

"Why he's your soul, Mr. Gallatin. Don't you recognize it when you are touched by your own soul?"

"My soul's warm and furry and has a tongue like a dog? I don't think so, Mr. Beef-low."

"Beeflow. You disappoint me, sir. Shall I give you a demonstration?"

"You can give me the key out of here."

"All right."

Suddenly the truck door opened—bam—and I didn't think twice. I ran for the daylight and jumped off the lip of the back of the truck. Something smart told me don't look back. Was there really a Beeflow or a Cyrus or anything else to further cook my already-barbecued brain? I didn't want to find out. The only thing on my mind at the moment was to get the fuck out of there.

When my feet touched pavement I started running. I was so bent on getting someplace, anyplace away from there that I didn't really look around. Why should I? This was my town. I'd lived here all my life. All I had to do was grab a quick glimpse of what was around me and I'd know exactly where I was. And just when the thought of taking that quick glimpse came to me, I heard something coming up very fast behind me. The sound it made scared me right down to the basement of my blood cells.

And whatever it was got closer while I ran faster, as fast as I could. Just as I cried out because I knew I was caught, doomed, the thing jumped on my back and knocked me flat on my face.

It was heavy. Huge. Whatever hit me had a lot of weight and that fact made it a ton more scary.

So I stayed down, a mouse with a cat on its back, my cheek flat against the hot street asphalt. I could smell it, along with other things. Something in my mouth was bleeding, my nose honked hurt. I tasted blood; pain flew around my face. I smelled the hot street.

"Pose, get down boy. Come back here." The man's voice wasn't familiar but just hearing the thing on my back had a name, a name I understood made me feel sort of better. But "Pose" stayed standing on me and did not move an inch of its heavy self.

"Damn it, dog, what'd I just say to you? Get over here!"

The weight left and I was free again. Looking up a little, I saw four large hairy paws moving away. Slowly I put my palms flat on the ground and pushed myself to my knees. My arms were shaking because I guess I wasn't finished being scared.

"Jeez buddy, I'm terribly sorry about that. Pose gets carried away sometimes when he sees someone running like you were. He wants to get in on the fun. Still pretty much a puppy." The voice tried to be friendly and apologizing at the same time. I was finally going to kick someone's ass: Pose's Daddy's.

Standing again, I brushed off my hands and looked up real slow, Clint Eastwood-style.

Five feet away a giant Irish wolfhound stood next to a nothing-looking man. Both of them were on fire. I mean, both man and dog were in big bright flames. The guy was smiling and came toward me. Before I could do anything he stuck out a burning hand to shake and said, "I'm Mel Shaveetz. Nice to meet you. We just moved in here a couple of days ago. Haven't met many people yet."

Taking one giant step back, I jammed both hands as deep into my pockets as they'd go. Through his flames Mel frowned until it dawned on him. "Oh for God's sake, I'm sorry!" He blew on his index finger. All the flames on him went out like he'd blown out a birthday candle. Like he was blowing himself out.

"I keep forgetting. Sorry about that."

"Who are you?"

Instead of answering, he reached down and squeezed the dog's nose. Its flames went out too. "Mel Shaveetz. And this is Posafega."

"You were on fire!"

"Yeah well, that happens where we come from."

"And where's that?"

"Hell."

"You mean you're dead?"

"Couldn't put on this kind of light show if I was alive. Did you think I was one of those monks who burn themselves alive?"

"You and the dog are dead?"

"No, I am. Pose is just a hound from Hell. He's my roommate."

"A Hellhound!"

"That's right."

"How come I didn't get burned when he was standing on my back?"

"Because you're not dead."

"It just looks like a big wolfhound to me."

Mel shrugged. "Nobody ever said what breed Hellhounds had to be. You want to come in the house and have a beer?"

"Which house do you mean? I know everyone who lives around here."

He pointed to a brown and white saltbox across the street. "You're looking at it—number eighty-eight."

"Eighty-eight? I know who lives in eighty-eight and it isn't you. Chris and Terry Rolfe live there."

He looked away and tried to make his eyes busy. "Yeah well, not anymore. They moved."

I remembered what our refrigerator movers had said about seeing piles of people's belongings left out on the street. And I remembered the Brothers saying that was because the dead were being moved back to earth from Hell.

"I went to school with Chris Rolfe. He's lived in this town as long as I have. I'd know if he was planning to leave."

"Look, you want that beer or not?"

I wanted to check out the inside of that house. I didn't believe for a minute what he was saying about Rolfe. As far as I knew, that house still belonged to a living guy I saw at least once a week for the past twenty years.

We walked slowly up to the front door, Posafega keeping us company all the way. Not only was that dog big, it was also seriously ugly. Its hair looked like stuffing out of an eighty-year-old mattress. Its face was thin enough to open a letter. The animal was so big that if it stood on its hind legs and had a good hook shot, it could have played pro basketball. So that was a Hellhound. I said the word inside my mouth to myself—Hellhound.

Just as we were walking in the door, I smelled smoke. Sure enough, Mel was beginning to go up in flames again. "Hey man, you're on fire."

"Yeah well, I'll fix it when we get inside." He kept moving while his flames kept rising. The big dog's, too.

Remember I said we love the movie *Back to the Future*? Well my wife and I are just overall big movie fans so it isn't the only video we own. And that's where my next problem arrived. I wasn't about to pass up the chance to see the inside of a dead man's house and look around for Chris Rolfe. Plus the invitation was offered on a silver platter. But when I think about it now, maybe going in there wasn't the best idea I ever had. Because here's what happened next: opening the front door, Mel and flame-dog marched in, no big deal. A lot more carefully I followed but got only a few feet into the place before I froze and my jaw dropped below sea level.

I recognized what I saw immediately because I'd seen it so often before and had always wished I could go there. Now I was. The inside of Mel's house, the house that used to belong to Chris Rolfe, was now Rick's American Bar from the movie *Casablanca*.

While my brain tried to swallow that fact, Mel sat down at the white piano and began playing the movie's theme song, "As Time Goes By." He wasn't bad either. Then he began to sing it but I was walking around the room so I didn't pay much attention. The dog plumped down on the floor and went to sleep. I was in such shock that I didn't realize until later that both of them lost their flames as soon as we got into the house. Like once they were home they were normal again. Although my idea of normal that day had taken a vacation to another planet.

As far as I could see every detail in the room was perfect, right down to the ashtrays on the table and full bottles behind the bar. The room was empty except for us, which gave it a whole different feeling from what it was like in the movie. Other than that though, this definitely was Rick's place. If Humphrey Bogart had walked in at that minute I would not have been one bit surprised.

Mel finished playing with a big right hand display—DONG!—and afterwards everything was very quiet in there. Naturally I was tempted to say real coolly, "Play it again, Sam," but I didn't.

Instead I asked, "What is all this?"

"It's Rick's. Don't you know *Casablanca*? The movie?"

"Yes I know *Casablanca*! That wasn't my question. How come you live in this house now and it looks like a movie set instead of someone's living room?"

"Before we come back, they ask us what kind of decor we would like where we live. We get to choose."

"Choose what?"

"The decor! What'd I just tell you?"

"I'm very confused, Mel."

He took a deep breath like I was the stupidest being he'd ever met and my dumbness was using up his air supply. "Before we come back here, to earth, they ask what kind of decor we'd like in the house they assign us. We get to choose. I said Rick's American Bar from the movie because that was the coolest place on earth."

"How long ago did you die?"

"Last Friday."

"How?"

"I drowned in Aqaba, scuba diving. I stepped on a poisonous sea urchin and had an allergic reaction. Pretty pathetic way to go."

"And you went to Hell?"

"Straight to. Do not pass go, do not collect two hundred dollars."

"But you're back here a week later?"

"Not by choice, pal. Not by choice." The doorbell rang. Mel held up one finger for quiet. "Let me just get that. What kind of beer do you want? I've got everything here. There's even a good Polish one. Zee-veetch or some name like that."

He left the room and the animal followed. I wondered if it was some kind of satanic chaperone. What kind of visitors did the dead have? That thought grew so fast and so horror-movie-ugly in my head that in the minute or so it took Mel to return, I was almost hyperventilating. What kind of visitors DID the dead have? Good God, what if they were—

"It's for you."

I opened my mouth, closed it, opened again. "Me? No one knows I'm here."

"Yeah well, obviously they do. They say they want to talk to you. Two goofy looking guys with shaggy haircuts."

"Brooks and Zin Zan!"

"Whatever." Mel shrugged.

I started out but stopped short when I thought of something. "Were—were you on fire when they saw you?"

"Sure. Anytime I step out of this house I start to burn. One of the many drawbacks of being back on earth again." He sounded angry about it, put out.

"Did you like it in Hell?"

"I can't say much about it because that's against the rules, you being alive and all." He looked left and right, as if some enemy might be listening. "But I will tell you this—ever think maybe that Hell stuff you've always heard is a bunch of crap? Maybe it's given all that bad press because they want to keep people OUT of there? That if people really knew what it was like, an awful lot of them might kill themselves to get there sooner?"

The dog started growling. It was not a sound you ever want to hear. Worse, it was staring at Mel while it snarled. That monster's lip was curled up and twitching like it was going to attack any second.

"Shut up, Pose. How about that cat you told the other day? Don't you think I was listening?"

"Whoa! You and the dog understand each other?"

"Different rules apply when you're dead. Yes we understand each other. He's pissed off at me for telling you about Hell. It doesn't matter. You'd better go see your friends. I'll get the beers." He went to the bar and I left the room.

Sure enough, Brooks and Zin Zan were standing just the other side of the open doorway. They lit up when they saw me. I gotta admit I was happy to see them too, considering everything that had been happening.

"Hi guys, what are you doing here?"

Both opened their mouths and started talking but I didn't hear a thing. Their faces and hand movements were busy, too, but came with no soundtrack. After a while I pointed to my ears and made a face that said nothing's coming through. They seemed to understand and gestured for me to step outside.

Just as I was about to do exactly that, Mel Shaveetz's voice said from about five inches behind my ear, "I wouldn't go out there if I were you."

Still looking at the Brothers, I asked why not? I don't like being told what to do; especially not by dead people who live on movie sets with burning dogs.

"Because once you do, you can't come back in here again."

"Why would I want to?"

"Because the answers you need are in here, not out there with them." Mel's voice was snotty and know-it-all, all "You dumbbell—I'm smarter than you are" tone. Which I hate. Without even bothering to look back at the asshole, I stepped toward the Brothers. I heard a terrible savage growl from back in the house. The hairy Devil dog was coming for me again.

Adding to that, the Brothers' eyeballs widened till they almost popped out of their heads at whatever it was they saw coming up behind me. Then those holy cowards turned on their four heels and ran. Me too. Not that I expected to get very far. I knew how that giant could run. I'd felt its weight pressing down on my back. Now I knew any second it'd be on me again doing a lot worse than before.

I'm running and know I'll be caught but I'll fight back. What else could I do? For the first sprint I ran looking at the ground. That's how I always ran fastest as a kid. No distractions, just watch the ground straight in front of you and move like lightning in front of thunder.

But eventually I realized even through all the fear that nothing had caught or eaten me yet. So I looked up, wondering why not? The Brothers were a hundred feet ahead, standing still now and facing me. Why had they stopped when a moment ago they were so scared? And where was that Posafega?

I looked over my shoulder cringing because it might just be waiting to give me a nasty shock. But the only surprise was that that dog wasn't there. "What is going on?"

"We were afraid we wouldn't be able to get you out of there, sir. That would have been big trouble for all concerned. But here you are—you made it!"

Zin Zan looked like he was about to kiss me, he was so happy.

Instead of answering, I looked at Rolfe's house again to make sure we were talking about the same thing. Only when I was bringing my eyes back around to the Brothers did I see a street sign: Pilot Hill. That's where we'd been planning to go in the first place before all this other shit started happening.

"Is this what you wanted to show me? Rolfe's house? Is that what this is all about?"

"No sir, actually it was someone else's house we wanted to show you up here. But I don't think you need to see it now to believe what we were saying before."

"True. So who else lost their house on this street?"

They looked at each other to see which of them was going to drop the next bad news bomb. Zin Zan said, "Everyone."

"What?"

"That's right." Brooks moved his arm in a way that took in the whole area. "Every house on Pilot Hill has been taken over."

"I don't believe it." I looked around again to make sure that dog wasn't sneaking up on me from some secret angle.

"It's true, Mr. Gallatin. If you'd like, go look in anyone's window here and you'll see."

"I will do exactly that." I crossed the street to my friend Carl Hull's house and looked in his window because I knew exactly what it looked like inside. What I noticed first was everything was black and white in there. Or I should say in black and white. I knew Carl's house and this wasn't it. I stepped back and looked at the facade. This was Hull's house, all right. So I looked in the window again. Carl's wife Naomi loves yellow things—furniture, pillows, rugs. But there wasn't an inch of yellow anything in there. No couch, curtains, nothing—only black and white.

The living room was full of old fat furniture; most of it covered in some thick material like velvet. Like your Grandma's house. Pure old people's furniture. The Hull house I knew had a few pieces of cheap yellow furniture, a round "Garfield" rug in front of a TV set as big as you could get. That machine was Carl's pride and you had to give the man credit—he didn't scrimp when it came to home entertainment. But where was that big Sony screen today?

"Sherlock Holmes."

I jumped. "Don't do that, Brooks! Don't sneak up on me. My eggs have been scrambled enough for one day. Besides, what are you talking about?"

"This house—the woman who moved in here chose the decor of the first Sherlock Holmes film. Starring Clive Brook, Ernest Torrence—"

"Where's Carl and Naomi?"

"At Lake of the Ozarks on vacation. They'll be coming back soon to this ugly surprise."

"Where's their stuff? Their belongings?"

"The new tenant had it hauled away this morning."

"Why is everything in black and white in there?"

Brooks seemed surprised at my question. "Because that film was in black and white. The new occupant wanted things to look exactly like the film."

"Well, *Casablanca* was black and white too. But Mel's house was in color. You saw it."

Brooks nodded. "He chose the colorized version. He's not a purist. I hope you don't mind me saying this, Mr. Gallatin, but it would be very good if we got a move on."

"Where to now?"

"Back to your house."

"What's at my house that wasn't there an hour ago?"

"A moving van."

Three sets of eyes bounced back and forth, back and forth like Flubber for a while before any of the mouths connected to them had more to say.

"They're taking over my house now?"

"Yes sir. That's why we came to warn you this morning."

"You knew about this? You knew it would happen?" We started walking—fast.

"We always know it'll happen—just not when. We didn't think it would be so soon and in such large numbers. That's why we go door to door. The problem is no one ever believes what we say until it's too late. So Beeflow decided to change the way we do things because the situation is now getting critical."

"Was that really Beeflow who talked to me back in the truck?"

"Yes sir. Was Cyrus there too?"

"How do you know about that? I thought it was my soul!"

"It is. Did it lick your hand in the dark?" He smiled and shook his head like he'd just found a fond memory in his pocket. "That's its way of greeting you, telling you it's there. It happens that way to us all. But 'Cyrus' is only Beeflow's nickname for it. The real name of the human soul is Kopum, pronounced Coepoom. You'll learn all about that later."

"Then why does he call it Cyrus?"

"It's easier to accept in the beginning. The name sounds a lot less strange than Kopum. People like feeling safe, especially when it comes to their souls."

We hurried back and only when we were halfway home did I think about what I was doing or the fact I had accepted everything they'd told me as cold hard fact. The name of my soul was Cyrus, but not really because it's actually Kopum. Okay. Dead people were moving into my house? If you say so. The craziness of it all made me slow some but not stop. I'd seen and heard enough in the last hour to know parts of my world had suddenly gone seriously damned wobbly, but this? Could it really be true?

"Look at that."

I was so deep into thinking about all of this that my brain didn't click until my eyes saw the scene in front of us. And then the first thing I did was burst out laughing. There's this guy I know and work with named Eric Dickey. Just saying that name makes my lips squinch up like I ate something bad. I hate that son of a bitch. You don't want to get me started on him because I've got a whole alphabet of reasons why I do not wish him well—in this life or any other. It's enough to say that we started disliking each other in ninth grade and only got better at it as the years passed.

Anyway, Eric Dickey and his stumpy wife Sue live in a nice house a few blocks from ours. And I've got to admit it is a handsome place. Eric is a foreman at my company who knows how to kiss ass well enough to get promotions while the rest of us are worrying half the time about what will happen if there are layoffs. But the fact of the matter is the Dickeys do have a really nice house and at work Eric is always bragging about the new this or new that they bought for their place. They don't have any kids so they go all-out buying top of the line air conditioners, lawnmowers, gas grills—the kind of expensive things that can be seen from the street and coveted by the rest of us slobs. A real asshole.

So anyway, I'm laughing now because what do you know—old Dickey's stuff is piled on the street in front of his beautiful house. This time seeing a pile like that doesn't surprise me so much as make my heart throw a fist in the air and yell ALL RIGHT! Maybe this Hell business isn't so bad after all. But that feeling was short lived because just as I was relishing seeing kiss-ass Dickey's stuff dumped out on the street, who should walk around from the back of his house but a caveman!

So help me God. That sounds totally nuts but it is the truth. And you've seen him before in every caveman movie you ever watched. The fucker is hunched over in a sort of monkey scrunch and has got so much hair growing on his body that you can't really make out where the head ends and the rest begins. I mean this fellow is ALL hair and even when he looks at you, his face is hard to make out because everything is so completely covered in fur.

Now if that wasn't enough, this whatever it is, this creature looks at us and growls like a monster. No, he more like roars like a lion and it's one loud ugly sound. Then he threw up two furry arms that looked like a couple of tree trunks with brown moss growing off them. I was sure he was going to come charging at us because he thought we were going to steal his place from him. But as far as I was concerned, he was the best neighbor in town if he had evicted Eric Dickey on his bragging ass. When I thought for sure Mr. Caveman was coming for us, I put up my hand—palm out. I was even about to say "How!" like cowboys do to Indians when they meet up on the prairie. Where that idea came from in my brain I do not know, except maybe I thought you greeted dinosaur eaters the same way you did Commanches. Even though the two groups were only about a few million years apart on the time line. When he roared again I thought it was time to get out of there so I started off.

"Wait, don't run. He can't bother you." Zin Zan called out. I stopped but my feet weren't convinced. They kept going up and down, sort of running in place just in case he was wrong. "How do you know that?"

"Because we're with you. We know how to keep him away. You're protected so long as you don't go into his house. That's why it was so dangerous when you went into that other man's place."

"But where's Dickey and his wife?"

"Hiding in their basement."

"No shit?" Ear to ear I was grinning. Ear to ear.

"You're going to have to stop using that kind of language, Mr. Gallatin. It just won't do."

I wanted to say "fuck you," but the picture of Eric hiding in his basement from a furry caveman, while all his high-priced possessions sat in a heap on the curb—that was happiness enough for the moment to keep my dirty words in my mouth. "So dead people from all the different ages are being sent back here? Not just recent ones like Mel?"

Brooks shook his head and frowned. "That is correct. It's totally chaotic but only part of the problem we face. Look! That is exactly what I'm talking about!" From behind the house smoke and flame started coming around the corner. And not just "too many burgers on the barbecue" stuff—these were big impressive clouds of brown smoke and some yellow flame coming fast and scary toward us.

"What's happening?"

Zin Zan pointed at the caveman. "He probably started a fire back there. He can't help it—guys like him don't know any better."

"Should we do something about it?"

From the distance came faint siren sounds.

"No, someone's obviously called it in already. We've got to get to your house now."

"Yeah, but what's going to happen when the firetrucks get here and have to deal with Mr. One Million B. C.?" I pointed at you-know-who.

"That's their problem, not ours. Right now we've got to get you back home."

We started walking again but I kept turning around to look at that hairy guy standing in front of Eric's house. He didn't move. Smoke was coming thick and fast behind him but he didn't move. The sirens got louder, nearer. Were those voices coming from inside the house? Was someone shouting in there?

"Come on, Mr. Gallatin. There's no time."

I looked at the Brothers. I looked at the caveman. I looked at the house, the smoke behind him. I knew I was about to do something really stupid and probably unnecessary.

"We can't just go."

Both Brothers turned toward the siren sounds and gestured toward them. "They're coming now. They'll be here any minute."

"But what happens in the meantime? Maybe they'll die down there of smoke inhalation or whatever. Don't you watch those emergency rescue shows on TV? Every minute counts."

"Every minute counts for you too. You have to save your home! Do you understand that? They are taking your house!"

I lowered my head and started walking in the wrong direction. One of them touched my arm. I shook him off. Eric Dickey was a turd but I wasn't going to let him die. Maybe I was being stupid because he probably would have been saved just fine without my help. But I don't want ugly things on my conscience. I don't want to live the rest of my life with a picture pinned to the inside of my brain of a man and his weasel-eyed wife lying face down forever in a smoky basement because I needed to get home.

"We won't be able to help if you go in there. We can't go with you!"

"Then just wait out here. I'll be right back." I kept walking. The caveman saw me but seemed to have his mind on other things. He lifted his head and sniffed the air like an animal—nose up high, making these little up and down jerks every now and again. Sniff-jerk-sniff-jerk. Then he turned and ran around the house to the back.

Which was just fine with me because it gave me free access to the front door. The moment B. C. disappeared from sight, I ran for it. Behind me the Brothers were hollering now, "Don't!" and, "Please come back!" But I was already there. The bad news was that door was locked. The good news? An aluminum baseball bat was leaning against the house. Without a second's hesitation I picked it up. Not a second too soon because I heard a rough animal grunt behind me. Not too close but close enough to have me bringing that bat up to "play ball!" height by the time I'd swiveled around to face that grunt. In shock I almost dropped the damned thing seeing what I did.

The caveman was about ten feet away. In his hands was the charred body of what could only have been a dog. In fact it was definitely a dog because the head wasn't as grilled as the rest of the black, still-smoking body. I could make out that it was once upon a time a beagle or some such. That's what the fire behind the house probably started off being: he was cooking some poor sucker's Lassie or Snoopy. Rest in Peace, Snoop. Bet you never thought you'd end up lunch.

I didn't have any time to think about it because B. C. dropped his Happy Meal and came at me. I swung the bat at his head. Lucky for him, he was able to turn a bit at the last second so instead of hitting a home run I only knocked him flat.

The clang of metal-on-head sounded like a cooking pot dropped on concrete. I knew I hadn't killed him because he was already dead, but also because he was twitching and frothing up ugly stuff out at the mouth. I stood over him a few seconds to see if he'd get up again. But most of him was on vacation and what wasn't, was busy jerking around.

So I swung that fine silver bat again, this time through one of the large windows into what I assumed was the Dickey living room. After the first crash of glass, I knocked out some slivers still stuck in the window frame and after a last glance at him just to be sure, I climbed in.

I've never been to a jungle. I've never been most places but that's okay because I don't speak other languages and the idea of a passport makes me nervous. But as soon as I put both feet down inside the Dickeys' house I was hit by a wet tropical heat the likes of which I'd never experienced. Everything around me was like this 3-D green. A green so strong it almost hurt my eyes. When I took a step forward, I was hit in the face by some kind of nasty thick vine that was a whole new scare in itself. When I managed to push that out of the way I tried to get my bearings looking left and right but all I saw was green everything and sounds that screamed and screeched and cawed and pretty much made me deaf. I was in a jungle somehow and as that sunk into my brain I somehow remembered a line from school that just popped up out of nowhere but said it all— the forest primeval.

Mel Shaveetz had said they got to choose a decor when they came back to earth. So of course a caveman would want one exactly like where he had been living. In the forest primeval. The earth a million years ago or fifty thousand or whenever.

Instead of Eric Dickey's living room, I was back on earth a zillion years ago, standing like a rabbit frozen in the headlights. And there were no walls in this "decor," it wasn't limited to a few closed-in rooms like Rick's Bar. Everywhere I looked was jungle that went out in every direction with no end in sight. This wasn't a room—this was forever. Right about then the next words came to my mind.

"Jurassic Park," I said out loud but couldn't hear very well for all the screeching going on around me.

"Dinosaurs!" Monsters with teeth as big as the baseball bat I still held. Walking houses with serious appetites for anything fleshy. I had to get out of here. In a panic I turned around, planning to go right back through the window into my world. But there was no window. Only trees and vines and green and noise.

Eventually my brain stopped its own screeching in fear. And although I was scared shitless of what might come stomping out of the trees at any minute, I was losing control so fast that there was only one thing left to do—close my eyes. A trick that almost always worked for me when things got so bad I could feel life unraveling. Close my eyes and say, "I am driving my life. I am steering this car. I CONTROL THINGS."

I started the "I am—" but it was drowned out by the terrible new sound of something very big—and near—coming my way through the jungle. THUMP THUMP THUMP. It was running! As huge as it sounded in the not so far distance, the speed of its footsteps said it was running at me. It was my turn to be lunch.

"What are the six questions?"

How did I hear that? The voice had spoken calmly and in no hurry. But I heard it clearly above everything else. What six questions? Who was this? Were they the last words I'd ever hear? WAS IT GOD?

"No, Mr. Gallatin, it's Beeflow. What are the six questions?"

Thump Thump Thump. I heard bushes crashing, birds crying out like they do when they're disturbed or attacked. This monster was closer, it was almost here.

"WHAT ARE THE SIX QUESTIONS?"

"I don't know what the fuck you're talking about! Get me out of here!"

And then the biggest shock of all—I heard him sigh! A disappointed sigh. The sigh of a teacher when you've answered a question wrong in class.

"All right, I'll help you this one time but not again. Name one experience from your past you wish you could repeat. That is the third question."

"Are you nuts? Now? The thing's coming! Get me out of here."

"Then answer the question, and quickly."

"An experience I want to repeat? I don't know. Jeez, I don't know. Help me, willya?" My voice sounded like one of the scared birds up in the trees.

"No, help yourself—answer that question."

And when he said that, an answer came so clear and calm to my mind that I was surprised I hadn't known it immediately. "I wish I could have sex again for the first time with Rae. That was the best night of my life."

"Very very good. Now look in your hand."

I looked, even though the bushes nearby rustled hard which meant whatever monster was coming had arrived. Instead of the silver baseball bat, I held a black metal cylinder about two feet long. The dinosaur burst out at me like a rocket with legs. Its teeth were even bigger than I had thought they'd be. Its open mouth looked ten feet wide. I didn't even have a chance to raise the cylinder up to do whatever it might do to fight off the thing. Because it was there.

And then gone.

That's right—it whizzed right by me. Whatever kind of prehistoric piece of shit it was, the creature ran by and went crashing on into the jungle behind me. It didn't even stop to have a look or say hello. Not that I was disappointed. I stood there looking after it and then I looked at the black cylinder in my hand, trying to figure out how it played into all of this. No answer came. It was just this metal thing that a while before had been a baseball bat.

I stood there listening while Tyrannosaurus-whatever galloped farther away into the jungle. And then it became quiet around me, or as quiet as a place like that is ever going to be. It took me some more time to de-tox from the scare that was still sending fireballs of adrenaline to all corners of my body. I stood a while longer and then sort of collapsed on the ground in a heap, dropping the cylinder as I did.

I looked at it and wondered what kind of magic had changed it from a baseball bat into this without my ever having felt it. I wondered if it had somehow saved me from being eaten. Or had answering Beeflow's question been the reason? What were these six questions he was talking about? What was this cylinder lying on the ground a foot away? How was I going to get out of the forest primeval and back to my world?

"Don't turn around."

I didn't but sure was tempted. It was Beeflow again. "Why can't I look at you?"

"Because I told you before, Mr. Gallatin, I am everything ugly about you. I'm your shit in the toilet, the dark side of your moon, the worst lies you've told, the hurt you dropped on others. I am everything bad about you and if you want to look that square in the face then go ahead. But I warn you, looking your own evil in the eye is as bad as looking at Medusa. It will wreck you, turn part of you into stone."

"And you say you're me?"

"Only in part. I've chosen to take on all that's bad in you for the time being so that you can face challenges other than your own."

"Are you, uh, human?"

"I was once, but am no longer. Years ago I had a vision and it changed me forever."

"What kind of vision?"

"You're looking at it now."

I happened to be looking at the cylinder next to me. "That thing? The baseball bat?"

"Yes. I was in a flea market in London and on a table amongst other junk was a brass object. I worked as a travel agent but my great hobbies were inventing and the history of tools. So I was well versed in the function of all sorts of machinery, archaic tools, and the like. I was no newcomer to obscure gadgets. But for the life of me I could not understand what purpose this gizmo served. Written on the side of it in thick letters were the words 'Heidelberg Cylinder.' I picked it up and turned it over and over in my hands but its purpose still baffled me. I was perplexed and fascinated, so I paid three pounds and put it in my pocket.

"When I returned home to America and was able to look through the reference books in my library, I discovered something staggering: The Heidelberg

Cylinder had been used in every great modern invention. The cotton gin, the first steam engine, the telephone, internal combustion engine. You name it and a version of the cylinder was one of the components. It was the essential piece in every one of those innovations. It was the thing that made them all work. I was astonished and then utterly skeptical so I researched further. Different versions of the cylinder were used in the first telegraph, the television, computers. Sometimes it was made of a different metal, or Bakelite, then plastic, carbon— you get the point. It was the part that made these earth-shaking inventions work, Mr. Gallatin, but no one had ever noted the connection. One manmade object made all of these things possible.

"I couldn't believe that no one had ever made the discovery. And then it hit me—no one was supposed to make the discovery! The Heidelberg Cylinder is meant to be invented again and again in its different guises and then put into the workings of whatever new different machines we dream up in the future.

"Because do you know what the cylinder really is? The concrete proof of our immortality. The result of the human mind and spirit working as one to solve problems and overcome them. Any problems. Physical proof of the fact we can do anything we want, even live forever if we choose, if we set our minds to it."

I looked at it and rubbed my mouth. "That thing?"

"Yes, that thing."

I picked it up, turned it over. It was black and there was nothing written on it. Definitely not any "Heidelberg Cylinder."

"How come it's black then and there's no writing on it?"

"Because once you realize what it is, it changes into something else. Something someone else will need to discover its importance. For me it was the brass object I described. For the person who had it before you it turned into a sixteenth-century Persian lock. For you it became a baseball bat."

"Then what is it now?"

"I don't know. Probably something from the future."

Reaching out to pick it up, I stopped when he said that. "But I didn't discover anything with the baseball bat. Definitely not any of that stuff you were saying about man's immortality: I just brained the caveman with it."

"Yes, but that's because I've chosen to intervene. There simply isn't enough time for it to happen in the slow and proper way it should. Mankind is in jeopardy and we must work quickly to avoid a catastrophe. I'll tell you the end of my story briefly and then you will understand.

"When I grasped the extraordinary importance of the Heidelberg Cylinder, I became obsessed with my search and found it again and again the further I looked. But what was I to do with my discovery? Who should I tell and in what context?"

I had to interrupt. "When did you turn into, uh, what you are?"

"Once we've learned about the Cylinder, all of us change eventually." That made me stand up. "What do you mean? Change how?"

"It varies from person to person. I can't say how it will affect you."

I was getting nervous again. "But what about Brooks and Zin Zan? They're both normal. They're weird but they're normal."

"For now, because both of them are new to the group. But sooner or later they will change and take on new forms. We call it 'hatching.' As I said, I can't tell you what forms either of them will take, but they will definitely metamorphose into something entirely different."

"Do they know that? Do they know they're going to change?"

"Of course Mr. Gallatin, and they welcome it."

"So that means now that I know, I'm going to change too?"

"Yes."

"But I don't want to change! I like my life."

"I'm afraid we need you more than you need your life. I want to show you something."

Before I had a chance to protest, everything changed. In an instant, a blink, half a breath, we went from jungle to paradise.

I'd heard it before but now I know it's true: paradise is what you want it to be. If you imagine angels with wings and harps sitting on gold clouds, that's what you'll see. Perfect gardens where lions dance the cha-cha while beautiful women serve you ice-cold rum? Then that's what it will be. I didn't know my paradise until I saw it. The moment I did, I knew this was it—nothing could be better.

An outdoor restaurant in the middle of the countryside somewhere. A few metal tables were set up under four big chestnut trees. The wind was blowing, tossing up the corners of the white tablecloths. The sun shone down through the leaves, flickering beautiful yellow, green and white light across everything.

A bunch of people were sitting at one of the tables having the best time laughing, eating and talking. A Black guy was sitting at one end of the table playing a Gibson Hummingbird guitar softly but really well. A woman nearby kept jumping up from her place, hugging him and then sitting back down again.

The different colors and variety of food spread out for them across the table was amazing. All kinds of meats and salads, vegetables piled high, soups, cakes and pies. The breads alone would have kept you busy for days making sandwiches. Once you saw it you couldn't take your eyes off this—plenty. My mouth started watering. I knew it had to be the greatest food that ever was and to taste any bit of it would bring you to tears.

"Hey Bill, why're you standing over there like you're hypnotized? Get your ass over here and say hello." The man who spoke didn't just look like my father, it was him. He'd been dead eleven years.

I didn't move but just assumed Beeflow was nearby so I asked out loud, "Is it real? Is that really my Dad?"

"Yes. Look around the table. You know everyone there."

It was true. A girl I'd known and liked who'd died in a water skiing accident, my Uncle Birmy next to my father, others. I did know everyone at that table. Some better than others but I had known them all—when they were alive. When my father called out my name they looked over and smiled like seeing me was the best thing that had happened to them all day. It made me feel good and gave me the damned creeps at the same time.

"Welcome to Hell, Mr. Gallatin," Beeflow said.

Why did I already know that? How did I know that's what he was going to say and it wouldn't surprise me?

"It's the most wonderful place in the world because it's your most wonderful place. Everything is familiar here, you know everyone, the food is gorgeous—"

He was interrupted by the sound of the drowned girl laughing. It was the most beautiful, innocent, sexy laugh I'd ever heard. Her head was thrown back and she was laughing and all I could focus on was her long slim neck. Like everything else there, it was almost too much to take. Since when could the sight of a woman's bare neck send me over the moon?

"You see, it's already beginning to affect you. That's what's so splendid about it. Because everything here is yours, it would be so easy to slide right into this world and never want to go home."

"It really is Hell? This is where you go when you've been bad?"

"Yes. That's what Mel Shaveetz was saying to you and why the dog started growling at him. If people knew how marvelous this is, do you think they'd work hard at living? Or at being good, achieving something, working for one another? Too many of them would throw up their hands and just wait to die. Or they would kill themselves for the stupidest reasons just so they could come here earlier than planned."

"Everyone's Hell is this good?"

"Yes it is."

"Then what's Heaven like?"

"Infinitely better. But it is extremely hard to get into Heaven, Mr. Gallatin. It is almost impossible."

"But a person wins either way: Hell is great and Heaven is better."

"That should make no difference to you when you're alive. There is a purpose to living that is far more important than ending up comfortably dead."

"So what is the purpose of living?"

The people at the table seemed to have forgotten I was standing there and had gone back to enjoying their party. Some of them were singing now. The Black guy was playing the Lovin' Spoonful song "Coconut Grove." Others were eating big fat chicken legs or steaks, slices of pie a la mode. More than anything I wanted to go over and join them. Like a hungry kid, I was itching to be at that table.

"Pay attention, Gallatin! Stop drooling over hamburgers. What I'm telling you is vitally important. People are alive because they have jobs to do. They are meant to improve and broaden the human experience as best they can. The Cylinder is concrete proof of that. After death, mankind comes here if they've failed, or to Heaven if they succeeded. But if they knew about this, it would change everything.

Dangerously few people would work hard, or dream, or love well and with all their hearts. Because no matter how they lived, they get this in the end.

"Mankind's progress has been slow but steady. But now Satan is attempting to change that. He says there is no more room in Hell and has begun moving the dead back to earth in greater and greater numbers. Those who have already been sent were told the move wouldn't be permanent. Life on earth is made as pleasant as possible for them by allowing them to create their environment.

"God cannot reason with Satan about this, but we know that is nothing new. This forced relocation has been going on for centuries, but until now God overlooked it because the few that were sent back to earth were regarded by the living as lunatics and ignored. Not anymore."

"Why? Why is it happening?"

"Because Mankind no longer accepts the idea of Damnation. He no longer feels he deserves eternal suffering for what he did or did not do on earth. Guilt has grown obsolete. In the past, people were so afraid of what would happen to them in the afterlife that they created the most frightening scenarios possible. So when they did die, naturally those things happened to them. They brought their worst nightmares along and they came true.

"No longer. For the common man today, a fire and brimstone Hell has become an old-fashioned idea, and Heaven is a child's dream."

"Because we live happier lives, we get to be happier dead?"

"Exactly, and Satan absolutely hates that. When suffering prevailed in Hell, he was satisfied. But since people create their own Hell from what they knew in life, in recent decades it has generally become a rather nice place. He cannot abide that. So he has changed the rules. He is sending the dead back to earth en masse. And it is clear what effect that will have on things there."

"Why doesn't God stop him?"

"Because God wants us to stop him. It is part of our ongoing task."

"How? How are we supposed to stop the Devil?"

"We must come up with a plan. Perhaps many plans before one works effectively. Obviously some of them will work, others won't."

"Jeez, Bill, are we going to have to drag you over to the table with a rope? We even got your favorite over there—potato salad with extra horseradish in the sauce." My father was suddenly standing in front of me smiling that great old smile that had always made me want to climb in his lap and stay there forever.

"Dad, where's Mom? Is she here?"

He smiled and threw a thumb over his shoulder for me to look there. Coming out of the restaurant was my mother. A cry rose up in my throat that I was just barely able to hold onto before it spilled out. There she was, looking like she did before the cancer ate her body. There she was in that red and white striped dress, all her black hair long and curly again. Best of all she was chubby like before—"pleasantly plump" as she called herself. Not the hairless stick-thin woman who turned to the wall one day while lying in her bed and never really turned back, choosing instead to disappear into her sickness and never come out again.

In her hands she held a whipped cream cake. Sort of pale pink on the sides, black bittersweet chocolate on the top. It was my favorite. She had always made it on special occasions. The last time I ever had it was on our wedding day. Rae got the recipe from her but was never able to make it right. All Moms have one secret recipe that can't be copied and this was hers. A whipped cream cake.

She went to the table and put it down in front of an empty seat. Reaching over, she arranged the silverware there. I knew she was setting it up for me. Come over and cut your cake, she was saying. Sit with your father and me and tell us what your life has been since we left. Tell us about Rae who we always liked and your job and how you've filled your days. Because we love you and want to hear everything. How many people on this earth want to hear everything about you? How many people—

"They're dead. Mr. Gallatin."

I blinked, looking from my mother to my father. I was in a trance. My mother, my father, her cake, this place—

"They're dead and you have things to do."

Beeflow's words struck my head like a hammer. They hurt that much. I didn't want to hear them; I didn't want this picture of my good parents to go away just because they were dead.

"What do you want from me? It's my parents! I haven't seen them—Can't I have five minutes together with my parents?"

"You're finding reasons to stay here. And the longer you stay, the more reasons you'll find. It's very tricky that way. Very seductive. But everything here is from your life, Gallatin, it is from life, do you understand? How lucky you've been to amass all these fine memories? How good life has been to you? It's been a good friend. Don't you owe it something?"

Furious, I turned toward his voice without thinking. And when I saw him, when I saw what he was I began to cry. Because he'd told the truth—he was everything I didn't want to know about myself. He had no special shape or size. You couldn't say it's a man or a monster or a Devil or whatever. He was just it, them, all those things you try to ignore or cover up or argue against or justify or put up a million defenses against just to keep from saying there I am, that is part of me.

But then something amazing happened and I don't even know if I can take credit for it. I turned away. I turned away from Mr. Beeflow and looked back at that table, my parents, and the things that made my life big rather than small and shitty. I saw the good people, the good stuff on the table, the trees blowing in the wind and the smell of spring and food and life. Despite having "seen" Beeflow, I still had managed to survive and bring all of these beautiful things along to the death that would someday be mine. I was grateful. And I knew he was right—painful as it was, I had to give all this up for now and go back to do what I could to try and keep life as it had always been for everybody.

"Son?" Dad's voice.

I closed my eyes. "All right, Mr. Beeflow, I understand. Take me back."

Immediately something warm and familiar licked my hand. This time I didn't open my eyes. Whatever it was took the hand and pulled it gently to the left. Blind, I walked a few steps, trusting it, knowing that it was Cyrus. It made so much sense—once you made your mind up to go, only your own soul could lead you back to where you began.

"Not so fast, Monsieur. Who's going to pay for this meal, Bill? The bill, Bill. When you eat at my table, you pay for my cooking."

The Devil wore a chef's cap. One of those stupid high white ones that look like something put on the end of a lamb chop at a ritzy restaurant. He wore that white hat and all the rest of his clothes were white too. His face was nothing special—just a face surrounded by lots of white. No, that's not true—there was one strange-looking thing about him—he had two moustaches. Slim little things, they sat one right under the other like lines on a paper.

"I see by your admiring eye that you're looking at my moustaches. Is this going to be the new trend or what?"

"It looks stupid if you ask me. Plus people can't grow two moustaches."

He shrugged and played with both of them. Top one, then the bottom. "But they can grow one really thick one and cut a space in the middle, making levels."

"It's still stupid."

"Every fool's entitled to his opinion. But let's get back to the facts—how do you plan on paying for this meal? P.S. I don't take VISA or Mastercard." He laughed and it sounded like someone unscrewing a tight plastic-on-plastic cap. I squinted at the sound but didn't look away. I guess my face said I was confused, so he took my arm. I tried to pull away but he wouldn't let me.

"You chose to come here, Bill boy, and now you want to leave, which, however, is a human no-no. Any person who sees this and wants to go back has to pay."

"Pay with what?"

"Something you love. I'll let you go back but the price for this meal, this little view you just had, is something you love in life. If you stay here you get to keep all this. But if you go back you've got to give me something from your life you never thought you could live without."

"Mr. Beeflow, are you there? Is this true?"

"Forget it, he can't help you. Anyway you saw what he looked like."

"You made Beeflow do this too?"

"Yup. He gave up his body. He was a handsome man. A very vain one too. Nothing he liked more than looking at himself in a mirror and admiring the view. I never thought he would do it but sometimes people surprise me."

Suddenly I remembered Cyrus and looked down at the hand he had been holding. No Cyrus—nothing was there. Only the ground. The ground in this beautiful Hell. Gathering myself together, gathering words in my mouth to make a sentence I never thought I would say in a million years, I took a deep breath and said, "Rae, take my love for Rae."

He didn't react immediately. He looked at me hard, like I was trying to trick him. But we both knew there was no way I could trick him.

"I thought you'd say something like that but it's not enough, Bill. Try again."

"I don't know anything else. That's about as bad as I can imagine. Not loving my wife anymore? What could be worse than not loving Rae?"

I climbed through the window of Eric Dickey's house back out into my world and my life. The first thing I smelled there was big thick smoke. It took only a second to remember I'd gone in there in the first place to save Eric and his wife from burning up in the caveman's fire. Jumping off the porch, I ran around to the back of the house. There was a high pile of wood and other things burning in the middle of their yard. Firemen had a hose turned on it, trying to get it under control. Both of the Dickeys were off to one side on their knees, taking oxygen. There was so much tussle and turmoil out there—people running around, fire being fought, police, firemen and the like. No one noticed me standing there. I couldn't help thinking that there had been absolutely no reason for me to go into that house because the fire had all been out here. But then if I hadn't gone in—

"Brother Bill?"

Brooks came up on one side of me, Zin Zan the other. Neither of them was smiling and neither was I.

"Are you all right?"

A fireman rushed by us and knocked into me hard as he passed but I didn't react.

"Now I'm your Brother? Is that what you call me from now on? Brother Bill?"

"We don't have to call you anything if that's what you'd prefer. Are you all right?"

"You know where I just was, don't you?"

They both nodded.

"And you both were there once and saw the Devil?"

Again, slow nods.

In the smoke and the fire and the confusion and the running around and the noise that was a hundred kinds of noise, I saw something I hadn't seen all afternoon although it had been right in front of me the whole time.

"My God, you're Brooks Collins!"

Half a smile crossed Brother Brooks's face and then died. He nodded again.

"I have all your albums."

"Better take care of them—there won't be any more."

"You gave that up?" A few beats passed until I understood. "That's what you gave the Devil? Your talent?"

"And the fame. He wasn't going to let me go just giving up the one. The world today is full of people who have no talent but are famous. No one recognizes me anymore. Only you, but that's because you've been to Hell. You perceive things other people don't."

"I guess we'd better get going."

It was not a far walk to my place but long enough to look around and appreciate things like I never had before. Now and then we'd pass a house and from just a glimpse, we knew if it had been taken over or not. But once I wasn't sure and crept to a window to look. I can't tell you how happy I was to see a normal family inside watching TV and eating popcorn.

"How come Mel Shaveetz and his dog were on fire when they left their house, but the caveman wasn't? All of them were dead."

"Because the Devil keeps changing the rules all the time. That's the reason why so many people are unhappy in life—the rules keep changing. There's really no way of knowing what will happen from one day to the next with this. That's why it's so hard for us to convince people of what's going on. And because it's happening so much faster now, that's why Beeflow has become more directly involved."

"Why doesn't the Devil stop him?"

"Arrogance. He doesn't see Beeflow or us as a threat. There's your house. Do you know what you're gonna do?"

"Stay here. I've got to see something."

They stood by a light pole while I went and opened the front door. Closing it quietly behind me as if someone nearby was sleeping and I didn't want to wake them, I just stood in the hallway a minute, being home, breathing home. My mother used to say after we'd come back from a trip, "At home, even the walls heal you." And that's just how I felt standing there, smelling my life in those near rooms, my eyes running over our possessions and photos on the walls that I knew the whole history of. Lucky me—all of them showed in different ways what a very good time I'd had right up until that day. Lucky me. But the

Brothers had earlier said a moving van had been in front of my house. That's why I'd come back in here—to see who had taken over our house and how they had changed things. I needed to see what was different so I could prepare my wife and somehow protect her from what was happening. But why then was nothing different in here?

Then I heard it—the zhunk of furniture being shoved hard across a floor. Someone else was in my house. Someone upstairs from the sound of it. The back of my neck prickled and my eyes opened wide of their own doing. I wore sneakers so I was able to cross the floor and climb the stairs with very little sound. While climbing I heard that same sound a few more times, sometimes louder and longer, sometimes short and sharp. Zhunk-silence-zhuuunk. Like that. I couldn't figure out what it was but it was definitely real and I needed to find out about it.

At the top of the stairs I stood still and waited till the next time it came.

It was down the hall in our bedroom. Zhunk. From where I stood I could see that door was open about a third and something white was on the floor just inside the bedroom. I couldn't make out what it was. Tiptoeing down the hall, I kept trying to focus in on what that white thing was. It came to me in stages. A piece of clothing—a shirt—a white T-shirt. And just when I realized that's what it was, I heard the other sounds. Sex. A woman having sex and liking it a lot.

Rae doesn't like sex. That's been the major problem in our marriage. Once in a while she's sort of in the mood, but it's like when you're sort of in the mood for pizza but can easily do without it if there's none around. I always get the feeling she's doing me a favor when she says yes and I can't tell you how dry and lonely that makes me feel. She's a woman I have always wanted to touch but it is more than clear she doesn't want that.

A T-shirt was on the floor and when I looked I saw writing on it and knew it said "Hard Rock Café." It was my shirt but it was very big and Rae liked that so she often slept in it. Her sounds kept up and they would have made any man hot. I'd known them once but not for a long time. Still, I recognized them instantly. I walked as close to the door as I could and looked in.

My wife was on our bed naked, straddling a guy whose face I couldn't see. She was working him so hard that their banging bodies made the bed slide on the floor. Zhunk.

Even when we did have sex, she'd never do it like that with me because she didn't like me seeing her whole naked. It was always in the dark and she'd wear some kind of clothes—a shirt or sweatshirt so she'd never be completely stripped. As if wearing something meant she was still distant from me and this act even when it was going on.

Did I watch? Yes. Did it make me hot? It sure did. I stood off to a side and watched her do to whoever was beneath her all the things I'd dreamt of her doing with me for as long as I could remember.

What had I given to the Devil to come back here? Rae's love for me. My love for her wasn't enough, or so he said. So I said take hers then.

Our relationship wasn't the best. We never had sex anymore, and we seemed to fight more than we should have. Still, I knew she loved me in her scared, mysterious way. I could see it in her eyes when she looked at me.

Sometimes. Plus there were other things she did that overall made up for what was missing. You get along and sometimes you get along so well that you don't think about what you're missing because you just love them there in your life, whatever way they've chosen to be.

As I stood there watching my wife fuck another man, I knew the Devil had changed the rules again: no dead people had moved into my house. No *Casablanca* backgrounds or jungles were needed here. Everything was the same except for the fact my wife's love for me was dead. What more proof did I need than what was right in front of me?

There was nothing to take. I turned and went back down the hall, down the stairs. I was planning to go right back out of the house but when I touched the front doorknob I stopped. I walked back to the kitchen and without thinking, kissed that new refrigerator. The thing that had started all this in the first place. That was all I wanted to do before leaving but don't ask me why. It just meant something to me and that was reason enough. I kissed our silver refrigerator and it was cool metal on my lips and then it was really time to go.

"Mr. Gallatin?" Beeflow's voice.

I stood and stared at the refrigerator. "What?"

"If it's of any comfort, he didn't make this happen. It's been going on for some time. Upstairs?"

"I know what you mean."

"You were never supposed to know about it. She was always very careful and discreet. But when you offered it to him, when you gave up her love for you—"

"I know what you're saying, Beeflow. I'm not that stupid. He shows me the truth, you show me the truth—both of you are killing me with all this truth about my life. Was that the plan? Because what good does it do? Seeing the truth just shows you how wrong you were about things and how ugly they really are."

"Sometimes. And sometimes it brings the genuinely good things into better focus."

I threw up my hands in disgust. "I don't want to hear any more. Okay? Don't say another word." I left my house for the last time and started walking over to the Brothers, not really knowing if what Beeflow had said made things better or worse.

But I didn't have any time to think about it. Suddenly from down the street came all these screams and sounds of people running. *Lots* of people running. I'd just gotten to Brooks and Zin Zan when this crowd arrived. First came a bunch of men in Roman gladiator uniforms—swords, shields, sandals up to their knees, the whole bit. They came stampeding down the street slap-slap-slapping on their sandals. Every last one of them looked scared shitless. They all kept looking over their shoulders at what was after them.

When they were gone, a few moments passed and then came the second wave. Maybe a hundred wild-looking, screaming women in leather and animal skins, wearing headdresses made out of crazy-colored bird feathers, carrying spears and swords and all kinds of other ugly weapons, some of their faces covered in war paint, went barreling after those scared gladiators. It was clear like they were going to catch up any minute.

454 ↔ Jonathan Carroll

After the last ones passed I said, "What the fuck was that?"

Brooks and Zin Zan started running after them. Brooks said, "Some dead fool chose the movie *Hercules and the Captive Women* to fill his house. But guess what—they escaped."

"And we're supposed to do something about it? Us? Just the three of us?"

We were already running after them when Zin Zan said, "Now it gets interesting."

Gone

Jack Ketchum is the author of such diverse novels as Off Season, Cover, The Girl Next Door, Red, Hide and Seek, Ladies' Night, and most recently, The Lost. This is his second story to appear in The Year's Best Fantasy and Horror—his first, "The Box," won a Bram Stoker Award for best short fiction of the year.

"I got to pondering," he says, "what kind of courage it took to lose a loved one to a world unknown and then start over again. My only personal experience of this was watching what a dear friend of mine went through when her old, beloved cat disappeared one night, no trace of him ever found. That awful not knowing. Did he suffer? Is he suffering? It was a long time before she found the heart to adopt another. And then I thought, trick or treat." "Gone" was first published in October Dreams: A Celebration of Halloween, edited by Richard Chizmar and Robert Morrish.

—E. D.

Seven-thirty and nobody at the door. No knock, no doorbell.

What am I? The wicked old witch from Hansel and Gretel.

The jack-o-lantern flickered out into the world from the window ledge, the jointed cardboard skeleton swayed dangling from the transform. Both there by way of invitation, which so far had been ignored. In a wooden salad bowl on the coffee table in front of her bite-sized Milky Ways and Mars Bars and Nestle's Crunch winked at her reassuringly—crinkly gleaming foil-wrap and smooth shiny paper.

Buy candy, and they will come.

Don't worry, she thought. Someone'll show. It's early yet.

But it wasn't.

Not these days. At least that's what she'd gathered from her window on Halloweens previous. By dark it was pretty much over on her block. When she was a kid they'd stayed out till eleven—twelve even. Roamed where they pleased. Nobody was afraid of strangers or razored apples or poisoned candy. Nobody's mother or father lurked in attendance either. For everybody but the real toddlers, having mom and dad around was ludicrous, unthinkable.

But by today's standards, seven-thirty was late.

Somebody'll come by. Don't worry.

ET was over and NBC was doing a marathon *Third Rock* every half hour from now till ten. What *Third Rock* had to do with Halloween she didn't know. Maybe there was a clue in the Mars Bars. But *Third Rock* was usually okay for a laugh now and then so she padded barefoot to the kitchen and poured herself a second dirty Stoli martini from the shaker in the fridge and lay back on the couch and picked at the olives and tried to settle in.

The waiting made her anxious, though. Thoughts nagged like scolding parents.

Why'd you let yourself in for this, idiot?

You knew it would hurt if they didn't come.

You knew it would hurt if they did.

"You've got a no-win situation here," she said.

She was talking to herself out loud now. Great.

It was a damn good question, though.

Years past, she'd avoided this. Turned off the porch light and the lights in the living room. *Nobody home.* Watched TV in the bedroom.

Maybe she should have done the same tonight.

But for her, holidays were all about children. Thanksgiving and New Year's Eve being the exceptions. Labor Day and the President's days and the rest didn't even count—they weren't *real* holidays. Christmas. *That was Santa.* Easter. *The Easter Bunny.* The Fourth of July. *Firecrackers, sparklers, fireworks in the night sky.* And none was more about kids than Halloween. Halloween was about dress-up and *trick or treat.* And *trick or treat* was children.

She'd shut out children for a very long time now.

She was trying to let them in.

It looked like they weren't buying.

She didn't know whether to be angry, laugh or cry.

She knew it was partly her fault. She'd been such a goddamn mess.

People still talked about it. Talked about *her.* She knew they did. *Was that why her house seemed to have PLAGUE painted on the door? Parents talking to their kids about the lady down the block?* She could still walk by in a supermarket and stop somebody's conversation dead in its tracks. Almost five years later and she *still* got that from time to time.

Five years—shy three months, really, because the afternoon had been in August—over which time the MISSING posters gradually came down off the store windows and trees and phone poles, the police had stopped coming around long before, her mother had gone from calling her over twice a day to only once a week—she could be glad of some things, anyhow—and long-suffering Stephen, sick of her sullenness, sick of her brooding, sick of her rages, had finally moved in with his dental assistant, a pretty little strawberry blonde named Shirley who reminded them both of the actress Shirley Jones.

The car was hers, the house was hers.

The house was empty.

Five years since the less than three minutes that changed everything.

All she'd done was forget the newspaper—a simple event, an inconsequential event, everybody did it once in a while—and then go back for it and come out of the 7-Eleven and the car was there with the passenger door open and Alice wasn't. It had occurred with all the impact of a bullet or head-on collision and nearly that fast.

Her three-year-old daughter, gone. Vanished. Not a soul in the lot. And she, Helen Teal, *nee* Mazik, went from pre-school teacher, homemaker, wife and mother to the three *p*'s—psychoanalysis, Prozac and paralysis.

She took another sip of her martini. Not too much.

Just in case they came.

By nine-twenty-five *Third Rock* was wearing thin and she was considering a fourth and final dirty martini and then putting it to bed.

At nine-thirty a Ford commercial brought her close to tears.

There was this family, two kids in the back and mom and dad in front and they were going somewhere with mom looking at the map and the kids peering over her shoulder and though she always clicked the MUTE button during the commercials and couldn't tell what they were saying they were a happy family and you knew that.

To hell with it, she thought, one more, the goddamn night was practically breaking her heart here, and got up and went to the refrigerator.

She'd set the martini down and was headed for the hall to turn out the porch light, to give up the vigil, the night depressing her, the night a total loss finally, a total waste, when the doorbell rang.

She stepped back.

Teenagers, she thought. *Uh-oh.* They'd probably be the only ones out this late. With teenagers these days you never knew. Teens could be trouble. She turned and went to the window. The jack-o-lantern's jagged carved top was caving slowly down into its body. It gave off a half-cooked musky aroma that pleased her. She felt excited and a little scared. She leaned over the windowsill and looked outside.

On the porch stood a witch in a short black cloak, a werewolf in plaid shirt and jeans, and a bug-eyed alien. All wearing rubber masks. The alien standing in front by the doorbell.

Not teenagers.

Ten or eleven, tops.

Not the little ones she'd been hoping for all night long in their ghost-sheets and ballerina costumes. But kids. *Children.*

And the night's thrill—the *enchantment* even—was suddenly there for her.

She went to the door and opened it and her smile was wide and very real.

"Trick or treat!"

Two boys and a girl. She hadn't been sure of the alien.

"Happy Halloween!" she said.

"Happy Halloween," they chorused back.

The witch was giggling. The werewolf elbowed her in the ribs.

"Ow!" she said and hit him with her black plastic broom.

"Wait right here, kids," she said.

She knew they wouldn't come in. Nobody came in anymore. The days of bobbing for apples were long over.

She wondered where their parents were. Usually there were parents around. She hadn't seen them on the lawn or in the street.

She took the bowl of candy off the coffee table and returned to them standing silent and expectant at the door. She was going to be generous with them, she'd decided that immediately. They were the first kids to show, for one thing. Possibly they'd be the *only* ones to show. But these also weren't kids who came from money. You only had to take one look to see that. Not only were the three of them mostly skin and bones but the costumes were cheap-looking mass-market affairs—the kind you see in generic cardboard packages at Walgreen's. In the werewolf's case, not even a proper costume at all. Just a shirt and jeans and a mask with some fake fur attached.

"Anybody have any preferences, candy-wise?"

They shook their heads. She began digging into the candy and dropping fistfuls into their black plastic shopping bags.

"Are you guys all related?"

Nods.

"Brothers and sister?"

More nods.

The shy type, she guessed. But that was okay. Doing this felt just right. Doing this was fine. She felt a kind of weight lifted off her, sailing away through the clear night sky. If nobody else came by for the rest of the night that was fine too. Next year would be even better.

Somehow she knew that.

"Do you live around here? Do I know you, or your mom and dad maybe?"

"No, ma'am," said the alien.

She waited for more but more evidently wasn't forthcoming.

They really *were* shy.

"Well, I love your costumes," she lied. "*Very* scary. You have a Happy Halloween now, okay?"

"Thank you." A murmured chorus.

She emptied the bowl. Why not? she thought. She had more in the refrigerator just in case. *Lots* more. She smiled and said *Happy Halloween* again and stepped back and was about to close the door when she realized that instead of tumbling down the stairs on their way to the next house the way she figured kids would always do, all three of them were still standing there.

Could they possibly want more? She almost laughed. *Little gluttons.*

"You're her, right, ma'am?" said the alien.

"Excuse me?"

"You're her?"

"Who?"

"The lady who lost her baby? The little girl?"

And of course she'd heard it in her head before he even said it, heard it from the first question, knew it could be nothing else. She just needed to hear *him* say it, hear the *way* he said it and determine what was there, mockery or pity or morbid curiosity but his voice held none of that, it was flat and indeterminate as a newly washed chalkboard. Yet she felt as if he'd hit her anyhow, as though they all had. As though the clear blue eyes gazing up at her from behind the masks were not so much awaiting her answer as awaiting an execution.

She turned away a moment and swiped at the tears with the back of her hand and cleared her throat and then turned back to them.

"Yes," she said.

"Thought so," he said. "We're sorry. G'night, ma'am. Happy Halloween."

They turned away and headed slowly down the stairs and she almost asked them to wait, to stay a moment, for what reason and to what end she didn't know but that would be silly and awful too, no reason to put them through her pain, they were just kids, children, they were just asking a question the way children did sometimes, oblivious to its consequences and it would be wrong to say anything further, so she began to close the door and almost didn't hear him turn to his sister and say, *too bad they wouldn't let her out tonight, huh? too bad they never do* in a low voice but loud enough to register but at first it *didn't* register, not quite, as though the words held no meaning, as though the words were some strange rebus she could not immediately master, not until after she'd closed the door and then when finally they impacted her like grapeshot, she flung open the door and ran screaming down the stairs into the empty street.

She thought when she was able to think at all of what she might say to the police.

Witch, werewolf, alien. Of this age and that height and weight.

Out of nowhere, vanished back into nowhere.

Carrying along what was left of her.

Gone.

JOHN CROWLEY

An Earthly Mother
Sits and Sings

John Crowley won the World Fantasy Award for Little, Big, *an absolutely brilliant work of contemporary magical fiction. His other fine novels and story collections include* The Deep, Beasts, Engine Summer, Novelty, Aegypt, Love and Sleep, *and most recently,* Daemonomania.

The following little piece is a brief but crystalline retelling of the folk song "The Gray Selchie of Sule Skerry," about a seal man and a mortal maid on the rugged north coast of Scotland. It was published as a limited edition chapbook by DreamHaven Books in Minneapolis, with illustrations by Charles Vess.

—T. W.

W hen she turned away from the seaward windows and looked through the window that faced the rocky way leading down toward the village she could see that someone was coming up toward the house. He was having some difficulty; at times the rainy wind snatched away his cloak entirely and he seemed on the point of taking flight, but he hauled it in and wrapped it around himself again, and, pulling himself up on stones and planting his feet heavily, he made progress up toward her. The rippled diamond panes of the mullioned window, streaked with rain, made the little figure seem to shift size and nature continually; sometimes when the wind threw a might slew across the window he disappeared from view entirely, as though he had been drowned.

Cormac, she thought. He was coming all the way up from the village to tell her what she already knew: that was like him. She, who always knew first whatever happened in the surrounding country and on the sea, because her house stood high up above the village and surveyed not only the road that wound down from the bens to the east but the sea-road and the long spit of beach as well; she who had little to do but watch, anyway. Yet he would always come to her with the cold news. That a curragh, which had gone out with four brothers in it, had come back on the tide stove in and empty, and lay overturned on the beach. That a line of English soldiery was coming from the east, with pieces of ordnance and a man in armor at its head. "Yes, Cormac," she would say patiently, for she had seen them already at dawn, and counted their cannon, and seen the armor glint in the red sun. It was only that he loved her, not that he was an idle gossip; the fiction that he was bringing her news was understood by both of them for what it was, and she didn't dislike him for it. Yet she did feel, as she turned away from the window, a small irritation. Why hadn't he more sense than to climb up here uselessly in a storm?

Out the seaward windows she could see that the great ships were coming, helplessly, nearer the shore. The black, white-fringed waves rose so high that now and then the ships were lost to sight entirely, as though swamped and sunk already, but then they would appear again: one, a fleck of white sail only, far off; the other due west and straining to keep to the open sea; and the third, seeming to have surrendered to its awful fate, nearest the land, near enough for her to see the red crosses on its sails, and its shrouds torn away and waving rhythmically, or was it only the spray of rain cast off its spars as it creased the storm? The waves that bore it landward seemed to rise with an unreal slowness, like the great crushing waves that rose in her dreams; they seemed to rise endlessly, black glass circles with pools of froth, each one shattering against the tormented beach only at that last moment before its movement upward would become unceasing and it would rise up and drown the world.

She, who had watched the sea most of her life, had never seen a catastrophe anything like this one, had never seen the sea attempt to destroy men on such a scale. She had seen storms as bad, and worse, but they spent themselves against the land, which she knew could always bear it. And the sea even in a mood of mild petulance could kill the fishermen of the village, singly or in pairs, and suck their curraghs to its bottom; and then she would feel a sickening anger at the unfairness of the sea. But she had never seen ships the size of these galleons, like mansions put to sea. There would be dozens of men aboard them; she could see now, with a thrill of terror, that tiny men actually clung to the masts and rigging of the nearest ship, trying to cut loose the luffing sails large as meadows, and as the sea canted the ship over suddenly, one man was flung into the sea.

What should she feel? Pity for them? She couldn't. Horror at the destruction of the floating castles? The pride of them, even in destruction, forbade it. She could only watch, fascinated, the two monstrosities, sea and galleon, contend.

The same winds that carried the ships toward shore tormented the house, hooting in the chimney and rattling the windows in their frames. Small winds, wet and salt, were in the house, couldn't be kept out. In the silences which came momentarily when the wind turned around she could hear her father, in the loft, praying. *Ave Maria gratia plena Dominus tecum benedictas tu in mulieribus.* If her father died this night, that would be right; she, caught up in the vast wasting of human life by the sea and somehow fiercely indifferent, unable to feel pity or shock, wouldn't feel then at her father's death all the guilty anguish she had long expected to feel when at last his strong mad ghost gave up its body. She almost, wrapped in a sudden draft of cold sea air, almost wished for it.

The nearest galleon had begun to break up on the drowned stones of the

causeway that lay beyond the spit. Farther off, the seaward ship had lost its
battle, and, a loose sail flapping with slow grace like a handkerchief, swept down
toward the cliffy places to the south. The third she could no longer see. The sea
had thrown it away.

At the other end of the house the unbarred door was opened and shut again.
She felt a gust of wind that made her shiver.

"Bar the door, Cormac," she said. She turned with reluctance from the window
and went into the narrow tangle of hallway that led to the door. "You're a fool,
Cormac Burke," she said, not quite as gently as she had intended, "to come all
the way up here in this weather, and to tell me about the ships, is it?"

She stopped then, because the man who turned to face her from barring the
door wasn't Cormac Burke. She didn't know him. The water coursing down his
mantle and the brim of his hat spattered rapidly on the floor; there was a puddle
around his booted feet, and when he stepped toward her the boots made a
sodden sound.

"Who are you?" she said, stepping back.

"Not the one you named. One very wet."

They stood facing each other for a long moment. In the darkness of the hall
she couldn't see his face. His Irish had a Scotch intonation, and sounded wet as
well, as though the water had got into his throat.

"Might I," he said at last, "claim some hospitality of this house? A fire, if you
have such a thing? I wouldn't trouble you long." He held up both hands, slowly,
as though to show he wasn't armed. The two hands seemed to glow faintly in
the dark hall, as silver objects or certain sea-shells do in dimness.

She came to herself, "Yes, come in," she said. "Warm yourself. I didn't mean
to refuse the house."

He stripped off his wet mantle, heavy with water, and followed her into the
comparative warmth and light of the main room of the house. He stood a moment looking around him, seeming to take inventory of the place, or as though
trying to remember if he had ever been in it before. Then he went to the chimney corner and hung his mantle and hat on a peg there.

"We get few guests," she said.

"I think that's odd," he said. His hair was lank and gray, and his face was
white like his hands, though now in the light of the fire and the rushes they
seemed not to glow spectrally as they had in the hall. His eyes were large and
pale and with some melancholy humorousness in them that was disconcerting.

"Odd? We're far off the traveled roads. It's a long climb up."

"But it's the finest house nearby. A traveler who put out the effort might be
likely to find more than a cup of water for himself."

She ought to have resented this calculation, but she couldn't, he said it so
frankly. "You must be a skilled traveler then," she said.

"Oh, I am."

"And from where?"

He said a mouth-filling Scotch name she didn't recognize and said his name
was Sorley.

"A kinsman of Sorley Boy?"

"No, not of that clan," he said with a faint smile that made her wonder if he
was lying, and then wonder why she wondered. "And what's your name?"

"Ineen," she said, and looked away.

"And right too," he said, for Ineen is only "girl" in Irish.

"Ineen Fitzgerald," she said. To another that would have stopped further inquiry. She felt it wouldn't with this Sorley; and in fact he asked her what one with such a name did living in this northwestern place.

"There's a tale in that," she said, and turned away to the window again. The Spanish ship was stove in now, the breach in its side was evident, it was shipping water and seemed to pant like a dying bull as it rose and fell on the foamy waves. There was a flotsam, boards, barrels. Did men cling to them? With a sudden fear she realized that the sea might not take them all, not all those dozens. Some might live, and gain the beach. Spanish men. Spanish soldiers. What would happen then?

"They are only men after all," said Sorley.

So intent was she, had she been all that day, on the ships that she didn't find it odd that he seemed to have read her thoughts.

"All up and down the coast," he said, "from Limerick to Inishowen, they've been putting in, or trying to; breaking up, most of them. Most of the men drowning."

"Why have they come? Why so many?"

"No reason of their own. They never wanted to. They meant to sail and conquer England. The sea and the wind drove them here."

She turned to him. The fire behind him seemed to edge his gray hair with light, to give him a faint, wavering outline.

"How do you come to know so much of it?" Ineen asked him.

"Travel with eyes and ears open."

"You came up from the south, then."

He answered nothing to this. The wind rose to a sudden shriek, and the rain made a fierce hissing in the thatch of the roof. Outside, something loose, a bucket, a rake, went blowing across the yard, making a noise that startled her. In the loft, her father groaned and began the Commination: *Cursed be he that putteth his trust in Man, that taketh Man for his salvation . . .*"

Sorley looked up toward the dimness of the loft. "What others are in the house?"

"My father. Ill." Mad and dying, the word meant. "Servants. Gone down now to the beach, to watch the ships."

"When the Spanish come on the beach, they will be murdered. Half-drowned they'll come out of the sea and each be struck by a mattock or an axe, or be stoned or sworded to death, till all those not drowned will be just as dead." He said all this calmly and with certainty, as though it had already happened, perhaps years ago. "Ill luck to come up out of the sea, alive, and speak no Irish."

"They never would!" She—a Geraldine, a Norman, of the oldest and highest Norman aristocracy Ireland had, however she might have fallen—had no illusions about the villagers below her; but to murder the Spanish, their true friends, only because they were Spanish—that was too monstrous, too ridiculously savage. Sorley only smiled, his thin fixed smile; she had begun to think he smiled only the way hawks frowned, out of his nature somehow and not his mood.

"Would you have anything to eat?" he said. "I seem to have come a long way on yesterday's dinner."

Called to herself again, reminded of how inhospitable she'd grown in her long exile, she blushed, and went to see what might be in the house. On an impulse she drew a jug of red wine from one of the remaining tuns. When she returned with this, and some herring and a loaf, he was sitting on a stool by the fire, looking at his long pale hands.

"You see how much sea has blown in today," he said. She looked more closely, and saw that his hands were dusted with a fine white glowing powder. "Salt," he said. His face was dusty the same way. She accepted his reason for this without thinking that, while stones and driftwood left long in the sea may become salt-encrusted like that, she had never been, though she often spent whole days walking in sea-spray along the beach. She brought him a bowl of water, and he dipped his hands into it; it seemed to hiss faintly. When he withdrew them wet, they had again become glistening and faintly opalescent.

"Now it's sea-water in the bowl," he said. "Look into it, Ineen Fitzgerald."

She did look in, apprehensive and not knowing why. The bowl was old dark crockery, thick and cracked. For a strange moment she did seem to see the whole sea, as though she were a gull, or God, looking down on it; the ripples Sorley's hands had made in it lapped its edge as tides lap the edges of the world. She saw something moving over the face of the waters, indistinct and multiform, as though the creatures might be rising to look up at her as she looked down; then she saw it was only a faint reflection of her own face.

She laughed, and looked at Sorley, who was smiling more broadly. Her apprehension was gone. She felt as if she had been playing a children's game with him, and it seemed to make an intimacy between them; an elation almost like the elation of nakedness, of childhood games played naked. It was the same fierce indifferent elation she had felt watching the ships. She was vaguely aware that a charm had been worked on her, a charm like the charm in fast sea breezes and scudding cloud, a charm to make her free.

Stop it now, mad girl, she told herself, too much alone, stop all that. She pulled her shawl around her. Sorley ate herring and bread, delicately, as though he didn't need it for sustenance. He poured wine into a battered cup and tasted it.

"Canary," he said. "And fine, too."

Without really considering it, she took a cup for herself and filled it. "What do you do abroad, Sorley?" she said.

"Looking for a wife, Ineen Fitzgerald," he said, and drank.

I am a man upon the land

On the beach, Cormac Burke stared helplessly at the oblique lines of waves folding together and dashing against the beach with a noise like a rising but never climaxing peal of thunder. His voice was raw from shouting against it. A few shards and pieces were still coming in on the tide: a window-frame, a barrel-stave. Strung out across the beach in tight, self-defensive knots, the villagers ran from one to another of these treasures and exclaimed over them.

He had tried to organize them into a troop of sorts, armed men in front, then other men, the women to salvage, a priest for the dying. Hopeless. He had tried to explain to them that there were three things that must be done: aid should be given to the hurt; the goods should be rounded up and put in piles; the soldiers must be disarmed and, for the moment, made prisoner, for the English would certainly see them as invaders and any Irish who helped them as rebels. Their arms could be taken from them and hidden; later . . . But it was useless. The sea was mad; and there was no organizing these kerns. They went their own way.

On the beach, now nearly covered in sand, lay three—four—bodies. If he had not known them to be Spaniards he wouldn't now as darkness came on have known they were men. But he knew; he had rushed toward them with the others when they came tumbling from the sea, staggering up like apes from the withdrawing water. They had reached out hands to him: *Auxilio. Succoro, Señores.* And the Irishmen with him, crying out like animals, their faces distended so that he seemed not to know them at all, had murdered them; had almost murdered Cormac when he tried to stop them.

Now he stood farther off, afraid to watch any longer to see more Spaniards come ashore, knowing he would not again try to interfere in the villagers' madness, yet unable to leave. If he had a gun. Tears of frustration and helpless rage mixed with the rain clouding his vision. He turned away from the sea and looked up to where, just raising itself above a coign of rock, the roof of the Fitzgeralds' house could be seen. Was there a light burning? He thought there was.

And what did you do when they came ashore, Cormac?

I could do nothing, and the Spanish were murdered, Ineen.

He pulled his feet from the muddy sand and began to work his way down the shingle, watching the sea and the knots of men, and, far off, the ship, whose masts were now parallel to the slabs of sea that bore it up.

Little ken I my bairn's father

It wasn't the wine, not entirely; though when she went to draw another jug she noticed that her lips and nose itched a little, growing numb, and that filling the jug she was slapdash; she spoke aloud to herself, saying she shouldn't have babbled on to this stranger, and laughed.

She had told him about her father, who had been a priest, and was a cousin of the Earl of Kildare, and how the English had persuaded him to come into the new dispensation and he would be made a bishop by the Queen; how he did so, despite all his kin's hatred of him for it; how he renounced his vows and the True Church, and married the frail daughter of an English lord in Dublin.

And was it that his family hated him for it; or that his wife despised him and lived in a continual state of loathing and shock at Irish ways and the Irish until she died, soon after Ineen was born, leaving her loathing behind her, solid as furniture; or that after their promises, and in spite of a hundred letters her father sent to London, and twenty visits to Dublin, the English never began raising her father toward the promised bishopric, not so much as a wardenship—apparently satisfied that promises had been enough to draw him out of his church; or was it that in the end he had lost even the false and empty parish the English had given him, where he preached to nearly nobody, because at last Desmond—his distant cousin too—rose up against the English and heresy, and her father had to be taken off by sea lest he be hanged by his flock: was it that terrible story, or was it God's vengeance at his defection, that had made him mad? The English, as though tossing him away, had placed him in this northern isolation and given him a piece of the wine trade—wine! that with his breath he had once altered in its red heart to the blood of Jesus!—and let him live on a tariff he collected, a useless middle-man. Was all that enough to make him mad? Or was God's vengeance needed?

"It hasn't made you mad, Ineen," Sorley said, and she saw that the story had washed over him without altering his features. "And Desmond is dead, who fought for Mother Church. Whose vengeance was that, then?"

She returned now with the brimming jug, and Sorley saluted it with his cup. She filled the cups; two drops splashed out and stained the linen of her sleeve as quick as blood. She dipped the sleeve in the bowl of water, pressing water through it absently. "I wouldn't like to drown," she said. "Not of any way."

"Avoid the sea."

"They say men drowning can see treasures lost in the sea—ships sunk, gold, jewels."

"Do they? And do they have candles with them to light up the darkness?"

She laughed, wiping her mouth. Her father cried out, dreaming; a sob, as though someone were stifling him with a pillow. Another cry, louder. He called her name; he was awake. She waited a moment, feeling vaguely ashamed. Maybe he would sleep again. But again he called her name, his voice edged now with that piteous panic she knew well, which grated on her senses like a rasp. "Yes, father," she said gently, and went to the press in the corner, from which she took a jar of powder; some of this she mixed into a cup of wine, and, having lit a rushlight at the fire, carried the wine and the light carefully up into the loft.

Her father's white face looked out from the bed curtains, his white cap and large pinkish eyes making him look like a terrified rabbit looking out from its burrow.

"Who is it in the house?" he whispered urgently. "Cormac?"

"Yes," she said, "only Cormac."

She had him drink the wine, and kissed him, and said a prayer with him; then when he groaned again she laid him firmly down, speaking calmly but with authority, as she might to a child. He lay back on the pillows, his stricken eyes still searching her face. She smiled, and drew his curtains.

Sorley sat unchanged by the fire, turning his cup in his fingers.

Why had she lied to her father?

"They say too," she said, taking a gulp of wine, "that there's a bishop under the sea. A fish bishop." She had seen a picture in a bestiary of her father's.

"Certainly," Sorley said. "To marry and bury."

"What rites does he use, do you think?"

"And the mackerel is the fish's bawd. Men!" He shook his head, smiling. "They think even the fish live by the laws they live by. A little handful of folk, huddled up on the dry land that's not a tenth part of the size of the seas, and dreaming of bishops for the fish."

"How is it, then, in the sea?" she said, for some reason not doubting he knew.

"Come with me and see," he said.

Far less the land that he goes in

Where they went, that night, was not seaward though. Cold as his touch was, it was strong, and she would not have been able to resist it even if she'd chosen to do that, which she did not choose. She thought to press her hand against his mouth so that he would not cry aloud, but he was not one who cried aloud.

She slept like one dead, and he was gone when she awoke, and her father too, calling from the loft, but she paid him no mind, and got up; felt run down the inside of her thigh a dribble of slime she thought might be blood, but no, she hadn't bled.

He was not gone far. How she knew it she could not have said. She wrapped herself in a warm mantle and went out into the day, where the storm-wrack still filled the sky and the sea. The ship she had watched could still be seen, dismasted and in fragments clinging to the rocks like unswallowed fragments in a mastiff's mouth. She went down along the way to the beach, and it wasn't long before she saw him striding ahead of her, holding his hat on his head for the offshore breeze. She passed the place where last night the men from the Spanish ship had come ashore; their bodies lay dark and shapeless as seals, half-buried in sand: no place a human soul could rest; they must be buried as Christian men, whatever. She would ask Cormac Burke to help.

He had not turned at all to look at the bodies of the men on the beach, kept on till the turn of the cove and the flat rocks that went out into the sea, where the seals did sometimes lie to bake their cold bodies. He was after tossing away his hat, and then his cloak, and when he came to the rocks he was as naked as he had been in her bed in the night. And when he bent to reach into the seaweed and the crusted stones wedged in the great split of the rocks and found something there to don, she knew whom she had had in her. She had known all along, but now she knew to see and to think: to think what would come of this, now and in the months and years to come.

> And he has tae'en a purse of gold
> And he has placed it on her knee
> Saying "Give to me my little young son
> And take thee up thy nurse's fee.
>
> "And though shalt marry a gunner good
> And a right fine gunner I'm sure he'll be
> And the very first shot that e'er he shoot
> Shall kill both my young son and me."

DAWN KARIMA PETTIGREW

Atasdi: Fish Story

Dawn Karima Pettigrew received a B.A. from Harvard University, an M.F.A. from Ohio State University, and is pursuing a doctorate from the University of Kentucky. Her work has appeared in numerous journals and anthologies, including Red Ink, Oklahoma Indian Times, Wicazo Sa, The Mythic Midwest, The Urban Midwest, Gatherings, *and* Twenty-five and Under: Fiction. *She is also an ordained minister serving the Qualla boundary reservation in Cherokee, North Carolina, and a correspondent for* News From Indian Country.

"Atasdi: Fish Story" is wonderfully rich in language, character, and magical imagery, particularly for a story of its brevity. It is reprinted from Through the Eye of the Deer: An Anthology of Native American Women Writers, *edited by Carolyn Dunn and Carol Comfort (Aunt Lute Books, San Francisco). Pettigrew is a writer of Cherokee/Creek/Chickasaw/Choctaw and other Native descent.*

—T. W.

I have never again eaten a fish. I owe them a debt and plan to pay. North Carolina trout have nothing to fear from me. So you want to hear a fish story, that takes some doing.

Some men have wealth. Others own land. Jack StandsStraight, my daddy, had Tennessee Jane. Tennessee Jane came at the end of the middle, where it is hard enough to be noticed, let alone first at much of anything. Even though God left her between our big sister Carolina and myself, He blessed her with a spectacular beauty. Young men dreamed dreams and old men hid and watched until Tennessee Jane grew up.

Tennessee Jane was useless. She never could cook and refused to learn. She wandered the roads between Cherokee and Birdtown, watching for the tear of a seam in the sky. Daddy let her alone, since daydreaming looks an awful lot like virtue and virtue in girls like Tennessee Jane is just the thing that makes bankers, doctors, even Hollywood come calling with blankets and cash money. My sister's smile on fire from heaven, stirred in with her tendency to chase after Jesus, were better for Daddy than an old-age retirement policy.

Me, I make things happen. It rains when I pray, thunders when I tantrum. I dream about ordering a bushel basket of rattlesnakes, then rebuking them, just for the practice. My cool hands cross broken bodies, reclaim hurt limbs from odd angles, pressing them into another day of service. Daddy calls me the daughter that made herself out of his last chance for a son.

People talk like life is solid, but it's not. Life is fluid as clear water, only harder to catch. There are moments when we dam it up, send it streaming a different way, and then wonder when the water falls into other folks' lives. That's how I see it. About half the time, a body isn't living just their own life, but swimming in somebody else's spillover.

How Tennessee Jane ended up hurt by the GoingBack boy is just like that. Daddy sent me everywhere with my older sister, made me watch over her. Keep her pure, he'd say, don't let her scratch her long legs on rocks or mar up her pretty face. Entertain her so she don't look out too far toward the world or take up with strangers. So you can imagine me, tearing through the woods, screaming for my sister, carried off by the GoingBack boy, the middle boy, not even the oldest, who had gone to the service and learned a trade, but the middle boy, who near as I could figure, had a way with cars, but couldn't write his name.

Daddy searched, took all nine of his brothers with him. Drove clear over to Sylva and Waynesville and back up to Bryson. Never did find them.

"You lost me my future," Daddy said squarely. He stared into his coffee, into the round eyes of eggs that Carolina fried. "If you want a place to stay other than the street, you get it back."

Now, you can judge me if you want. It's easy to convict a body of all kinds of things. What I did may not have been all right, but you tell me, if you had been thirteen and not much to look at, wouldn't you have done pretty much the same thing?

Wore my shoes out searching the mountains. Stumbled through Yellowhill and Soco. Wrapped my feet in cold ashes and cotton and kept on. The rising of the sun and setting came and went seventy-seven times as I walked the mountains, checked every cove. Didn't find her.

Funny how most of your prayers get answered on the way home. Following the Oconaluftee River back toward our homeplace, I noticed a red ribbon of blood in the water. I ran against the river, upstream and into my sister. At least the leavings of her.

Tennessee Jane's magnificent face was swollen with water. Her eyes were inked with bruises. I pressed my hands against her torn fingers, matching every inch of her body with one of mine.

"Please don't be dead," I begged. "God, please." My tears watered my sister's eyes. I whispered every name of God.

Tennessee Jane whimpered. I rejoiced. That is, until I looked up and there was Isaac Earl GoingBack sitting on the far side of the bank. Fishing.

It is something what a body can do mad. My sister's broken body felt like a sack of down across my back. I would carry her home, away from hands that shatter bone. As I turned, there was Isaac Earl GoingBack, fishing away, like he hadn't wronged Tennessee Jane one bit.

"Someday, Isaac Earl GoingBack," I whispered, "you will catch a fish that will talk to you."

The rest of it, I heard this way. Isaac Earl caught a fish that day. Swam right alongside him and jumped up onto the shore, clear into the bucket.

"I don't want to catch you," Isaac Earl said.

"Well, you did," replied the fish, just as natural as if fish are prone to talking all the time.

So Isaac Earl picked him up, going against everything in his natural mind. Stopped by his mama's house and asked her to clean his trout.

"No, sir." There went the fish chit-chatting again, which surprised Isaac Earl's mama something terrible. "You caught me, now you clean me."

Isaac Earl's hands moved themselves. Scales and bones spread blood across his no-account fingers and onto the floor. Isaac Earl asked his mama, who can't hardly move for horror, to cook the fish for him.

"Excuse me, but no." There goes that fish speaking out again. "You cleaned me, now you cook me."

Isaac Earl's mama says she never will forget the pain on her son's face as he floured and fried that fish. She said it was as if he was watching his own self work, not wanting to and still doing it.

"Mama!" Isaac Earl cried out, realizing that this fish wasn't no ordinary one. "Mama, come eat this fish with me!" Like that would keep him from getting his comeuppance.

Isaac Earl's mama couldn't budge. The fish cleared its throat and sighed.

"No," it answered. "You know you cooked me. You better eat me."

Isaac Earl choked on the first bite. Fell down dead as dead gets in the middle of the floor.

They laid him in the ground Tuesday evening. Tennessee Jane woke on Wednesday morning with the face of an angel. Married a Holiness preacher, and they took Daddy circuit riding with them. I get along pretty good, tend to my business. I'm in church now, but people still stay out of my way. I never go fishing.

You asked for a fish story and there it is. Things have a way of working out one way or the other. Life is like that. You always catch the fish that you deserve.

AMY WACK

Tooth Fairy and The Sandman

Amy Wack was born in Florida, raised in California, and attended the writing program at Columbia University in New York City. She currently lives in Cardiff, Wales, where she is poetry editor for Seren Books and reviews editor for Poetry Wales *magazine. Her delightful poems, "Tooth Fairy" and "The Sandman," first appeared in* Agenda, *vol.37, number 4.*

—T. W.

Tooth Fairy

Not Titania or Tinkerbell, not minute
with dragonfly wings a dimple,
but fleshly and glamorously, her hair,
a blonde waterfall, her breath, a mint
chill. She moves like Ginger Rodgers
in that white feather dress she wore to
dance with Fred Astaire in Top Hat.
Perfume sizzles on her skin, she eats
candyfloss and drinks gin with a twist
poured over diamond-shards of ice.
She's uncanny as a ghost or alien,
and strangely craven, this apparition,
color of the cloud's bright lining.
But to a small child she is an angel,
almost a mother, an aura, an air,
her song higher than the mosquito,
her touch invisible, beneficent, pure.
Her coins glitter as they fall to the pillow.
She fingers each small tooth like a jewel,
puts it in a silken sack that she slings

over her wings as she dissipates like mist.
What does she do with them all?
They warm her throat like pearls,
they fasten her dress, stud her shoes,
spark in circlets on her wrists and gleam
in the spikes of her tiara like a smile.
Somewhere there must be a white throne
in a white palace, in a white city,
—all a vast unholy mosaic of milk-teeth.
She waits there for her lover to finish
his equally huge and punishing shift.
She calls to him softly, "Hey, Sandman."

Sandman

At first he is bodiless, roomy as a dune
or stretch of shoreline, fluid as grains
in an hourglass. At dusk he arises,
assumes his shape: tall, suave, blonde,
austere, and with the wryest of smiles.
He is underplayed by an Englishman
like Leslie Howard or Alec Guinness.
Stoic, heroic, like Capt. Oates in a crisis,
he may step outside and be some time.
She wears whatever merges with shadow:
suits of black cashmere, sand-washed
silk skirts the color of storm-clouds
with no cuffs to catch the sand spills,
shoes with a dull polish of carbon,
nothing that shines or catches the light,
except his silver hip flask of whiskey
(each sip is smooth like a fiery honey).
He eats proscuitto, slivers of red flesh
on the thinnest and saltiest of crackers.
He's got a job to do, to procure the sand,
his special recipe, his own admixture
of potent and subtle opiates refined
almost to dust. He needs a ton of it
each night, pours it into burlap sacks
and sets off for where the earth's edge
dips into shadow. He'll sprinkle a pinch
into your eyes at the brink of sleep.
Almost an angel, harbinger of dreams,
he's not invisible, but you'll never see him.
He slips off as you head for oblivion,
leaving a gift of grit in your tear-duct.

LEONE ROSS

Tasting Songs

Leone Ross is the author of two fine novels: Orange Laughter *and* All the Blood is Red, *the latter of which was short-listed for the 1997 Orange Prize for Women. Her short fiction has been published in anthologies in England and Canada.*

"Tasting Songs," like much of Ross's work, draws upon the author's English-Jamaican heritage. This lush, beautifully written tale of contemporary fantasy first appeared in Dark Matter: A Century of Speculative Fiction from the African Diaspora, *edited by Sheree R. Thomas (Warner Aspect).*

—T. W.

At the time, the only problem I had sleeping with another woman in my wife's bed was the sweat.

I make no apologies for the affair. No, actually, that's not true. I apologize, even today. When I say that, I don't mean the days that screamed with silence, when all you could hear in our house was the click-click of Sasha's heels and the taunt of her zippers, her snap fastenings, swear I could even hear her fingers against the buttons of her shirts as she walked around me, "through" me, dressing, sitting in front of the fridge spearing cold akee and saltfish into her mouth because she didn't have the energy to cook, packing Jake's little bag, all in awful silence, handing him, wordless, to her sister, whose disapproving back called out to me as she left with my son, yelling, "Adulterer, adulterer," with every self-righteous step, as Sasha turned back to the battle, one only she could win. I don't mean the sound of my pleas that eventually became whimpers and soared into shouting and then dipped down to the indignity of whispered pleas once more, begging her to forgive me, "Please, just talk to me, say anything, I'm sorry, I'm so sorry, Sash." I don't mean any of those things. I mean the apology inside of me. To Sasha and to Brianna. To both of them.

I'm putting this all down, sitting on the veranda of our new house. For Jake, I think. He should know, and I realize that having him read it as an addendum to our will is a damned cowardly way, but I can think of no other.

This is still the new house to me, even though we've been here twenty years; Jake departed for college two years ago. Jake, do you dream of this house? When my subconscious pulls down images of home, it always chooses the old house, the house of my own childhood, the one my mother left for me. On Hope Road, the dogs howling over the fence, cats mating at night, bunches of hibiscus laden with crazed humming-birds, clumps of love bush, splayed in orange chaos across the hedges at the front, a difficult driveway that Sasha could never reverse into. But my son's dreams must be strident with this new house, the only one he's ever known, the place where his parents embarrassed him by laying their hands on each other, even in their disgraceful forties. When he comes out from Miami on Spring Break I see him watch ghosts here: ghosts of himself, hurting his knees and knuckles, playing marbles, doing homework.

But it's still the new house to me; it reveals none of my childhood. Or my sins.

It's the house Sasha insisted on, after Brianna. "Number One," she said. "I can never live in this old house," she said. "I don't care if you first walked here and your fucking mother breastfed you here. Buy a new one." I remember those words because they were the first ones she said to me after she found me and Brianna grappling like lost animals in her bed, the sheets stinking with good-byes. Sasha made it clear: "Moving out of this house is the first step. And then I will think about me and you." I could smell victory; I blew my savings on a deposit immediately, put the old house on the market, bought new furniture, decorated. Sasha would have nothing to do with it. It was penance. She swigged Red Stripe and watched me pack our clothes, wrangle on the phone with estate agents, laying one imperious, broken nail on the fabric swatches I placed before her, a yes or a no handed down from her hurt high. My patience and sorrow were tested in those weeks, with the inquiring looks from decorators who could not understand how a man with broad shoulders could walk on glass around his matchbox wife. She's small, Sasha. Small with a strength that makes her taller than me, and if you strike her, she burns.

She said that she could smell the sweat everywhere, that it was like some oil slick that had infected the old house, as if the liquid had touched each surface, had dived into her underwear drawer, insidious in the folds of frothy G-strings and off-white panties for long-gone heavy period days, as if it poured itself among the cutlery and evaporated into the air, contaminating her. I told her that Brianna only ever came to the house that one time, but she didn't believe me. There were times when I found her washing herself like a woman after rape, scrubbing at her skin until brown was red, watching Brianna disappear down the plug hole of the sunken shower, then reinfecting herself as she stepped onto the bath mat. And, of course, the photographs had to go. God help me, it hurt to destroy them. Simply, some of the most inspired work I've ever done, seasoned with desire and the eroticism of guilt. "How would you feel if I fucked someone else, Jerry?" She said it to me conversationally, our second day in the new house, Jake playing with a star-covered mobile in his cot, her moving closer to him, despite herself, smiling at his first smiles that were really gas. Yes, a casual tone, over my son: "I should. I should go to one of Lillian's sick parties and fuck the first man I meet. Can you see that in your mind's eye, Jerry? Sure you can. That's Number Two. Picture it for me." Sasha. She knows me, and she says it like it is. I suppose that I understand why her first words came out of her sore, and why they hurt my ears. She could see the way I coveted Brianna. I still, yes, even now, feel an old stirring when I think of Brianna, her body, the way she moved, my inability to bring her peace.

I was twenty-eight, and we'd been married for a year. I left my wife for weeks at a time, to work. It was June, hot, but less than ninety degrees in the shade, when I returned to Jamaica and her from a harried, thirsty tour of Central America, rolls of film stuffed into every orifice. They were full of female pulchritude: a woman who told me she couldn't remember her age, who covered her face the first three times I spoke to her, whose wrinkles I made into journeys; her daughter, blind, who lived on her tiptoes and the money she made kissing men; a twelve-year-old with burnt sienna skin and eerie eyes, yellow and green, like a cat's, that she rolled back until there was nothing there but the whites, a habit from childhood days when she was teased as a *temba*, a goddess fallen from the sky; another girl whose face had been torn apart by jealous acid. It's my gift: to hold up women's beauty and show it to them, to revisit the faces and breasts and feet that they'd judged wanting, old, withered, not enough, too much, and have them see them anew. And they cleaved to me, eagerly, afraid, I suppose, that they'd forget that they were beautiful once I was gone.

My mother often told me that my sweet mouth would get me into trouble, that no love followed a man whose lips dripped honey. My mother died having only ever seen one photograph that I'd taken of her, despite my irritation: She said it frightened her enough. I'd made her beautiful after a lifetime of "You never gwine get a man, man goin' breed you an' lef' you fe pretty gyal, yes him ah beat you, but tek it an' pray, after all, where you gwine get one next man?"— all about my father, an empty soul, defined only by his fine Chinese origins that he wore as if he'd made them himself, and his splendid cruelty to my mother. And to me. Years of blood and invisibility. But I don't want to talk about that.

I met Brianna at one of Lillian's parties. I remember that I walked up to the door and laughed. It was covered with purple balloons and silver condoms: someone's idea of convenience and questionable humor. I pushed it open and played Name That Drug as weed and coke competed with the smell of women's thighs and the orange peel that simmered in oil-filled, antique vats. Along the brittle corridor, couples kissed and groped, twisting hands in the shadow of thighs, their laughter and moans tinkling on the air. One man, resplendent in a heart-shaped eye patch, pushed peach chiffon aside to bite his partner's neck under the dark ceiling. Somewhere, bass buzzed insidiously.

As I walked through the house, groups of beautiful people chatted and paused to nod at me; a woman masturbated in a far-off corner, her groans unheard by the rest; a man lifted a sodden mouth from his companion's vagina and waved. He was the only person I recognized; I'd taken pictures of him in the moonlight last year, his two-year-old son in his arms, his love for the child marred only by my knowledge of his promiscuity. I'd spent three months in the company of Jamaica's high-red, most debauched crowd, all happy to be captured on film by a young, up-and-coming, feted, new photographer. They'd amused me, and I'd amused Sasha, telling her the outrageous gossip I collected every night. She wasn't interested in that kind of scene. As I stood in the middle of the bacchanalia, I breathed deeply, trying to get clean air into my lungs, regretting my decision to come. It was the kind of place that made me stop feeling.

Lillian passed me by, and stopped to air-kiss my cheeks. She was so covered in gold that she clanked as she moved: countless gold loops fell down her face; they were in her eyebrows, her cheeks, lips, and ears, drowning her delicate throat. Bracelets, like sand-colored spaghetti hoops, dangled from her arms, and twisted bunches of jewels glinted around both ankles. I wasn't surprised when she opened her mouth and gave me a glimpse of rubies, embedded in her teeth like flecks of ketchup.

"Nice to see you, Jerry," she purred.

"And you're as gorgeous as usual, Lil." I felt like squinting in her opulence.

"Not as gorgeous as you, baby!" She slipped a hand between us and squeezed me. "Want to take some pictures of me later?" I murmured an excuse; she wanted me as a lover, but I was a good boy, my wife's boy, and embarrassingly faithful. Besides, I had all the pictures I wanted of Lillian.

She was a shallow woman, made even worse by her overt sexuality. Those were the days when I liked to chase the mystery of a woman, when obvious was no challenge for my art.

"Another time, eh?" She grinned, undefeated, and then clapped her hands. The busy, frenzied lovers around us paused in their play and looked up. She spread her arms. "This evening's entertainment will begin in five minutes. By the pool."

Brianna sat on the steps of the swimming pool, her hands, skirt, and bare feet soaked in water. We gathered around her, our fashionable cynicism held like a weapon before us. I wondered what she was doing there. She was too clean for us.

She was the barest woman I've ever seen. Her fragile skull was nearly bald, newly shaved. She wore no makeup, no jewelry. Her skin was enough decoration, buffed and unblemished, like squeaky, gleaming leather. It was as if she'd never played as a child, never skinned her knee, or eaten too-green mangoes and stained herself on their flesh, as if she'd never brushed a market woman's arm, taking with her the rebellion or camaraderie of daily higglering. She was very still. A man called out, "What a pretty gyal, to rass!" crinkling her brow with what looked like embarrassment. I'm sure my mouth was open. My fingers itched. I wanted to squeeze her for juice.

The night lay down on us as Brianna Riley began to sing. A slice of moon soared above the trees as the sound of her took me back to my childhood bed, the pillows soaked with sweat and tears as my father denounced my dreams. I let her stretch her gift along the length of my spine, pausing to touch each bone, sweeping around to cup her music to my face, the sound of her filling my eyes, kicking at the cotton clouds, silencing the crickets. Jamaicans, as she would have known, are a demanding audience, but in the middle of the seediness, we were suddenly, pathetically eager. She was that good. She pushed our facades aside with her gentle, crooning melody and she reminded me of drunken Christmas cake on a Sunday morning, of cricket matches in perfect whites, of children on their way home from church, of tamarind balls searing the mouth, of Chinese skipping in Kingston playgrounds. Three men shambled from the poolside and fled to the parking lot. I could hear the rumble of their car engines as her voice fell silent. I clapped until my fingertips felt scalded, and watched as the island's strangest elite surround her like mosquitoes.

Later that evening, Lillian and I entertained her, long after the last of the crowd slipped away. She listened to us intently, balanced in the middle of the pool, her elbows on a plastic float. Her dress drifted around her, like a huge lily. Her big, seal eyes flickered over us both.

"Lillian is the one who gave me the money to do my demo tapes," she said. Her speaking voice was pleasant, but normal. I restrained my disbelief; I didn't know Lillian to be a generous woman. I glanced at our hostess. Surely she could tell that this woman would never become part of her sordid little circle of adorers.

"And now you have a deal?" I asked.

"Yes. Well . . . almost. Warner Brothers are very interested," she said.

"Of course they are. She's so cute!" said Lillian. I wanted to swat her, like a fly.

"They like my . . . voice." She stopped. I noticed that she half answered, or ignored questions, as if she was unused to idle chitchat. "Jerry, can I ask you about your parents' background? You have a very . . . interesting . . . look."

"My father is a Chinese Jamaican and my mother is Indian and black. Hence the eyes." She tilted her head.

"Yes, my dear, Jerry is our favorite onlooker," said Lillian. "We all want him, but he won't play our little games with wifey at home." Her laughter disturbed the pool water. "I must check the locks." She rose, tinkling.

Brianna looked dismayed. "Oh—I'll go. I'm keeping you from your bed. I'm so sorry." She reached out a long, sinuous arm and paddled to the poolside, shot me a look that I didn't understand. "It's just nice to talk. . . ." I watched her take a breath before she stepped out of the water. "Could I call a taxi?"

Lillian shook her head. "No, no. Stay if you want. . . ."

"I can take you home," I said.

I watched her struggle. "All right," she said, finally.

In my car, after she'd dried and changed, she was silent. I made up for it, coaxing laughter from her like a pathetic court jester, driving as slowly as I could. I didn't want the night to end. I nearly crashed into a tattered goat strolling through Half Way Tree in my efforts to watch her and drive at the same time. She was so calm, even regal, and yet she'd carelessly taken Lillian's monogrammed towel with her, holding it in her lap as if it were a purse.

We reached her home too quickly. I followed her out, making sure that she was safe. Dawdled at the door, looking for the words to delay her. I can honestly say that in that moment, I became two men. One, the faithful husband, a man I pushed aside. The other, totally led by desire. I wanted to kiss Brianna until sunrise, because she looked like the kind of woman who would have liked that. I gestured at the towel. "Lillian will want that back," I joked.

"Oh, yes. I'll . . . take it to her." She twisted the damp cloth in her hands. I could tell that she wanted to stay, and yet something greater urged her away.

"I could come back and take you up there," I offered inanely.

"No. No. I'll do it."

Desperately, I reached through the bullshit.

"Brianna. I'm a photographer. Would you consider . . ."

She looked alarmed. "No, I don't like taking photographs. I'm sorry. I have to go."

I sat in the car outside her house for half an hour, imagining her under my lens.

I said at the beginning that I make no apologies. What I meant was that I make no excuses. I drove home fantasizing. I hugged my wife. My sexual interest in Brianna had nothing to do with Sasha. Women will dismiss this as cliché, but I know it's one of those clichés that is utterly true. I can understand why women feel betrayed by the deceit of infidelity, how conned they feel at a change of plan, of structure, without their being involved, how their men change the rules, lie, dip, dive, curve underneath them, avoiding discovery. I can see how foolish they feel, why the idea of their man naked with another somebody offends the ego and the heart. But I don't understand why they think that sexual arousal for another woman has anything to do with them. Wanting to possess a different pussy does not reflect on the beloved. So I went home and kissed my wife.

Jake hadn't been born yet, and we spent a quiet night together, regrouping. She wanted to hear my stories of San Jose and Costa Rica and Brazil. She said that she missed me, and I knew it was true, in between her job as senior editor at Randall Publishers. She rolled a spliff for us as she spoke, sifting the ganja between her fingers, discarding tiny seeds and debris in a silver-colored ashtray. Real weed. The first time I showed her hash in London, we both laughed. She'd turned the black clump between her palms, wondering. The first time I met her, at her sister's house, she was rolling a spliff. She looked up at me as I walked into the living room, and I wondered how anyone could be so compact, so complete. Watching Sasha lick the edge of a piece of Rizla comforts me. Watching her lids weighed down by the buzz makes me feel safe. As moths burnt themselves on the lamplight, I looked at my wife's face, half in shadow, and let myself resent the comfort and the safety.

"Sash, how do you feel about the women I take pictures of?"

She put her head to one side. Inhaled. I could see her shoulders relaxing.

"What do you mean?"

"I spend a lot of time with other women."

"So?" She passed the spliff to me. I took a puff, felt it glide inside me.

"Some women would be jealous. Have you ever been jealous?"

She laughed and coughed. "They're no competition."

"Seriously, Sash."

"Would you give them up?"

I shook my head.

"Do you sleep with them?"

Again, a shake of the head. Part of me wishes that she'd asked the question differently, that she'd allowed herself to stop trusting me in that moment. If she'd asked me if I was considering it, I would have said yes, laid my head on her knee, and confessed like a child, sought ways to go past Brianna. But she didn't.

"I don't worry about it, Jerry. Really. I know you love me, and I know we're friends. I know you wouldn't mess with that, so I married you. You told me that . . . the other thing . . . didn't matter. First man who ever said that to me. So, I married you, knowing that I was 'enough.'"

I didn't notice her pain. It was so familiar. Let the weed paint pictures of Brianna Riley in my head. I suppose I pretended that I had permission.

We take sweat for granted. I remember what I was told at school, that sweat was the body's way of cooling itself; I suppose everyone remembers that. Brianna used to say that if that was the case, a volcano lived inside her, constantly waiting to be cooled. I liked that image; when we became lovers, I would imagine, when I was inside her, that I touched that inferno and made her sweat all the more. She sweated and hummed when we made love. Song and sweat. To be defined by such things. To love one and hate the other so much that you can't see your own reflection in the eyes of others. But I knew what it was like to be defined in twos: pictures and need. I didn't admit it when I was a young man, but I loved the women I took pictures of, needing me. One wasn't enough. I believed in quantity over quality.

Two days later, I went back to Brianna's house and knocked on the door. She opened it and looked at me as if I had never left.

"Hello," she said. I felt absurd.

"Can I come in?" I said.

Her stance was odd, her hands behind her back, breasts pushed forward, like a kid hiding a present. Her face worked.

"Tell me you're not attracted to me, B, and I'll leave." An old approach, but sometimes they're the best.

"Please try and understand." Her voice was low. "I can't have a relationship with you or anybody. Can't you accept that?"

"Are you attracted to me?" I grinned. "What happen, babylove? I don't look 'nice' to you?"

"I have to go—"

"Don't I?" I said.

"Yes, okay? That what you want to hear? Yes."

I reached for her, but she backed away, her hands still behind her. There was a kind of mute appeal in her face.

"Brianna, what are you holding—"

I stared. Water pattered around her bare feet, drenching them. Fat, unceasing drips, like the leaks we'd had in the roof at high school. Faster and faster.

"Brianna, you're spilling something—what—"

Her voice broke into pieces.

"I'm spilling *myself*. Okay?"

She raised her hands to my eyes.

"It's called hyperhydrosis."

We were sitting in her apartment. Like her, it was bare. The plastic-covered sofa was the only piece of furniture in her living room. The floorboards were naked, too. I glanced up at a light switch. It was shrouded with plastic. I wondered what her bed looked like.

"Most people with it get very clammy palms, but I'm a severe case."

"Have you always had it?" I asked.

She nodded hesitantly, then plunged forward. "When I was a little girl, no one wanted to play with me. Even grown-ups said I was nasty. I couldn't do anything about it . . . I hid my hands in my pockets. I wore gloves that got soaked in twenty minutes." She laughed softly, bitterly. "I learned to live in twenty-minute increments, which is as long as it takes before they . . . start getting bad. Then I had to sit on them. I rubbed them on my clothes. The kids laughed."

She held her slightly cupped hands in a glass bowl on her lap, as if they didn't belong to her. I watched the water bubble to the surface of her skin and roll over her fingers. The bowl was half full.

"I can't imagine how you felt," I said.

"No, you can't," she snapped. "My parents took me to a dermatologist, and she gave me something that looked like roll-on, to put on my fingers, but it didn't help. Then they sent me for a kind of electric shock treatment, but afterwards I couldn't eat or drink . . . or talk, because there wasn't any saliva in my mouth. It made me dry for about a week, and I was happy. But it gave me heart palpitations. I could've dealt with that. But my parents said it cost too much money for the treatment. My mother said it was God's way, and I had to accept it. But I hate it. *Hate* it!"

"But there must be something—"

"Yes there is, there always is. An operation, but I can't afford it. When I got the money from Lillian and Warners were interested, I was going to have it done. But the guy at Warners keeps jumping up and down—he loves my voice, but he calls the sweat a 'hook.' He thinks it'll fascinate the fans."

"I can see that," I said.

"I don't care." The bowl tilted, spilling drops on her bare knees.

"People think I'm nasty. They think I smell. They think it's my fault. You know how Jamaican people are scornful. They point at me: 'Is time you clean up youself, mi' dear.' Like I can't see what I am! I won't let anyone feel 'sorry' for me!"

I sat beside her. She scrambled to get away, the bowl wavering dangerously. She grabbed for it, but it slipped out of her hands and shattered on the floor. She leapt to her feet, ignoring the glass.

"Brianna, you'll cut yourself."

"Get out of my house!"

"No." I moved toward her, trying to get her out of the way of the shards, but she shrank from me, scrubbing her hands against her T-shirt. Big wet splotches stained her chest, soaking through to her nipples.

"Please, please, Jerry, please go. It gets worse. It gets worse—"

"When you're upset?"

"Yes!" She sounded as if she wanted to cry. I watched her hands weep, instead. They were all but gushing now, their merciless flow darkening her wooden floor. "I have to get something to hold my hands over—"

I grabbed her shoulders. "No. We can clean it up afterwards. I can. Move out of the way of the glass and stay here." She pushed at my chest with her elbows, sweat pumping from her palms, coursing down her wrists onto my shirt.

I grabbed her face and held it. I made her look at me. "This is 'part' of you. You've got wet hands, B. You can't even push me away. Why not? You want to. What's the worse thing about this? Huh?"

Her face crumpled. "That . . . I can't touch anybody, not even my . . . mother . . ."

"Touch me," I said.

Her hands circled my neck. I felt water soak my back as I gave Brianna Riley her first kiss. I felt like the hero in some cynically penned drama. It was what I needed in those days. Extremes. Drama. Don't we all?

I took pictures of Brianna and carried them home for Sasha to admire. Hundreds of them. She was as fascinated as me by the woman's strange condition. Sometimes I caught her bending over them in my darkroom and workspace, thoughtful. She came over to me for a hug. "Oh, I understand her so much, y'know? She must feel so out of control, like her body just does things and she can't change it. I know how she feels." I held her close and tried to remember which shirt I'd left at Brianna's house.

I transformed Brianna's apartment into a studio and worked furiously, my new lover stepping around the equipment, anxious that she not damage anything. I slid my lens across her gleaming skin. I shot her bald head from the depths of a coconut tree. I cross-referenced her pores with her eyes and caught her as whizzing demigoddess; a wanton tease; a child; running across the parking lot; naked, rolled in dirt and sand like a zebra; tiptoed, capturing the sweet arch of her back; rough and ready as a ragamuffin; as dance hall queen; as prostitute; as maid. She was the most adaptable model I'd ever had. And water, yes, water everywhere. I poured food coloring into her palms and together we watched, enthralled, as she made a mauve waterfall in her back garden, the liquid pouring from her, spraying into the air in lovely droplets, in sumptuous curves, simmering in the heat of our country. I made her lift her hands above her head and clicked my shutter as she rained on herself, and it was amazing to watch her laugh. To watch my wife laugh, delighted that I had found a muse, happy in the smoky pretense of her husband's growing ability. I never thought she would find out. Truly. If she couldn't see it in the glow of Brianna's eyes, I guessed that I'd done all I could do.

"Jerry, I need some money."

"What for?" I rolled over and tweaked her nipple, then brought one of her fingers up and watched liquid mount her aureole.

"The operation," she said. I looked at her, startled. "I've decided to do it anyway. My voice is what's most important, and Warners is just going to have to take that."

"Ah . . ." I was shocked now. "You still want the operation?"

She frowned. "I always told you that."

"Yes, but . . ." I was suddenly embarrassed. I thought that my old magic had transformed her, that the pictures were enough. Hadn't I excised my mother's pain with a single photograph?

She looked at me, suddenly comprehending. She laughed, splashing my cheek. "You actually think pretty pictures make it all okay?"

"No, no, I mean, this has been a problem all your life . . ." I lied. I fixed my face into sympathy.

She laughed again. "You are so arrogant, baby. So sweet with the arrogance." She got off the bed, her body twisting into parenthesis. "There's another reason why I need money."

"Yes?"

"I'm pregnant."

A *New York Times* critic once damned me to hell, in the days before my computer was crammed with kiss-kiss e-mails from my agent: "The way that Jeremy Butler brings his models to the frame suggests coercion of the lowest kind. Underneath the smiles are screaming women, if you can only bend close enough to hear them." I crumpled the review and dismissed him. But after Brianna I've often wondered whether I cured any of the women I captured. I wonder if I truly did cure my mother, or whether I just wanted to believe that I had. I realized that I imagined all of them changed, confident, careless in the knowledge of their beauty forever, a swath behind me, all made up of whole and hearty ladies, purring in the knowledge of the wondrousness that Jerry Butler showed them. Now I wonder if I made it worse; whether the magic faded and left them emptier than before. I used them. I may not have touched any of them except Brianna, but I look at my old work and see how I masturbated with their souls.

"Sasha will just have to hold her corner and chill," said Lillian. We sat in her living room. She was a dread by then, her fake locks twisted and alien down her back, wrapped in scarlet, amber, and jade, her skirt long and wide, hiding her feet. I knew she was the wrong person to talk to as soon as I said it, but I needed someone to tell me it wasn't a big deal, and Lillian's carelessness was stunning in its consistency.

"Shit," I said, out loud.

Lillian sucked her teeth, waved the air. "How many men you know in Jamaica that have children out of doors? Nearly all of them. C'mon, Jerry. And anyway, what does Sasha expect?"

"I'm not that kind of man," I said.

"Of course you are, my dear."

I didn't tell Sasha. Denial is such a convenient thing. Just kept on going. But I watched my wife, paying our bills, giving the maid daily instructions, cutting her toenails, reading me manuscripts in bed. I listened to her whisper into my ear at night: "I can't take it, God, I can't take it." I once read a survey of what Caribbean women said at the point of orgasm. Jamaican women say that a lot, apparently: "I can't take it." Bajan women say, "Do me so, oh Lord." Grenadian women say, "Ram me, Jesus Christ, ram me, boy." I wonder if God looks down and asks what the hell He has to do with it.

I watched Brianna swell and sweat. I gave her money. As the baby grew inside her, she grew obsessed. She wanted, she said, to hold this baby in dry arms, and sing to it. It was the sum of all her thoughts: holding her child, moistened only by the blood of the birth, introducing herself with the sound of her voice. She'd told the record company that she was having the operation, and, reluctantly, they agreed that they would sign the deal without it. But after the baby, they said. When she shaped up, they'd start recording. I was proud of her determination.

We booked her in for the operation six weeks before her due date. It was a simple procedure, but it was expensive. I crept off to New York for my latest exhibition. I walked around the exhibiting hall, discussing mounting, lighting, which shots would be made available to the public as three-hundred-dollar prints, which ones would make two-dollar postcards. The curator fluttered around me, lip-glossed, his vocabulary studded with "darlings." "Brianna is just the best of your work, hon," he said. "You just get better and better. Who is she, anyway?"

I looked at the pictures and thought about my lover, my mistress. She was nervous the morning I'd left, and I'd only been able to steal a little while with her. Sasha couldn't understand where I had to go just hours before she drove me to the airport.

"You can't be here? You can't cancel?"

"B, I have to make some money. Come on, now."

She was propped up in bed, bulbous, like a big, naked moon. She had me pile her houseplants around her on the sheets, and began to water them, dipping her busy fingers into their pots and feeding them with herself, roots up. I'd seen her do it countless times, and wasn't amused anymore. Recently, each time she did something bizarre with her hands, I loved Sasha more. I had begun to think of ways of extricating myself.

She looked up. "They're going to collapse my lungs." She was near tears.

Groaning, contrite, I pushed a plant out of the way and stroked her face. I could give her comfort—it wasn't so much to ask for. The operation was keyhole surgery. The specialist would work through each armpit, cauterizing the nerve that induced sweating. To get to the nerve he would deflate her lungs, left side, right side. I thought of Sasha and her breasts: her nipples always hardened alternately, as if they were playing hide and seek with my mouth.

"Think of holding the baby, sweetheart." Wincing, I checked my watch. Sasha would be raising her eyebrows at me by the time I got back.

"All right," Brianna said. She sighed. She let the tears dry. She never wiped her face. It was silly to do so. She was lucky that she didn't need makeup. "Yes. It's going to be a girl, y'know. That's what the doctor said."

"I know." I refused to think of my child coming into the world in a month. Perhaps if Brianna had been the kind of woman who threatened taking the kid into Sasha's face, I would have fallen out of denial. But she wasn't. So I didn't.

A week later, I unlocked the burglar bars around our veranda. Our maid, Michelle, stood waiting for me, her face impassive. She'd been picking the parasitic love bush off the hedges in the garden. Her hands were stained orange.

"Hello, Mr. Jerry," she said.

"Hello, Michelle. Where's Mrs. Butler?"

"She not here. She gone down to the office, say she comin' back late."

Something in her tone made me look up from the padlock I was twisting into place. She was pushing her lips out in that kissing gesture that Jamaicans do when they want to point at something, but don't want to use their hands.

"S'maddy here to see you, Mr. Jerry," she said.

Brianna was sitting on our bed. She wore a red T-shirt with a rip under one arm, and close-fitting jeans. I stared at her flat stomach, uncomprehending. Part of me was poised to snatch her from my marital bed the minute liquid threatened. Another part was utterly aroused by her in that marital bed, those miles of perfect skin, remembering how each time I touched her it felt new. Yet another part was outraged at her audacity. How could she come to my home? Dimly, I realized that she'd started weeping when I stepped into the room. The outrage died. Curiosity and lust and pity took over. I held her.

"Did you lose the baby?"

"No. The baby's at home. I had it early. You weren't here."

I looked down at her hands, reached to touch them, but she pulled away, was down on her knees before I could stop her, dragging arid palms across the electric sockets, across the carpet.

"So you're dry! Great! So what—"

"Look at what I can do." She began to slap herself. Big, open-handed, full-palmed slaps, cracking across her face, faster and faster. I could feel Michelle listening at the door as I stumbled to Brianna's side, nearly tearful myself. I grabbed her hands and forced them down. The skin of her fingers was cracking. It was eerie to touch them.

Her skin was bone-dry, like my throat.

She told me that she went into labor half an hour after her surgery. In fifteen hours she held her baby boy, exhausted, wanting me, but looking down at this little person, neat and dry and safe in her arms. "Boy, we musta missed that penis," the nurse chuckled at her. Brianna watched the Jamaican dawn playing with the windows of her room, and she thought how nice it was that I'd gotten her a private room, away from the labor ward screams. She opened her mouth and waited for the taste of her song. What came out was less than a bark. The surgeons said they couldn't do anything. "An unfortunate side effect," they said. "Never seen anything like it."

She climbed into my arms and I forgot about Michelle as Brianna scratched and wailed and pulled me inside her, thrusting her hips at me, our wet cheeks sliding against each other as I cried, too, telling her I was sorry, so sorry that she was sad, between whining and groans and acres of curious dryness and the sound of her coming over and over, like she'd never stop, and in all of it I don't know how I heard that tiny gasp behind me, my wife standing at the bedroom door, her eyes so big that they suddenly saw all the world. I turned, I tell you, from my lover, God knows how I heard that small, hurt sound in between Brianna's orgasmic sorrow, but I did. I can hear it now.

I'm glad that I've written it all down. I'll ask Sasha whether she thinks I should keep it for Jake. I'll trust her feelings on the matter. Perhaps she won't want to change his dreams. Perhaps they would be twisted, like my own. I dream of Brianna, not smooth, or burnished, or wet, but surrounded by options: was it a knife, a rope, a razor blade, drugs, did she vomit, did she hate me, did she bleed, did it hurt? Lillian got the news on the wind and came up to the house, dragged me into the yard to tell me. It made page five of the *Daily Gleaner*: SINGER

SUICIDE AFTER BOTCHED OPERATION. The *Gleaner* was never subtle, and they spread my lover's face all over their pages, frozen in a death mask. I know something. I know she wouldn't have killed herself if I had followed her that day. But I chose. I chose my wife's disbelieving eyes, and that small sound of hurt. I chose to heal the only thing I could heal.

My wife always wanted a son. When we came to the new house, Jake in my arms, she finally threw out her off-white underwear, saved for heavy periods, the ones she hadn't worn for years. I remember her words: "Number Three, Jerry: Let this be enough. Will it be enough? It has to be enough." I said yes, that my son was enough. That I'd never touch another woman.

Jake is coming home tomorrow. He's grown to be a fine man. Bright, responsible, not at all interested in photography: he has Sasha's feeling for words, and he's studying linguistics and sociology. He's had the same girl since he was sixteen. They cuddle and wind love bush in each other's hair when they're here. Sometimes, when she thinks we're not looking, his girl sucks salt water off his fingers and teases him about another one of her shirts ruined. But she doesn't mind the sweat. Neither does Jake. He waters the plants at the front of the yard with his hands, and Sasha smiles.

DENNIS ETCHISON

My Present Wife

Dennis Etchison has been selling stories since the early 1960s. He is one of the horror genre's most respected and distinguished practitioners, a multiple winner of both the British Fantasy Award and the World Fantasy Award. The Death Artist, published by DreamHaven Books, is his fourth story collection illustrated by J. K. Potter. A forty-year retrospective of Etchison's short fiction, Talking in the Dark, was recently published by Stealth Press. In addition to having published four novels, he has also edited several acclaimed anthologies, including Cutting Edge and Metahorror. He is the editor of the recently published official HWA anthology, The Museum of Horrors. Etchison, a longtime resident of Los Angeles, has put his familiarity with its paranoia and obsessions to excellent use in a series of stories that he's written over the past few years (four of which have been reprinted in previous volumes of our series).

About the following tale, he says: "The late Robert Bloch had a deliciously mordant sense of humor. Always the wicked jokester, his mischief found expression in public and private conversation as well as in his writing. I once heard him introduce his lovely spouse Elly, to whom he had been happily married for many years, as 'my present wife,' a remark she somehow did not find amusing. When I followed his example and tried to introduce 'my first wife' (first and only, I should add) on a couple of occasions, for some reason mine did not like that one any better. So, since I do not share Bloch's love of risk in matters of domestic harmony, I decided that it might be safer to write about a character given to such remarks." "My Present Wife" was originally published in Dark Terrors 5, edited by Stephen Jones and David Sutton.

—E. D.

T he road was wide and well-lighted for the first mile or so, then narrowed to a single lane and led into the foothills, where the signs were impossible to read even with her high beams. That was almost enough to make Lesley turn around and go home, especially when the other car sped up and began to close the distance. It had been on her tail since she left the freeway. She tried to ignore the headlights and stopped under the first streetlamp in several long blocks, took the invitation out of her purse and looked at it one more time.

The hand-drawn map on the back was useless. It might have been a child's sketch of a tree made with black crayon, the branches leading off the page into unknown territory. The lines were not labeled and there was only an X at the top, a house number and the words *Saddleback Circle.*

When the headlights glared in her rearview mirror she had to glance up.

The other car slowed, pulling even and hovering for a moment. Her side window was milky with frost. She reached for the button and rolled the glass down.

"Richard," she shouted, "leave me alone or I'll call the police! I mean it this time."

Then she got a good look at the other car. It was a brand new Chrysler, shiny black and heavy with chrome fittings, so dark inside that she could not see the driver. Embarrassed, she held up the invitation and waved it, accidentally brushing the controls by the steering wheel.

"Sorry, I—I thought you were someone else. Do you know where—"

But now her wipers were on, skittering back and forth across the windshield, drowning out her own voice. The tinted passenger window on the other car remained closed.

"Wait, please! I think I'm lost . . ."

The Chrysler glided silently past her to the next corner, a plume of white exhaust billowing up behind it.

She spotted the same car a few minutes later, its turn signals winding uphill in a pattern that vaguely resembled part of the hand-drawn map. Then there was an entire row of red taillight reflectors ahead, stopped along both sides of the road, so many that there could be no doubt she had finally found the party. It took a few minutes more to locate a parking space next to the split-rail fence on Saddleback Circle.

A sharp wind blew out of the canyon, gathering force and turning back on itself as if chilled by the cul-de-sac at the end. Lesley walked toward the glow of a big house, while heavy steps sounded beyond the fence and white breath condensed in the air between the trees. A riderless horse, pale and steaming against the darkness, stood snorting and pawing the earth. She closed her collar and hurried on.

The house shone like iced gingerbread, all the doors and windows sparkling with color and movement. The gravel driveway was still full of cars. Someone stepped forward from the shadows and she put her hand up to shield her eyes from the glare of Christmas lights over the porch.

"Hello?" she called out, shivering.

"Les, you made it."

"Coral? It feels like it's going to snow!"

"Don't say that in L.A. It's bad luck."

"Am I too late?"

"Come on in, for God's sake." Coral led her up the wooden steps. "Get yourself some eggnog and I'll introduce you around."

A dozen people were jammed around the coatrack in the foyer, the faces of the taller ones blurring as they moved aside for their hostess. The air was warm with body heat but Lesley's fingers trembled as she undid the button at her throat and smoothed her collar.

"I can't stay."

"You have a late date?"

"Right, Coral."

"Then stick with me. I'll fix you up."

"No, really, I'll just mingle . . ."

Lesley squinted in the sudden brightness, gazing through crêpe paper and popcorn strung from the vaulted living room ceiling. The party was close to breaking up but a few tanned women in satin and denim stood talking to men with cowboy boots and silver belt buckles, while long-legged teenagers whispered behind a table full of empty pie tins and half-eaten cookies. When she turned around Coral was not there.

She rubbed her hands together and wandered into the hall, past matted photographs of her friend in a black hunt cap and coat jumping a chestnut mare over hurdles. A man's voice droned from one of the bedrooms, describing how he had broken his ankle during a flying dismount the previous year. Only his broad shoulders and pressed Levi's were visible through the doorway. Three women sat on the edge of the bed, listening with lips parted. Lesley continued down the hall before he could roll up the leg of his jeans to show them the scar.

In the den, Coral took her arm and led her to a balding man on the sofa.

"Ed, you remember Les, from the Tri-Valley meet. We went out for dinner after."

"Oh, right," he said, half-standing, the top of his head a pink smear. "Did you ever sell that Hermès saddle?"

"Not yet," said Lesley.

"How much do you want for it?" asked a drunk woman on the other end of the sofa.

"I haven't decided."

"Where's your friend?" said the balding man.

"Who?"

"Big guy, longrider coat. What's his name?"

Coral said in a low voice, "Honey, that was last summer."

"Richie, that's it." He looked around. "Is he here?"

Coral rolled her eyes. "They're not together anymore."

"Oh. Too bad. Nice fellow."

"Sit down, Ed." When they were back in the hall, Coral whispered, "I'm so sorry. I told him, but he doesn't listen."

"It's okay. I'm over it." They passed the bedroom, now empty. "Who was that man?"

"You know my husband!"

"I mean in there, with those women."

"What did he look like?"

"I couldn't see his face. Tall, black hair . . ."

"Sounds familiar."

"I don't know what you're talking about."

"Don't you?" Coral steered her toward a table of *hors d'oeuvres* in the dining room. "Do yourself a favor. Try a different type, for once?"

Lesley blinked and lowered her head, fumbling for a paper plate. The first chafing dish contained a few wieners floating in water. Before she could open the next one small feet thundered behind her and five or six children ran to the table and filled the last of the hot dog buns. When they were gone she set her plate aside, reached for a cut-glass cup and dipped some punch out of the bowl.

"Do you have any vodka to go with this?" she asked, but Coral had already gone on to the living room.

Lesley explored the rest of the downstairs.

She passed several couples. There were a few single men leaning in doorways or working the halls, their faces indistinct as she squeezed by them with her head down. In an enclosed back porch the teenaged girls were busy rehearsing a skit of some sort. The yard was illuminated by floodlights and the trees shook silently beyond the glass, teasing a view of absolute darkness. She listened to the girls for a minute, then found her way to the TV room.

A young mother held her sleepy son on her lap, stroking his forehead as they watched a tape of *The Man from Snowy River*, and a woman in a short black cocktail dress stood in the corner talking to a slim, sandy-haired man. Lesley was about to move on when the woman spotted her.

"Les?"

"Hi, Jane." Lesley started out of the porch, but the woman was already at her side.

"I haven't seen you in so long."

"I don't ride anymore."

"Why not?"

"I moved."

"So where are you taking lessons?"

"Nowhere. I can't, till my arm heals."

Jane seemed not to hear her and turned to the man in the corner. "Do you know—?"

"I was looking for Judy," said Lesley as he came over to join them. "Is she . . . ?"

"This is Les," the woman told him. "Ask her. She has a fabulous horse."

Lesley avoided his eyes. "I used to."

"What happened?" the man asked.

"I had to sell him."

"You should have seen her in the Tri-Valley Finals," said Jane.

"That was one of Suzie's horses. She let me take him out for the day."

"Who paid?" he said. "Or did you go Dutch?"

Jane laughed too loudly and said, "Have you met—?"

"Michael."

"I don't think so." His fingers were soft, smooth and unknotted. She withdrew her hand and reached for her purse, but it was not at her side. She had left it on the coatrack in the foyer.

"Where do you ride?"

"Shady Acres. I mean, I did."

"How do you like it?"

"Beautiful!" said Jane. "You'll have to come out sometime."

"I should. My wife wants to ride, but I'm afraid I'll get rug-burns."

Jane cracked up.

Lesley could not quite meet his eyes, which stood out in an otherwise ordinary, almost uncompleted face. "Hunters and jumpers?"

"Not that advanced. She's only been on a horse a few times."

"Well," said Jane, "I can show you some easy trail rides. It's right by the State Park."

"Great. I'll tell her all about it."

"Where is your wife?"

"She's on her way She had to work late." He turned his attention to Lesley again. "What does a decent horse go for?"

She averted her gaze. "That depends on what you're looking for, I guess."

"Well . . ." Jane pulled at her lip as she waited for his eyes to fall on her again. "I'm not supposed to talk about it, but Suzie told me about a steal up in Ventura Country. An eight-year-old, A-circuit champion, for—"

Just then a bell clanged.

Lesley went to the hall, following the sound.

Coral held up a metal triangle and beat it with a soup ladle as though calling ranch hands to a chuckwagon dinner. When the remaining guests had assembled in the dining room she announced a special treat, a one-act play written and performed by the Junior Class girls. Lesley saw the teenagers through the open kitchen door, waiting with handwritten notebook pages, practicing their lines one last time. She took a position along the wall nearest the living room, as a pretty blond girl stepped in front of the buffet table and began speaking.

"Kind ladies and gentlemen, I pray you, do not judge me! I was but a poor maid who lost her way . . ."

"The girl held out her arms, palms up, in a gesture of supplication. From the foyer came the rustling of coats as a few more couples took this opportunity to slip away. Lesley watched the girl, not looking at the hall to see if Jane and the fair-haired man had followed her.

". . . so when *he* came to Sparta and offered me such a fine mount, how could I resist?"

Now a crude horse's head bobbed out of the kitchen, followed by a second half made of brown paper with a real horsehair tail. A high-pitched whinnying came from under the paper and the two halves of the horse reared up and bumped the girl, who fell onto her back.

Next to Lesley, a woman nearly spilled her glass of wine.

The audience giggled and applauded. The horse took a premature bow. The woman held her husband's arm to keep from losing her balance.

"Is this R-rated?" she said, convulsed with laughter. "Her mother's going to die!"

"It's all right," said her husband behind the brim of his Stetson. "I think it's *Equus*."

"I think it's the Trojan Horse," said another voice.

Lesley raised her eyes and saw that a man wearing a camel's hair sportcoat and a bolo tie had squeezed in next to her.

"Don't you?" he asked her, leaning closer.

"I really don't know."

"What are you drinking, little lady?"

She shook her head. "Nothing, thank you."

She let herself out onto the wide front porch and felt for her purse, but it was still inside. Couples walked down the steps to the gravel, blowing on their hands, jingling keyrings, unlocking cars in the driveway. Headlights flashed and for a second the blond girl from the play was silhouetted against the split-rail fence, imprisoned by the arms of a teenaged boy. The headlights moved on and there was the sound of laughter in the dark. Lesley leaned on the railing as footsteps passed behind her from the other end of the porch.

"Excuse me," she said without turning, "but do you have a cigarette, by any chance?"

"Well, let's just see here once." It was the one Jane had introduced as Michael. He checked his shirt pocket and came up with a crushed pack of Marlboros. "Hey, you scored."

"I don't want to take your last one."

He straightened the cigarette for her. "My wife says I should quit, anyway. You can help me get rid of the evidence."

She cupped her fingers around the flame, careful not to touch his hand. "Did she finally make it?"

"She'll be here. She promised."

"What does she do?"

"Legal work," he said.

"I'd like to meet her."

"You need a lawyer?"

She inhaled and blew out a cone of smoke. "Oh, I guess not."

"Sexual harassment, or a quickie divorce? Let's see, you keep the house and car . . ."

"I'm not married."

"Palimony? That's easy. But first you have to stop calling and hanging up. Leaving notes on his car."

"It's not me."

"You found a dead horse in your bed?"

"Not yet." She smiled at him and coughed.

"Smooth, huh?"

"This is the first one I've had in a long time."

"Why did you stop?"

"Someone I know—knew—didn't like it."

"He should meet my present wife."

"How many times have you been married?"

"Only once. It's a joke. I used to call her my first wife, but she didn't like it. So now I introduce her as my present wife. She doesn't think that's funny, either."

"I wonder why."

"You're a lot like her."

"What's her name?"

"Sometimes I forget," he said with a twinkle in his eye.

A burst of whistles and applause from inside the house.

"I'd better go in," she said. "Thanks."

"The first one's free." His eyes shone out of the shadows. "Seriously. She can get you a restraining order."

"Who, your present wife?"

"If that doesn't work, we'll tie him up and dump him on a trail somewhere. State Parks are always good."

They laughed.

Mothers hugged their shiny-faced daughters, who made desperate hand signals to each other across the dining room. Lesley touched the blond one's arm.

"You were wonderful."

"Thanks!" the girl said in a sweet, breathless voice.

"You're Tara, aren't you?"

"Um, yeah." The girl looked over her head, scanning the room with restless green eyes. She had a broad forehead and skin that almost glowed.

"You probably don't remember me," said Lesley. "I helped you train for your first Junior Class meet."

The girl pretended not to hear and swept by her to the hall, where the two halves of the horse, now in riding clothes, led her away. They were all legs and gangly arms, their silken hair pinned to the backs of long necks above collarless dressage shirts, their clean faces mouthing words that could almost be read from across the room. Lesley smiled after them and went into the kitchen.

Coral and three other women were putting food into stainless steel bowls.

"Well, it's about time," said the one with the short haircut.

"Judy? I was looking for you!"

"We had a bet you wouldn't show."

"Michelle! And Jeannie . . ." Lesley embraced them. "Sorry I'm late. I saw Tara—she's adorable. What a great Helen."

"Next week she'll be Joan of Arc," said Michelle. "All she does is watch that movie over and over."

"Does she still ride?"

"She will, if I get her some chain-mail."

"Judy has a bone to pick with you," said Jeannie, covering a bowl with plastic wrap.

"What about?"

"When's the last time I saw you at Shady Acres?" asked the one with short hair.

"A few months."

"Try six. Right?" she asked Jeannie, pouring the leftover eggnog back into a carton.

"I had to sell Kahlua when I moved out."

"That's no excuse. You're the best rider I've ever seen."

"No, I'm not . . ."

"And you know darn well you can ride Jack any time. All you have to do is ask."

Lesley blushed. "That's really, really nice of you, Jude. I will, as soon as my arm's healed."

"It's healed now, and so are you. Got it? You dumped the jerk and you're back in the mix. What are you doing Saturday?"

"I'm not sure yet."

"The Grand Prix at Oak Ridge. Box seats."

"I'll call you." Lesley glanced over Judy's shoulder at the kitchen window, as a tall dark figure passed in the yard outside. She put her hand to her throat. "Who else did you invite?"

"Friends only."

"I mean tonight," she said to Coral.

"Is it cold in here?"

"No, I'm fine."

"Then why are you shivering?" Coral put the last bowl away and closed the refrigerator door. "Come on. I can't let you leave like this."

There were plates, half-eaten hot dog buns and torn wrapping paper on every surface. A few sportcoats and plaid Pendletons still prowled the edges of the living room. Coral led her upstairs, past small children bundled like teddy bears for the ride home. She thanked the mothers and fathers for coming, then steered Lesley into the master bedroom.

"I'll help you clean up."

"No, you won't." Coral rummaged in the closet, pulled out a suede jacket with sheepskin lining. "Here. Put this on."

"I'll bring it back."

"Saturday. The old gang will be there." She helped Lesley get her bad arm into the jacket and looked at her. "I know it's been a rough year for you. But it's over."

"I guess so."

Lesley turned away and opened the curtains above a table that held Coral's trophies and ribbons, just enough to see down into the backyard.

"Did you ever find out who she was?" said Coral.

Below, the yard was empty, the gate latched. There was no one on the side of the house next to the kitchen. In the distance taillights wound slowly up the canyon road like blood cells through a clogged artery. She let the curtains fall closed.

"He never admitted it. He told me I was paranoid, and after a while I almost believed him. But I know I did the right thing. It's just that sometimes . . ."

"You don't call him, do you?"

"He calls me."

"What does he say?"

"Nothing."

"Then how do you know?"

"Well, if it's not him, then that means he was right. And I *am* paranoid."

"My God, Les."

"Sometimes I think he's following me. Like tonight."

"I definitely did not invite Richard!"

"There was a car behind me, on the way."

"If he's stalking you—"

"It wasn't even his car. But when I saw it I thought . . ."

Coral sat her down on the bed.

"Listen. There are plenty of men out there. You could have met a few tonight, if you'd take those damned blinders off."

"I don't want another relationship."

"Who's talking about that? Take them for what they are: fun and games. I'll tell you a secret. The rest of it isn't that great."

"Then why did you get married again?"

"Ed's a good man. And I love our new house. But there's only one first time." She pressed Lesley's fingers. "You're lucky. Everything's still right there in front of you, like a candy store—all you have to do is enjoy. Like the song says, love the one you're with, right? What's the first thing you do when you get thrown? Pull yourself together and get back on! So give yourself a chance. For me?"

At the foot of the stairs her husband was busy picking loose popcorn out of the rug. His body was thick around the middle and when he got up he had to hold the banister for support. Coral helped him stand.

"Leave that," she said, resting her head on his shoulder. "You're such a neatness freak."

He kissed her with a noisy smack. His pink face was detailed in this light, with kindly lines etched around the eyes.

"I'll do it," said Lesley. She found a paper cup and began collecting the popcorn.

"It can wait till morning."

Michelle and Judy came in from the dining room.

"Who's here?" Coral asked them.

"Just some guys," said Judy. "The kind that never give up."

"Jeannie's in the kitchen," said Michelle. "She drank too much eggnog."

"Put her in the guest bedroom. She can sleep it off."

"The junior girls are there."

"What are they doing?"

"Talking about boys and horses."

"Are there any boys?"

"Only that trainer, with the story about his leg. He has one boot off."

"Pervert," said Ed and headed for the back of the house.

Lesley crossed the dining room. There were candy canes and sugared peanuts on the carpet, cookie crumbs folded in napkins by every chair. As she gathered them up colorful holiday sweaters and turquoise watchbands flashed beyond the arches. The faces of the men who had stayed were no longer blurred but easy to see now, weathered and tan or pale but interesting, professionals and jocks from the city or the country, each with a story to tell. Easy laughter lilted from every direction. It would take a few more minutes for them all to say their goodbyes. She grabbed as much trash as she could and took it to the kitchen.

As she emptied her arms, a low moaning came from the floor by the butcher block table.

"Jeannie, what are you doing down there?"

"Sitting."

Michele and Judy came in with a crumpled paper tablecloth. They stepped around Jeannie and found the trash can.

"How are we going to get her on her feet?"

"Tell her Hap Hanson's in the other room."

"He's too old."

"He's not, is he?" said Lesley.

"Too old?"

"No, in the other room."

"Sure."

"Who is?" Lesley asked.

They both turned from the sink and looked at her. Michelle winked at Judy. "There might be a couple of single guys out there."

"Like?"

"Chris, from the barn. And Jason the baby doctor, and that guy from Westlake Village, the lawyer—"

"His wife's the lawyer," said Lesley.

"Which one is he?" asked Judy.

"Curly hair, five-eight or nine . . ."

"That's him. He's definitely married."

"To his first wife!"

"I know. I was just wondering."

"If he fools around?"

"No. He's nice, though. Funny. Is he a friend of Coral's?"

"She didn't invite him."

"His wife, then," said Michelle. "She rides."

"Not yet," Lesley told them. "She wants to take lessons."

"I heard she works for a TV station."

"She's a vet," said Judy.

"They just moved here," Michelle said. "From Phoenix."

"Texas," said Judy.

"He told me San Diego . . ." Jeannie mumbled from the floor.

"Maybe he crashed the party."

"Why would he do that?"

"Looking for his present wife!"

"Remember, he's off-limits."

"I *know*," said Lesley, "okay?"

She made coffee and helped her friends walk Jeannie to a sofa in the living room, then left them and joined Coral and her husband. The front door was open just enough to show the blond girl at the edge of the porch, kissing someone goodnight in the shadows. It was not the same boy she had been with earlier. Lesley lingered in the foyer as the last guests put on their coats. Michelle made her promise to meet for lunch next week, then went outside to find her daughter.

"You finally stopped shivering," said Coral.

"I feel better now."

"Good."

"Glad you could make it," said Ed.

Lesley met his eyes without flinching. "Thanks for inviting me. You don't know."

"Any time," said Coral and held her. "I mean it," she whispered. "See you Saturday?"

"I'd love to."

She went back to the living room. Judy would take Jeannie home and bring her back to pick up her car in the morning. Then Lesley remembered her purse. It was on the rack, behind a long black leather coat.

"Whose is this?"

"Mine," said Ed.

"It was my present to him," Coral said. "Because he's my sweetie."

"Oh." Lesley hooked her arm through the strap of the purse.

"You drive carefully, now," Ed told her.

Lesley started out, then came back and hugged him, too.

"I will," she said.

She closed the door. Now the moon shone down like a huge streetlamp, illuminating the fence and the tops of the trees beyond the front yard. There were no more cars or shadows in the driveway. She started down the steps.

Behind her, the boards squeaked and a man's voice said, "Need a ride?"

"No, thanks."

"Sure?"

"I have a car."

"Where? I'll drive you."

She noticed a black Chrysler still parked by the curb at the end of the driveway and walked faster, digging for her keys. She shook her purse but nothing jingled. When she stopped to open it he bumped into her and the purse fell to the ground.

"Let me get that, little lady."

"I can do it."

She knelt before a pair of snakeskin boots. They belonged to the one with the camel's hair coat and bolo tie.

"Wonder what happened to those keys?" he said with a grin.

"How did you know . . . ?"

"I got it, honey," said another voice.

"Over here," she called as the sandy-haired man came down from the porch. "Where were you, Michael?"

"Looking for you." To the tall men he said, "We're okay here, pardner."

When the other man left she said, "You have wonderful timing."

"You, too."

"I feel so stupid. Now I can't find my keys." She kept sifting through the gravel with her fingers. "I left my purse for a while. You don't suppose that man . . . ?"

"Let's just see here once."

He put his hand in his pocket and clinked his own keys. Then he leaned down and raked the gravel, and suddenly her keyring glinted there in the moonlight.

"Oh, God, thanks!"

"Where are you parked?"

"All the way at the end."

"I'll walk you." He helped her up. "Do you have a long way to go?"

"A few miles. Once I get to the freeway I'm okay."

"Left at the first street, then follow it till you see the on-ramp."

"Got it." When he patted his pockets she reached into her purse. "How about a menthol?"

"Just like my wife."

"I thought she didn't smoke."

"She used to."

"I hope she's all right. Did she call?"

In the flare of the lighter his hair was red and his smile ironic. He cupped his hands over the flame, enclosing her fingers.

"She wouldn't know the number here."

"Does she have a cell phone?"

"No. She doesn't want people bugging her when she's away from the clinic."

Lesley lit her own cigarette and blew out a cloud of smoke, white as frost from the chill in the air. "I thought she was a lawyer."

"The office, I mean."

They came to the end of the driveway. Ahead the trees were so tall that the rest of the canyon was black.

"Do you mind if I follow you?" she said.

"Sounds like a plan."

"In case I get lost again." She fingered her keys, took a deep breath, held it and finally let it out. "Look, would you like to have coffee or something? It's so cold. I was thinking about stopping, before I get on the freeway."

"There's a Denny's by the underpass."

"Is that the only place open?"

"Something wrong with Denny's?"

"I just meant . . ."

A car drove out of the canyon and he turned to her, the headlights blazing in his eyes. "Not good enough for you?"

"What?"

"Nothing's ever good enough, is it?"

She tried to step back but he had hold of her wrist, the one that was almost healed.

"You're hurting me!"

"Sometimes I wonder why I married you in the first place," he said, his breath steaming until his face was only a blur again. "Well, listen up, bitch. Tonight you're going to do exactly what I tell you and like it! Got that? I might even take you to the State Park afterward. There's never anybody around . . ."

Then, jerking her so violently that her feet left the ground and her toes scraped the dirt and the rocks, he dragged her the rest of the way down into the cul-de-sac.

JEFFREY THOMAS

The Flaying Season

Jeffrey Thomas's short stories have been published in numerous small press magazines, and in such books as Quick Chills II: The Best Horror Fiction from the Specialty Press, New Mythos Legends, *and Karl Edward Wagner's* The Year's Best Horror Stories XXII. *The year 2000 saw two collections of his fiction released—*Terror Incognita, *published by Delirium Books, and* Punktown, *published by The Ministry of Whimsy Press, from which "The Flaying Season" is taken.*

The author tells us, " 'The Flaying Season' was inspired in part by two authors—Thomas Hardy and Yukio Mishima. I wanted to create a story in which the protagonist's psychological state would be reflected/externalized in her environment, as in Hardy's Tess of the d'Urbervilles. *And Mishima's story 'Patriotism,' a harrowing account of self annihilation, plays an active role in my tale. I've been setting stories in the futuristic Everycity of Punktown since 1980. It's become my all-purpose fantasy world—my Oz, my Arkham, my Bradbury's Mars."*

The author lives in Westborough, Massachusetts, with one wife, one child, a newt, and the ghost of an elderly lady.

—E. D.

T he flukes, as the great beasts were called, had skins of malachite, swirled green and black and smoothly sheened, which the Antse people flayed from the carcasses inside ceramic block garages or hangar-like structures with scrap metal roofs, and their watery yellow blood would run down the streets of the neighborhood into grates, and dry to a crust along the gutters when the season of flaying was over.

Kohl had once watched a team of Antse capture a fluke; she had never been able to watch more than once. The swollen, tadpole-like form had been called out of its dimension into this one, lured by means she didn't understand, but the Antse themselves had settled in Punktown from that same place conterminous with this one. Before the whole of its body had even passed through, the Antse had hooks in its flanks, cords around it, had lodged barbed metal pikes in its various apertures, which fluttered and snorted in pain and distress as the rest of the body, thrashing back and forth in empty air ten feet off the street, was hauled out with a jarring thud. The huge creature had squirmed, flailed several cord-like forelimbs, but the Antse had quickly finished it without much marring its hide.

Now Kohl drew the shade when a fluke was caught in the street below, put on music to drown out the sounds of slaughter, some jangly fast-tempoed Middle Eastern music to distract her. But it was hard to avoid the spectacle of the flaying season altogether, in this neighborhood that the Antse had congregated in. The Antse hung out vast sheets of malachite hide to dry like laundry, rustling in the night breeze, smelling like tar either naturally or due to some tanning process, beautifully translucent when the sun was behind them. And then, the Antse applied those skins to their own bodies, adhering them by some means Kohl had never witnessed nor comprehended, so that the normally smooth gray skins of these naked settlers were covered every inch by the tightly form-fitting leather of the flukes. The Antse would then resemble skeletons carved of malachite, for the next season, until for whatever reason—religious, she assumed, which she found explained most unexplainable behaviors—the flesh was peeled or shed until the next flaying season.

To be fair, perhaps the skins kept them warm during a cold season in their own world, though the flaying season occurred in summer, here. But the effigies had to have a religious meaning. Even now, a cup of tea in hand, her music turned low, Kohl stood at the window gazing across at one of these fleshy mannikins swaying in an early evening breeze. It hung from a pole protruding from a second floor window, just over the heads of those who might pass below. There would be dozens throughout the neighborhood, now that it was flaying time. It was a loosely anthropomorphic figure, hewn from the translucent white flesh beneath the lovely hide of some fluke. To be fair, the Antse ate this white meat. Though Kohl did not eat meat, or wear animal flesh, she knew that the customs were not by any means peculiar to the Antse. But the mannikins were more a mystery to her than the wearing of fluke flesh; the Antse were secretive about the meaning of their customs, if not shy about the products of their customs being seen. These suspended totems were filled with thick spikes and long thin nails, and bound in strings of something like barbed wire, so that they were like suffering saints carved from God's own underbelly.

Birds would gingerly land among the forests of cruel thorns to pick at them. Stray dogs would find scraps of them fallen to the street. When they crumbled or smelled too much they were replaced with new effigies, until the flaying season was over.

Kohl regarded the hanging figure opposite her window, and it seemed to regard her back, spikes for eyes.

The neighborhood was tightly packed buildings in every color of gray, their night flanks slick with rain but abruptly bleached with strobe lightning from the sparking of the old shunt lines on which carriages lashed to and from the Canberra Mall. Kohl had just returned to her neighborhood on one of those shunts; she worked at one of the mall's several coffee shops. Her clothing had smelled too strongly of coffee; she had never thought she would ever have too much of its scent. She had showered, made a cup of tea (she had never imagined she'd grow tired of the taste of coffee, either). Kohl could only just afford these four small rooms (bath included), but once had had a better job. She had been a net researcher for a large conglomerate, its head offices on earth, and she had clear memories of the job. She did not, however, have memories of being raped in the parking lot of the company. That was all she knew of it: that she had been raped in the company parking lot. She had been traumatized by her rape. The men had never been caught. She had become so troubled, so afraid to venture from her apartment, to go out at night, even to go to work, that she had lost her job.

But that was for the best, the doctor she ultimately consulted assured her. She should start life anew, put all the nightmare behind her. And yet it was he who really put it from her mind. Her attack had been delicately, precisely burned from her memory. It had been burned from the entire record of thought that followed the incident itself, tracked stealthily by complex brain scan. Even her memories of her physical wounding were gone, so that she did not know what the men had done to injure her in the course of the rape itself.

She stood again at the window, again with tea, in her robe, and watched the rain course down the pane. A shunt whooshed from the distant mall, and the sparking burst lit the face of the tenement opposite. The effigy glared in at her, its spikes looking all the blacker in the flesh made bright—almost luminous—by the stark flash. Then, a ghost, it was gone, and Kohl stepped back from the window, dropped the curtain. Setting aside her tea, she opened her robe and gazed down at her body. Smooth, white, the small neat dent of her navel the only scar, looking like a deep puncture. What had the shadow men done? How much had she been repaired?

Jazz played almost inaudibly. Kohl resumed her tea drinking, wandered back to the bathroom, where the mirror was losing its obscuring mist. Her reflection regarded her. Hair, dyed dark red, in wet tangles . . . the thick black makeup she favored washed away, making her eyes look stripped, she felt weak and faded. Why did she like to dye her hair, and paint her lips a dark brown shade? Had her husband liked her that way, found it alluring? All memory of him was gone, but was it possible that the scan, the burning, had left behind clues to their relationship? Might she like a certain film director because her husband had originally introduced her to his work? Might even the jazz she was listening to be from a chip he had bought her? She tried to remember purchasing this one and found that she couldn't.

A shunt passed and the shade lit up, then went dark again like a closed eyelid.

"I love the smell in here," the customer said, a smile in his voice behind Kohl's back as she prepared him his mocha cappuccino. She set it before him, rang it up. He dumped all his change in the tip cup, as if to impress her. "Quiet night in the mall, huh? Everybody home watching the big game, you think?"

"Big game?" Kohl asked without interest.

"Never mind," the man chuckled. "That's how I feel about it, too. Much rather read." He lifted a bag from the book store a bit further down the main hall. "You like books?"

Kohl pushed a stray strand of hair out of her face, then regretted it, as the man might take it as a gesture of flirtation. "I read on the net," she replied blandly.

"Aww . . . you don't get that smell of paper. You can't sink down into a bath tub with . . ."

"I do, sometimes; I have a headset." But she regretted discussing her private life. Especially referring to any activities that involved her being naked. Thankfully, a new customer had just entered the shop, and was perusing the bags of fresh beans. Kohl prayed for her to hurry up and approach the counter.

"Well," the young man sighed, taking up his coffee, "time to head home before the game gets over and all the drunks leave the bars, eh? You be careful yourself, tonight."

"Thanks," said Kohl. She was careful, leaving the mall every night, waiting for a shunt. She had bought nightvision glasses that looked like regular sunglasses, and carried a small pistol in her shoulder bag.

She watched the man leave, a bit surprised that he had dropped his flirtation without asking her out. Had the new customer made him self-conscious, or had it never been his intent to ask her out? Or even flirt; perhaps he had only meant to be friendly. Whereas a minute ago Kohl had resented his attentions, now she felt a bit disappointed, she was surprised to realize. He had been an attractive man. Intelligent, obviously, probably sensitive.

But wouldn't her husband have been those things, too, if those were qualities that attracted her? And he must have shown a darker side, in time. Maybe he had cheated on her, become a drunk. Beat her. Even raped her. He must have hurt her badly, if she had returned to her doctor and paid him to obliterate all memories of her husband, after first divorcing him, after first removing all photographs and vids of him, after changing her name and moving to a new neighborhood where the nonhuman immigrants did not trouble her, did not find her attractive, even with her red hair and brown lips.

Kohl even felt insulted, hurt, that the man had lost interest in her, or never really had it in the first place. But it was for the best, no doubt.

An hour later, and her shop closed up for the night. She sat on a bench in the main hall reading a magazine. A group of teenage boys drifted past, eyeing her and making lip-smacking noises. She slid one hand in her shoulder bag as she continued to read, but a security robot came rumbling along, dented and covered in graffiti, and rolled after the boys, urging them onward. Kohl removed her hand from the now slick grip of her pistol.

Her sister was late, but at last here she was: Terr, so pretty, with her thick black eyebrows and perfectly shaped head shaved down to a mere dark stubble. She kissed Kohl lightly and they began to walk the half closed mall.

"Traitor," Kohl said, nodding at the coffee cup Terr carried; not her shop's brand.

"Sorry, couldn't wait . . ."

Kohl asked how Terr's wedding plans were going. Her fiance seemed like a nice enough man; attractive, sensitive, artistic. Kohl worried about her sister but was afraid to darken her enthusiasm in any way. She just wished her sister had known the man longer.

"How are you doing?" Terr now asked her in turn, as she drove Kohl to a restaurant where they planned to have a late meal and a few drinks.

Kohl stared straight ahead through the windshield at the night city; buildings so black they seemed windowless, like solid obelisks, others lit brightly but no more warmly. One great scalloped Tikkihotto temple was of blue stone and lit with blue floodlights and struck Kohl as particularly lonely-looking. Some local journalists spoke of the exciting blend of cultures in Punktown, the fascinating ethnic melting pot. Kohl felt that the buildings were not a rich diversity but a silent cacophony, disharmonious, so many unalike strangers forced to stand shoulder-to-shoulder.

"Terr," she asked in a dull voice, "did you like my husband?"

"Jesus, Kohl!" Terr said. "Jesus!"

"What?"

"Are you trying to get us in an accident?" Terr composed herself, sat up straighter at the controls. "You know I can't talk about him. You asked me to never talk about him . . . or the other thing! You paid a lot to have that work done. Why would you even want to know?"

"I don't know, I just . . . it bothers me . . . sometimes."

"It bothered you when you knew; that's why you wanted to forget. First the rape, then him. You were hurting, so you wanted to take away the hurt. You're getting your life back now, so don't walk backwards."

"I'm just curious, sometimes. How can I not be? Does he still live in town? Has he ever asked you where I am? Did he hurt me . . . physically?"

"Shut up, Kohl! I'm just honoring what you made me promise before, so shut up."

"Just one thing, Terr. Please. Did he hurt me? Physically?"

Terr said nothing; wagged her head.

"Please, Terr. Just that one thing."

"No. Not physically. All right? Happy? Not physically."

"How, then? Why would I leave him? Or did he leave me? Maybe he wasn't bad to me, but good to me, huh? Maybe that's why I wanted to forget him . . . because I loved him so much . . ."

"It doesn't matter either way. It doesn't matter if I liked him or not, if he's alive or he's dead. You wanted this, and I gave my word, and that's that. Move along. You were purged clean, you have a fresh start. You should concentrate on getting your old job back or suing those bastards and forget about the rape and your marriage."

"I was married two years, and dated him before that. Three years gone. I remember my job, in that time, but not him. I remember the dental work I had in that time, but not him. It's just . . . strange, Terr."

"I'm sure it is. But not as strange as being raped."

Kohl was quiet again for a few moments. Then: "Sometimes I try to remember. I think a song will remind me, or a smell, or . . ."

"That's not possible. It won't come, so don't wait for it. Memories physically alter the brain. Your brain was physically altered to erase all that. You will never remember, okay? It's as gone as if it never happened . . . like it should be. It's the closest we can come to going back in time and making things so they never were. I'd like to go back and touch up a few painful memories myself, sometime when I have the money. Not Dad altogether, but just the times he teased me; he could be really sadistic, the way he teased. And some stuff from school; that too." Terr nodded, her intense face underlit by the vehicle's dash displays. "It's a good thing to forget. Life hurts too much."

"I know," Kohl conceded softly. "It's just . . . it feels funny to have . . . holes like that. Three years. Even . . . even the rape. It's something important that happened to me . . ."

Terr glared over at her sister. "It's a horrible thing that happened to you! You learned nothing from it, gained nothing from it, you don't need it, so forget it, you hear me? You forget it!"

"It's a hole. It feels more scary, sometimes, not knowing how bad it was! Sometimes I imagine one nightmare and sometimes another. My husband, too. I try to fill in the hole and it scares me!"

"The doctor can only do so much. The rest is up to you. You aren't trying hard enough. You have to move on, and don't look back. You know, Dad used to tease you a lot, too. Probably damaged your self-esteem. You should go back and have that stuff cleaned out, too. That might help. You know?"

"It wouldn't be a real memory of Dad! It would be a censored version!"

"It would be the way he should have been," Terr muttered.

"I remember when we were kids you and me got in a fight and you started strangling me with your hands until I couldn't breathe, and I got really scared. Maybe I should get that erased, too, huh?"

"We were just kids!" Terr snapped. "But if it still bothers you, hey, by all means do so."

"I wouldn't have anything much left," Kohl murmured. "We waste so much time sleeping. It feels like losing so much more time . . ."

"Bad time. You don't need it. It's better this way. How can it not be?"

Kohl watched the moon lower over the spires and monuments of the city's jagged silhouette. It was a three-quarter moon, and looked to Kohl as if someone had taken a big bite out of it.

Kohl had originally moved here at the end of last year's flaying season, and now she could tell with relief that this year's time of slaughter was nearly finished. It was a few months early, but she guessed that the Antse year was shorter. The gutters stopped running with blood, and the effigies were not replaced; were left to fall into ruin and wither and mummify in the hot sun.

She was more willing to walk in the neighborhood now, and one Sunday in the early evening made a trip to a corner market. On her way back to her apartment, she paused at the front of a building. She had stopped here before.

It was an old, crumbling brick structure, native Choom in origin, predating colonization of this planet named Oasis. But there was a fossil in its brick that was not an ancient one. It was the mummified figure of an Earth man; a teleportation accident had fused the poor soul half into the gray brick. There was a painted arrow above his head, like a marking made on the street to indicate where a water pipe lay for repair, as if such were needed to point him out. The half of him that showed had never been claimed or removed, however. His clothing was mostly torn or worn away, and his one hand was gone, probably taken by young pranksters like whoever had spray-painted genitals where his own had withered.

His whole right side from crown to foot was lost in the wall. Half of his head absorbed into the brick so that only a skull socket and half a lipless grimace remained. A few strands of gray hair stirred in the languid summer air.

Kohl reached out and lightly touched his shoulder as if to comfort him in his solitary, silent anguish. Then, self-consciously, she looked around her, and there was an Antse male watching her from a window in the brick building itself, his face so close and his deeply recessed eyes so fixed on her that she started. Whether he was merely curious or found a cruel amusement in observing her sentimentality, she couldn't tell from the apparition's skeletal face aswirl in green and black. But he withdrew immediately upon being spotted, as if embarrassed himself, and despite their being of such radically different races, his furtive actions led Kohl to wonder if he might even have been surreptitiously admiring her.

Disturbed by this thought, she hurried on toward her apartment before it could grow dark.

"Hello again," the good-looking young man said, leaning on the counter. Had he lurked outside the shop until he saw that no one else was inside? "How about a mocha cappuccino, extra large?"

Kohl smiled faintly and turned her back on him. Reluctantly.

This was the third time this month he had come in here. The second time, she had been secretly gratified to see him again. But then, after they had chatted briefly and he had left, doubts had begun to surface. Even fears.

What if he knew her from before her treatments? What, in short, if this were her husband, who had succeeded in seeking her out, tracking her down? Her husband, who had somehow learned that she would not recognize him? Her husband, who was finding a perverse satisfaction in courting his ex-wife again, as if for the first time, who wanted to show her that she could not escape him as easily as that . . .

Her eyes flicked to her shoulder bag, resting on the back counter. Her pistol was in there. If he tried to come around the counter . . .

Placing the coffee before him, Kohl asked, "So what are we going to read now?"

"A collection of short stories by a twentieth-century writer, Yukio Mishima." The man showed her the book. "He committed suicide by ritual disembowelment."

"Yuck," Kohl chuckled nervously, accepting his money. "Well, enjoy it."

"You should read him . . . he's great." The ritual dumping of change into her tip cup. "Well, see you next time, huh?"

"Right. Bye."

Kohl watched him leave. And that evening she closed up the shop fifteen minutes early, rushed down to the book shop, and bought a volume of the Mishima stories. She brought it home that night to read, beginning on the shunt ride. There might be some clues in it, even that he meant for her to catch. Something that might indicate his true identity, his true intentions.

Whether he was her husband. Whether he was one of the rapists, even, from the parking lot . . .

"Yes . . . I remember that," Kohl said to the vidphone, her right hand absently riffling the pages of the Mishima collection. "Dr. Rudy did inform me of the option to have the memories recorded in case I changed my mind . . . at an extra cost. But I didn't think I'd ever want that, at the time, and I wanted to save some money, and so . . ."

"So you opted not to have those patterns recorded," said Dr. Rudy's receptionist, her face turned from the screen as she examined another monitor.

"Right," Kohl said. "But I was hoping . . . I wondered if maybe he records these things anyway, and saves them for a while after the procedure in case someone changes their mind." Kohl tried to joke, "Or wants their mind changed back."

"No, that isn't Dr. Rudy's system, I'm sorry. And even if it were, it has been over a year now since your first session. But no—" the woman swiveled back to face Kohl "—I gave it a look anyway and I don't see any indication that he ever made a recording of what you had removed. I'm sorry."

Kohl smiled, shrugged. "That's okay . . . I didn't really think he would have. I was just wondering. Thanks anyway."

"Sorry I couldn't help you."

"It's not important. Thanks again." Kohl tapped a key, and a screen saver replaced the woman's face.

Kohl more consciously thumbed through the Mishima book now. One story, "Patriotism," related in agonizing, loving detail the double suicide—called shinju—of a Japanese military officer and his wife. Particularly the man's disembowelment; Kohl could almost imagine that Mishima had penned it while cutting his own belly open, writing down his observations. Picturing the slicing, the bleeding made her so light-headed as she read the story that she had to set the book down for a few moments to calm her breathing.

What might the young man be suggesting to her, through this book? Was he indeed her husband, obsessed with her, having tracked her down at last . . . and now suggesting that they perform this most devoted of romantic acts together? Die united in the ritual of shinju?

Kohl lifted her gaze again to the vidphone's mindless swirlings of color. How carefully had that receptionist really checked? Should she try to talk to Dr. Rudy himself?

What if Rudy had kept the recording for his own purposes? His own entertainment? Even now, might he be watching Kohl and her husband on their wedding night, through Kohl's eyes?

Might he be watching her rape in the parking lot, finding excitement in it?

The concept so horrified her that she was startled. But men were like that, weren't they? In polls they freely admitted they would rape if they thought they could get away with it. That it was their foremost sexual fantasy. Men hungered, men consumed. She thought again of the staring Antse in the window, his face the face of all men, stripped of the deceitful flesh, the facade of civilization, leaving only the gaping eyes and Death's head grin.

The night fell. Kohl played music. She made tea. She went to the window.

Tomorrow she would return to work. And she would bring her gun, as she always did . . . though lately she had taken to carrying it in her dress pocket, rather than her shoulder bag. And if the young man came in again, she would point the gun at him and demand that he reveal his identity.

If he was a rapist, she would shoot him in the face. And if he were her husband, she would shoot him in the heart, and then she would shoot herself in the heart, because shinju meant "inside the heart." And then she and her husband would be united, linked again forever in death. They would be whole.

A shunt passed. A burst of sparks illuminated, for one second, the flesh scarecrow suspended from the window opposite . . . now barely recognizable, a bundle of tattered scraps, all but fallen away.

PAUL J. MCAULEY

Bone Orchards

Paul J. McAuley, who lives in London, has published nine novels, including Child of the River, Ancients of Days, and Shrine of Stars, which form the Confluence trilogy. His most recent novel, The Secret of Life, has just been published in the U.S. His forthcoming novel is called Whole Wide World. Although McAuley is best known for his science fiction, he also writes the occasional fantasy or horror story.

The protagonist of "Bone Orchards" made an appearance in "Naming the Dead," which was in last year's volume of this series. "Bone Orchards" was originally published in Time Out London Short Stories Volume 2, edited by Nicholas Royle. He says, "I'm growing quite fond of Mr. Carlyle, a man of very Victorian sensibility who is helping me understand the strange and wonderful city (its present incarnation very much dominated by the Victorians) where I live."

—E. D.

Cemeteries are fine, private, quiet places, for it is the living, not the dead, who make ghosts. It is the living who slough shells of anger or terror, shed shivers of joy or ooze sullen residues of hate, sticky as spilled crude oil. Only the living, at the crucial moment of transition, cast off yearning or puzzled phantoms, and because most ghosts do not know they are dead, they do not often stray into the gardens of the dead. And so it is that I go to cemeteries to find respite from the blooming, buzzing confusion of the city.

Usually my clients must seek me out, and I make sure that I am not easy to find because I am their last hope, not their first. But, rarely, I discover someone I can help, and this was one such affair, begun in the peace of a bone orchard.

It was in the spring of 199-. Collective manias and delusions at the end of this dreadful century had set loose a host of strange and wild things. I had taken to walking about the city, trying to understand the redrawn maps of influence. It was a transformation as slow but sure as the yielding of winter to spring, but more profound, more permanent. It was as if the climate was changing.

My walks were not entirely random. I made a point of stopping for an hour or two of peaceful contemplation in the sanctuary of one or another of the city's

cemeteries. The secret garden of the Moravian cemetery, entered by an unmarked door next to a public house off the King's Road. Kensal Green Cemetery,
with its great Doric arch and graveled roads wide enough for carriages. The
ordered plots of Brompton Cemetery, radiating from the central octagonal
chapel. The City of London Cemetery, its drained lake now a valley of catacombs. Even Bunhill Cemetery, its weathered tombs protected by prissy green
municipal railings, could afford a little tranquillity as long as one avoided the
lunchtime crowds of office workers.

That day, I had walked north up the Kingsland Road, past the new mosque
(although my family has a long and honorable tradition in the matter of the
dead, I am not a religious man, but any sign of communal faith gives me hope),
through the brawl and tacky commerciality of Dalston (the Santería shop was
closed down; I wondered if that had been caused by a minor fluctuation of the
new climate), to Stoke Newington and Abney Park Cemetery.

Abney Park:

Beyond the modest entrance off Church Street, hard by the fire station, beyond the imposing graves of Salvation Army generals, paths divide and divide
again, leading you away from city noise. The place is thick with trees, and sap-
lings push up between close-set graves or are even rooted in the graves themselves, as if the dead are sprouting at skull or ribs or thigh. There are angels and
pyramids and obelisks and hundreds of ordinary headstones. There is a lion.
There are anchors cast on a rough boulder. Many graves are tilted, as if the dead,
restless for Judgment Day, have been pounding on the roofs of their tombs. At
the center is the derelict chapel of rest, a gothic ruin surprisingly free of graffiti,
its windows boarded up or covered in bright new corrugated iron, every bit of
glass smashed from the rose at the apex of the square tower. Boards have been
prised away from one window; the scraps of the trespassers' spent lust curl within
like exhausted snakes.

That day, yellow daffodils nodded in the mild breeze above some graves—the
last land our lives leave, our final plot, is a garden the size of our bodies—and
others were bright with rainwashed silk flowers. I wandered the paths, munching
chocolate bourbons from the packet I had purchased at a Turkish corner shop.
The blue sky was netted by a web of bare branches. Birds sang, defining their
territories. A man in a grubby T-shirt and a wrinkled leather jacket led an eager
mongrel on a string and a carried a can of strong beer; imps hid from me in the
tangled rat-tails of his hair. An art student in black was hunched on a bench,
sketching one of the angels (its left arm had been broken off at the elbow; fresh
stone showed as shockingly white as bone against its weathered gray skin). A
man and a woman in identical shell suits sat at another bench, talking quietly.
A young woman pushed her baby in an old-fashioned perambulator.

And an old woman in a shabby gray anorak knelt like a penitent at a grave.
Something about her made me stop and sit at a bench nearby. I took out my
book (a badly foxed copy of Abellio's *La Fin de l'ésotérisme*), and pretended to
ruffle through its pages while raking her with covert glances. She was bathed in
sunlight that fell at an angle between close-laced branches, like a saint in
a medieval woodcut. A quite unremarkable woman in her late sixties, with a
pinched, exhausted face devoid of make-up, coarse gray hair caught under a

flowery scarf. Her anorak, her rayon trousers and her cheap flat shoes had all been bought in the same high street emporium. She was tidying the grave with slow, painful care, raking its green gravel, straightening the silk roses in their brass pot, washing city dirt from the white headstone. She did not see me; nor did she see what seemed to be a small child running about the old graves in the distance.

No one could see it but me.

At last, the woman pulled a shiny black purse from the pocket of her anorak, opened it, and took out a piece of paper. She lifted up a smooth beach pebble, removed something, and tucked the paper underneath. Then she laboriously got to her feet, one hand on the small of her back, dusted her hands, and hobbled away down the path.

I shut my book and went to the grave and retrieved the paper. It was a sheet torn from a cheap, lined writing pad, as soft as newspulp, folded twice into a square. I was about to unfold it when something said, "That's mine."

It presented as a girl of ten or eleven, thin, determined, petulant, in a pale dress fifty years out of date. A scarf was knotted at her skinny neck. Eyes that were no more than dark smudges were half-hidden by tangled hair that stirred in a breeze I could not feel. It stamped ineffectively and said again, "That's mine."

I held out the folded sheet of paper.

"I don't want it now, not now you've touched it, you smelly old thing."

"I will read it for you, if you like."

"Smelly old fat thing," it said spitefully, and turned and took a few steps along the path the old woman had taken before stopping and looking at me over its shoulder, hesitant, unsure.

"I can read it for you," I said again. "I am not like the others. I speak for people like you."

The pale child ran up to me and swiped at the paper with fingers crooked into talons. It failed to take it, of course, and was suddenly dancing in fury. "Fat fucker! Smelly fat fucking fucker!"

The sun seemed to darken, and the child grew in definition, as a candle flame steadies after it has been lit. Branches moved overhead like bony fingers rubbing together.

"You fucking fat smelly fuck!"

Stuff like drool slicked the child's chin, dripped onto the path.

I waited, holding out the paper. When the child was quiet again, I said, "I can read it for you. I do not think you can."

"Fuck you."

Quieter now.

"Is she your mother?"

"She's mine. She's always been mine. You can't have her."

And then the child was chasing away through the trees after the old woman like smoke blown from a gun. There was a wetness on the path, frothy as the mucus shed by a salted slug.

I unfolded the sheet of paper, read the few lines written in painstaking copperplate, then looked at the headstone of the grave.

Jennifer Burton
28th November 1933—28th November 1944
Taken from us, she sleeps in peace

I had thought the grave only a few years old. It had been faithfully tended for over fifty years.

I wrote down the particulars in the flyleaf of my book, copied the lines on the sheet of paper, and tucked it back under the pebble.

"She was murdered," Detective-Superintendent Rawles told me. "Strangled by the scarf her mother gave her for her birthday. Murdered, but not sexually assaulted. Her sister was found wandering the streets nearby, with scratches on her arms and face. She had been attacked too, but she must have managed to get away when her sister was strangled, and she couldn't remember anything. You don't think of ordinary crimes happening then, with the war going on, but there it is. The case is still open."

"Like a wound," I said, remembering the scarf around the little girl's neck.

We were sitting in the snug of *The Seven Stars*, the comfortable old pub just around the corner from Lincoln Inn Fields. Rawles was due to give evidence at a murder trial in an hour. He was uncharacteristically nervous, and had kept stealing glances at his watch as I described my encounter and worked my way through a steak and kidney pie. Around us, sleek lawyers in dark suits talked loudly about chambers gossip and old and forthcoming cases. The sad quiet shade of a pot boy was drifting about a dark corner of the bar; out of courtesy, we pretended to ignore each other.

Rawles passed a hand over his close-cropped white hair and sighed. My old friend and ally looked worn out. There were deep lines either side of his mouth, and nests of hair in his ears. The skin on the backs of his hands was as loose as a lizard's, and crazed with a diamond pattern. He said, "Do you really think you should be prying into this, Carlyle?"

"How long is it until you retire, Robert?"

"Three months, as you know very well. I'm dreading it."

"The bungalow in Essex? Your roses?"

"I can't wait to get out of the city. What I dread is the party they're going to give me."

"I will be there in spirit."

Rawles drained his pint glass and said, "The bungalow is brand new. No ghosts at all."

"There are ghosts everywhere, Rawles. I can look at your bungalow, if you like. You might be surprised."

"I'd rather live in ignorant bliss. That's going to be my motto from now on. See nothing, hear nothing. What about you, Carlyle? Why the interest in this?"

"Think of it as spring cleaning. It is the time of year when you do all those little jobs that in the depths of winter you always meant to get around to but never quite did. Now the world wakes, and you do too."

"I've seen your place," Rawles said. "I don't think you've ever dusted in your life."

"It is merely a metaphor. In these strange times, a small bit of work like this will do me some good. Think of it as a charitable case."

Rawles said. "I'm going to be out of it soon, thank Christ," and pushed the brown folder across the table. It was tied with faded green string. "I'll want this back. And if the animal that killed her is still alive, I suppose I'll have to do something about it."

Jennifer Burton had been murdered a few streets from where she lived, on a bombsite where, according to the police report, the local kids had made a kind of camp or den. She had been found amidst candle stubs and broken bits of furniture, strangled by her birthday scarf.

It was amongst the anonymous streets just to the east of the British Museum and Bloomsbury, where cheap tourist hotels, student hostels, council blocks, red brick mansions blocks and university offices crowd together along treeless streets where the sun never quite reaches. There was a block of flats—white concrete and metal-framed windows—where the bombsite had been. I rang bells at random. When at last someone answered, I said, "It's me," and shouldered aside the door when it was buzzed open.

I found a stair down to the basement, and stood a while in the dim light that seeped from a pavement grill, amongst bicycles and boxes of discarded belongings, under pipes that snaked across the ceiling. There was nothing there, but I had not expected anything. The ghost of the murdered girl had fled with her sister, I thought, and she had carried that burden ever since.

My Darling Jennifer, the old woman had written. *It is a lovely spring day and so I came to visit you, and see that you were nice and tidy. It will soon be the next century, the new millennium, and I wonder how it is that I am still alive. I carry you with me always, my darling.*

The fierce deep anguish that burned through these banal sentiments!

I had learned little from the old police files. Jennifer Burton had been eleven when she had died, older by a half hour than her twin, Joan. The police had interviewed known sex offenders and every soldier arrested in London for drunkenness or desertion in the weeks following the murder, but with no result. Joan had been interviewed three times, but remembered nothing of that day. The case had gone cold.

I left that quiet basement and found the address where the two girls had been living with their mother. They had only recently returned from the village in Devon to which they had been evacuated at the beginning of the Blitz. The building had been made over into offices, with a stark modern foyer behind big plate glass windows. A security guard sat behind a bleached oak desk. I could have worked up some plausible bluff, but someone who could help me was nearby, and I went to find him instead.

Coram's Fields, in the middle of the parish of St. Pancras, is one of the happiest places I know. There is a playground where the only adults allowed in are those who bring their children, and there is an adjoining park, St. George's Gardens, where I sometimes sit for a while. The playground is built on the site of the Foundling Hospital; the gardens are laid out on what was once a cemetery. I know only too well how much of London is built on her dead.

That the park and playground are unmarked by darkness is due in large part to its unofficial and unacknowledged guardian. Harry Wright was a pacifist who became a volunteer fireman during the war. He was killed at the height of the Blitz, when the front of a burning house collapsed on him as he went in to rescue three children trapped inside. I sat on a bench amongst clipped, mulched rose beds in cold sunlight. The shrieks and laughter of children at play was clear and sharp. Presently Harry drifted over, tentative and curious.

"It's you, Mr. Carlyle," he said, smiling with relief. "For a moment, I thought it might be trouble."

"I am afraid that I have brought a little trouble, Harry. Sit down, and I will tell you about it."

"I'll keep watch if you don't mind, Mr. Carlyle, and I do it better standing."

He was a small, tough, bantam-rooster of a man in his mid thirties, in shirt and braces, his honest face smudged and indistinct, like a half-erased sketch. He drifted around the bench, head cocked for any trouble, as I explained my encounter at Abney Park Cemetery.

"Oh, I couldn't go all the way up there," he said, when I had finished. "I have enough of a job here."

"I understand. What I have in mind is much closer to home."

"I don't know if I could, Mr. Carlyle."

"There is a child to be helped, Harry, and it will take only a little of your time."

"Still," he said doubtfully, "things are difficult at the moment. It all seems so hopeless sometimes, as if the whole world is bearing down on me and my little patch."

"Things are changing, Harry. We all feel it."

"I saw that librarian chap a while ago," Harry said. He was still patrolling my bench, keeping watch on the perimeters of the park. "Was it last week? Anyway, he felt the same thing."

Like many of his kind, Harry was vague about time. I knew it must have been at least several months ago, for that was when the Librarian had been devoured. It had been my fault. I had sent him against something whose strength I had underestimated. I still carried the guilt, like an ink stain on my soul.

I said, "I am afraid that he has passed on."

"That's a shame. Him and me, we had some interesting talks. Very well educated, he was, and polite as anyone I've met. Perhaps it was for the best, Mr. Carlyle. I don't suppose he would have liked the changes to his place."

The old Reading Room of the British Library was closed; its books had been transferred to the new red brick building on Euston Road. When I had last been there, I had stood a while in the wood-paneled room where the autographed manuscripts had once been on view, and where display boards and glass-cased models of the new extension now stood, mantled with a fine layer of concrete dust from the building works, disturbed only by the occasional tourist who had taken a wrong turning. I had waited a long time, but he had not come.

I told Harry Wright's restlessly circling ghost, "You are quite right. He would have hated it."

"He was a man of his time, Mr. Carlyle. Now, I think I can help you, but I'll have to be quick. Even the day isn't safe anymore."

I was glad that I did not have to compel him. I waited outside the office building while Harry made his search. I waited more than an hour, pretending to read my book under the gaze of a security camera, and I grew so anxious that I almost cried out in amazement when at last Harry appeared with his burden.

"We'll take the poor mite to my place," he said, brisk and matter-of-fact. "Safer that way."

I lost him when I had to wait for a gap in the traffic shuddering angrily down Judd Street, but he was waiting for me in the rose garden. He was still holding the child he had rescued. Her face was pressed against his shoulder. There was a scarf around her neck, and she wore the same dress as the venomously angry thing I had confronted in Abney Park.

"She's scared," Harry said. "She was hiding in a cupboard. It's all right now, darling," he added, speaking softly to the child. "You're safe here."

It took a while to coax her around. At last, Harry set her on her feet and resumed his patrol while she scampered about, stopping every minute to look up at the sky. I waited until she drifted back to me, shy and sidelong.

"You're a funny man," she said.

She stood on one foot, twisting the other behind her calf. A breeze could have blown her away.

"I know I am," I said.

A woman walking her dog glanced at me as she went past; I suppose she would have seen an overweight man in a black raincoat, hunched over and talking to himself. Hardly an uncommon sight in these troubled times.

The girl said, "So many people came at first, and they were making such a fuss, that I hid. But then they went away and after that I couldn't make anyone hear me. I thought Joan would find me. I waited and waited. Will you take me to her?"

"I cannot do that. But I can help you, if you will help me. I want to know what happened to you. Do you understand?"

She nodded. She said, "It was like being filled with black boxes. The dark came flying in, and it had corners. It filled me up."

"Did you see who brought the dark, Jennifer?"

The child's hands had gone to her throat, plucking at the knotted scarf. She said, "I don't want to cause trouble."

"None of that matters, not anymore."

"That's what the nice man told me," the child said, and added, "He said that he was a fireman."

"So he is. And a very good one. We both want to help you, Jennifer. I think that I know what happened, but I need to be sure. Will you tell me?"

"Joan was cross. She wanted my scarf because she said that it was nicer than hers. She said I always got nicer things because I was older. She wanted it, and I wouldn't give it to her because it was mine!"

She ran then. I did not try to follow her, and at last Harry brought her back. She would not talk, but it did not matter, because I knew now how wrong I had been. I told the little girl that she could rest. That she could sleep. And then I sent her away.

Harry said, "Is it like that, Mr. Carlyle? Like going to sleep?"

"I do not know," I said. "But that is what everyone wants to believe."

Harry brushed his hands together. "There's no rest for the wicked, as my gran used to say. I'll be back to work. It's getting dark, and there can be trouble, after dark."

A week later, I was sitting on the bench in Abney Park Cemetery, near Jennifer Burton's grave. I had been coming here every day, waiting for Jennifer's sister, and her burden. Every day, at dusk, when I knew that the old woman would not come, I passed by her mean little basement flat in Albion Road on my way home. I once saw her coming up the steps in her gray coat and her neat scarf, moving slowly and painfully, bowed under the weight of her burden, which had hissed like a cat when it spied me across the street.

It was another sunny day. The buds were beginning to break on the trees, so that the stark outlines of their branches were blurred by a ghostly scantling of green. The old woman came just after noon, and her burden came with her, circling us both at a distance, hardly more than broken shadow and sunlight. At last, the old woman finished tidying her sister's grave. She took out a piece of folded paper and tucked it under the pebble, and crumpled up the note I had carefully replaced.

The ghost circled through the trees as the old woman went away down the path. I called its name and told it to come to me and it did, glaring at me through the tangle of its hair.

"You fat old fucker," it said. "You don't scare me."

"I know why you did it, Joan. You wanted the scarf. You did not realize that you had hurt your sister so badly."

"She messed her knickers," the thing said, with a vicious smile. "She made a funny sound and messed her knickers, the smelly silly."

It was the ghost Joan Burton had cast off in a moment of sudden and intense anger. It was the memory that she could never acknowledge, the memory of murdering her own sister. She had been imprisoned by it ever since, a longer sentence than any court would have imposed.

It glared at me through its tangled hair and hissed, "Keep away from me, you fat fucker. I'll hurt you. I will."

"Enough," I said, and gathered it to me. It was like lifting up an armful of icy briars, but only for a moment.

"So you found nothing," Detective-Superintendent Rawles said. "That's not like you, Carlyle. You usually like to see things through to the end."

Once again, we had met in The Seven Stars. Once again, Rawles was stealing glances at his watch. The jury in his case was expected to announce its verdict that afternoon.

I said, "Times are changing."

"Times change, Carlyle, but you don't. You're more or less the same as when I met you back in '64."

"Ah, but I was already old then."

"You do have a bit of a spring in your step today," Rawles said. "I noticed when I came in."

"I did? I suppose it is the season. Everything seems hopeful at this time of year."

I had passed Joan Burton on the way out of the cemetery. She was still stooped, but I think it was out of habit, not necessity. I said, "A nice day, is it not?"

She glanced at me and smiled, and I saw in that smile the pretty girl she had once been. "I hadn't noticed," she said, "but yes, you're right. Isn't it beautiful?"

NEIL GAIMAN

Instructions

Neil Gaiman, best known for his award-winning Sandman *series of graphic novels, is also the author of magical novels (*Stardust, Neverwhere, *etc.), novellas (*The Dream Hunters*), and children's books (*The Day I Swapped My Dad for Two Goldfish*), as well as short stories and poetry collected in* Visitations *and* Smoke and Mirrors. *He has won the World Fantasy Award, the Mythopoeic Award, and the Julia Verlanger Award for Best Novel published in France. Born and raised in England, Gaiman now lives in the American Midwest.*

"Instructions" is a gorgeous poem written for the fairy-tale anthology A Wolf at the Door. *It's a poem that begs to be read aloud, and not just to the children.*

—T. W.

Touch the wooden gate in the wall you never saw before.
Say "please" before you open the latch,
go through,
walk down the path.
A red metal imp hangs from the green-painted front door,
as a knocker,
do not touch it; it will bite your fingers.
Walk through the house. Take nothing. Eat nothing.
However,
if any creature tells you that it hungers,
feed it.
If it tells you that it is dirty,
clean it.
If it cries to you that it hurts,
if you can,
ease its pain.

From the back garden you will be able to see the wild wood.
The deep well you walk past leads to Winter's realm;
there is another land at the bottom of it.

If you turn around here,
you can walk back, safely;
you will lose no face. I will think no less of you.

Once through the garden you will be in the wood.
The trees are old. Eyes peer from the undergrowth.
Beneath a twisted oak sits an old woman. She may ask for something;
give it to her. She
will point the way to the castle.
Inside it are three princesses.
Do not trust the youngest. Walk on.
In the clearing beyond the castle the twelve months sit about a fire,
warming their feet, exchanging tales.
They may do favors for you, if you are polite.
You may pick strawberries in December's frost.
Trust the wolves, but do not tell them where you are going.
The river can be crossed by the ferry. The ferry-man will take you.
(The answer to his question is this:
If he hands the oar to his passenger, he will be free to leave the boat.
Only tell him this from a safe distance.)

If an eagle gives you a feather, keep it safe.
Remember: that giants sleep too soundly; that
witches are often betrayed by their appetites;
dragons have one soft spot, somewhere, always;
hearts can be well-hidden,
and you betray them with your tongue.

Do not be jealous of your sister.
Know that diamonds and roses
are as uncomfortable when they tumble from one's lips as toads and frogs:
colder, too, and sharper, and they cut.

Remember your name.
Do not lose hope—what you seek will be found.
Trust ghosts. Trust those that you have helped to help you in their turn.
Trust dreams.
Trust your heart, and trust your story.
When you come back, return the way you came.
Favors will be returned, debts be repaid.
Do not forget your manners.
Do not look back.
Ride the wise eagle (you shall not fall)
Ride the silver fish (you will not drown)
Ride the gray wolf (hold tightly to his fur).

There is a worm at the heart of the tower; that is why it will not stand.

When you reach the little house, the place your journey started,
you will recognize it, although it will seem much smaller than you remember.

Walk up the path, and through the garden gate you never saw before but
   once.

And then go home. Or make a home.

Or rest.

ESTHER M. FRIESNER

Hallowmass

*Esther M. Friesner is a prolific author of magical tales both light and dark.
She has published* The Silver Mountain, Druid's Blood, Yesterday We Saw
Mermaids, Wishing Season, The Sherwood Game, Mustapha and His Wise
Dog, New York by Knight, Here Be Demons, Majyk by Accident, Up the
Wall and Other Tales of King Arthur and His Knights, *and numerous other
books in the fantasy field. Friesner is a graduate of Vassar College, and lives
in Connecticut.*

*Although best known for sparkling stories and novels of humorous fantasy,
Friesner's darker works (such as her novel* The Psalms of Herod, *and the
following tale) are imagistic, folkloric, and gorgeously poetic. The inspiration
for "Hallowmass" came, says the author, during a trip to Chartres cathedral,
where a young man with a flute created "silvery threads of music that seemed
to spiral down from no visible source in the shadows above." The story was
first published in the January issue of* The Magazine of Fantasy & Science
Fiction.*

—T. W.

Master, the heart of these things came to pass in the autumn of the
year that the great cathedral neared completion. Beyond the town
walls the fields were nearly bare and the forest put on splendor. Bright
leaf crowns of bronze and purple, scarlet and gold flung themselves
over the secret fastnesses of the wood where terrors crouched. In the shorn
fields asters winked blue among the stubble. And everywhere, in the streets
and on the narrow track slipping between the hills to the outlying villages, there
was song.

The countryfolk sang because their harvest was done and the war had slithered
its huge, armored body far into the south that year. Mothers sang cradle songs
to cradles where for once no spectral hand of famine or illness or whetted steel
had crept to touch and take their babes. Farmers bellowed drinking songs in the
taverns because singing drowned out the noise of backbones that creaked and
snapped when honest working men at last unbent their spines from the labor of
reaping and stacking, threshing and winnowing the grain.

Giles was a man who made his songs with stone. He was well past the middle years of Adam's sons, his raven hair streaked and stippled with gray, his beard blazed silver like the back of a badger. When he first arrived, over fifteen Easters agone, no one in the town knew where he came from or who paid out his wages. He presented himself to the widow Agnes who had a small house hard by the cathedral's growing shadow and offered her a fair price for the rental of a room, food to fill his belly, and the free use of her modest yard. The yard stood behind the house and was supposed to contain the widow's humble garden, but the plastered walls of the house itself hoarded sunlight from what few plants struggled their way out of the sour soil, and in time the cathedral's rising walls shouldered aside almost everything but shadows.

The widow Agnes therefore did not complain too loudly when the nature of Giles's intent for her property was made known. The very next day after his arrival, a dust-faced man named Paul the Brown presented himself at her door driving a cart with a load of fresh timber. She recognized him as one of the bishop's lowest-ranked servants and kept her thoughts to herself when Giles rushed out to greet him eagerly. Together the two men transported the lumber into the widow's yard and from it built a spacious, slant-roofed shed on ground where flowers often had been planted but never had lived to bloom.

In the days that followed, the widow Agnes witnessed more strange shipments arrive on her doorstep for her new boarder. There was a small, sturdy table, a stool standing on four fat legs, a coarse hempen sack that clanked demons out of the widow's white cat Belle, and lengths of sailcloth, thick with pale dust and neatly folded. All of these effects were trundled out to the shed in the yard where some were put in place and others put into ironbound chests of wood that locked with a *snick-clack* sound like jackdaws laughing. Last of all came the stones.

A squadron of servants showed their yellowed teeth to the widow when she answered their thunderous summons on the day the first more-than-man-size block of stone arrived. As with the first servant, Paul the Brown, their faces were all familiar to her—work-creased vizards of skin glimpsed in passing on market day, or when the widow's curious eye wandered during mass, or in the shadow of the tavern sign.

The leader of that burly crew doffed a cap frosty with dust and asked, "Where'll Master Giles have it?" He gestured to the block of raw-hewn stone on the cart behind him.

"*Master* Giles?" the widow echoed. Her commerce with the man until this had been scant and small (and she a woman whose inquisitive tongue could winkle out a fellow's life history in the time it takes to break a tinker's promise!). She knew him by that name but not that title.

"Aye, this is the first of 'em," the servant said. He might have said more, but Master Giles was there, white Belle a mewing ghost at his ankles. He spoke with brief courtesy to his landlady, begging her pardon for not having forewarned her of this visitation while at the same time telling her no more about it. Then he hustled forward to direct the men to move the block of stone into the widow's yard, under the shelter of the shed.

Some days later the widow Agnes found the form of a man emerging from the great stone. Crude as God's first tentative pinchings in the red clay that would be Adam, Master Giles's man lacked the features of a face (unless the first hint of a high-bridged nose could be reckoned to that credit) and could be said to possess human hands only as a courtesy to the lumpy mass of rock at the ends of what *might* have been arms.

Master Giles saw the widow staring at his work and grinned. His thick hair and beard were now all white with the breath of chiseled rock, as if the stone were sucking away his allotted lifespan, but he worked bare-armed and bare-chested in the pleasant summer weather and the knotted muscles moving sleekly beneath the skin cried *liar!* to any who dared to call him old.

"Good day to you, goodwife," he said, still swinging the hammer, still holding the steel-edged cutting tool to its task. The tapping blows and the chinking sound of the stone's thousand small surrenders underlay his words in a smooth, steady rhythm. "What do you think of my Saint Clement?" He lowered the hammer and gestured at a protruding lump of rock with the chisel. "Here's the anchor that dragged him to a glorious martyr's death. I would have given him a stonecutter's tools, but my lord bishop would discover my vanity all the earlier then." His hearty laugh was for himself and for all the petty conceits of a fragile world.

The widow crept nearer, but she could see neither the offered anchor nor the stonecutter's point. His smile did not mock her when she confessed herself either bewildered by the light or merely bewitched by her own ignorance.

"You will see the anchor in time," Master Giles said kindly, setting his tools down on the worktable and taking her plump hand in his calloused palm. "The saint is still being born. You see, my lord bishop has brought me here for the cathedral's sake. I am to adorn the south porch below the great rose window with twelve figures in stone, and since Master Martin whose province is the north porch has already laid claim to the Twelve Apostles, I have a free hand in the choice of my saints. I thought to begin well by invoking the protection of Saint Clement. He has always been a friend to those of my trade. The Emperor Trajan tore him from the papal throne and sent him as a slave to the marble quarries of Russia, but even there he made conversions and worked miracles. Once, they say, his faith called forth water from a rock for the sake of his fellow-slaves' thirst. Soon after, he was flung into a great sea, the anchor around his neck. The angels themselves built him a stone tomb beneath the waves. That is beyond me, so I do this, to his glory."

The widow Agnes bobbed her head. She loved the tales of saints' lives, for she was a devout woman—all the more so since her husband had gone to sleep in a churchyard bed. He took with him to eternal rest the staff with which he used to beat his bride, but he forbore to fetch away his money. If this was not proof of divine grace, it would do for the widow Agnes. "Which saints will you choose for the other—" She did a quick tally "—eleven?"

"I don't know," said master Giles. "Saint Barbara, perhaps, to keep the peril of fire far from the holy place, and Saint George to aid the farmer and protect good horses. Who can say?" His smile was whiter than the fresh-cut stone as he glimpsed Belle's pointed face staring boldly out at him from behind the widow's skirts. "I might even carve a likeness of Saint Anthony to mind the fortunes of some small animals in need of watching."

The widow Agnes laughed out loud and told him he was a sorry rogue, and

that she would warn my lord bishop of the jackanapes he'd hired for the adorn-
ment of the south porch. Then she brought Master Giles the good wine from
the cellar and when the sun's setting cheated the eyes of gossips everywhere, she
took him to her bed.

The years ran and the cathedral grew. The shapes of saints blossomed in the
widow's yard and were duly bundled away to their places in the niches of the
south porch. The widow and Master Giles lay down together many times with
only simple human comfort in mind and awoke one morning startled to find
love had slipped between the sheets. They did not marry, for the talk would
crumble Master Giles's favor with the bishop as surely as it would destroy the
widow's fame for piety and prayer. There did come a time in that first mad year
when the widow had cause to travel south to settle a matter of inheritance
among her distant kin, but she returned within a sixmonth and all was as before.

The little white cat Belle birthed many litters and died, leaving the wardship
of the widow's house to her daughter Candida, who was also furred with snow.
And one hot August day the widow died of a sweating fever that carried off
many souls besides her own, leaving the care of her house to a distant relative
and the care of Candida to Master Giles.

The distant relative turned out to be a spinster of the breed that seem born
crones from their mothers' wombs. She was called Margaret, dead Agnes's far-
removed cousin, a woman who had never married and therefore begrudged the
joy of any woman who had. She was able, for charity, to forgive those who found
themselves bound in miserable, loveless matches, and so for a time she had made
Agnes her favorite. But when Agnes's husband died leaving the lady young
enough and rich enough to live on sweetly content, Margaret came near to
choking on the injustice of it all. Or perhaps it was only her own bile that rose
to fill her throat.

Margaret lived with her parents in a village whose chief product was stink.
After they died, Agnes sent her cousin plentiful support, the only fact which
allowed Margaret to reconcile herself somewhat to Agnes's good fortune. She
had less trouble reconciling herself to her own when the news reached her of
Agnes's death and her own inheritance.

She arrived on a raw December day when Master Giles was just finishing work
on his ninth saint. She came mounted on a fat donkey, purchased with the first
portion of Agnes's bequest. (A clerk of the cathedral was guardian and messenger
of the widow's estate. He it was who took word of Agnes's death and final
testament to Margaret, along with a sum of money to finance the spinster's
journey to her new demesne. Agnes had made a sizable gift to the cathedral as
well as to her cousin, and so it was plain courtesy to see that good woman's
affairs well settled.)

Margaret drove the donkey on to the timpani of her bony heels against the
animal's heaving sides, a stout stick in her hand playing counterpoint on his
rump. The poor beast's brayed petition of mercy to heaven roused every street
through which they passed. So loud was her advent, and so well heralded by the
urchins running along beside her, that Master Giles himself was lured from his
beloved stone to see what nine-days' wonder was invading his emptied life.

When she drew up abreast of the late widow Agnes's house, the spinster
Margaret jerked on the donkey's rope bridle and slid from the saddle-blanket

with poor grace. The throng of merrymaking children who had joined in her processional swarmed around her, offering to guide her, to hold the donkey's bridle, to perform any of a dozen needless errands to justify their continued presence underfoot. Master Giles saw with horror how the woman raised her stick, threatening to treat the children after a fashion that was unfit to treat a donkey.

"Go home, children," he said gently, stepping into their midst and placing his towering body as a shield between them and Margaret's stick. "Off with you now, you're wanted home." The children giggled and darted away, all save one.

"Who are you?" Margaret demanded of the stonecutter, her lips thin as meat cut at a poor man's table.

"I am Master Giles, in the service of my lord bishop."

"Oh." Her mouth was small and hard as a prunepit. "You. The clerk said you pay rent and you work to finish the cathedral. My lord bishop would rather not have you moved."

"My lord bishop is kind," said Master Giles in such a way that he let her know how alien he thought kindness was to her heart.

"My lord bishop may command me," Margaret said dryly. "So you are to stay, then, since it does nothing to inconvenience *him*. How much longer *must* you live here?"

"Until I have finished birthing my saints."

"*Birthing*? How dare you speak so of the holy ones?" Margaret squawked like a goose caught under a style. "As if they were slimed with the foulness of a sinful woman's blood? Ugh! I will report this blasphemy to the bishop and you will be made to leave my house before another sun sets."

Master Giles's eyes lost their tolerant warmth. "You may say what you like into whatever ears will hear it. I will deny it all. Do you think my lord bishop will risk the promised beauty of his cathedral for the sake of a lone woman's rantings?"

"I have truth to speak for me," Margaret said, stiffer than the carven draperies that clothed Master Giles's stone children.

"That's as may be," he replied. "But I have my saints, and my saints have my lord bishop's ear." He turned from her proudly and almost sprawled over the huddled body of the boy who crouched against the doorframe of dead Agnes's house.

"Go home, child," Master Giles told him. "Why do you linger here?" The boy looked up at the stonecutter with eyes as stony and unseeing as those of the master's carved saints and a face as beautiful as heaven. A blind man's staff leaned against his hollow shoulder but he did not have the shabby air of a beggar. His garb was well worn, simple, sufficient, and there was a bundle of belongings at his feet.

Margaret gave a harsh sniff. "This is Benedict," she said, and she seized the boy roughly by the wrist and thrust the lead-rope of her donkey into his hand. She barged into the window Agnes's house without another word, leaving Master Giles to stare at the boy as blankly as if he himself were the sightless one.

The boy leaned on his staff and got to his feet, holding fast to the donkey's rope. "Is there a stable?" he asked, stooping to juggle rope and staff so that he might hold these and still take up his bundle.

"I will take care of the beast," Master Giles said, his tongue stumbling over the words as a score of unasked questions struggled for precedence. He tried to disengage the boy's hand from the donkey's lead, but Benedict refused to relinquish it.

"This is my work," he said. "I am always the one with the beasts."

Master Giles considered the boy's reply as no stranger than his bearing. He did not seem a servant, yet Margaret did not treat him as kin. "This way, then," he said at last, and set his hand on the boy's shoulder to guide him to the shack that served dead Agnes's house for a stable.

The house that once had warmed itself with love now steeped itself in ice. The house that once had rung with the sweet tempo of iron on stone, keeping time to a well-loved woman's morning song, now sheltered only silence. Margaret provided Master Giles with food and shelter and free use of the yard in accordance, to the letter, with dead Agnes's first agreement with the man. No less. Certainly no more. The stonecutter could find no matter for complaint in the quality and quantity of his victuals, and yet he rose from the table empty, burning with a hunger of the heart, a thirst of the soul.

As promised, the boy Benedict was the one with the beasts. He took care of the donkey and later, when Margaret purchased a family of chickens and a brown milk-goat, he looked after these too. He was up early each day, leading his charges off to graze on what few mouthfuls of dry grass the town green afforded in the harsh weather. Master Giles heard his staff tap across the paving stones, falling into its own cadence somewhere between the quicktime of the goat's hooves and the steady clop of the donkey's feet.

Winter closed over the town. It was a cruel season. Work on the cathedral slowed, with labor limited to only those artisans whose hands touched the interior of the sanctuary. Unfinished walls put on a penitent's shirt of thatch to keep the bitter weather from setting its teeth into the stone. Master Giles set up canvas walls around his shed and worked on in all weathers, so long as the frost did not grow deep enough to affect the fiber of the rock.

One morning soon after Candlemas, before even the whisper of dawn had touched the sky, he was roused from his lonely sleep by the voice of the stone. The hour was too early even for country-bred Margaret to be padding about. Master Giles tossed aside his blankets, did up his hose, and pulled on a wooden smock over his tunic. His bones cried out for a cloak, but he hushed them with the reminder that work would warm them soon enough.

He loped silently down the stairs and came into the kitchen. A breath of light from the fading moon silvered the edges of the shutters. Master Giles fetched a small iron pot and filled it with coals plucked from the hearth's neatly banked ashes. This would be all the heat he'd have in the shed, for a greater fire might cause the stone to split. It was enough to keep his hands from stiffening at his art, and that was all he asked.

The house was very still. He felt as if he were Lazarus leaving the tomb. Margaret kept the place clean as boiled bones, yet she did not speak with Master Giles except to return his perfunctory salutations, to summon him at mealtimes, to give him messages from the cathedral, and to answer any questions he might ask. But while she tithed her words to him, the boy Benedict paid out none at all.

There was frost on the earth. Master Giles stood in the yard with his back to the house and raised his eyes to the great cathedral. "Five years or six and it will be done," he said, weaving white veils with his breath on the darkness. "Two years or three and it may be consecrated to use while the last touches are made on the outside. Had you lived to see it, Agnes—!" And his leathery thumb brushed the tears away before they could freeze into stars against the gray and black cloud of his beard.

It was then he heard the song. Thin and reedy, borne on a voice wobbling over words and music like a newborn calf trying its legs, it came so softly to the sculptor's ear that he almost doubted he heard it. But it was there. It was coming from the shed.

Master Giles felt something brush his leg. He looked down into Candida's flower-face. The white cat mewed inquisitively and he, feeling only a little foolish, motioned for her to keep still. He moved with the cat's own stealth to where the canvas walls were pierced by a loose-hung flap of sailcloth that kept out the wind. The song praised God for His all-sheltering love as the stonecutter crept through the doorway.

The boy Benedict sat on a heap of straw that warmed the feet of Master Giles's newest saint. The carven lamb that pressed itself against the carven lady's robes permitted thin young arms to wreath its rocky neck, made no objection to a dark head pillowed on its curlicued flank, did not protest the tears staining its gray fleece like the tracks of the rain. The boy sang through tears, his voice leaping and falling, trembling on a cusp of music and slipping from the precarious perch of a high note not quite grasped.

Master Giles held the music in his mouth and let the lovely, imperfect taste of it melt sweetly over his tongue. He could not take his eyes from the boy. His mind did not want to know the things his eyes finally told his heart. The stone face of the saintly virgin Agnes smiled down on the bowed head of a child whose face was the image of her own.

The white cat was not enthralled by human music. She ambled past the stonecutter, bright eyes of gold on the small, gray, squeaking temptations which all that straw might hide. Seeing a tuft tremble, she crouched, haunches bunched, tail stiffly twitching, lips silently writhing over her race's ceremonial curse upon the whole tribe of vermin. Then she sprang.

If there had been a mouse in hiding there, he escaped her, but the boy's foot did not. Benedict shouted with surprise and flung himself backward as Candida's paws captured his ankle. His whole weight struck the statue.

Master Giles shot through the doorway, throwing himself forward to embrace the boy with one arm and to steady the statue with the other. Straw flew up in a sunburst of golden dust. The boy yelled again to feel Master Giles's strong hand on his arm. He flailed his limbs wildly, fingers groping for his staff.

"Ouch!" cried the stonecutter as the boy's heel struck his thigh. "Hush, hush, don't be afraid, it's only me." His words worked. The boy was still. Empty eyes could yet hold questions. Master Giles replied, "I couldn't sleep, so I came out here to work. When I saw the cat pounce on you, and you hit the statue, I was afraid you were going to knock . . . it . . . o. . . ." Realization stole over him as he spoke, and he saw the same dawn on the boy's face as a smile.

The statue was nine feet of solid rock, Benedict a scant five feet of flimsy flesh and bone. "*Me* knock *her* over?" the boy asked lightly, dimples showing in a smile that belonged to the beloved phantom of the house.

"Why, yes," Master Giles said, falling gladly into the straightfaced fool's part. "With all your muscle, my poor saint would never have a chance to stand against you." And they both laughed.

He could tell the boy what he knew, then; what he had just then come to know. Shared laughter made shared hearts easier. The evidence of Master Giles's eyes did not come as much news to Benedict.

"I never knew you were my father, but I knew she was my mother," the boy said. "Margaret called me bastard so often when I was small that I grew up thinking it was my name. But when I knew the difference and heard her call her cousin Agnes whore, I knew that must be another way for Margaret to say that Agnes was the bastard's mother."

"I'll kill her." Master Giles forced the words out between gritted teeth. Benedict could not hope to see his father's knuckles whiten, but he could not help feel the stonecutter's corded arms tense with cold rage.

"Let her be," said Benedict softly, and his voice held the peace of Christ. It was then that Master Giles knew there would never be anything he could refuse his son.

"She never told me she was with child," the stonecutter said, stroking the last of the tears from Benedict's cheeks. "If she had—" He shook his head regretfully for all things small and lost and loveless. The two of them sat in the straw at the feet of the stone Saint Agnes. Her arms reached out, turning her cloak to sheltering wings above them. The irreverent cat bounded onto the table and thence up to perch on the saint's crown of martyrdom. Cold dawn paled the canvas walls.

The boy ran his hand over the lamb's petrified curls. "You are carving this for her."

Master Giles nodded, then realized such silent signs were useless with his son. "Yes," he said. "This saint is hers. She will stand with Saint Clement and Saint George, Barbara and Anthony, Martin for my good friend Master Martin, Giles in thanks to my patron saint for his many blessings, Mathurin for all the fools of this world and sweet Saint Cecilia for music."

"Music," breathed the boy.

"You sing—you sing well." Master Giles was ill at ease with compliments. Even in dead Agnes's arms he could not put his tongue to lovers' words but let moans and kisses and the touch of hands speak her praises for him. "I heard you when I came out here this morning. I did not know the song."

"She taught it to me," said Benedict.

"Margaret?" he could not fathom that dry stick teaching a child anything but a catechism of bitterness.

Benedict laughed. "Can you really think such a thing? No, no, I mean the other."

"Your. . . . mother?" Master Giles cudgeled his brains, trying to recall another time besides the secret months of Benedict's awaited birth when his lost love had left the town. He could bring none to mind.

The boy said, "No. I mean the lady." And he said no more, as if having said this was enough.

Master Giles felt like one of good Saint Mathurin's protected fools. "What lady is this? The wife of the lord of Margaret's old village? His daughter? A kinswoman?"

Benedict snorted all of these away. "If you could hear her sing, you would know. I met her in the woods, when Margaret sent me there to pasture the pigs. There were tumbled stones, and the broken tooth of a ridged column. In spring-time I could feel tiny chips of rock like little slick scales under my bare feet, and places between them where the mortar had cracked and violets grew."

"A ruin," said Master Giles, who had passed many such places as he moved from town to town, following his calling. One time he had thought to spend the night in the shelter of half-vanished walls, sleeping on a mosaic of dolphins and vines, until his eye fell upon a toppled statue in the empty basin of a fountain. Lichens crawled across enameled eyes, moss clothed wanton nakedness, and still this work of a dead man's hands outshone Master Giles's finest endeavors. He fled the place, ashamed and aching with envy.

"She was there," the boy said. "I didn't know, at first. Then I heard the music. The words praised God, yet sounded . . . I cannot say how they sounded, not truly. Can praise hold sorrow? I called out, 'Who's there?' The music stilled. All I could hear was the snuffle and grunt of Margaret's pigs. I thought I'd frightened the lady away."

"How could you tell she was a lady?" Master Giles asked. "She might have been a peasant's daughter sent, like you, on an errand."

"You would not say so if you'd heard the daintiness of her song. A voice like that never called pigs home or shooed chickens," Benedict countered. "Besides, I caught her scent, all flowers, dewy and clean. When she returned, she gave me reason not to doubt, proof of what I already knew."

"She returned?"

"That very day. The wood was growing cooler; it must have been near sunset. I was whistling up my pigs—they're bright, obedient beasts or Margaret never would have trusted them to me—when I heard her song again. This time it was a different one, a hymn to the Virgin. I'd never heard the like. There was a year when the pigs bred so well, Margaret allowed me to accompany her to a fair at Saint Jerome's abbey. I heard the monks in choir and stood captured by the sound until Margaret gave me a knock on the head to hurry me along. I thought then that there could be nothing more beautiful in all the world than the sound of so many voices interwoven so perfectly." A wistful look crossed his face. "I was wrong."

There was something in his son's expression that troubled Master Giles to the heart. Blind, his boy must keep company with fancies more than most. Some fancies fevered the brain, bringing madness. What was all this talk of ladies met in the wildwood? The forest was no haven for the gently bred. It welcomed none.

The woods around this town were shrouded in dark legends, tales of the Fey with their cold immortal beauty who begrudged men their frail immortal souls. Their chief delight was robbery, pure and simple, snatching away the precious few comforts mortals could claim. With their deceiving ghost-lights they robbed the weary workman of his way home to rest when he crossed their lands by night. Their heartless swains led maidens to believe themselves beloved, let them wake to find themselves abandoned. Not even the innocent babe in the cradle was safe from their malice, their schemes at once bereaving mother of child and child of human love.

Was stealing a poor blind boy's sanity beyond them?

"My boy," said the stonecutter, trying to hold his voice as steady as he held his chisel. "My boy, think. What would a lady do in such a place, so late, so lone? Are you sure of what you heard? Perhaps it was the wind."

"Does the wind sing Christ's hosannas?" The saintly stone children born of Master Giles's hand had faces less set and stern than Benedict's.

"I mean, perhaps the wind brought you the sound of human voices from a distance," the man suggested. "There are convents in the wood, and the holy sisters—"

"I touched her sleeve. It flowed over my fingertips like water. I touched her hand. It was softer than the muzzle of a newborn foal."

"How did she come to permit these liberties?"

"The second time I heard her song, I rushed forward calling on her to reveal herself, in Christ's name. I couldn't bear to have that sound taken from me again. I imagined that if she was a Christian, she must heed my plea, and if she was not then the power of Our Lord's name would break her glamour and hold her where she stood." His look was rueful as he added: "When I ran, I tripped over a pig."

The agitation of Master Giles's spirit almost broke free as laughter. He smothered it. "She came to your aid, then?" The boy confirmed this. "And was that when you learned who this lady was?"

"She said she was called the lady Oudhalise." The boy pronounced the outlandish name as easily as if it were plain Mary. "She told me that her kin lived nearby, but that I had found her at home."

"At home! In a ruin? A place with no stone left atop another? She must have been mad." The stonecutter was aghast at the thought of his son in such company.

Fresh tears trembled in the boy's milky eyes. "Then I wish I were as mad as she."

Master Giles cast his arms around Benedict and held him tight. "Don't speak so! For the sake of your soul, don't."

The boy was stiff in his father's embrace. "For the sake of my soul, she taught me her songs. We sat there until the night was cold around us and she sang for me until I had them all by heart. She told me, 'The women here once heard a man who told them that they could not enter heaven except as children. I can never be a child, but I long for the promise of your heaven. My songs are my offering to the Lord I seek, though the lord I serve would destroy me if he knew I give them to you. Take them into your heart. Take me with you to the gates of paradise.' "

Master Giles shook his head. *Madness*, he thought, but all he said was: "Poor lady."

"Yes," the boy agreed. "I have her face here, in my hands. She let me touch her face and left me after. I came back to that same place in the forest many times, but I never met with her again. All I have left is what she gave me." And now he loosed the longing of his tears.

Later that day Margaret could do nothing but mutter "Lackwit, madman,

fool," when Master Giles announced he'd taken the blind boy to be his apprentice. Others said the same when the news went 'round.

"How can you do this thing?" Master Martin demanded as the two stonecut-
ters sat in the tavern over wine. Outside the wind howled early March's chill
damnation and blew away lost souls' last grasp on their graves. "He can't see the
stone. How will he shape it?"

"You mind your Apostles and leave me to mind my saints," was all Master
Giles replied.

All that he knew was the need to shelter his son from a world that would
destroy him if it heard his tale of the lady in the wood. The only way he could
see to prevent this was to take the boy into his care, and the one path open to
him there was to name him apprentice.

In time, it might have been forgotten, but for Margaret.

The bishop did not care if Master Giles apprenticed himself a wild dog so
long as his chisel continued to shape saints for the glorification of the cathedral.
He praised the sweetness of Master Giles's Saint Agnes and could not commend
the sculptor's skill highly enough when his next creation, the beautiful Saint
Sebastian, drew the hearts as well as the eyes of all who saw it. (And if the saint's
face was the image of the man's apprentice lad, what of that? Time enough to
inquire into such matters after all twelve niches of the south porch held their
treasures.)

It was Margaret kept things on the boil, Margaret whose tongue wagged free
in the marketplace, the tavern, the church, the street. When Master Giles took
Benedict for his apprentice, he stole away not only that woman's unpaid servant
but the butt at which she shot her wormwood-tipped barbs. How could the
loveless woman feel superior to the beloved dead if she could no longer hurl
abuse at love's living proof? Her tongue had lost its whetstone and its target. All
that remained to her was to hound Master Giles with a madman's reputation as
punishment for his having taken away her sport.

"Let him be as mad as Nebuchadnezzar," said the bishop. "But let him give
me saints." So Master Giles gave him next Saint Catherine of Alexandria. "That
face!" the bishop cried when the sculptor and his workmen brought the finished
statue to the cathedral grounds. "Twisted as an old grapevine's root. The holy
legends rated her a beauty, but this is a shrew."

"Ah well . . ." Master Giles shrugged. "So many centuries, looking after the
affairs of spinsters—" He patted the spiked wheel of her martyrdom. "That
would turn nectar to vinegar, my lord, given the temperament of some of her
congregation."

The bishop squinted up at the saint. "That face . . . Do I know it?" And weeks
later, when his processional happened to pass Margaret in the street, the way he
stared at her became her shame and the talk of the town for days.

Saint Catherine was Master Giles's eleventh saint. There was now only one
niche below the great rose window of the south porch that wanted its tenant.

How strangely it all turned out! One day the boy who could not see to swing
a hammer against a chisel's head came across a lump of raw clay on his father's
workbench. It was Master Giles's habit to mold his creatures out of clay before
giving them their bodies of stone. Benedict felt the cool, pliable earth beneath
his fingers and began to work it. As he worked, he sang one of his alien songs.

His voice had mellowed with the years, learned steadiness, could hold to a tune the way a good hound held to a trail. It was a pleasure to hear him so melodiously praising all things holy, even if the music that fell from his lips was like nothing that ever rang out beneath the church rafters nor in the taverns nor in the distant fields.

"What's this?" cried Master Giles, coming up behind his boy and seeing the red mass under his hands. He reached over Benedict's shoulder and plucked the nearly finished figure from its creator's grasp. The stonecutter sucked in his breath in awe. The face of an infant angel dimpled up at him.

It was perfection. He had never seen the like. That cherub's countenance contained just enough of the earthly child's essence to give a man hope that even his stained soul might someday soar with the hosts of heaven.

"Is it good, Father?" Benedict asked softly.

"Is it good . . ." Master Giles could only stare at his son's handmade marvel while tears of wonder brimmed his eyes. "I will copy it out in stone, my boy, and lay it before my lord bishop himself."

So he did. The bishop was a canny man who knew the work of each of his cathedral worker's hands the way a falconer knows each of his birds by flight, when they are no more than specks against the sun. The bishop knew this angel was not Master Giles's work.

Master Giles said, "It was made by my apprentice, who is blind. He worked it in clay. All I did was give it a body of stone."

"The Lord closes only the eyes of the body," the bishop replied. "In His mercy, He has opened for this lad the eyes of the soul. Bring him to me. I am minded to see this miracle."

Master Giles did as he was bidden, his heart light. He knew, you see, that soon enough his work on the great cathedral would be done. Already he was considering the final saint he must carve, and once that was accomplished there would be no further call for him in this town. If it fell out that another town had use for his skills, all would be well, but if not—He had gone the roads in idleness before this, sometimes for weeks, sometimes for months, once for over a year. When there was only himself to think of, the roads held no terror, but now—

Now the devil's fork held him: He could not subject a blind boy to the road. He could not abandon his son to the absent mercies of Margaret.

A miracle, my lord bishop calls him, he thought. *Let it be so! What churchman would not be proud to keep a tame miracle in his court, especially now that there is a great cathedral to support? The relics of the saints will bring some pilgrims, but many more will flock to see beauty spring from the hands of the blind.* Then and there he resolved to do everything he could to advance Benedict in favor with my lord bishop.

The first thing that he did was to bring the lad before the bishop, as the bishop had commanded.

"Well, my child, you must tell me how you did it," the bishop said, seated on his great chair of state while Master Giles helped his son to kneel and kiss the ring and rise again.

"What would you have me tell?" Benedict asked.

"Why, how you came to do this." The bishop held up the cherub's head.

Then he realized that the lad could not know his meaning, lacking sight. "How you knew to make so exquisite a thing as this angel," he amended.

"Oh," said Benedict, nodding. "That was easy. She sang him for me."

The bishop sat a little straighter in his chair. "She?" he asked, and also: "Sang?"

Master Giles's hands tightened on his son's shoulders. "It is a true miracle, my lord bishop," he said hastily. "The lad himself told me of it. The Virgin Mary appeared to him in a vision of the soul, for which no man needs eyes, and sang of the glories of heaven. Thus he was divinely inspired."

"Ah." It was the bishop's turn to nod. He was a man willing to understand miracles, but not wonders. "And do you think this was a solitary vision, or might we expect more?"

"More," said Master Giles emphatically. "God willing," he added, seeing the bishop's eye turn hard and cold and narrow as the chisel's blade.

"Let us pray that so it may be," the bishop said dryly, and laid aside the angel. "It were a pity to spend all the inspiration of a vision on grasping so small a portion of heaven."

Later, as they were walking home, Master Giles asked his son, "What rubble was that you gave the bishop? 'She *sang* him for me'? He will think you a lunatic."

"She did." The boy was sullen. "My lady of the forest. I slept and saw her. It's happened before this, only I never had cause to speak of it. She was seated at a fountainside, singing praise to God. Oh Father, the colors! How sweetly they sounded on my ear!" His sulky look melted in the bliss of his remembered vision. "With her voice alone she built a stair of silver and gold to the very throne of glory, and up and down its length the angels climbed. Father, I think that I saw my mother among the blest. My lady sang her face for me so that I could feel it to my heart!" He embraced himself as if wings of joy had enfolded him. Then his shoulders sagged, his head drooped. "But she is dead, my poor lady of the forest, and kept from hope of heaven. Her songs of praise and her salvation are locked away from her Redeemer as deeply as if they were encased in stone."

Master Giles pressed his calloused hand to the boy's brow. "Have you fever?" he asked, feeling his heart drum panic. "This is no holy vision, but a sending from the damned. Don't speak of it! Not before any, man or woman!"

"But you asked," the boy replied simply. "And so did the bishop. I tell you, that is how I came to make the angel. Her song opened the vault of heaven to my eyes and left the shapes of all the saints and angels in my hands. I cannot forget them. I cannot forget her, or her pain, or her song."

"I am your father," Master Giles said severely. "I command you to forget." They walked the rest of the way home in silence.

Like most parents, Master Giles mistook silence for consent. So it was that by the time they reached dead Agnes's house he was convinced that his child was in no further danger of being branded mad for the indiscretions of his tongue. Indeed, the stonecutter felt secure enough in his dominion over the boy to revert to planning for Benedict's future.

"My son," he said the next day, "here is clay." He placed the boy's hands on a lump of the stuff that was at least five times as big as the quantity he was used to employ to make his models. "Make a saint."

"Father . . . ?" Benedict turned toward Master Giles's voice.

"The twelfth saint for the south porch," Master Giles went on. "I want it to be of your design, just as you made the angel. Then I will carve it. You can do this, my boy." *You must do this, for your life's sake*, his heart implored silently.

Benedict sighed and rested his hands on the clay. "I can try," he said. And he began.

There passed a shiftless several weeks for Master Giles. Unable to work until he had Benedict's model before him, he roamed the town, fidgety as a dog with a skinful of fleas. He was not used to idleness, and so made himself a pest on the cathedral site, diverting the workmen with japes and stories, discussing problems in design with the master architect that had not been problems until he suggested otherwise. Mostly he knew the tavern.

But at last there came a morning when Benedict shyly asked his father to see what it was that lay hidden beneath the damp rag on the worktable in the shed. Master Giles removed the clay-stained cloth with the reverence a lover might accord the last veil between himself and the enjoyment of his lady's favors.

And then he stood as one taken by the immanence of angels.

Words flew through the town streets, darting from house to house like a flight of swallows. Rumor soared and dipped beneath a hundred roofs, coming at last to nest in the bishop's palace: The last saint was more than stone, more than flesh. The last saint of Master Giles's carving was the beauty of a blessed soul made visible.

Oh, how many came to see her, this incredible apparition! Hard Margaret stood ward at the gates of the house and used her broom to shoo away all comers save the highest as if they had been poultry. The bishop's grace she admitted, of course, though that churchman still had the tendency to steal shuddersome sideways looks at her in a way that got beneath her skin and itched.

"Magnificent!" the bishop breathed when Master Giles swept aside the cloth he'd used to shroud the last saint from prying eyes. "Is it Magdalen you've chosen to bless our final vacancy?"

"My apprentice chose her," Master Giles replied, growing fat with pride in his son's accomplishment and the bishop's obvious approval. But had that worthy of the church been paying any sort of heed, he might have heard that Master Giles did not truly answer his inquiry as to the identity of this wonder caught in stone.

And so the bishop's servants came to carry off the last of the twelve statues and set her in her place along with all the rest, above the south porch of the cathedral. With her came the news that the holy place might now be consecrated, and all the town rejoiced with preparations for the great day.

Master Giles sat with his son in the now-empty shed. "The bishop is much taken with your work, Benedict," he said. A bowl of blushing grapes and shiny apples sat on the table between them, the first fruits of the coming harvest. "He would have you move into his palace and work for him."

"How shall I do that, Father?" Benedict asked, his fingers wandering over the boards until they encountered a plump grape and popped it into his mouth. "I can only work the clay."

"There are plenty of men who can copy out in stone what others make in clay," Master Giles replied. "There are precious few who can copy out in clay what exists only in visions. My lord bishop knows talent and has the power to shape the world around you into a most comfortable place indeed, if you will simply place that talent in his service. Your saint has stolen his heart."

"As she stole mine," the boy murmured. His father bit into an apple then, and the crisp report of teeth in white flesh kept him from hearing Benedict's words.

So it came to be, in that harvest season, that the countryside buzzed louder than a hundred hives with the great doings of the town. (The highborn must be called purposely, but the poor always hear the chink of alms and follow.) Peddlars and mountebanks and wandering priests carried the news out of the gates, into the fields. (Who would not come who could? Which farmer's dreary nights and drudging days would not be enlivened for his being able to boast, in after years, *I was there!*) Word spread from the stone walls over the ploughlands and into the darkest recesses of the wildwood, where once a blind boy had pastured pigs among ruins. (In the twilight of a day that saw the town roads thick with travelers bound to witness the next dawn's consecration rites, a tall figure of inhuman slenderness and grace rose from his place beside a shallow, harebell-covered grave and called his vassals home.)

On the day of the consecration, Margaret rose grumpily from her bed and stumbled to the window, scrubbing the smut of sour-hearted dreams from her eyes. She pushed the shutters open and gave a cross look down into the street where already the populace was flooding the narrow thoroughfare, heading for the cathedral. Somewhere the bell of a smaller church was ringing. Water sloshed over stone. Roosters stretched their necks to the blade of the rising sun and crowed mortality's defiance of death.

Margaret tossed her woolen gown over her head and went downstairs without the formality of a face-wash.

Master Giles and Benedict were already up and about their business. Margaret's chill eyes swallowed the boy's beauty as an insult to all her fixed ideas of sin and punishment. Not even his blindness could assuage her offended sense of morality this day. He was going to live in the bishop's palace—a bastard to live in luxury and ease who should have suffered and died for his mother's sins! Was this fair? Was this the reward her stale virginity had earned in this world? Only by setting her thoughts on the pious hope of fiery eternal torment awaiting the child hereafter was she able to enjoy her breakfast.

The three ill-sorted souls, whose only common ground was the shelter of dead Agnes's roof, walked out that morning in company. Together they made their way to the open space before the cathedral where the ceremonies would commence. There was a special place set aside for certain of the bishop's favored ones—Master Giles and Benedict among them. For this reason alone Margaret consorted with them, sticking so close they could not hope to escape her. She smiled grimly, knowing that a real man would have sent her on her way with a cuff, but that this great fool of a Master Giles never would do, because he was weak and silly.

It was as splendid a spectacle as ever any townsman could have hoped. The villeins who had come to gawp were well content with all there was to gawp at. Highborn men were there, and ladies so white they looked like milk poured into samite skins. Faces like painted eggs nodded beneath headdresses of terrifying weight and unpredictable balance. Gusts of musk and spiced orange puffed from tight-laced bosoms, little cloth-caged breasts seeming hard as cobblestones.

There was to be a procession, it was said. Sweet-voiced children garbed in white would march with pure beeswax tapers in their chubby pink hands, singing hymns and anthems. The bishop would come gowned in music, every glint of his jeweled robes tossing a garland of notes against the sky. Or so the whispers ran.

There were many whispers, many murmurings. The crowd bumped and jostled all along the route the bishop and his suite were supposed to follow. The nobles and the peasantry alike would not be still for fear that they might miss the chance to pass along the all-important cry of "There they are!"

As it happened, they need never have worried.

Where did it come from, that uncanny hush that fell so suddenly over all the town, like the stillness before a thunderstorm? The ripe, red-gold sunlight of October drained to gray. Men looked up and could not tell the stone bastions of the cathedral from the sky that stood behind. Even the rooks who had haunted the cathedral since its inception were quiet. A lady dropped her rosary. Pearls clattered over the stones like the bones of martyrs tossed out of their tombs.

And then, a lone, sharp cry to shatter the stillness: "There they are!"

There were horses. There were never supposed to be horses. The bishop's procession was supposed to be afoot, a show of humility for the people to remember. Yet here were horses! Indeed, for an instant those who saw the tall, proud mounts doubted their eyes, for the beasts made no sound at all as their silver-shod hooves passed over the pavement. The open space before the cathedral filled with them—black and smoke and roan—and the richness of their trappings would have left the bishop's robes looking like a beggar's rags had my lord bishop been anywhere in sight.

Where was he? No one thought to ask; no one cared to answer. The eyes of all present were devoured by the sight before them, for if the mounts of that eerie parade were worth noting, the riders were impossible to ignore.

High and haughty the lords of elven sat their gemmed and lacquered saddles. Hair like hoarfrost streamed down in gossamer falls that overlay their horses' trappings with a mantle more glorious than any weaving from a mortal loom. Lords and ladies of the Fey came riding, tiny winged dragons perched on their slim wrists as ordinary men might sport a favorite falcon. They rode up to the very steps of the cathedral and there they stopped and stayed.

"What blasphemy is this?" boomed the bishop. He seemed to have come out of nowhere, all his splendor made invisible by the awe which the Fey had conjured so casually from the people. He was not a man who relished being overlooked. He stood between the elven host and the bulky fortress of his faith, gilded crozier in hand, as if to offer them battle. "Begone, you soulless rabble! May the devil claim his own!"

"May we all claim our own this day," said the foremost elvenlord, and his soft words lilted with such melody that the bishop's promised child-choir would have sounded like a clash of copper pans beside him.

"What do you seek here?" the bishop demanded, eyeing the elvenlord with the narrow mind's suspicion of beauty.

"We know our quarry," came the cool reply. And the elvenlord flicked the bridle of his mount just enough to make it resume its leisurely pace around to the south porch of the cathedral.

The crowd did not seem to move, and yet somehow the passage of the Faerie host drew mortals along with it the way a stream in flood will carry all manner of oddments along in its course. Master Giles certainly did not know how he came to be there, yet there he was, in full sight of the south porch with his son's shoulder under his guiding hand and even Margaret's stack-o'-sticks body a comforting presence at his side.

The elvenlord was pointing up. His slender hand made bright with diamonds, blue and white, was pointing at the row of saints above the porch, below the rose window.

"Give her back to us," he said, "and we will go."

They knew whom he meant, mortals and elves alike. There was no need for him to stipulate. She stood apart from her eleven companions as a dove among jackdaws. Her lips were parted as if her stony body were a spell that had overcome her at her prayers, freezing on her tongue all her pleas for divine clemency, her petitions for heaven's compassion.

Not for herself, that mercy she implored, no, much as she might require it. There was that in her face to tell any with heart (if not eyes) to see that all her unsaid, unsung prayers were for the outcast, the helpless, the one who does not even know he stands in need.

"Do you know," the bishop was heard to remark, "on second glance I don't think that's the Magdalen after all."

"She is my sister, the lady Oudhalise," said the elvenlord. "A fool, but still a lady of the Fey. She broke her heart with hankering after your mortal talk of heaven. There was no need for her to perish. We are immortal, when we own the wit to enjoy immortality. Still, she died, she pined and died, fading from our court like a frost-struck flower. She lies buried in woodland earth, poor witling, and there let her lie. This likeness is an insult and a desecration."

"I never thought I'd stand in agreement with an elf," the bishop muttered.

"Give her back," repeated the elvenlord.

"Take her, then," the bishop spat. But his venom was all in his eyes, and these were aimed elsewhere. Master Giles saw the poisonous look he and his son received from my lord bishop, and he felt his bowels go cold.

"I may not," the lady's lordly brother replied. "If it were so easy, would I have troubled your petty rites? She may not be taken unless she is freely given."

"Well, then, consider it so. I give her back to you more than freely—gladly!" The bishop used his crozier in the same style that Margaret had used her broom to shoo away unwanted visitors. A child in the mob giggled.

Still the elvenlord demurred. "She is not yours to give." His eyes scanned the press and met eyes that could not tell that they were sought. "She is his. Let him give her up and we will go."

They tore Benedict from his father's grasp and hustled the lad before the bishop, before the Faerie host. The boy's unseeing gaze rose as the elf-lord uttered his demand again: "Release her, boy, and we may yet depart leaving you as we found you."

Master Giles wrung his hands, for he knew his son's response even before the words left Benedict's lips: "That I will not. I can't give what isn't any man's to hold."

They fell upon him with words at first—both sides of the quarrel, elven and mortal. The bishop and all his suite exhorted the lad not to be a fool, to speak sense, to give this unholy congregation of visitants whatever it took to effect their banishment. Only do that, they told him, and his insane blasphemy (Who-ever heard of an elvenlady in the company of saints? Merciful God above!) might in time be absolved. On their side the elves spoke less and said more. Would he choose to give them what they asked or did he want to die? It was that simple.

Then all fell silent again, and Benedict replied, "I've already said all I can say: I can't give what isn't mine. Her soul is her own, God have it in keeping. I have only offered it a haven, a shell of stone it must outgrow, soon or late, as surely as the flower breaks the seed that holds it safely through the winter."

The elvenlord's laughter was like perfect music with the heart torn from it, all a fair seeming, but meaningless. "You speak of souls in the same breath with our kind, boy? Are you so ignorant, or do you play some idiot game? I am in no sportive mood, I would be gone quickly. I tell you, it is like an agony of cold iron in my eyes to have to remain in your midst, seeing the crudeness of your mortal cities, the ugliness of your mortal faces. I have not come here for pleasure; I have come for my own."

"If she were your own, you'd have her," the boy replied mildly.

"Come now!" the bishop cried, thumping Benedict smartly on the shoulder with his square-fingered hand. "It's common knowledge that these creatures of fire and air are soulless as stone!"

The boy turned his face toward the bishop's voice and said, "Then this knowl-edge is very common, but knows nothing at all, either of souls or stones." His head swung back vaguely in the direction of the elvenlord. "You were her kin, yet you never knew her. If you dreamed you loved her at all, you loved her as a mirror of yourself. But I—I have no use for mirrors. I held her image not before my eyes, but in my heart. She knew love, forgiveness, mercy, prayer. Knowing all these, could she help but know God? Could she do other than own a soul? I have heard it preached how the rich man Dives turned the beggar Lazarus from his palace gate and burned in hell for his sins. Will the same God who judged Dives thus for uncharity lack charity Himself? Will He turn her from the gate of His cathedral now?"

"Boy, you walk dangerous ground," the bishop said harshly. "Who taught you it was your place to speak of Scripture? Your elven woman is of no importance to our Lord. How can He even be aware of her presence, when it takes a human soul to call upon His mercy and be seen?"

"I do not ask Him to see," said Benedict. "Nor did she. Only to listen." And he closed his sightless eyes, pressed his hands together, and opened his mouth in song.

It was the song that Master Giles had heard the boy sing while his fingers worked the clay. It entered his body not by the ears but by the bones, the blood, the pulsing of the heart. Note by tremulous note, it was a song meant to ascend the golden steps of Paradise.

And then it was gone, sharply, abruptly, with no warning. Benedict sprawled face-down on the stones before the south porch of the cathedral, a little trickle of blood running from his head. Over him stood Margaret.

"Damn you, you bastard limb of Satan, give this creature what it wants and let it be gone!" she shrieked, waving the cudgel with which she'd struck the boy. It was a piece of wood garnered from the trash of the street, bristling with splinters. Master Giles stood as one lightning-struck, unable to believe the brutality he'd just witnessed. Margaret ranted on at the unconscious boy: "You'll have us all killed by faerie magic, else turned over to the Church courts for harboring a heretic like you!" She whirled to face the elvenlord. "Take your sister! Take her! Have no more dealings with the boy—he's mad! I am his guardian and I speak for him. Take her! She is freely given!"

The paralysis left Master Giles's limbs in a rush of red hate. He leaped forward with a roar, hands hungering for Margaret's skinny neck. She shrieked and threw herself for the bridle of the elf-lord's steed, hoping perhaps to merit his protection as his good and faithful servant. The elf-lord merely tugged at the reins and caused his mount to step primly back, out of the way between Master Giles and Margaret. The stonecutter's hands met the woman's papery flesh and closed tightly around her windpipe. The egg-faced highborn ladies chirped and twittered, fine hands fluttering like doves in delight over the unexpected treat of spectacle and death.

And then the miracle.

They could not tell—none of them who stood there in the great cathedral's shadow that day—they could not say just when they first heard the music. It was simply there, like the air and the sunlight and the smells of the town. Some claimed it fell from heaven, a shower of angelic voices. Some raised work-hardened hands to thick, ungainly lips and dreamed that the voices they heard were their own, transformed by some greater power, raised in a song whose words and music they had never been taught but had always known.

It was a healing, that music. It stole Master Giles's hands from around Margaret's neck and set them to raise up the body of his son instead. It set the bishop's heart and not just the words of his mouth on forgiveness, love, salvation. It was a song kin and child of many songs: A mother's voice rejoicing over a blessed cradle; a husbandman's rough cheer over a day's work done and well done; a virgin lass weaving dreams of love into the melody that springs unbidden to her lips when she first sees a young man's smile that is meant for her alone; an old woman crooning a low, contented tune by the fireside where even her dwindling life is beloved and welcomed by those around her.

Master Giles was the first to recognize the true source of that song. "The statue!" he cried. "The statue is singing!" He held his son's limp body to his breast with one strong arm and with his free hand gestured wildly at the stone he had carved to match his son's clay model, the saint who was called soulless sister to a lord of Faerie.

His words said all and said far too little. More than a single miracle had put on a skin of music there that day. More than the single statue molded prayer into melody as a blind boy molds beauty into clay. The lady's image did not sing alone. All the stone saints sang together with her, and all the people of the town, and all the stones of the cathedral too until the heavens could not help but hear the sweet, pious petition of one yearning heart.

All the people of the town? No. Margaret stood cold and still as any stone, unmoved by the chorus of life and love surging up around her. "Fools!" she bellowed, red-faced, into the faces of the noblewomen. "Idiots!" she roared into my lord bishop's own enraptured gaze and moving lips. "Break this spell, shatter this glamour, burst this evil enchantment into a thousand pieces!"

But all that broke was the twelfth statue in its niche. It burst from the inside out, like a bubble, and something small and pure and brilliant flew from its shattered core and soared into the waiting smile of heaven.

Silence held the square before the great cathedral, silence and all its awesome host, flourishing their smoke-streaked banners. Neither elf nor mortal dared to break the holy reign of that innumerable army that laid ghostly swords to living lips and stole away all chance of speech.

But all sounds are not speech, and often it is the unarmed scout who steals from the city gates and breaks the encircling army's hold. A sob rang out in the bright fall air, and the sound of a man falling to his knees on stone, in his arms the still, pale body of his son.

It seemed like such a little hurt, the blow cold Margaret dealt blind Benedict. Yet who has the eyes capable of seeing beneath the skin? Whose sight can discern the tracings of mortality's doorways on the smiling skull? Who among us can tell at which of these gates of blood and bone a single knock will open a wide way for the dark-winged angel of death?

Benedict sagged in his father's arms, the warmth fast leaving those thin limbs, his lips still parted in a song he would never finish. Master Giles cradled him close and let his tears water eyes now sightless forever.

At length his raw grief eased and he became aware of a slim, strong hand on his shoulder. Reluctantly he lifted his face from his boy's stone visage and turned to meet the gaze of the elvenlord.

"Mortal man," said the master of the Fey, holding his wondrous steed by its golden bridle, "I do not pretend to understand your miracles. As I am soulless, I have no need of your heaven, no fear of your hell, and all your past and future are a single summer's day to me. I have never tried to understand your kind any more than your kind have tried to see the world through the eyes of the cow you drive to the slaughter, or the donkey whose back you break with burdens, or the stray dog you kick away from the fire. And yet—" His voice, so flawless, caught itself upon the bramble of a sob. "And yet this—this I think I understand."

Master Giles's, voice rasped over the elvenlord's words. "What good is all your understanding when I have lost my son?"

They gathered around him then, all the lords and ladies of Faerie, all the masters of the Church, the people of the town. Some kissed his cheek, some only touched his hand, some begged blessing of dead Benedict's fragile corpse, others stared at the little body with the relic-hunter's rapacious hunger, biding time and opportunity. Those mortals who could not find a way through the press to reach the body looked angrily about for the hand that had struck down the child. Not because to take so small a life was horror enough; for them such losses were a common thing, an immutable fact of life's harsh rule, to be clucked over and tidily forgotten when they raised a stick against their own younglings. No, these good folk wanted Margaret's blood because she had robbed them of a living saint, of fresh miracles his song might have made their due, of the chance for their own reflected glory. A great clamor arose from the crowd, a cry of hounds.

It was a very lucky thing for Margaret that the bishop's entourage ringed her first, or she would have been raw strands of flesh and bloody bone by the time the mob was through with her. She stood between two men-at-arms—shaking with fear, weeping for her own fate—until the stronger of the two dealt her a backhand blow to buckle her knees and make her keep still.

The bishop called for peace, but all he got was silence. His robes, stiff with their fine embroidery of gold and silver and pearl, cut a furrow through the mob like a plough's wooden tooth tearing up the soil. He stood over Master Giles and said, "God's mercy is great, His judgments beyond question. For your son's life, we have purchased sight of a miracle."

"Sight . . ." The word rang hollow in Master Giles's throat and the laughter that followed left many men thinking of the echoing grave.

The bishop was not one to be belittled by his servant's inattention. He meant to do a great thing here, before his new cathedral, so that ever afterward his action might be linked to the miracle and his name remembered. "Life is God's to give," he said with proper solemnity. "We cannot restore what He, in His wisdom, has chosen to take. Yet this much I can do: You shall cut me a new statue to stand in the twelfth niche and it shall be the image of your son." He beamed down on the desolation of Master Giles's heart as if further tears from the stonecutter would be an act of basest ingratitude.

Ingrate that he was, Master Giles wept on.

The bishop's smile shriveled. "What ails you, man? What more would you have of us? I tell you, life lies beyond my power to restore! The woman who has done this shall be punished, be assured of it. We will hold her imprisoned until your son's image has been raised to its proper place, then carry out her sentence on these very stones, so that her death may be under his eyes!"

The ruler of the Fey, once more astride the saddle, moved his steed a few steps nearer to my lord bishop's bejeweled person. The churchman's blazing splendor dwindled to an ailing firefly's light beside the elf's cool beauty. "I too would make a remembrance of this day," he said.

The elven lord spoke words like the sounding of glass chimes and a cold, silvery mist fell over the square.

Master Giles gave a small, sharp cry and rose to his feet, his arms empty. The mist drew in, gathering itself over Benedict's dead body like a winding sheet of frost-struck churchyard moss, molding itself to breathless flesh until all the child's seeming was gray and cold.

And then the mist was gone, and Master Giles knelt again beside his lost love's child to touch his fingers to a smile now forever set. "Stone," he breathed. "He is stone."

He only half-heard the Faerie spell that next touched the image. The stone figure of the blind boy rose upon the hands of a thousand airy servants to settle itself at last into the embrace of the vacant niche below the great rose window. So lovingly did they bear the boy's frozen shape that they barely stirred the shining rubble that remained from that other, shattered statue. In truth, only a single fragment of stone fell when they set Benedict in his final resting place.

It was very small, that bit of rock, but it had far to fall. Some say it fell. Some say it flew, guided by a ghostly hand, to strike its only proper target: Margaret. Fallen or flung, it struck her hard enough, where she stood between the bishop's men. It brought her down.

At first they thought she was dead, but that might have been because her heart had hardened itself pulseless long ago. Then someone felt her breath against his skin and cried out, "She lives!" There was a murmur from the crowd then, a confused grumble of voices. They did not know whether to be disappointed that she had not died outright or pleased that she was still theirs to hold for the burning.

Then she opened her eyes. They were stone. Not blind, my lord—I mean no clever jongleur's trick of words and meaning—but stone as hard and gray and smooth as a carved saint's hand. Here was another miracle, but one the people fled, even the hosts of the Fey, even my lord bishop's men, whose swords had known the taste of blood in Christ's name.

Only Master Giles remained behind with Margaret. None know what he said to her, or if words passed between them at all. All know that when the next day's dawning came, she crept out of dead Agnes's house, her hand on the stonecutter's arm. And so it was each day until he died.

She begs before the cathedral now, a clump of rags and sorrow seated beneath the niche that holds blind Benedict's image. Bereft of Master Giles's aid she was soon the prey of every passing rogue, every marketplace sharper, a summer sheep swiftly shorn of all she had. No man or woman of this city ever raised a hand to prevent this, piously pointing out that it would be wrong to interfere in heaven's manifest judgment against the woman.

There are always too many, Master, who will harp readily to no other verse than God's vengeance. And yet these are the same who stood before the great cathedral and witnessed proof of His unbounded mercy! Ah, me.

Some say her punishment came as holy penitence, others whisper how it was a shifty trick of the Faerie host, done more by way of mischief than morality. Who knows? Give her some coins, Master, if your heart is not made of the same stuff as her eyes, and listen to the ringing sound the coppers make when they drop into her begging bowl. And then, as she is blind, be blind yourself and let your charity also fall into the empty bowls of all who huddle in the shadow of God's house for mercy's sake.

There. Do you hear it? Some say it comes from the dead child's image, that sweet song, the soul's own, the melody that breaks open the hard shells that hold us here, that shatters the stone that forms around our hearts, that anchors us to earth when we yearn for heaven: the song of the soulless who truly know the value of a soul.

Or do you not hear it yet? Will you ever hear it at all? I have heard the wise men teach that in the Gospel's tongue *charity* is but another word for *love*. More coins, my lord—an open hand, an open heart. Let them fall like angel voices, let them chime out the hope of a full belly, a warm cloak, a roof against the rain. From those few notes must arise that wondrous melody that rises from us all whenever we give the poor more than a rag or a dish of scraps or the cold lecture that they are themselves to blame for their poverty. More love, my lord, more kindness, more music of the soul redeemed!

And that is all my song.

Honorable Mentions: 2000

Alexander, Michael, "Beowulf Reduced" (poem), *Agenda*, Spring-Summer.
Allen, Karen Jordan, "Heartlines," *Century*, Winter.
Anderson, Barth, "Landlocked," *Talebones* 18.
Anderson, Robert, "Schism," *Ice Age*.
———, "Slight Return," Ibid.
Arnott, Marion, "Prussian Snowdrops," *Crimewave 4: Mood Indigo*.
Ashley, Allen, "Somme-Nambula," *The Third Alternative* 24.
Austin, Alan, "The Deerstalker Hat," *Enigmatic Tales*, Autumn.
Bailey, Dale, "The Anencephalic Fields," *The Magazine of Fantasy & Science Fiction*, Jan.
———, "Heat," *F & SF*, Sept.
Bailey, Robin Wayne, "The Woman Who Loved Death," *Spell Fantastic*.
Banker, Ashok, "Blood Mangoes," *Gothic.net*, December.
Barker, Trey R., "The Ghost of Her," *Noirotica* 3.
Barnes, Steven, "The Woman in the Wall," *Dark Matter*.
Baumer, Jennifer Rachel, "Another Arm Moving," *Talebones* 18.
———, "The Party Over There," *Ghost Writing*.
Beaumont, Charles, "Fallen Star," *A Touch of the Creature*.
———, "The Indian Piper," Ibid.
———, "Resurrection Island," Ibid.
Bell, M. Shayne, "The Road to Candarei," *Realms of Fantasy*, June.
Bennett, Nancy, "Familiar" (poem), *Black Petals*, Winter.
Bischoff, David, "May Oysters Have Legs," *Mardi Gras Madness*.
Bishop, Michael, "How Beautiful With Banners," *Century*, Spring.
———, "Tithes of Mint and Rue," *Lisa Snelling's Strange Attraction*.
Blaylock, James P., "The Other Side," *SCIFI.COM*, October 18.
Blumlein, Michael, "Fidelity: A Primer," *F & SF*, Sept.
Boston, Bruce, "The Kissing of Frogs" (poem), *Weird Tales* 319.
Bovberg, Jason, "Crush," *Noirotica* 3.
Boyczuk, Robert, "Tabula Rasa," *Queer Fear*.
Bradshaw, Paul, "At Riley's Bar," *Not One of Us 23/The Reservoir of Dreams*.
———, "The Dreamer of No Dreams," *The Reservoir of Dreams*.

Braunbeck, Gary A., "Iphigenia," *Brainbox*.

Brenchley, Chaz, "Everything, in All the Wrong Order," *Dark Terrors 5*.

————, "The Insolence of Candles Against the Light's Dying," *Taps and Sighs*.

————, "Junk Male," *Crimewave 4*.

————, "Up the Airy Mountain," *Crime Wave 3: Burning Down the House*.

Brite, Poppy Z., "Lantern Marsh," *October Dreams*.

Brooke, Keith & Brown, Eric, "The Denebian Cycle," *Interzone* 152.

Brown, Adam, "The Nativity Plague," *Aurealis* 25/26.

Bryant, Ed, "Mr. Twisted," *Strange Attraction*.

Buckell, Tobias S., "Spurn Babylon," *Whispers From the Cotton Tree Root*.

Burke, John, "We've Been Waiting for You," *We've Been Waiting for You*.

Burkett, Joshua, "The Wall Kissers," *Black Petals*, Winter.

Burns, Cliff, "Daughter," *Crimewave 4*.

Burt, Steve, "Casino Night," *Psychotrope* 8.

————, "The Strand," *Dread April*.

————, "The Witness Tree," *Shadows and Silence*.

Byrne, Michelle, "The dead," (poem), *Poetry East* 49/50.

Cacek, P. D., "A Rag, a Bone, and a Hank of Hair," *Extremes* CD-Rom.

————, "Reflections in the Water," *Whispered from the Grave*.

————, "Second Chance," *Noirotica 3*.

————, "The Toy Box," *Imagination Fully Dilated II*.

Cadnum, Michael, "Where July Went: A Halloween Memory," *October Dreams*.

Campbell, Ramsey, "Return Journey," *Taps and Sighs*.

Cantú, Ricardo Martinez, "Emergent Biology: A Corrupted Text," translated from the Spanish by Geoff Hargreaves, *The Malahat Review*, Fall.

Carroll, Siobhan, "Killer of Men," *On Spec*, Fall.

Carson, Pat, "How a Cartoon Deals With Loss" (poem), *Calyx*, Vol. 19, #2.

Case, David, "Pelican Cay" (novella), *Dark Terrors 5*.

Cash, Debra, "Briar Rose" and "Witch" (poems), *Black Heart, Ivory Bones*.

Casil, Amy Sterling, "Mad for the Mints," *F & SF*, July.

Castle, Mort, "Bird's Dead," *Moon on the Water*.

Castro, Adam-Troy, "The Magic Bullet Theory," *Skull Full of Spurs*.

Cave, Hugh B., "Littler," *Shadows and Silence*.

Chaffee, Karen, "Yekaterinburg, 1918" (poem), *Penny Dreadful* 13.

Charles, Paul, "Frankie and Johnny Were Lovers?" *Fresh Blood 3*.

Chiang, Ted, "Seventy-Two Letters," *Vanishing Acts*.

Chizmar, Richard T. "The Night Shift," *Imagination F. D. II*.

Christian, M., "Wanderlust," *Graven Images*.

Clark, Alan M., & Edwards, Mark, "Just How Expensive a Free Lunch Can Be," *Imagination F. D. II*.

Clark, Simon, "On Wings that So Darkly Beat . . . ," *Bad News*.

————, "The Whitby Experience," *October Dreams*.

Clegg, Douglas, "Piercing Men," *Queer Fear*.

————, "Purity," (novella) C D Pubs. Novella series.

Cobb, William, "Brother Bobby's Eye," *Shenandoah*, Fall.

Collins, Nancy A., "Calaverada," *Skull Full of Spurs*.

————, "The Serpent Queen," *Strange Attraction*.

Cooper, Louise, "St Gumper's Feast," *The Spiral Garden*.

Coward, Mat, "Jilly's Fault," *Gothic.net*, April.

——, "Now I Know its Name," *Fearsmag.com*, August.

Cox, F. Brett, "The Light of the Ideal," *Century*, Winter.

Crabtree, Deborah, "Murder of Crows," *Aurealis* 25/26.

Craig, John, "Dance of the Dead," *On Spec*, Summer.

Crew, Gary, "Another Rumour From the Wasteland," *Tales From the Wasteland*.

Crow, Jennifer, "Beauty for Ashes" (poem), *Edgar: Digested Verse*, Winter.

——, "Martha Speaks" (poem), *Talebones* 19.

Crowther, Peter, "Days of the Wheel," *Strange Attraction*.

——, "Dream a Little Dream For Me . . . ," *Perchance to Dream*.

——, "Fallen Angel," *Hideous Progeny*.

——, "Grandad Cohen and the Land at the End of the Working Day," Subterranean Press chapbook.

D'Ammassa, Don, "Dark Paris," *Extremes* (CD-Rom).

Dacey, Philip, "The Ghost Lover" (poem), *Tar River Poetry*, Spring.

Darby, Iain, "Bits and Pieces," *Hideous Progeny*.

Davis, Kathryn, "Floggings," *Ghost Writing*.

de Lint, Charles, "Big City Littles," Triskell Press chapbook.

——, "Many Worlds Are Born Tonight," *Strange Attraction*.

——, "Wingless Angels," *Black Gate* Vol. 1, #1.

——, "The Words that Remain," *Taps and Sighs*.

De Winter, Corrine, "Of Wings" (poem), *Icarus Ascending*, Fall/Winter.

Deane, John F., "The Seven Year Trance," *An Irish Christmas*.

Dedman, Stephen, "Beholder," *Embraces*.

——, "The Devotee," *Eidolon* 29/30.

——, "A Sentiment Open to Doubt," *Ticonderoga Online*.

——, "What you Wished For," *Weird Tales* 319.

Del Carlo, Eric, "Abrasions," *Talebones* 18.

——. "Blood Culture," *Talebones* 20.

Dellamonica, A. M., "Nevada," *SCI.FICTION*, October 11.

Denny, Thomas, "Déjà vu," *Enigmatic Tales* 10.

Denton, Bradley, "Blackburn's Lady," *The 26th World Fantasy Convention Program Book*.

Di Filippo, Paul, "Each to Each," *Interzone* 155.

——, "Stealing Happy Hours," *Interzone* 153.

——, "Rare Firsts," *Realms of Fantasy*, Dec.

DiMartino, Nick, "The Other Side of the Bay," *Shadows and Silence*.

Doig, James "Hands Touched by Chrism," *Enigmatic Tales* 9.

——, "Waiting," *Enigmatic Tales* 8.

Dondrup, Tsering, "A Show to Delight the Masses," translated from the Tibetan by Lauren Hartley, *Persimmon*, Vol. 1, #3.

Doyle, Arthur Conan, "The Haunted Grange of Goresthorpe," Ash-Tree Press.

Due, Tananarive, "Patient Zero," *F & SF*, August.

Duffy, Steve, "The Rag-and-Bone Men," *Shadows and Silence*.

Duncan, Andy, "From Alfano's Reliquary," *Weird Tales/Beluthahatchie and Other Stories*.

——, "Lincoln in Frogmore," *Beluthahatchie . . .*

Duncan, Sydney, "Clarion" (poem), *Uncommon Places: Poems of the Fantastic*.

Dunn, Carolyn, "Salmon Creek Road Kill," *Through the Eye of the Deer*.

Dunyach, Jean-Claude, "All the Roads to Heaven," *Interzone* 156.

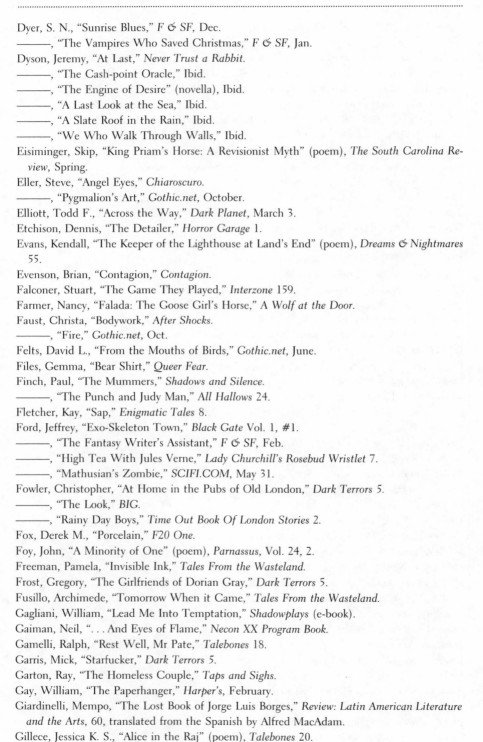

Dyer, S. N., "Sunrise Blues," *F & SF*, Dec.

———, "The Vampires Who Saved Christmas," *F & SF*, Jan.

Dyson, Jeremy, "At Last," *Never Trust a Rabbit*.

———, "The Cash-point Oracle," Ibid.

———, "The Engine of Desire" (novella), Ibid.

———, "A Last Look at the Sea," Ibid.

———, "A Slate Roof in the Rain," Ibid.

———, "We Who Walk Through Walls," Ibid.

Eisiminger, Skip, "King Priam's Horse: A Revisionist Myth" (poem), *The South Carolina Review*, Spring.

Eller, Steve, "Angel Eyes," *Chiaroscuro*.

———, "Pygmalion's Art," *Gothic.net*, October.

Elliott, Todd F., "Across the Way," *Dark Planet*, March 3.

Etchison, Dennis, "The Detailer," *Horror Garage* 1.

Evans, Kendall, "The Keeper of the Lighthouse at Land's End" (poem), *Dreams & Nightmares* 55.

Evenson, Brian, "Contagion," *Contagion*.

Falconer, Stuart, "The Game They Played," *Interzone* 159.

Farmer, Nancy, "Falada: The Goose Girl's Horse," *A Wolf at the Door*.

Faust, Christa, "Bodywork," *After Shocks*.

———, "Fire," *Gothic.net*, Oct.

Felts, David L., "From the Mouths of Birds," *Gothic.net*, June.

Files, Gemma, "Bear Shirt," *Queer Fear*.

Finch, Paul, "The Mummers," *Shadows and Silence*.

———, "The Punch and Judy Man," *All Hallows* 24.

Fletcher, Kay, "Sap," *Enigmatic Tales* 8.

Ford, Jeffrey, "Exo-Skeleton Town," *Black Gate* Vol. 1, #1.

———, "The Fantasy Writer's Assistant," *F & SF*, Feb.

———, "High Tea With Jules Verne," *Lady Churchill's Rosebud Wristlet* 7.

———, "Mathusian's Zombie," *SCIFI.COM*, May 31.

Fowler, Christopher, "At Home in the Pubs of Old London," *Dark Terrors* 5.

———, "The Look," *BIG*.

———, "Rainy Day Boys," *Time Out Book Of London Stories* 2.

Fox, Derek M., "Porcelain," *F20 One*.

Foy, John, "A Minority of One" (poem), *Parnassus*, Vol. 24, 2.

Freeman, Pamela, "Invisible Ink," *Tales From the Wasteland*.

Frost, Gregory, "The Girlfriends of Dorian Gray," *Dark Terrors* 5.

Fusillo, Archimede, "Tomorrow When it Came," *Tales From the Wasteland*.

Gagliani, William, "Lead Me Into Temptation," *Shadowplays* (e-book).

Gaiman, Neil, ". . . And Eyes of Flame," *Necon XX Program Book*.

Gamelli, Ralph, "Rest Well, Mr Pate," *Talebones* 18.

Garris, Mick, "Starfucker," *Dark Terrors* 5.

Garton, Ray, "The Homeless Couple," *Taps and Sighs*.

Gay, William, "The Paperhanger," *Harper's*, February.

Giardinelli, Mempo, "The Lost Book of Jorge Luis Borges," *Review: Latin American Literature and the Arts*, 60, translated from the Spanish by Alfred MacAdam.

Gillece, Jessica K. S., "Alice in the Raj" (poem), *Talebones* 20.

Gilman, Megan, "Eat Flounderly," *Shenandoah*, Winter.

Glass, Alexander, "The Language of the Dead," *Interzone* 161.

———, "The Lonely Ones," *The Third Alternative* 24.

———, "A View from the Cage," *Albedo One* 21.

Glass, James C., "The Mask of Eridani," *Talebones* 19.

Glassco, Bruce "Thrushbeard," *Realms of Fantasy*, December.

———, "When Beasts Eat Roses," *Realms of Fantasy*, April.

Glover, Douglas, "A Piece of the True Cross," *Ghost Writing*.

Golden, Christopher, "Runaway," *Cemetery Dance* 33.

Gonzalez, Ray, "Collecting Parrots," *Flyway*, Spring.

González, Francisco Rojas, "Our Lady of Nequeteje," *The Medicine Man*, translated from the Spanish by Robert S. Rudder and Gloria Arjona.

Gorman, Ed, "The Broker," *Fantastic*, Summer.

———, "Ghosts," *Taps and Sighs*.

———, "The Gun Show," *Be Afraid!*

———, "On the Run," *Bad News*.

Graves, Rain, "The Drunkard's Coin," *Daughter of Dangerous Dames*.

Green, Scott E., "The Breath of Sharks" (poem), *Dreams & Nightmares* 57.

Green, Terence M. and Weiner, Andrew, "Wavelength," *Northern Horror*.

Greenwood, Ed, "The Witch of the Dawn," *Be Afraid!*

Greenwood, Gary, "The Hollow Stones," *Enigmatic Tales* 10.

Gregg, Eric, "Stadium Square," *Bell, Book & Beyond*.

Grey, Ian, "Matchbox Screamers," *Embraces*.

Grey, John, "Madness, Please" (poem), *Icarus Ascending*, Fall/Winter.

Guffey, Robert, "The Infant Kiss," *After Shocks*.

Guilbeau, Kim, "Linger," *Cemetery Sonata II*.

Gunson, Catharine S., "The Adelaide Effect," *Tessellations*.

Guthridge, George, "The Silence of Phii Krasue," *Extremes* CD-Rom.

Hand, Elizabeth, "Chip Crockett's Christmas Carol," *SCIFI.COM*, Dec. 6–27.

Hardin, Rob, "Before the White Asylum," *Embraces*.

Harman, Christopher, "A Better Place," *Ghosts & Scholars* 31.

Harrison, M. John, "The Neon Heart Murders," *F & SF*, April.

Hearon, Shelby, "Order," *Ghost Writing*.

Helfers, John, "FILS," *Cemetery Dance* 33.

Hennessy, John, "Ophelia's Regrets" (poem), *Connecticut Review*, Spring.

Hicok, Bob, "Bedtime Story" (poem), *Poetry East*, 49/50.

Higgins, John, "A Mother's Eyes," *Aurealis* 25/26.

Hodge, Brian, "Before the Last Snowflake Falls," *Imagination F. D. II*.

———, "Forbidden Fruits, that Rot Upon the Vine," *Horror Garage* 1.

———, "Now Day was Fled as the Worm Had Wished," *Dark Terrors 5*.

———, "Pages Stuck by a Bowie Knife to a Cheyenne Gallows," *Skull Full* . . .

———, "Syndromes," *Noirotica* 3.

Hoffman, Nina Kiriki, "Night Life," *F & SF*, Aug.

———, "Shaped Stones," *Graven Images*.

Hoing, Dave, "The Only Shake-scene in the Country," *Century*, Winter.

Holder, Nancy, "You Give me Fever," *Embraces*.

———, "The Heart in Darkness," *After Shocks*.

———, "Skeleton Krewe," *Mardi Gras Madness*.

Hood, Robert, "That Old Black Graffiti," *Tales From the Wasteland*.

Hoornaert, Edward, "Devil, Devil," *On Spec*, Fall.

Hope, Akua Lezli, "The Becoming," *Dark Matter*.

Hopkins, Brian A., "Crocodile Gods," *Brainbox*.

———, "The Trouble With the Truth," *Unnatural Selection*.

———, "Wrinkles at Twilight," *Wrinkles at Twilight*.

Hopkinson, Nalo, "The Glass Bottle Trick," *Whispers from the Cotton Tree Root*.

Houarner, Gerard, "Born from the Womb of Forever," *Enigmatic Electronic*, March.

———, "Bui Doi," *Indigenous Fiction* 5.

———, "I Love you and There is Nothing You Can Do about It," *I Love You and There is Nothing You Can Do about It*.

Howkins, Elizabeth, "The Caretaker" (poem), *Penny Dreadful* 13.

Huff, Tanya, "Now Entering the Ring," *On Spec*, Winter 99.

Hughes, Monica, "The Gift," *Be Afraid!*

Hughes, Rhys, "The Banker of Ingolstadt," *A Nasty Piece of Work* 14.

———, "Depressurized Ghost Story," *The Smell of Telescopes*.

———, "The Haunted Womb," *A Nasty Piece of Work* 14.

———, "Mah Jong Breath," Ibid.

———, "The Orange Goat," Ibid.

———, "Spermaceti Whiskers," Ibid.

Humphrey, Kate, "Falling From Grace" (poem), *Altair* V.

Hunter, C. Bruce, "Changes," *Dark Terrors* 5.

Hunter, Ian, "A Little Something for a Job Well Done," *A Nasty Piece of Work* 14.

Hurry, Graeme & Meikle, William, "The Blue Hag," *Millenium Macabre*.

Irvine, Alexander C., "Rosetti Song," *F & SF*, March.

Jackson-Adams, Tracina, "Fairytale: The Beast" (poem), *The Magazine of Speculative Poetry*, Spring.

Jacob, Charlee, "Firmament," *The Third Alternative* 24.

———, "Flesh of Leaves, Bones of Desire," *Brainbox*.

———, "The Pentacles of their Hands," *New Genre* 1.

———, "Up, Out of the Cities that Blow Hot and Cold," *Up, Out of the Cities that Blow Hot and Cold*.

———, "White Moths" (poem), *Space and Time* 92.

Jacobi, Carl, "Dyak Reward," *Arkham's Masters of Horror*.

Jakeman, Jane, "Frosted Glass," *Shadows and Silence*.

———, "The House With no History," *Ghosts & Scholars* 31.

Jeffers, Honorée Fanonne, "Sister Lilith," *Dark Matter*.

Jens, Tina L., "Damned Fool Man," *Whispered from the Grave*.

Jeske, Brad, "Swamp Bodies," *Cemetery Sonata II*.

Jeter, K.W., "Straight Shot," *The 26th World Fantasy Con Prog. Bk.*

Jones, Gwyneth, "Destroyer of Worlds," *Dark Terrors* 5.

Jones, Lee, "The Offering," *Sackcloth & Ashes* 7.

Jordan, Ceri, "Mad Jack," *Hideous Progeny*.

———, "Playing Mother," *Crime Wave* 3.

Joyce, Graham, "Candia," *Taps and Sighs*.

Kandel, Michael, "Multum in Parvo," *Amazing Stories*, Summer.

Kane, Donna, "The Man With a Hand Transplant" (poem), *The Malahat Review*, Spring.

Keller, David H., "The Beautiful Lady," *Arkham's Masters of Horror*.

Kelly, Michael, "Comes a Cool Rain," *Northern Horror*.

Kennett, Rick, "The Last of Mr. Benjimen," *Shadows and Silence*.

Kenny, Wilma, "The Wedding," *On Spec*, Fall.

Kenworthy, Christopher, "The Frequency of You," *The Third Alternative* 24.

Ketchum, Jack, "The Best," *Bad News*.

————, "Forever," *Imagination F. D. II*.

————, "Luck," *Skull Full of Spurs*.

————, "Sunday," *Necon XX Program Book*.

Kiernan, Caitlín R., ". . . Between the Gargoyle Trees," *Tales of Pain and Wonder*.

————, "In the Water Works (Birmingham, Alabama 1888)," *Dark Terrors* 5.

————, "Lafayette," *Horror Garage* 1.

————, "A Redress for Andromeda," *October Dreams*.

————, "San Andreas," *Horror Garage* 1.

————, "Valentia," *Dark Terrors* 5.

Kilworth, Garry, "Bonsai Tiger," *Spectrum SF* 1.

Klasky, Mindy L., "Saving the Sky Children," *Realms of F.*, Oct.

Knez, Dora, "Vaster Than Empires," *Five Forbidden Things*.

Koja, Kathe, "Jackson's Novelties," *Horror Garage* 1.

Kritzer, Naomi, "The Price," *Tales of the Unanticipated* 21.

Kucera, Ann MacKinnon, "Falling out of the Sky," *Songs of Innocence* 3.

Kuzminski, Tina, "The Goddamned Tooth Fairy," *F&SF*, Oct./Nov.

Lamsley, Terry, "An Evening with Harrod," *Dark Matters*.

Lane, Joel, "The Bootleg Heart," *Dark Terrors* 5.

————, "Cash in Hand," *Hideous Progeny*.

Lannes, Roberta, "Pearl," *Dark Terrors* 5.

Laymon, Richard, "Boo," *October Dreams*.

————, "Double Date," (novella) *Bad News*.

Lebbon, Tim, "The Butterfly," *As the Sun Goes Down*.

————, "Curves and Sharp Edges," *F20 One*.

————, "Dust," *As the Sun Goes Down*.

————, "The Empty Room," *Ibid*.

————, "King of the Dead," *Ibid*.

————, "Life Within," *A Nasty Piece of Work* 14.

————, "Naming of Parts" (novella), PS Publishing.

————, "The Origin of Truth," *SCIFI.COM*, October 4.

————, "Pay the Ghost," *October Dreams*.

————, "Recent Wounds," *As the Sun Goes Down*.

————, "Reconstructing Amy," *Ibid*.

————, "Repulsion," *Extremes* CD-Rom.

————, "The Unfortunate," (novella) *As the Sun Goes Down*.

Lee, Tanith, "The Children of His Old Age," *Realms of Fantasy*, Oct.

————, "The Eye in the Heart," *F&SF*, March.

————, "Rapunzel," *Black Heart, Ivory Bones*.

————, "The Woman in Scarlet," *Realms of Fantasy*, April.

Leeflang, Ed, "He" (poem), translated from the Dutch by Pleuke Boyce, *The Malahat Review*, Summer.

————, "Sleeping Beauty" (poem), *Ibid*.

Leslie, Scott, "Phantom," *All Hallows* 25.

Ligotti, Thomas, "I Have a Special Plan for this World," *Horror Garage* 2.

Linaweaver, Brad, "Chump Hoist," *Strange Attraction.*

Lindow, Sandra J., "Eating the Bones" (poem), *Talebones* 19

Lindsay, Sarah, "Laser Palmistry: The Early Days" (poem), *The Atlantic Monthly*, July.

Lindskold, Jane, "Sacrifice," *Mardi Gras Madness.*

Link, Kelly, "Shoe and Marriage," *4 Stories.*

———, "Swans," A *Wolf at the Door.*

Litt, Toby, "Unhaunted," *Time Out London Sh.St.* 2.

Little, Bentley, "Tree Hugger," *Bad News.*

Locascio, Phil, "Not a Nickel More," *Cemetery Sonata II.*

Lockey, Paul, "True Love," *Roadworks* 8.

Lockley, Steve, "An Act of Faith," *Hideous Progeny.*

Lockley, Steve & Lewis, Paul, "The Winter Hunt," *F20 One.*

Logan, Sean, "Fiesta," *Deadbolt Magazine* 6.

Louvish, Simon, "Saddam Hussein on Ice," *Descant* 108.

Lozada, Antonio Garcia, "The Beggar," *Connecticut Review*, Spring.

Lunde, David, "Vampire Villanelle" (poem), *Uncommon Places.*

Mackey, Heather, "The Alchemist," *The South Carolina Review*, Spring.

MacLeod, Catherine, "The Other Dead," *On Spec*, Summer.

MacLeod, Ian R., "The Dragon Gift" (poem), *Asimov's SF*, Sept.

Mann, Anthony, "Shopping," *Crime Time* 4.

Marshall, Paul, "For Michael," *Enigmatic Tales* 8.

———, "The Tragedy of Power," *Ibid.*

Martin, George R. R., "Path of the Dragon," *Asimov's SF*, Dec.

Massin, Kain, "Wrong Dreaming," *On Spec*, Fall.

Masson, Sophie, "Bells Underwater," *Tales From the Wasteland.*

Masterton, Graham, "The Ballyhooly Boy," *Cemetery Dance* 33.

———, "Spirits of the Age," *Taps and Sighs.*

———, "The Sympathy Society," *Feelings of Fear.*

———, "Witch-Compass," *Dark Terrors* 5.

Masud, Naiyer, "Essence of Camphor," translated from the Urdu by Moazzam Sheikh and Elizabeth Bell, *Essence of Camphor.*

Matheson, Richard Christian, "Barking Sands," *Dark Terrors* 5.

———, "Bedlam," *Dystopia.*

———, "Dead of Winter," *Ibid.*

———, "Water Child," *Ibid.*

Mayhew, Michael, "Everything You Need to Know About Agatha," *Dark Planet*, March 3.

———, "The Symbiote," *Talebones* 19.

Maynard, L. H. & Sims, M. P. N., "The Nice House," *Bell, Book & Beyond.*

———, "Beware the Beckoning Stranger," *Jobs in Hell.*

McAuley, Paul J., "Straight to Hell," *The Third Alternative* 24.

McAvoy, Paul, "The Last Door down the Hall," *Kimota* 12.

McDonald, Ian, "White Noise," *Taps and Sighs.*

McDonald, Keris, "The Spirit Mirror," *Shadows and Silence.*

McKillip, Patricia A., "The Twelve Dancing Princesses," A *Wolf at the Door.*

McLaughlin, Mark, "Our Anne, Paxton Catafalque, and the Infante Sarkazein," *Gothic.net*, Feb.

Mihesuah, Devon A., "Kowi Annukasha: The Little People," *The Roads of my Relations.*

Mina, Denise, "Helena and the Babies," *Fresh Blood* 3.

Minier, Samuel, "Quiet Flickings, Milky Darkness," *Crimson Online* 12.

Mohanraj, Mary Anne, "Would You Live for Me?" *A Taste of Midnight*.

Mohn, Steve, "Not Plowed or Sanded in Winter," *On Spec*, Fall.

Morales, John, "Monsters," *Hideous Progeny*.

Morgan, Edwin, "Gilgamesh and Ziusara" (poem), *Poetry Nation Review* 133.

Morris, Mark, "Copying Cannibals," *The Third Alternative* 23.

Morton, Lisa, "El Cazador," *After Shocks*.

Mrozek, Slawomir, "Three Stories," translated from the Polish by Ela Ktkowska-Atkinson and Karen Underhill, *Chicago Review*, Fall-Winter.

Navarro, Yvonne, "Divine Justice," *Skull Full of Spurs*.

———, "Santa Alma," *Extremes* CD-Rom.

Nayler, Ray "Cutting Wood, Carrying Water," *Crime Time* 4.

Nestor, Daniel M., "Three Versions of an Iranian Death Game" (poem), *The South Carolina Review*, Spring.

Newland, Courttia, "Suicide Note," *Time Out London Sh. St.* 2.

Newman, Kim, "Castle in the Desert: Anno Dracula 1977," *SCIFI.COM*, June 14.

———, "Going to Series," *Dark Terrors* 5.

———, "Is There Anybody There?" *The New Engl. Lib. Bk. of Internet Stories*.

———, "The Man on the Clapham Omnibus," *Time Out London Sh. St.* 2. Nickle, David, "The Bird Feeders," *Queer Fear*.

———, "Mrs. Thurston's Instrument of Justice," *Northern Horror*.

O'Connell, John, "Gone to Earth," *Time Out London Sh. St.* 2.

O'Donnell, William, "Endemoniada," *Bell, Book & Beyond*.

O'Leary, Patrick, "Goetheanum" (poem), *Uncommon Places*.

O'Neill, Gene, "Counting Backwards," *Cemetery Sonata II*.

Oates, Joyce Carol, "In Shock," *F&SF*, June.

———, "You, Little Match-girl," *Black Heart, Ivory Bones*.

Okorafor, Nnedi, "The Palm Tree Bandit," *Strange Horizons*, Dec. 12.

Oliver, Frances, "The Black Mare Midnight," *All Hallows* 25.

———, "The Man in the Blue Mercedes," *Shadows and Silence*.

Olivieri, Michael, "The Burden," *Black Petals* Volume III, #2.

Ong, Alistair, "Can You Hear the Angels Sing?" *Aurealis* 25/26.

Painter, Pamela, "Doors," *Ghost Writing*.

Palwick, Susan, "Wood and Water," *F&SF*, Feb.

Park, Severna, "The Golem," *Black Heart, Ivory Bones*.

Parker, Ward, "The Power Doctor," *Bell, Book & Beyond*.

Parks, Richard, "The God of Children," *Asimov's SF*, December.

Partridge, Norman, "The Big Man," *Horror Garage* 1.

Peiffer-Willett, Jody Nokwisa, "hungry is the wolf," *Through the Eye . . . Deer*.

Pelan, John, "Spider," *Shadows and Silence*.

Phalen, David, "Playing in the Dark," *Realms of Fantasy*, Aug.

Phillips, Holly, "No Such Thing as an Ex-Con," *On Spec*. Summer.

Pinn, Paul, "Bangala Ruse," *Roadworks* 8.

Platt, John R., "That Old Black Magic," *Bell, Book & Beyond*.

Pond, Whitt. "The Island," *Bell, Book & Beyond*.

Pryor, Michael, "Sewercide," *Aurealis* 25/26.

Ptacek, Kathryn, "The Grotto," *Graven Images*.

———, "The Lake," *Necon XX Program Book*.

Raine, Steven C., "Her Dust Grimed Eyes," *Tessellations*.

Rainey, Stephen Mark, "Orchestra," *October Dreams*.

Raleigh, Richard, "The Hanged Man," *turtleneck.net*, Spring.

Rand, Ken, "Refuge," *Weird Tales* 320.

———, "The Find," *Extremes* CD-Rom.

Rath, Tina, "The Pied Piper of Milltown," *All Hallows* 25.

Rathbone, Wendy, "Rebirth Day" (poem), *Dreams and Nightmares* 55.

Read, William I. I., "The Bogle Ring," *Degrees of Fear*.

———, "The Phantom Pudding," Ibid.

———, "The Winkle Inheritance," Ibid.

Reed, Kit, "Precautions," *F&SF*, August.

Reed, Robert, "Due," *F&SF*, Feb.

———, "Grandma's Jumpman," *Century*, Spring.

Reisman, Jessica, "The Arcana of Maps," *The Third Alternative* 23.

Rensun, Jin, "A Story of Koryo," translated from the Chinese by Chen Haiyan, *Chinese Literature Press*.

Resnick, Mike, "Redchapel," *Asimov's SF*. Dec.

Riedel, Kate, "The Seventh Sleeper," *Realms of Fantasy*, June.

Roach, Kathryn, "Divine Nature," *Indigenous Fiction* 6.

Roden, Barbara, "Tourist Trap," *Shadows and Silence*.

Rogers, Bruce Holland, "King Corpus," *Mardi Gras Madness*.

———, "Little Brother™," *One Evening a Year*.

Rogers, Lenore K., "More than Music," *Cemetery Sonata II*.

Rojas, Andrew, "Cain's Curse" (poem), *New England Review*, Vol. 21, #1.

Ross, Leone, "Mud Man," *Time Out London Sh. St. 2*.

Rossi, Christina Peri, "Indicios pánicos," translated from the Spanish by Mercedes Rowinksky, *Southwest Review*, Vol. 85, #3.

Rowand, Richard & Wilson, David Niall, "Moon Like a Gambler's Face," *Gothic.net*. Nov.

Royle, Nicholas, "The Proposal," *Dark Terrors 5*.

Rucker, Lynda E., "Beneath the Drops," *The Third Alternative* 25.

Rusch, Kristine Kathryn, "Burial Detail," *Realms of Fantasy*, Feb.

———, "Kindred Souls," *Fictionwise.com*, Sept. 25.

———, "Saving Face," *Spell Fantastic*.

Russell, Jay, "First Love," *Embraces*.

Russo, Patricia, "Le Demon Riant," *Space and Time*, Spring.

———, "Skin," *Not One of Us* 24.

———, "Velvet," *Indigenous Fiction* 6.

Rutherford, Jeff, "Espalier," *Horrorfind.com*.

Samuels, Mark. "The Grandmaster's Final Game." *Enigmatic Tales* 10.

Sandner, David, "The Cry of Those Waiting under the Bridge," (poem) *Weird Tales* 318.

Sarban, "Number Fourteen," (novella) *Ringstones and other Curious Tales*.

Saunders, George C., "Pastorialia," *The New Yorker* April 5.

Sawyer, Robert J., "Fallen Angel," *L.S.'s Strange Attraction*.

———, "Last but Not Least," *Be Afraid!*

Scarborough, Elizabeth Ann, "Worse Than the Curse," *Such a Pretty Face*.

Schoenfeld, Yael, "The Collection Treatment," *Playboy*, Oct.

Schow, David J., "2 cents worth," *Gothic.net*, Jan.

———, "Blessed Event," *Vanishing Acts*.

———, "Calendar Girl," *ThePosition.com*, June.

———, "Holiday," *Horror Garage* 2.

———, "Why Rudy Can't Read," *Dark Terrors* 5.

Schroeder, Randy, "The Skeleton Crows," *On Spec*, Winter 99.

Schweitzer, Darrell, "Appeasing the Darkness," *L.S.'s Strange Attraction*.

———, "The Fire Eggs," *Interzone* 153.

———, "The House-Guest's Ghost Story" (poem), *Fantasy Commentator*, Spring.

———, "In the Street of the Witches," *Weird Tales*, 320.

———, "Vandibar Nasha in the College of Shadows," *Adventures of Swords & Sorcery* 7.

Scott, Manda, "99%," *Fresh Blood* 3.

Sellers, Peter, "Dents," *Whistling Past the Graveyard*.

———, "Freak Attraction," Ibid.

Senior, Olive, "Mad Fish," *Whispers from the Cotton Tree Root*.

Shannon, Lorelei, "The Virgin Spring," *Embraces*.

Shea, Michael, "For Every Tatter in Its Mortal Dress," *F&SF*, April.

Sheckley, Robert, "The New Horla," *F&SF*, July.

Sherman, Delia, "The Months of Manhattan," *A Wolf at the Door*.

Shiner, Lewis, "The Circle," *October Dreams*.

———, "Primes," *F&SF*, Oct./Nov.

Shirley, John, "Mask Game," *October Dreams*.

———, "Nineteen Seconds," *Horror Garage* 1.

———, "Sweetbite Point," *Imagination F. D. II*.

Shockley, Gary W., "Skullcracker," *F&SF*, June.

Shrayer-Petrov, David, "Dismemberers," translated from the Russian by Maxim D. Shrayer and Victor Terras, *Southwest Review*, Vol. 85, #1.

Sieber, Carl, "Jack Be Nimble," *On Spec*, Fall.

Silva, David B., "Out of the Dark," *October Dreams*.

Simonds, Merilyn, "The Lion in the Room Next Door," *The Lion in the Room Next Door*.

———, "Nossa Senhora dos Remédios," Ibid.

Sinclair, Iain, "The Keeper of the Rothenstein Tomb," *Time Out Lond. Sh. St.* 2.

Smith, Michael Marshall, "Charms," *Taps and Sighs*.

———, "Some Witch's Bed," *October Dreams*.

Smith, R. S., "The Dead Room," *Penny Dreadful* 13.

Sonde, Susan, "Break-Up," *Crime Time* 4.

Spark, Muriel, "The Young Man Who Discovered the Secret of Life," *Partisan Review*, Winter.

Spencer, William Browning, "The Foster Child," *F&SF*, June.

Springer, Nancy, "Know Your True Enemy," *Sherwood*.

Stableford, Brian, "Chanterelle," *Black Heart, Ivory Bones*.

———, "The Mandrake Garden," *F&SF*, July.

Steiber, Ellen, "The Cats of San Martino," *Black Heart, Ivory Bones*.

Steinbach, Meredith, "The Third Visitor," *Southwest Review*, Vol. 85, #2.

Stevens, Bryce, "Sisters of the Moss," *Orb Speculative Fiction* 1.

Stewart, Dolores, "The Old Medicine Song" (poem), *Poetry*, May.

Stone, Del, Jr., "Sitters," *Northern Horror*.

Stuart, Kiel, "Mr. Darkmore's Neighborhood," *Weird Tales* 321.

———, "Road Map of the Last Day" (poem), *Potomac Review*, Winter 1999–2000.

Suggs, Rob, "The Cherokee Rose," *All Hallows* 25.

Sullivan, Tim, "Hawk on a Flagpole," *Asimov's SF*, July.

Sussex, Lucy, "The Gloaming," *Eidolon* 29/30.

———, "The Morgue," *Tales From the Wasteland*.

Taylor, Lucy, "Girl Under Glass," *Bad News*.

———, "Stiletto," *Noirotica 3*.

Tem, Melanie, "Alicia," *Dark Terrors 5*.

Tem, Steve Rasnic, "Bad Dogs Come out of the Rain," *Horror Garage* 2.

———, "A Condemned Man" (non-fic), *October Dreams*.

———, "Cubs," *Hideous Progeny*.

———, "Eggs," *City Fishing*.

———, "Jake's Body," *Be Afraid!*

———, "Pareidolia," *City Fishing*.

———, "The Sadness of Angels," *Ibid*.

———, "The Slow Fall of Dust in a Quiet Place," *Shadows and Silence*.

Tessier, Thomas, "Figures in Scrimshaw," *Ghost Music*.

———, "Nocturne," *Ghost Music*.

———, "The Ventriloquist," *Horror Garage* 2.

———, "Wax," *Ghost Music*.

Thomas, Jeffrey, "Adoration," *Terror Incognita*.

———, "Crimson Blues," Ibid.

———, "Immolation," *Punktown*.

———, "The Library of Sorrows," Ibid.

———, "Precious Metal," Ibid.

———, "Wakizashi," Ibid.

Thompson, Philip, "Lonesome Mary," *Space and Time* 92.

Tiedemann, Mark W., "Politics," *F&SF*, Sept.

Tremblay, Erin Elizabeth, "Frostbitten" (poem), *The Louisville Review*, Winter-Summer.

Trotter, William R., "Honeysuckle" (novella), *Dark Terrors 5*.

Troy, Pamela, "Red World," *Crimson Online Magazine* 7.

Troy-Castro, Adam, "The Magic Bullet Theory," *Skull Full of Spurs*.

Tumasonis, Don, "The Graveyard," *Shadows and Silence*.

Tuttle, Lisa, "Haunts," *Dark Terrors 5*.

Umland, C. Mark, "The Nightguard," *Queer Fear*.

Urban, Scott H., "The Transaction," *Northern Horror*.

———, "The Wounds that Don't Bleed," *Blood Moon Zine*, Vol 2, #2.

van Belkom, Edo, "To be More Like Them," *Be Afraid!*

Van Pelt, James, "Parallel Highways," *After Shocks*.

———, "Road Decoy," *Space and Time*, Spring.

———, "Savannah is Six," *Dark Terrors 5*.

Vanderbes, Jennifer C., "Child of Mine," *F&SF*, May.

VanderMeer, Jeff, "Ghost Dancing with Manco Tupac," *Imagination F. D. II*.

Vernon, Steve, "Rolling Stock," *Not One of Us* 24.

Viscosi, James, "Caller ID," *Dread* Jan.

Volk, Stephen, "Blitzenstein," *Hideous Progeny*.

———, "The Chapel of Unrest," *Shadows and Silence*.

Wagoner, David, "Frankenstein's Garden" (poem), *The American Poetry Review*, Vol. 29, #3.

Wahl, Sharon, "I Also Dated Zarathustra," *Pleiades*, Vol. 20, #2.

Wakefield, H. R., "An Air of Berlioz," *Reunion at Dawn*.

———, "The Assignation," Ibid.

————, "At World's End," Ibid.

————, "The Bodyguard," Ibid.

————, "The Fall of the House of Gilpin," Ibid.

————, "Family Spirit," Ibid.

————, "The Fire-Watcher's Story," Ibid.

————, "The Latch-Key," Ibid.

————, "The Library of Sorrows," Ibid.

————, "Parrot Cry," Ibid.

————, "Reunion at Dawn," Ibid.

————, "The Sandwich," Ibid.

————, "Surprise for Papa," Ibid.

Waldrop, Howard, "Our Mortal Span," *Black Heart, Ivory Bones.*

Walters, John, "Under Calcutta," *Talebones* 19.

Walther, Paul, "The Toll," *New Genre* 1.

Warburton, Geoffrey, "Merry Roderick," *All Hallows* 23.

Ward, C. E., "Not Found Among You," *Ghosts & Scholars* 30.

Ward, Clive E., "One Over the Twelve," *Shadows and Silence.*

Ward, James, "The Smell of Scruffy Kids," *Roadworks* 8.

Watson, Ian, "Tales from Weston Willow," *Weird Tales* 319.

Weighell, Ron, "The Counsels of Night," *Shadows and Silence.*

West, Mark, "Empty Souls, Drowning," *Enigmatic Tales* 10.

————, "Speckles," *Sackcloth & Ashes*, March.

Westgard, Sten, "Shovel Them Under and Let Me Work," *Crime Wave* 3.

Whitbourn, John, "Culloden 2," *All Hallows* 23.

————, "Excuse Me . . ." *Shadows and Silence.*

————, "The Way, the Truth. . . ." *F&SF*, Jan.

Wild, Dean H. "Harm None," *Bell, Book & Beyond.*

Wilder, Cherry, "Saturday," *Dark Terrors* 5.

Wilhelm, Kate, "Earth's Blood," *F&SF*, Oct./Nov.

Williams, Conrad, "Excuse the Unusual Approach," *The Third Alternative* 25.

————, "Known," *Time Out London Sh. Sts 2.*

Williams, Liz, "Dog Years," *Interzone* 152.

Williamson, Chet, "A Collector of Magic," *Imagination F. D. II.*

Williamson, Neil, "The Bone Farmer," *Albedo One* 21.

Willrich, Chris, "The Thief with Two Deaths," *F&SF*, June.

Wilson, David Niall, "Defining Moments," *Gothic.net.* May.

Wilson, F. Paul, "Anna," *Imagination F. D. II.*

Wilson, Mehitobel, "Madeline in Effigy," *Brainbox.*

Wilson, Robert Charles, "The Fields of Abraham," *The Perseids and Other Stories.*

Wolfe, Gene, "The Eleventh City," *Graven Images.*

————, "The Fat Magician," *Such a Pretty Face.*

————, "Pocketsful of Diamonds," *Strange Attraction.*

————, "The Walking Sticks," *Taps and Sighs.*

Woodbury, Katherine, "Golden Hands," *Space and Time*, Spring.

Worley, Alec, "A Curious Incident," *Enigmatic Tales* 9.

Worozbyt, Theodore, "Heaven" (poem), *Poet Lore*, Vol. 95, #1.

ya Salamm, Kalamu, "Can You Wear My Eyes," *Dark Matter.*

Yolen, Jane, "Fat is Not a Fairy Tale," (poem), *Such a Pretty Face.*

————, "Green" (poem), *Color Me a Rhyme*.

————, "Our Lady of the Greenwood," *Sherwood*.

————, "Snow in Summer," *Black Heart, Ivory Bones*.

————, "Speaking to the Wind," *Sister Emily's Lightship and other Stories*.

Yolen, Jane and Harris, Robert J., "Requiem Antarctica," *Asimov's SF*, May.